AMBERGRIS

CITY OF SAINTS AND MADMEN

SHRIEK: AN AFTERWORD

FINCH

MCD FARRAR, STRAUS AND GIROUX NEW YORK

AMBERGRIS

JEFF VANDERMEER

MCD

Farrar, Straus and Giroux

120 Broadway, New York 10271

City of Saints and Madmen was originally published in 2002 by Prime Books.
Shriek: An Afterword was originally published in 2006 by Tor Books.
Finch was originally published in 2009 by Underland Press.

Owing to limitations of space, illustration credits can be found on page 869.

Library of Congress Cataloging-in-Publication Data

Names: VanderMeer, Jeff, author.

Title: Ambergris / Jeff VanderMeer.

Description: First edition. | New York : MCD / Farrar, Straus and Giroux, 2020. | City
of Saints and Madmen was originally published in 2002 by Prime Books; Shriek:
An Afterword was originally published in 2006 by Tor Books; Finch was originally
published in 2009 by Underland Press.

Identifiers: LCCN 2020028189 | ISBN 9780374103170 (hardcover)

Subjects: GSAFD: Fantasy fiction.

Classification: LCC PS3572.A4284 A84 2020 | DDC 813/.54—dc23

LC record available at https://lccn.loc.gov/2020028189

Designed by Abby Kagan

Our books may be purchased in bulk for promotional, educational, or business use. Please contact
your local bookseller or the Macmillan Corporate and Premium Sales Department at 1-800-221-7945,
extension 5442, or by e-mail at MacmillanSpecialMarkets@macmillan.com.

www.mcdbooks.com • www.fsgbooks.com

Follow us on Twitter, Facebook, and Instagram at @mcdbooks

1   3   5   7   9   10   8   6   4   2

for Ann

CONTENTS

City of Saints
and Madmen

"What can be said about Ambergris that has not already been said? Every minute section of the city, no matter how seemingly super-fluous, has a complex, even devious, part to play in the communal life. And no matter how often I stroll down Albumuth Boulevard, I never lose my sense of the city's incomparable splendor — its love of ritual, its passion for music, its infinite capacity for the beautiful cruelty."

—Voss Bender, *Memoirs of a Composer*, Vol. No. 1, page 558, Ministry of Whimsy Press

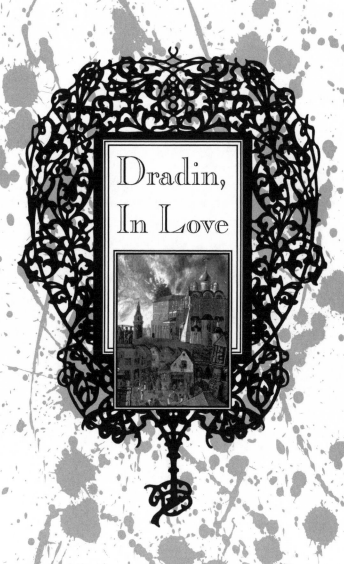

Dradin, In Love

radin, in love, beneath the window of his love, staring up at her while crowds surge and seethe around him, bumping and bruising him all unawares in their rough-clothed, bright-rouged thousands. For Dradin watches *her*, she taking dictation from a *machine*, an inscrutable block of gray from which sprout the earphones she wears over her delicate egg-shaped head. Dradin is struck dumb and dumber still by the seraphim blue of her eyes and the cascade of long and lustrous black hair over her shoulders, her pale face gloomy against the glass and masked by the reflection of the graying sky above. She is three stories up, ensconced in brick and mortar, almost a monument, her seat near the window just above the sign that reads HOEGBOTTON & SONS, DISTRIBUTORS. Hoegbotton & Sons: the largest importer and exporter in all of lawless Ambergris, that oldest of cities named for the most valuable and secret part of the whale. Hoegbotton & Sons: boxes and boxes of depravities shipped for the amusement of the decadent from far, far Surphasia and the nether regions of the Occident, those places that moisten, ripen, and decay in a blink. And yet, Dradin surmises, she looks as if she comes from more contented stock, not a stay-at-home, but uncomfortable abroad, unless traveling on the arm of her lover. Does she have a lover? A husband?

Are her parents yet living? Does she like the opera or the bawdy theater shows put on down by the docks, where the creaking limbs of laborers load the crates of Hoegbotton & Sons onto barges that take the measure of the mighty River Moth as it flows, sludge-filled and torpid, down into the rapid swell of the sea? If she likes the theater, I can at least afford her, Dradin thinks, gawping up at her. His long hair slides down into his face, but so struck is he that he does not care. The heat withers him this far from the river, but he ignores the noose of sweat round his neck.

Dradin, dressed in black with dusty white collar, dusty black shoes, and the demeanor of an out-of-work missionary (which indeed he is), had not meant to see the woman. Dradin had not meant to look up at all. He had been looking *down* to pick up the coins he had lost through a hole in his threadbare trousers, their seat torn by the lurching carriage ride from the docks into Ambergris, the carriage drawn by a horse bound for the glue factory, perhaps taken to the slaughter yards that very day—the day before the Festival of the Freshwater Squid as the carriage driver took pains to inform him, perhaps hoping Dradin would require his further services. But it was all Dradin could do to stay seated as they made their way to a hostel, deposited his baggage in a room, and returned once more to the merchant districts—to catch a bit of local color, a bite to eat—where he and the carriage driver parted company. The driver's mangy beast had left its stale smell on Dradin, but it was a necessary beast nonetheless, for he could never have afforded a mechanized horse, a vehicle of smoke and oil. Not when he would soon be down to his last coins and in desperate need of a job, the job he had come to Ambergris to find, for his former teacher at the Morrow Religious Institute—a certain Cadimon Signal—preached from Ambergris's Religious Quarter, and surely, what with the festivities, there would be work?

But when Dradin picked up his coins, he regained his feet rather too jauntily, spun and rattled by a ragtag gang of jackanapes who ran past him, and his gaze had come up on the gray, rain-threatening sky, and swung through to the window he now watched with such intensity.

The woman had long, delicate fingers that typed to their own peculiar rhythms, so that she might as well have been playing Voss Bender's Fifth, diving to the desperate lows and soaring to the magnificent highs that Voss Bender claimed as his territory. When her face became, for the moment, revealed to Dradin through the glare of glass—a slight forward motion to advance the tape, perhaps—he could see that her features, a match for her hands, were reserved, streamlined, artful. Nothing in her spoke of the rough rude world surrounding Dradin, nor of the great, unmapped southern jungles from which he had just returned; where the black panther and the blacker mamba waited with such malign intent; where he had been so consumed by fever and by doubt and by lack of converts to his religion that he had come back into the charted territory of laws and governments, where, sweet joy, there existed women like the creature in the window above him. Watching her, his blood simmering within him, Dradin wondered if he was dreaming her, she a haloed, burning vision of salvation, soon to disappear mirage-like, so that he might once more be cocooned within his fever, in the jungle, in the darkness.

But it was not a dream and, of a sudden, Dradin broke from his reverie, knowing she might see him, so vulnerable, or that passersby might guess at his intent and reveal it to her before he was ready. For the real world surrounded him, from the stink of vegetables in the drains to the *sweet* of half-gnawed ham hocks in the trash; the clip-clop-stomp of horse and the rattled honk of motored vehicles; the rustle-whisper of mushroom dwellers disturbed from daily slumber and, from somewhere hidden, the sound of a baroque and lilting music, crackly as if played on a phonograph. People knocked into him, allowed him no space to move: merchants and jugglers and knife salesmen and sidewalk barbers and tourists and prostitutes and sailors on leave from their ships, even the odd pale-faced young tough, smiling a gangrenous smile.

Dradin realized he must act and yet he was too shy to approach her, to fling open the door to Hoegbotton & Sons, dash up the three flights of stairs and, un-announced (and perhaps unwanted) and unwashed, come before her dusty and smitten, a twelve-o'clock shadow upon his chin. Obvious that he had come from the Great Beyond, for he still stank of the jungle rot and jungle excess. No, no. He must not thrust himself upon her.

But what, then, to do? Dradin's thoughts tumbled one over the other like distraught clowns and he was close to panic, close to wringing his hands in the way his mother had disapproved of but that indicated nothing unusual in a missionary, when a thought came to him and left him speechless at his own ingenuity.

A bauble, of course. A present. A trifle, at his expense, to show his love for her. Dradin looked up and down the street, behind and below him for a shop that might hold a treasure to touch, intrigue, and, ultimately, keep her. Madame Lowery's Crochets? The Lady's Emporium? Jessible's Jewelry Store? No, no, no. For what if she were a Modern, a woman who would not be kept or kept pregnant, but moved in the same circles as the artisans and writers, the actors and singers? What an insult such a gift would be to her then. What an insensitive man she would think him to be—and what an insensitive man he *would* be. Had all his months in the jungle peeled away his common sense, layer by layer, until he was as naked as an orangutan? No, it would not do. He could not buy clothing, chocolates, or even flowers, for these gifts were too forward, unsubtle, uncouth, and lacking in imagination. Besides, they—

—and his roving gaze, touching on the ruined aqueduct that divided the two sides of the street like the giant fossilized spine of a long, lean shark, locked in on the distant opposite shore and the modern sign with the double curlicues and the bold lines of type that proclaimed BORGES BOOKSTORE, and right there, on Albumuth

Boulevard, the filthiest, most sublime, and richest thoroughfare in all of Ambergris, Dradin realized he had found the perfect gift. Nothing could be better than a book, or more mysterious, and nothing could draw her more perfectly to him.

Still dusty and alone in the swirl of the city—a voyeur among her skirts—Dradin set out toward the opposite side, threading himself between street players and pimps, card sharks and candy sellers, through the aqueduct, and, braving the snarl of twin stone lions atop a final archway, came at last to the BORGES BOOKSTORE. It had splendid antique windows, gilt embroidered, with letters that read:

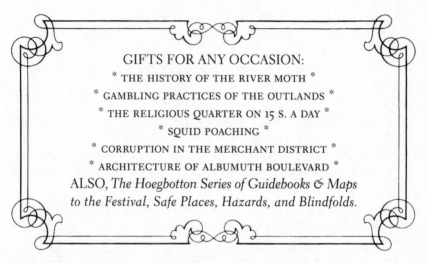

GIFTS FOR ANY OCCASION:
* THE HISTORY OF THE RIVER MOTH *
* GAMBLING PRACTICES OF THE OUTLANDS *
* THE RELIGIOUS QUARTER ON 15 S. A DAY *
* SQUID POACHING *
* CORRUPTION IN THE MERCHANT DISTRICT *
* ARCHITECTURE OF ALBUMUTH BOULEVARD *
ALSO, *The Hoegbotton Series of Guidebooks & Maps to the Festival, Safe Places, Hazards, and Blindfolds.*

Book upon piled book mentioned in the silvery scrawl and beyond the glass the quiet, slow movements of bibliophiles, feasting upon the genuine articles. It made Dradin forget to breathe, and not simply because this place would have a gift for his dearest, his most beloved, the woman in the window, but because he had been away from the world for a year and, now back, he found the accoutrements of civilization comforted him. His father, that tortured soul, was still a great reader, between the bouts of drinking, despite the erosion of encroaching years, and Dradin could remember many a time that the man had, honking his red, red nose—a monstrosity of a nose, out of proportion to anything in the family line—read and wept at the sangfroid exploits of two poor debutantes named Juliette and Justine as they progressed from poverty to prostitution, to the jungles and back again, weepy with joy as they rediscovered wealth and went on to have wonderful adventures up and down the length and breadth of the River Moth, until finally pristine Justine expired from the pressure of tragic pleasures wreaked upon her.

It made Dradin swell with pride to think that the woman at the window was more beautiful than either Juliette or Justine, far more beautiful, and likely more stalwart besides. (And yet, Dradin admitted, in the delicacy of her features, the pale gloss of her lips, he espied an innately breakable quality as well.)

Thus thinking, Dradin pushed open the glass door, the lacquered oak frame a-creak, and a bell chimed once, twice, thrice. On the thrice chime, a clerk dressed all in dark greens, sleeves spiked with gold cufflinks, came forward, shoes soundless on the thick carpet, bowed, and asked, "How may I help you?"

To which Dradin explained that he sought a gift for a woman. "Not a woman I know," he said, "but a woman I should like to know."

The clerk, a rake of a lad with dirty brown hair and a face as subtle as mutton pie, winked wryly, smiled, and said, "I understand, sir, and I have *precisely* the book for you. It arrived a fortnight ago from the Ministry of Whimsy imprint—an Occidental publisher, sir. Please follow me."

The clerk led Dradin past mountainous shelves of history texts perused by shriveled prunes of men dressed in orange pantaloons—buffoons from university, no doubt, practicing for some baroque Voss Bender revival—and voluminous mantels of fictions and pastorals, neglected except by a widow in black and a child of twelve with thick glasses, then exhaustive columns of philosophy on which the dust had settled thicker still, until finally they reached a corner hidden by "Funerals" entitled "Objects of Desire."

The clerk pulled out an elegant eight-by-eleven book lined with soft velvet and gold leaf. "It is called *The Refraction of Light in a Prison* and in it can be found the collected wisdom of the last of the Truffidian monks imprisoned in the Kalif's dark towers. It was snuck out of those dark towers by an intrepid adventurer who—"

"Who was not a son of Hoegbotton, I hope," Dradin said, because it was well known that Hoegbotton & Sons dealt in all sorts of gimmickry and mimicry, and he did not like to think that he was giving his love an item she might have unpacked and cataloged herself.

"Hoegbotton & Sons? No, sir. Not a son of Hoegbotton. We do not deal with

Hoegbotton & Sons (except inasmuch as we are contracted to carry their guide-books), as their practices are . . . how shall I put it? . . . *questionable*. With neither Hoegbotton nor his sons do we deal. But where was I? The Truffidians.

"They are experts at the art of cataloging passion, with this grave distinction: that when I say to you, sir, 'passion,' I mean the word in its most general sense, a sense that does not allow for intimacies of the kind that might strike the lady you *wish to know better* as too vulgar. It merely speaks to the general—the *incorporeal*, as one more highly witted than I might say. It shall not offend; rather, it shall lend to the gift-giver an aura of mystery that may prove permanently alluring."

The clerk proffered the book for inspection, but Dradin merely touched the svelte cover with his hand and said no, for he had had the most delightful thought: that he could explore those pages at the same time as his love. The thought made his hands tremble as they had not trembled since the fever ruled his body and he feared he might die. He imagined his hand atop hers as they turned the pages, her eyes caressing the same chapter and paragraph, the same line and word; thus could they learn of passion together but separate.

"Excellent, excellent," Dradin said, and, after a tic of hesitation—for he was much closer to penniless than penniful—he added, "but I shall need two," and as the clerk's eyebrows rose like the startled silhouettes of twin seagulls upon finding that a fish within their grasp is actually a snark, he stuttered, "A-a-and a map. A map of the city. For the Festival."

"Of course," said the clerk, as if to say, *Converts all around, eh?*

Dradin, dour-faced, said only, "Wrap this one and I will take the other unwrapped, along with the map," and stood stiff, brimming over with urgency, as the clerk dawdled and digressed. He knew well the clerk's thoughts: *a rogue priest, ungodly and unbound by any covenant made with God.* And perhaps the clerk was right, but did not canonical law provide for the unforeseen and the estranged, for the combination of beauty and the bizarre of which the jungle was itself composed? How else could one encompass and explain the terrible grace of the Hull Peoples, who lived within the caves hewn by a waterfall, and who, when dispossessed by Dradin and sent to the missionary fort, complained of the silence, the silence of God, how God would not talk to them, for what else was the play of water upon the rocks but the voice of God? He had had to send them back to their waterfall, for he could not bear the haunted looks upon their faces, the disorientation blossoming in their eyes like a deadly and deadening flower.

Dradin had first taken a lover in the jungles: a sweaty woman priest whose kisses smothered and suffocated him even as they brought him back to the world of flesh. Had she infected his mission? No, for he had tried so very hard for conversions, despite their scarcity. Even confronted by savage beast, savage plant, and just plain savage he had persevered. Perhaps persevered for too long, in the face of too many obstacles, his hair proof of his tenacity—the stark black streaked with white or, in certain light, stark white shot through with black, each strand of white attributable to the jungle fever (so cold it burned, his skin glacial), each strand of black a testament to being alive afterward.

Finally, the clerk tied a lime-green bow around a bright red package: gaudy but serviceable. Dradin dropped the necessary coin on the marble counter, stuck the map in the unwrapped copy and, with a frown to the clerk, walked to the door.

Out in the gray glare of the street, the heat and the bustling confusion struck Dradin and he thought he was lost, lost in the jungles that he had only just fled, lost so he would never again find his lady. His breaths came ragged and he put a hand to his temple, for he felt faint yet giddy.

Gathering his strength, he plunged into the muddle of sweating flesh, sweating clothes, sweating cobblestones. He rushed past the twin lions, their asses waggling at him as if they knew very well what he was up to, the arches, and then a vanguard of mango sellers, followed by an army of elderly dowager women with brimming stomachs and deep-pouched aprons, determined to buy up every last fruit or legume; young pups in play nipped at his heels, and, lord help him, he was delivered pell-mell in a pile, delivered with a stumble and a bruise to the opposite sidewalk, there to stare up once again at his lady love. Could any passage be more perilous than that daylight passage across Albumuth Boulevard, unless it was to cross the Moth at flood time?

Undaunted, Dradin sprang to his feet, his two books secure, one under each arm, and smiled to himself.

The woman had not moved from her station on the third floor; Dradin could tell, for he stood exactly as he had previous, upon the same crack in the pavement, and she was exactly as before, down to the pattern of shadows across the glass. Her rigid bearing brought questions half-stumbling to his lips. Did they not give her time for lunch? Did they make a virtue out of vice and virtually imprison her, enslave her to a cruel schedule? What had the clerk said? That Hoegbotton practices were *questionable*? He wanted to march into the building and talk to her superior, be her hero, but his dilemma was of a more practical kind: he did not wish to reveal himself as yet and thus needed a messenger for his gift.

Dradin searched the babble of people and his vision blurred, the world simplified to a sea of walking clothes: cufflinks and ragged trousers, blouses dancing with skirts, tall cotton hats and shoes with loose laces. How to distinguish? How to know whom to approach?

Fingers tugged at his shoulder and someone said, "Do you want to buy her?"

Buy her? Glancing down, Dradin found himself confronted by a singular man. This singular soul looked to be, it must be said, almost one muscle, a squat man with a low center of gravity, and yet a source of levity despite this: in short, a dwarf. How could one miss him? He wore a jacket and vest red as a freshly slaughtered carcass and claribel pleated trousers dark as crusted blood and shoes tipped with steel. A permanent grin molded the sides of his mouth so rigidly that, on second glance, Dradin wondered if it might not be a grimace. Melon bald, the dwarf was tattooed from head to foot.

The tattoo—which first appeared to be a birthmark or fungal growth—rendered Dradin speechless so that the dwarf said to him not once, but twice, "Are you all right, sir?"

While Dradin just stared, gap-jawed like a young jackdaw with naive fluff for wing feathers. For the dwarf had, tattooed from a point on the top of his head, and extending downward, a precise and detailed map of the River Moth, complete with the names of cities etched in black against the red dots that represented them. The river flowed a dark blue-green, thickening and thinning in places, dribbling up over the dwarf's left eyelid, skirting the midnight black of the eye itself, and down past taut lines of nose and mouth, curving over the generous chin and, like an exotic snake act, disappearing into the dwarf's vest and chest hair. A map of the lands beyond spread out from the River Moth. The northern cities of Dradin's youth—Belezar, Stockton, and Morrow (the last where his father still lived)—were clustered upon the dwarf's brow and there, upon the lower neck, almost the back, if one were to niggle, lay the jungles of Dradin's last year: a solid wall of green drawn with a jeweler's precision, the only hint of civilization a few smudges of red that denoted church enclaves. Dradin could have traced the line that marked his own dismal travels. He grinned, and he had to stop himself from putting out a hand to touch the dwarf's head for it had occurred to him that the dwarf's body served as a time line. Did it not show Dradin's birthplace and early years in the north as well as his slow descent into the south, the jungles, and now, more southern still, Ambergris? Could he not, if he were to see the entire tattoo, trace his descent farther south, to the seas into which flowed the River Moth? Could he not chart his future, as it were? He would have laughed if not aware of the impropriety of doing so.

"Incredible," Dradin said.

"Incredible," echoed the dwarf, and smiled, revealing large yellowed teeth scattered between the gaping black of absent incisors and molars. "My father, Alberich, did it for me when I stopped growing. I was to be part of his show—he was a riverboat pilot for tourists—and thus he traced upon my skin the course he plotted for them. It hurt like a thousand devils curling hooks into my flesh, but now I am, indeed, incredible. Do you wish to buy her? My name is Dvorak Nibelung." From within this storm of information, the dwarf extended a blunt, whorled hand that, when Dradin took it, was cool to the touch, and very rough.

"My name is Dradin."

"Dradin," Dvorak said. "Dradin. I say again, do you wish to buy her?"

"Buy who?"

"The woman in the window."

Dradin frowned. "No, of course I don't wish to buy her."

Dvorak looked up at him with black, watery eyes. Dradin could smell the strong musk of river water and silt on the dwarf, mixed with the sharp tang of an addictive, *ghittlnut*.

Dvorak said, "Must I tell you that she is only an image in a window? She is no more real to you. Seeing her, you fall in love. But, if you desire, I can find you a woman who looks like her. She will do anything for money. Would you like such a woman?"

"No," Dradin said, and would have turned away if there had been room in the swirl of people to do so without appearing rude. Dvorak's hand found his arm again.

"If you do not wish to buy her, what do you wish to do with her?" Dvorak's voice was flat with miscomprehension.

"I wish to . . . I wish to woo her. I need to give her this book." And, then, if only to be rid of him, Dradin said, "Would you take this book to her and say that it comes from an admirer who wishes her to read it?"

To Dradin's surprise, Dvorak began to make huffing sounds, soft but then louder, until the River Moth changed course across the whorls of his face and something fastened to the inside of his jacket clicked together with a hundred deadly shivers.

Dradin's face turned scarlet.

"I suppose I will have to find someone else."

He took from his pocket two burnished gold coins engraved with the face of Trillian the Great Banker, and prepared to turn sharply on his heel.

Dvorak sobered and tugged yet a third time on his arm. "No, no, sir. Forgive me. Forgive me if I've offended, if I've made you angry," and the hand pulled at the gift-wrapped book in the crook of Dradin's shoulder. "I will take the book to the woman in the window. It is no great chore, for I already trade with Hoegbotton & Sons, see," and he pulled open the left side of his jacket to reveal five rows of cutlery: serrated and double-edged, made of whalebone and of steel, hilted in engraved wood and thick leather. "See," he said again. "I peddle knives for them outside their offices. I know this building," and he pointed at the solid brick. "Please?"

Dradin, painfully aware of the dwarf's claustrophobic closeness, the reek of him, would have said no, would have turned and said not only no, but *How dare you touch a man of God?*, but then what? He must make acquaintance with one or another of these people, pull some ruffian off the dusty sidewalk, for he could not do the deed himself. He knew this in the way his knees shook the closer he came to Hoegbotton & Sons, the way his words rattled around his mouth, came out mumbled and masticated into disconnected syllables.

Dradin shook Dvorak's hand off the book. "Yes, yes, you may give her the book." He placed the book in Dvorak's arms. "But hurry about it." A sense of relief lifted the weight of heat from his shoulders. He dropped the coins into a pocket of Dvorak's jacket. "Go on," and he waved a hand.

"Thank you, sir," Dvorak said. "But, should you not meet with me again, to-morrow, at the same hour, so you may know her thoughts? So you may gift her a second time, should you desire?"

"Shouldn't I wait to see her now?"

Dvorak shook his head. "No. Where is the mystery, the romance? Trust me: better that you disappear into the crowds. Better indeed. Then she will wonder at your appearance, your bearing, and have only the riddle of the gift to guide her. You see?"

"No, I don't. I don't see at all. I must be confident. I must allow her to—"

"You are right—you do not see at all. Sir, are you or are you not a priest?"

"Yes, but—"

"You do not think it best to delay her knowing of this until the right moment? You do not think she will find it odd a priest should woo her? Sir, you wear the clothes of a missionary, but she is no ordinary convert."

And now Dradin did see. And wondered why he had not seen before. He must lead her gently into the particulars of his occupation. He must not boldly announce it for fear of scaring her off.

"You are right," Dradin said. "You are right, of course."

Dvorak patted his arm. "Trust me, sir."

"Tomorrow then."

"Tomorrow, and bring more coin, for I cannot live on goodwill alone."

"Of course," Dradin said.

Dvorak bowed, turned, walked up to the door of Hoegbotton & Sons, and—quick and smooth and graceful—disappeared inside.

Dradin looked up at his love, wondering if he had made a mistake. Her lips still called to him and the entire sky seemed concentrated in her eyes, but he followed the dwarf's advice and, lighthearted, disappeared into the crowds.

2

Dradin, happier than he had been since dropping the fever at the Sisters of Mercy Hospital, some five hundred miles away and three months in the past, sauntered down Albumuth, breathing in the smell of catfish simmering on open skillets, the tangy broth of codger soup, the sweet regret of overripe melons, pomegranates, and leechee fruit offered for sale. Stomach grumbling, he stopped long enough to buy a skewer of beef and onions and eat it noisily, afterward wiping his hands on the back of his pants. He leaned against a lamppost next to a sidewalk barber and—aware of the sour effluvium from the shampoos, standing clear of the trickle of water that crept into the gutter—pulled out the map he had bought at Borges Bookstore. It was cheaply printed on butcher paper, many of the street names drawn by hand. Colorless, it compared unfavorably with Dvorak's tattoo, but it was accurate and he easily found the intersection of streets that marked his hostel. Beyond the hostel lay the valley of the city proper; north of it stood the religious district and his old teacher, Cadimon Signal. He could make his way to the hostel via one of two routes. The first would take him through an old factory district, no doubt littered with the corpses of rusted out motored vehicles and railroad cars, railroad tracks cut up and curving into the air with a profound sense of futility. In his childhood in the city of Morrow, Dradin, along with his long-lost friend Anthony Toliver (Tolive the Olive, he had been called, because of his fondness for the olive fruit or its oil), had played in just such a district, and it did not fit his temperament. He remembered how their play had been made somber by the sight of the trains, their great, dull heads upended, some staring glassily skyward while others drank in the cool, dark earth beneath. He was in no mood for such a death of metal, not with his heartbeat slowing and rushing, his manner at once calm and hyperactive.

No, he would take the second route—through the oldest part of the city, over one thousand years old, so old as to have lost any recollection of itself, its stones worn smooth and memory-less by the years. Perhaps such a route would settle him, allow him this bursting joy in his heart and yet not make his head spin quite so much.

Dradin moved on—ignoring an old man defecating on the sidewalk (trousers down around his ankles) and neatly sidestepping an Occidental woman around whom flopped live carp as she, armed with a club, methodically beat at their heads until a spackle of yellow brains glistened on the cobblestones.

After a few minutes of walking, the wall-to-wall buildings fell away, taking the smoke and dust and babble of voices with them. The world became a silent place except for the scuff of Dradin's shoes on the cobblestones and the occasional muttering chug-chuff of a motored vehicle, patched up and trundling along, like as not burning more oil than fuel. Dradin ignored the smell of fumes, the angry retort of tailpipes. He saw only the face of the woman from the window—in the pattern of lichen on a gray-stained wall, in the swirl of leaves gathered in a gutter.

The oldest avenues, thoroughfares grandfatherly when the Court of the Mourning Dog had been young and the Days of the Burning Sun had yet to scorch the land, lay a-drowning in a thick soup of honeysuckle, passion fruit, and bougainvillea, scorned by bee and hornet. Such streets had the lightest of traffic: old men on an after-lunch constitutional; a private tutor leading two children dressed in Sunday clothes, all polished shoes and handkerchief-and-spit-cleaned faces.

The buildings Dradin passed were made of a stern, impervious gray stone and separated by fountains and courtyards. Weeds and ivy smothered the sides of these stodgy, baroque halls, their windows broken as if the press of vines inward had smashed the glass. Morning glories, four-o'clocks, and yet more ivy-choked moldering stone street markers, trailed from rusted balconies, sprouted from pavement cracks, and stitched themselves into fences or gates scoured with old fire burns. Whom such buildings had housed, or what business had been conducted within, Dradin could only guess. They had, in their height and solidity, an atmosphere of states-craft about them, bureaucratic in their flourishes and busts, gargoyles and stout columns. But a bureaucracy lost to time: sword-wielding statues on horseback overgrown with lichen, the features of faces eaten away by rot deep in the stone; a fountain split down the center by the muscular roots of an oak. There was such a staggering sense of lawlessness in the silence amid the creepers.

Certainly the jungle had never concealed such a cornucopia of assorted fungi, for between patches of stone burned black Dradin now espied rich clusters of mushrooms in as many colors as there were beggars on Albumuth Boulevard: emerald, magenta, ruby, sapphire, plain brown, royal purple, corpse white. They ranged in size from a thimble to an obese eunuch's belly.

Such a playful and random dotting delighted Dradin so much that he began to follow the spray of mushrooms.

Their trail led him to a narrow avenue blocked in by ten-foot-high gray stone walls, and he was soon struck by the notion that he traveled down the throat of a serpent. The mushrooms proliferated, until they not only grew in the cobblestone cracks, but also from the walls, speckling the gray with their bright hoods and stems.

The sun dimmed between clouds. A wind came up, brisk on Dradin's face. Trees loured ever closer, darkening the sky. The street continued to narrow until it was wide enough for two men, then one man, and finally so narrow—narrow as any narthex Dradin had ever encountered—that he moved sideways crab-like, and still tore a button.

Eventually, the street widened again. He stumbled out into the open space— only to be met by a *crack!* loud as the severing of a spine, a sound that shot up, over, and past him. He cried out and flinched, one arm held up to ward off a blow, as a sea of wings thrashed toward the sky.

He slowly brought his arm down. Pigeons. A flock of pigeons. Only pigeons.

Ahead, when the flock had cleared the trees, Dradin saw, along the street's right-hand side, the rotting columbary from which the birds had flown. Its many covey holes had the bottomless gaze of the blind. The stink of pigeon droppings made his stomach queasy. Beside the columbary, separated by an alleyway, stood a columbarium, also rotting and deserted, so that urns of ashes teetered on the edge of a windowsill, while below the smashed window two urns lay cracked on the cobblestones, their black ash spilling out.

A columbary and a columbarium! Side by side, no less, like old and familiar friends, joined in decay.

Much as the sight intrigued him, the alley between the columbary and columbarium fascinated Dradin more, for the mushrooms that had crowded the crevices of the street and dotted the walls like the pox now proliferated beyond all imagining, the cobblestones thick with them in a hundred shades and hues. Down the right-hand side of the alley, ten alcoves had been carved, complete with iron gates, a hundred hardened cherubim and devils alike caught in the metalwork. The gate of the nearest alcove stood open and from within spilled lichen, creepers, and mushroom dwellers, their red flags droopy. Surrounded by the vines, the mushroom dwellers resembled human headstones or dreamy, drowning swimmers in a green sea.

Beside Dradin—and he jumped back as he realized his mistake—lay a mushroom dweller that he had thought was a mushroom the size of a small child. It mewled and writhed in half-awakened slumber as Dradin looked at it with a mixture of fascination and distaste. Stranger to Ambergris that he was, still Dradin knew of the mushroom dwellers, for, as Cadimon Signal had taught him in Morrow, "they form the most outlandish of all known cults," although little else had been forthcoming from Cadimon's dried and withered lips.

Mushroom dwellers smelled of old, rotted barns and spoiled milk and vegetables mixed with the moistness of dark crevices and the dryness of day-dead dung beetles. Some folk said they whispered and plotted among themselves in a secret language so old that no one else, even in the far, far Occident, spoke it. Others said they came from the subterranean caves and tunnels below Ambergris, that they were escaped convicts who had gathered in the darkness and made their own singular religion and purpose, that they shunned the light because they were blind from their many years underground. And yet others, the poor and the undereducated, said that newts, golliwogs, slugs, and salamanders followed in their wake by land, while above bats, nighthawks, and whip-poor-wills flew, feasting on the insects that crawled around mushroom and mushroom dweller alike.

Mushroom dwellers slept on the streets by day, but came out at night to harvest the fungus that had grown in the cracks and shadows of graveyards during sunlit hours. Wherever they slept, they planted the red flags of warning, and woe to the man who, as Dradin had, disturbed their wet and lugubrious slumber. Sailors on the docks had told Dradin that the mushroom dwellers were known to rob graves for compost, or even murder tourists and use the flesh for their midnight crop. If no one questioned or policed them, it was because during the night they tended to the garbage and carcasses that littered Ambergris. By dawn the streets had been picked clean and lay shining and innocent under the sun.

Fifty mushroom dwellers now spilled out from the alcove gateway, macabre in their very peacefulness and the even hum-thrum of their breath: stunted in growth, wrapped in robes the pale gray-green of a frog's underbelly, their heads hidden by wide-brimmed gray felt hats that, like the hooded tops of their name-sakes, covered them to the neck. Their necks were the only exposed part of them— incredibly long, pale necks; at rest, they did indeed resemble mushrooms.

And yet, to Dradin's eye, they were disturbingly human rather than inhuman—a separate race, developing side by side, silent, invisible, chained to ritual—and the sight of them, on the same day that he had fallen so irrevocably in love, unnerved Dradin. He had already felt death upon him in the jungles and had known no fear, only pain, but here fear burrowed deep into his bones. Fear of death. Fear of the unknown. Fear of knowing death before he drank deeply of love. Morbidity and sullen curiosity mixed with dreams of isolation and desolation. All those obses-sions of which the religious institute had supposedly cured him.

Positioned as he was, at the mouth of the alley, Dradin felt as though he were spying on a secret, forbidden world. Did they dream of giant mushrooms, gray caps agleam with the dark light of a midnight sun? Did they dream of a world lit only by the phosphorescent splendor of their charges?

Dradin watched them for a moment longer and then, his pace considerably faster, made his way past the alley mouth.

Eventually, under the cloud-darkened eye of the sun, the maze of alleys gave way to wide, open-ended streets traversed by carpenters, clerks, blacksmiths, and broad-sheet vendors, and he soon came upon the depressing but cheap Holander-Barth Hostel. (In another, richer, time he never would have considered staying there.) He had seen all too many such establishments in the jungles: great mansions rotted down to their foundations, occupied by the last inbred descendants of men and women who had thought the jungle could be conquered with machete and fire, only to find that the jungle had conquered them; where yesterday they had hacked down a hundred vines a thousand now writhed and interlocked in a fecundity of life. Dradin could not even be sure that the Sisters of Mercy Hospital still stood, untouched by such natural forces.

The Holander-Barth Hostel, once white, now dull gray, was a salute to pretentiousness, the dolorous inlaid marble columns crumbling from the inside out and laundry spread across ornately filigreed balconies black with decay. Perhaps once, jaded aristocrats had owned it, but now tubercular men walked its halls, hacking their lungs out while fishing in torn pockets for cigars or cigarettes. The majority were soldiers from long-forgotten campaigns who had used their pensions to secure lodging, blissfully ignorant (or ignoring) the cracked fixtures, curled wallpaper, communal showers and toilets. But, as the hansom driver had remarked on the way in, "It is the cheapest" and had added, "It is also far away from the Festival." Luckily, the proprietors respected a man of the cloth, no matter how weathered, and Dradin had managed to rent one of two second-story rooms with a private bath.

Heart pounding now not from fear, but rather from desire, Dradin dashed up the warped veranda—past the elderly pensioners, who bowed their heads or made confused signs of Truffidian ritual—up the spiral staircase, came to his door, fumbled with the key, and once inside, fell on the bed with a thump that made the springs groan, the book thrown down beside him. The cover felt velvety and smooth to his touch. It felt like her skin must feel, he thought, and promptly fell asleep, a smile on his lips, for it was still near midday and the heat had drained his strength.

3

Mouth dry, hair tousled, and chin scratchy with stubble, Dradin woke to a pinched nerve in his back that made him moan and turn over and over on the bed, his perspective notably skewed, though not this time by the woman. Still, he could tell that the sun had plummeted beneath the horizon and where the sky had been gray with clouds, it now ranged from black to a bruised purple, the moon mottled, the light measured out in rough dollops. Dradin yawned and scrunched his shoulders together to cure the pinchedness, then rose and walked to the tall but slender windows. He unhooked the latch and pulled the twin panes open to let in the smell of approaching rain, mixed with the sweet stink of garbage and honeysuckle.

The window looked down on the city proper, which lay inside the cupped hands of a valley veined with tributaries of the Moth. It was there that ordinary people slept and dreamt not of jungles and humidity and the lust that fed and starved men's hearts, but of quiet walks under the stars and milk-fat kittens and the gentle hum of wind on wooden porches. They raised families and doubtless missionaries never moved among their ranks, but only full-fledged priests, for they were already converted to a faith. Indeed, they—and people like them in other cities—paid their tithes and, in return, had emissaries sent out into the wilderness to spread the word, such emissaries nothing more than the physical form of their own hopes, wishes, fears; their desires made flesh. Dradin found the idea a sad one, sadder still, in a way he hesitated to define, that were it not for his chosen vocation, he could have had such a life: settling down into a daily rhythm that did not include the throbbing of the jungles, twinned to the beating of his heart. Anthony Toliver had chosen such a life, abandoning the clergy soon after graduation from the religious institute.

Around the valley lay the fringe, like a roughly circular smudge of wine and vulgar lipstick. The Holander-Barth Hostel marked the dividing line between the valley and fringe, just as the beginning of Albumuth Boulevard marked the end of the docks and the beginning of the fringe. It was here, not truly at a city's core, that Dradin had always been most comfortable, even back in his religious institute days, when he had been more severe on himself than the most pious monks who taught him.

On the fringe, jesters pricked and pranced, jugglers plied their trade with babies and knives (mixing the two as casually as one might mix apples and oranges). The life's blood swelled at a more exhilarating pace, a pace that quickened beyond the fringe, where the doughty sailors of the River Moth sailed on barges, dhows, frigates, and the rare steamer: anything that could float and hold a man without sinking into the silt.

Beyond the river lay the jungles, where the pace quickened into madness. The jungles hid creatures that died after a single day, their lives condensed beyond comprehension, so that Dradin, in observation of their own swift mortality, had sensed his body dying, hour by hour, minute by minute, a feeling that had not left him even when he lay down with the sweaty woman priest.

Dradin let the breeze from the window brush against him, cooling him, then returned to the bed, circling around it to the bed lamp, turned the switch, and lo!, a brassy light to read by. He plopped down on the bed, legs akimbo, and opened the book to the first page. Thus began the fantasy: that in some other room, some other house—perhaps even in the valley below—the woman from the window lay in her own bed by some dim light and turned these same pages, read these same words. The touch of the pages to his fingers was erotic; they felt damp and charged his limbs with the short, sharp shock of a ceremonial cup of liqueur. He became hard, but resisted the urge to touch himself. Ah, sweet agony! Nothing in his life had ever felt half so good, half so tortuous. Nothing in the bravely savage world beyond the Moth could compare: not the entwining snake dances of the Magpie Women of the Frangipani Veldt, nor the single, aching cry of a Zinfendel maid as she jumped headfirst into the roar of a waterfall. Not even the sweaty woman priest before the fever struck, her panting moans during their awkward love play more a testimonial to the humidity and ever-present mosquitoes than any skill on his part.

Dradin looked around his room. How bare it was for all that he had lived some thirty years. There was his red-handled machete, balanced against the edge of the dresser drawers, and his knapsack, which contained powders and liquids to cure a hundred jungle diseases, and his orange-scuffed boots beside that, and his coins on the table, the gold almost crimson in the light, but what else? Just his suitcase with two changes of clothes, his yellowing, torn diploma from the Morrow Institute of Religiosity, and daguerreotypes of his mother and father, them in their short-lived youth, Dad not yet a red-faced, broken-veined lout of an academic, Mom's eyes not yet squinty with surrounding wrinkles and sharp as bloodied shards of glass.

What did the woman's room look like? No doubt it too was briskly clean, but not bare, oh no. It would have a bed with white mosquito netting and a place for a glass of water, and her favorite books in a row beside the bed, and beyond that a white and silver mantel and mirror, and below that, her dresser drawers, filled to bursting with frilly night things and frilly day things, and filthily frilly twilight things as well. Powders and lotions for her skin, to keep it beyond the pale. Knitting needles and wool, or other less feminine tools for hobbies. Perhaps she kept a vanilla kitten close by, to play with the balls of wool. If she lived at home, this might be the extent of her world, but if she lived alone, then Dradin had three, four, other rooms to fill with her loves and hates. Did she enjoy small talk and other chatter? Did she dance? Did she go to social events? What might she be thinking as she read the book, on the first page of which was written:

THE REFRACTION OF LIGHT IN A PRISON
(Being an Account of the Truffidian Monks Held in the
Dungeons of the Kalif, for They Have Not Given Up
Sanity, or Hope)
BY:
Brother Peek
Brother Prowcosh
Brother Witamoor
Brother Sirin
Brother Grae
(and, held unfortunately in separate quarters,
communicating to us purely by the force of her
will, Sister Stalker)

And, on the next page:

BEING CHAPTER ONE:
THE MYSTICAL PASSIONS

The most mystical of all passions are those practiced by the water people of the Lower Moth, for though they remain celibate and spend most of their lives in the water, they attain a oneness with their mates that bedevils those lesser of us who equate love with intercourse. Surely, their women would never become the objects of their desire, for then these women would lose an intrinsic eroticism.

Dradin read on impatiently, his hands sweaty, his throat dry, but, no, no, he would not rise to drink water from the sink, nor release his tension, but must burn, as his love must burn, reading the self-same words. For now he was in truth a missionary, converting himself to the cause of love, and he could not stop.

Outside, along the lip of the valley, lights began to blink and waver in phosphorescent reds, greens, blues, and yellows, and Dradin realized that preparations for the Festival of the Freshwater Squid must be under way. On the morrow night, Albumuth Boulevard would be cleared for a parade that would overflow onto the adjacent streets and then the entire city. Along the avenues, candles wrapped in boxes of crepe paper would appear, so that the light would be like the dancing of the squid, great and small, upon the midnight salt water where it met the mouth of the Moth. A celebration of the spawning season, when males battled mightily for females of the species and the fisherfolk of the docks would set out for a month's trawling of the lusting grounds, hoping to bring back enough meat to last until winter.

If only he could be with her on the morrow night. Among the sights the hansom driver had pointed out on the way into Ambergris was a tavern, the Drunken Boat, decked out with the finest in cutlery and clientele, and featuring, for the Festival only, the caterwauling of a band called the Ravens. To dance with her, her hands interwoven with his, the scent of her body on his, would make up for all that had happened in the jungle and the humiliations since: the hunt for ever more miserable jobs, accompanied by a general lightening of coin in his pockets.

The clocks struck the insomniac hours after midnight and, below the window, Dradin heard the moist scuttle of mushroom dwellers as they gathered offal and refuse. Rain followed the striking of the clocks, falling softly, as light in touch as Dradin's hand upon *The Refraction of Light in a Prison*. The smell of rain, fresh and sharp, came from the window.

Drawn by that smell, Dradin put the book aside and rose to the window, watched the rain as it caught the faint light, the drops like a school of tiny silver-scaled fish, here and gone, back a moment later. A vein of lightning, a boom of thunder, and the rain came faster and harder.

Many times Dradin had stared through the rain-splashed windows of the old gray house on the hill from his childhood in Morrow (the house with the closed shutters like eyes stitched shut) while relatives came up the gray, coiled road: the headlights of expensive motored vehicles bright in the sheen of rain. They resembled a small army of hunched black, white, and red beetles, like the ones in his father's insect books, creeping up the hill. Below them, where it was not fogged over, the rest of Morrow: industrious, built of stone and wood, feeding off the River Moth.

From one particular window in the study, Dradin could enjoy a double image: inside, at the end of a row of three open doors—library, living room, dining room—his enormous opera singer of a mother (tall and big-boned) stuffed into the kitchen. No maid helped her, for they lived, the three of them, alone on the hill, and so she would be delicately placing mincemeats on plates, cookies on trays, splashing lemonade and punch into glasses, trying very hard to keep her hands clean and her red dress of frills and lace unstained. She would sing to herself as she worked, in an unrestrained and husky voice (it seemed she never spoke to Dradin, but only sang) so that he could hear, conducted through the various pipes, air ducts, and passageways, the words of Voss Bender's greatest opera:

> Come to me in the spring
> When the rains fall hard
> For you are sweet as pollen,
> Sweet as fresh honeycomb.
>
> When the hard brown branches
> Of the oak sprout green leaves,
> In the season of love, come to me.

Into the oven would go the annual pheasant, while outside the window Dradin could see his father, thin and meticulous in tuxedo and tails, picking his way through the puddles in the front drive, carrying a big, ragged black umbrella. Dad would *walk precisely*, as if by stepping first *here* and then *there*, he might escape the rain drops, slip between them because he knew the umbrella would do no good, riddled as it was with rips and moth holes. But, oh, what a pantomime for the guests!, while Dradin laughed and his mother sang. Apologies for the rain, the puddles, the tattered appearance of the umbrella. In later years, Dad's greetings became loutish, slurred by drink and age until they were no longer generous. But back then he would unfold his limbs like a good-natured mantis and with quick movements of his hands switch the umbrella from left to right as he gestured his apologies. All the while, the guests would be half-in, half-out of the car—Aunt Sophie and Uncle Ken, perhaps—trying hard to be polite, but meanwhile drenched to the skin. Inside, Mom would have time to steel herself, ready a greeting smile by the front door, and—one doomful eye on the soon-to-be-burnt pheasant—call for Dradin.

In a much more raging rain, Dradin had first been touched by a force akin to the spiritual. It occurred on a similarly dreary day of visiting relatives, Dradin only nine and trapped: trapped by dry pecks on the cheek; trapped by the smell of damp, sweaty bodies brought close together; trapped by the dry burn of cigars and by the alarming stares of the elderly men, eyebrows inert white slugs, mustaches wriggly, eyes enormous and watery through glasses or monocles. Trapped, too, by the ladies, even worse at that advanced age, their cavernous grouper mouths intent on devouring him whole into their bellies.

Dradin had begged his mother to invite Anthony Toliver and, against his father's wishes, she had said yes. Anthony, a fearless follower, was a wiry boy with sallow skin and dark eyes. They had met in public school, odd fellows bonded together by the simple fact that both had been beaten up by the school bully, Roger Gimmell.

As soon as Tony arrived, Dradin convinced him to escape the party. Off they snuck, through a parlor door into a backyard bounded only at the horizon by a tangled wilderness of trees. Water pelted them, splattered on shirts, and pummeled flesh, so that Dradin's ears rang with the force of it and dull aches woke him the morning after. Grass was swept away, dirt dissolving into mud.

Tony fell almost immediately and, scrabbling at Dradin, made him fall too, into the wet, grasping at weeds for support. Tony laughed at the surprised look on Dradin's face. Dradin laughed at the mud clogging Tony's left ear. Splash! Slosh! Mud in the boots, mud in the trousers, mud flecking their hair, mud coating their faces.

They grappled and giggled. The rain fell so hard it stung. It bit into their clothes, cut into the tops of their heads, attacked their eyes so they could barely open them. In the middle of the mud fight they stopped battling each other and started battling the rain. They scrambled to their feet, no longer playing, then lost touch with each other, Tony's hand slipping from Dradin's, so that Tony said only, "Come on!" and ran toward the house, never looking back at Dradin, who stood still as a frightened rabbit, utterly alone in the universe.

As Dradin stands alone in the sheets of rain, staring at the heavens that have opened up and sent the rains down, he begins to shake. The rain, like a hand on his shoulders, presses him down; the electric sensation of water on his skin rinses away mud and bits of grass, leaves him cold and sodden. He shudders convulsively, sensing the prickle of an immensity up in the sky, staring down at him. He knows from the rush and rage of blood, the magnified beat of his heart, that nothing this *alive*, this out of control, can be random.

Dradin closes his eyes and a thousand colors, a thousand images, explode inside his mind, one for each drop of rain. A rain of shooting stars, and from this conflagration the universe opening up before him. For an instant, Dradin can sense every throbbing artery and arrhythmic heart in the city below him—every darting quicksilver thought of hope, of pain, of hatred, of love. A hundred thousand sorrows and a hundred thousand joys ascending to him.

The babble of sensation so overwhelms him that he can hardly breathe, cannot feel his body except as a hollow receptacle. Then the sensations fade until, closer at hand, he feels the pinprick lives of mice in the nearby glades, the deer like graceful shadows, the foxes clever in their burrows, the ladybugs hidden on the undersides of leaves, and then nothing, and when it is gone, he says, shoulders slumped, but still on his feet, *Is this God?*

When Dradin—a husk now, his hearing deafened by the rain, his bones cleansed by it—turned back toward the house; when he finally faced the house with its shuttered windows, as common sense dictated he should, the light from within fairly burst to be let out. And Dradin saw (as he stood by the window in the hostel) not Tony, who was safely inside, but his mother. His mother. The later memory fused to the earlier seamlessly, as if they had happened together, one, of a piece. That he had turned and she was there, already leveling a blank stare toward him; that, simple as breath, the rain brought redemption and madness crashing down on both their heads, the time span no obstacle and of no importance.

. . . he turned and there was his mother, on her knees in the mud, in her red dress spattered brown. She scooped the mud up with her hands, regarded it, and began to eat, so ravenously that she bit into her little finger. The eyes on the face of stone—the face as blank as the rain—looked up at him with the most curious expression, as if trapped as Dradin had felt trapped inside the house, trapped and asking Dradin . . . to do something. And him, even then, already fourteen, not knowing what to do, calling for Dad, calling for a doctor, while the mud smudged the edges of her mouth and, unconcerned, she ate more and stared at him after each bite, until he cried and came to her and hugged her and tried to make her stop, though nothing in the world could make her stop, or make him stop trying. What unnerved him more than anything, more than the mud in her mouth, was the complete silence that surrounded her, for he had come to define her by her voice, and this she did not use, even to ask for help.

Dradin again heard the mushroom dwellers below and closed the window abruptly. He sat back on the bed. He wanted to read more of the book, except that now his thoughts floated, rose and fell like waves and, before he realized it, before he could stop it, he was, as it were, not quite dead, but merely asleep.

✻

In the morning, Dradin rose rested and spry, his body almost certainly recovered from the jungle fever. For months he had risen to the ache of sore muscles and bruised internal organs; now he had only a fever of a different sort. Every time Dradin glanced at *The Refraction of Light in a Prison*—as he washed his face in the green-tinged basin, as he dressed, not looking at his pant legs so it took him several tries to put them on—he thought of her. What piece of glitter might catch her eye for him? For now, surely, if she had read the book, was the time to appraise her worth to him, to let her know that serious is as serious does. In just such a manner had his dad wooed his mom, Dad a rake-thin but puff-bellied proud graduate of Morrow's University of Arts & Facts (which certainly defined Dad). She, known by the maiden name of Barsombly, the famous singer with a voice like a pit bull—almost baritone, but husky enough, Dradin admitted, to conceal a sultry sexuality. He could not remember when he had not either felt the *thrulling* vibrations of his mother's voice or heard the voice itself. Or a time when he had not watched as she applied raucous perfumes and powders to herself, after putting on the low-bodiced, gold-satin costumes that rounded her taut bulk like an impenetrable wall. He could remember her taking him into theaters and music halls through the back entrance, bepuddled and muddened, and as some helpful squire would escort him sodden to his seat, so too would she be escorted atop the stage, so that as Dradin sat, the curtain rose, simultaneous with the applause from the audience—an ovation like the crashing of waves against rock.

Then she would sing, and he would imagine the thrull of her against him, and marvel at the power of her voice, the depths and hollows of it, the way it matched the flow and melody of the orchestra only to diverge, coursing like a secret and perilous undertow, the vibration growing and growing until there was no longer any music at all, just the voice devouring the music.

Dad did not go to any of her performances and sometimes Dradin thought she sang so loud, so full of rage, that Dad might still hear her faintly, him up late reading in the study of the old house on the hill with the shutters like eyes stitched shut.

His mother would have been proud of his attempts to woo, but, alas, she had been gagged and trussed for her own good and traveled now with the Bedlam Rovers, a cruising troupe of petty psychiatrists—sailing down the Moth on a glorified houseboat under the subtitle of "Boat-Bound Psychiatrists: Miracle Workers of the Mind"—to whom, finally, Dad had given over his dearest, the spiced fig of his heart, Dradin's mother—for a fee, of course; and didn't it, Dad had raged and blustered, come to the same thing? In a rest home or asylum; either situated in one place, or on the move. It was not so bad, he would say, slumping down in a damp green chair, waving his amber bottle of Smashing Todd's Finest; after all, the sights she would see, the places she would experience, and all under the wise and benevolent care of trained psychiatrists who *paid* to take that care. Surely, his father would finish with a belch or burp, there is no better arrangement.

Youngish Dradin, still smarting from the ghost of the strap of a half an hour past, dared not argue, but thought often: yes, but all such locutions of thought are reliable and reliant upon one simple supposition—to whit, that she be insane. What if not insane but sane "south by southwest" as the great Voss Bender said? What if, inside the graying but leopardesque head, the burgeoning frame, lay a wide realm of sanity, with only the outer shell susceptible to hallucinations, incantations, and inappropriate metaphors? What then? To be yanked about thus, like an animal on a chain, could this be stood by a sane individual? Might such parading and humiliation lead a person to the very insanity hitherto avoided?

And, worse thought still, that his father had driven her to it with his cruel, carefully planned indifference.

But Dradin—remembering the awful silence of that day in the rain when Mom had stuffed her mouth full of mud—refused to dwell on it. He must find a present for his darling, this accomplished by rummaging through his pack and coming up with a necklace, the centerpiece an uncut emerald. It had been given to him by a tribal chieftain as a bribe to go away ("There is only One God," Dradin had said. "What's his name?" the chieftain asked. "God," replied Dradin. "How bloody boring," the chieftain said. "Please go away.") and he had taken it initially as a donation to the church, although he had meant to give it to the spiced fig of his heart, the sweaty woman priest, only to have the fever overtake him first. As he held the necklace in his hand, he recognized the exceptional workmanship of the blue-and-green beads. If he were to sell it, he might pay the rent at the hostel for another week. But, more attractive, if he gave it to his love, she would understand the seriousness of his heart's desire.

With uncharacteristic grace and a touch of inspired lunacy, Dradin tore the first page from *The Refraction of Light in a Prison* and wrote his name below the name of the last monk, like so:

> Brother Dradin Kashmir—
> Not truly a brother, but devout
> in his love for you alone

Dradin looked over his penmanship with satisfaction. There. It was done. It could not be undone.

4

Over breakfast, his sparse needs tended to by a gaunt waiter who looked like a malaria victim, Dradin examined his dull gray map. Toast without jam for him, nothing richer like sausages frying in their own fat, or bacon with white strips of lard. The jungle climate had, from the start, made his bowels and bladder loosen up and pour forth their bile like the sludge of rain in the most deadly of monsoon seasons. Dradin had avoided rich foods ever since, saying no to such jungle delicacies as fried grasshopper, boiled pig, and a local favorite that baked huge black slugs into their shells.

From dirty gray table-clothed tables on either side, war veterans coughed and harrumphed, their bloodshot eyes perked into semi-awareness by the sight of Dradin's map. Treasure? War on two fronts? Mad, drunken charges into the eye-teeth of the enemy? No doubt. Dradin knew their type, for his father was the same, if with an academic bent. The map would be a mystery of the mind to his father.

Ignoring their stares, Dradin found the Religious Quarter on the map, traced over it with his index finger. It resembled a bird's-eye view of a wheel with interconnecting spokes. No more a "quarter" than drawn. Cadimon Signal's mission stood near the center of the spokes, snuggled into a corner between the Church of the Fisherman and the Church of the Seven-Pointed Star. Even looking at it on the map made Dradin nervous. To meet his religious instructor after such a time. How would Cadimon have aged after seven years? Perversely, as far afield as Dradin had gone, Cadimon Signal had, in that time, come closer to the center, his home, for he had been born in Ambergris. At the religious institute Cadimon had extolled the city's virtues and, to be fair, its vices many times after lectures, in the common hall. His voice, hollow and echoing against the black marble archways, gave a raspy voice to the gossamer-thin cherubim carved into the swirl of white marble ceilings. Dradin had spent many nights along with Anthony Toliver listening to that voice, surrounded by thousands of religious texts on shelves gilded with gold leaf.

The question that most intrigued Dradin, that guided his thoughts and bedeviled his nights, was this: Would Cadimon Signal take pity on a former student and find a job for him? He hoped, of course, for a missionary position, but failing that a position which would not break his back or tie him in knots of bureaucratic red tape. Dad was an unlikely ally in this, for Dad had recommended Dradin to Cadimon and also recommended Cadimon to Dradin.

Before the fuzzy beginnings of Dradin's memory, Dad had, when still young and thin and mischievous, invited Cadimon over for tea and conversation, surrounded in Dad's study by books, books, and more books. Books on culture and civilization, religion and philosophy. They would, or so Dad told Dradin later, debate every topic imaginable, and some that were unimaginable, distasteful, or all too real until the hours struck midnight, one o'clock, two o'clock, and the lanterns dimmed to an ironic light, brackish and ill-suited to discussion. Surely this bond would be enough? Surely Cadimon would look at him and see the father in the son?

After breakfast, necklace and map in hand, Dradin wandered into the Religious Quarter, known by the common moniker of Pejora's Folly after Midan Pejora, the principal early architect, to whose credit or discredit could be placed the slanted walls, the jumble of Occidental and accidental, northern and southern, baroque and pure jungle, styles. Buildings battled for breath and space like centuries-slow soldiers in brick-to-brick combat. To look into the revolving spin of a kaleidoscope while heavily intoxicated, Dradin thought, would not be half so bad.

The rain from the night before took the form of sunlit droplets on plants, windowpanes, and cobblestones that wiped away the dull and dusty veneer of the city. Cats preened and tiny hop toads hopped while dead sparrows lay in furrows of water, beaten down by the storm's ferocity.

He snorted in disbelief as he observed followers of gentle Saint Solon the De-crepit placing the corpses of rain victims such as the sparrows into tiny wooden coffins for burial. In the jungle, deaths occurred in such thick numbers that one might walk a mile on the decayed carcasses, the white clean bones of deceased animals, and after a time even the most fastidious missionary gave the crunching sound not a second thought.

As he neared the mission, Dradin tried to calm himself by breathing in the acrid scent of votive candles burning from alcoves and crevices and doorways. He tried to imagine the richness of his father's conversations with Cadimon— the plethora of topics discussed, the righteous and pious denials and arguments. When his father mentioned those conversations, the man would shake off the weight of years, his voice light and his eyes moist with nostalgia. If only Cadimon remembered such encounters with similar enthusiasm.

The slap-slap of punished pilgrim feet against the stones of the street pulled him from his reverie. He stood to one side as twenty or thirty mendicants slapped on past, cleansing their sins through their calluses, on their way to one of a thou-sand shrines. In their calm but blank gaze, their slack mouths, Dradin saw the shadow of his mother's face, and he wondered what she had done while his father and Cadimon talked. Gone to sleep? Finished up the dishes? Sat in bed and lis-tened through the wall?

At last, Dradin found the Mission of Cadimon Signal. Set back from the street, the mission remained almost invisible among the skyward-straining cathe-drals surrounding it—remarkable only for the emptiness, the silence, and the swirl of swallows skimming through the air like weightless trapeze artists. The build-ing that housed the mission was an old tin-roofed warehouse reinforced with mortar and brick, opened up from the inside with ragged holes for skylights, which made Dradin wonder what they did when it rained. Let it rain on them, he supposed.

Christened with fragmented mosaics that depicted saints, monks, and mar-tyrs, the enormous doorway lay open to him. All around, acolytes frantically lifted sandbags and long pieces of timber, intent on barricading the entrance, but none challenged him as he walked up the steps and through the gateway; no one, in fact, spared him a second glance, so focused were they on their efforts.

Inside, Dradin went from sunlight to shadows, his footfalls hollow in the si-lence. A maze of paths wound through lush green Occidental-style gardens. The gardens centered around rock-lined pools cut through by the curving fins of corpulent carp. Next to the pools lay the eroded ruins of ancient, pagan temples, which had been reclaimed with gaily colored paper and splashes of red, green, blue, and white paint. Among the temples and gardens and pools, unobtrusive as lampposts, acolytes in gray habits toiled, removing dirt, planting herbs, and watering flowers. The air had a metallic color and flavor to it and Dradin heard the buzzing of bees at the many poppies, the soft *scull-skithing* as acolytes wielded their scythes against encroaching weeds.

The ragged, bluegrass-fringed trail led Dradin to a raised mound of dirt on which stood a catafalque, decorated with gold leaf and the legend SAINT PHILIP THE PHILANDERER printed along its side. In the shadow of the catafalque, amid the grass, a gardener dressed in dark green robes planted lilies he had set on a nearby bench. Atop the catafalque, halting Dradin in mid-step, stood Signal. He had changed since Dradin had last seen him, for he was bald and gaunt, with white tufts of hair sprouting from his ears. A studded dog collar circled his withered neck. But most disturbing, unless one wished to count a cask of wine that dangled from his left hand—no doubt shipped in by those reliable if questionable purveyors of spirits Hoegbotton & Sons, perhaps even held, caressed, by his love— *the man was stark staring naked!* The object of no one's desire bobbed like a length of flaccid purpling sausage, held in some semblance of erectitude by the man's right hand, the hand currently engaged in an up-and-down motion that brought great pleasure to its owner.

"Ccc-Cadimon Ssss-sigggnal?"

"Yes, who is it now?" said the gardener.

"I beg your pardon."

"I said," repeated the gardener with infinite patience, as if he really would not mind saying it a third, a fourth, or a fifth time, "I said 'Yes, who is it now?'"

"It's Dradin. Dradin Kashmir. Who are you?" Dradin kept one eye on the naked man atop the catafalque.

"I'm Cadimon Signal, of course," the gardener said, patiently pulling weeds, potting lilies. *Pull, pot, pull.* "Welcome to my mission, Dradin. It's been a long time." The small, green-robed man in front of Dradin had mannerisms and features indistinguishable from any wizened beggar on Albumuth Boulevard, but looking closer Dradin thought he could see a certain resemblance to the man he had known in Morrow. Perhaps.

"Who is he, then?" Dradin pointed to the naked man, who was now ejaculating into a rosebush.

"He's a Living Saint. A professional holy man. You should remember that from your theology classes. I know I must have taught you about Living Saints. Unless, of course, I switched that with a unit on Dead Martyrs. No other kind, really. That's a joke, Dradin. Have the decency to laugh."

The Living Saint, no longer aroused, but quite tired, lay down on the smooth cool stone of the catafalque and began to snore.

"But what's a Living Saint doing here? And naked?"

"I keep him here to discomfort my creditors who come calling. Lots of upkeep to this place. My, you have changed, haven't you?"

"What?"

"I thought I had gone deaf. I said you've changed. Please, ignore my Living Saint. As I said, he's for the creditors. Just trundle him out, have him spill his seed, and they don't come back."

"I've changed?"

"Yes, I've said that already." Cadimon stopped potting lilies and stood up, examined Dradin from crown to stirrups. "You've been to the jungle. A pity, really. You were a good student."

"I have come back from the jungle, if that's what you mean. I took fever."

"No doubt. You've changed most definitely. Here, hold a lily bulb for me." Cadimon crouched down once more. *Pull, pot, pull.*

"You seem . . . you seem somehow less imposing. But healthier."

"No, no. You've grown taller, that's all. What are you now that you are no longer a missionary?"

"No longer a missionary?" Dradin said, and felt as if he were drowning, and here they had only just started to talk.

"Yes. Or no. Lily please. Thank you. Blessed things require so much dirt. Good for the lungs exercise is. Good for the soul. How is your father these days? Such a shame about your mother. But how is he?"

"I haven't seen him in over three years. He wrote me while I was in the jungle and he seemed to be doing well."

"Mmmm. I'm glad to hear it. Your father and I had the most wonderful conversations a long time ago. A very long time ago. Why, I can remember sitting up at his house—you just in a crib then, of course—and debating the aesthetic value of the Golden Spheres until—"

"I've come here looking for a job."

Silence. Then Cadimon said, "Don't you still work for—"

"I quit." Emphasis on *quit*, like the pressure on an egg to make it crack just so.

"Did you now? I told you you were no longer a missionary. I haven't changed a bit from those days at the academy, Dradin. You didn't recognize me because you've changed, not I. I'm the same. I do not change. Which is more than you can say for the weather around here."

It was time, Dradin decided, to take control of the conversation. It was not enough to counterpunch Cadimon's drifting dialogue. He bent to his knees and gently placed the rest of the lilies in Cadimon's lap.

"Sir," he said. "I need a position. I have been out of my mind with the fever for three months and now, only just recovered, I long to return to the life of a missionary."

"Determined to stick to a point, aren't you?" Cadimon said. "A point stickler. A stickler for rules. I remember you. Always the sort to be shocked by a Living Saint rather than amused. Rehearsed rather than spontaneous. Oh well."

"Cadimon . . ."

"Can you cook?"

"Cook? I can boil cabbage. I can heat water."

Cadimon patted Dradin on the side of his stomach. "So can a hedgehog, my dear. So can a hedgehog, if pressed. No, I mean cook as in the Cooks of Kalay, who can take nothing more than a cauldron of bilge water and a side of beef three days old and tough as calluses and make a dish so succulent and sweet it shames the taste buds to eat so much as a carrot for days afterward. You can't cook, can you?"

"What does cooking have to do with missionary work?"

"Oh, ho. I'd have thought a jungle veteran would know the answer to that! Ever heard of cannibals? Eh? No, that's a joke. It has nothing to do with missionary work. There." He patted the last of the lilies and rose to sit on the bench, indicating with a wave of the hand that Dradin should join him.

Dradin sat down on the bench next to Cadimon. "Surely, you need experienced missionaries?"

Cadimon shook his head. "We don't have a job for you. I'm sorry. You've changed, Dradin."

"But you and my father . . ." Blood rose to Dradin's face. For he could woo until he turned purple, but without a job, how to fund such adventures in pocketbook as his new love would entail?

"Your father is a good man, Dradin. But this mission is not made of money. I see tough times ahead."

Pride surfaced in Dradin's mind like a particularly ugly crocodile. "I am a good missionary, sir. A very good missionary. I have been a missionary for over five years, as you know. And, as I have said, I am just now out of the jungle, having nearly died of fever. Several of my colleagues did not recover. The woman. The woman . . ."

But he trailed off, his skin goose-pimpled from a sudden chill. Layeville, Flay, Stern, Thaw, and Krug had all gone mad or died under the onslaught of green, the rain and the dysentery, and the savages with their poison arrows. Only he had crawled to safety, the mush of the jungle floor beneath his chest a-murmur with leeches and dung bugs and "molly twelve-step" centipedes. A trek into and out of hell, and he could not even now remember it all, or wanted to remember it all.

"Paugh! Dying of fever is easy. The jungle is easy, Dradin. I could survive, frail as I am. It's the city that's hard. If you'd only bother to observe, you'd see the air is overripe with missionaries. You can't defecate out a window without fouling a brace of them. The city bursts with them. They think that the Festival signals opportunity, but the opportunity is not for them! No, we need a cook, and you cannot cook."

Dradin's palms slickened with sweat, his hands shaking as he examined them. What now? What to do? His thoughts circled and circled around the same unanswerable question: How could he survive on the coins he had yet on his person and still woo the woman in the window? And he must woo her; he did not feel his heart could withstand the blow of *not* pursuing her.

"I am a good missionary," Dradin repeated, looking at the ground. "What happened in the jungle was not my fault. We went out looking for converts and when I came back the compound was overrun."

Dradin's breaths came quick and shallow and his head felt light. Suffocating. He was suffocating under the weight of jungle leaves closing over his nose and mouth.

Cadimon sighed and shook his head. In a soft voice he said, "I am not unsympathetic," and held out his hands to Dradin. "How can I explain myself? Maybe I cannot, but let me try. Perhaps this way: Have you converted the Flying Squirrel People of the western hydras? Have you braved the frozen wastes of Lascia to convert the ice cube–like Skamoo?"

"No."

"What did you say?"

"No!"

"Then we can't use you. At least not now."

Dradin's throat ached and his jaw tightened. Would he have to beg, then? Would he have to become a mendicant himself? On the catafalque, the Living Saint had begun to stir, mumbling in his half sleep.

Cadimon rose and put his hand on Dradin's shoulder. "If it is any consolation, you were never really a missionary, not even at the religious academy. And you are definitely not a missionary now. You are . . . something else. Extraordinary, really, that I can't put my finger on it."

"You insult me," Dradin said, as if he were the gaudy figurehead on some pompous yacht sailing languid on the Moth.

"That is not my intent, my dear. Not at all."

"Perhaps you could give me money. I could repay you."

"Now *you* insult *me*. Dradin, I cannot lend you money. We have no money. All the money we collect goes to our creditors or into the houses and shelters of the poor. We have no money, nor do we covet it."

"Cadimon," Dradin said. "Cadimon, I'm desperate. I need money."

"If you are desperate, take my advice—leave Ambergris. And before the Festival. It's not safe for priests to be on the streets after dark on Festival night. There have been so many years of calm. Ha! I tell you, it can't last."

"It wouldn't have to be much money. Just enough to—"

Cadimon gestured toward the entrance. "Beg from your father, not from me. Leave. Leave now."

Dradin, taut muscles and clenched fists, would have obeyed Cadimon out of respect for the memory of authority, but now a vision rose into his mind like the moon rising over the valley the night before. A vision of the jungle, the dark green leaves with their veins like spines, like long, delicate bones. The jungle and the woman and all of the dead . . .

"I will not."

Cadimon frowned. "I'm sorry to hear you say that. I ask you again, leave."

Lush green, smothering, the taste of dirt in his mouth; the smell of burning, smoke curling up into a question mark.

"Cadimon, I was your student. You owe me the—"

"Living Saint!" Cadimon shouted. "Wake up, Living Saint."

The Living Saint uncurled himself from his repose atop the catafalque.

"Living Saint," Cadimon said, "dispense with him. No need to be gentle." And, turning to Dradin: "Goodbye, Dradin. I am very sorry."

The Living Saint, spouting insults, jumped from the catafalque and—his penis purpling and flaccid as a sea anemone, brandished menacingly—ran toward Dradin, who promptly took to his heels, stumbling through the ranks of the gathered acolytes and hearing directly behind him as he navigated the bluegrass trail not only the Living Saint's screams of "Piss off! Piss off, you great big baboon!" but also Cadimon's distant shouts of: "I'll pray for you, Dradin. I'll pray for you." And, then, too close, much too close, the unmistakable hot and steamy sound of a man relieving himself, followed by the hands of the Living Saint clamped down on his shoulder blades, and a much swifter exit than he had hoped for upon his arrival, scuffing his fundament, his pride, his dignity.

"And stay out!"

When Dradin stopped running he found himself on the fringe of the Religious Quarter, next to an emaciated macadamia salesman who cracked jokes like nuts. Out of breath, Dradin put his hands on his hips. His lungs strained for air. Blood rushed furiously through his chest. He could almost persuade himself that these symptoms were only the aftershock of exertion, not the aftershock of anger and desperation. Actions unbecoming a missionary. Actions unbecoming a gentleman. What might love next drive him to?

Determined to regain his composure, Dradin straightened his shirt and collar, then continued on his way in a manner he hoped mimicked the stately gait of a mid-level clergy member, to whom all such earthly things were beneath and below. But the bulge of red veins at his neck, the stiffness of fingers in claws at his sides, these clues gave him away, and knowing this made him angrier still. How dare Cadimon treat him as though he were practically a stranger! How dare the man betray the bond between his father and the church!

More disturbing, where were the agents of order when you needed them? No doubt the city had ordinances against public urination. Although that presupposed the existence of a civil authority, and of this mythic beast Dradin had yet to convince himself. He had not seen a single blue, black, or brown uniform, and certainly not filled out with a body lodged within its fabric, a man who might symbolize law and order and thus give the word flesh. What did the people of Ambergris do when thieves and molesters and murderers traversed the thoroughfares and alleyways, the underpasses and the bridges? But the thought brought him back to the mushroom dwellers and their alcove shrines, and he abandoned it, a convulsion traveling from his chin to the tips of his toes. Perhaps the jungle had not yet relinquished its grip.

Finally, shoulders bowed, eyes on the ground, in abject defeat, he admitted to himself that his methods had been grotesque. He had made a fool of himself in front of Cadimon. Cadimon was not beholden to him. Cadimon had only acted as he must when confronted with the ungodly.

Necklace still wrapped in the page from *The Refraction of Light in a Prison*, Dradin came again to Hoegbotton & Sons, only to find that his love no longer stared from the third-floor window. A shock traveled up his spine, a shock that might have sent him gibbering to his mother's side aboard the psychiatrists' houseboat, if not that he was a rational and rationalizing man. How his heart drowned in a sea of fears as he tried to conjure up a thousand excuses: she was out to lunch; she had taken ill; she had moved to another part of the building. Never that she was gone for good, lost as he was lost; that he might never, ever see her face again. Now Dradin understood his father's addiction to sweet-milled mead, beer, wine, and champagne, for the woman was his addiction, and he knew that if he had only seen her porcelain-perfect visage as he suffered from the jungle fevers, he would have lived for her sake alone.

The city might be savage, stray dogs might share the streets with grimy urchins whose blank eyes reflected the knowledge that they might soon be covered over, blinded forever, by the same two pennies just begged from some gentleman, and no one in all the fuming, fulminous boulevards of trade might know who actually ran Ambergris—or, if anyone ran it at all, but, like a renegade clock, it ran on and wound itself heedless, empowered by the insane weight of its own inertia, the weight of its own citizenry, stamping one, two, three hundred thousand strong; no matter this savagery in the midst of apparent civilization—still the woman in the window seemed to him more ruly, more disciplined and in control and thus, perversely, malleable to his desire, than anyone Dradin had yet met in Ambergris: this priceless part of the whale, this overbrimming stew of the sublime and the ridiculous.

It was then that his rescuer came: Dvorak, popping up from betwixt a yardstick of a butcher awaiting a hansom and a jowly furrier draped over with furs of auburn, gray, and white. Dvorak, indeed, dressed all in black, against which the red dots of his tattoo throbbed and, in his jacket pocket, a dove-white handkerchief stained red at the edges. A mysterious, feminine smile decorated his mutilated face.

"She's not at the window," Dradin said.

Dvorak's laugh forced his mouth open wide and wider still, carnivorous in its red depths. "No. She is not at the window. But have no doubt: she is inside. She is a most devout employee."

"You gave her the book?"

"I did, sir." The laugh receded into a shallow smile. "She took it from me like a lady, with hesitation, and when I told her it came from a secret admirer, she blushed."

"Blushed?" Dradin felt lighter, his blood yammering and his head a puff of smoke, a cloud, a spray of cotton candy.

"Blushed. Indeed, sir, a good sign."

Dradin took the package from his pocket and, hands trembling, gave it to the dwarf. "Now you must go back in and find her, and when you find her, give her this. You must ask her to join me at the Drunken Boat at twilight. You know the place?"

Dvorak nodded, his hands clasped protectively around the package.

"Good. I will have a table next to the Festival parade route. Beg her if you must. Intrigue her and entreat her."

"I will do so."

"U-u-unless you think I should take this gift to her myself?"

Dvorak sneered. He shook his head so that the green of the jungle blurred before Dradin's eyes. "Think, sir. Think hard. Would you have her see you first out of breath, unkempt, and, if I may be so bold, there is a slight smell of *urine*. No, sir. Meet her first at the tavern, and there you shall appear a man of means, at your ease, inviting her to the unraveling of further mysteries."

Dradin looked away. How his inexperience must show. How foolish his suggestions. And yet, also, relief that Dvorak had thwarted his brashness.

"Sir?" Dvorak said. "Sir?"

Dradin forced himself to look at Dvorak. "You are correct, of course. I will see her at the tavern."

"Coins, sir."

"Coins?"

"I cannot live on kindness."

"Yes. Of course. Of course." Damn Dvorak! No compassion there. He stuck a hand into his pants pocket and pulled out a gold coin, which he handed to Dvorak. "Another when you return."

"As you wish. Wait here." Dvorak gave Dradin one last long look and then scurried up the steps, disappearing into the darkness of the doorway.

Dradin discovered he was bad at waiting. He sat on the curb, got up, crouched to his knees, leaned on a lamppost, scratched at a flea biting his ankle. All the while, he looked up at the blank window and thought: If I had come into the city today, I would have looked up at the third floor and seen nothing and this frustration, this impatience, this *ardor*, would not be practically bursting from me now.

Finally, Dvorak scuttled down the steps with his jacket tails floating out behind him, his grin larger, if that were possible, positively a leer.

"What did she say?" Dradin pressed. "Did she say anything? Something? Yes? No?"

"Success, sir. Success. Busy as she is, devout as she is, she said little, but only that she will meet you at the Drunken Boat, though perhaps not until after dusk has fallen. She looked quite favorably on the emerald and the message. She calls you, sir, a gentleman."

A *gentleman*. Dradin stood straighter. "Thank you," he said. "You have been a great help to me. Here." And he passed another coin to Dvorak, who snatched it from his hand with all the swiftness of a snake.

As Dvorak murmured goodbye, Dradin heard him with but one ear, cocooned as he was in a world where the sun always shone bright and uncovered all hidden corners, allowing no shadows or dark and glimmering truths.

5

Dradin hurried back to the hostel. He hardly saw the flashes of red, green, and blue around him, nor sensed the expectant quality in the air, the huddled groups of people talking in animated voices, for night would bring the Festival of Freshwater Squid and the streets would hum and thrum with celebration. Already, the clean smell of fresh-baked bread, mixed with the treacly promise of sweets, began to tease noses and turn frowns into smiles. Boys let out early from school played games with hoops and marbles and bits of brick. The more adventurous imitated the grand old King Squid sinking ships with a single lash of tentacle, puddle-bound toy boats smashed against drainpipes. Still others watched the erection of scaffolding on tributary streets leading into Albumuth Boulevard. Stilt men with purpling painted faces hung candy and papier-mâché heads in equal quantities from their stilts.

At last, Dradin came to his room, flung open the door, and shut it abruptly behind him. As the citizens of Ambergris prepared for the Festival, so now he must prepare for his love, putting aside the distractions of joblessness and decreasing coin. He stripped and took a shower, turning the water on so hot that needles of heat tattooed his skin red, but he felt clean, and more than clean, cleansed and calm, when he came out after thirty minutes and wiped himself dry with a large green towel. Standing in front of the bathroom mirror in the nude, Dradin noted that although he had filled out since the cessation of his fever, he had not filled out into fat. Not even the shadow of a belly, and his legs thick with muscle. Hardly a family characteristic, that, for his randy father had, since the onset of Mom's river adventures, grown as pudgy as raw bread dough. Nothing for Dad to do but continue to teach ethics at the university and hope that the lithe young things populating his classes would pity him. But for his son a different fate, Dradin was sure.

Dradin shaved, running the blade across his chin and down his neck, so that he thrilled to the self-control it took to keep the blade steady; and yet, when he was done, his hand shook. There. Now various oils worked into the scalp so that his hair became a uniform black, untainted by white except at the outer provinces, where it grazed his ears. Then a spot of rouge to bring out the muddy green of his eyes—a scandalous habit, perhaps, learned from his mother of course, but Dradin knew many pale priests who used it.

For clothing, Dradin started with clean underwear and followed with fancy socks done up in muted purple and gold serpent designs. Then the trousers of gray—gray as the slits of his father's eyes in the grip of spirits, gray as his mother's listless moods after performances at the music halls. Yes, a smart gray, a deep gray, not truly conservative, followed by the shirt: large on him but not voluminous, white with purple and gold buttons, to match the socks, and a jacket over top that mixed gray and purple thread so that, from heel to head, he looked as distinguished as a debutante at some political gala. It pleased him—as much a uniform as his missionary clothes, but the goal a conversion of a more personal nature. Yes, he would do well.

Thus equipped, his pockets jingly with his last coins, his stomach wrapped in coils of nerves (an at-sea sensation of *notenoughmoney, notenoughmoney* beating inside his organs like a pulse), Dradin made his way out onto the streets.

The haze of twilight had smothered Ambergris, muffling sounds and limiting vision, but everywhere also: lights. Lights from balconies and bedrooms, signposts and horse carriages, candles held by hand and lanterns swinging on the arms of grizzled caretakers who sang out, from deep in their throats, "The dying of the light! The dying of the light! Let the Festival begin."

Wraiths riding metal bars, men on bicycles swished past, bells all a-tinkle, and children in formal attire, entow to the vast and long-suffering barges of nannies, who tottered forward on unsteady if stocky legs. Child mimes in white face approached Dradin, prancing and pirouetting, and Dradin clapped in approval and patted their heads. They reminded him of the naked boys and girls of the Nimbly-tod Tribe, who swung through trees and ate birds that became lost in the forest and could not find their way again into the light.

Women in the red and black of hunters' uniforms crossed his path. They rode hollow wooden horses that fit around their waists, fake wooden legs clacking to either side as their own legs cantered or galloped or pranced, but so controlled, so tight and rigid, that they never broke formation despite the random nature of their movements. The horses had each been individually painted in grotesque shades of green, red, and white: eyes wept blood, teeth snarled into black fangs. The women's lips were drawn back against the red leer of lipstick to neigh and nicker. Around them, the gathering crowd shrieked in laughter, the riders so entranced that only the whites of their eyes showed, shockingly pale against the gloom.

Dradin passed giant spits on which spun and roasted whole cows, whole pigs, and a host of smaller beasts, the spits rotated by grunting, muscular, ruddy-faced men. Everywhere, the mushroom dwellers uncurled from slumber with a yawn, picked up their red flags, and trundled off to their secret and arcane rites. Armed men mock-fought with saber and with knife while youths wrestled half naked in the gutters—their bodies burnished with sweat, their eyes focused not on each other but on the young women who watched their battles. Impromptu dances devoid of form or unified steps spread among the spectators until Dradin had to struggle through their spider's webs of gyrations, inured to the laughter and chatter of conversations, the tap and stomp of feet on the rough stones. For this was the most magical night of the year in Ambergris, the Festival of the Freshwater Squid, and the city lay in trance, spellbound and difficult, and everywhere, into the apparent lull, glance met glance, eyes sliding from eyes, as if to say, "What next? What will happen next?"

At last, after passing through an archway strung with nooses, Dradin came out onto a main boulevard, the Drunken Boat before him. How could he miss it? It had been lit up like an ornament so that all three stories of slanted dark oak decks sparkled and glowed with good cheer.

A crowd had lined up in front of the tavern, waiting to gain entrance, but Dradin fought through the press, bribed the doorman with a gold coin, and ducked inside, climbing stairs to the second level, high enough to see far down the boulevard, although not so high that the sights would be uninvolving and distant. A tip to the waiter secured Dradin a prime table next to the railing of the deck. The table, complete with lace and embroidered tablecloth, engraved cutlery, and a quavery candle encircled by glass, lay equidistant from the parade and the musical meanderings of the Ravens, four scruffy-looking musicians who played, respectively, the mandolin, twelve-string guitar, the flute, and the drums:

> In the city of lies
> I spoke in nothing
> but the language of spies.
>
> In the city of my demise
> I spoke in nothing
> but the language of flies.

Their music reminded Dradin of high tide crashing against cliffs and, then, on the down-tempo, of the back-and-forth swell of giant waves rippling across a smooth surface of water. It soothed him and made him seasick both, and when he sat down at the table, the wood beneath him lurched, though he knew it was only the surging of his own pulse, echoed in the floorboards.

Dradin surveyed the parade route, which was lined with glittery lights rimmed with crepe paper that made a crinkly sound as the breeze hit it. A thousand lights done up in blue and green, and the crowd gathered to both sides behind them, so that the street became an iridescent replica of the Moth, not nearly as wide, but surely as deep and magical.

Around him came the sounds of laughter and polite conversation, each table its own island of charm and anticipation: ladies in white and red dresses that sparkled with sequins when the light caught them, gentlemen in dark blue suits or tuxedos, looking just as ridiculous as Dad had once looked, caught out in the rain.

Dradin ordered a mildly alcoholic drink called a Red Orchid and sipped it as he snuck glances at the couple to his immediate right: a tall, thin man with aquiline features, eyes narrow as paper cuts, and rich, gray sideburns, and his con-sort, a blond woman in an emerald dress that covered her completely and yet also revealed her completely in the tightness of its fabric. Flushed in the candlelight, she laughed too loudly, smiled too quickly, and it made Dradin cringe to watch her make a fool of herself, the man a bigger fool for not putting her at ease. The man only watched her with a thin smile splayed across his face. Surely when the woman in the window, his love, came to his table, there would be only traces of this awk-wardness, this ugliness in the guise of grace?

His love? Glass at his lips, Dradin realized he didn't know her name. It could be Angeline or Melanctha or Galendrace, or even—and his expression darkened as he concentrated *hard*, felt an odd tingling in his temples, finally expelled the name—"Nepenthe," the name of the sweaty woman priest in the jungle. He put down his glass. All this preparation, his nerves on edge, and he didn't even know the name of the woman in the window. A chill went through him, for did he not know her as well as he knew himself?

Soon, the procession made its way down the parade route: the vast, engulfing cloth kites with wire ribs that formed the shapes of giant squid, paper streamers for tentacles running out behind as, lit by their own inner flames, they bumped and spun against the darkened sky. Ships followed them—floats mounted on the rusted hulks of mechanized vehicles, their purpose to reenact the same scene as the boys with their toy boats: the hunt for the mighty King Squid, which made its home in the deepest parts of the Moth, in the place where the river was wide as the sea and twice as mad with silt.

Dradin clapped and said, "Beautiful, beautiful," and, with elegant despera-tion, ordered another drink, for if he was to be starving and penniless anyway, what was one more expense?

On the parade route, performing wolfhounds followed the floats, then jugglers, mimes, fire-eaters, contortionists, and belly dancers. The gangrenous moon began to seep across the sky in dark green hues. The drone of conversations grew more urgent and the cries of the people on the street below, befouled by food, drink, and revelry, became discordant: a fragmented roar of fragmenting desires.

Where was his love? Would she not come? Dradin's head felt light and hollow, yet heavy as the earth spinning up to greet him, at the possibility. No, it was not a possibility. Dradin ordered yet another Red Orchid.

She would come. Dressed in white and red she would come, around her throat a necklace of intricate blue and green beads, a rough emerald dangling from the center. He would stand to greet her and she would offer her hand to him and he would bow to kiss it. Her skin would be warm to the touch of his lips and his lips would feel warm and electric to her. He would say to her, "Please, take a seat," and pull out her chair. She would acknowledge his chivalry with a slight leftward tip of her head. He would wait for her to sit and then he would sit, wave to a waiter, order her a glass of wine, and then they would talk. Circling in toward how he had first seen her, he would ask her how she liked the book, the necklace. Perhaps both would laugh at the crudity of Dvorak, and at his own shyness, for surely now she could see that he was not truly shy. The hours would pass and with each minute and each witty comment, she would look more deeply into his eyes and he into hers. Their hands would creep forward across the table until, clumsily, she jostled her wineglass and he reached out to keep it from falling—and found her hand instead.

From there, her hand in his, their gaze so intimate across the table, everything would be easy, because it would all be unspoken, but no less eloquent for that. Perhaps they would leave the table, the tavern, traverse the streets in the aftermath of the Festival. But, no matter what they did, there would be this bond between them: that they had drunk deep of the desire in each other's eyes.

Dradin wiped the sweat from his forehead, took another sip of his drink, looked into the crowd, which merged with the parade, crashing and pushing toward the lights and the performers.

War veterans were marching past: a grotesque assembly of ghost limbs, memories disassembled from the flesh, for not a one had two arms and two legs both. They clattered and shambled forward in their odd company with crutches and wheelchairs and comrades supporting them. They wore the uniforms of a hundred wars and ranged in age from seventeen to seventy; Dradin recognized a few from his hostel. Those who carried sabers waved and twirled their weapons, inciting the crowd, which now pushed and pulled and divided among itself like a replicating beast, to shriek and line the parade route ever more closely.

Then, with solemn precision, four men came carrying a coffin, so small as to be for a child, each lending but a single hand to the effort. On occasion, the leader would fling open the top to reveal the empty interior and the crowd would moan and stamp its feet.

Behind the coffin, in a cage, came a jungle cat that snarled and worked one enormous pitch paw through bamboo bars. Looking into the dulled but defiant eyes of the cat, Dradin gulped his Red Orchid and thought of the jungle. *The moist heat, the ferns curling into their fetid greenness, the flowers running red, the thick smell of rich black soil on the shovel, the pale gray of the woman's hand, the suddenness of coming upon a savage village, soon to be a ghost place, the savages fled or struck down by disease, the dark eyes, the questioning looks on the faces of those he disturbed, bringing his missionary word, the way the forest could be too green, so fraught with scents and tastes and sounds that one could become intoxicated by it, even become feverish within it, drowning in black water, plagued by the curse of no converts.*

Dradin shuddered again from the cold of the drink, and thought he felt the deck beneath him roll and plunge in time to the music of the Ravens. Was it possible that he had never fully recovered from the fever? Was he even now stone cold mad in the head, or was he simply woozy from Red Orchids? Or could he be, in his final distress, drunk on love? He had precious little else left, a realization accompanied by a not unwelcome thrill of fear. With no job and little money, the only element of his being he found constant and unyielding, undoubting, was the strength of his love for the woman in the window.

He smiled at the couple at the next table, though no doubt it came out as the sort of drunken leer peculiar to his father. Past relationships had been of an unfortunate nature; he could admit that to himself now. Too platonic, too strange, and always too brief. The jungle did not approve of long relationships. The jungle ate up long relationships, ground them between its teeth and spat them out. Like the relationship between himself and Nepenthe. Nepenthe. Might the woman in the window also be called Nepenthe? Would she mind if he called her that? Now the deck beneath him really did roll and list like a ship at sea, and he held himself to his chair, pushed the Red Orchid away when he had come once more to rest.

Looking out at the parade, Dradin saw Cadimon Signal and he had to laugh. Cadimon. Good old Cadimon. Was this parade to become like Dvorak's wonderfully ugly tattoo? A trip from past to present? For there indeed was Cadimon, waving to the crowds from a float of gold and white satin, the Living Saint beside him, diplomatically clothed for the occasion in messianic white robes.

"Hah!" Dradin said. "Hah!"

The parade ended with an elderly man leading a live lobster on a leash, a sight that made Dradin laugh until he cried. The lights along the boulevard began to be snuffed out, at first one by one, and then, as the mob descended, ripped out in swathes, so that whole sections were plunged into darkness at once. Beyond them, the great spits no longer turned, abandoned, the meat upon them blackened to ash, and beyond the spits bonfires roared and blazed all the more brightly, as if to make up for the death of the other lights. Now it was impossible to tell parade members from crowd members, so clotted together and at-sea were they, mixed in merriment under the green light of the moon.

Around Dradin, busboys hastily cleaned up tables, helped by barkeepers, and he heard one mutter to another, "It will be bad this year. Very bad. I can feel it." The waiter presented Dradin with the check, tapping his feet while Dradin searched his pockets for the necessary coin, and when it was finally offered, snatching it from his hand and leaving in a flurry of tails and shiny shoes.

Dradin, hollow and tired and sad, looked up at the black-and-green-tinged sky. His love had not come and would not now come, and perhaps had never planned to come, for he only had the word of Dvorak. He did not know how he should feel, for he had never considered this possibility, that he might not meet her. He looked around him—at the table fixtures, the emptying tables, the sudden lull. Now what could he do? He could take a menial job and survive on scraps until he could get a message to his father in Morrow—who then might or might not take pity on him. But for salvation? For redemption?

Fireworks wormholed into the sky and exploded in an umbrella of sparks so that the crowds screamed louder to drown out the noise. Someone jostled him from behind. Wetness dripped down his left shoulder, followed by a curse, and he turned in time to see one of the waiters scurry off with a half-spilled drink.

The smoke from the fireworks descended, mixed with the growing fog traipsing off the River Moth. It spread more quickly than Dradin would have thought possible, the night smudged with smoke, thick and dark. And who should come out of this haze and into Dradin's gloom but Dvorak, dressed now in green so that the dilute light of the moon passed invisibly over him. His head cocked curiously, like a monkey's, he approached sideways toward Dradin, an appraising look on his face. Was he poisonous like the snake, Dradin thought, or edible, like the insect? Or was he merely a bit of bark to be ignored? For so did Dvorak appraise him. A spark of anger began to smolder in Dradin, for after all Dvorak had made the arrangements and the woman was not here.

"You," Dradin said, raising his voice over the general roar. "You. What're you doing here? You're late . . . I mean, she's late. She's not coming. Where is she? *Did you lie to me, Dvorak?*"

Dvorak moved to Dradin's side and, with his muscular hands under Dradin's arms, pulled Dradin halfway to his feet with such suddenness that he would have fallen over if he hadn't caught himself.

Dradin whirled around, intending to reprimand Dvorak, but found himself speechless as he stared down into the dwarf's eyes—dark eyes, so impenetrable, the entire face set like sculpted clay, that he could only stand there and say, weakly, "You said she'd be here."

"Shut up," Dvorak said, and the stiff, coiled menace in the voice caught Dradin between anger and obedience. Dvorak filled the moment with words: "She is here. Nearby. It is Festival night. There is danger everywhere. If she had come earlier, perhaps. But now, now you must meet her elsewhere, in safety. For her safety." Dvorak put a clammy hand on Dradin's arm, but Dradin shook him off.

"Don't touch me. Where's safer than here?"

"Nearby, I tell you. The crowd, the Festival. Night is upon us. She will not wait for you."

On the street below, fistfights had broken out. Through the haze, Dradin could hear the slap of flesh on flesh, the snap of bone, the moans of victims. People ran hither and thither, shadows flitting through green darkness.

"Come, sir. *Now.*" Dvorak tugged on Dradin's arm, pulled him close, whispered in Dradin's ear like an echo from another place, another time, the map of his face so inscrutable Dradin could not read it: "You must come *now.* Or not at all. If not at all, you will never see her. She will only see you now. Now! Are you so foolish that you will pass?"

Dradin hesitated, weighing the risks. Where might the dwarf lead him?

Dvorak cursed. "Then do not come. Do not. And take your chances with the Festival."

He turned to leave but Dradin reached down and grabbed his arm.

"Wait," Dradin said. "I will come," and taking a few steps found to his relief that he did not stagger.

"Your love awaits," Dvorak said, unsmiling. "Follow close, sir. You would not wish to become lost from me. It would go hard on you."

"How far—"

"No questions. No talking. Follow."

6

Dvorak led Dradin around the back of the Drunken Boat and into an alley, the stones slick with vomit, littered with sharp glass from broken beer and wine bottles, and guarded by a bum muttering an old song from the equinox. Rats waddled on fat legs to eat from half-gnawed drumsticks and soggy buns.

The rats reminded Dradin of the Religious Quarter and of Cadimon, and then of Cadimon's warning: *"It's not safe for priests to be on the streets after dark during Festival."* He stopped following Dvorak, his head clearer.

"I've changed my mind. I can see her tomorrow at Hoegbotton & Sons."

Dvorak's face clouded like a storm come up from the bottom of the sea as he turned and came back to Dradin. He said, "You have no choice. Follow me."

"No."

"You will never see her then."

"Are you threatening me?"

Dvorak sighed and his overcoat shivered with the blades of a hundred knives.

"You will come with me."

"You've already said that."

"Then you will not come?"

"No."

Dvorak punched Dradin in the stomach. The blow felt like an iron ball. All the breath went out of Dradin. The sky spun above him. He doubled over. The side of Dvorak's shoe caught him in the temple, a deep searing pain. Dradin fell heavily on the slick slime and glass of the cobblestones. Glass cut into his palms, his legs, as he twisted and groaned. He tried, groggily, to get to his feet. Dvorak's shoe exploded against his ribs. He screamed, fell onto his side where he lay unmoving, unable to breathe except in gasps. Clammy hands put a noose of hemp around his neck, pulled it taut, brought his head up off the ground.

Dvorak held a long, slender blade to Dradin's neck and pulled at the hemp until Dradin was on his knees, looking up into the mottled face. Dradin gasped despite his pain, for it was a different face than only moments before.

Dvorak's features were a sea of conflicting emotions, his mouth twisted to express fear, jealousy, sadness, joy, hatred, as if by encompassing a map of the world he had somehow encompassed all of worldly experience, and that it had driven him mad. In Dvorak's eyes, Dradin saw the dwarf's true detachment from the world and on Dvorak's face he saw the beatific smile of the truly damned, for the face, the flesh, still held the memory of emotion, even if the mind behind the flesh had forgotten.

"In the name of God, Dvorak," Dradin said.

Dvorak's mouth opened and the tongue clacked down and the voice came, distant and thin as memory, "You are coming with me, sir. On your feet."

Dvorak pulled savagely on the rope. Dradin gurgled and forced his fingers between the rope and his neck.

"On your feet, I said."

Dradin groaned and rolled over. "I can't."

The knife jabbed into the back of his neck. "Soft! Get up, or I'll kill you here."

Dradin forced himself up, though his head was woozy and his stomach felt punctured beyond repair. He avoided looking down into Dvorak's eyes. To look would only confirm that he was dealing with a monster

"I am a priest."

"I know you are a priest," Dvorak said.

"Your soul will burn in hell," Dradin said.

A burst of laughter. "I was born there, sir. My face reflects its flames. Now, you will walk ahead of me. You will not run. You will not raise your voice. If you do, I shall choke you and gut you where you stand."

"I have money," Dradin said heavily, still trying to let air into his lungs. "I have gold."

"And we will take it. Walk! There is not much time."

"Where are we going?"

"You will know when we get there."

When Dradin still did not move, Dvorak shoved him forward. Dradin began to walk, Dvorak so close behind he imagined he could feel the point of the blade against the small of his back.

The green light of the moon stained everything except the bonfires the color of toads and dead grass. The bonfires called with their siren song of flame until crowds gathered at each one to dance, shout, and fight. Dradin soon saw that Dvorak's route—through alley after alley, over barricades—was intended to avoid the bonfires. There was now no cool wind in all the city, for around every corner they turned, the harsh rasp of the bonfires met them. To all sides, buildings sprang up out of the fog—dark, silent, menacing.

As they crossed a bridge, over murky water thick with sewage and the flotsam of the festivities, a man hobbled toward them. His left ear had been severed from his head. He cradled part of someone's leg in his arms. He moaned and when he saw Dradin, Dvorak masked by shadow, he shouted, "Stop them! Stop them!" only to continue on into the darkness, and Dradin helpless anyway. Soon after, following the trail of blood, a hooting mob of ten or twelve youths came a-hunting, tawny-limbed and fresh for the kill. They yelled catcalls and taunted Dradin, but when they saw that he was a prisoner they turned their attentions back to their own prey.

The buildings became black shadows tinged green, the street under foot rough and ill hewn. A wall stood to either side.

A deep sliver of fear pulled Dradin's nerves taut. "How much further?" he asked.

"Not far. Not far at all."

The mist deepened until Dradin could not tell the difference between the world with his eyes shut and the world with his eyes open. Dradin sensed the scuffle of feet on the pavement behind and in front, and the darkness became claustrophobic, close with the scent of rot and decay.

"We are being followed," Dradin said.

"You are mistaken."

"I hear them!"

"Shut up! It's not far. Trust me."

"*Trust me?*" Did Dvorak realize the irony of those words? How foolish that they should converse at all, the knife at his back and the hushed breathing from behind and ahead, stalking them. Fear raised the hairs along his arms and heightened his senses, distorting and magnifying every sound.

Their journey ended where the trees were less thick and the fog had been swept aside. Walls did indeed cordon them in, gray walls that ended abruptly ten feet ahead in a welter of shadows that rustled and quivered like dead leaves lifted by the wind, but there was no wind.

Dradin's temples pounded and his breath caught in his throat. On another street, parallel but out of sight, a clock doled out the hours, one through eleven, and revelers tooted on horns or screamed out names or called to the moon in weeping, distant, fading voices.

Dvorak shoved Dradin forward until they came to an open gate, ornately filigreed, and beyond the gate, through the bars, the brooding headstones of a vast graveyard. Mausoleums and memorials, single tombs and groups, families dead together under the thick humus, the young and the old alike feeding the worms, feeding the earth.

The graveyard was overgrown with grass and weeds so that the headstones swam in a sea of green. Beyond these fading statements of life after death writ upon the fissured stones, riven and made secretive by the moonlight, lay the broken husks of trains, haphazard and strewn across the landscape. The twisted metal of engines, freight cars, and cabooses gleamed darkly green and the patina of broken glass windows, held together by moss, shone especially bright, like vast, reflective eyes. Eyes that still held a glimmer of the past when coal had coursed through their engines like blood and brimstone, and their compartments had been busy with the footsteps of those same people who now lay beneath the earth.

The industrial district. Dradin was in the industrial district and now he knew that due south was his hostel and southwest was Hoegbotton & Sons, and the River Moth beyond it.

"I do not see her," Dradin said, to avoid looking ahead to the squirming shadows.

Dvorak's face as the dwarf turned to him was a sickly green and his mouth a cruel slit of darkness. "Should you see her, do you think? I am leading you to a graveyard, missionary. Pray, if you wish."

At those words, Dradin would have run, would have taken off into the mist, not caring if Dvorak found him and gutted him, such was his terror. But then the creeping tread of the creatures resolved itself. The sound grew louder, coming up behind and ahead of him. As he watched, the shadows became shapes and then figures, until he could see the glinty eyes and glinty knives of a legion of silent, waiting mushroom dwellers. Behind them, hopping and rustling, came toads and rats, their eyes bright with darkness. The sky thickened with the swooping shapes of bats.

"Surely," Dradin said, "surely there has been a mistake."

In a sad voice, his face strangely mournful and moonlike, Dvorak said, "There have indeed been mistakes, but they are yours. Take off your clothes."

Dradin backed away, into the arms of the leathery, stretched, musty folk behind. Cringing from their touch, he leapt forward.

"I have money," Dradin said to Dvorak. "I will give you money. My father has money."

Dvorak's smile turned sadly sweeter and sweetly sadder. "How you waste words when you have so few words left to waste. Remove your clothes or they will do it for you," and he motioned to the mushroom dwellers. A hiss of menace rose from their assembled ranks as they pressed closer, closer still, until he could not escape the dry, piercing rot of them, nor the sound of their shambling gait.

He took off his shoes, his socks, his trousers, his shirt, his underwear, folding each item carefully, until his pale body gleamed and he saw himself in his mind's eye as switching positions with the Living Saint. How he would have loved to see the hoary ejaculator now, coming to his rescue, but there was no hope of that. Despite the chill, Dradin held his hands over his penis rather than his chest. What did modesty matter, and yet still he did it.

Dvorak hunched nearer, hand taut on the rope, and used his knife to pull the clothes over to him. He went through the pockets, took the remaining coins, and then put the clothes over his shoulder.

"Please, let me go," Dradin said. "I beg you." There was a tremor in his voice but, he marveled, only a tremor, only a hint of fear.

Who would have guessed that so close to his own murder he could be so calm?

"I cannot let you go. You no longer belong to me. You are a priest, are you not? They pay well for the blood of priests."

"My friends will come for me."

"You have no friends in this city."

"Where is the woman from the window?"

Dvorak smiled with a smugness that turned Dradin's stomach. A spark of anger spread all up and down his back and made his teeth grind together. The graveyard gate was open. He had run through graveyards once, with Anthony—graveyards redolent with the stink of old metal and ancient technologies—but was that not where they wished him to go?

"In the name of God, what have you done with her?"

"You are too clever by half," Dvorak said. "She is still in Hoegbotton & Sons."

"At this hour?"

"Yes."

"W-w-why is she there?" His fear for her, deeper into him than his own anger, made his voice quiver.

Dvorak's mask cracked. He giggled and cackled and stomped his foot. "Because, because, sir, sir, I have taken her to pieces. I have dismembered her!" And from behind and in front and all around, the horrible, galumphing, harrumphing laughter of the mushroom dwellers.

Dismembered her.

The laughter, mocking and cruel, set him free from his inertia. Clear and cold he was now, made of ice, always keeping the face of his beloved before him. He could not die until he had seen her body.

Dradin yanked on the rope and, as Dvorak fell forward, wrenched free the noose. He kicked the dwarf in the head and heard a satisfying howl of pain, but did not wait, did not watch—he was already running through the gate before the mushroom dwellers could stop him. His legs felt like cold metal, like the churning pistons of the old coal-chewing trains. He ran as he had never run in all his life, even with Tony. He ran like a man possessed, recklessly dodging tombstones and high grass, while behind came the angry screams of Dvorak, the slithery swiftness of the mushroom dwellers. And still Dradin laughed as he went—bellowing as he jumped atop a catacomb of mausoleums and leapt between monuments, trapped for an instant by abutting tombstones, and then up and running again, across the top of yet another broad sepulcher. He found his voice and shouted to his pursuers, "Catch me! Catch me!", and cackled his own mad cackle, for he was as naked as the day he had entered the world and his beloved was dead and he had nothing left in the world to lose. Lost as he might be, lost as he might always be, yet the feeling of freedom was heady. It made him giddy and drunk with his own power. He crowed to his pursuers, he needled them, only to pop up elsewhere, thrilling to the hardness of his muscles, the toughness gained in the jungle where all else had been lost.

Finally, he came to the line of old trains, byzantine and convoluted and dark, surrounded by the smell of dank, rusting metal. One backward glance before entering the maze revealed that the mushroom dwellers, led by Dvorak, had reached the last line of tombstones, fifty feet away.

—but a glance only before he swung himself into the side door of an engine, walked on the balls of his feet into the cool darkness. Hushed quiet. This was what he needed now. Quiet and stealth in equal measures so that he could reach the relative safety of the street beyond the trains. His senses heightened, he could hear *them* coming, the whispers between them as they spread out to search the compartments.

Spiderlike, Dradin moved as he heard them move, shadowing them but out of sight—into their clutches and out again with a finesse he had not known he possessed—always working his way farther into the jungle of metal. Train tracks. Dining cars. Engines split open by the years, so that he hid among their most secret parts and came out again when danger had passed him by, a pale figure flecked with rust.

Ahead, when he dared to take his gaze from his pursuers, Dradin could see the uniform darkness of the wall and, from beyond, the red flashes of a bonfire. Two rows of cars lay between him and the wall. He crept forward through the gaping doorway of a dining car—

—just as, cloaked by shadow, Dvorak entered the car from the opposite end. Dradin considered backing out of the car, but no: Dvorak would hear him. Instead, he crouched down, hidden from view by an overturned table, a salt-and-pepper shaker still nailed to it.

Dvorak's footsteps came closer, accompanied by raspy breathing and the shivery threat of the knives beneath his coat. A single shout from Dvorak and the mushroom dwellers would find him.

Dvorak stopped in front of the overturned table. Dradin could smell him now, the *must* of mushroom dweller, the *tang* of Moth silt.

Dradin sprang up and slapped his left hand across Dvorak's mouth, spun him around as he grunted, and grappled for Dvorak's knife. Dvorak opened his mouth to bite Dradin. Dradin stuck his fist in Dvorak's mouth, muffling his own scream as the teeth bit down. Now Dvorak could make no sound and the dwarf frantically tried to expel Dradin's fist. Dradin did not let him. The knife seesawed from Dvorak's side up to Dradin's clavicle and back again. Dvorak thrashed about, trying to dislodge Dradin's hold on him, trying to face his enemy. Dradin, muscles straining, entangled Dvorak's legs in his and managed to keep him in the center of the compartment. If they banged up against the sides, it would be as loud as a word from Dvorak's mouth. But the knife was coming too close to Dradin's throat. He smashed Dvorak's hand against a railing, a sound that sent up an echo Dradin thought the mushroom dwellers must surely hear. No one came as the knife fell from Dvorak's hand. Dvorak tried to grasp inside his jacket for another. Dradin pulled a knife from within the jacket first. As Dvorak withdrew his own weapon, Dradin's blade was already buried deep in his throat.

Dradin felt the dwarf's body go taut and then lose its rigidity, while the mouth came loose of his fist and a thick, viscous liquid dribbled down his knife arm.

Dradin turned to catch the body as it fell, so that as he held it and lowered it to the ground, his hand throbbing and bloody, he could see Dvorak's eyes as the life left them. The tattoo, in that light, became all undone, the red dots of cities like wounds, sliding off to become merely a crisscross of lines. Dark blood coated the front of his shirt.

Dradin mumbled a prayer under his breath from reflex alone, for some part of him—the part of him that had laughed to watch the followers of Saint Solon placing sparrows in coffins—insisted that death was unremarkable, undistinguished, and, ultimately, unimportant, for it happened every day, everywhere. Unlike the jungle, Nepenthe's severed hand, here there was no amnesia, no fugue. There was only the body beneath him and an echo in his ears, the memory of his mother's voice as she *thrulled* from deep in her throat a death march, a funeral veil stitched of words and music. How could he feel hatred? He could not. He felt only emptiness.

He heard, with newly preternatural senses, the movement of mushroom dwellers nearby and, resting Dvorak's head against the cold metal floor, he left the compartment, a shadow against the deeper shadow of the wrecked and rotted wheels.

Now it was easy for Dradin, slipping between tracks, huddling in dining compartments, the mushroom dwellers blind to his actions. The two rows of cars between him and the wall became one row and then he was at the wall. He climbed it tortuously, the rough stone cutting into his hands and feet. When he reached the top, he swung up and over to the other side.

Ah, the boulevard beyond, for now Dradin wondered if he should return to the graveyard and hide there. Strewn across the boulevard were scaffolds and from the scaffolds men and women had been hung so that they lolled and, limp, had the semblance of rag dolls. Rag dolls in tatters, the flesh pulled from hindquarters, groins, chests, the red meeting the green of the moon and turning black. Eyes stared sightless. The harsh wind carried the smell of offal. Dogs bit at the feet, the legs, the bodies so thick that as Dradin walked forward, keen for the sound of mushroom dwellers behind him, he had to push aside and duck under the limbs of the dead. Blood splashed his shoulders and he breathed in gasps and held his side, as if something pained him, though it was only the sight of the bodies that pained him. When he realized that he still wore a noose of his own, he pulled it over his head with such speed that it cut him and left a burn.

Past the hanging bodies and burning buildings and flamed out motored vehicles, only to see . . . stilt men carrying severed heads, which they threw to the waiting crowds, who kicked and tossed them . . . a man disemboweled, his intestines streaming out into the gutter as his attackers continued to hack him apart and he clutched at their legs . . . a woman assaulted against a brick wall by ten men who held her down as they cut and raped her . . . fountains full of floating, bloated bodies, the waters turned red-black with blood . . . glimpses of the bonfires, bodies stacked for burning in the dozens . . . a man and woman decapitated, still caught in an embrace, on their knees in the murk of rising mist . . . the unearthly screams, the taste of blood rising in the air, the smell of fire and burning flesh . . . and the female riders on their wooden horses, riding over the bodies of the dead, their eyes still turned inward, that they might not know the horrors of the night.

Oh, that he could rip his own eyes from his sockets! He did not wish to see and yet could not help but see if he wished to live. In the face of such carnage, his killing of Dvorak became the gentlest of mercies. Bile rose in his throat and, sick with grief and horror, he vomited beside an abandoned horse buggy. When the sickness had passed, he gathered his wits, found a landmark he recognized, and by passing through lesser alleys and climbing over the rooftops of one-story houses set close together, came once again to his hostel.

The hostel was empty and silent. Dradin crept, limping from glass in his foot and the ache in his muscles, up to the second floor and his room. Once inside, he did not even try to wash off the blood, the dirt, the filth, did not put on clothes, but stumbled to his belongings and stuffed his pictures, *The Refraction of Light in a Prison*, and his certificate from the religious college into the knapsack. He stood in the center of the room, knapsack over his left shoulder, the machete held in his right hand, breathing heavily, trying to remember who he might be and where he might be and what he should do next. He shuffled over to the window and looked down on the valley. What he saw made him laugh, a high-pitched sound so repugnant to him that he closed his mouth immediately.

The valley lay under a darkness broken by soft, warm lights. No bonfires raged in the valley below. No one hung from scaffolding, tongues blue and purpling. No one bathed in the blood of the dead.

Seeing the valley so calm, Dradin remembered when he had wondered if, perhaps, his beloved lived there, amid the peace where there were no missionaries. No Living Saints. No Cadimons. No Dvoraks. He looked toward the door. It was a perilous door, a deceitful door, for the world lay beyond it in all its brutality. He stood there for several beats of his heart, thinking of how beautiful the woman had looked in the third-story window, how he had thrilled to see her there. What a beautiful place the world had been then, so long ago.

Machete held ready, Dradin walked to the door and out into the night.

7

When Dradin had at last fought his way back to Hoegbotton & Sons, Albumuth Boulevard was deserted except for a girl in a ragged flower print dress. She listened to a tattered phonograph that played Voss Bender tunes.

> *In the deep of winter:*
> *Snatches of song*
> *Through the branches*
> *Brittle as bone.*
>
> *You'll not see my face*
> *But there I'll be,*
> *Frost in my hair,*
> *My hunger hollowing me.*

The sky had cleared and the cold, white pricks of stars shone through the black of night, the green-tinge of moon. The black in which moon and stars floated was absolute; it ate the light of the city, muted everything but the shadows, which multiplied and rippled outward. Behind Dradin, sounds of destruction grew nearer, but here the stores were ghostly but whole. And yet here too men, women, and children hung from the lampposts and looked down with lost, vacant, and wondering stares.

The girl sat on her knees in front of the phonograph. Over her lay the shadow of the great lambent eye, shiny and saucepan blind, of one of the colorful cloth squid, its tentacles rippling in the breeze. Bodies were caught in its fake coils, sprawled and sitting upright in the maw and craw of the beast, as if they had drowned amid the tentacles, washed ashore still entangled and stiffening.

Dradin walked up to the girl. She had brown hair and dark, unreadable eyes with long lashes. She was crying, although her face had long ago been wiped clean of sorrow and of joy. She watched the phonograph as if it were the last thing in the world that made sense to her.

He nudged her. "Go. Go on! Get off the street. You're not safe here."

She did not move, and he looked at her with a mixture of sadness and exasperation. There was nothing he could do. Events were flowing away from him, caught in an undertow stronger than that of the Moth. It was all he could do to preserve his own life, his bloody machete proof of the dangers of the bureaucratic district by which he had come again to Albumuth. The same languid, nostalgic streets of daylight had become killing grounds, a thousand steely-eyed murderers hiding among the vetch and honeysuckle. It was there that he had rediscovered the white-faced mimes, entangled in the ivy, features still in death.

Dradin walked past the girl until Hoegbotton & Sons lay before him. The dull red brick seemed brighter in the night, as if it reflected the fires burning throughout the city.

And so it ends where it began, Dradin thought. In front of the very same Hoegbotton & Sons building. Were he not such a coward, he should have ended it there much sooner.

Dradin stole up the stairs to the door. He smashed the glass of the door with his already mangled fist, grunting with pain. The pain pulsed far away, disconnected from him in his splendid nakedness. *Pinpricks on the souls of distant sinners.* Dradin swung the door open and shut it with such a clatter that he was sure someone had heard him and would come loping down the boulevard after him. But no one came and his feet, naked and dirty and cut, continued to slap the steps inside so loudly that surely she would run away if she was still alive, thinking him an intruder. But where to run? He could hear his own labored breathing as he navigated the stairs: the sound filled the landing; it filled the spaces between the steps; and it filled him with determination, for it was the most vital sign that he still lived, despite every misfortune.

Dradin laughed, but it came out ragged around the edges. His mind sagged under the weight of carnage: the cries of looting, begging; the sound of men swinging by their necks or their feet. Swinging all across a city grown suddenly wise and quiet in their deaths.

But that was out there, in the city. In here, Dradin promised, he would not lose himself to such images. He would not lose the thread.

Curious, but on reaching the door to the third floor, Dradin paused, halted, did not yet grasp the iron knob. For this door led to the window. He had engraved her position so perfectly on the interstices of his memory that he knew exactly where she must be . . . One moment more of hesitation, and then Dradin entered.

A room. Darkened. The smell of sawdust packing and boxes. Not the right room. Not her room. The antechamber only, for receiving visitors, perhaps, the walls lined with decadent art objects, and beyond that, an open doorway, leading to . . .

The next room was lined with Occidental shadow puppets that looked like black scars, seared and shaped into human forms: bodies entwined in lust and devout in prayer, bodies engaged in murder and in business. Harlequins and pierrots with bashful red eyes and sharp teeth lay on their backs, feet up in the air. Jungle plants trellised and cat's cradled the interior, freed from terrariums, while a clutter of other things hidden by the shadows beckoned him with their strange, angular shapes. The smell of moist rot mixed with the stench of mushroom dweller and the sweet bitter of sweat, as if the very walls labored for the creation of such wonderful monstrosities.

She still faced the window, but set back from it, in a wooden chair, so that the curling curious fires ravaging the city beyond could not sear her face. The light from these fires created a zone of blackness and Dradin could see only her black hair draped across the chair.

It seemed to Dradin as he looked at the woman sitting in the chair that he had not seen her in a hundred, a thousand, years; that he saw her across some great becalmed ocean or desert, she only a shape like the shadow puppets. He moved closer.

His woman, the woman of his dreams, gazed off into the charred red-black air, the opposite street, or even toward the hidden River Moth beyond. He thought he saw a hint of movement as he approached her—a slight uplifting of one arm—she no longer concerned with the short view, but with the long view, the perspective that nothing of the moment mattered or would ever matter. It had been Dvorak's view, with the map that had taken over his body. It was Cadimon's view, not allowing the priest to take pity on a former student.

"My love," Dradin said, and again, "My love," as he walked around so he could see the profile of her face. A white sheet covered her body, but her face, oh, her face . . . her eyebrows were thin and dark, her eyes like twin blue flames, her nose small, unobtrusive, her skin white, white, white, but with a touch of color that drew him down to the sumptuous curve of her mouth, the bead of sweat upon the upper lip, the fine hairs placed to seduce, to trick; the way in which the clothes clung to her body and made it seem to curve, the arms placed upon the arms of the chair, so naturally that there was no artifice in having done so. Might she . . . could she . . . still be . . . alive?

Dradin pulled aside the white sheet—and screamed, for there lay the torso, the legs severed and in pieces beneath, but placed cleverly for the illusion of life, the head balanced atop the torso, dripping neither blood nor precious humors, but as dry and slick and perfect as if it had never known a body. Which it had not. From head to toe, Dradin's beloved was a mannequin, an artifice, a deception. *Hoegbotton & Sons, specialists in all manner of profane and Occidental technologies . . .*

Dradin's mouth opened and closed but no sound came from him. Now he could see the glassy finish of her features, the innate breakability of a creature made of papier-mâché and metal and porcelain and clay, mixed and beaten and blown and sandpapered and engraved and made up like any other woman. A testimony to the clockmaker's craft, for at the hinges and joints of the creature dangled broken filaments and wires and gimshaw circuitry. Fool. He was thrice a fool.

Dradin circled the woman, his body shivering, his hands reaching out to caress the curve of cheekbone, only to pull back before he touched skin. The jungle fever beat within him, fell away in *decrescendo*, then again *crescendo*. Twice more around and his arm darted out against his will and he touched her cheek. Cold. So cold. So monstrously cold against the warmth of his body. Cold and dead in her beauty despite the heat and the bonfires roaring outside. Dead. Not alive. Never alive.

As he touched her, as he saw all of her severed parts and how they fit together, something small and essential broke inside him; broke so he couldn't ever fix it. Now he saw Nepenthe in his mind's eye in all of her darkness and grace. Now he could see her as a person, not an idea. Now he could see her nakedness, remember the way she had felt under him—smooth and moist and warm—never moving as he made love to her. As he took her though she did not want to be taken. If ever he had lost his faith it was then, as he lost himself in the arms of a woman indifferent to him, indifferent to the world. He saw again the flash of small hand, severed and gray, and saw again his own hand, holding the blade. Her severed hand. His hand holding the blade. Coming to in the burning missionary station, severed of his memory, severed from his faith, severed from his senses by the fever. Her severed gray hand in his and in the other the machete.

Dradin dropped the machete and it landed with a clang next to the mannequin's feet.

Feverish, he had crawled back from his jungle expedition, the sole survivor, only to find that the people he had gone out to convert had come to the station and burned it to the ground . . . fallen unconscious, and come to with the hand in his, Nepenthe naked and dead next to him. Betrayal.

The shattered pieces within came loose in an exhalation of breath. He could not contain himself any longer, and he sobbed there, at the mannequin's feet. As he hugged her to him, the fragile balance came undone and her body scattered into pieces all around him, the head staring up at him from the floor.

"I killed her I did I killed her I didn't kill her I didn't mean to I meant to I didn't mean to she made me I let her I wanted her I couldn't have her I never wanted her I wanted her not the way I wanted I couldn't I meant to I couldn't have meant to but I did it I don't know if I did it—*I can't remember!*"

Dradin slid to the floor and lay there for a long while, exhausted, gasping for breath, his mouth tight, his jaw unfamiliar to him. He welcomed the pain from the splinters that cut into his flesh from the floorboards. He felt hollow inside, indifferent, so fatigued, so despairing that he did not know if he could ever regain his feet.

But, after a time, Dradin looked full into the woman's eyes and a grim smile spread across his face. He thought he could hear his mother's voice mixed with the sound of rain thrumming across a roof. He thought he could hear his father reading the adventures of Juliette and Justine to him. He knelt beside the head and caressed its cheek. He lay beside the head and admired its features.

He heard himself say it.

"I love you."

He still loved her. He could not deny it. Could not. It was a love that might last a minute or a day, an hour or a month, but for the moment, in his need, it seemed as permanent as the moon and the stars, and as cold.

It did not matter that she was in pieces, that she was not real, for he could see now that she was his salvation. Had he not been in love with what he saw in the third-story window, and had what he had seen through that window changed in its essential nature? Wasn't she better suited to him than if she had been real, with all the avarices and hungers and needs and awkwardnesses that create disappointment? He had invented an entire history for this woman and now his expectations of her would never change and she would never age, never criticize him, never tell him he was too fat or too sloppy or too neat, and he would never have to raise his voice to her.

It struck Dradin as he basked in the glow of such feelings, as he watched the porcelain lines of the head while shouts grew louder and the gallows jerked and swung merrily all across the city. It struck him that he could not betray this woman. There would be no decaying, severed hand. No flowers sprayed red with blood. No crucial misunderstandings. The thought blossomed bright and blinding in his head. He could not betray her. Even if he set her head upon the mantel and took a lover there, in front of her, as his father might once have done to his mother, those eyes would not register the sin. This seemed to him, in that moment, to be a form of wisdom beyond even Cadimon, a wisdom akin to the vision that had struck him as he stood in the backyard of the old house in Morrow.

Dradin embraced the pieces of his lover, luxuriating in the smooth and shiny feel of her, the precision of her skin. He rose to a knee, cradling his beloved's head in his shaking arms. Was he moaning now? Was he screaming now? Who could tell?

With careful deliberateness, Dradin took his lover's head and walked into the antechamber, and then out the door. The third-floor landing was dark and quiet. He began to walk down the stairs, descending slowly at first, taking pains to slap his feet against each step. But when he reached the second-floor landing, he became more frantic, as if to escape what lay behind him, until by the time he reached the first floor and burst out from the shattered front door, he was running hard, knapsack bobbing against his back.

Down the boulevard, seen through the folds of the squid float, a mob approached, holding candles and torches and lanterns. Stores flared and burned behind them . . .

Dradin spared them not a glance, but continued to run—past the girl and her phonograph, still playing Voss Bender, and past Borges Bookstore, in the shadow of which prowled the black panther from the parade, and then beyond, into the unknown. Sidestepping mushroom dwellers at their dark harvest, their hands full of mushrooms from which spores broke off like dandelion tufts, and the last of the revelers of the Festival of the Freshwater Squid, their trajectories those of pendulums and their tongues blue if not black, arms slack at their sides. Through viscera and the limbs of babies stacked in neat piles. Among the heehaws and gimgobs, the drunken dead and the lolly lashers with their dark whips. Weeping now, tears without end. Mumbling and whispering endearments to his beloved, running strong under the mad, mad light of the moon—headed forever and always for the docks and the muscular waters of the River Moth, which would take him and his lover as far as he might wish, though perhaps not far enough.

The Hoegbotton Guide

to the

EARLY HISTORY OF THE CITY OF

Ambergris

BY

DUNCAN SHRIEK

he history of Ambergris, for our purposes, begins with the legendary exploits of the whaler-cum-pirate Cappan John Manzikert[1,2,3], who, in the Year of Fire—so called for the catastrophic volcanic activity in the Southern Hemisphere that season—led his fleet of 30 whaling ships up the Moth River Delta into the River Moth proper. Although not the first reported incursion of Aan whaling clans into the region, it is the first incursion of any importance.

Manzikert's purpose was to escape the wrath of his clansman Michael Brueghel, who had decimated Manzikert's once-proud 100-ship fleet off the coast of the Isle of Aandalay. Brueghel meant to finish off Manzikert for good, and so pursued him some 40 miles upriver, near the current port of Stockton, before finally giving up the chase. The reason for this conflict between potential allies is unclear—our historical sources are few and often inaccurate; indeed, one of the most infuriating aspects of early Ambergrisian history is the regularity with which

1. By Manzikert's time, the rough southern accent of his people had permanently changed the designation "Captain" to "Cappan." "Captain" referred not only to Manzikert's command of a fleet of ships, but also to the old Imperial titles given by the Saphants to the commander of a *see* of islands; thus, the title had both religious and military connotations. Its use, this late in history, reflects how pervasive the Saphant Empire's influence was: 200 years after its fall, its titles were still being used by clans that had only known of the Empire secondhand.

2. A footnote on the purpose of these footnotes: This text is rich with footnotes to avoid inflicting upon you, the idle tourist, so much knowledge that, bloated with it, you can no longer proceed to the delights of the city with your customary mindless abandon. In order to hamstring your predictable attempts—once having discovered a topic of interest in this narrative—to skip ahead, I have weeded out all of those cross references to other Hoegbotton publications that litter the rest of this pamphlet series like a plague of fungi.

3. I should add to footnote 2 that the most interesting information will be included only in footnote form, and I will endeavor to include as many footnotes as possible. Indeed, information alluded to in footnote form will later be expanded upon in the main text, thus confusing any of you who have decided not to read the footnotes. This is the price to be paid by those who would rouse an elderly historian from his slumber behind a desk in order to coerce him to write for a common travel guide series.

truth and legend pursue separate courses—but the result is clear: in late summer of the Year of Fire, Manzikert found himself a full 70 miles upriver, at the place where the Moth forms an inverted "L" before straightening out both north and south. Here, for the first time, he found that the fresh water flowing south had completely cleansed the salt water seeping north.[4]

Manzikert anchored his ships at the joint of the "L," which formed a natural harbor, at dusk of the day of their arrival. The banks were covered in a lush undergrowth very familiar to the Aan, as it would have approximated the vegetation of their own native southern islands.[5] They had, encouragingly enough, seen no signs of possibly hostile habitation, but could not muster the energy, as dusk approached, to launch an expedition. However, that night the watchmen on the ships were startled to see the lights of campfires clearly visible through the trees and, as more than one keen-eared whaler noticed, the sound of a high and distant chanting. Manzikert immediately ordered a military force to land under cover of darkness, but the Truffidian monk Samuel Tonsure persuaded him to rescind the order and await the dawn.

Tonsure—who, following his capture from Nicea (near the mouth of the Moth River Delta), had persuaded the Cappan to convert to Truffidianism and thus gained influence over him—plays a major role, perhaps the major role, in our understanding of Ambergris's early history.[6] It is from Tonsure that most histories

4. Today, the salinity of the river changes to fresh water a mere 25 miles upriver; the reason for this change is unknown, but may be linked to the buildup of silt at the river's mouth, which acts as a natural filter.

5. Almost 500 years later, the Petularch Dray Mikal would order the uprooting of native flora around the city in favor of the northern species of his youth, surely among the most strikingly arrogant responses to homesickness on record. The Petularch would be dead for 50 years before the transplantation could be ruled a success.

6. And yet, what is our understanding of the monk's early history? Obscure at best. The records at Nicea contain no mention of a Samuel Tonsure, and it is possible he was just passing through the city on his way elsewhere and so did not actively preach there. "Samuel Tonsure" may also be a name that Tonsure created to disguise his true identity. A handful of scholars, in particular the truculent Mary Sabon, argue that Tonsure was none other than the Patriarch of Nicea himself, a man who is known to have disappeared at roughly the same time Tonsure appeared with Manzikert. Sabon offers as circumstantial evidence the oft repeated story that the Patriarch sometimes traversed his city incognito, dressed as a simple monk to spy on his subordinates. He could easily have been captured without knowledge of his rank—which, if revealed, would have given Manzikert such leverage over Nicea that he might well have been able to take the city and settle behind its walls, safe from Brueghel. If so, however, why didn't the Patriarch make any attempt to escape once he had gained Manzikert's trust? The case, despite some of Sabon's other evidence, seems wrong-headed from its inception. My own research, corroborated by the Autarch of Nunk, indicates that the Patriarch's disappearance coincides with that of the priestess Caroline of the Church of

descend—both from the discredited (and incomplete) *Biography of John Manzikert I of Aan and Ambergris,*[7] obviously written to please the Cappan, and from his secret journal, which he kept on his person at all times and which we may assume Manzikert never saw since otherwise he would have had Tonsure put to death.

The journal contains a most intricate account of Manzikert, his exploits, and subsequent events. That this journal appeared (or, rather, reappeared) under somewhat dubious circumstances should not detract from its overall validity, and does not explain the derision directed at it from certain quarters, possibly because the name "Samuel Tonsure" sounds like a joke to a few small-minded scholars. It certainly was not a joke to Samuel Tonsure.[8]

At daybreak, Manzikert ordered the boats lowered and with 100 men, including Tonsure, set off on a reconnaissance mission to the shore. It must have been a somewhat ridiculous sight, for as Tonsure writes of Manzikert, a man possessed of a cruel and mercurial temper, "he must occupy one boat himself, save for the oarsman, such a large man was he and the boat beneath him a child's toy."[9] Here, as Manzikert is rowed toward the site of the city he will found, it is appropriate to quote in full Tonsure's famous appraisal of the Cappan:

> I myself marveled at the man; for nature had combined in his person all the qualities necessary for a military commander. He stood at the height of almost seven feet, so that to look at him men would tilt back their heads as if toward the top of a hill or a high mountain. Possessed of startling blue eyes and furrowed brows, his countenance was neither gentle nor pleasing, but put one in mind of a tempest; his

---

the Seven-Pointed Star, and that the Patriarch and Caroline eloped together, the ceremony performed by a traveling juggler hastily ordained as a priest.

7. For reasons which will become clear, Tonsure could no longer complete it; therefore, 10 years later, Manzikert's son had another Truffidian monk summoned from Nicea for this purpose. Unfortunately, this monk, whose name is lost to us, believed in wearing hair shirts, daily flagellation, and preaching "the abomination of the written word." He did indeed complete the biography, but he might as well have spared himself the effort. Although edited by Manzikert II himself, it contains such prose as "And his highly exhulted majesty set foot on land like a swaggorin conquor from daes of your." Clearly this abominator's abominations against the Written Word far outweigh any crimes It may have perpetrated upon him.

8. If the careful historian needs further proof that Sabon is wrong, he need look no further than the inscription on the monk's journal: "Samuel Tonsure." Why would he bother to maintain the pretense since the contents of the journal itself would condemn him to death? And why would he, if indeed the Patriarch (a learned and clever man by all accounts), choose such a clumsy and obvious pseudonym?

9. All quotes without attribution are from Tonsure's journal, not the biography.

voice was like thunder and his hands seemed made for tearing down walls or for smashing doors of bronze. He could spring like a lion and his frown was terrible. Those who saw him for the first time discovered that every description that they had heard of him was an understatement.[10]

Alas, the Cappan possessed no corresponding wisdom or quality of mercy. Tonsure obviously feared his master's mood on this occasion, for he tried to persuade Manzikert to remain onboard his flagship and allow the more reasonable of his lieutenants—perhaps even his son John Manzikert II,[11] who would one day govern his people brilliantly—to lead the landing party, but Manzikert, Truffidian though he was, would have none of it. The Cappan also actively encouraged his wife, Sophia, to accompany them. Unfortunately, Tonsure tells us little about Sophia Manzikert in either the biography or the journal (her own biography has not survived), but from the little we do know Tonsure's description of her husband might fit her equally well; the two often waxed romantic on the pleasures of being able to pillage together.

And so, Manzikert, Sophia, Tonsure, and the Cappan's men landed on the site of what would soon be Ambergris. At the moment, however, it was occupied by a people Tonsure christened "gray caps," known today as "mushroom dwellers."

Tonsure reports that they had advanced hardly a hundred paces into the underbrush before they came upon the first inhabitant, standing outside of his "rounded and domed single-story house, built low to the ground and seamless, from which issued a road made of smooth, shiny stones cleverly mortared together." The building might have once served as a sentinel post, but was now used as living quarters.

Clearly Tonsure found the building more impressive than the native standing outside of it, for he spends three pages on its every minute detail and gives us only this short paragraph on the building's inhabitant:

> Stout and short, he came only to the Cappan's shoulder: swathed from head to foot in
> a gray cloak that covered his tunic and trousers, these made from lighter gray swatches

---

10. Quote taken from the biography. One wonders: if the Cappan was so fierce, how much more fearsome must Michael Brueghel have been to make him flee the south?

11. The Cappan's appending "II" to his son's name gives us an early indication that he meant to settle on land and found a dynasty. The Aan clan would have thought the idea of a dynasty odd, for usually cappans were chosen from among the ablest sailors, with hereditary claims a secondary consideration.

of animal skin stitched together. Upon his head lay a hat the color of an Oliphaunt's skin: a tall, wide contrivance that covered his face from the sun. His features, what could be seen of them, were thick, sallow, innocent of knowledge. When the Cappan inquired as to the nature and name of the place, this unattractive creature could not answer except in a series of clicks, grunts, and whistles that appeared to imitate the song of the cricket and locust. It could not be considered speech or language. It was, as with insects, a warning or curious sound, devoid of other meaning.[12]

We can take a farcical delight from imagining the scene: the giant leaning down to communicate with the dwarf, the dwarf speaking a language so subtle and sophisticated that it has resisted translation to the present day, while the giant spits out a series of crude consonants and vowels that must have seemed to the gray cap a sudden bout of apoplexy.

Manzikert found the gray cap repellent, resembling as it did, he is quoted as saying, "both child and mushroom,"[13] and if not for his fear of retaliation from a presumed ruling body of unknown strength, the Cappan would have run the native through with his sword. Instead, he left the gray cap to its incomprehensible

---

12. I find it necessary to interject three observations here. First, that the paragraph on the gray caps written for the Cappan's biography is far worse, describing as it does "small, piglike eyes, a jowly jagged crease for a mouth, and a nose like an ape." The gray caps actually looked much like the mushroom dwellers of today—which is to say, like smaller versions of ourselves—but the Cappan was already attempting to dehumanize them, and thus create a justification, a rationalization, for depriving them of life and property. Second, and surprisingly, evidence suggests that the gray caps wove their clothing from the cured pelts of field mice. Third, Tonsure appears to have given away a secret—if, in fact, the gray cap they met came "only to the Cappan's shoulder" and the gray caps averaged, by Tonsure's own admission, three and one-half feet in height (as do the modern mushroom dwellers), then the Cappan could only have stood four and one-half feet to five feet in height, something of a small person himself. (Is it of import that in a letter concerning future trade relations written to the Kalif, Brueghel calls Manzikert "my insignificant enemy," since "insignificant" in the Kalif's language doubles as a noun meaning "dwarf" and Brueghel, who wrote his own letters of state, loved word play?) Perhaps Tonsure's description of Manzikert in the biography was dictated by the Cappan, who wished to conceal his slight stature from History. Unfortunately, the Cappan's height, or lack thereof, remains an ambiguous subject, and thus I will stay true to the orthodox version of the story as related by Tonsure. Still, it is delicious to speculate. (If indeed Manzikert was short, we might have hoped he would look upon the gray caps as long-lost cousins twice removed. Alas, he did not do so.)
13. We can only speculate as to why Manzikert should find children and mushrooms repulsive. He certainly ate mushrooms and had had a child with Sophia. Perhaps, if indeed undertall, his nickname growing up had been "little mushroom"?

vigil, still clicking and whistling to their backs,[14] and proceeded along the silvery road until they reached the city.

Although Tonsure has, criminally, neglected to provide us with the reactions of Manzikert and Sophia upon their first glimpse of the city proper—and, from the monk's description of aqueducts, almost certainly the future site of Albumuth Boulevard—we can imagine that they were as impressed as Tonsure himself, who wrote:

> The buildings visible beyond the increasingly scanty tree cover were decorated throughout by golden stars, like the very vault of heaven, but whereas heaven has its stars only at intervals, here the surfaces were entirely covered with gold, issuing forth from the center in a never-ending stream. Surrounding the main building were other, smaller buildings, themselves surrounded completely or in part by cloisters. Structures of breathtaking complexity stretched as far as the eye could see. Then came a second circle of buildings, larger than the first, with lawns covered in mushrooms of every possible size and color—from gigantic growths as large as the Oliphaunt[15] to delicate, glassy nodules no larger than a child's fingernail. These mushrooms—red capped and blue capped, their undersides dusted with streaks of silver or emerald or obsidian—gave off spores of the most varied and remarkable fragrances, while the gray caps themselves tended their charges with, in this one instance, admirable delicacy and loving concern . . .[16] There were also

14. As this is the first and last time the gray caps actively attempted to communicate with the Aan, one wonders just what the gray cap was saying to Manzikert. A friendly greeting? A warning? The very loquaciousness of this particular gray cap in relation to the others they were to encounter has led more than one historian to assume that he (or she—contrary to popular opinion, there are as many female gray caps as male; the robes tend to make them all look unisexual) had been assigned to greet the landing party. What opportunities did Manzikert miss by not trying harder to understand the gray cap's intent? What tragedies might have been averted?

15. Tonsure was criminally fond of Oliphaunts. References to them, usually preceded by mundanea like "as large as" or "as gray as," occur 30 times in the journal. Possessed of infinite mercy, I shall spare you 28 of these comparisons.

16. Tonsure's description in the biography also includes a series of mushroom drawings by Manzikert—an attempt to "appear sensitive," Tonsure sneers in his journal—from which I provide three samples for the half dozen of you who are curious as to the Cappan's illustrative skills:

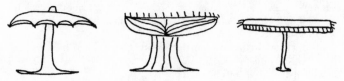

fountains which filled basins of water; gardens, some of them hanging, full of exotic mosses, lichens, and ferns, others sloping down to the level ground; and a bath of pure gold that was beautiful beyond description.[17]

We can only imagine the slavering delight of Manzikert and his wife upon seeing all that gold; unfortunately, as they would soon find out, much of the "gold" covering the buildings was actually a living organism similar to lichen that the gray caps had trained to create decorative patterns; *not* only was it not gold, it wasn't even edible.

Nonetheless, Manzikert and his men began to explore the city. The most elemental details about the buildings they ignored, instead remarking upon the abundance of tame rats as large as cats,[18] the plethora of exotic birds, and, of course, the large quantities of fungus, which the gray caps appeared to harvest, eat, and store against future famine.[19]

While Manzikert explores, I shall pass the time by relating a few facts about the city. According to the scant gray cap records that have been found and, if not translated, then haltingly understood, they called the city "Cinsorium," although the meaning of the word has been lost, or, more accurately, never been found. It is estimated by those who have studied the ruins lying beneath Ambergris[20] that at one time Cinsorium could have housed 250,000 souls, making it among the largest

17. Apparently, since Tonsure fails to describe it.
18. The mammologist Xaver Daffed maintains that these were "actually cababari, a stunted relation of the pig that resembles a rat." (Quote taken from *The Hoegbotton Guide to Small, Indigenous Mammals*.) If so, then, as subsequent events will show, the rats of Ambergris have managed something of a public relations coup; the poor cababari are today extinct in the southern climes.
19. James Lacond has suggested that the fungus had hallucinogenic qualities. Tonsure, for his part, sampled a "fungus that resembled an artichoke" and found it tasted like unleavened bread; he reports no side effects, although Lacond claims that the rest of Tonsure's account must be considered a drug-induced dream. Lacond further claims that Tonsure's later account of Manzikert's men glutting themselves on the fungi—some of which tasted like honey and some like chicken—explains their sudden mercilessness. But Lacond contradicts himself: if the rest of Tonsure's account is a fever dream, then so is his description of the men eating the fungus. As always when discussing the gray caps, debate tends to describe the same circles as their buildings. (A similar circularity drove a subdivided Lacond, late in his life, to declare that the world as we know it is actually a product of the dream dreamt by Tonsure. Since our knowledge of our identity as Ambergrisians, where we came from, is so dependent on Tonsure's journal, this is close to the heresy of madness.)
20. Admittedly, a perilous and notoriously inaccurate undertaking; the mushroom dwellers tend to look unkindly upon intrusions into their territory.

of all ancient cities. Cinsorium also boasted highly advanced plumbing and water distribution systems that would be the envy of many a city today.[21]

However, at the time Manzikert stumbled upon Cinsorium, Tonsure argued, it was well past its glory years. He based this conclusion on rather shaky evidence: the "undeniable decadence" of its inhabitants. Surely Tonsure is prejudicial beyond reason, for the city appeared fully functional—the high domed buildings in sparkling good repair, the streets swept constantly, the amphitheaters looking as if they might, within minutes, play host to innumerable entertainments.

Tonsure ignored these signs of a healthy culture, perhaps fearing to admit that an almost certainly heretical people might be superior. Instead, he argued, in the biography especially, but also in his journal, that the current inhabitants—numbering no more, he estimates, than 700—had no claim to any greatness once possessed by their ancestors, for they were "clearly the last generations of a dying race," unable to understand the processes of the city, unable to work its machines, unable to farm, "reduced to hunting and gathering."[22] Their watch fires scorched the interiors of great halls, whole clans wetly bickering with one another within a territory marked by the walls of a single building. They did not a one of them, according to Tonsure, comprehend the legacy of their heritage.

Tonsure's greatest argument for the gray caps' degeneracy may also be his weakest. That first day, Manzikert and Sophia entered what the monk described as a library, a structure "more immense than all but the most revered ecclesiastical institutions I have studied within." The shelves of this library had rotted away before the onslaught of a startling profusion of small dark purple mushrooms with white stems. The books, made from palm frond pulp in a process lost to us, had all spilled out upon the main floor—thousands of books, many ornately engraved with strange letters[23] and overlaid by the now familiar golden lichen. The use the current gray caps had made of these books was as firewood, for as Manzikert

21. The question of where the gray caps came from and why they were concentrated only in Cinsorium remains a mystery. The subject has frustrated many a historian and, to avoid a similar fate, I shall pass over it entirely.
22. But surely they farmed the fungus?
23. Tonsure reports the following symbol showed up repeatedly:

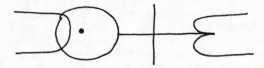

watched in disbelief, gray caps came and went, collecting the books and condemning them to their cooking fires.

Did Tonsure correctly interpret what he saw in the "library"? I think not, and have published my doubts in a monograph entitled "An Argument for the Gray Caps and Against the Evidence of Tonsure's Eyes."[24] I believe the "library" was actually a place for religious worship, the "books" prayer rolls. Prayer rolls in some cultures, particularly in the far Occident, are consigned to the flames in a holy ritual. The "shelves" were rotted wooden planks specifically inserted into the walls to foster the growth of the special purple mushrooms, which grew nowhere else in Cinsorium and may well have had religious significance.[25] Another clue lay in the large, mushroom-shaped stone erected just beyond the library's front steps, since determined to have been an altar.

Sophia chose this moment to remark upon what she termed the "primitivism" of the natives, chiding her husband for his "cowardice." Faced with such a rebuke, Manzikert became more aggressive and free of any moral restraints. Fortunately, it took several days for this new attitude to manifest itself, during which time Manzikert moved more and more of his people off the ships and onto the lip of the bay, where he commenced building docks. He also appropriated several of the round, squat structures on the fringes as living quarters, evicting the native inhabitants who, burbling to themselves, complacently walked into the city proper.

Not only were Manzikert's clan members glad to stretch their legs, but the land that awaited them proved, upon exploration, to be ideal. Abundant springs and natural aquifers fed off the Moth, while game, from pigs to deer to a flightless bird called a "grout," provided an ample food source. The curve of the river accentuated the breeze that blew from the west, generally cooling the savage climate, and with the breeze came birds, swallows in particular, to swoop down at dusk and devour the vast clouds of insects that hovered over the water.

Tonsure spent these five or six days wandering the city, which he still found a marvel. He had, he wrote in his journal, "squandered" much of his early life in the realm of the Kalif, where architectural marvels crowded every city, but never

24. Volume XX, Issue 2, of *The Real History Newsletter*, published by the Ambergrisians for the Original Inhabitants Society.
25. In a city otherwise so pristine, such blatant "disorder" should have made Tonsure suspicious. Was he now so completely set, as was his master, on the goal of discrediting and dehumanizing the gray caps, that he could see it no other way?

had he seen anything like Cinsorium.[26] First of all, the city had no corners, only curves. Its architects had built circles within circles, domes within domes, and circles within domes. Tonsure found the effect soothing to the eye, and more importantly to the spirit: "This lack of edges, of conflicting lines, makes of the mind a plateau both serene and calm." The possible truth of this observation has been confirmed by modern-day architects who, on review of the reconstructed blueprint of Cinsorium, have described it as the structural equivalent of a tuning fork, a vibration in the soul.

Just as delightful were the huge, festive mosaics lining the walls, most of which depicted battles or mushroom harvesting, while a few consisted of abstract shiftings of red and black; these last gave Tonsure as much unease as the lack of corners had given him comfort, although again he could not say why. The mosaics were made from lichen and fungus skillfully placed and trained to achieve the desired effect. Sometimes fruits, vegetables, or seeds were also used to form decorative patterns—cauliflower to depict a sheeplike creature called the "lunger," for example—with the gray caps replacing these weekly. If Tonsure can be believed, one mosaic used the eggs of a native thrush to depict the eyes of a gray cap; when the eggs hatched, the eyes appeared to be opening.

The library yielded the most magnificent of Tonsure's discoveries: a mechanized golden tree, its branches festooned with intricate jeweled shrikes and parrots, while on the circular dais by which it moved equally intricate deer, stalked by lions, pawed the golden ground. By use of a winding key, the birds would burst simultaneously into song while the lions roared beneath them. The gray caps maintained it in perfect working condition, but had no appreciation for its beauty, as if they "were themselves clockwork parts in some vast machine, fated to retrace the same movements year after year."

Yet, as Tonsure's appreciation for the city grew, so too did his loathing of its inhabitants. Runts, he calls them—cripples. In their ignorance of the beauty of their own city, he wrote (in the biography), they "had become unfit to rule over it, or even to live within its boundaries." Their "pallor, the sickly moistness of their skin, even the rheumy discharge from their eyes," all pointed to the "abomination of their existence, mocking the memory of what they once had been."[27]

26. Unfortunately, this claim strengthens Sabon's assertion with regard to the Patriarch of Nicea—see footnote 6.
27. Poor Tonsure. Just preceding this diatribe, the monk describes a kind of hard mushroom, about seven inches tall, with a stem as thick as its head. When squeezed, this mushroom suddenly

Why the normally tolerant Tonsure came to espouse such ideas we may never know; certainly, there is none of the element of pity that marks his journal comments about Manzikert, whom he calls "a seething mass of emotions, a pincushion of feelings who would surely be locked away if he were not already a leader of men." Although Tonsure's disparaging comments in his journal seem overwrought, similar comments in the biography are easily attributed to Manzikert himself, for if the monk reviled the natives, the Cappan hated them with an intensity that can have no rational explanation. Tonsure records that whenever Manzikert had cause to walk through the city, he would casually murder any gray cap in his path. Perhaps even more chilling, other gray caps in the vicinity ignored such unprovoked murder, and the mortally wounded themselves expired without a struggle.[28]

At the end of the first week, Manzikert and Sophia held a festival not only to celebrate the completion of the docks, but also "this new beginning as dwellers on the land." Due to its timing, this celebration must be considered the forerunner of the Festival of the Freshwater Squid.[29] During the festivities, Manzikert christened the new settlement "Ambergris," after the "most secret and valuable part of the whale"[30]—over Sophia's objections, who, predictably enough, wanted to call the settlement "Sophia."

---

throbs to an even greater size. While walking innocently between the "library" and the amphitheater, Tonsure came across a group of gray cap women using these mushrooms in what he calls a "lascivious way." So perhaps we should forgive him his hyperbole. Still, shocked or not—and he was a more worldly monk than many—Tonsure should have noticed that for every such "perversion," the gray caps had developed a dozen more useful wonders. For example, another type of mushroom stood two feet tall and had a long, thin stem with a wide hood that, when plucked, could be used as an umbrella; the hood even collapsed into the stem for easy storage.

28. Here Lacond proves useful. He puts forth two theories for the gray caps' passivity: first, that Manzikert had landed in the midst of a religious festival during which the gray caps were forbidden to take part in any aggressive acts, even to defend themselves; second, that the gray cap society resembled that of bees or ants, and thus none of the "units" in the city had free will, being extensions of some hive intellect. This second theory by Lacond seems extreme to some historians, but the idea of passivity being bred into particular classes of gray cap society cannot be ruled out. This would support my own theory that the entire city of Cinsorium was a religious artifact, a temple, if you will, in which violence was not permitted to be inflicted by its keepers. Were Manzikert's actions tantamount to desecration?

29. Typically, Sabon cannot bite her tongue and disagrees, citing the Calabrian Calendar used by the Aan as schismatic—most definitely not synchronized with the modern calendar. However, Sabon fails to take into account that Tonsure, as the non-Aan author of the biography and the journal, would have used the Kalif's calendar, which is identical to our own.

30. Cynically, Tonsure reports, "Better to name a city after the nether parts of a whale than to actually go whaling, for Manzikert, lazy as he is, finds piracy much easier than whaling: when you

The next morning, Manzikert, groggy from grog the night before, got up to relieve himself and, about to do so beside one of the gray caps' round dwellings, noticed on the wall a small, flesh-colored lichen that bore a striking resemblance to the Lepress Saint Kristina of Malfour, a major icon in the Truffidian religion. Menacing the Saint was a lichen that looked uncannily like a gray cap. Manzikert fell into a religious rage, gathered his people and told them of his vision. In the biography, Tonsure dutifully reports the jubilant reaction of Manzikert's men upon learning they were going to war because of a maliciously shaped fungus,[31] but neglects to mention this reaction in his journal, presumably out of shame.[32]

Late in the afternoon, Sophia and Tonsure at his side, Cappan Manzikert I of Aan and Ambergris led a force of 200 men into the city. The sun, Tonsure writes, shone blood red, and the streets of Cinsorium soon reflected red independent of the sun, for at Manzikert's order, his men began to slaughter the gray caps. It was a horribly mute affair. The gray caps offered no resistance, but only stared up at their attackers as they were cut down.[33] Perhaps if they had resisted, Manzikert might have shown them mercy, but their silence, their utter willingness to die rather than fight back, infuriated the Cappan, and the massacre continued unabated until dusk. By this time "the newly christened city had become indistinguishable from a charnel house, so much blood had been spilled upon the streets; the smell of the slaughter gathered in the humid air, and the blood itself clung to us like sweat."

---

harpoon an honest sailor, he is less likely to drag you 300 miles across open water and then, turning, casually devour you and drown your companions." Other names Manzikert considered include "Aanville," "Aanapolis," and "Aanburg," so we may be fairly certain that Tonsure suggested "Ambergris," despite his ridicule of the name.

31. Or, as Sabon put it, "how cunning a fungus."

32. Tonsure does, in his journal, write that the lichen in question "more closely resembled one blob rutting with another blob, but who is to doubt the vision of cappans?" Are we to believe that the carnage to come was all the result of two unfortunately shaped lichen? Sabon points to the Holy Visitation of Stockton (alternately known by historians as the Sham Involving Jam), where a stain of blueberry jam resembling the heretic Ibonof Ibonof sparked seven days of riots. Lacond, in agreement with Sabon, relates the story that the Kalif's order to attack the Menite town of Richter was the direct result of a Richter lemon squirting him in the eye when he cut it open. Unfortunately, Sabon and Lacond have joined forces to support an idea that lacks merit given the context. It is my opinion that, lichen or no lichen, Manzikert would have attacked the gray caps.

33. Tonsure never indicates what he did during the massacre—whether to participate or intervene; later circumstantial evidence indicates he may have tried to intervene. Nonetheless, Tonsure's description of the massacre has a disturbingly cold, disinterested edge to it. Predictably, the biography account speaks of Manzikert's bravery as, surrounded by "dangerous gray caps armed to the teeth," (read: "wide-eyed, weaponless small folk") he managed to cut his way through them to safety.

The bodies were so numerous that they had to be stacked in piles so that Manzikert and his men could navigate the streets back to the docks.

Except that Manzikert, as the sunset finally bled into night and his men lit their torches, did *not* return to the docks.

For, as they passed the great "library" and the inert shapes sprawled on its front steps, Manzikert espied a gray cap dressed in purple robes standing by the red-stained altar. This gray cap not only clicked and whistled at the Cappan, but, after making an unmistakably rude gesture, fled up the stairs. At first shocked, Manzikert pursued with a select group of men,[34] shouting out to Sophia to lead the rest back to the ships; he would follow shortly. Then he and his men—including, for some reason, Tonsure, journal in his pocket—disappeared into the "library." Sophia, always a good soldier, followed orders and returned to the docks.

The night passed without event—except that Manzikert did not return. At first light, Sophia immediately reentered the city with a force of 300 men, larger by a half than the small army that had slaughtered the gray caps the evening before.

It must have been an odd sight for Sophia and the young Manzikert II.[35] The morning sun shone down upon an empty city. The birds called out from the trees, the bees buzzed around their flowers, but nowhere could be found a dead gray cap, a living man—not even a trace of blood, as if the massacre had never happened and Manzikert himself had never walked the earth. As they walked through the silent streets, fear so overcame them that by the time they had reached the library, which lay near the city's center, more than half the men had broken ranks and headed back to the docks. Although Sophia and Manzikert II did not lose their nerve, it was a close thing. Manzikert II writes that:

> Not only had I not seen my Mother so afrightened before, I had never thought to see the day; and yet it was undeniable: she shook with fear as we went up the library steps. Her hands whitest white, her eyes nervous in her head, that something might any moment leap out of bluest sky, the gentle air, the unshadowed dwellings, and set upon her. Seeing my Mother so afeared, I thought myself no coward for my own fear.

34. The bersar, an honorary title peculiar to the Aan and awarded only to men who had shown great bravery in combat.

35. All the information we have about the events that follow comes from Manzikert II, who is not nearly as entertaining as Tonsure, lacking both his wit and powers of description. Manzikert II was serious and 17—a disastrous combination for historical writing, as I can attest—and I have resisted direct quotation for the most part.

Within the library, which had been emptied of its books, its mushrooms, its "shelves," they found only a single chair,[36] and sitting in that chair, Manzikert I,[37] who wept and covered his face with his hands. Behind him, in the far wall: a gaping hole with stairs that led down into Cinsorium's extensive network of underground tunnels. Into this hole the night before, Manzikert I would later divulge, he, Tonsure, and his bersar had entered in pursuit of the fleeing gray cap.

But at the moment, all Manzikert I could do was weep, and when Sophia finally managed to pry his hands from his face, she could see that there were no tears, for his "eyes had been plucked from their sockets so cleanly, so expertly, that to look at him, this pitiable man, one might think he had been born that way." Of Tonsure, of the Cappan's men, there was no sign, and no sign of any except for the monk would ever turn up. They had effectively vanished for all time.

Manzikert I remained incoherent for several days, screaming out in the night, vomiting, and subject to fits that appear to have been epileptic in nature. He also had lost his bearings, for he claimed to have been underground for more than a month, when clearly he had only just gone underground the night before.

During this difficult time—her husband incapacitated, her son stricken with immobility by the double trauma of his father's condition and Tonsure's disappearance—Sophia's grief and fear turned into rage. On the third day after discovering her husband in the library, she reached a decision that has divided historians throughout the ages: she put Cinsorium to the torch.[38]

The conflagration began in the library, and she is said to have expressed great regret that no "books" remained to feed to the fire. The city burned for three days, during which time, due to a miscalculation, the Aan were forced to work long hours protecting the docks which, when the winds shifted, were in serious danger of going up in flame as well. Finally, though, the city burned to the ground, leaving behind only the fleeting descriptions in Tonsure's journal, a few other scattered accounts from Manzikert I's clan, and a handful of buildings that proved resistant

36. The gray caps must also have taken the fabulous golden tree, for there is no mention of it in Manzikert II's account, or in any future chronicle. It defies the laws of probability that such a remarkable invention would not be mentioned somewhere, in some account, had it not already been taken back by the gray caps.

37. I will call him Manzikert I from this point on, so as to avoid confusing him with his son.

38. Lacond: "An act of utter barbarism, destroying the finest artifacts of a culture that has never been found anywhere else in the known world and destroying a people both peaceful and advanced. Genocide is too kind a word." Sabon: "Without Sophia's bravery, the newborn city of Ambergris would soon have perished, undone by the treachery of the gray caps."

to the blaze.[39] Chief among these were the walls of the library itself, which proved to have been made of a fire-repellent stone, the aqueducts, and the altar outside of the library (these last two still stand today). Sophia realized the futility, not to mention the economic consequences, of dismantling the aqueducts, and so took out her frustrations on the altar and the library. The altar was made of a stone so strong they could not crack it with their hammers and other tools. When they tried to dig it out, they discovered it was a pillar that descended at least 100 feet, if not farther, and thus impregnable. The library, however, she had taken apart until "not one stone stood upon another stone." As for the entrances to the underground sections of the ancient city, Sophia had these blocked up with several layers of burned stones from the demolished buildings, and then topped this off with a crude cement fashioned from mortar, pebbles, and dirt. This layer was reinforced with wooden planks stripped from the ships. Finally, Sophia posted sentries, in groups of ten, at each site, and five years later we find a description of these sentries in Manzikert II's journal, still manning their posts.

By this time, Sophia's husband had regained his senses—or, rather, had regained as much of them as he ever would . . .

Manzikert I refused to discuss what had occurred underground, so we will never know whether he even remembered the events that led up to his blinding. He would talk of nothing but the sleek, fat rats that, hiding from the carnage and the fires, had reemerged to wander the cindered city, no doubt puzzled by the changes. Manzikert I claimed the rats were the reincarnated spirits of saints and martyrs, and as such must be worshipped, groomed, fed, and housed to the extent that they had known such comforts in their former lives.[40] These claims drove Sophia to distraction, and many were the screaming matches aboard the flagship over the next few weeks. However, when she realized that her husband had not recovered, but had, in a sense, died underground, she installed him near the docks, in the very building beside which he had met his first gray cap. There she allowed him to indulge his mania to his heart's content.

Although no longer a fearsome sight, short or tall, Manzikert I lived out his remaining years in a state of perpetual happiness, his gap-toothed grin as prominent

39. Sophia, in the biography, would have us believe that she destroyed all of the buildings, but since we find Manzikert II, 10 years later, using several of them for defensive and storage purposes, this seems unlikely.

40. We begin to wonder if Manzikert did believe in his heart of hearts that he should massacre the gray caps because of two oddly shaped lichens.

as his frown had been in previous years. It was common to see him, with the help of a walking stick, blindly leading his huge charges—sleek, well-fed, and increasingly tame—around the city he had named. At night, the rats all crowded into his new house, and to his son's embarrassment, slept by his side, or even on his bed. Such reverence as he showed the rats, whether the result of insanity or genuine religious epiphany, greatly impressed many of the Aan, especially those who still worshipped the old icons and those who had participated in the slaughter of the gray caps. Soon, he had many helpers.[41] One morning, eight years after the fires, these helpers found Manzikert in his bed, gnawed to death by his "saints and martyrs," and yet, if Manzikert II is to be believed, "with a smile upon his eyeless face."

Thus ended the oddly poignant life of Ambergris's first ruler—a man who thoroughly deserved to be gnawed to death by rats, as a year had not gone by before his blinding when he had not personally murdered at least a dozen people. Brave but cruel, a tactical genius at war but a failure at peace, and an enigma in terms of his height, Manzikert I is today remembered less as the founder of Ambergris, than as the founder of a religion which still has its adherents today in the city's Religious Quarter and which is still known as "Manziism."[42]

2[43]

To Manzikert I's son, Cappan Manzikert II, would fall the monumental task of converting a pirate/whaling fleet into a viable land-based culture that could supplement fishing with extensive farming and trade with other communities.[44]

41. So many that Manzikert II had to ban the feeding of rats during a time of famine.

42. Much to the disgust of Truffidians everywhere, Manziists often claim to be the Brothers and Sisters of Truff, a claim that has led to riots—and dozens of rats cooked on spits—in the Religious Quarter.

43. The impatient, feckless reader, possessed of no glimmer of intellectual or historical curiosity, should do an old historian a favor and skip the next few pages, proceeding directly to the Silence itself (Part III). I would assume that, in these horrid modern times, that will include most of you. Of course, those readers least likely to read these footnotes, and thus least likely to appreciate the next few pages, will skip this note and bore themselves upon the ennui of history . . .

44. Sophia was never the same after Manzikert I returned to her blinded and deranged—she died soon after him and while alive expressed little or no interest in governing, although she did on at least two occasions, at her son's insistence and with great success, lead punitive expeditions against the southern tribes. Sophia had truly loved her brute of a man, although not in the maudlin terms described by Voss Bender in his first and least successful opera, *The Tragedy of John &*

Luckily, Manzikert II possessed virtues his father lacked, and although never the military leader his father had been, neither did he have the impulsive nature that had led to their exile in the first place.[45] He also had the ghost of Samuel Tonsure at his disposal, for he had taken the monk's teachings to heart.

Above all else, Manzikert II proved to be a builder—whether it was establishing a permanent town within the old city of Cinsorium or creating friendships with nearby tribes.[46] When peace proved impossible—with, for example, the western tribe known as the Dogghe—Manzikert II showed no reluctance to use force. Twice in the first ten years, he abandoned his rebuilding efforts to battle the Dogghe, until, in a decisive encounter on the outskirts of Ambergris itself, he put to flight and decimated a large tribal army and, using his naval strength to its best effect, annihilated the rest as they took to their canoes. The chieftain of the Dogghe died of extreme gout during the fighting and with his death the Dogghe had no choice but to come to terms.

Thus, in Manzikert II's eleventh year of rule, he was finally able to focus exclusively on building roads, promoting trade, and, most importantly, designing the layers of efficient bureaucracy necessary to govern a large area. He himself never conquered much territory, but he laid the groundwork for the system that would reach its apogee 300 years later during the reign of Trillian the Great Banker.[47]

Manzikert II also laid the groundwork for Ambergris's unique religious flavor by building churches in what would become the Religious Quarter—and, less to his credit, by active plundering of other cities. Obsessed with relics, Manzikert II was forever sending agents to the south and west to buy or steal the body parts of saints, until by the end of his reign he had amassed a huge collection of some

---

Sophia; it is difficult not to laugh while John dances with a man in a rat suit, which he has mistaken in his madness for Sophia, toward the end of Act III.

45. He was, by all accounts, a handsome man, if not possessed of the swarthy, thick handsomeness of his father; he had a slender frame and a head topped with a tangle of black hair, beneath which his green eyes shone with a cunning fierceness.

46. For a long time, these tribes avoided the city and accorded the new settlement an undue measure of respect—until they began to realize the gray caps had left, apparently for good, after which a vigorous contempt for the Aan became the norm.

47. For a thorough overview of the early political and economic systems, as well as particulars on crops, etc., see Richard Mandible's excellent "Early Ambergrisian Finance and Society," recently published in Vol. XXXII, Issue 3, of *Historian's Quarterly*. Such detailed information lies beyond the brief of this particular essay, not to mention the patience of the reader and the endurance of an old historian with creaky joints.

70 mummified noses, eyelids, feet, kneecaps, fingers, hearts, and livers.[48] Housed in the various churches, these relics attracted thousands of pilgrims (along with their money), some of whom stayed in the city, thus helping to spark the rapid growth that made Ambergris a thriving metropolis only 20 years after its foundation. Remarkably, Manzikert II's astute diplomacy averted catastrophe in at least four instances where his thievery of relics so infuriated the plundered cities that they were ready to invade Ambergris.

On the architectural front, Manzikert II built many remarkable structures with the help of his chief architect Midan Pejora, but none so well-known as the Cappan's Palace, which would exist intact until, 350 years later, the Kalif's Grand Vizir, upon his temporary occupation of Ambergris, dismantled much of it.[49] The palace was, by all accounts, a rather peculiar building. The exterior inspired the noted traveler Alan Busker to write:

> The walls, the columns rise until, at last, as if in ecstasy, the crests of the arches break into a marble foam, and toss themselves far into the blue sky in flashes and wreaths of sculptured spray, as if the breakers on the shore had been frost bound before they fell, and the river nymphs had inlaid them with diamonds and amethyst.

However, the interior prompted him to write: "We shall find that the work is at least pure in its insipidity, and subtle in its vice; but this monument is remarkable

48. A catalog kept during Manzikert II's reign indicates that at least two of these relics were taken from saintly men while still living, and that although the Cappan's agents bargained long and hard for the purchase from the Kalif of the "penis and left testicle of Saint George of Assuf," they managed only to procure the testicle. (We can only imagine the bizarre sight of the testicle's triumphant entrance to the city, borne upon a perfumed, gold-embroidered pillow held high by a senior Truffidian priest while the crowds cheered wildly.) At the height of the religious frenzy, the Church of the Seven-Pointed Star even put together an array of different saints' body parts—a head here, an ear there—to make a creature they called the "The Saint of Saints," a sort of super saint. This was put on display for 20 years until several other churches, on the verge of bankruptcy due to their own lack of relics, launched a joint raid and "dismembered" this early golem.

49. The rebuilt palace elicited neither condemnation nor praise; indeed, its most interesting features were its many interior murals and portraits, several of which commemorate victories against the Kalif created out of thin air by Ambergrisian historians. Worse, the first two portraits in the Great Hall depict cappans who never existed, to gloss over the Occupation, a period when the city was under the Kalif's control. To this day, Ambergrisian schoolchildren are taught the exploits of Cappan Skinder and Cappan Bartine. Braver if less substantial leaders have rarely trod upon the earth . . .

as showing the refuse of one style encumbering the embryo of another, and all principles of life entangled either in diapers or the shroud." The actual bust of Manzikert II pleased Busker even less: "A huge, gross, bony clown's face, with the peculiar sodden and sensual cunning in it which is seen so often in the countenances of the worst Truffidian priests; a face part of iron and part of clay. I blame the sculptor, not the subject."

Manzikert II ruled for 43 years and sired a son on his sickly wife Isobel when he was already a gray beard of 45 years. During his reign, he had managed the impossible task of both consolidating his position and preparing for future growth. If his religious fervor led him to bad decisions, then at least his gift for diplomacy saved him from the consequences of those decisions.

Following the death of Manzikert II,[50] Manzikert III duly took his place as ruler of lands that now stretched some 40 miles south of Ambergris and 50 miles north.[51] Manzikert III suffered from mild oliphauntitus[52] that apparently affected his internal organs, yet oddly enough he died, after six tumultuous years, of jungle rot[53] received while on a southern expedition to procure lemur eyelids and kidneys for an exotic meat pie. The Cappan's condition was not immediately diagnosed, perhaps due to his oliphauntitus, and by the time doctors had discovered the nature of his condition, it was too late. Displaying a fine disregard for mercy, Manzikert III's last

50. Evidence suggests he may have been poisoned by his ambitious son, whom he was always careful to bring on campaign with him, so as to keep the boy under a watchful eye. Manzikert II died suddenly, with no apparent symptoms, his body quickly cremated on his son's order. If there was little protest, this may have been because he had never been a popular leader, despite his excellent record. He lacked the necessary charisma for men to follow him unthinkingly.

51. In the north, the Cappandom of Ambergris, as it was now officially known, encountered implacable resistance from the Menites, adherents to a religion that saw Truffid as heresy. The Menites would subsequently establish a vast northern commercial empire, based in the city of Morrow, some 85 miles upriver from Ambergris.

52. Sabon insists it was leprosy, while others believe it was epilepsy. Regardless, we can choose from three spectacular diseases with very different symptoms.

53. Jungle rot can have various manifestations, but, according to an anonymous observer, Manzikert III's jungle rot was among the nastiest ever recorded: "Suddenly an abscess appeared in his privy parts then a deep-seated fistular ulcer; these could not be cured and ate their way into the very midst of his entrails. Hence there sprang an innumerable multitude of worms, and a deadly stench was given off, since the entire bulk of his members had, through gluttony, even before the disease, been changed into an excessive quantity of soft fat, which then became putrid and presented an intolerable and most fearful sight to those who came near it. As for the physicians, some of them were wholly unable to endure the exceeding and unearthly stench, while those who still attended his side could not be of any assistance, since the whole mass had swollen and reached a point where there was no hope of recovery."

order before he died was for every last member of the Institute of Medicine to be boiled alive in an eel broth; evidently, he had thought up a new recipe.[54]

Manzikert III had not been a good cappan.[55] During his reign, he had launched numerous futile assaults on the Menites, and although no one ever doubted his personal bravery, he had all of his grandfather's impatience and impulsiveness, but none of that man's charisma or shrewdness. A grotesque gastronome, he put on decadent banquets even during the famine that struck in the third year of his reign.[56] About all that can be said in Manzikert III's defense is that he provided monies for research that resulted in refinements of the mariner's compass and the invention of the double-ruddered ship (useful for maneuvering in narrow tributaries). However, Manzikert III is best remembered for his poor treatment of the poet Maximillian Sharp. Sharp came to Ambergris as an emissary of the Menites, and when it came time for him to leave, Manzikert III would not allow him safe passage by the most convenient route. He was consequently obliged to make his way back through malarial swampland, as a result of which this greatest of all ancient masters caught a fever and died.[57] Manzikert III, when brought news of

54. Although Manzikert III's order (rescinded after his death) was extreme, his charge that the city's doctors knew little of their craft is, unfortunately, true. In an attempt to upgrade its service, the Institute sent representatives to the Kalif's court, as well as to the witch doctors of native tribes. The Kalif's physicians refused to reveal their methodology, but the witchdoctors proved very helpful. The Institute incorporated such native procedures as applying the freshwater electric flounder as a local anesthetic during surgery. Another procedure, perhaps even more ingenious, solved the problem of infection during the stitching up of intestines. Large senegrosa ants, placed along the opening, clamped the wounds shut with their jaws; the witch doctor then cut away the bodies, leaving only the heads. After replacing the intestines in the stomach, the witch doctor would sew up the abdomen. As the wound healed, the ant heads would gradually dissolve.

55. Although I have certainly devoted enough footnotes to him.

56. One menu for such a banquet included calf's brain custard, roast hedgehog, and a dish rather cruelly known as Oliphaunt's Delight, the incomplete recipe for which was uncovered by the Ambergrisian Gastronomic Association just last year:

    1 scooped out oliphaunt's skull
    1 pureed oliphaunt's brain
    1 gallon of brandy
    6 oysters
    2 very clean pigs' bladders
    24 eggs
    salt, pepper, and a sprig of parsley

I am unhappy to report that the search is on for the missing ingredients.

57. In all fairness to Manzikert III, Sharp had an insufferable ego. His autobiography, published from the unedited manuscript found on his body, contains such gems as, "From East and West

Sharp's death, is said to have joked, "Consider this my contribution to the Arts."[58] Another year and Manzikert III might have exhausted both the treasury and his people's patience. As it was, he managed little permanent damage and all of this was put right by his successor: Manzikert II's illegitimate son by a distant third cousin, the handsome and intelligent Michael Aquelus, arguably the greatest of the Manzikert cappans.[59] If not for Aquelus's firm hand, Ambergris, cappandom and city, might well have crumbled to dust within a generation.

We now stand on the threshold of the event known as the Silence. Almost 70 years have passed since the massacre of the gray caps and the destruction of the ancient city of Cinsorium. The new Cappandom of Ambergris has begun to thrive over its ruins and no gray caps have been seen since the day of the massacre. An initial population that may well have flinched in anticipation of some terrible reprisal for genocide has given way to people who have never seen a gray cap, many of them Aan clans folk from the south who also wish to resettle on land. Manzikert

---

alike my reputation brings them flocking to Morrow. The Moth may water the lands of the Kalif, but it is my golden words that nourish their spirit. Ask the Brueghelites or the followers of Stretcher Jones: they will tell you that they know me, that they admire me and seek me out. Only recently there arrived an Ambergrisian, impelled by an insurmountable desire to drink at the fountain of my eloquence."

58. The Scathadian novelist George Leopran had an experience almost as bad, returning to Scatha only after much tribulation: "I boarded my vessel and left the city that I had thought to be so rich and prosperous but is actually a starveling, a city full of lies, tricks, perjury, and greed, a city rapacious, avaricious, and vainglorious. My guide was with me, and after 49 days of ass-riding, walking, horse-riding, fasting, thirsting, sighing, weeping, and groaning, I arrived at the Kalif's court. Even this was not the end of my sufferings, for upon setting out for the final stretch of my journey, I was delayed by contrary winds at Paust, deserted by my ship's crew at Latras, unkindly received by a eunuch bishop and half-starved on Lukas and subjected to three consecutive earthquakes on Dominon, where I subsequently fell in among thieves. Only after another 60 days did I finally return to my home, never again to leave it." If he had known that an arthritic Ambergrisian historian would someday find his account hilarious, he might have cheered up. Or perhaps not. In any event, we can certainly understand historical novelists' tendency to vilify Manzikert III beyond even his due.

59. We will never know why Aquelus was accepted so readily, unless Manzikert III had proclaimed him ruler on his deathbed or Manzikert II, knowing his son's sickly nature, had already decreed that if Manzikert III died, Aquelus should take his place. The story that, in his childhood, a golden eagle alighted at Aquelus's bedroom window and told him he would one day be cappan is almost certainly apocryphal.

II has already, during an exceedingly long reign, overseen the painful transition to a permanent settlement—already, too, a prosperous middle class of merchants, shopkeepers, and bankers has sprung up, supplemented by farmers who have settled in Ambergris and the outlying minor towns.[60] River trade is booming, and has made the city rich in a short period of time. Compulsory two-year military service has proven a success—the army is strong but civic-minded while Ambergris's enemies appear few and impotent. Units of barter based on a gold standard have been introduced and these coins form the principal form of currency, followed closely by the southern Aan sel, which will gradually be phased out. All of Ambergris's rulers—including Manzikert III—have successfully foiled attempts by the upper classes (mostly descendants of Manzikert I's lieutenants) to form a ruling aristocracy by parceling out most of the land to small farmers. Thus, there are no serious internal threats to the succession. Finally, we are on the cusp of a period of inspired building and invention known as the Aquelus Age.

Everywhere, new ideas take root. The refurbished whaling fleet has focused its efforts on the giant freshwater squid, with great success. Aquelus will not just make freshwater squid products a national industry, but part of the national identity, inadvertently introducing the Festival of the Freshwater Squid, which will remain a peaceful event throughout the rule of the Manzikerts.[61] The old aqueducts have been made functional again and extensive settlement has occurred in the valley beyond the city proper, creating a separate town of craftspeople. Every day a new house goes up and a new street is dedicated, and by the time of Aquelus there

60. Three centuries later, city mayors all along the Moth would cast off the yoke of cappans and kings and create a league of city-states based on trade alliances—eventually plunging Ambergris into its current state of "functional anarchy."

61. The first festival, held by Manzikert I, had been a simple affair: a two-course feast attended by an elderly swordswallower who managed to impale himself. More elaborate entertainments would mark the reign of Aquelus in particular. Such celebrations included a representation of the Gardens of Nicea, 300 yards across, built on rafts between the two banks of the Moth, complete with flowers, trees of brightly colored crystal, and an artificial lake stocked with fish, from which guests were to choose their dinner before retiring to a banquet. In the year after the Silence, at a touch from the Cappaness's hand, an outsized artificial owl sped around the public courtyard, sparking off a hundred torches as it, finally, came to rest on an 80-foot-high replica of the Kalif's Arch of Tarbut. But perhaps the most audacious presentation occurred during the reign of Manzikert VII, who resurrected the gray caps' old coliseum, sealed it off, had the arena flooded with water, and re-created famous naval battles using ships built to 2/3 scale. All this pomp and circumstance served as genuine celebration, but also, in later years, to hide the city's growing poverty and military weakness.

are over 30,000 permanent residents in Ambergris: approximately 13,000 men and 17,000 women and children.[62]

And yet, as Aquelus enters his sixth year in power, there is something *dreadfully wrong*, and although no one knows the source of this wrongness, perhaps a few suspect, at least a little. First, there is the sinister way in which the gray caps have entered the collective consciousness of the city: parents tell tales of the old inhabitants of Cinsorium to children at bedtime—that the gray caps will creep up out of the ground on their clammy pale hands and feet, crawl in through an open window, and *grab you* if you don't go to sleep.

Or, more frequently now, the term "mushroom dweller" is used instead of "gray cap," no doubt become more common because, rather disturbingly, the only major failure of the civil government and private citizens has been the war against the fungus that has overgrown many areas of Ambergris: cascades of dark and bright mushrooms, gaily festooned with red and green, or somber in jackets of gray or brown, sometimes as thick as the very grass. Public complaints proliferate, for certain types exude a slick poison which, when it comes into contact with legs, feet, arms, hands, leaves the victim in extreme pain and covered with purple splotches for up to a week. More alarmingly, a new type of mushroom with a stem as thick as an oak and four or five feet tall, begins to spring up in the middle of certain streets, wrenching free from the cobblestones. These blue-tinged "white whales,"[63] as some wag nicknamed them, have to be chopped down by either fire emergency workers or the civil police department, causing hours of inconvenience and lost work time. They also smell so strongly of rotten eggs that whole neighborhoods have to be evacuated, sometimes for days.

Certainly the afflicted areas had grown more numerous in those last years before the Silence, almost as if the fungi formed a vast, nonsentient advance guard . . . but for what? At least one prominent citizen, the inventor Stephen

---

62. Fourth Census—on file in the old bureaucratic quarter.

63. Lacond's most delicious "theory" according to most historians (and therefore well worth relating) postulates that some mushroom dwellers actually gestated within such mushrooms. This explains both why the axe blows to fell them caused the mushrooms to shriek and why their centers often proved to be composed of a dark, watery mass reminiscent of afterbirth or amniotic fluid. I myself now believe they "shrieked" because this is the sound a certain rubbery consistency of fungi flesh makes when an axe cleaves it; as for the "afterbirth," many fungi contain a nutrient sac. We could wish that Lacond had done more research on the subject before venturing an opinion, but then we would be bereft of this marvelous conjecture.

Bacilus[64]—the great-great-great grandfather of the influential statistician Gort—appears to have known what for, and to have recognized a potential danger. As he put it to the Home Council, a body created to address issues of citywide security:

> The very fact that we cannot stop their proliferation, that every poison only makes them thrive the more, should alarm us. For it indicates the presence of another, superior, force determined that these fungi should live. The further observation, made by many in this room tonight, that some fungi, after we have uprooted them and placed them in the appointed garbage heaps for burning, mysteriously find their way back to their former location—this should also shock us into action . . . and, finally, I need not remind you, except that so many of us today have short memories, that several of these mushrooms are purple in hue. Until a few years ago, a purple mushroom could not be found in all the city. Somehow, I find this fact more sinister than any other . . .

Unfortunately, the Council dismissed his evidence as based on old wives' tales, and placed an edict on Bacilus that forbid him to speak about "mushrooms, fungi, lichen, moss, or related plants so as not to unwittingly and unnecessarily cause a general panic among the populace."[65] After all, the Home Council was responsible for security in the city.

64. By now in his late sixties, Bacilus was a fiery old man with a smoking white beard who must have made quite a spectacle in public.

65. In the Council's defense, Bacilus had a rather checkered reputation in Ambergris. We have, today, the luxury of distance, but the Council had no time to expunge from memory such Bacilus innovations as artificial legs for snakes, mittens for fish, or the infamous Flying Jacket. Bacilus reasoned that if trapped air will make an object float upon the water, then trapped air might also allow an object, in this case a man, to float upon the air. Therefore, Bacilus created a special body suit he called the Flying Jacket. Made from hollowed out pig and cow stomachs, it consisted of three dozen air sacs sewn together. Without prior testing, Bacilus persuaded his cousin Brandon Map to don the Flying Jacket and, in front of some of Aquelus's foremost ministers, to jump from the top of the new Truffidian Cathedral. After the poor man had plummeted to his death, it was generally observed within Bacilus's earshot, if only to make the loss appear not completely pointless, that yes, perhaps his cousin had flown a little bit before the end. Another minister, less kindly, remarked that if Bacilus himself, surely a natural windbag if ever he'd seen one, had donned the jacket, the results might have been different, for it was obvious that Brandon had no air within him anymore, nor blood, nor bones . . . The Truffidians were, of course, horrified that their new cathedral had been christened with such a splatter of blood—and even more upset when they discovered Brandon had been an atheist. (I should note, however, that Truffidians have spent the last seven centuries being horrified by some event or other.)

But did Bacilus have cause for alarm? Perhaps so. According to police reports, three years before the Silence the city experienced 76 unexplained or unsolved break-ins, up from only 30 the previous year. Two years before the Silence this figure rose to 99 break-ins, and in the year before the Silence, almost 150 unexplained break-ins occurred within the city limits. No doubt some of these burglaries can be attributed to the large number of unassimilated immigrant adventurers flooding into Ambergris, and no doubt the authorities' failure to show undue concern means they had reached a similar conclusion. However, the victims in an astonishing number of these cases claim, when they saw anyone at all, that the intruder was a *small person*, usually hidden by shadow and almost always *wearing a large felt hat*. These mystery burglars most often made off with cutlery, jewelry, and food items.[66]

It is unfortunate indeed that the urban legend of the mushroom dwellers had spread so widely, because, reduced to stories to scare children, no one took them seriously. The police passed off such accounts as hysterical or as bald-faced lies, while criminals complicated the situation by disguising themselves in gray cap "garb" when committing burglaries.[67]

66. This police report filed by Richard Krokus provides a typical example: "I woke in the middle of the night to a humming sound from the kitchen. It must have been two in the morning and my wife was by my side, and we have no children, so I knew no one who was supposed to be in the house was fixing themselves a midnight snack. So I go into the kitchen real quiet-like, having picked up a plank of wood for a weapon that I was going to use to reinforce the mantel, but hadn't gotten around to on account of my bad back—I served like everyone in the army and messed up my back when I fell during training exercises and even got disability payments for a while, until they found out I'd slipped on a tomato—and my wife had been nagging me to fix the mantel so I picked up the wood—from the store, first, I mean, and then that night I picked it up, but not so as to fix the mantel, you know, but to defend myself. Where was I? Oh, yes. So I go into the kitchen and I'm already thinking about making myself a sandwich with the leftover bread, so maybe I'm not paying as much attention as I should to the situation, and I'll be f— if there isn't this little person, this wee little person in a great big felt hat just sitting on the countertop, stuffing its face with the missus's chocolate cake. I looked at it and it looked at me, and I didn't move and it didn't move. It had great big eyes in its head, and a small nose, and a grin like all get out, only it had teeth, too, real big teeth, so it kind of spoiled the cheerfulness. Of course, it had already spoiled my wife's cake, so I was going to hit it with my plank of wood, only then it threw a mushroom at me and next thing I know it's morning and not only is the cake completely gone, but my wife is slapping my face and telling me to get up have I been drinking again don't I know I'm late for work. And later that day, when I'm setting the plates for dinner, I can't find any of the knives or forks. They're all gone. Oh, yes, and I almost forgot—I couldn't find the mushroom that hit me, either, but I'm telling you, it was heavier than it looked because it left this great big bump on top of me head. See?"

67. A few local souvenir shops, hoping to cash in on the pilgrim business, had begun to sell small statues and dolls of the mushroom dwellers, as well as potpourris made from mushrooms; a

Worse still, the efficient government and the network of peace treaties Manzikert II and Aquelus had created proved to be built on a fragile foundation.

At the time of the Silence, it would have seemed that Ambergris was not only secure but richer than ever before. Indeed, Aquelus had just formed an even stronger alliance with the Menites[68]—and took the first step toward the continuation of his bloodline by marrying the old Menite King's daughter Irene,[69] who by all accounts was not only beautiful but intelligent and could be expected to rule jointly with Aquelus, much as had, in their fashion, Sophia and Manzikert I.[70]

The same year, Aquelus secured his western borders against possible attacks by the Kalif [71] with the signing of a treaty in which Ambergrisian merchants would

---

singular tavern called "The Spore of the Gray Cap" even sprouted up. (This tavern still exists today and serves some of the best cold beer in the city.)

68. Aquelus, in a brilliant maneuver, sent, along with his ambassador suggesting marriage, a bevy of Truffidian monks to Morrow, to negotiate a religious compromise that would allow the Menite kingdom and the Truffidian cappandom to reconcile their differences. Many of the arguments were extremely obscure. For example, the Menites believed God was to be found in all creatures, while the Truffidians, in their attempts to disassociate themselves from Manziism, believed rats were "of the Devil"; after weeks of ridiculous testimony on the merits ("their fur is pleasant to stroke") and deficiencies ("they spread disease") of rats, the compromise was that "of the Devil" should be struck from the Truffidian literature and replaced with the language "not of God" (originally changed to "made of God, but perhaps strayed from His teachings," but the Truffidians would not accept this). After a tortuous year of negotiation, and possibly more from exhaustion and boredom than because anyone actually believed in it, a settlement was reached, much to the relief of both rulers (who, although religious, had a strong streak of pragmatism). This agreement would last for 70 years, until made void by the Great Schism, and even then the dissolution of the contract transpired through the offices of the main Truffidian Church in the lands of the Kalif.

69. Chroniclers of the period call the marriage one of convenience, as evidence suggests Aquelus liked men. But if begun in convenience, it soon deepened into mutual love. Certainly nothing rules out the possibility of Aquelus being bisexual, much as the gay scholar cappan of Ambergris, Meriad, writing two centuries later, would have us believe Aquelus was as bent as a broken bow.

70. Given Sophia and Manzikert I's example, it is not surprising that, until the fall of Trillian the Great Banker and his Banker Warriors, women served in the army, many of them attaining the highest ranks. Irene herself excelled as a hunter, could outrun and outfight the fastest of her five brothers, and had studied strategy with no less a personage than the Kalif's brilliant general, Masouf.

71. Please note that in these several references to the Kalif over the past 60 years, I have been referring to more than one ruler. The Kalif was chosen by secret ballot, and his identity never revealed, so as to protect against assassination attempts. Each Kalif was called simply "the Kalif." It is little wonder that the position of Royal Genealogist has so few rewards and so many frustrations.

receive preferential treatment (especially the waiver of export taxes) and in return Aquelus promised to hold Ambergris in vassalage to the Kalif.[72]

The depth of Aquelus's deviousness is best illustrated by his response when the Kalif asked Aquelus to help suppress the southern rebellion of Stretcher Jones in return for further trade concessions. The Kalif, a devious man himself, also wrote that Aquelus's two half-brothers, closest successors to the cappanship, had been awarded the honor of studying in the Kalif's court, under the tutelage of his most able instructors, "among the most learned men in the civilized world." Aquelus, who had remained neutral in the conflict, replied that a Brueghelite armada of 100 sail already threatened Ambergris—a fleet actually some 200 miles away, contentedly plundering the southern islands—and he could not spare any ships to attack a friendly Truffidian power in the west; nonetheless, he gratefully accepted the privileges so generously offered by the Kalif. As for the invitation to his half-brothers, Aquelus returned his "devout and immense thanks," but they never went. Had they gone, the Kalif would almost certainly have kept them as hostages.[73]

However pleased Aquelus may have been at the adroit deflection of these potential threats, he still, as the annual freshwater squid expedition came ever closer, had two other dangerous situations that required swift resolution. First, the clear shortfall in the spring crops, combined with the influx of new settlers (which he had no wish to see slacken) meant the possibility of famine. Second, the Haragck, a warlike clan of nomads who rode sturdy mountain ponies into battle, had begun to make inroads on his western borders.[74] Aquelus had no cavalry, but the Haragck

72. If this arrangement seems extreme, we should consider that in effect the vassalage meant nothing—the Kalif was far too busy consolidating his recent eastern conquests (rebellions in these lands secretly funded by Aquelus, who left nothing to chance) to exact tribute or even send his own administrators to oversee the Cappandom. However, the Kalif may have outmaneuvered Aquelus in this regard, since in later centuries his successors would claim that the Cappandom of Ambergris belonged by right to them and would wage war to "liberate" it.

73. When Stretcher Jones was finally defeated, in a bloody battle that consolidated the Kalif's western supremacy for 300 years, Aquelus responded with the following words: "Being a friend of both sovereigns, I can only say, with God: I rejoice with them that do rejoice and weep with them that weep."

74. Even before Stretcher Jones's fall these fierce warriors had been driven east by the slowly advancing armies of the Kalif, who most certainly wished for them to weaken Ambergris. They have since passed out of history in a manner both shocking and absurd, but tangential to the concerns of this essay; suffice it to say that exploding ponies do not a pretty sight make, and that no one knows who was responsible for the worms.

had no fleet, and if it came to armed confrontation, Aquelus must have been confident—now that Morrow, in firm control of the northern Moth, was an ally— that he could stop the barbarians from crossing the river in force.

If the Haragck had been Aquelus's only enemy, he would still have had cause to thank his good fortune, but to the south an old adversary chose this moment to reassert itself: the Aan descendants of the same Brueghel who had chased Manzikert I upriver. Drawn by the Aan exodus to the rich suburbs of Ambergris, these Brueghelites, as they called themselves, had begun to make trouble in the south. Understandably, they resented the loss of so much potential manpower when they found themselves beset by the still more southerly Gray Tribes. Most damaging, in light of the famine, the Brueghelites waged a trade war instead of a military war, which might at least have been resolved quickly. Some of their weapons included transit dues on Ambergrisian goods, heavy tolls on produce bound for the southern islands, and customs houses (backed by large, well-armed garrisons) along the Moth.[75]

Eventually, Aquelus would find a way to set the Haragck against the Brueghelites, eliminating both as a threat to Ambergris,[76] but as the freshwater squid season approached, Aquelus could not know that his bribes and political maneuverings would bear fruit. Thus, he made the fateful decree that three times as many ships would participate in the hunt as usual. His purpose was to offset the shortfall of crops with squid meat and by-products, and to provide enough extra food to withstand a siege by either the Brueghelites or the Haragck.[77] In the event there was no siege, these provisions could accommodate the continuing flow of immigrants. The maneuvers to catch the squid, coincidentally, required a prowess and skill level far greater than necessary during an actual war, and so Aquelus also looked to toughen up his navy.

75. With access to the sea blocked in this way, it is hardly surprising that Ambergris did not become the dominant naval power in the region until the days of Manzikert V, who established the Factory: a world-renowned shipbuilding center that could produce a galley in 12 hours, a fully armed warship in two days.

76. And, coincidentally, providing Aquelus with an excellent example of what happens when an army with a strong cavalry fights a primarily naval force: nothing.

77. To this end, Aquelus built land walls to protect against an assault from the north, south, or east. He also set out defensive fortifications on the riverside that included provisions for converting ships into floating barricades. Very little remains of any of these structures, as the contractor who won the bid, purportedly a former Brueghelite, used inferior materials; the extreme eastern side of the Religious Quarter still abuts the last nub of the land walls.

At the appointed time, Aquelus, at the head of nearly 5,000 men and women, took to the river in his 100 ships.[78] They would be gone for two weeks, the longest period of time Aquelus thought he could safely remain away from the capital. His new wife stayed behind. No two turns of fate—Irene's choice to stay at home and the enormity of the fleet that set off for the southern hunting grounds—would have a more profound effect on Ambergris during its early history.

3

Any historian must take extreme care when discussing the Silence, for the enormity of the event demands respect. But when the historian in question, myself, explains the Silence for a paltry pamphlet series, he must display a degree of solemnity in direct inverse proportion to the frivolity of the surrounding information. I find it unacceptable that you, the reader, should flip—a most disagreeably shallow word—from this pamphlet to the next, which may concern Best Masquerade Festivals or Where to Procure a Prostitute, without being made to grasp the awful ramifications of the Event. This requires no melodramatic folderol on my part, for the facts themselves should suffice: *upon Aquelus's return, the city of Ambergris lay empty, not a single living soul to be found upon any of its boulevards, alleyways, and avenues, nor within its many homes, public buildings, and courtyards.*

Aquelus's ships landed at docks where the only sound was the lapping of water against wood. Arrived in the early morning, having raced home to meet the self-imposed two-week deadline, the Cappan found the city cast in a weak light, wreathed in mist come off the river. It must have been an ethereal scene—perhaps even a terrifying one.

At first, no one noticed the severity of the Silence, but as the fleet weighed anchor and the crews walked out onto the docks, many thought it odd no one had come out to greet them. Soon, they noticed that the river defenses lay unmanned, and that the boats in the harbor around them, as they came clear of the mist, drifted, under no one's control.

When Aquelus noticed these anomalies, he feared the worst—an invasion by

78. Even if there had been no famine, Aquelus would have been obliged to take nearly as many ships with him, for they would have to pass through the outer edge of Brueghelite waters in order to hunt the squid.

the Brueghelites during his absence—and ordered the crews back onto the ships. All ships but his own sailed back out into the middle of the River Moth, where they remained, laden with squid, at battle readiness.

Then Aquelus, anxious to find his new bride, personally led an expedition of 50 men into the city.[79] His fears of invasion seemed unfounded, for everywhere they went, Ambergris was as empty of enemies as it was of friends.

We are lucky indeed that among the leaders of the expedition was one Simon Jersak, a common soldier who would one day serve as the chief tax collector for the western provinces. Jersak left us with a full account of the expedition's journey into Ambergris, and I quote liberally from it here:

> As the mist, which had hidden the true extent of the city's emptiness from us, dissipated, and as every street, every building, every shop on every corner, proved to have been abandoned, the Cappan himself trembled and drew his cloak about him. Men from among our ranks were sent randomly through the neighborhoods, only to return with the news that more silence lay ahead: meals lay on tables ready to eat, and carts with horses stood placidly by the sides of avenues that, even at the early hour, would normally have been abustle. But nowhere could we find a soul: the banks were unlocked and empty, while in the Religious Quarter, the flags still weakly fluttered, and the giant rats meandered about the courtyards, but, again, no people; even the fungi that had been our scourge had gone away. We quickly searched through the public baths, the granaries, the porticos, the schools— nothing. When we reached the Cappan's palace and found no one there—not his bride, not the least retainer—the Cappan openly wept, and yet underneath the tears his face was set as if for war. He was not the only man reduced to tears, for it soon became clear that our wives, our children, had all disappeared, and yet left behind all the signs of their presence, so we knew we had not been dreaming our lives away—they had existed, they had lived, but they were no longer in the city . . . And so, disconsolate, robbed of all power to act against an enemy whose identity he did not know, my Cappan sat upon the steps of the palace and stared out across the city . . . until such time as one of the men who had been sent out discovered

79. Aquelus's one weakness was a penchant for taking personal command of military expeditions. Such bravery often helped him win the day, but it would also be the cause of his death a few days shy of his 67th birthday, when, although incapacitated as we shall see, he insisted on riding a specially trained horse into battle against the Skamoo, who had come down from the frozen tundra to attack Morrow. Aquelus never saw the northern giant who felled him with a battle-axe.

certain items on the old altar of the gray caps. At this news, the Cappan donned his cloak once more, wiped the tears from his face, drew his sword and sped to the site with all haste. As we followed behind our Cappan, through that city once so full of lives and now as empty as a tomb, there were none among us who did not, in our heart of hearts, fear what we would find upon the old altar . . .

What did they find upon the altar? An old weathered journal and two human eyeballs preserved by some unknown process in a solid square made of an unknown clear metal. Between journal and squared eyeballs blood had been used to draw a symbol:[80]

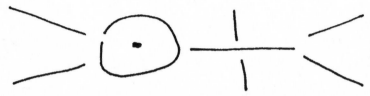

More ominous still, the legendary entrance, once blocked up, boarded over, lay wide open, the same stairs that had enticed Manzikert I beckoning now to Aquelus.

The journal was, of course, the one that had disappeared with Samuel Tonsure 60 years before. The eyes, a fierce blue, could belong to no one but Manzikert I. Who the blood had come from, no one cared to guess, but Aquelus, finally confronted with an enemy—for who could now doubt the return of the gray caps and their implication in the disappearance of the city's citizens?[81]—acted decisively.

Those commanders who argued that a military force should attack the underground found themselves overruled by Aquelus, who, in the face of almost overwhelming opposition, ordered all of his military commanders back to the ships, there to speed up the disembarkation so as to simultaneously process the squid, which otherwise would have rotted, and take up defensive positions throughout the city. Aquelus knew that the Haragck, upon hearing of the developments in Ambergris, might well attack, followed by the Brueghelites. Worse still,

80. Note the difference between this symbol and the one accompanying footnote 23. No one has yet deciphered the original symbol, nor the meaning of its "dismemberment."

81. Who but Sabon, of course. Sabon claims the Menites herded up the city's residents, massacred them some fifty miles from the city, and then left behind evidence to implicate the gray caps. She supports this ridiculous theory by pointing out the Cappaness's fate (soon to be revealed).

if the Cappaness could not be found, the political consequences—regardless of his love for her—would be disastrous. Might not the King of the Menites blame Aquelus for the death of his daughter?

Once the commanders had taken their leave, Aquelus transferred power to his minister of finance, one Thomas Nadal,[82] and announced that he intended to go down below himself.[83] The Cappan's decision horrified his ministers.[84] In addition to their personal affection for Aquelus, they feared losing their Cappan after all else that had been taken from them. Many, Nadal included, also feared the Haragck and the Brueghelites, but Aquelus countered these arguments by pointing out, truthfully enough, that his military commanders could easily lead any defense of the city—after all, they had drawn up a plan for just such a situation months ago. However, when Nadal then asked, "Yes, but who other than you can lead us to rebuild the morale of this shattered city?" Aquelus ignored him. Clearly, only he or

---

82. Aquelus's lover for many years. What Irene thought of this arrangement we do not know, but we do know that she treated Nadal with much more kindness and respect than he treated her. Later, he would lose his position for it.

83. The reason for this decision appears to have been both political and personal. Although Aquelus never commented on the decision either in public or private, Nadal wrote after the Cappan's death that (much to Nadal's distress) the Cappan truly loved Irene and, in the madness of his grief, was convinced she still lived underground. However, Nadal's account must be considered somewhat disingenuous, for if Aquelus believed his wife was alive, surely he would have allowed the military to send a large force after her? No, his sacrifice served several other purposes: if he did not go, then in the current state of anger and anguish, these men would surely take their own actions, possibly overthrowing him if he tried to stop them again. (Further, if his descent was seen as taken on behalf of Irene, perhaps the Menite king would look more kindly upon the Cappan.) Most importantly, Aquelus was an ardent student of history and must have known the details of the gray cap massacre and the subsequent burning of Cinsorium. No doubt he interpreted the gray caps' actions as revenge, and what must be avoided at all costs were reprisals against them, which would only lead to further retaliation on both sides, permanently destabilizing the city and making it impossible to rule. For, if the gray caps could make 25,000 people disappear without a trace, then Aquelus had only two choices: to leave the city forever, or reach some sort of accommodation. Perhaps perceiving that, having taken their revenge, the gray caps might be persuaded to negotiate, knowing also that some action must be taken, and even now hoping against hope to rescue his wife, he must have felt he had no choice. If Aquelus saw the situation in this light, then he was among the most selfless leaders Ambergris would ever have; such selflessness would carry a heavy price.

84. In the unlikely event that you are wondering how so many ministers survived the Silence, let me draw aside the veils of ignorance: Ministers were in no way exempted from periodic military service—in fact, their positions demanded it, since Aquelus was determined to keep the army as "civilian" as possible. Therefore, at least seven major ministers or their designees had sailed with the fleet.

his disappeared wife could make Ambergris a viable, living metropolis again. Still, down below he went, and down below he stayed for three days.[85]

Aboveground, Aquelus's military commanders might well have staged a coup if not for the arrival that first night of Irene, only 12 hours after Aquelus's descent into the domains of the mushroom dwellers. By a quirk of chance both cruel and kind, she had left the capital for a two-day hunting trip in the surrounding countryside.[86]

Faced with the double-edged horror of the Silence and her husband's underground sojourn, Cappaness Irene never faltered, taking quick, decisive action. The rebellious commanders—Seymour, Nialson, and Rayne—she had thrown in prison. Simultaneously, she sent a fast boat to Morrow with a message for her father, asking for his immediate military support.[87] The Cappaness might have thought this ended her immediate problems, but she had severely underestimated the mood of the men and women who had returned to the city. The soldiers guarding the rebel commanders freed their prisoners[88] and led a drunken mob of naval cadets to the front steps of the palace.

Inside, the Cappan's ministers had succumbed to panic—burning documents,

---

85. Peter Copper, in his biography *Aquelus*, provides a poignant account of the Cappan's departure for the nether regions. Copper writes: "And so down he went, down into the dark, not as Manzikert I had done, for blood sport, but after much thought and in the belief that no other action could deliver his city from annihilation physical and spiritual. As the darkness swallowed him up and his footsteps became an ever fainter echo, his ministers truly believed they would never see him again."

86. Near Baudux, where the old ruins of Alfar still stand; grouse and wild pigs are plentiful in the region.

87. At the time she meant for such help to strengthen her internal position, not to defend the city from external threats.

88. That the Cappaness even managed to have the commanders imprisoned is testimony not only to Irene's strength of character, but to the civil service system put into place by Manzikert II. Most survivors of the Silence, when the Cappan's decision and the rumor of the mushroom dwellers' involvement became common knowledge, were for an all-out assault on the underground areas of the city. Indeed, despite the Cappaness's reiteration of Aquelus's orders, Red Martigan, a lieutenant on the Cappan's flagship, did lead a clandestine operation against the mushroom dwellers while the Cappan was still below ground. He took some 50 men to the city's extreme southeastern corner and entered the sewer system through an open culvert. Some days later, a friend who had not joined Martigan's expedition went down to the culvert to check on them. He found, neatly set out across the top of the culvert, the heads of Red Martigan and his 50 men, their eyes scooped out, their mouths to a one set in a kind of "grimacy" smile that was more frightening than the sight of the heads themselves. As to whether this action on Martigan's part hurt Aquelus's efforts underground, I can only offer the by now familiar, and irritating, refrain of "alas, we shall never know."

stripping murals for their gold thread, and preparing to abandon the city under cover of darkness. When they came to the Cappaness with news of the insurrection and told her she must flee too, she refused and, as reported by Nadal, said to them:

> Every man who is born into the light of day must sooner or later die; and how could I allow myself the luxury of such cowardice when my husband took all our sins upon himself and went underground? May I never willingly shed the colors of Ambergris, nor see the day when I am no longer addressed by my title. If you, my noble ministers, wish to save your skins, you will have little difficulty in doing so. You have plundered the palace's riches and with luck you can reach the river and your boats moored there. But consider first whether when you reach safety you will not regret that you did not choose death. For those who remain, I shall ask only that you contain your fear, for we must present a brave face if we are to survive this night.

Shamed by these words, Nadal and his colleagues had no choice but to follow the Cappaness out to the front steps of the palace. What followed must be considered the crowning achievement of early Ambergrisian nationalism—a moment that even today sends "chills down the spine" of the least patriotic city dweller. This daughter of Menites, this Cappaness without a Cappan, made her famous speech in which she called upon the mob to lay down its arms "in the service of a greater good, for the greater glory of a city unique in the history of the world. For if we can overcome this strife now, we shall never fear ourselves ever again."[89] She then detailed in cold-blooded fashion exactly who the rebels would have to kill to gain power and the full extent of the repercussions for a severely divided Ambergris: instant assimilation by the Brueghelites.[90] Further, she promised to strengthen the elected position of city mayor[91] and not to pursue reprisals against the mob itself, only its leaders.

Such was the magnetism of her personality and the passion of her speech that the mob turned on its leaders and brought them to the Cappaness in chains. Thus

89. While we can trust Nadal on the contents of the speech, he is a less trustworthy reporter of the actual verbiage: in his mouth, even the word "nausea" becomes both vainglorious and tediously melodramatic. He is, however, our only source.
90. In reality, the Haragck were the greater threat.
91. With the result that in later years, under weak cappans, the mayor actually had equal status.

was the most severe internal crisis in the cappandom's short history diffused by Irene—the daughter of a foreign state with a heretical (to the Truffidians) religion. The people would not soon forget her.

But the Cappaness and her people had no time to draw breath, for on the second day of Aquelus's disappearance, 7,000 Haragck crossed the Moth and attacked Ambergris.[92] The Cappaness's forces, although taken by surprise, managed to keep the Haragck pinned down in the region of the docks, except for a contingent of 2,000, whom Irene allowed to break through to the city proper; she rightly sought to split the Haragck army in two, and in the labyrinthine streets of Ambergris, her own troops had a distinct advantage.[93]

Outflanked by the Ambergrisian ships behind them, which they had neglected

92. How did the Haragck cross over in such numbers? Atrocious swimmers, they somehow managed to make 7,000 inflatable animal skins—not, as rumor has it, made from their ponies, which they loved—and, fully armed, floated/dog paddled across the Moth. The reliefs that depict this event are among the only surviving examples of Haragck artwork:

The more perplexing question is: How did the Haragck know to attack so soon? Until recent times, it remained a mystery. Even a good rider could not have reached Ambergris's western borders in less than three days, and it would take three days to return after receiving the news—to say nothing of crossing the Moth itself. Five years ago, a carpenter in the western city of Nysimia accidentally unearthed a series of stone tablets carved with Haragck folk legends, and among these is one, dating from the right time period, that tells of a mushroom that sprang suddenly from the ground, and from which emerged an old man who told them to attack their "eastern enemies." Could it be that the mushroom dwellers managed to coordinate the Haragck attack with their Silence? And could the old man have been Tonsure himself?

93. Seeking to redeem themselves, some rebel Ambergrisian commanders asked to be put in charge of the dangerous street-to-street fighting, and accounted themselves well enough that although they were deprived of their rank and returned to civilian life after the emergency, their lands were not confiscated, and neither were their lives.

to secure before establishing their beach head, the rest of the Haragck floundered; bereft of their ponies, they fought hand-to-hand on the shore while the Ambergrisian sailors assaulted them from behind with arrows and burning faggots. If the Haragck had managed to fire the ships, they might still have won the day, but instead they tried to capture them (rightly perceiving that without a navy they would never be able to conquer the region). Even so, the defenders barely managed to hold their positions through the night. But at dawn of the third day an advance guard of light horsemen arrived from Morrow and turned the fortunes of the defenders, who, tired and disheartened by all they had lost, would soon have given way to Haragck pressure.

By nightfall, the surviving Haragck had either tried to bob back over the Moth on their inflated animal skins or run north or south. Those who swam were slaughtered by the navy (the inflated animal skins were neither maneuverable nor inflammable);[94] those who fled south ended up as slaves to the Archduke of Malid[95] (who, in his turn, would be enslaved by the encroaching Brueghelites); those who fled north managed to evade the Menite army marching south, but then ran into the ferocious Skamoo with their spears made of ice.[96]

That night, Cappan Aquelus made his way back to the surface on his hands

94. Worse still, whatever animal they had made their floats from had wide pores and the skins, hastily prepared, suffered slow leakage; although the vast majority had survived the initial crossing, many sank upon the return trip.

95. A notorious cannibal with a taste for the western tribes; that Aquelus kept him on retainer as a buffer against the Brueghelites may have been a political necessity, but it was still morally reprehensible.

96. The only reason the Haragck regrouped so quickly—they would pose a threat to Ambergris again a mere three years later—is that their great general Heckira Blgkkydks escaped the Skamoo with seven of his men and, his anger fearsome to behold (more fearsome than that of Manzikert I), eventually reached the fortress of Gelis, where the Haragck Khan Grnnck (who had ordered the amphibious attack on Ambergris) had taken refuge. Starving, shoeless, his clothes in tatters, Blgkkydks burst into the Khan's court, reportedly roared out, *"Inflatable animal skins?!"*, cut off his ruler's head with a single blow of his sword, and promptly proclaimed himself Khan; he would remain Khan for 20 years before the destruction of the Haragck as a political/cultural entity. Luckily, he spent the next three years annihilating the Skamoo, for he had suffered terribly at their hands, and by the time he refocused on Ambergris, the city had sufficiently recovered to defend itself. (One long-term effect on the Haragck as a consequence of their failed attack on Ambergris was a crucial lack of good translators, almost all of whom had been killed by the burning faggots of Ambergris. Thus, when Blgkkydks issued a formal demand for Ambergrisian surrender as a pretense for declaring war, the threat which accompanied the demand read, "I will put fried eggs up your armpits," when the old Haragck saying *should* have read, "I will tear you armpit to armpit like a chicken.")

and knees, his hair a shocking white and his eyes plucked from him;[97] they would never, even posthumously, be returned to him.[98] Weak with hunger and delirium, Aquelus soon recovered under the personal ministrations of his wife, who was also a noted surgeon. Like Manzikert I, he would never discuss what had happened to him. Unlike Manzikert I, he would rule again, but in the three days of his absence, the dynamics of power had undergone a radical shift. His Cappaness had proven herself quite capable of governing and had demonstrated remarkable toughness in the face of catastrophe. The Cappandom was also indebted to the Menite King for his help.

Finally, not only had Aquelus been blinded, but even many of his own ministers concluded that his underground adventure had been an act of rashness and/or cowardice. Never again would Aquelus be the sole ruling authority; from now on it would be his wife who, backed by her father, ruled in matters of defense and foreign diplomacy. More and more, Aquelus would oversee building projects and provide valuable advice to his wife. That she ever intended to usurp the cappanship is unlikely,[99] but once she had it, the people would not let her abdicate it.[100]

The problem went deeper than this, however. Although Aquelus had sacrificed

97. Some horticulturists—none of the ones consulted for this travel guide—have pointed out that the tissue in eyeballs provides excellent nutrient value for fungi.

98. We cannot forget the late Voss Bender's opera about the Silence, *The King Underground*, which—although it contains a patently idiotic wish fulfillment sequence in which the Cappan single-handedly slays two dozen children dressed as mushroom dwellers, after which "all quaver before him"—has a rather profound and singular beauty to it, especially in the scene where the Cappan crawls back up the steps to the surface, hears the voice of his Irene, and, his hand upon her cheek (aft, not nether), sings:

My fingers are not blind,
and they hunger still
for the sight of you;
and you, not seen but seeing,
can you bear the sight of me?

As Bender's opera is more popular than any history book, his vision has become the popular conception of the event, conveniently ignoring the unfortunate Nadal's passion for the Cappan. Luckily, many subjects—including the Haragck's use of floating animal skins—Bender thought to be unsuitable for opera, and it is in such low domains, far below the public eye, that creatures such as myself are still allowed to crawl about while muttering our "expert" opinions.

99. Although the Menite king did pressure her to annex Ambergris for Morrow; already firmly committed to her adopted people, she put him off by invoking the specter of intervention by the Kalif should the Cappandom fall into Menite hands.

100. That Aquelus still loved her is undeniable, and he himself made no complaint, although many of his ministers, who effectively lost power as a result, did complain—vociferously.

his sight for them—indeed, many have speculated that Aquelus reached a pact with the mushroom dwellers that saved the city—the people no longer trusted him, and would never regain their former love for him. That he had gone below and survived when so many had not was proof enough for the common naval cadet that their Cappan had conspired with the enemy. Tales circulated that he snuck out at midnight to seek counsel with the mushroom dwellers. It was said that a tunnel had been dug from his private chambers to the mushroom dwellers' underground lair. Most ridiculous of all, some claimed that Aquelus was actually a doppelganger, made of fungus, under the mushroom dwellers' control; he had, after all, forbidden anyone from attacking them.[101]

The latter part of Aquelus's "reign" was marked by increasingly desperate attempts to regain the respect of his subjects. To this end, he would have himself led out into the city disguised as a blind beggar and listen to the common laborers and merchants as they walked by his huddled form. He also gave away huge sums of money to the poor, so seriously draining the treasury that Irene was forced to order a halt to his largesse. Aquelus's spending, combined with the promises made to entice people to settle in Ambergris, led to the selling of titles and, in later years, a landed aristocracy that would prove a constant source of treasonous ambition.

Despite these failings, Aquelus managed partial redemption by having four children with Irene, although surely the irony of the Cappaness being the instrument of his salvation was not lost on him. These children—Mandrel, Tiphony, Cyril, and Samantha—became Aquelus's delight and main reason for living. While Irene ruled, he doted on them, and the people doted on them too. In Aquelus's love for his children, Ambergrisians saw the shadow of their former love for him, and many forgave him his involvement with the mushroom dwellers—a charge almost certainly false anyway.

Thus, although in many ways tragic, the partnership of Cappaness and Cappan would define and redefine Ambergris—both internally and in the world beyond—for another 30 years.[102] They would be haunted years, however, for the legacy of

101. Nadal, who had stuck by Aquelus through all of this, reports to us a conversation in which the Cappan chastised Nadal for his anger at the many slurs, saying, "They have suffered a terrible loss. If to heal they must remake me in the image of the villain, let them."
102. It is outside the scope of this essay to tell of the continuation of the Manzikert line or of the mushroom dwellers; suffice it to say, the mushroom dwellers are still with us, while the Manzikerts exist only as a borderline religion and as a rather obnoxious model of black, beetle-like motored vehicle.

the Silence would permeate Ambergris for generations—in the sudden muting of the voices of children, of women, of those men who had stayed behind. For those inhabitants who had lost their families, their friends, the city was nothing more than a giant morgue, and no matter how they might console one another, no matter how they might set to their tasks with almost superhuman intensity, the better to block out the memories, they could never really escape the Silence, for the "City of Remembrance and Memorial," as one poet called it, was all around them.[103] It was common in those early, horrible years—still scarred by famine, despite the reduction in the population—for men and women to break down on the street in a sudden flux of tears.

The Truffidian priest Michael Nysman came to the city as part of a humanitarian mission the year after the Silence and was shocked by what he found there. In a letter to his diocese back in Nicea, he wrote:

> The buildings are gray and their windows often like sad, empty eyes. The only sound in the street is that of weeping. Truly, there is a great emptiness to the city, as if its heart had stopped beating, and its people are a grim, suspicious folk. They will hardly open their doors to you, and have as many locks as can be imagined . . . Few of them sleep more than two or three hours at a time, and then only when someone else is available to watch over them. They abhor basements, and have blocked up all the dirt floors with rocks. Nor will they suffer the slightest section of wall to harbor fungus of any kind, but will scrape it off immediately, or preferably, burn it. Some neighborhoods have formed Watches during the night that go from home to home with torches, making sure that all within are safe. Most eerie and discomfiting, the citizens of this bleak city leave lanterns burning all through the night, and in such proliferation that the city, in such a hard, all-seeing light, cannot fail to

---

103. Little wonder that many moved away, to other cities, and that their places were taken by settlers from the southern Aan islands and, north, from Morrow. Additional bodies were drummed up among the tribes neighboring the city; Irene offered them jobs and reduced taxation in return for their relocation. The influx of these foreign cultures into the predominantly Aan city forever diversified and rejuvenated the local culture . . . We might well ask why so many people were willing to reinhabit a place where 25,000 souls had disappeared, but, in fact, the government deliberately spread misinformation, blaming the invading Haragck and the Brueghelites for the loss of life. In the confusion of the times, it appears many outside of the city did not even hear the real story. Others chose not to believe it, for it was not, after all, a very believable story. Thus, for several centuries, historians who should have known better promulgated false stories of plague and civil war.

seem already enveloped in the flames of Hell, it only remaining for the Lord of the Nether World to take up his throne and scepter and walk out upon its streets. Just yesterday some unfortunate soul tried to rob a watchmaker and was torn to pieces before it was discovered he was not a gray cap . . . Worst of all: no children; the schools have closed down and their radiant, innocent voices are no longer heard in the church choirs. The city is childless, barren—it has only visions of the happy past, and what parent will bring a child into a city that contains the ghosts of so many children? Some parents—although usually only one parent has survived— believe that their children will return, and some tried to unblock the hole by the old altar before the Cappaness made it a hanging offense. Still others wait by the door at dinner, certain that a familiar small shape will walk by. It breaks my heart to see this. Can such a city ever now lose a certain touch of cruelty, of melancholy, a lingering hint of the macabre? Is this, then, the grief of the gray caps 70 years later given palpable form? I fear I can do little more here at this time; I am caught up in their sadness, and thus cannot give them solace for it, although unscrupu- lous priests sell dispensations, which they say will protect the user from the mush- room dwellers while simultaneously absolving the disappeared of their sins.

What are we, in this modern era, to make of the assertion that 25,000 people simply disappeared, leaving no trace of any struggle? Can it be believed? If the number were 1,000 could we believe it? The answer the honest historian reluc- tantly comes to is that the tale must be believed, because it happened. Not a single person escaped from the mushroom dwellers. More hurtful still, it left behind a generation known simply as the Dispossessed.[104] The city recovered, as all cities do, and yet for at least 100 years,[105] this absence, this silence, insinuated itself into the happiest of events: the coronations and weddings of cappans, the extraordi- narily high birth rate (and low mortality rate), the victories over both Haragck and Brueghelite. The survivors retook their homes uneasily, if at all, and some areas, some houses, stood abandoned for a generation, never reentered, so that dinners set out before the Silence rotted, moldered, and eventually fossilized.[106] There

104. Given the magnitude of the loss, remarkably few survivors killed themselves. We must credit the industriousness of Irene and Aquelus—the example they set and the work they provided.
105. For, at the 100-year mark, the mushroom dwellers first began to integrate themselves with Ambergrisian society, albeit as garbage collectors.
106. As recently as 50 years ago, a few homes were found in this state: they had been boarded up and then built over, and were discovered by accident during a survey expedition to install streetlamps. The surveyors found the atmosphere within these rooms (the dust over everything,

remained the terrible conviction among the survivors that they had brought this upon themselves through Manzikert I's massacre of the gray caps and Sophia's torching of Cinsorium. It was hard not to feel that it was God's judgment to see Ambergris destroyed soul by soul.[107]

Worst of all, there was never any clue as to the fate of the Disappeared, and in the absence of information, imaginations, as always, imagined the worst. Soon, in the popular folklore of the times, the Disappeared had not only been killed, but had been subjected to terrible tortures and defilements. Although some still claimed the Brueghelites had carried off the 25,000, most people truly believed the mushroom dwellers had been responsible. Theories as to how cropped up much more frequently than why because, short of revenge, no one could fathom why. It was said that the ever-present fungus had released spores that, inhaled, put all of the city's inhabitants to sleep, after which the mushroom dwellers had come out and dragged them underground. Others claimed that the spores had not put the Disappeared to sleep, but had actually, in chemical combination, formed a mist that corroded human flesh, so that the inhabitants had slowly melted into nothing. The truth is, we shall never know unless the mushroom dwellers deign to tell us.

4[108]

But what of Samuel Tonsure's journal? What, after all these years, did it contain? Aquelus wisely had it placed in the care of the librarians at the Manzikert Memo-

---

the plates and kitchen implements corroded, the smell dry as death, the dried flowers set out as a memorial) so oppressive that after a brief reconnaissance, they not only boarded them back up, but filled them in, despite a vigorous protest from myself and various other old farts at the Ambergrisian Historical Society.

107. If so, then the Devil has saved it several times over.

108. At this point in the narrative I begin to make my formal farewells, for those of you who ever even noticed my marginal existence. By now the blind mechanism of the story has surpassed me, and I shall jump out of its way in order to let it roll on, unimpeded by my frantic gesticulations for attention. The time-bound history is done: there is only the matter of sweeping the floors, taking out the garbage, and turning off the lights. Meanwhile, I shall retire once more to the anonymity of my little apartment overlooking the Voss Bender Memorial Square. This is the fate of historians: to fade ever more into the fabric of their history, until they no longer exist outside of it. Remember this while you navigate the afternoon crowd in the Religious Quarter, your guidebook held limply in your pudgy left hand as your right hand struggles to balance a half-pint of bitter.

rial Library.[109] In effect, the book disappeared again, as—hidden and known by only a few—it was not part of the public discourse.[110] Aquelus made the librarians swear not to reveal the contents of the journal, or even hint at its existence to anyone, on pain of death. The journal was kept in a locked strongbox, which was then put inside another box. We can certainly understand why Aquelus kept it a secret, for the journal tells a tale both macabre and frightening. If the general populace had, at the time, known of its contents, they would no longer have had anything to fear from their imaginations—only to have their worst nightmares given validation. The burden on Aquelus and Irene of not releasing this information was terrible—Nadal, who was privy to most state secrets, reports that the two frequently fought over whether the journal should be made public, often switching sides in mid-argument.

To head librarian Michael Abrasis fell the task of examining the journal, and luckily he kept notes. Abrasis describes the journal as:

> . . . leather-bound, 6 x 9, with at least 300 pages, of which almost all have been used. The leather has been contaminated by a green fungus that, ironically, has helped to preserve the book; indeed, were the lichen to be removed, the covers would disintegrate, so ingrained and so uniform are these green "shingles." Of the ink, it would appear that the first 75 pages are of a black ink easily recognizable as distilled from whale's oil. However, the sections thereafter are written using a purple ink that, after careful study, appears to have been distilled from some sort of fungus. These sections exude a distinctly sweet odor.[111]

Abrasis had copies of the journal made and secreted them away—which accounts for the existence of the text in the city to this day—but, unfortunately, the original was pawned to the Kalif during the tragic last days of Trillian.

We have already discussed the early days of Ambergris as recounted in Ton-

---

109. The library already housed a number of unique manuscripts, including the anonymous Dictionary of Foreplay, Stretcher Jones's Memories, a few sheets of palm-pulp paper with mushroom dweller scrawls on them, and 69 texts on preserving flesh, stolen from the Kalif, that had been of great use to Manzikert II while conducting his body parts shopping spree among the saints.

110. As it is, when copies were made available 50 years later, it forced Cappan Manzikert VI to abdicate and join a monastery.

111. Alas, Abrasis never commented on the consistency of the handwriting!

sure's journal, but what of the last portion of the journal? The first entry Tonsure managed to make following his descent[112] reads:

> Dark and darker for three days. We are lost and cannot find our way to the light. The Cappan still pursues the gray caps, but they remain flitting shadows against the pale, dead glow of the fungus, the mushrooms that stink and writhe and even seem to speak a little. We have run out of food and are reduced to eating from the mushrooms that rise so tall in these caverns we must seek sustenance from the stem alone—maddeningly aware of succulent leathery lobes too high to reach. We know we are being watched, and this has unnerved all but the strongest men. We can no longer afford to sleep except in shifts, for too often we have woken to find another of our party missing. Early yesterday I woke to find a stealthy gray cap about to murder the Cappan himself, and when I gave the alarm, this creature smiled most chillingly, made a chirping sound, and ran down the passageway. We gave chase, the Cappan and I and some 20 others. The gray cap escaped, and when we returned our supplies were gone, as were the 15 men who had remained behind. The gray caps' behavior here is as different as night is to day—here they are fast and crafty and we hardly catch sight of them before they strike. I do not believe we will make it to the surface alive.

Tonsure's composure is admirable, although his sense of time is certainly faulty—he writes that three days had passed, when it must still have been but a single night, for Manzikert I was found in the library the very next morning.[113] Another entry, dated just a few "days" later, is more disjointed and, one feels, soaked through with terror:

> Three more gone—taken. In the night. Morning now. What do we find arranged around us like puppet actors? We find arranged around us the heads of those who have been taken from us. Ramkin, Starkin, Weatherby, and all the rest. Staring. But they cannot stare. They have no eyes. I wish I had no eyes. Cappan long ago

112. With the exception of his entry describing the massacre and Manzikert I's decision to go underground.
113. No less a skeptic than Sabon half-heartedly documents the folktale that the Manzikert I who reappeared in the library was actually a construct, a doppelganger, created out of fungus. Although ridiculous on the face of it, we must remember how often tales of doppelgangers intertwine with the history of the mushroom dwellers.

gave up on all but the idea of escape. And it eludes us. We can taste it—the air sometimes fresher, so we know we are near the surface, and yet we might as well be a hundred miles underground! We must escape these blind staring heads. We eat the fungus, but I feel it eats us instead. Cappan near despair. Never seen him this way. Seven of us. Trapped. Cappan just stares at the heads. Talks to them, calls them by name. He's not mad. He's not mad. He has it easier in these tunnels than I.[114] And still they watch us . . .

Tonsure then describes the deaths of the men still with the Cappan and Tonsure—two by poisoned mushrooms, two by blow dart, and one by a trap set into the ground that cut the man's legs off and left him to bleed to death. Now it is just the Cappan and Tonsure, and, somehow, Tonsure has recovered his nerve:

We wonder now if there ever were such a dream as aboveground, or if this place has always been the reality and we simply deluding ourselves. We shamble through this darkness, through the foul emanations of the fungus, like lost souls in the Nether World . . . Today, we beseeched them to end it, for we could hear their laughter all around us, could glimpse the shadows of their passage, and we are past fear. End it, do not toy with us. It is clear enough now that here, on their territory, they are our Masters. I looked over my notes last night and giggled at my innocence. "Degenerate traces of a once-great civilization" indeed. We have passed through so many queer and ominous chambers, filled with otherworldly buildings, otherworldly sights—the wonders I have seen! Luminous purple mushrooms pulsing in the darkness. Creatures that can only be seen when they smile, for their skin reflects their surroundings. Eyeless, pulsating, blind salamanders that slowly ponder the dead darkness through other senses. Winged animals that speak in voices. Headless things that whisper our names. And ever and always, the gray caps. We have even spied upon them at play, although only because they disdain us so, and seen the monuments carved from solid rock that beggar the buildings aboveground. What I would give for a single breath of fresh air. Manzikert resists even these fancies; he has become sullen, responding to my words with grunts and clicks and whistles . . . More disturbing still, we have yet to retrace our steps; thus, this underground land must be several times larger than the aboveground city, much as the submerged portion of an iceberg is larger than the part visible to a sailor.

114. Another indication Manzikert was a little man.

Clearly, however, Tonsure never regained his time-sense, for on this day, marked by him as the sixth, Manzikert would already have been five days aboveground, eyeless but alive. Perhaps Tonsure deluded himself that Manzikert remained by his side to strengthen his own resolve, or perhaps the fringe-historians have for once been too conservative: instead of a golem Manzikert being returned to the surface, perhaps the underground Manzikert was replaced with a golem. Tonsure certainly never tells us what happened to Manzikert; his entries simply do not mention him after approximately the ninth day. By the twelfth day, the entries become somewhat disjointed, and the last coherent entry, before the journal dissolves into fragments, is this pathetic paragraph:

> They're coming for me. They've had their fun—now they'll finish me. To my mother: I have always tried to be your obedient son. To my illegitimate son and his mother: I have always loved you, although I didn't always know it. To the world that may read this: know that I was a decent man, that I meant no harm, that I lived a life far less pious than I should have, but far better than many. May God have mercy on my soul.[115]

And yet, apparently, they did not "finish" him,[116] for another 150 pages of writing follow this entry. Of these 150 pages, the first two are full of weird scribbles punctuated by a few coherent passages,[117] all written using the strange purple ink described by Abrasis as having been distilled from fungus. These pages provide

---

115. Then as now, bastards were a sel-a-dozen among the clergy; how much more interesting to know where this mother and child resided—Nicea, perhaps?

116. Sabon dryly writes, "Tonsure was already the most finished man in the history of the world. How then could they improve upon perfection?"

117. Most of the scribbles are erotic in nature and superfluous. Of the writings, the following lines appear in no known religious text and are accompanied by the notation "d.t.," meaning "dictated to." Scholars believe that the lines are an example of mushroom dweller poetry translated by Tonsure.

We are old.
We have no teeth.
We swallow what we chew.
We chew up all the swallows.
Then we excrete the swallows.
Poor swallows—they do not fly
once they are out of us.

damning evidence of a mind gone rapidly deranged, and yet they are followed by 148 lucid pages of essays on Truffidian religious rituals, broken infrequently by glimpses into Tonsure's captivity.

The essays have proven invaluable to present-day Truffidians who wish to read an "eyewitness" account of the early church, but baffle those of us who naturally want answers to the mysteries inherent in the Silence and the journal itself. The most obvious question is, why did the mushroom dwellers suffer Tonsure to live? On this subject, Tonsure at least provides his own theory, the explanation inserted into the middle of a paragraph on the Truffidian position on circumcision:[118]

> Gradually, as they come to me time after time and rub my bald head, it has struck me why I have been spared. It is such a simple thing that it makes me laugh even to contemplate it: I look like a mushroom. Quick! Alert the authorities! I must send a message aboveground—tell them all to shave their heads! I can hardly contain my laughter even now, which startles my captors and makes it hard to write legibly.

Later, stuck between a discussion on the divine properties of frogs and a diatribe against interspecies marriages, Tonsure provides us with another glimpse into the mushroom dwellers' world that entices the reader like a flash of gold:

> They have led me to a vast chamber unlike any place I have ever seen, above or below. There stands before me a palace of shimmering silver built entirely of interlocking mushrooms and festooned with lichen and moss of green and blue. A sweet, sweet perfume hangs pungent in the air. The columns that support this dwelling are, it appears, made of living tissue, for they recoil at the touch . . . from the doorway steps the ruler of the province, who is herself but a foot soldier compared to the mightiest ranks that can be found here. All glows with an unearthly splendor and supplicant after supplicant kneels before the ruler and begs for her blessing. I am made to understand that I must come forward and allow the ruler to rub my head for luck. I must go.

If this is indeed mushroom dweller poetry, then we must conclude that either the translator—under stress and with insufficient light—did a less than superlative job, or that the mushroom dwellers had a spectacular lack of poetic talent.

118. They're for it, by the way.

Other entries hint that Tonsure made at least two attempts to escape, each followed by harsh punishment, the second of which may have been partial blinding,[119] and at least one sentence suggests that afterward he was led secretly to the surface: "Oh, such torture, to be able to hear the river chuckling below me, to feel the night wind upon my face, to smell the briny silt, but to see *nothing*." However, Tonsure may have been blindfolded or been so old and have existed in darkness for so long that his eyes could not adapt to the outside, day or night. Tonsure's sense of time being suspect, we can only guess as to his age when he wrote that entry.

Finally, toward the end of the journal, Tonsure relates a series of what surely must be waking dreams, created by his long diet of fungus and the attendant fumes thereof:

> They wheeled me into a steel chamber and suddenly a window appeared in the side of the wall and I saw before me a vision of the city that frightened me more than anything I have yet seen below ground. As I watched, the city grew from just the docks built by my poor lost Cappan to such immense structures that half the sky was blotted out by them, and the sky itself fluxed light, dark, and light again in rapid succession, clouds moving across it in a flurry. I saw a great palace erected in a few minutes. I saw carts that moved without horses. I saw battles fought in the city and without. And, in the end, I saw the river flood the streets, and the gray caps came out once again into the light and rebuilt their old city and everything was as before. The one I call my Keeper wept at this vision, so surely he must have seen it too?[120]

Then follow the last 10 pages of the journal, filled with so concrete and frenzied a description of Truffidian religious practices that we can only conclude that he wrote these passages as a bulwark against insanity and that, ultimately, when he

---

119. Lacond's pet theory, sneered at by Sabon: the two shall continue to make war, history itself their battlefield, hands caressing each other's necks, legs entwined for all eternity, and yet neither shall ever win in such a subjective area as theoretical history. (Although my pet theory is that Lacond and Sabon are the conflicting sides of the same hopelessly divided historian. If only they could reach some understanding?)

120. Sabon has suggested that the mushroom dwellers had a form of zoetrope or "magic lantern" that could project images on a wall. As for the reference to a "Keeper," it appears nowhere else in the text and thus is frustratingly enigmatic. Many a historian has ended his career dashed to pieces on the rocks of Tonsure's journal; I refuse to follow false beacons, myself.

ran out of paper, he ran out of hope—either writing on the walls[121] or succumbing to the despair that must have been a tangible part of every one of his days below ground. Indeed, the last line of the journal reads: "An inordinate love of ritual can be harmful to the soul, unless, of course, in times of great crisis, when ritual can protect the soul from fracture."

Thus passes into silence one of the most influential and mysterious characters in the entire history of Ambergris. Because of Tonsure, Truffidianism and the Cappandom cannot, to this day, be separated from each other. His tutorials informed the administrative genius of Manzikert II, while his counsel both inflamed and restrained Manzikert I. Aquelus studied his journal endlessly, perhaps seeking some clue to which only he, with his own experience below ground, was privy. Tonsure's biography of Manzikert I (never out of print) and his journal remain the sources historians turn to for information about early Ambergris and early Truffidianism.

If the journal proves anything it is that another city exists below the city proper, for Cinsorium was not truly destroyed when Sophia razed its aboveground manifestation. Unfortunately, all attempts to explore the underground have met with disaster,[122] and now that the city has no central government, it is unlikely that there will be further attempts—especially since such authority as does exist would prefer the mysteries remain mysteries for the sake of tourism.[123] It would seem that two separate and very different societies shall continue to evolve side by side, separated by a few vertical feet of cement. In our world, we see their red flags and how thoroughly they clean the city, but we are allowed no similar impact on their world except through the refuse that goes down our sewer pipes.

The validity of the journal has been called into question several times over the years—lately by the noted writer Sirin, who claims that the journal is actually a forgery based on Manzikert I's biography. He points to the writer Maxwell

121. I have a certain affection for Lacond's theory that Tonsure's journal is merely the introduction to a vast piece of fiction/nonfiction scrawled on the walls of the underground sewer system, and that this work, if revealed to the world aboveground, would utterly change our conception of the universe. Myself, I believe such a work might, at best, change our conception of Lacond—for, if it existed, at least one of his theories might be accepted by mainstream historians.
122. The most recent, 30 years ago, resulting in the loss of the entire membership of the Ambergrisian Historical Society, and two of its dog mascots.
123. Until recently you could take an ostensible tour of the mushroom dwellers' tunnels run by a certain Guido Zardoz. After tourists had imbibed refreshments laced with hallucinogens, Zardoz would lead them down into his basement, where several dwarfs in felt hats awaited the signal to leap out from hiding and say "Boo!" Reluctantly, the district councilor shut the establishment down after an old lady from Stockton had a heart attack.

Glaring, who lived in Ambergris some 40 years after the Silence. Glaring, Sirin says, carefully studied the biography written by Tonsure, incorporated elements of it into his fake, invented the underground accounts, used an odd purple ink distilled from the freshwater squid[124] for the last half, and then "produced" the "journal" via a friend in the administrative quarter who spread the rumor that Aquelus had suppressed it for 50 years. Sirin's theory has its attractions—Glaring, after all, forged a number of state documents to help his friends embezzle money from the treasury, and his novels often contain an amount of desperate derring-do in keeping with the fragments of reason found in the latter portion of the journal.[125] Adding to the controversy, Glaring was murdered—his throat cut as he crossed a back alley on his way to the post office—shortly after the release of the journal.

Sabon prefers the alternate theory that, yes, Glaring *did* forge parts of the journal, but only the sections on obscure Truffidian religious practices[126]—these pages inserted to replace pages removed by the government for national security reasons. Glaring was then killed by the Cappan's operatives to preserve the secret. Unfortunately, a fire gutted part of the palace's administrative core, destroying the records that might have provided a clue as to whether Glaring was on the national payroll. Sabon further speculates that Glaring's embezzlement had been discovered and was used as leverage to make him forge the journal pages, for otherwise, some of his relatives having disappeared in the Silence, he would have been disinclined to suppress evidence as to mushroom dweller involvement.[127] Sabon explains away the few paragraphs dealing with Tonsure's captivity as Glaring's genius in knowing that a good forgery must address issues of its authenticity—the journal must therefore contain some evidence of Tonsure's underground experiences. These paragraphs, meanwhile, *Lacond* claims are genuine, pulled from the real journal.[128]

124. And since discontinued—too runny.
125. A passage from his *Midnight for Munfroe* reads "It was in this cloying darkness, the lights from Krotch's house stabbing at me from beyond the grave, that I could no longer hold onto the idea that I was going to be all right. I would have to kill the bastard. I would have to do it before he did it to me. Because if he did it to me, there would be no way for me to do it to him."
126. Certainly possible—Glaring could have interviewed any number of Truffid monks or read any number of books, few now surviving, on the subject.
127. Sabon notes that Glaring kept copies of his forgeries. Further, that a letter Glaring wrote to a friend mentions "a rather unusual memoir of sorts I've been told to duplicate." Sabon believes Glaring made a true copy of the original pages. If so, no one has found this true copy.
128. It is perhaps too cruel to think of Tonsure not only struggling to express himself, to communicate, underground, but also struggling aboveground to be heard as Glaring tries equally hard to snuff him out.

Another claim, which has taken on the status of popular myth, suggests that the mushroom dwellers skillfully rewrote and replaced many pages, to keep inviolate their secrets, but this theory is rendered ridiculous by the fact that the journal was left on the altar—a fact confirmed by Nadal, the then minister of finance. This eyewitness account also nixes the first of Sabon's theories: that the entire journal is a forgery.[129]

To further complicate matters, an obscure sect of Truffidians who inhabit the ruined fortress of Zamilon near the eastern approaches to the Kalif's empire claim to possess the last true page of Tonsure's journal. According to legend, Trillian's men once stayed at the fortress on their way to the Kalif, bearing the journal that, the careful reader will remember, was hocked by the Cappandom. A monk crept into the room where the journal was kept and stole the last page, apparently as revenge for the left femur of their leader having been spirited away by agents of Cappan Manzikert II 300 years before.

The front of the page consists of more early Truffidian religious ritual, but the back of the page reads as follows:

> We have traveled through a series of rooms. The first rooms were tiny—I had to crawl into them, and even then barely squeezed through, banging my head on the ceiling. These rooms had the delicate yet ornate qualities of an illuminated manuscript, or one of the miniature paintings so beloved by the Kalif. Golden lichen covered the walls in intricate patterns, crossed through with a royal red fungus that formed star shapes. Strangely, in these rooms I felt as if I had unlimited space in which to move and breathe. Each room we entered was larger and more elaborate than its predecessor—although never did I have the sense that anyone had ever lived in the rooms, despite the presence of chairs, tables, and bookshelves—so that I found myself bedazzled by the light, the flourishes, the engraved ceilings. And yet, oddly enough, as the curious rooms expanded, my sense of claustrophobia expanded too, so that it took over all my thoughts . . . This continued for days and days, until I had become numb to the glamour and dulled to the claustrophobia. When hungry, we broke off pieces of the walls and ate of them. When thirsty, we squeezed the chair arms and greedily drank the drops of mossy elixir that came from them. Eventually, we would push open the now immense doors leading to

129. Although Sabon, predictably, claims Nadal's eyewitness account could also have been forged by Glaring.

the next room and see only distantly the far wall . . . Then, just when I thought this journey might never end—and yet surely could not continue—I was brought through one final door (as large as many of the rooms we had passed through). Beyond this door, it was night, lit vaguely by the stars, and we had come out upon a hill of massive columns, through which I could see, below us, a vast city that looked uncannily like Cinsorium, surrounded by a forest. A sweet, sweet breeze blew through the trees and lifted the grass along the hill. Above, the immense sky—and I thought, I thought, that I had been brought aboveground, for the entire world seemed to spread out before me. But no, I realized with sinking heart, for far above me I could see, when I squinted, that, luminous blue against the blackness, the lines of strange constellations had been set out there, using some instrument more precise than known of aboveground. And yet the stars themselves *moved* in phosphorescent patterns of blue, green, red, yellow, and purple, and after a moment I discovered that these "stars" were actually huge moths gliding across the upper darkness . . . My captors intend to leave me here; I am given to understand that I have reached the end of my journey—they are done with me, and I am free. I have but a few more minutes to write in this journal before they take it from me. What now to do? I shall not follow the light of the moths, for it is a false light and wanders where it will. But, in the lands that spread out before me, a light beckons in the distance. It is a clear light, an even light, and because light still, to me, means the surface, I have decided to walk toward it in hopes, after all this time, of regaining the world I have lost. I may well simply find another door when I find the source of the light, but perhaps not. In any event, God speed say I.

Surely, *surely*, such visions indicate Tonsure's advanced delirium or, more probably, monkish forgery, but one is almost convinced by the holy reverence in which the inhabitants of Zamilon hold their page, for it means more to them than any other of their possessions, and even now, after many a reading, it moves more than one monk to tears.[130]

To attempt to put the controversy to rest[131]—after all, Tonsure has become a saint to the Truffidians by virtue of his faith in the face of adversity—a delegation from the Morrow-based Institute of Religiosity,[132] led by the distinguished

130. I myself have journeyed to Zamilon to see the page and am cagey enough at this stage of my bizarre career to decline comment on its authenticity or fakery.
131. Admittedly confined to the pages of obscure history journals and religious pamphlets.
132. Then called the Morrow Religious Institute.

head instructor Cadimon Signal,[133] journeyed 20 years ago to the lands of the Kalif, under guarantee of safe passage, to examine the journal in its place of honor in Lepo.

The conditions under which the delegation could view the journal—conditions set after their arrival—could not have been more rigid: they could examine the book for an hour, but, due to the book's fragile condition, they themselves could not touch it; they must allow an attendant to do so for them. Further, the attendant would flip through *all* of the pages once, and then the delegation would be able to study up to 10 individual pages, but no more than 10—and they must name the page numbers in question on the basis of the first flip through.[134] The delegation had no alternative but to accept the ridiculous conditions,[135] and resolved to make the most of their time. After half an hour, they found it appeared parts of the book *had* been replaced with different paper, and that the penmanship appeared, in places, somewhat different from Tonsure's own (as compared against the biography). Alas, at the half-hour mark, news reached the Kalif by carrier pigeon that the then mayor of Ambergris had tendered a major personal insult to the Kalif, and he immediately expelled the delegation from the reading room and sent them via fast horses to his borders, where they were unceremoniously dumped with their belongings. Their notes had been taken from them, and they could not remember any useful particulars about the page they had seen. No further examination has been allowed as of the date of this writing.

Thus, although we have copies of the journal, we may never know why pages were replaced in this invaluable primary source of history. We are left with the difficult task of either repudiating the entire document or, as I believe, embracing it all. If you do believe in Samuel Tonsure's journal, in its validity, then your plea-

133. Cadimon Signal was a friend of mine and so, to avoid a conflict of interest, I shall not expound upon his many virtues—his strength of character, his fine sense of humor, the pedigree of the wines hidden in his basement.

134. The Kalif had had golden page numbers added for his convenience.

135. Signal reports that the attendant "flipped through the pages at such incredible speed that we could hardly see them. When it came time for us to present the 10 page numbers, which we simply chose at random, a great ceremony was made of taking them to the attendant, who made an equally great show of finding the right page, during which we were made to wait outside, for fear we might see a forbidden page. By the time the first page was located and presented to us some 20 minutes had elapsed, and it turned out to be blank, except for the words 'see next page.'"

sure will be enhanced as you pass the equestrian statue of Manzikert I[136] in the Banker's Courtyard and as you survey the ruined aqueducts on Albumuth Boulevard that are, besides the mushroom dwellers themselves, the only remaining sign of Cinsorium, the city before Ambergris.[137]

136. Suitably tall, although the statue's torso and legs (and the horse itself—Manzikert never saw a horse, let alone rode on one) are not of Manzikert I, but the remains of an equestrian statue dating from the period of the Kalif's brief occupation of the city—onto which someone has rather crudely attached Manzikert's head. The original statue of Manzikert I was of an unknown height and showed Manzikert I surrounded by his beloved rats, rendered in bronze. An enterprising but none too bright bureaucrat sold the statue, sans head, for scrap to the Archduke of Banfours a century before the Kalif's invasion; the Archduke promptly recast the statue as a cannon affectionately christened "Old Manzikert" and bombarded the stuffing out of Ambergris with it. As for the rats, they now decorate a small altar near the aqueduct, and if they look more like cats than rats, this is because the sculptor's models died halfway through the commission and he had to use his tabby to complete it.

137. Surely, after all, it is more comforting to believe that the sources on which this account is based are truthful, that this has not all, in fact, been one huge, monstrous lie? And with that pleasant thought, O Tourist, I take my leave for good.

THE
CAGE

he hall contained the following items, some of which were later cataloged on faded yellow sheets constrained by blue lines and anointed with a hint of mildew:

- 24 moving boxes, stacked three high. Atop one box stood
- 1 stuffed black swan with banded blood-red legs, its marble eyes plucked, the empty sockets a shock of outrushing cotton (or was it fungus?), the bird merely a scout for the
- 5,325 specimens from far-off lands placed on shelves that ran along the four walls and into the adjoining corridors—lit with what he could only describe as a black light: it illuminated but did not lift the gloom. Iridescent thrush corpses, the exhausted remains of tattered jellyfish floating in amber bottles, tiny mammals with bright eyes that hinted at the memory of catastrophe, their bodies frozen in brittle poses. The stink of chemicals, a whiff of blood, and
- 1 Manzikert-brand phonograph, in perfect condition, wedged beside the jagged black teeth of 11 broken records and
- 8 framed daguerreotypes of the family that had lived in the mansion. On vacation in the Southern Isles. Posed in front of a hedge. Blissful on the front porch. His favorite picture showed a boy of seven or eight sticking his tongue out, face animated by some wild delight. The frame was cracked, a smudge of blood in the lower left corner. Phonograph, records, and daguerreotypes stood atop
- 1 long oak table covered by a dark green cloth that could not conceal the upward thrust that had splintered the surface of the wood. Around the table stood
- 8 oak chairs, silver lion paws sheathing their legs. The chairs dated to before the reign of Trillian the Great Banker. He could not help but wince noting the abuse to which the chairs had been subjected, or fail to notice
- 1 grandfather clock, its blood-spattered glass face cracked, the hands frozen at a point just before midnight, a faint repressed ticking coming from somewhere

within its gears, as if the hands sought to move once again—and beneath the clock

- 1 embroidered rug, clearly woven in the north, near Morrow, perhaps even by one of his own ancestors. It depicted the arrival of Morrow cavalry in Ambergris at the time of the Silence, the horses and riders bathed in a halo of blood that might, in another light, be seen as part of the tapestry. Although no light could conceal
- 1 bookcase, lacquered, stacked with books wounded, ravaged, as if something had torn through the spines, leaving blood in wide furrows. Next to the bookcase
- 1 solicitor, dressed all in black. The solicitor wore a cloth mask over his nose and mouth. It was a popular fashion, for those who believed in the "Invisible World" newly mapped by the Kalif's scientists. Nervous and fatigued, the solicitor, eyes blinking rapidly over the top of the mask, stood next to
- 1 pale, slender woman in a white dress. Her hooded eyes never blinked, the ethereal quality of her gaze weaving cobwebs into the distance. Her hands had recently been hacked off, the end of the bloody bandage that hid her left nub held by
- 1 pale gaunt boy with eyes as wide and twitchy as twinned pocket watches. At the end of his other arm dangled a small blue-green suitcase, his grasp as fragile as his mother's gaze. His legs trembled in his ash-gray trousers. He stared at
- 1 metal cage, three feet tall and in shape similar to the squat mortar shells that the Kalif's troops had lately rained down upon the city during the ill-fated Occupation. An emerald-green cover hid its bars from view. The boy's gaze, which required him to twist neck and shoulder to the right while also raising his head to look up and behind, drew the attention of
- 1 exporter-importer, Robert Hoegbotton, 35 years old: neither thin nor fat, neither handsome nor ugly. He wore a drab gray suit he hoped displayed neither imagination nor lack of it. He too wore a cloth mask over his (small) nose and (wide, sardonic) mouth, although not for the same reasons as the solicitor. Hoegbotton considered the mask a weakness, an inconvenience, a superstition. His gaze followed that of the boy up to the high perch, an alcove set halfway up the wall where

the cage sat on a window ledge. The dark, narrow window reflected needlings of rain through its tubular green glass. It was the season of downpours in Ambergris.

The rain would not let up for days on end, the skies blue-green-gray with moisture. Fruiting bodies would rise, fat and fecund, in all the hidden corners of the city. Nothing in the bruised sky would reveal whether it was morning, noon, or dusk.

The solicitor was talking and had been for what seemed to Hoegbotton like a rather long time.

"That black swan, for example, is in bad condition," Hoegbotton said, to slow the solicitor's relentless chatter.

The solicitor wiped his beaded forehead with a handkerchief tinged a pale green.

"The bird itself. The bird," the solicitor said, "is in superb condition. Missing eyes, yes. Yes, this is true. But," he gestured at the walls, "surely you see the richness of Daffed's collection."

Thomas Daffed. The last in a long line of famous zoologists. Daffed's wife and son stood beside the solicitor, last remnants of a family of six.

Hoegbotton frowned. "But I don't really need the collection. It's a fine collection, very fine"—and he meant it; he admired a man who could so single-mindedly, perhaps obsessively, acquire such a diverse yet unified assortment of *things*—"but my average customer needs a pot or an umbrella or a stove. I stock the odd curio from time to time, but a collection of this size?" Hoegbotton shrugged his famous shrug, perfected over several years of haggling.

The solicitor stared at Hoegbotton as if he did not believe him. "Well, then, what *is* your offer? What *will* you take?"

"I'm still calculating that figure."

The solicitor loosened his collar with one sharp tug. "It's been more than an hour. My clients are not well!" He was sweating profusely. A greenish pallor had begun to infiltrate his skin. Despite the sweat, the solicitor seemed parched. His mask puffed in and out from the violence of his speech.

"I'm sorry for your loss—all of your losses," Hoegbotton said, turning to the mother and child who stood in mute acceptance of their fate. "I won't keep you much longer." The speech never sounded sincere, no matter how sincerely he meant it.

The solicitor made a noise between a groan and a choke that Hoegbotton did not bother to catalog.

His thoughts had returned to the merchandise—rug, clock, bookcase, phonograph, table, chairs. What price might they accept?

Hoegbotton would not have included the cage in his calculations if the boy's stare had not kept flickering wildly toward it and back down again, gliding like Hoegbotton's own over the remnants of a success that had become utter failure. For all the outlandish things in the room—the boy's own mother to be counted among them—the boy most feared the cage, an object that could no more hurt him than the green suitcase that hung from his arm.

A reflexive sadness for the boy ran through Hoegbotton, even as he noted the delicacy of the silver engravings on the chair legs; definitely pre-Trillian.

He stared at the boy until the boy stared back. "Don't you know you're safe now?" Hoegbotton said a little too loudly, the words muffled by the cloth over his mouth. An echo traveled up to the high ceiling, encountered the skylight, and descended at a higher pitch.

The boy said nothing. As was his right. Outside, the bodies of his father, brother, and two sisters were being burned as a precaution, the bodies too mutilated to have withstood a Viewing anyway. The boy's fate, too, was uncertain. Sometimes survivors did not survive.

Nothing could make one safe. There had been a great spasm of buying houses without basements or with stone floors, but no one had yet proven that such a measure, or any measure, helped. The random nature of the events, combined with their infrequency, had instilled a certain fatalism in Ambergris's inhabitants.

The solicitor had run out of patience. He stood uncomfortably close to Hoegbotton, his breath sour and thick. "Are you ready yet? You've had more than enough time. Should I call Slattery or Ungdom instead?" His voice seemed more distorted than the mask could explain, as if he were in the grip of a new, perhaps deadly, emotion.

Hoegbotton took a step back from the ferocity of the solicitor's gaze. The names of his chief rivals made a little vein in Hoegbotton's left eyelid pulse in and out. Especially Ungdom—towering John Ungdom, he of the wide belly, steeped in alcohol and pork lard.

"Call for them, then," he said, looking away.

The solicitor's gaze bored into his cheek and then the foul presence was gone. The solicitor had slumped into one of the chairs, a great smudge of a man.

"Anyway, I'm almost ready," Hoegbotton said. The vein in his eyelid would not stop pulsing. It was true: neither Slattery nor Ungdom would come. Because they were afraid. Because their devotion to their job was incomplete, insufficient, inadequate. Hoegbotton imagined them both taken up into the rain and torn to pieces by the wind.

"Tell me about the cage," Hoegbotton said suddenly, surprising himself. "The cage up there"—he pointed—"is it for sale, too?"

The boy stiffened, stared at the floor.

To Hoegbotton's surprise, the woman turned to look at him. Her eyes were black as an abyss; they did not blink and reflected nothing. He felt for a moment as if he stood balanced precariously between the son's alarm and the mother's regard.

"The cage was always open," the woman said, her voice gravelly, something stuck in her throat. "We had a bird. We always let it fly around. It was a pretty bird. It flew high through the rooms. It—No one could find the bird. After." The terrible pressure of the word *after* appeared to be too much for her and she fell back into her silence.

"We've never had a cage," the boy said, the dark green suitcase swaying. "We've never had a bird. They left it here. *They* left it."

A chill ran through Hoegbotton that was not caused by a draft. The sleepy gaze of a pig embryo floating in a jar caught his eye. Opportunity or disaster? The value of an artifact *they* had left behind might be considerable. The risks, however, might also be considerable. This was the third time in the last nine months that he had been called to a house visited by the gray caps. Each of the previous times, he had escaped unharmed. In fact, he had come to believe that late arrivals like himself were impervious to any side effects. Yet even he had experienced moments of discomfort, as when, at the last house, he had walked down a white hallway to the room where the merchandise awaited him and found a series of dark smudges and trails and tracks of blood. Halfway down the hallway, he had spied a dark object, shaped like a piece of dried fruit, glistening from the floor. Curious, he had leaned down to examine it, only to recoil and stand up when he realized it was a human ear.

This time, the solicitor had experienced the most unease. According to the talkative messenger who had summoned Hoegbotton, the solicitor had arrived in the early afternoon to find the bodies and survivors. Arms and legs had been stuck into the walls between specimen jars, arranged in intricate poses that displayed a perverse sense of humor.

The light glinted softly off the windows. The silence became more absolute. All around, dead things watched one another, from wall to wall—a cacophony of gazes that saw everything but remembered nothing. Outside, the rain fell relentlessly.

A tingling sensation crept into Hoegbotton's fingertips. A price had material-ized in his mind, manifested itself in glittering detail.

"Two thousand sels—for everything."

The solicitor sighed, almost crumpled in on himself. The woman blinked rap-idly, as if puzzled, and then stared at Hoegbotton with a hatred more real for being so distant. All the former protests of the solicitor, even the boy's fear, were nothing next to that look. The red at the end of her arms had become paler, as if the white bandages had begun to heal her.

He heard himself say, "Three thousand sels. If you include the cage." And it was true, he realized—he wanted the cage.

The solicitor, trying to mask some small personal distress now, giggled and said, "Done. But you must retrieve it yourself. I'm not feeling well." The cloth of the man's mask moved in and out almost imperceptibly as he breathed. A sour smell had entered the room.

On the ladder, Hoegbotton had a moment of vertigo. The world spun, then righted itself as he continued to the top. When he peered onto the windowsill, two eyes stared up at him from beside the cage.

"Manzikert!" he hissed. He recoiled, almost lost his balance as he flailed at empty air, managed to fall back against the ladder . . . and realized that they were just the missing marble eyes of the swan, placed there by some prankster, although it did not pay to think of who such a prankster might be. He caught his breath, tried to swallow the unease that pressed down on his shoulders, his tongue, his eyelids.

The cage stood to the right of the ladder and he was acutely conscious of having to lock his legs onto the ladder's sides as he slowly leaned toward the cage.

Below, the solicitor and the boy were speaking, but their voices seemed dulled and distant. He hesitated. What might be in the cage? What horrible thing far worse than a severed human ear? The odd idea struck him that he would pull the cord to reveal Thomas Daffed's severed head. He could see the bars beneath the cloth, though, he told himself. Whatever lived inside the cage would remain inside the cage. Now that it was his property, his acquisition, he refused to suffer the same failure of nerve as Slattery and Ungdom.

The cover of the cage, which in the dim light appeared to be sprinkled with a luminous green dust, had a drawstring and opened like a curtain. With a sharp yank on the drawstring, Hoegbotton drew aside the cover—and flinched, again nearly fell, a sensation of displaced air flowing across his face, as of *something* moving. He cried out. Then realized the cage was empty. He stood there for an instant, breathing heavily, staring into the cage. Nothing. It contained nothing. Relief came burrowing out of his bones, followed by disappointment. Empty. Except for some straw lining the bottom of the cage and, dangling near the back, almost as an afterthought, a perch, swaying back and forth, the movement no doubt caused by the speed with which he had drawn back the cover. A latched door extended the full three feet from the base to the top of the cage and could be slid back on special grooves. Stained green, the metal bars featured detail work as fine as he had ever seen—intricate flowers and vines with little figures peering out of a background rich with mushrooms. He could sell it for 4,000 sels, with the right sales pitch.

Hoegbotton looked down through a murk diluted only by a few lamps.

"It's empty," he shouted down. "The cage is empty. But I'll take it."

An unintelligible answer floated up. As his sight adjusted to the scene below, the distant solicitor in his chair, the other two still standing, he thought for a horrible second that they were melting. The boy seemed melded to his suitcase, the green of it inseparable from the white of the attached arm. The woman's nubs were impossibly white, as if she had grown new bones. The solicitor was just a splash of green.

When he stood on solid ground again, he could not control his shaking.

"I'll have the papers to you tomorrow, after I've cataloged all of the items," he said.

All around, on the arms of the chairs, on the table, atop the bookcase, white mushrooms had risen on slender stalks, their gills tinged red.

The solicitor sat in his chair and giggled uncontrollably.

"It was nice to meet you," Hoegbotton said as he walked to the door that led to the room that led to the next room and the room after that and then, hopefully, the outside, by which time he would be running. The woman's stubs had sprouted white tendrils of fungus that lazily wound their way around the dried blood and obscured it. Her eyes were slowly filling with white.

Hoegbotton backed into the damaged table and almost fell. "As I say, a pleasure doing business with you."

"Yes, yes, yes, yes," the solicitor said, and giggled again, his skin as green and wrinkly as a lizard's.

"Then I will see you again, soon," Hoegbotton said, edging toward the door, groping behind him for the knob, "and under . . . under better . . ." But he could not finish his sentence.

The boy's arms were dark green, fuzzy and indistinct, as if he were a still life made of points of paint on a canvas. His suitcase, once blue, had turned a blackish green, for the fungi had engulfed it much as ivy had engulfed the eastern wall of the mansion. All the terrible knowledge of his condition shone through the boy's eyes and yet still he held his mother's arm as the white tendrils wound round both their limbs in an ever more permanent embrace.

Hoegbotton later believed he would have stood at the door forever, hand on the knob, the solicitor's giggle a low whine in the background, if not for what happened next.

The broken clock groaned and struck midnight. The shuddering stroke reverberated through the room, through the thousands of jars of preserved animals. The solicitor looked up in sudden terror and, with a soft popping sound, exploded into a lightly falling rain of emerald spores that drifted to the floor with as slow and tranquil a grace as the seeds of a dandelion. As if the sound had torn him apart.

✿

Outside, Hoegbotton tore off his mask, knelt, and threw up beside the fountain that guarded the path to Albumuth Boulevard. Behind him, across a square of dark green grass, the bodies of Daffed, his daughters, his other son, smoldered gray and black. The charred smell mixed with mildew and the rain that stippled his back. Hoegbotton's arms and legs trembled with an enervating weakness. His mouth felt hot and dry. For a long time, he sat in the same position, watching pinpricks break his reflection in the fountain. He shivered as the water shivered.

He had never come this close before. Either they had died long before he arrived or long after he left. The solicitor's liquid giggle trickled through his ears, along with the soft pop of the spores. He shuddered, relaxed, shuddered again.

When his assistant Alan Bristlewing questioned, as he often did, the wisdom of taking on such hazardous work, Hoegbotton would smile and change the subject. He could not choose between two conflicting impulses: the upswelling of excitement and the desire to flee Ambergris and return to Morrow, the city of his birth. As each new episode receded into memory, his nerve returned, somehow stronger.

The boy's arm, fused to his suitcase.

Holding on to the lichen-flecked stone lip of the pool, Hoegbotton plunged his head into the smooth water. The chill shocked him. It prickled his skin, cut through the numbness to burn the inside of his nose. A sob escaped him, and another, and then a third that bent him over the water again. The back of his neck was suddenly cool. When he pulled away, he looked down at his reflection—and the mask he had made to hide his emotions was gone. He was himself again.

Hoegbotton stood up. Across the courtyard, the Cappan's men had abandoned the bodies to begin the task of nailing boards across the doors and windows of the mansion. No one pulled the shades open to protest being trapped inside. No one banged on the door, begging to be let out. They had already begun their journey.

One look at his face as he staggered to safety had told the Cappan's men everything. No doubt they would have boarded him in too, if not for the bribes and his previous record of survival.

Hoegbotton wiped his mouth with his handkerchief. The merchandise he had bought would molder in the mansion, unused and unrecorded except in his ledger of "Potential Acquisitions: Lost." Depending on which hysteria-induced procedure the Cappan had adopted this fortnight, the mansion grounds might be cordoned off or the mansion itself might be put to the torch.

The clock struck midnight.

The cage stood beside him, slick with rain. Hoegbotton had gripped its handle so hard during his escape—from every corner, Daffed's infernal collection of dead things staring innocently at him—that he had been branded where the skin had not been rubbed off his palm. He bore the mark of the handle: a delicate filigree of unfamiliar symbols from behind which strange eyes peered out. In the fading light, with the rain falling harder, the fungi appeared to have been washed off the cover of the cage. Perversely, this fact disappointed him. With each new encounter, he had come to expect further revelations.

Blinking away the rain, Hoegbotton let out a deep breath, stuffed his mask in a pocket, wrapped the cloth around his injured hand, and picked up the cage. It was heavier than he remembered it, and oddly balanced. It made him list to the side as he started walking up the path to the main road. He would have to hurry if he was to make the curfew imposed by the Cappan.

Ambergris at dusk, occluded and darkened by the rain that splattered on sidewalks, rattled against rooftops, struck windows, hinted at a level of debauchery almost as unnerving to Hoegbotton as the way, whenever he stopped to switch the cage from his left to his right hand and back again, the weight never seemed the same.

The city that flourished from wholesome activity by day became its opposite by night. Orgies had been reported in abandoned churches. Grotesque and lewd water puppet shows were staged down by the docks. Weekly, the merchant quarter held midnight auctions of paintings that could only be termed obscene. The fey illustrated books of Collart and Slothian enjoyed a popularity that placed the authors but a single step below the Cappan in status. In the Religious Quarter, the hard-pressed Truffidian priests tried to wrest back authority from the conflicting prophets Peterson and Stratton, whose dueling theologies infected ever-more violent followers.

At the root of this immorality: the renewed presence of the gray caps, who in recent years came and went like the ebb and flow of a tide—now underground, now aboveground, as if in a perpetual migration between light and dark, night and day. Always, the city reacted to their presence in unpredictable ways. What choice did the city's inhabitants have but to go about their business, hoping they would not be next, blind to all but their own misfortunes? It was now one hundred years since the Silence, when thousands had vanished without a trace, and people could be forgiven their loss of memory. Most people no longer thought of the Silence on a daily basis. It did not figure into the ordinary sorrows of Ambergris's inhabitants so much as into the weekly sermons of the Truffidians or into the worries of the Cappan and his men.

As Hoegbotton walked home, streetlamps appeared out of the murk, illuminating fleeting figures: a priest holding his robe up as he ran so he wouldn't trip on the hem; two Dogghe tribesmen hunched against the closed doors of a bank, their distinctive green spiraled hats pulled down low over their weathered faces. Of the recent Occupation by the Kalif, no sign remained except for painted graffiti urging the invaders to go home. But Hoegbotton still came upon the faintly glowing, six-foot-wide purplish circles that showed where, before the Silence, huge mushrooms had been chopped down by worried authorities.

Hoegbotton's wife was already asleep when he walked up the seven flights of stairs and entered their apartment. She had turned off the lamps because it gave her the advantage in case of an intruder. The faint scent of lilacs and honeysuckle told him the flower vendor from the floor above them had been by to see Rebecca.

A dim half-light shone from the living room to his left as he set down the cage, took off his shoes and socks, and hung his raincoat on the coat rack. Directly ahead lay the dining room, with its mold-encrusted window, the purple sheen burning darkly as the rain fed it. He had checked the fungi guard just a week ago and found no leakage, but he made a mental note to check it again in the morning.

Hoegbotton found a towel in the hall closet and used it to dry his face, his hair, and then the outside of the cage. Again picking up the uncomfortable weight of the cage, he tiptoed into the living room, the rug beneath his feet thick but cold. A medley of dark shapes greeted him, most of them items from his store: lamps and side tables, a couch, a long low coffee table, a bookcase, a grandfather clock. Beyond them lay the balcony, long lost to fungi and locked up as a result.

The fey light almost transformed the living room's contents into the priceless artifacts he had told her they were. He had chosen them not for their value but for their texture, their smell, and for the sounds they made when moved or sat upon or opened. Little of it appealed visually, but she delighted in what he had chosen and it meant he could store the most important merchandise at the shop, where it was more secure.

Hoegbotton set the cage down on the living room table. The palms of his hands were hot and raw from carrying it. He took off the rest of his clothes and laid them on the arm of the couch.

The light came from the bedroom, which lay to the right of the living room. He walked into the bedroom and turned to the left, the closed window above the bed reflecting back the iridescent light that came from her and her alone. Rebecca lay on her back, the sheets draped across her body, exposing the long, black, vaguely tear-shaped scar on her left thigh. He ran his gaze over it lustfully. It glistened like obsidian.

Hoegbotton walked around to the right side and eased himself into the bed. He moved up beside her and pressed himself against the darkness of the scar. An image of the woman from the mansion flashed through his mind.

Rebecca turned in her sleep and put an arm across his chest as he moved onto his back. Her hand, warm and soft, was as delicate as the starfish that glided through the shallows down by the docks. It looked so small against his chest.

The light came from her open eyes, although he could tell she was asleep. It was a silvery glow awash with faint phosphorescent sparks of blue, green, and red: shivers and hiccups of splintered light, as if a half-dozen tiny lightning storms had welled up in her gaze. What rich worlds did she dream of? And, for the thousandth time: What did the light mean? He had met her on a business trip to Stockton, after the fungal infection that had resulted in the blindness, the odd light, the scar.

Who was this stranger, so pale and silent and beautiful? A joyful sorrow rose within him as he watched the light emanating from her. They had argued about having children just the day before. Every word he had thrown at her in anger had hurt him so deeply that finally he had been wordless, and all he could do was stare at her. Looking at her now, her face unguarded, her body next to his, he could not help loving her for the scar, the eyes, even if it meant he wished her to be this way.

2

The next morning, Hoegbotton woke to the fading image of the woman's bloody bandages and the sounds of Rebecca making breakfast. She knew the apartment better than he did—knew its surfaces, its edges, the exact number of steps from table to chair to doorway—and she liked to make meals in a kitchen that had become more familiar to her than it could ever be to him. Yet she also asked him to bring back more furniture for the living room and bedroom or rearrange existing furniture. She became bored otherwise. "I want an unexplored country. I want a hint of the unknown," she said once and Hoegbotton agreed with her.

To an extent. There were things Hoegbotton wished would stay unknown. On the mantel opposite the bed, for example, lay those of his grandmother's possessions that his relatives in Morrow had sent to him: a pin, a series of portraits of family members, a set of spoons, a poorly copied family history. A letter had accompanied the heirlooms, describing his grandmother's last days. The package had been waiting for him on the doorstep of the apartment one evening a month ago. His grandmother had died six weeks before that. He had not gone to the funeral. He had not even brought himself to tell Rebecca about the death. All she knew of it was the crinkling of the envelope as he smoothed out the letter to read it. She might even have picked up the pin or the spoons and wondered why he had brought them home. Telling her would mean explaining why he hadn't gone to the funeral and then he would have to talk about the bad blood between him and his brother Richard.

The smell of bacon and eggs spurred him to throw back the covers, get up, put on a bathrobe, and stumble bleary-eyed through the living room to the kitchen. A dead sort of almost-sunlight—pale and green and lukewarm—suffused the kitchen window through the purple mold and thin veins of green. A watermark of the city appeared through the glass: gray spires, forlorn flags, the indistinct shapes of other anonymous apartment buildings.

Rebecca stood in the kitchen, spatula in hand, framed by the dour light. Her black hair was brightly dark. Her dress, a green-and-blue sweep of fabric, fit her loosely. She was intent on the skillet in front of her, gaze unblinking, mouth pursed.

As he came up behind Rebecca and wrapped his arms around her, a sense of guilt made him frown. He had come so close last night, almost as close as the boy, the woman. Was that as close as he could get without . . . ? The question had haunted him throughout his quest. A sudden deep swell of emotion overcame him and he found that his eyes were wet. What if, what if?

Rebecca snuggled into his embrace and turned toward him. Her eyes looked almost normal during the day. Flecks of phosphorescence shot lazily across the pupils.

"Did you sleep well?" she asked. "You came home so late."

"I slept. I'm sorry I was late. It was a difficult job this time."

"Profitable?" Her elbow nudged him as she turned the eggs over with the spatula.

"Not very."

"Really? Why not?"

He stiffened. Would Rebecca have realized the mansion had become a death trap? Would she have smelled the blood, tasted the fear? He served as her eyes, her contact with the world of images, but would he truly deprive her by not describing its horrors to her in every detail?

"Well . . ." he began. He shut his eyes. The sick gaze of the solicitor flickering over the scene of his own death washed over him. Even as he held Rebecca, he could feel a distance opening up between them.

"You don't need to shut your eyes to see," she said, pulling out of his embrace.

"How did you know?" he said, although he knew.

"I heard you close them." She smiled with grim satisfaction.

"It was just sad," he said, sitting down at the kitchen table. "Nothing horrible. Just sad. The wife had lost her husband and had to sell the estate. She had a boy with her who kept holding on to a little suitcase."

The remnants of the solicitor floating to the ground, curling up like confetti. The boy's gaze fluttering between him and the cage.

"I felt sorry for them. They had some nice heirlooms, but most of it was already promised to Slattery. I didn't get much. They had a nice rug from Morrow, from before the Silence. Nice detail of Morrow cavalry coming to our rescue. I would have liked to have bought it."

She carefully slid the eggs and bacon onto a plate and brought it to the table.

"Thank you," he said. She had burned the bacon. The eggs were too dry. He never complained. She needed these little sleights of hand, these illusions of illumination. It was edible. He couldn't do better.

"Mrs. Bloodgood took me down to the Morhaim Museum yesterday," she said. "Many of their artifacts are on open display. The textures were amazing. And the flower vendor visited, as you may have guessed."

Rebecca's father, Paul, was the curator for a small museum in Stockton. Paul liked to joke that Hoegbotton was just the temporary caretaker for items that would eventually find their way to him. Hoegbotton had always thought museums just hoarded that which should be available on the open market. Rebecca had been her father's assistant until the disease stole her sight. Now Hoegbotton sometimes took her down to the store to help him sort and catalog new acquisitions.

"I noticed the flowers," he said. "I'm glad the museum was nice."

For some reason, his hand shook as he ate his eggs. He put his fork down.

"Isn't it good?" she asked.

"It's very good," he said. "I just need water."

He got up and walked to the sink. The faucet had been put in five weeks ago, after a two-year wait. Before, they had gotten jugs of water from a well down in the valley. He watched with satisfaction as the faucet spluttered and his glass gradually filled up.

"It's a nice bird or whatever," she said from behind him.

"Bird." A vague fear shot through him. "Bird?" The glass clinked against the edge of the sink as he momentarily lost his grip on it.

"Or lizard. Or whatever it is. What is it?"

He turned, leaned against the sink. "What are you talking about?"

"That cage you brought home with you."

The vague fear crept up his spine. "There's nothing in the cage. It's empty." Was she joking?

Rebecca laughed: a pleasant, liquid sound. "That's funny, because your empty cage was rattling earlier. At first, it scared me. Something was rustling around in there. I couldn't tell if it was a bird or a lizard or I would have reached through the bars and touched it."

"But you didn't."

"No."

"There's nothing in the cage."

Her face underwent a subtle change and he knew she thought he doubted her on something at which she was expert: the interpretation of sound. On a calm day, she had told him, she could hear a boy skipping stones down by the docks. This was in jest, he felt, but could not know.

For a moment, he said nothing. He couldn't stay quiet for long. She couldn't read his face without touching it, but he suspected she knew the difference between types of silence.

He laughed. "I'm joking. It's a lizard—but it bites. So you were wise not to touch it."

Suspicion tightened her features. Then she relaxed and smiled at him. She reached out, felt for his plate with her left hand, and stole a piece of his bacon. "I knew it was a lizard!"

He longed to go into the living room where the cage stood atop the table. But he couldn't, not just yet.

"It's quiet in here," he said softly, already expecting the reply.

"No it's not. It's not quiet at all. It's loud."

The left corner of his mouth curled up as he replied by rote: "What do you hear, my love?"

Her smile widened. "Well, first, there's your voice, my love—a nice, deep baritone. Then there's Hobson downstairs, playing a phonograph as low as he can to avoid disturbing the Potaks, who are at this moment in an argument about something so petty I will not give you the details, while to the side, just below them"—her eyes narrowed—"I believe the Smythes are also making bacon. Above us, old man Clox is pacing and pacing with his cane, muttering about money. On his balcony, there's a sparrow chirping, which makes me realize now that the animal in your cage must be a lizard, because it sounds like something clicking and clucking, not chirping—unless you've got a chicken in there?"

"No, no—it's a lizard."

"What kind of lizard?"

"It's a Saphant Click-Spitting Fire Lizard from the Southern Isles," he said. "It only ever grows in cages, which it makes itself by chewing up dirt, changing it into metal, and regurgitating it. It can only eat animals that can't see it."

She laughed in appreciation and got up and hugged him. Her scent made him forget his fear. "It's a good story, but I don't believe you. I do know this, though—you are going to be late to work."

Once on the ground floor, where he did not think it would make a difference if Rebecca heard, Hoegbotton set down the cage. The awkwardness of carrying it, uneven and swaying, down the spiral staircase had unnerved him. He was sweating under his raincoat. His breath came hard and fast. The musty quality of the lobby, the traces of tiny rust mushrooms that had spread along the floor like mouse tracks, the mottled green-orange mold on the windows in the front door, did not put him at ease.

Someone had left a worn umbrella leaning against the front door. He grabbed it and turned back to stare at the cage. Was this the moment that Ungdom and Slattery's ill wishes caught up with him? He drove the umbrella tip between the bars. The cover gave a little, creasing, and then regained its former shape as he withdrew the umbrella. Nothing came leaping out at him. He tried again.

No response.

"Is something in there?" he asked the cage. The cage did not reply.

Umbrella held like a sword in front of him, Hoegbotton pulled the cover aside—and leapt back.

The cage was still empty. The perch swung back and forth madly from the violence with which he had pulled aside the cover. The woman had said, "The cage was always open." The boy had said, "We never had a cage." The solicitor had never offered an opinion. The swinging perch, the emptiness of the cage, depressed him. He could not say why. He drew the cover back across the cage.

Footsteps sounded on the stairs behind him and he whirled around, then relaxed. It was just Sarah Willis, their landlady, walking down from her second floor apartment.

"Good morning, Mrs. Willis," he said, leaning on the umbrella.

Mrs. Willis did not bother to respond until she was standing in front of him, staring up at him through her thick glasses. A flower-patterned hat covered her balding head. A matching flower dress, faded, covered her ancient body, even her presumably shoed feet.

"No pets allowed," she said.

"Pets?" Hoegbotton was momentarily bewildered. "What pets?"

Mrs. Willis nodded at the cage. "What's in there?"

"Oh, that. It's not a pet."

"No animals allowed, pets or meat." Mrs. Willis cackled and coughed at her own joke.

"It's not . . ." He realized it was useless. "I'm taking it out now. It was just there for the morning."

Mrs. Willis grunted and pushed past him.

At the door, just as she walked out into the renewed patter of rain, apparently counting on her hat to protect her, she offered Hoegbotton the following advice: "Miss Constance? On the third floor? She'll have your head if you don't put back her umbrella."

Located on Albumuth Boulevard, halfway between the docks and the residential sections that descended into a valley ever in danger of flooding, Hoegbotton's store—ROBERT HOEGBOTTON & SONS: QUALITY IMPORTERS OF FINE NEW & USED ITEMS FROM HOME & ABROAD—took up the first floor of a solid two-story wooden building owned by a monk in the Religious Quarter. The sign exhibited optimism; there were no sons. Not yet. The time was not right, the situation too uncertain, no matter what Rebecca might say. Someday his shop might serve as the headquarters for a merchant empire, but that wouldn't happen for several years. Always in the back of his mind, spurring him on: his brother Richard's threat to swoop down with the rest of the Hoegbotton clan to save the family name should he fail.

The display window, protected from the rain by an awning, held a battered mauve couch, an opulent, gold leaf–covered chair (nicked by Hoegbotton, along with several other treasures, during the panicked withdrawal of the Kalif's troops), a phonograph, a large red vase, an undistinguished-looking saddle, and Alan Bristlewing, his assistant.

Bristlewing knelt inside the display, carefully placing records in the stand beside the phonograph. He had already wiped the window clean of fungi that had accumulated the night before. The detritus of the cleaning lay on the sidewalk in curled-up piles of red, green, and blue. A sour smell emanated from these remnants, but the rain would wash it all away in an hour or two.

When Bristlewing saw Hoegbotton, he waved and inched his wiry frame out of the window. A moment later, shielding his head from the rain with a newspaper, he was opening the huge lock in the iron grille of the door, his mouth set in the familiar laconic grin that itself displayed some antiques, courtesy of a sidewalk dentist. A few button-shaped mushrooms, a fiery red, tumbled out of the lock as the key withdrew, rolling to a stop on the wet sidewalk.

Bristlewing was a scruffy, short, animated man who smelled of cigar smoke and often disappeared for days on end. Stories of debaucheries with prostitutes and weeklong fishing trips down the River Moth buzzed around Bristlewing without settling on him. Hoegbotton could not afford to hire more dependable help.

"Morning," Bristlewing said.

"Good morning," Hoegbotton replied. "Any customers last night?"

"None with any money . . ." Bristlewing's grin vanished as he saw the cage. "Oh. I see you went to another one."

Hoegbotton set the cage down in front of Bristlewing and took the ring of keys from him at the same time. "Just put it in the office. Are the inventory books up-to-date?" Hoegbotton's hand still stung from where the imprint of the handle had branded itself on his skin.

"Course they're current," Bristlewing said, turning stiffly away as he picked up his new burden.

By design, the way to Hoegbotton's office at the back of the store was blocked by a maze of items, from which rose a collective must-metal-rotted-dusty smell that to him formed the most delicate of perfumes. This smell of antiquity validated his selections as surely as any papers of authenticity. That customers tripped and frequently lost their bearings as they navigated the arbitrary footpaths mattered little to Hoegbotton. The received family wisdom said that thus hemmed in the customer had no choice but to buy something from the stacks of chairs, umbrellas, watches, pens, fishing rods, clothes, enameled boxes, deer racks, plaster casts of lizards, elegant mirrors of glass and copper, reading glasses, Truffidian religious icons, boards for playing dice made of oliphaunt ivory, porcelain water jugs, globes of the world, model ships, old medals, sword canes, musical clocks, and other ephemera from past lives or distant places. Hoegbotton loved knowing that a customer might, in seeking out a perfectly ordinary set of dinner plates, come face-to-face with the flared nostrils and questing tongue of an erotic mask. An over-whelming sense of the secret history of these objects could sometimes send him into a trance-like state. Thankfully, Rebecca understood this feeling, having been exposed to it from an early age.

Emerging from this morass of riches, Hoegbotton's office lay open to the rest of the store like an oasis of sparseness. Five steps led down to its sunken carpeting—crimson with gold threads, bought from the old Threnody Larkspur Theater before it burned to the ground—and a simple rosewood desk whose only flourishes were legs carved into the shape of writhing squid. A matching chair, two worktables against the far wall, and a couch for visitors rounded out the furniture. To the left of the office space stood two doors. The first led to a private bathroom, recently installed, much to Bristlewing's delight.

The desk lay beneath an organized clutter of books of inventory, a blotter, a selection of fountain pens, stationery with the H&S logo emblazoned upon it, folders full of invoices, a metal message capsule with a curled-up piece of paper inside, a slice of orange mushroom in a small paper bag, a shell he had found while on vacation in the Southern Isles when he was six, and the new Frankwrithe & Lewden edition of *The Mystery of Cinsorium* by Blake Clockmoor. Daguerreotypes of Rebecca, his brother Stephen (lost to the family now, having signed up for the Kalif's cavalry on a monstrous but historically common whim) and his mother Gertrude standing on the lawn of someone else's mansion in Morrow added a personal touch.

Bristlewing had already made himself scarce—Hoegbotton could hear him pulling some artifact out from behind a row of old bookcases stacked high with cracked flowerpots—and the cage stood on the sideboard of his desk as if it had always been there.

Hoegbotton hung his raincoat on one of the six coat racks lined up like soldiers in the farthest corner of the office. Then he took the past day's book of inventory and purchases and walked to the door that led to the room next to the bathroom. The door was very old, wormholed, and studded with odd metal symbols that Hoegbotton had taken from an abandoned Manziist shrine.

Hoegbotton unlocked the door and went inside. The door shut silently behind him and he was alone. The light that cast its yellowing glare upon the room came from an old-fashioned squid oil lamp nailed into the room's far wall.

Nothing, at first glance, distinguished the room from any other room. It contained a tired-looking dining table around which stood four worn chairs. To one side, plates, cups, bowls, and utensils sat atop a cabinet with a mirror that served as a backboard. The mirror was veined with a purplish fungus that had managed to infiltrate minute fractures in the glass. He had worried that the Cappan's men might confiscate the mirror on one of their weekly inspections of his store, but they had ignored it, perhaps recognizing the age of the mirror and the way mold had itself begun to grow on the fungus.

The table held three place settings, the faded napkins unfolded and haphazard. Across the middle of the table lay a parchment of faded words, so old that it looked as if it might disintegrate into dust at the slightest touch. A bottle of port, half-full, stood on the table next to a bare space in front of the fourth chair.

By tradition, recently established, Hoegbotton sat there for his daily readings from the books of inventory. Bound in red leather, the books were imported from Morrow. The off-white pages were thin as tissue paper to accommodate as many sheets as possible. The two books Hoegbotton had taken with him represented the inventory for the past three months. Sixteen others, as massive and unwieldy, had been wrapped in a blanket and carefully hidden beneath the floorboards in his office. (Two separate notebooks to record unfortunate but necessary dealings with Ungdom and Slattery, suitably yellow and brown, had been tossed into an unlocked drawer of his desk.)

Yesterday had been slow—only five items sold, two of them phonograph records. He frowned when he read Bristlewing's description of the buyers as "Short lady with walking stick. Did not give a name." And "Man looked sick. Took forever to make up his mind. Bought one record after all that time." Bristlewing did not respect the system. By contrast, a typical Hoegbotton-penned buyer entry read like an investigative report: "Miss Glissandra Beckle, 4232 East Munrale Mews, late 40s. Gray-silver hair. Startling blue eyes. Wore an expensive green dress but cheap black shoes, scuffed. She insisted on calling me 'Mr. Hoegbotton.' She examined a very expensive Occidental vase and commented favorably on a bone hairpin, a pearl snuffbox, and a watch once worn by a prominent Truffidian priest. However, she only bought the hairpin."

If Bristlewing disliked the detail required by Hoegbotton for the ledgers, he disliked the room itself even more. After carefully cataloging its contents upon their arrival three years before, Hoegbotton had asked Bristlewing a question.

"Do you know what this is?"

"Old musty room. No air."

"No. It's not an old musty room with no air."

"Fooled me," Bristlewing had said and, scowling, left him there.

3

But Bristlewing was wrong. Bristlewing did not understand the first thing about the room. How could he? And how could Hoegbotton explain that the room was perhaps the most important room in the world, that he often found himself inside it even while walking around the city, at home reading to his wife, or buying fruit and eggs from the farmers market?

The history of the room went back to the Silence itself. His great-great-grandfather, Samuel Hoegbotton, had been the first Hoegbotton to move to Ambergris, much against the wishes of the rest of his extended family, including his twenty-year-old son, John, who stayed in Morrow.

For a man who had uprooted his wife and daughter from all that was familiar to take up residence in an unknown, sometimes cruel, city, Samuel Hoegbotton became remarkably successful, establishing three stores down by the docks. It seemed only a matter of time before more of the Hoegbotton clan moved down to Ambergris.

However, this was not to be. One day, Samuel Hoegbotton, his wife, and his daughter disappeared, just three of the thousands of souls who vanished from Ambergris during the episode known as the Silence—leaving behind empty buildings, empty courtyards, empty houses, and the assumption among those who grieved that the gray caps had caused the tragedy. Hoegbotton remembered one line in particular from John's diary: "I cannot believe my father has really disappeared. It is possible he could have come to harm, but to simply disappear? Along with my mother and sister? I keep thinking that they will return one day and explain what happened to me. It is too difficult to live with, otherwise."

Sitting in his mother's bedroom with the diary open before him, the young Robert Hoegbotton had felt a chill across the back of his neck. What had happened to Samuel Hoegbotton? He spent many summer afternoons in the attic, surrounded by antiquities, speculating on the subject. He combed through old letters Samuel had sent home before his disappearance. He visited the family archive. He wrote to relatives in other cities. His mother disapproved of such inquiries; his grandmother just smiled and said sadly, "I've often wondered myself." He could not talk to his father about it; that cold and distant figure was rarely home.

His sister also found the mystery intriguing. They would act out scenarios with the house as the backdrop. They would ask the maids questions to fill gaps in their knowledge and thus uncover the meaning of words like "gray cap" and "Cappan." His grandmother had even given them an old sketch that showed the apartment's living room—Samuel Hoegbotton surrounded by smiling relatives on a visit. But for his sister it was just relief of a temporary boredom and he was soon so busy learning the family business that the mystery faded from his thoughts.

When he reached the age of majority, he decided to leave Morrow and travel to Ambergris. No Hoegbotton had set foot in Ambergris for ninety years and it was precisely for this reason that he chose the city, or so he told himself. In Morrow, under the predatory eye of Richard, he had felt as if none of his plans would ever be successful. In Ambergris, he had started out poor but independent, operating a sidewalk stall that sold fruit and broadsheets. At odd times—at an auction, looking at jewelry that reminded him of something his mother might wear; sneaking around Ungdom's store examining all that merchandise, so much richer than what he could acquire at the time—thoughts of the Silence wormed their way into his head.

The day after he signed the lease on his own store, Hoegbotton visited Samuel's apartment. He had the address from some of the man's letters. The building lay in a warren of derelict structures that rose from the side of the valley to the east of the Merchant Quarter. It took Hoegbotton an hour to find it, the carriage ride followed by progress on foot. He knew he was close when he had to climb over a wooden fence with a sign on it that read OFF LIMITS BY ORDER OF THE CAPPAN. The sky was overcast, the sunlight weak yet bright, and he walked through the tenements feeling ethereal, dislocated. Here and there, he found walls where bones had been mixed with the mortar and he knew by these signs that such places had been turned into graveyards.

When he finally stood in front of the apartment—on the ground level of a three-story building—he wondered if he should turn around and go home. The exterior was boarded up, fire scorched and splotched with brown-yellow fungi. Weeds had drowned the grass and other signs of a lawn. A smell like dull vinegar permeated the air. The facing rows of buildings formed a corridor of light, at the end of which a stray dog sniffed at the ground, picking up a scent. He could see its ribs even from so far away. Somewhere, a child began to cry, the sound thin, attenuated, automatic. The sound was so unexpected, almost horrifying, that he thought it must not be a baby at all, but *something* mimicking a baby, hoping to lure him closer.

After a few more moments, he reached a decision and took a crowbar from his pack. Half an hour later, he had unpried the boards and the door stood revealed, a pale "X" running across the dark wood. He realized he was breathing in shallow gasps, anticipation laced with fear. No one could help him if he opened the door and needed help, but he still wanted whatever was inside the apartment. It could be anything, even the end of his life, and yet the adrenaline rushed through him.

Hoegbotton pulled the door open and stepped inside, crowbar held like a weapon.

It took a moment for his eyes to adjust to the darkness. The air was stale. Windows to the right and left of the hallway, although boarded up, let in enough light to make patches of dust on the floor shine like colonies of tiny, subdued fireflies. The hallway was oddly ordinary, nothing out of place. In the even more dimly lit living room, Hoegbotton could make out that some vagrant had long ago set up digs and abandoned them. A sofa had been overturned and a blanket used as a roof for a makeshift tent, broadsheets strewn across the floor for a bed. Dog droppings were more recent, as were the bones of small animals piled in a corner. A rabbit carcass, withered but caked with dried blood, might have been as fresh as the week before. The wallpaper had collapsed into a mumbling senility of fragments and strips. Paintings that had hung on the wall lay in tumbled flight against the floor, their hooks having long since given out. A faint, bitter smell rose from the room—a sourness that revealed hidden negotiations between wood and fungi, the natural results of decay. Hoegbotton relaxed. The gray caps had not been in the apartment for a long time. He let the crowbar dangle in his hand.

Hoegbotton entered the dining room. Brittle fragments of newsprint lay scattered across the dining room table, held in place by a bottle of port with glass beside it. Colonized by cobwebs, by dust, by mottled fragments of wood that had drifted down from the ceiling, the table also held three plates and place settings. The stale air had preserved the contents of the plates in a mummified state. Three plates. Three pieces of ossified chicken, accompanied by a green smear of some vegetable long since dried out. Samuel Hoegbotton. His wife Sarah. His daughter Jane. All three chairs, worm-eaten and rickety, were pulled out slightly from the table. A fourth chair lay off to the side, smashed into fragments by time or violence.

Hoegbotton stared at the chairs for a long time. Had they been moved at all in the last hundred years? Had freak winds blowing through the gaps in the boarded-up windows caused them to move? How could anyone know? And yet, their current positioning teased his imagination. It did not look as if Samuel Hoegbotton's family had gotten up in alarm—unfolded napkins lay on the seats of two of the chairs. The third—that of the person who would have been reading the newspaper—had not been used, nor had the silverware for that setting. The silverware of the other two was positioned peculiarly. On the right side, the fork lay at an angle near the plate, as if thrown there. Something dark and withered had been skewered by the fork's tines. Did it match an irregularity in the dry flesh of the chicken upon the matching plate? The knife was missing entirely. On the left side of the table, the fork was still stuck into its piece of chicken, the knife sawing into the flesh beside it.

It appeared to Hoegbotton as if the family had been eating and simply . . . disappeared . . . in mid-meal. A prickly, cold sensation spread across Hoegbotton's skin. The fork. The knife. The chairs. The broadsheet. The meals uneaten, half eaten. The bottle of port. The mystery gnawed at him even as it became ever more impenetrable. Nothing in the scenarios his sister and he had drawn up in their youth could account for it.

Hoegbotton took out his pocketknife and leaned over the table. He carefully pulled aside one leaf of the broadsheet to reveal the date: the very day of the Silence. The date transfixed him. He pulled out the chair where surely Samuel Hoegbotton must have sat, reading his papers, and slowly slid into it. Looked down the table to where his daughter and wife would have been sitting. Continued to read the paper with its articles on the turmoil at the docks, preparing for the windfall of squid meat due with the return of the fishing fleet; a brief message on blasphemy from the Truffidian Antechamber; the crossword puzzle. A sudden shift, a dislocation, a puzzled look from his wife, and he had stared up from his paper in that last moment to see . . . what? To see the gray caps or a vision much worse? Had Samuel Hoegbotton known surprise? Terror? Wonder? Or was he taken away so swiftly that he, his daughter, and his wife, had no time for any reaction at all.

Hoegbotton stared across the table again, focused on the bottle of port. The glass was half full. He leaned forward, examined the glass. The liquid inside had dried into sludge over time. A faint imprint of tiny lips could be seen on the edge of the glass. The cork was tightly wedged into the mouth of the bottle. A further mystery. Had the port been poured long after the Silence?

Beyond the bottle, the fork with the skewered meat came into focus. It did not, from this angle, look as if it came from the piece of chicken on the plate.

He pulled back, as much from a thought that had suddenly occurred to him as from the fork itself. A dim glint from the floor beside the chair caught his eye. Samuel Hoegbotton's glasses. Twisted into a shape that resembled a circle attached to a line and two "U" shapes on either end. As he stared at the glasses, Hoegbotton felt the questions multiply, until he was not just sitting in Samuel Hoegbotton's chair, but in the chairs of thousands of souls, looking out into darkness, trying to see what they had seen, to know what they came to know.

The baby was still screaming as Hoegbotton stumbled outside, gasping. He ran over bits of brick and rubble. He ran through the long weeds. He ran past the buildings with mortar made from bones. He scrambled over the fence that said he should not have been there. He did not stop running until he had reached the familiar cobblestones of Albumuth Boulevard's farthest extreme. When he did stop, gasping for breath, the pressure in his temples remained, the stray thought lodged in his head like a disease. What had Samuel Hoegbotton seen? And was it necessary to disappear to have seen it?

That was how it had started—following a cold, one-hundred-year-old trail. At first, he convinced himself that he was just pursuing a good business opportunity: buying up the contents of boarded-up homes, fixing what was in disrepair, and reselling it from his store. He had begun with Samuel Hoegbotton's apartment, hiring workmen to take the contents of the dining room and transplant it to the room next to his office. They had arranged it exactly as it had been when he first entered it. He would sit in the room for hours, scrutinizing each element—the bottle of port, the plates, the silverware, the napkins haphazard on the chairs—but no further insight came to him. After a few months, he dusted it all and repaired the table, the chairs, restoring everything but the broadsheet to the way it must have been the day of the Silence. In his darker moments, he felt as if he might be ushering in a new Silence with his actions, but still he came no closer to an answer.

Soon even the abandoned rooms of the Silence lost their hold on Hoegbotton. He would go in with the workmen and find old, dimly lit spaces from which whatever had briefly imbued them with a ghastly intensity had long since departed. He stopped acquiring such properties, although in a sense, it was too late. Ungdom, Slattery, and their ilk had already begun to slander him, spreading rumors about his intent and his sanity. They made life difficult for him, but by ignoring their barbs, he had survived it.

Hoegbotton did not give up. Whenever he could, he bought items that had some connection to the gray caps, hoping to find the answers necessary to quell his curiosity. He read books. He spoke to those who remembered, vaguely, the tales their elders had told them about the Silence. And then, finally, the breakthrough: a series of atrocities at one mansion after the other, bringing him closer than ever before.

Hoegbotton finished reading the ledger, took a last sip of the port he had poured for himself, and walked out of the room in time to hear the bell that announced the arrival of a customer. He put the books back in their place and was about to lock the door to Samuel Hoegbotton's dining room when it occurred to him that the cage might be more secure inside the room. He picked it up—the handle seemed hot to the touch—walked back into the room, and placed the cage on the far end of the table. Then he locked the door, put the key in his desk, and went to attend to the needs of his customer.

4

That night, he made love to Rebecca. Her scar gleamed by the light from her eyes, which, at the height of her rapture, blazed so brightly that the bedroom seemed transported from night to day. As he came inside of her, he felt a part of her scar enter him. It registered as an ecstatic shudder that penetrated his muscles, his bones, his heart. She called out his name and ran her hands down his back, across his face, her eyes sparking with pleasure. At such moments, when the strangeness of her seeped through into him, he would suffer a sudden panic, as if he was losing himself, as if he no longer knew his own name. He would sit up, as now, all the muscles in his back rigid.

She knew him well enough not to ask what was wrong, but, sleep besotted, the light from her eyes dimming to a satisfied glow, said, simply, "I love you."

"I love you, too," he said. "Your eyes are full of fireflies."

She laughed, but he meant it: entire cities, entire worlds, pulsed inside those eyes, hinting at an existence beyond the mundane.

Something in her gaze reminded him suddenly of the woman with the missing hands and he looked away, toward the window that, though closed, let in the persistent sound of rain. Beside the window, his grandmother's possessions still lay in shadows on the mantel.

The next day, as he sat in Samuel Hoegbotton's room writing out invoices for the past week's exports—Saphant carnival masks, rare eelwood furniture from Nicea, necklaces made by yet another indigenous tribe discovered at the heart of the great southern rainforests, all destined for Morrow—he noticed something odd. He drew his breath in sharply. He pushed his chair back and stood up.

There, growing at a right angle from the green cloth that covered the cage, was a fragile, milk-white fruiting body on a long stem, the gills tinged red. It was identical to the mushrooms that had appeared in Daffed's mansion. He cast about for a weapon, his gaze fixed on the cage. There was nothing but the bottle of port. Beyond the cage, the fungus that had infiltrated the cracks of the mirror appeared to have darkened and thickened. Irrationally, he decided he had to remove the cage from the room. The room had caused the fruiting body. Picking up a napkin, he wound it around the handle of the cage and carried it out of the room, to his desk.

He stared across the store, trying to locate Bristlewing. His assistant stood in a far corner helping an elderly gentleman decide on a chair. Hoegbotton could just see the back of Bristlewing's head, nodding at something the potential customer had said, both of them obscured by a column of school desks.

Slowly, as if the mushroom was watching him, Hoegbotton slid his hand over to the top drawer of his desk, pulled it open and took out a silver letter opener. Holding it in front of him, he approached the cage. Images of the woman and her son flickered in his mind. He couldn't keep his hand still. He hesitated, wavered. A vision of the mushroom multiplying into two, three, four came to him. Hoegbotton leaned over his desk, chopped the mushroom off the side of the cage. It fell onto his desk, leaving behind only a small, circular white spot on the green cover, as innocent as a bird dropping.

Hoegbotton pulled his handkerchief out of his breast pocket and squashed the mushroom in its folds, careful not to touch any part of it. Then he stuffed the handkerchief into the wastebasket at his side. A moment's hesitation. He fished it out. Decided against it and placed the handkerchief back into the wastebasket. Fished it out again.

Hoegbotton realized that both Bristlewing and his customer were now standing a few feet away, staring at him. He froze, then smiled.

"My dear Bristlewing," he said. "What can I help you with?"

Bristlewing gave him a disgusted look. "Mr. Sporlender here was interested in a writing desk, for his son. We've a good, solid chair but nothing appropriate in a desk. Anything in storage?"

Hoegbotton smiled, extremely aware of the dead mushroom in his hand. The irritation caused by the handle of the cage flared up, pulsing across his palm. "Yes, actually, Mr. Sporlender, if you would come back tomorrow, I believe we might have something to show you . . ." Or not. Just so long as he left the shop—now.

Hoegbotton nudged Bristlewing out of the way and guided the man toward the door, through the crowded stacks of artifacts—babbling about the rain, about the importance of a writing desk, about anything at all, while Bristlewing's disgusted stare burned into the back of his skull. Hoegbotton had never been more impatient to reach the rain-scoured street. When it came, it was like a wave—of light, of fresh air. It hit him with such force that he gasped, drawing a sharp look from Mr. Sporlender.

As they stood there, on the cusp of the street, the iron door at Hoegbotton's back, the man stared at him through narrowed eyes. "Really, Mr. Hoegbotton— should I come back tomorrow? Would you truly advise that?"

Hoegbotton stared down at his hand, which was about to rebel and throw the handkerchief and mushroom as far away as possible. Some of the early afternoon passersby already stared curiously at the two of them.

"I suppose you shouldn't, actually. We don't have a desk in storage or anywhere else . . . I have a condition of sudden claustrophobia. It comes and goes. I cannot control it."

The man sneered. "I saw what you put in the handkerchief. I know what it is. Will I tell? Why bother—you'll be dead soon enough." The man stalked off.

Hoegbotton immediately began to fast-walk in the opposite direction, past sidewalk vendors, a thin stream of pedestrians, and an even thinner stream of carts and carriages, which the rain rendered in smudges and humid smells. Only after three or four blocks, soaked to the skin, did he feel comfortable tossing the handkerchief and its contents into a public trashcan. He already had an image in his head of the Cappan's men searching his store for traces of fungi.

A man was throwing up into the gutter. A woman was yelling at her husband. The sky was a uniform gray. The rain was unending, as common as the very air. He couldn't even feel it anymore. Everywhere, in the cracks of the sidewalk, in the minute spaces between bricks in shop fronts, new fungi were growing. He wondered if anything he did mattered.

Back at the store, Bristlewing was grumpily moving some boxes around. He spared Hoegbotton only a quick glance—watchful, wary. Hoegbotton brushed by him and headed for the bathroom, where he scrubbed his hands red before coming out again to examine the cage. It looked just as he had left it. The green cover was unblemished but for the white spot. There had been no proliferation of mushrooms in his absence. This was good. This meant he had done the right thing. (Why, then, was it so hard to draw breath? Why so difficult to stop shaking?)

He sat down behind the desk, staring at the cage. The inside of his mouth felt dry and thick. Nothing happened without a reason. The mushroom had not appeared by coincidence. This he could not believe. How could he?

Almost against his will, he reached over to the cage and pulled the cover aside, the green giving way to the finely etched metal bars, the shadows of the bars letting the light slide around them so that he saw the perch, gently swinging, and, below it, a pale white hand. Slender and delicate. The end a mass of dried blood. A vision overtook him: that he was Samuel Hoegbotton, staring across the dining room table at the cage, which was the last thing he ever saw . . . The hand, he had no doubt, was from Daffed's wife. What would it take to make it go away?

But then his mind registered a much more important detail, one that made him bite down hard on his lower lip to stop from screaming. The cage door was open, slid to the side as neatly as the cover. He sat there, motionless, staring, for several seconds. Throughout the store, he could hear the hands of myriad clocks clicking forward. No mask could help him now. The hand. The open cage. The fey brightness of the bars. A *rippling* at the edges of his vision.

Somewhere, Hoegbotton found the nerve. He reached out and slid the door back into position with both hands, worked the latch shut—just as he felt a sudden weight on the other side, rushing up to meet him. It brushed against his fingers and chilled them. He drew back with a gasp. The door rattled once, twice, fell still. The perch began to swing violently back and forth as if something had pushed up against it. Then it too fell still. Suddenly.

He could not breathe. He could not call out for help. His heart was beating so fast, he thought it might burst. This was not how he had imagined it. This was not how he had imagined it.

Something invisible picked up the hand and forced it through the bars. The hand fell onto his blotter, rocked once, twice, and was still.

It took five or six tries, his fingers nimble as blocks of wood, but he managed to find the cord to the cover and slide it back into position.

Then he sat there for a long time, staring at the green cover of the cage. Nothing happened. Nothing bad. The sense of weight on the other side of the bars had vanished with the drawing of the veil. The hand that lay on his blotter did not seem real. It looked like alabaster. It looked like wax. It was a candle without a wick. It was a piece of a statue.

An hour could have passed, or a minute, before he found a paper bag, nudged the hand into it using the letter opener, and folded the bag shut.

Bristlewing appeared in his field of vision some time later.

"Bristlewing," Hoegbotton said. "I'm glad. You're here."

"Eh?"

"You see this cage?"

"Yes."

"I need you to take it to Ungdom."

"Ungdom?" Bristlewing's face brightened. He clearly thought this was a joke.

"Yes. To Ungdom. Tell him that I send it with my compliments. That I offer it as a token of renewed friendship." Somewhere inside, he was laughing at Ungdom's future discomfort. Somewhere inside, he was screaming for help.

Bristlewing snorted. "Is it wise?"

Hoegbotton stared up at him, as if through a haze of smoke. "No. It isn't wise. But I would like you to do it anyway."

Bristlewing waited for a moment, as if there might be something more, but there was nothing more. He walked forward, picked up the cage. As Bristlewing bent over the cage, Hoegbotton thought he saw a patch of green at the base of his assistant's neck, under his left ear. Was Bristlewing already infected? Was Bristlewing the threat?

"Another thing. Take the rest of the week off. Once you've delivered the cage to Ungdom." If his assistant was going to dissolve into spores, let him do it elsewhere. Hoegbotton suppressed a giggle of hysteria.

Suspicious, Bristlewing frowned. "And if I want to work?"

"It's a vacation. A vacation. I've never given you one. I'll pay you for the time."

"All right," Bristlewing said. Now the look he gave Hoegbotton was, to Hoegbotton's eye, very close to a look of pity. "I'll give the cage to Ungdom and take the week off."

"That's what I said."

"Right. Bye then."

"Goodbye."

As Bristlewing negotiated the tiny flotsam-lined pathway, Hoegbotton could not help but notice that his assistant seemed to list to one side, as if the cage had grown unaccountably heavy.

Five minutes after Bristlewing had left, Hoegbotton closed up the shop for the day. It only took seven tries for him to lock the door behind him.

5

When he arrived at the apartment, Hoegbotton told Rebecca he was home early because he had learned of his grandmother's death. She seemed to interpret his shakes and shudders, the trembling of his voice, the way he needed to touch her, as consistent with his grief. They ate dinner in silence, her hand in his hand.

"Tell me about it," she said after dinner and he cataloged all the symptoms of fear as if they were the symptoms of loss, of grief. Everywhere he turned, the woman from the mansion confronted him, her gaze now angry, now mournful. Her wounds bled copiously down her dress but she did nothing to stanch the flow.

They went to bed early and Rebecca held him until he found a path toward sleep. But sleep held a kaleidoscope of images to torment him. In his dreams, he walked through Samuel Hoegbotton's apartment until he reached a long, white hallway he had never seen before. At the opposite end of the hallway, he could see the woman and the boy from the mansion, surrounded by great wealth, antiques fit for a god winking at him in their burnished multitudes. He was walking across a carpet of small, severed hands to reach them. This fact revolted him, but he could not stop walking: the promise of what lay ahead was too great. Even when he began to see his head, his arms, his own legs, crudely soldered to the walls using his own blood, he could not stop his progress toward the end of the hallway. The hands were cold and soft and pleading.

Despite the dreams, Hoegbotton woke the next morning feeling energetic and calm. The cage was gone. He had another chance. He did not feel the need to follow in Samuel Hoegbotton's footsteps. Even the imprint on his hand throbbed less painfully. The rain clattering down made him happy for obscure, childhood reasons—memories of sneaking out into thunderstorms to play under the dark clouds, of taking to the water on a rare fishing trip with his father while drops sprinkled the dark, languid surface of the River Moth.

At breakfast, he even told Rebecca that perhaps he had been wrong and they should start a family. Rebecca laughed, hugged him, and told him they should wait to talk about it until after he had recovered from his grandmother's death. When she did not ask him about the funeral arrangements, he wondered if she knew he had lied to her. On his way out the door, he held her close and kissed her. Her lips tasted of honeysuckle and rose. Her eyes were, as ever, a mystery, but he did not mind.

Once at work, Bristlewing blissfully absent, Hoegbotton searched the store for any sign of mushrooms. Donning long gloves and a fresh mask, he spent most of his time in the old dining room, scuffing his knees to examine the underside of the table, cleaning every surface. The fungus embedded in the mirror had lost its appearance of renewed vigor. Nevertheless, he took an old toothbrush and knife and spent half an hour gleefully scraping it away.

Then, divesting himself of mask and gloves, he went through the same routines with his ledgers as in the past, this time reading the entries aloud since Bristlewing was not there to frown at him for doing so. Fragments of disturbing images fluttered in his mind like caged birds, but he ignored them, bending himself to his routine that he might allow himself no other thoughts.

By noon, the rain had turned to light hail, discouraging many erstwhile customers. Those who did enter the store alighted like crows escaping bad weather, shaking their raincoat wings and unlikely to buy anything.

By one o'clock, he had only made one hundred sels. It didn't matter. It was almost liberating. He was beginning to think he had escaped great danger, even caught himself wondering if another rich family might experience a gray cap visitation.

At two o'clock, his spirits still high, Hoegbotton received a shock when a grim-faced member of the Cappan's security forces entered the store. The man was in full protective gear, clothed from head to foot, a gray mask covering his entire face except for his eyes. What could they know? It wasn't time for an inspection. Had the man looking for a desk talked to them? Hoegbotton scratched at his wounded palm.

"How can I help you?" he asked.

The man stared at him for a moment, then said, "I'm looking for a purse for my mother's birthday."

Hoegbotton burst out laughing and had to convince the man it was not directed at him before selling him a purse.

No customers entered the store for half an hour after the Cappan's man left. Hoegbotton had worked himself into a fever pitch of calm by the time the messenger arrived around three o'clock: a boy on a bicycle, pinched and drawn, wearing dirty clothes, who knocked at the door and waited for Hoegbotton to arrive before letting an envelope flutter to the welcome mat outside the door. The boy pulled his bicycle back to the sidewalk and pedaled away, ringing his bell.

Hoegbotton, softly singing to himself, leaned down to pick up the envelope. He opened it. The letter inside read, in a spidery scrawl:

> Thank you, Robert, for your very fine
> gift, but your bird has flown away home.
> I couldn't keep such a treasure. My
> regards to your wife.—John Ungdom.

Hoegbotton stared at the note, chuckling at the sarcasm. Read it again, a frown closing his lips. Flown away home. Read it a third time, his stomach filling with stones. My regards to your wife.

He dropped the note, flung on his raincoat, and, not bothering to lock the store behind him, ran out onto the street—into the blinding rain. He headed up Albumuth Boulevard, through the Bureaucratic Quarter, toward home. He felt as if he were running in place. Every pedestrian hindered him. Every horse and cart blocked his path. As the rain came down harder, it beat a rhythmic message into Hoegbotton's shoulders. The raindrops sounded like tapping fingers. Through the haze, the dull shapes of buildings became landmarks to anchor his staggering progress. Passersby stared at him as if he were crazy.

By the time he reached the apartment building lobby, his sides ached and he was drenched in sweat. He had fallen repeatedly on the slick pavement and bloodied his hands. He took the stairs three at a time, ran down the hallway to the apartment shouting "Rebecca!"

The apartment door was ajar. He tried to catch his breath, bending over as he slowly pushed the door open. A line of white mushrooms ran through the hallway, low to the ground, their gills stained red. Where his hand held the door, fungus touched his fingers. He recoiled, straightened up.

"Rebecca?" he said, staring into the kitchen. No one. The inside of the kitchen window was covered in purple fungi. A cane lay next to the coat rack, a gift from his father. He took it and walked into the apartment, picking his way between the white mushrooms as he pulled the edge of his raincoat up over his mouth. The doorway to the living room was directly to his left. He could hear nothing, as if his head were stuffed with cloth. Slowly, he peered around the doorway.

The living room was aglow with fungi, white and purple, green and yellow. Shelves of fungi jutted from the walls. Bottle-shaped mushrooms, a deep burgundy, wavering like balloons, were anchored to the floor. Hoegbotton's palm burned fiercely. Now he was in the dream, not before.

Looking like the exoskeleton shed by some tropical beetle, the cage stood on the coffee table, the cover drawn aside, the door open. Beside the cage lay another alabaster hand. This did not surprise him. It did not even register. For, beyond the table, the doors to the balcony had been thrown wide open. Rebecca stood on the balcony, in the rain, her hair slick and bright, her eyes dim. Strewn around her, as if in tribute, the strange growths that had long ago claimed the balcony: orange strands whipping in the winds, transparent bulbs that stood rigid, mosaic patterns of gold-green mold imprinted on the balcony's corroded railing. Beyond: the dark gray shadows of the city, dotted with smudges of light.

Rebecca was looking down at . . . nothing . . . her hands held out before her as if in supplication.

"Rebecca!" he shouted. Or thought he shouted. His mouth was tight and dry. He began to walk across the living room, the mushrooms pulling against his shoes, his pants, the air alive with spores. He blinked, sneezed, stopped just short of the balcony. Rebecca had still not looked up. Rain splattered against his boots.

"Rebecca," he said, afraid that she would not hear him, that the distance between them was somehow too great. "Come away from there. It isn't safe." She was shivering. He could see her shivering.

Rebecca turned to look at him and smiled. "Isn't safe? You did this yourself, didn't you? Opened the balcony for me before you left this morning?" She frowned. "But then I was puzzled. You had the cage sent back even though Mrs. Willis said we couldn't keep pets."

"I didn't open the balcony. I didn't send back the cage." His boots were tinged green. His shoulders ached.

"Well, someone brought it here—and I opened it. I was bored. The flower vendor was supposed to come and take me to the market, but he didn't."

"Rebecca—it isn't safe. Come away from the balcony." His words were dull, unconvincing. A lethargy had begun to envelop his body.

"I wish I knew what it was," she said. "Can you see it? It's right here—in front of me."

He started to say no, he couldn't see it, but then he realized he could see it. He was gasping from the sight of it. He was choking from the sight of it. Blood trickled down his chin where he had bitten into his lip. All the courage he had built up for Rebecca's sake melted away.

"Come here, Rebecca," he managed to say.

"Yes. Okay," she said in a small, broken voice.

Tripping over fungi, she walked into the apartment. He met her at the coffee table, drew her against him, whispered into her ear, "You need to get out of here, Rebecca. I need you to go downstairs. Find Mrs. Willis. Have her send for the Cappan's men." Her hair was wet against his face. He stroked it gently.

"I'm scared," she whispered back, arms thrown around him. "Come with me."

"I will, Rebecca. Rebecca, I will. In just a minute. But now, I need you to leave." He was trembling from mixed horror at the thought that he might never say her name again and relief, because now he knew why he loved her.

Then her weight was gone as she moved past him to the door and, perversely, his burden returned to him.

The thing had not moved from the balcony. It was not truly invisible but camouflaged itself by perfectly matching its background. The bars of a cage. The spaces between the bars. A perch. He could only glimpse it now because it could not mimic the rain that fell upon it fast enough.

Hoegbotton walked out onto the balcony. The rain felt good on his face. His legs were numb so he lowered himself into an old rotting chair they had never bothered to take off the balcony. While the thing watched, he sat there, staring between the bars of the balcony railing, out into the city. The rain trickled through his hair. He tried not to look at his hands, which were tinged green. He tried to laugh, but it came out as a rasping gurgle. The thought came to him that he must still be back in the mansion with the woman and the boy—that he had never really left—because, honestly, how could you escape such horror? How could anyone escape something like that?

The thing padded up to him on its quiet feet and sang to him. Because it no longer mattered, Hoegbotton turned to look at it. He choked back a sob. He had not expected this. It was beautiful. Its single eye, so like Rebecca's eyes, shone with an unearthly light, phosphorescent flashes darting across it. Its mirror skin shimmered with the rain. Its mouth, full of knives, smiled in a way that did not mean the same thing as a human smile. This was as close as he could get, he knew now, staring into that single, beautiful eye. This was as close. Maybe there was something else, something beyond. Maybe there was a knowledge still more secret than this knowledge, but he would never experience that.

The thing held out its clawed hand and, after a time, Hoegbotton took it in his own.

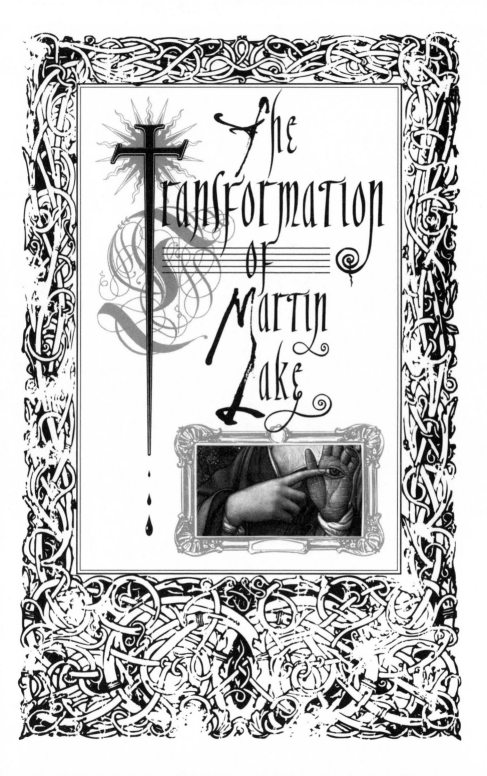

The Transformation of Martin Lake

A fresh river in a beautiful meadow
Imagined in his mind
The good Painter, who would someday paint it

> —Comanimi

If I was strange, and strange was my art,
Such strangeness is a source of grace and strength;
And whoever adds strangeness here and there to his style,
Gives life, force, and spirit to his paintings . . .
  —Engraved at Lake's request on his memorial in Trillian Square

ew painters have risen with such speed from such obscurity as Martin Lake, and fewer still are so closely identified with a single painting, a single city. What remains obscure, even to those of us who knew him, is how and why Lake managed the extraordinary transformation from pleasing but facile collages and acrylics, to the luminous oils—both fantastical and dark, moody and playful—that would come to define both the artist and Ambergris.

Information about Lake's childhood has a husk-like quality to it, as if someone had already scooped out the meat within the shell. At the age of six he contracted a rare bone disease in his left leg that, exacerbated by a hit-and-run accident with a Manzikert motored vehicle at age twelve, made it necessary for him to use a cane. We have no other information about his childhood except for a quick glimpse of his parents: Theodore and Catherine Lake. His father worked as an insect catcher outside of the town of Stockton, where the family lived in a simple rented apartment. There is some evidence, from comments Lake made to me prior to his fame, and from hints in subsequent interviews, that a tension existed between Lake and his father, created by Lake's desire to pursue art and his father's desire that the boy take up the profession of insect catcher.

Of Lake's mother there is no record, and Lake never spoke of her in any of his few interviews. The mock historian Samuel Gorge has put forth the theory that Lake's mother was a folk artist of considerable talent and also a fierce proponent of Truffidianism—that she instilled in Lake an appreciation for mysticism. Gorge believes the magnificent murals that line the walls of the Truffidian cathedral in Stockton are the anonymous work of Lake's mother. No one has yet confirmed Gorge's theory, but if true it might account for the streak of the occult, the macabre, that runs through Lake's art—stripped, of course, of the underlying religious aspect.

Lake's mother almost certainly gave him his first art lesson, and urged him to pursue lessons at the local school, under the tutelage of a Mr. Shores, who unfortunately passed away without ever being asked to recall the work of his most famous (indeed, *only* famous) student. Lake also took several anatomy classes when young; even in his most surreal paintings the figures often seem hyperreal—as if there are layers of paint unseen, beneath which exist veins, arteries, muscles, nerves, tendons. This hyperreality creates tension by playing against Lake's assertion that the "great artist swallows up the world that surrounds him until his whole environment has been absorbed in his own self."

We may think of the Lake who arrived in Ambergris from Stockton as a contradictory creature: steeped in the technical world of anatomy and yet well versed in the miraculous and ur-rational by his mother—a contradiction further enriched by his guilt over not following his father into the family trade. These are the elements Lake brought to Ambergris. In return, Ambergris gave Lake the freedom to be an artist while also opening his eyes to the possibilities of color.

Of the three years Lake lived in Ambergris prior to the startling change in his work, we know only that he befriended a number of artists whom he would champion, with mixed results, once he became famous. Chief among these artists was Jonathan Merrimount, a lifelong friend. He also met Raffe Constance, who many believe was his lifelong romantic companion. Together, Lake, Merrimount, and Constance would prove to be the most visible and influential artists of their generation. Unfortunately, neither Merrimount nor Constance has been willing to shed any illumination on the subject of Lake's life—his inspiration, his disappointments, his triumphs. Or, more importantly, how such a middle-class individual could have created such sorrowful, nightmarish art.

Thus, I must attempt to fill in details from my own experience of Lake. It is with some hesitancy that I reveal Lake first showed his work at my own Gallery of Hidden Fascinations, prior to his transformation into an artist of the first rank. Although I cannot personally bear witness to that transformation, I can at least give the reader a pre-fame portrait of a very private artist who was rarely seen in public.

Lake was a tall man who appeared to be of average height because, in using his cane, he had become stooped—an aspect that always gave him the impression of listening intently to you, although in reality he was a terrible listener and never hesitated to rudely interrupt when bored by what I said to him.

His face had a severe quality to it, offset by a firm chin, a perfect set of lips, and eyes that seemed to change color but which were, at base, a fierce, arresting green. In either anger or humor, his face was a weapon—for the narrowness became even more narrow in his anger and the eyes lanced you, while in laughter his face widened and the eyes admitted you to their compelling company. Mostly, though, he remained in a mode between laughter and anger, a mood which aped that of the "tortured artist" while at the same time keeping a distance between himself and any such passion. He was shy and clever, sly and arrogant—in other words, no different from many of the other artists I handled at my gallery.—From Janice Shriek's *A Short Overview of the Art of Martin Lake and His Invitation to a Beheading*, for *The Hoegbotton Guide to Ambergris*, 5th edition.

One blustery spring day in the legendary metropolis of Ambergris, the artist Martin Lake received an invitation to a beheading.

It was not an auspicious day to receive such an invitation and Lake was nursing several grudges as he made his way to the post office. First and foremost, the Reds and Greens were at war; already, a number of nasty skirmishes had spread disease-like up and down the streets, even infecting portions of Albumuth Boulevard itself.

The Reds and Greens as a phenomenon simultaneously fascinated and repulsed Lake. In short, the Greens saw the recent death of the (great) composer Voss Bender as a tragedy while the Reds thought the recent death of the (despotic) composer Voss Bender a blessing. They had taken their names from Bender's favorite and least favorite colors: the green of a youth spent in the forests of Morrow; the red flags of the indigenous mushroom dwellers who he believed had abducted his cousin.

No doubt these two political factions would vanish as quickly as they had appeared, but in the meantime Lake kept a Green flag in his right pocket and a Red flag in his left pocket, the better to express the correct patriotic fervor. (On a purely aural level, Lake sympathized with the Reds, if only because the Greens polluted the air with a thousand Bender tunes morning, noon, and night. Lake had hardly listened to Bender while the man was alive; he resented having to change his habits now the man was dead.)

Confronted by such dogma, Lake suspected his commitment to his weekly walk to the post office indicated a fatal character flaw, a fatal artistic curiosity. For he knew he would pull the wrong flag from the right pocket before the day was done. And yet, he thought, as he limped down Truff Avenue—even the blood-clot clusters of dog lilies, in their neat sidewalk rows, reminding him of the conflict—how else was he to exercise his left leg? Besides, no vehicle for hire would deliver him through the disputed areas to his objective.

Lake scowled as a youth bejeweled in red buttons and waving a huge red flag ran into the street. In the wake of the flag, Lake could see the distant edges of the post office, suffused with the extraordinary morning light, which came down in sheets of gold.

The secondary tier of Reasons Why I Should Have Stayed at Home concerned, much to Lake's irritation, the post office itself. He had no sympathy for its archaic architecture and only moderate respect for its function; the quality of a monopolistic private postal service being poor, most of his commissions arrived via courier. He also found distasteful the morbid nature of the building's history, its stacks of "corpse cases" as he called the postal boxes. These boxes, piled atop each other down the length and breadth of the great hall, climbed all the way to the ceiling. Surely any of the children previously shelved there had, on their ascent to heaven, found themselves trapped by that ugly yellow ceiling and to this day were banging their tiny ectoplasmic heads against it.

But, as the post office rounded into view—looming and guttering like some monstrous, senile great aunt—none of these objections registered as strongly as the recent change of name to the "Voss Bender Memorial Post Office." A shockingly *rushed* development, as the (great, despotic) composer and politician had died only three days before—rumors as to cause ranging from heart attack to poison— his body sequestered secretly, yet to be cremated and the ashes cast into the River Moth per Bender's request. (Not to mention that a splinter faction of the Greens, in a flurry of pamphlets and broadsheets, had advertised the resurrection of their beloved Bender: he would reappear in the form of the first child born after midnight in one year's time. Would the child be born with arias bursting forth from his mouth like nightingales, Lake wondered.)

The renaming alone made Lake's teeth grind together. It seemed, to his absurdly envious eye—he *knew* how absurd he was, but could not control his feelings—that every third building of any importance had had the composer's name rudely slapped over old assignations, with no sense of decorum or perspective. Was it not enough that while alive Bender had been a virtual tyrant of the arts, squashing all opera, all theater, that did not fit his outdated melodramatic sensibilities? Was it not enough that he had come to be the de facto ruler of a city that simultaneously abhorred and embraced the cult of personality? Did he now have to usurp the *entire* city—every last stone of it—forever and always as his mausoleum? Apparently so. Apparently everyone soon would be permanently lost, for every avenue, alley, boulevard, dead end, and cul-de-sac would be renamed "Bender." "Bender" would be the name given to all newborns; or, for variety's sake, "Voss." And a whole generation of Benders or Vosses would trip and tangle their way through a city which from every street corner threw back their name at them like an impersonal insult.

Why—Lake warmed to his own vitriol—if another Manzikert flattened him as he crossed this very street, he would be lucky to have his own name adorn his own gravestone! No doubt, he mused sourly—but with satisfaction—as he tested the post office's front steps with his cane, his final resting place would display the legend "Voss Bender Memorial Gravestone" with the words "(occupied by Martin Lake)" etched in tiny letters below.

Inside the post office, at the threshold of the great hall, Lake walked through the gloomy light cast by the far windows and presented himself to the attendant, a man with a face like a knife; Lake had never bothered to learn his name.

Lake held out his key. "Number 7768, please."

The attendant, legs propped against his desk, looked up from the broadsheet he was reading, scowled, and said, "I'm busy."

Lake, startled, paused for a moment. Then, showing his cane, he tossed his key onto the desk.

The attendant looked at it as if it were a dead cockroach. "That, sir, is your key, sir. Yes it is. Go to it, sir. And all good luck to you." He ruffled the broadsheet as he held it up to block out Lake.

Lake stared at the fingers holding the broadsheet and wondered if there would be a place for the man's sour features in his latest commission—if he could immortalize the unhelpfulness that was as blunt as the man's knuckles. After the long, grueling walk through hostile territory, this was really too much.

Lake peered over the broadsheet, using his cane to pull it down a little. "You *are* the attendant, aren't you? I haven't been giving you my key all these months only to now discover that you are merely a conscientious volunteer?"

The man blinked and put down his broadsheet to reveal a crooked smile.

"I *am* the attendant. That *is* your key. You *are* crippled. Sir."

"Then what is the problem?"

The man looked Lake up and down. "Your attire, sir. You are dressed somewhat . . . ambiguously."

Lake wasn't sure if the answer or the comfortable use of the word "ambiguously" surprised him more. Nonetheless, he examined his clothes. He had thrown on a blue vest over a white shirt, blue trousers with black shoes and socks.

The attendant wore clothes the color of overripe tomatoes.

Lake burst out laughing. The attendant smirked.

"True, true," Lake managed. "I've not *declared* myself, have I? I must have a coming out party. What am I? Vegetable or mineral?"

In clipped tones, his eyes cold and empty, the attendant asked, "Red or Green: which is it, sir."

Lake stopped laughing. The buffoon was serious. This same pleasant if distant man he had seen every week for over two years had succumbed to the dark allure of Voss Bender's death. Lake stared at the attendant and saw a stranger.

Slowly, carefully, Lake said, "I am green on the outside, being as yet youthful in my chosen profession, and red on the inside, being, as is everyone, a mere mortal." He produced both flags. "I have your flag—and the flag of the other side." He dangled them in front of the attendant. "Did I dislike Voss Bender and abhor his stranglehold on the city? Yes. Did I wish him dead? No. Is this not enough? Why must I declare myself when all I wish is to toss these silly flags in the River Moth and stand aside while you and your cohorts barrel through bent on butchery? I am neutral, sir." (Lake thought this a particularly fine speech.)

"Because, sir," the attendant said, as he rose with a great show of exertion and snatched up Lake's key, "Voss Bender is not dead."

He gave Lake a stare that made the little hairs on the back of his neck rise, then walked over to the boxes while Lake smoldered like a badly lit candle. Was the whole city going to play such games? Next time he went to the grocery store would the old lady behind the counter demand he sing a Bender aria before she would sell him a loaf of bread?

The attendant climbed one of the many ladders that leaned against the stacks like odd wooden insects. Lake hoped his journey had not been in vain—let there at least be a missive from his mother which might stave off the specter of homesickness. His father was, no doubt, still encased in the tight-lipped silence that covered him like a cicada's exoskeleton.

The attendant pulled Lake's box out, retrieved something from it, and climbed back down with an envelope.

"Here," the attendant said, glaring, and handed it to Lake, who took both it and his key with unintended gentleness, his anger losing out to bewilderment.

Bare of place and time, the maroon envelope displayed neither a return address nor his own address. More mysterious, he could find no trace of a postmark, which could only mean someone had hand-delivered it. On the back, Lake discovered a curious seal imprinted in an orange-gold wax that smelled of honey. The seal formed an owllike mask which, when Lake turned it upside down, became transformed into a human face. The intricate pattern reminded Lake of Trillian the Great Banker's many signature casts for coins.

"Do you know how this letter got here?" Lake started to say, turning toward the desk, but the attendant had vanished, leaving only the silence and shadows of the great hall, the close air filtering the dust of one hundred years through its coppery sheen, the open door a rectangle of golden light.

From the broadsheet on the desk the name "Voss Bender," in vermilion ink, winked up at him like some infernal, recurring joke.

※❀※

With only this feeble skeleton of a biography as our background material, we must now approach the work that has *become* Martin Lake: "Invitation to a Beheading." The piece marks the beginning of the grotesqueries, the controlled savagery of his oils—the slashes of emerald slitting open the sky, the deft, tinted green of the windows looking in, the moss green of the exterior walls: all are vintage Lake.

The subject is, of course, the Voss Bender Memorial Post Office, truly among the most imposing of Ambergris's many eccentric buildings. If we can trust the words of Bronet Raden, the noted art critic, when he writes

> The marvelous is not the same in every period of history—it partakes in some ob-
> scure way of a sort of general revelation only the fragments of which come down
> to us: they are the romantic ruins, the modern mannequins, or any other symbol
> capable of affecting the human sensibility for a period of time,

then the first of Lake's many accomplishments was to break the post office down into its fragments and re-create it from "romantic ruins" into the dream-edifice that, for thirty years, has horrified and delighted visitors to the post office.

The astute observer will note that the post office walls in Lake's painting are created with careful crosshatching brushstrokes layered over a dampened whiteness. This whiteness, upon close examination, is composed of hundreds of bones—skulls, femurs, ribs—all compressed and rendered with a pathetic delicacy that astounds the eye.

On a surface level, this imagery surely functions as a symbolic nod to the building's former usage. Conceived to house the Cappan and his family, the brooding structure that would become the Voss Bender Memorial Post Office was abandoned following the dissolution of the Cappandom and then converted into a repository for the corpses of mushroom dwellers and indigent children. After a time, it fell into disuse—as Lake effectively shows with his surfaces beneath surfaces: the white columns slowly turning gray-green, the snarling gargoyles blackened from disrepair, the building's entire skin pocked by lichen and mold.

Lake frequently visited the post office and must have been familiar with its former function. When the old post office burned down and relocated to its present location in what was little better than an abandoned morgue, it is rumored that the first patrons of the new service eagerly opened their post boxes only to find within them old and strangely delicate bones—the bones Lake has "woven" into the "fabric" of his painting.

Lake's interpretation of the building is superior in its ability to convey the post office's psychic or spiritual self. As the noted painter and instructor Leonard Venturi has written:

> Take two pictures representing the same subject; one may be dismissed as illustration if it is dominated by the subject and has no other justification but the subject, the other may be called painting if the subject is completely absorbed in the style, which is its own justification, whatever the subject, and has an intrinsic value.

Lake's representation of the post office is clearly a painting in Venturi's sense, for the subject is riddled through with wormholes of style, with layers of meaning.—From Janice Shriek's *A Short Overview of the Art of Martin Lake and His Invitation to a Beheading*, for *The Hoegbotton Guide to Ambergris*, 5th edition.

Lake lived farthest from the docks and the River Moth, at the eastern end of Albumuth Boulevard, where it merged with the warren of middle-class streets that laboriously, some thought treacherously, descended into the valley below. The neighborhood, its narrow mews crowded with cheap apartments and cafés, was filthy with writers, artists, architects, actors, and performers of every kind. Two years ago it had been resplendently fresh and on the cutting edge of the New Art. Street parties had lasted until six in the morning, and shocking conversations about the New Art, often destined for the pages of influential journals, had permeated the coffee-and-mint-flavored air surrounding every eatery. By now, however, the sycophants and hangers-on had caught wind of the little miracle and begun to masticate it into a safe, stable "community." Eventually, the smell of rot—rotting ideas, rotting relationships, rotting art—would force the real artists out, to settle new frontiers. Lake hoped he would be going with them.

Lake's apartment, on the third floor of an old beehive-like tenement run by a legendary landlord known alternately as "Dame Tuff" or "Dame Truff," depending on one's religious beliefs, was a small studio cluttered with the salmon, saffron, and sapphire bluster of his art: easels made from stripped birch branches, the blank canvases upon them flap-flapping for attention; paint-splattered stools; a chair smothered in a tangle of shirts that stank of turpentine; and in the middle of all this, like a besieged island, his cot, covered with watercolor sketches curled at the edges and brushes stiff from lazy washings. The sense of a furious mess pleased him; it always looked like he had just finished attacking some new work of art. Sometimes he added to the confusion just before the arrival of visitors, not so self-deluded that he couldn't laugh at himself as he did it.

Once back in his apartment, Lake locked the door, discarded his cane, threw the shirts from his chair, and sat down to contemplate the letter. Faces cut from various magazines stared at him from across the room, waiting to be turned into collages for an as-yet-untitled autobiography in the third person written (and self-published) by a Mr. Dradin Kashmir. The collages represented a month's rent and he was late completing them. He avoided the faces as if they all wore his father's scowl.

Did the envelope contain a commission? He took it out of his pocket, weighed it in his hand. Not heavy. A single sheet of paper? The indifferent light of his apartment made the maroon envelope almost black. The seal still scintillated so beautifully in his artist's imagination that he hesitated to break it. Reluctantly—his fingers must be coerced into such an action—he broke the seal, opened the flap, and pulled out a sheet of parchment paper shot through with crimson threads. Words had been printed on the paper in a gold-orange ink, followed by the same mask symbol found on the seal. He skimmed the words several times, as if by rapid review he might discover some hidden message, some hint of closure. But the words only deepened the mystery:

Invitation to a Beheading
You Are Invited to Attend:
45 Archmont Lane

7:30 in the evening
25th Day of This Month
Please arrive in costume

Lake stared at the message. A masquerade, but to what purpose? He suppressed an impulse to laugh and instead walked over to the balcony and opened the windows, letting in fresh air. The sudden chaos of voices from below, the rough sounds of street traffic—on foot, on horses, or in motored vehicles—gave Lake a comforting sense of community, as if he were debating the mystery of the message with the world.

From his balcony window he could see, on the right, a green-tinged slice of the valley, while straight ahead the spires and domes of the Religious Quarter burned white, gold, and silver. To the left, the solid red brick and orange marble of more apartment buildings.

Lake liked the view. It reminded him that he had survived three years in a city notorious for devouring innocents whole. Not famous, true, but not dead or defeated either. Indeed, he took a perverse pleasure from enduring and withstanding the city's countless petty cruelties, for he believed it made him stronger. One day he might rule the city, for certainly it had not ruled him.

And now this—this letter that seemed to have come from the city itself. Surely it was the work of one of his artist friends—Kinsky, Raffe, or that ruinous old scoundrel, Sonter? A practical joke, perhaps even Merrimount's doing? "Invitation to a Beheading." What could it mean? He vaguely remembered a book, a fiction, with that title, written by Sirin, wasn't it? Sirin, whose pseudonyms spread through the pages of literary journals like some mad yet strangely wonderful disease.

But perhaps it meant nothing at all and "they" intended that he waste so much time studying it that he would be late finishing his commissions.

Lake walked back to his chair and sat down. Gold ink was expensive, and the envelope, on closer inspection, was flecked with gold as well, while the paper for the invitation itself had gold threads. The paper even smelled of orange peel cologne. Lake frowned, his gaze lingering on the shimmery architecture of the Religious Quarter. The cost of such an invitation came to a sum equal to a week's commissions. Would his friends spend so much on a joke?

His frown deepened. Perhaps, merriest joke of all, the letter had been misdelivered, the sender having used the wrong address. Only, it *had no* address on it. Which made him suspect his friends again. And might the attendant, if he went back to the post office, recall who had slipped the letter through the front slot of his box? He sighed. It was hopeless; such speculations only fed the—

A pebble sailed through the open window and fell onto his lap. He started, then smiled and rose, the pebble falling to the floor. At the window, he looked down. Raffe stared up at him from the street: daring Raffe in her sarcastic red-and-green jacket.

"Good shot," he called down. He studied her face for any hint of complicity in a plot, found no mischief there, realized it meant nothing.

"We're headed for the Calf for the evening," Raffe shouted up at him. "Are you coming?"

Lake nodded. "Go on ahead. I'll be there soon."

Raffe smiled, waved, and continued on down the street.

Lake retreated into his room, put the letter back in its envelope, stuffed it all into an inner pocket, and retired to the bathroom down the hall, the better to freshen up for the night's festivities. As he washed his face and looked into the moss-tinged mirror, he considered whether he should remain mum or share the invitation. He had still not decided when he walked out onto the street and into the harsh light of late afternoon.

By the time he reached the Café of the Ruby-Throated Calf, Lake found that his fellow artists had, aided by large quantities of alcohol, adopted a cavalier attitude toward the War of the Reds and the Greens. As a gang of Reds ran by, dressed in their patchwork crimson robes, his friends rose together, produced their red flags and cheered as boisterously as if at some sporting event. Lake had just taken a seat, generally ignored in the hubbub, when a gang of Greens trotted by in pursuit, and once again his friends rose, green flags in hand this time, and let out a roar of approval.

Lake smiled, Raffe giving him a quick elbow to the ribs before she turned back to her conversation, and he let the smell of coffee and chocolate work its magic. His leg ached, as it did sometimes when he was under stress, but otherwise, he had no complaints. The weather had remained pleasant, neither too warm nor too cold, and a breeze ruffled the branches of the potted zindel trees with their jade leaves. The trees formed miniature forests around groups of tables, effectively blocking out rival conversations without blocking the street from view. Artists lounged in their iron latticework chairs or slouched over the black-framed round glass tables while imbibing a succession of exotic drinks and coffees. The night lanterns had just been turned on and the glow lent a cozy warmth to their own group, cocooned as they were by the foliage and the soothing murmur of conversations.

The four sitting with Lake he counted as his closest friends: Raffe, Sonter, Kinsky, and Merrimount. The rest had become as interchangeable as the bricks of Hoegbotton & Sons' many trading outposts, and about as interesting. At the moment, X, Y, and Z claimed the outer tables like petty island tyrants, their faces peering pale and glinty-eyed in at Lake's group, one ear to the inner conversation while at the same time trying to maintain an uneasy autonomy.

Merrimount, a handsome man with long, dark lashes and wide blue eyes, combined elements of painting and performance art in his work, his life itself a kind of performance art. Merrimount was Lake's on-again, off-again lover, and Lake shot him a raffish grin to let him know that, surely, they would be on-again soon? Merrimount ignored him. Last time they had seen each other, Lake had made Merri cry. "You want too much," Merri had said. "No one can give you that much love, not and still be human. Or sane." Raffe had told Lake to stay away from Merri but, painful as it was to admit, Lake knew Raffe meant *he* was bad for Merri.

Raffe, who sat next to Merrimount—a buffer between him and Lake—was a tall woman with long black hair and dark, expressive eyebrows that lent a needed intensity to her light green eyes. Raffe and Lake had become friends the day he arrived in Ambergris. She had found him on Albumuth Boulevard, watching the crowds, an overwhelmed, almost defeated, look on his face. Raffe had let him stay with her for the three months it had taken him to find his city legs. She painted huge, swirling, passionate cityscapes in which the people all seemed caught in mid-step of some intricate and unbearably graceful dance. They sold well, and not just to tourists.

Lake said to Raffe, "Do you think it wise to be so . . . careless?"

"Why, whatever do you mean, Martin?" Raffe had a deep, distinctly feminine voice that he never tired of hearing.

The strong, gravelly tones of Michael Kinsky, sitting on the other side of Merrimount, rumbled through Lake's answer: "He means, aren't we afraid of the donkey asses known as the Reds and the monkey butts known as the Greens."

Kinsky had a wiry frame and a sparse red beard. He made mosaics from discarded bits of stone, jewelry, and other gimcracks discovered on the city's streets. Kinsky had been well liked by Voss Bender and Lake imagined the composer's death had dealt Kinsky's career a serious blow—although, as always, Kinsky's laconic demeanor appeared unruffled by catastrophe.

"We're not afraid of anything," Raffe said, raising her chin and putting her hands on her sides in mock bravado.

Edward Sonter, to Kinsky's right and Lake's immediate left, giggled. He had a horrible tendency to produce a high-pitched squeal of amusement, in total contrast to the sensuality of his art. Sonter made abstract pottery and sculptures, vaguely obscene in nature. His gangly frame and his face, in which the eyes floated unsteadily, could often be seen in the Religious Quarter, where his work enjoyed unusually brisk sales.

As if Sonter's giggle had been a signal, they began to talk careers, gauge the day's fortunes and misfortunes. They had tame material this time: a gallery owner—no one Lake knew—had been discovered selling wall space in return for sexual favors. Lake ordered a cup of coffee, with a chocolate chaser, and listened without enthusiasm.

Lake sensed familiar undercurrents of tension, as each artist sought to ferret out information about his or her fellows—weasels, bright-eyed and eager for the kill, that their own weasel selves might burn all the brighter. These tensions had eaten more than one conversation, leaving the table silent with barely suppressed hatred born of envy. Such a cruel and cutting silence had even eaten an artist or two. Personally, Lake enjoyed the tension because it rarely centered around him; he was by far the most obscure member of the inner circle, kept there by the strength of Raffe's patronage. Now, though, he felt a different tension, centered around the letter. It lay in a pocket against his chest like a second heart in his awareness of it.

As the shadows deepened into early dusk and the buttery light of the lanterns on their delightfully curled bronze posts held back the night, the conversation, lubricated by wine, became to Lake's ears tantalizingly anonymous, as will happen in the company of people one is comfortable with, so that Lake could never remember exactly who had said what, or who had argued for what position. Lake later wondered if anything had been said, or if they had sat there, beautifully mute, while inside his head a conversation took place between Martin and Lake.

He spent the time contemplating the pleasures of reconciliation with Merri—drank in the twinned marvels of the man's perfect mouth, the compact, sinuous body. But Lake could not forget the letter. This, and his growing ennui, led him to direct the conversation toward a more timely subject:

"I've heard it said that the Greens are disemboweling innocent folk near the docks, just off of Albumuth. If they bleed red, they are denounced as sympathizers against Voss Bender; if they bleed green, then their attackers apologize for the inconvenience and try to patch them up. Of course, if they bleed green, they're likely headed for the columbarium anyhow."

"Are you trying to disgust us?"

"It wouldn't surprise me if it *were* true—it seems in keeping with the man himself: self-proclaimed Dictator of Art, with heavy emphasis on 'Dic.' We all know he was a genius, but it's a good thing he's dead . . . unless one of you is a Green with a dagger . . ."

"Very funny."

"Certainly it is rare for a single artist to so thoroughly dominate the city's cultural life—"

"—Not to mention politics—"

("Who started the Reds and the Greens anyhow?")

"And to be discussed so thoroughly, in so many cafés—"

("It started as an argument about the worth of Bender's music, between two professors of musicology on Trotten Street. Leave it to musicians to start a war over music; now that you're caught up, listen for God's sake!")

"—Not to mention politics, you say. And isn't it a warning to us all that Art and Politics are like oil and water? To comment—"

"—'oil and water'? Now we understand why you're a painter."

"How clever."

"—as I said, to comment on it, perhaps, if forced to, but not to participate?"

"But if not Bender, then some bureaucratic businessman like Trillian. Trillian, the Great Banker. Sounds like an advertisement, not a leader. Surely, Merrimount, we're damned either way. And why not let the city run itself?"

"Oh—and it's done such a good job of that so far—"

"Off topic. We're bloody well off topic—again!"

"Ah, but what you two *don't* see is that it is precisely his audience's passionate connection to his *art*—the fact that people believe the operas are the man—that has created the crisis!"

"Depends. I thought his *death* caused the crisis?"

At that moment, a group of Greens ran by. Lake, Merrimount, Kinsky, and

Sonter all raised their green flags with a curious mixture of derision and drunken fervor. Raffe sat up and shouted after them, "He's dead! He's dead! He's dead!" Her face was flushed, her hair furiously tangled.

The last of the Greens turned at the sound of Raffe's voice, his face ghastly pale under the lamps. Lake saw that the man's hands dripped red. He forced Raffe to sit down: "Hush now, hush!" The man's gaze swept across their table, and then he was running after his comrades, soon out of sight.

"Yes, not so obvious, that's all."

"Their spies are everywhere."

"Why, I found one in my nose this morning while blowing it."

"The morning or the nose?"

Laughter, and then a voice from beyond the inner circle, muffled by the dense shrubbery, offered, "It's not certain Bender is dead. The Greens claim he is alive."

"Ah yes." The inner circle deftly appropriated the topic, slamming like a rude, massive door on the outer circle.

"Yes, he's alive."

"—or he's dead and coming back in a fortnight, just a bit rotted for the decay. Delay?"

"—no one's actually seen the body."

"—hush hush secrecy. Even his friends didn't see—"

"—and what we're witnessing is actually a *coup*."

"Coo coo."

"Shut up, you bloody pigeon."

"I'm not a pigeon—I'm a cuckoo."

"Bender hated pigeons."

"He hated cuckoos too."

"He was a cuckoo."

"Boo! Boo!"

"As if *anyone* really controls this city, anyway?"

"O fecund grand mother matron, Ambergris, bathed in the blood of versions under the gangrenous moon." Merrimount's melodramatic lilt was unmistakable, and Lake roused himself.

"Did I hear right?" Lake rubbed his ears. "Is this poetry? Verse? But what is this gristle: bathed in the blood of *versions*? Surely, my merry mount, you mean *virgins*. We all were one once—or had one once."

A roar of approval from the gallery.

But Merrimount countered: "No, no, my dear Lake, I *meant* versions—I protest. I meant versions: Bathed in the blood of the city's many *versions* of itself."

"A nice recovery"—Sonter again—"but I still think you're drunk."

At which point, Sonter and Merrimount fell out of the conversation, the two locked in an orbit of "version"/"virgin" that, in all likelihood, would continue until the sun and moon fell out of the sky. Lake felt a twinge of jealousy.

Kinsky offered a smug smile, stood, stretched, and said, "I'm going to the opera. Anyone with me?"

A chorus of boos, accompanied by a series of "Fuck off's!"

Kinsky, face ruddy, guffawed, threw down some coins for his bill, and stumbled off down the street which, despite the late hour, twitched and rustled with foot traffic.

"Watch out for the Reds, the Greens, and the Blues," Raffe shouted after him.

"The Blues?" Lake said, turning to Raffe.

"Yes. The Blues—you know. The sads."

"Funny. I think the Blues are more dangerous than the Greens and the Reds put together."

"Only the Browns are more deadly."

Lake laughed, stared after Kinsky. "He's not serious, is he?"

"No," Raffe said. "After all, if there is to be a massacre, it will be at the opera. You'd think the theater owners, or even the actors, would have more sense and close down for a month."

"Shouldn't we leave the city? Just the two of us—and maybe Merrimount?"

Raffe snorted. "And maybe Merrimount? And where would we go? Morrow? The Court of the Kalif? Excuse me for saying so, but I'm broke."

Lake smirked. "Then why are you drinking so much."

"Seriously. Do you mean you'd pay for a trip?"

"No—I'm just as poor as you." Lake put down the drink. "But, I would pay for some advice."

"Eat healthy foods. Do your commissions on time. Don't let Merrimount back into your life."

"No, no. Not that kind of advice. More specific."

"About what?"

He leaned forward, said softly, "Have you ever received an anonymous commission?"

"How do you mean?"

"A letter appears in your post office box. It has no return address. Your address isn't on it. It's clearly from someone wealthy. It tells you to go to a certain place at a certain time. It mentions a masquerade."

Raffe frowned, the corners of her eyes narrowing. "You're serious."

"Yes."

"I've never gotten a commission like that. You have?"

"Yes. I think. I mean, I think it's a commission."

"May I see the letter."

Lake looked at her, his best friend, and somehow he couldn't share it with her. "I don't have it with me."

"Liar!"

As he started to protest, she took his hand and said, "No, no—it's all right. I understand. I won't take an advantage from you. But you want advice on whether you should go?"

Lake nodded, too ashamed to look at her.

"It might be your big break—a major collector who wants to remain anonymous until he's cornered the market in Lake originals. Or . . ."

She paused and a great fear settled over Lake, a fear he knew could only overwhelm him so quickly because it had been there all along.

"Or?"

"It could be a . . . special assignation."

"A *what?*"

"You don't know what I mean?"

He took a sip of his drink, set it down again, said, "I'll admit it. I've no idea what you're talking about."

"Naive, naive Martin," she said, and leaned forward to ruffle his hair.

Blushing, he drew back, said, "Just tell me, Raffe."

Raffe smiled. "Sometimes, Martin, a wealthy person will get a filthy little idea in a filthy little part of their mind—and that idea is to have personalized pornography done by an artist."

"Oh."

Quickly, she said, "But I'm probably wrong. Even if so, that kind of work pays very well. Maybe even enough to let you take time off from commissions to do your own work."

"So I should go?"

"You only become successful by taking chances . . . I've been meaning to tell you, Martin, as a friend and fellow artist—"

"What? What have you been meaning to tell me?"

Lake was acutely aware that Sonter and Merrimount had fallen silent.

She took his hand in hers. "Your work is small."

"Miniatures?" Lake said incredulously.

"No. How do I say this? Small in ambition. Your art treads carefully. You need to take bigger steps. You need to paint a bigger world."

Lake looked up at the clouds, trying to disguise the hurt in his voice, the ache in his throat: *"You're saying I'm no good."*

"I'm only saying *you* don't think you're any good. Why else do you waste such a talent on facile portraits, on a thousand lesser disciplines that *require* no discipline. You, Martin, could be the Voss Bender of artists."

"And look what happened to him—he's dead."

"Martin!"

Suddenly he felt very tired, very . . . small. His father's voice rang in his head unpleasantly.

"There's something about the quality of the light in this city that I cannot capture in paint," he mumbled.

"What?"

"The quality of light is deadly."

"I don't understand. Are you angry with me?"

He managed a thin smile. "Raffe, how could I be angry with you? I need time to think about what you've said. It's not something I can just agree with. But in the meantime, I'll take your advice—I'll go."

Raffe's face brightened. "Good! Now escort me home. I need my sleep."

"Merrimount will be jealous."

"No I won't," Merrimount said, with a look that was half scowl, half grin. "You just *wish* I'd be jealous."

Raffe squeezed his arm and said, "After all, no matter what the commission is, you can always say no."

However, once we have explored Lake's own exploration of the post office as building and metaphor, how much closer are we to the truth? Not very close at all. If biography is too slim to help us and the post office itself too superficial, then we must turn to other sources—specifically Lake's other paintings of note, for in the differences and similarities to "Invitation" we may uncover a kind of truth.

We can first, and most generally, discuss Lake's work in terms of architecture, in terms of his love for his adopted home. If "Invitation to a Beheading" marked Lake's emergence into maturity, it also inaugurated his fascination with Ambergris. The city is often the sole subject of Lake's art—and in almost every case the city encloses, crowds, or enmazes the people sharing the canvas. Further, the city has a palpable *presence* in Lake's work. It almost *intercedes* in the lives of its citizens.

Lake's well-known "Albumuth Boulevard" triptych consists of panels that ostensibly show, at dawn, noon, and dusk, the scene from a fourth-story window, looking down over a block of apartment buildings beyond which lie the domes of the Religious Quarter (shiny with the transcendent quality of light that Lake first perfected in "Invitation to a Beheading"). The painting is quite massive, the predominant colors yellow, red, and green. The one human constant to the three panels is a man standing on the boulevard below, surrounded by pedestrians. At first, the architecture appears identical, but on closer inspection, the streets, the buildings, clearly change or shift in each scene, in each panel further encroaching on the man. By dusk, the buildings have grown gargoyles where once perched pigeons. The people surrounding the man have become progressively more animallike, their heads angular, their noses snouts, their teeth fangs. The expressions on the faces of these people become progressively sadder, more melancholy and tragic, while the man, impassive, with his back to us, has no face. The buildings themselves come to resemble sad faces, so that the overall effect of the final panel is overwhelming . . . and yet, oddly, we feel sad not for the people or the buildings, but for the one immutable element of the series—the faceless man who stands with his back to the viewer.

This, then, is where Lake parts company with such symbolists as the great Darcimbaldo—Lake refuses to lose himself in his grotesque structures, or to abandon himself solely to an imagination under no causal restraints. All of his mature paintings possess a sense of overwhelming sorrow. This sorrow lifts his work above that of his contemporaries and provides the depth, the mystery, that so captivates the general public.—From Janice Shriek's *A Short Overview of the Art of Martin Lake and His Invitation to a Beheading*, for *The Hoegbotton Guide to Ambergris*, 5th edition.

Lake slept fitfully that moonless night, but when he woke the moon blossomed obscenely bright and red beyond his bed. His sheets had become, in that crimson light, violet waves of rippled fabric slick with his sweat. He smelled blood. The walls stank of it. A man stood in front of the open balcony windows, almost eclipsed by the weight of the moon at his back. Lake could not see the man's face. Lake sat up in bed.

"Merrimount? Merrimount? You've returned to me after all."

The man stood at the side of the bed. Lake stood by the balcony window. The man lay in the bed. Lake walked to the balcony. The man and Lake stood a foot apart in the middle of the room, the moon crepuscular and blood-engorged behind Lake. The moon was breathing its scarlet breath upon his back. He could not see the man's face. He was standing right in front of the man and could not see his face. The apartment, fixed in the perfect clarity of the bleeding light cried out to him in the sharpness of its detail, so that his eyes cut themselves upon such precision. Every bristle on his dried-out brushes surrendered to him its slightest imperfection. Every canvas became porous with the numbing roughness of its gesso.

"You're not Merrimount," he said to the man.

The man's eyes were closed.

Lake stood facing the moon. The man stood facing Lake.

The man opened his eyes and the ferruginous light of the moon shot through them and formed two rusty spots on Lake's neck, as if the man's eyes were just holes that pierced his skull from back to front.

The moon blinked out. The light still streamed from the man's eyes. The man smiled a half-moon smile and the light trickled out from between his teeth.

The man held Lake's left hand, palm up.

The knife sliced into the middle of Lake's palm. He felt the knife tear through the skin, and into the palmar fascia muscle, and beneath that, into the tendons, vessels, and nerves. The skin peeled back until his entire hand was flayed and open. He saw the knife sever the muscle from the lower margin of the annular ligament, then felt, almost heard, the lesser muscles snap back from the bones as they were cut—six for the middle finger, three for the ring finger—the knife now grinding up against the os magnum as the man guided it into the area near Lake's wrist—slicing through extensor tendons, through the nerves, through the farthest outposts of the radial and ulnar arteries. He could see it all—the yellow of the thin fat layer, the white of bone obscured by the dull red of muscle, the gray of tendons, as surely as if his hand had been labeled and diagrammed for his own benefit. The blood came thick and heavy, draining from all of his extremities until he only had feeling in his chest. The pain was infinite, so infinite that he did not try to escape it, but tried only to escape the red gaze of the man who was butchering him while he just stood there and let him do it. The thought went through his head like a dirge, like an epitaph, *I will never paint again.*

He could not get away. He could not get away.

Lake's hand began to mutter, to mumble . . .

In response, the man sang to Lake's hand, the words incomprehensible, strange, sad.

Lake's hand began to scream—a long, drawn out scream, ever higher in pitch, the wound become a mouth into which the man continued to plunge the knife.

Lake woke up shrieking. He was drowning in sweat, his right hand clenched around his left wrist. He tried to control his breathing—he sucked in great gulps of air—but found it was impossible. Panicked, he looked toward the window. There was no moon. No one stood there. He forced his gaze down to his left hand (he had done nothing, nothing, nothing while the man cut him apart) and found it whole.

He was still shrieking.

In "Invitation to a Beheading," the sorrow takes the form of two figures: the insect catcher outside the building and the man highlighted in the upper window of the post office itself. (If it seems that I have kept these two figures a secret in order to make of them a revelation, it is because they *are* a revelation to the viewer—due to the mass of detail around them, they are generally the last seen, and then, in a tribute to their intensity, the *only* things seen.)

The insect catcher, his light dimmed but for a single orange spark, hurries off down the front steps, one hand held up behind him, as if to ward off the man in the window. Is this figure literally Lake's father, or does it represent some mythical insect catcher—*the* Insect Catcher? Or did Lake see his father as a mythic figure? From my conversations with Lake, the latter interpretation strikes me as most plausible.

But to what can we attribute the single clear window in the building's upper story, through which we see a man who stands in utter anguish, his head thrown back to the sky? In one hand, the man holds a letter, while the other is held palm up by a vaguely stork-like shadow that has driven a knife through it. The scene derives all of its energy from this view through the window: the greens radiate outward from the pulsing crimson spot that marks where the knife has penetrated flesh. Adding to the effect, Lake has so layered and built up his oils that a trick of perspective is created by which the figure simultaneously exists inside and outside the window.

Although the building that houses this intricate scene lends itself to fantastical interpretation, and Lake might be thought to have re-created some historical event in phantasmagorical fashion, the figure with the pierced palm is clearly a man, not a child or mushroom dweller, and the letter held in the man's right hand indicates an admission of the building's use as a post office rather than as a morgue (unless, under duress, we are forced to acknowledge the weak black humor of "dead letter office").

Further examination of the man's face reveals two disturbing elements: (1) it bears a striking resemblance to Lake's own face, and (2) under close scrutiny with a magnifying glass, there is a second, almost translucent set of features transposed over the first. This "mask," its existence disputed by some critics, mimics, like a mold made from life, the features of the first, except in two particulars: this man has teeth made of broken glass and he, unlike his counterpart, smiles with unnerving brutality. Is this the face of the faceless man from "Albumuth Boulevard"? Is this the face of Death?

Regardless of Lake's intent, all of these elements combine to create in the viewer—even the viewer who only subconsciously notes certain of the more hidden elements—a true sense of unease and dread, as well as the release of this dread through the anguished, voiceless cry of the man in the window. The man in the window provides us with the only movement in the painting, for the insect catcher, hurrying away, is already in the past, and the bones of the post office are also in the past. Only the forlorn figure in the window is still alive, caught forever in the present. Further, although forsaken by the insect catcher and pierced by a shadow that may be a manifestation of his own fear, the *light* never forsakes or betrays him. Lake's tones are, as Venturi has noted, "resonant rather than bright, and the light contained in them is not so much a physical as a psychological illumination."— From Janice Shriek's A *Short Overview of the Art of Martin Lake and His Invitation to a Beheading*, for The *Hoegbotton Guide to Ambergris*, 5th edition.

Lake spent the next day trying to forget his nightmare.

To rid himself of its cloying atmosphere, he left his apartment—but not before receiving a stern lecture from Dame Truff on how loud noises after midnight showed no consideration for other tenants, while behind her a few neighbors, who had not come to his aid but obviously had heard his screams, gave him curious stares.

Then, punishment over, he made his way through the crowded streets to the Gallery of Hidden Fascinations, portfolio under one arm. The portfolio contained two new paintings, both of his father's hands, as he remembered them, open wide like wings as a cornucopia of insects—velvet ants, cicadas, moths, butterflies, walking sticks, praying mantises—crawled over them. It was a study he had been working on for years. His father had beautifully ruined hands, bitten and stung countless times, but as polished, as smooth, as white marble.

The gallery owner, Janice Shriek, greeted him at the door; she was a severe, hunched woman with calculating, cold blue eyes. This morning she had thrown on foppishly male trousers, and a jacket over a white shirt, the sleeves of which ended in cuffs that looked as if they had been made from doilies. Shriek rose up on tiptoe to plant a ceremonial kiss on his cheek while explaining that the short, portly gentleman currently casting his round shadow over the far end of the gallery had expressed interest in one of Lake's pieces, how fortunate that he had stopped by, and that while she continued to enflame that interest—she actually said "enflamed," much to Lake's amazement; was he to be some artistic gigolo now?—Lake should set down his portfolio and, after a decent interval, walk over and introduce himself, that was a dear—and back she scamper-lurched to the potential customer, leaving Lake rather breathless on her behalf. No one could ever say Janice Shriek lacked energy.

Lake placed his portfolio on a nearby table, the art of his countless rivals glaring down at him from the walls. The only good art (besides Lake's, of course) was a miniature entitled "Amber in the City" by Shriek's great find, Roger Mandible, who, unbeknownst to Shriek, had created his subtle amber shades from the earwax of a well-known diva who had had the misfortune to fall asleep at a café table where Mandible was mixing his paints. It made Lake snicker every time he saw it.

After a moment, Lake walked over to Shriek and the gentleman and engaged in the kind of obsequious small talk that nauseated him.

"Yes, I'm the artist."

"Maxwell Bibble. A pleasure to meet you."

"Likewise . . . Bibble. It is exceedingly rare to meet a true lover of art."

Bibble stank of beets. Lake could not get over it. Bibble stank of beets. He had difficulty not saying *Bibble imbibes bottled beets beautifully* . . .

"Well, you do . . . you do so well with, er, *colors*," Bibble said.

"How discerning you are. Did you hear what he said, Janice," Lake said.

Shriek nodded nervously, said, "Mr. Bibble's a businessman, but he has always wanted to be a—" *Beet?* thought Lake; but no: ". . . a critic of the arts," Shriek finished.

"Yes, marvelous colors," Bibble said, this time with more confidence.

"It is nothing. The *true artiste* can bend even the most stubborn light to his will," Lake said.

"I imagine so. I thought this piece might look good in the kitchen, next to the wife's needlepoint."

"'In the kitchen, next to the wife's needlepoint,'" Lake echoed blankly, and then put on a frozen smile.

"But I'm wondering if maybe it is too big . . ."

"It's smaller than it looks," Shriek offered, somewhat pathetically, Lake thought.

"Perhaps I could have it altered, cut down to size," Lake said, glaring at Shriek.

Bibble nodded, putting a hand to his chin in rapt contemplation of the possibilities.

"Or maybe I should just saw it in fourths and you can take the fourth you like best," Lake said. "Or maybe eighths would be more to your liking?"

Bibble stared blankly at him for a moment, before Shriek stepped in with, "Artists! Always joking! You know, I really don't think it will be too large. You could always buy it and if it doesn't fit, return it—not that I could refund your money, but you could pick something else."

Enough! Lake thought, and disengaged himself from the conversation. Leaving Shriek to ramble on convincingly about the cunning strength of his brushstrokes, a slick blather of nonsense that Lake despised and admired all at once. He could not complain that Shriek neglected to promote him—she was the only one who would take his work—but he hated the way she appropriated his art, speaking at times almost as if she herself had created it. A failed painter and a budding art historian, Shriek had started the gallery through the largesse of her famous brother, the historian Duncan Shriek, who had also procured for her many of her first and best clients. Lake felt that her drive to push, push, push was linked to a certain guilt at not having had to start at the bottom like everyone else.

Eventually, as Lake gave a thin-lipped smile, Bibble, still reeking of beets, announced that he couldn't possibly commit at the moment, but would come back later. Definitely, he would be back—and what a pleasure to meet the artist.

To which Lake said, and was sorry even as the words left his mouth, "It is a pleasure to *be* the artist."

A nervous laugh from Shriek. An unpleasant laugh from the almost-buyer, whose hand Lake tried his best to crush as they shook goodbye.

After Bibble had left, Shriek turned to him and said, "That was wonderful!"

"What was wonderful?"

Shriek's eyes became colder than usual. "That smug, arrogant, better-than-thou artist's demeanor. They like that, you know—it makes them feel they've bought the work of a budding genius."

"Well haven't they?" Lake said. Was she being sarcastic? He'd pretend otherwise.

Shriek patted him on the back. "Whatever it is, keep it up. Now, let's take a look at the new paintings."

Lake bit his lip to stop himself from committing career suicide, walked over to the table, and retrieved the two canvases. He spread them out with an awkward flourish.

Shriek stared at them, a quizzical look on her face.

"Well?" Lake finally said, Raffe's words from the night before buzzing in his ears. "Do you like them?"

"Hmm?" Shriek said, looking up from the paintings as if her thoughts had been far away.

Lake experienced a truth viscerally in that moment which he had only ever realized intellectually before: he was the least of Shriek's many prospects, and he was boring her.

Nonetheless, he pressed on, braced for further humiliation: "Do you like them?"

"Oh! The paintings?"

"No—the . . ." *The earwax on your walls?* he thought. *The beets?* "Yes, the paintings."

Shriek's brows furrowed and she put a hand to her chin in unconscious mimicry of the departed Bibble. "They're very . . . interesting."

Interesting.

"They're of my father's hands," Lake said, aware that he was about to launch into a confession both unseemly and useless, as if he could help make the paintings more appealing to her by saying *this happened*, this is a person *I know*, it is *real* therefore it is *good*. But he had no choice—he plunged forward: "He is a startlingly nonverbal man, my father, as most insect catchers are, but there was one way he felt comfortable communicating with me, Janice—by coming home with his hands closed—and when he'd open them, there would be some living jewel, some rare wonder of the insect world—sparkling black, red, or green—and his eyes would sparkle too. He'd name them all for me in his soft, stumbling voice— lovingly so; how they were all so very different from one another, how although he killed them and we often ate them in hard times, how it must be with respect and out of knowledge." Lake looked at the floor. "He wanted me to be an insect catcher too, but I wouldn't. I couldn't. I had to become an artist." He remembered the way the joy had shriveled up inside his father when he realized his son would not be following in his footsteps. It had hurt Lake to see his father so alone, trapped by his reticence and his solitary profession, but he knew it hurt his father more. He missed his father; it was an ache in his chest.

"That's a lovely story, Martin. A lovely story."

"So you'll take them?"

"No. But it is a lovely story."

"But see how perfectly I've rendered the insects," Lake said, pointing to them.

"It's a slow season and I don't have the space. Maybe when your other work sells."

Her tone as much as said not to press her too far.

When Lake returned to his apartment to work on Mr. Kashmir's commission, he was decidedly out of sorts. In addition to his disappointing trip to the gallery, he had spent money on greasy sausage that now sat in his belly like an extra coil of intestines. It did not help that the image of the man from his nightmares blinked on and off in his head no matter how hard he tried to suppress it.

Nevertheless, he dutifully picked up the pages of illustrations he had torn from discarded books bought cheap at the back door of the Borges Bookstore. He set about cutting them out with his rusty paint-speckled scissors. Ideas for his commissions came to him not in flashes from his muse but as calm re-creations of past work. Lately, he knew, he had become lazy, providing literal "translations" for his commissions, while suppressing any hint of his own imagination.

Still, this did not explain why, following a period of work during which he stared at the envelope and the invitation where it lay on his easel, he looked down to find that after carefully cutting out a trio of etched dancing girls, he had just as carefully sliced off their heads and then cut star designs out of their torsos.

In disgust, Lake tossed the scissors aside and let the ruins of the dancing girls flutter to the floor. Obviously, Mr. Kashmir's assignment would have to await a spark of inspiration. In the meantime, the afternoon still young, he would take Raffe's advice and work on something for himself.

Lake walked over to the crowded easel, emptied it by placing four or five canvases on the already chaotic bed, pulled his stool over, retrieved a blank canvas, and pinned it up. Slowly, he began to brushstroke oils onto the canvas. Despite three years of endless commissions, the familiar smell of fresh paint excited his senses and, even better, the light behind him was sharp, clear, so he did not have to resort to borrowing Dame Truff's lantern.

As he progressed, Lake did not know the painting's subject, or even how best to apply the oils, but he continued to create layers of paint, sensitive to the pressure of the brush against canvas. Raffe had forced the oils upon him months ago. At the time, he had given her a superior, doubtful look, since her last gift had been special paints created from a mixture of natural pigments and freshwater squid ink. Lake had used them for a week before his first paintings began to fade; soon his canvases were as blank as before. Raffe, always trying to find the good in the bad, had told him, when next they met at a café, that he could become famous selling "disappearing paintings." He had thrown the paint set at her. Fortunately, it missed and hit a stranger—a startled and startlingly handsome man named Merrimount.

This time, however, Raffe's idea appeared to be a good one. It had been several years since he had used oils and he had forgotten the ease of creating texture with them, how the paint built upon itself. He especially liked how he could blend colors for gradations of shadow. Assuming the current troubles were temporary—and that a drop cloth would suffice until that time—and even now giving a quick look over his shoulder, he worked on building color: emerald, jade, moss, lime, verdigris. He mixed all the shades in, until he had a luminous, shining background. Then, in dark green, he began to paint a face . . .

Only the Religious Quarter's evening call to prayer—the solemn tolling of the bell five times from the old Truffidian Cathedral—roused Lake from his trance. He blinked, turned toward the window, then looked back at his canvas. In shock and horror, he let the brush fall from his hand.

The head had a brutish mouth of broken glass teeth through which it smiled cruelly, while above the ruined nose, the eyes shone like twin flames. Lake stared at the face from his nightmare.

For a long time, Lake examined his work. His first impulse, to paint over it and start fresh, gradually gave way to a second, deeper impulse: to finish it. Far better, he thought, that the face should remain in the painting than, erased, once more take up residence in his mind. A little thrill ran through him as he realized it was totally unlike anything he had done before.

"I've trapped you," he said to it, gloating.

It stared at him with its unearthly eyes and said nothing. On the canvas it might still smile, but it could not smile only at him. Now it smiled at the world.

He worked on it for a few more minutes, adding definition to the eyelids and narrowing the cheekbones, relieved, for now that he had come around to the idea that the face *belonged* in the world, that perhaps it had always been in the world, he wanted it perfect in every detail, that no trace of it should ever haunt him again.

As the shadows lengthened and deepened, falling across his canvas, he put aside his palette, cleaned his brushes with turpentine, washed them in the sink across the hall, and quickly dressed to the sounds of a busker on the street below. After he had put on his jacket, he stuck his sketchbook and two sharpened pencils into his breast pocket—in case his mysterious host should need an immediate demonstration of his skills—and, running his fingers over the ornate seal, deposited the invitation there as well.

A few moments of rummaging under his bed and he had fished out a collapsible rubber frog head he had worn to the Festival of the Freshwater Squid a year before—it would have to do for a costume. He stuffed it in a side pocket, one bulbous yellow eye staring up at him absurdly. Further rummaging uncovered his map. Every wise citizen of Ambergris carried a map of the city, for its alleys were legion and seemed to change course of their own accord.

He spent a nervous moment adjusting his tie, then locked his apartment door behind him. He took a deep breath, descended the stairs, and set off down Albumuth Boulevard as the sky melted into the orange-green hue peculiar to Ambergris and Ambergris alone.

We find this quality of illumination in almost all of Lake's paintings, but nowhere more strikingly than in the incendiary "The Burning House," where it is meshed to a comment on his fear of birds—the only painting with any hint of birds in it besides "Invitation to a Beheading" and "Through His Eyes" (which I will discuss shortly). "The Burning House" blends reds, yellows, and oranges much as "Invitation" blends greens, but for a different effect. The painting shows a house with its roof and front wall torn away—to expose an owl, a stork, and a raven that are burning alive, while the totality of the flames themselves form the shadow of a fire bird, done in a style similar to Lagach. Clearly, this is as close to pure fantasy as Lake ever came, a wish fulfillment work in which his fear of birds is washed away by fire. As Venturi wrote, "The charm of the picture lies in its mysteriously suggestive power—the sigh of fatality that blows over the strangely contorted figures." Here we may hold another piece of the puzzle that describes the process of Lake's transformation. If so, we do not know quite where to place it—and whether it should be placed near or far away from the puzzle piece that is "Invitation to a Beheading."

A less ambiguous link to "Invitation" can be found in the person of Voss Bender, the famous opera composer née politician, and the tumult following his death—a death that occurred only three days before Lake began "Invitation." In later interviews, the usually taciturn Lake professed to hold Voss Bender in the highest regard, even as an inspiration (although, when I knew him, I cannot recall him ever mentioning Bender). More than one art historian, noting the repetition of Bender themes in Lake's work, has wondered if Lake obsessed over the dead composer. Perhaps "Invitation" represents a memorial to Voss Bender. If so, it is the first in a trilogy of such paintings, the last two, "Through His Eyes" and "Aria to the Brittle Bones of Winter," clear homages to Bender.—From Janice Shriek's *A Short Overview of the Art of Martin Lake and His Invitation to a Beheading*, for *The Hoegbotton Guide to Ambergris*, 5th edition.

The dusk had a mingled blood-and-orange-peel scent, and the light as it faded left behind a faint golden residue on the brass doorknobs of bank entrances, on the coppery flagpoles outside the embassies of foreign dignitaries, and on the Fountain of Trillian, with its obelisk at the top of which perched a sad rose-marble cherub, one elbow propped atop a leering black skull. Crowds had gathered at the surrounding lantern-lit square to hear poets declaim their verse while standing on wooden crates. Nearby taverns shed music and light in equal quantities, the light breaking against the cobblestones in thick shafts, while sidewalk vendors plied passersby with all manner of refreshments, from Lake's ill-starred sausages to flagrantly sinful pastries. Few outside of Ambergris realized that the great artist Darcimbaldo had created his fruit and seafood portraits from life—stolen from the vendors, who arranged oranges, apples, figs, and melons into faces with black grapes for eyes, or layered crayfish, trout, crabs, and the lesser squid into the imperious visage of the mayor; these vendors were almost as popular as the sidewalk poets, and had taken to hanging wide-angle lanterns in front of their stalls so that passersby could appreciate their ephemeral art. Through this tightly packed throng, occasional horse-and-carriages and motored vehicles lurched through like lighthouses for the drunk and disorderly, who would push and rock them at every opportunity.

Here, then, in the flushed faces, in the mixing of dark and light, in the swirling, shadowy facades of buildings, were a thousand scenes that lent themselves to the artist's eye, but Lake, intent on his map, saw them only as hindrances now.

And more than hindrances, for the difficulty of circumnavigating the crowds with his cane convinced Lake to flag down a for-hire motored vehicle. An old, sumptuous model, nicer than his apartment and prudently festooned with red and green flags, it had only two drawbacks: the shakes—almost certainly from watered down petrol—and a large, very dirty sheep with which he was forced to share the back seat. Man and sheep contemplated each other with equal unease while the driver smiled and shrugged apologetically (to him or the sheep?), his vehicle racing through the narrow streets. Nonetheless, Lake left the vehicle first, deposited at the edge of the requested neighborhood. The nervous driver sped off at top speed as soon as Lake had paid him. No doubt the detour to deliver Lake had made the sheep late for an appointment.

As for the neighborhood, located on the southeastern flank of the Religious Quarter, Lake had rarely seen one grimmer. The buildings, four and five stories high, had a scarcity of windows that made them appear to face away from him—inward, toward the maze of houses and apartments that contained his destination.

Such stark edifices gave Lake a glimpse of the future, of the decay into which his own apartment building might fall when the New Art moved on and left behind only remnants of unkept promises. The walls were awash in fire burns, the ground level doors rotted or broken open, the balconies that hung precariously over them black with rust. In some places, Lake could see bones worked into the mortar, for there had been a time when the dead were buried in the walls of their own homes.

Lake took out his invitation, ran his hand across the maroon-gold threads. Perhaps it *was* all a practical joke. Or perhaps his host just wanted to be discreet. He wavered, hesitated, but then his conversation with Raffe came back to him, followed by the irritating image of Shriek's face as she said, "Interesting." He sighed, and began to walk between two of the buildings, uncomfortable in the shadow of their height, under the blank or cracked windows whose dust-covered panes were somehow predatory. His cane clacked against rocks, a plaintive sound in that place.

Eventually, he emerged from the alleyway onto a larger street, strewn with rubbish. A few babarusa pigs, all grunts and curved tusks, fought with anemic-looking mushroom dwellers for the offal. The light had faded to a deep blue colder in its way than the temperature. The distant calls to prayer from the Religious Quarter sounded like the cries of men drowning fifty feet underwater.

By the guttering light of a public lamp, Lake made out the name of the street—Salamander—but could not locate it on his map. For a long time, the darkness broken by irregularly posted lamps, he walked alone, examining signs, finding none of the streets on his map. He kept himself from thinking *lost!* by trying to decide how best the surrounding shadows could be captured on canvas.

Gradually, he realized that the darkness, which at least had been broken by the lamps, had taken on a hazy quality through which he could see nothing at all. Fog, come off the River Moth. He cursed his luck. First, the stars went out, occluded by the weight of the shadows and by the dull, creeping rage of the fog. It was an angry fog, a sneering fog that ate its way through the sky, through the spaces between things, and it obscured the night. It smelled of the river: of silt and brackish water, of fish and mangroves. It rolled through Lake as if he did not exist. And because of this, the fog made Lake ethereal, for he could no longer see his arms or legs, could feel nothing but the cloying moisture of the fog as it clung to and settled over him. He was a ghost. He was free. There could be no reality to this fog-ridden world. There could be no reality to him while in it.

Lost and lost again, turning in the whiteness, not sure if he had walked forward or retraced his steps. The freedom he had felt turned to fear—fear of the unknown, fear that he might be late. So when he became aware of a dimly bobbing light ahead, he began to fast-walk toward it, heedless of obstacles that might make him turn an ankle or fall on his face.

A block later, he came upon the source of the light: the tall, green-hooded, green-robed figure of an insect catcher, his great, circular slab of glass attached to a round, buoy-shaped lantern that swung below it. As with most insect catchers, who are products of famine, this one was thin, with bony but strong arms. The glass was so large that the man had to hold on to it with both gloved hands, while grasshoppers, moths, beetles, and ant queens smacked up against it, trying to get to the light.

The glass functioned like a sticky lens inserted into a circular brass frame; when filled with insects, the lens would be removed and placed in a bag. The insect catcher would then insert a new lens and repeat the process. Once home, the new catch would be carefully plucked off the lens, then boiled or baked and salted, after which the insects would hang from his belt on strings for sale the next day. Many times Lake had spent his evening tying insects into strings, using a special knot taught to him by his father.

Steeped in such memories and in the fog, his first thought was that this man *was* his father. Why couldn't it be his father? They would be ghosts together, sailing through the night.

His first words to the insect catcher were tentative, respectful of his own past.

"Excuse me? Excuse me, sir?"

The man turned with a slow grace to peer down at this latest catch. The folds of the insect catcher's robes covered his face, but for a jutting nose like a scythe.

"Yes?" The man had a deep, sonorous voice.

"Do you know which way to Archmont Lane? My map is no help at all."

The insect catcher raised one bony finger and pointed upward.

Lake looked up. There, above the insect catcher's light, was a sign for Archmont Lane. Lake stood on Archmont Lane.

"Oh," he said. "Thank you."

But the insect catcher had already shambled on into the fog, little more than a shadow under a lantern that had already begun to fade . . .

———

From there, it was relatively easy to find 45 Archmont Lane—unlike the other entrances to left and right, it suffered few signs of disrepair and a lamp blazed above the doorway. The numerals "4" and "5" were rendered in glossy gold, the door painted maroon, the steps swept clean, the door knocker a twin to the seal on the envelope—all permeated by a sudsy smell.

Reassured by such cleanliness, Raffe's advice still whispering in his ear, Lake raised the doorknocker and lowered it—once, twice, thrice.

The door opened a crack, light flooded out, and Lake caught sight of a wild, staring eye, rimmed with crusted red. It was an animal's eye, the reflection in its black pupil his own distorted face. Lake took a quick step back.

The voice, when it came, sounded unreal, falsified: "What do you want?"

Lake held up the invitation. "I have this."

A blink of the horrible eye. "What does it say?"

"An invitation to a—"

"Quick! Put on your mask!" hissed the voice.

"My mask?"

"Your mask for the masquerade!"

"Oh! Yes. Sorry. Just a moment."

Lake pulled the rubber frog mask out of his pocket and put it over his head. It felt like slick jelly. He did not want it next to his skin. As he adjusted the mask so he could see out of the eyeholes that jutted from the frog's nostrils, the door opened, revealing a splendid foyer and the outstretched arm of the man with the false voice. The man himself stood to one side and Lake, his vision restricted to what he could see directly in front of him, had to make do with the beckoning white-gloved hand and a whispered, *"Enter now!"* He walked forward. The man slammed the door behind him and locked it.

Ahead, through glass paneled doors, Lake saw a staircase of burnished rosewood and, at the foot of the stairs, a globe of the world upon a polished mahogany table with lion paws for feet. Candles guttered in their slots, the wavery light somehow religious. On the left he glimpsed tightly stacked bookcases hemmed in by generous tables, while to the right the house opened up onto a sitting room, flanked by portraits. Black drop clothes covered the name plate and face of each portrait: a line of necks and shoulders greeted him from down the hall. The smell of soap had faded, replaced by a faint trace of rot, of mildew.

Lake turned toward the front door and the person who had opened it—a butler, he presumed—only to find himself confronted by a man with a stork head.

The red-ringed eyes, the cruel beak, the dull white of the feathered face, merged with a startlingly pale neck atop a gaunt body clothed in a black-and-white suit.

"I see that you are dressed already," Lake managed, although badly shaken. "And, unfortunately, as the natural predator of the frog. Ha ha. Perhaps, though, you can now tell me why I've been summoned here, Mister . . . ?"

The joke failed miserably. The attempt to discover the man's name failed with it. The Stork stared at him as if he came from a foreign, barbaric land. The Stork said, "Your jacket and your cane."

Lake disliked relinquishing his cane, which had driven off more than one potential assailant in its day, but handed both it and his jacket to the Stork. After placing them in a closet, the Stork said, "Follow me," and led Lake past the stairs, past the library, and into a study with a decorative fireplace, several upholstered chairs, a handful of glossy black wooden tables and, adorning the walls, eight paintings by masters of the last century: hunting scenes, cityscapes, still lifes—all genuine and all completely banal.

The Stork beckoned Lake to a couch farthest from the door. The couch was bounded by a magnificent, if unwieldy, rectangular box of a table that extended some six feet down the width of the room. It had decorative handles, but no drawers.

As Lake sat, making certain not to bang his leg against the table, he said, "Who owns this house?" to the Stork's retreating back.

The Stork spun around, put a finger to its beak, and said, "Don't speak! Don't speak!"

Lake nodded in a gesture of apology. The master of the house obviously valued his privacy.

The Stork stared at Lake a moment longer, as if afraid he might say something more, then turned on his heel.

Leaving Lake alone in his frog mask, which had become uncomfortably hot and scratchy. It smelled of a familiar cologne—Merri must have worn it since the Festival and not cleaned it out.

Claustrophobia battled with a pleasing sense of anonymity. Behind the mask he felt as if he would be capable of actions forbidden to the arrogant but staid Martin Lake. Very well, then, the new Martin Lake would undertake an examination of the room for more clues as to his host's taste—or lack thereof.

A bust of Trillian stared back at him from a far table, its white marble infiltrated by veins of some cerise stone. Also on this table lay a book entitled *The Architect of Ruins*, above which stood the stuffed and bejeweled carcass of a tortoise. Across from it, upon a dais, stood a telescope which, in quite a clever whimsy, faced a map of the world upon the wall. Atlases and other maps were strewn across the tables, but Lake had the sense that these had been placed haphazardly as the result of cold calculation. Indeed, the room conveyed an aura of artificiality, from the burgundy walls to the globe-shaped fixtures that spread a pleasant, if pinkish, light. Such a light was not conducive to reading or conversation. Despite this, the study had a rich warmth to it, both relaxing and comfortable.

Lake sat back, content. Who would have thought to find such refinement in the midst of such desolation? It appeared Raffe had been right: some wealthy patron wished to commission him, perhaps even to collect his art. He began to work out in his head an asking price that would be high enough, even if eventually knocked down by hard bargaining, to satisfy him. He could buy new canvases, replace his old, weary brushes, perhaps even convince an important gallery to carry his work.

Gradually, however, as if the opening notes of a music so subtle that the listener could not at first hear it, a tap-tap-tapping intruded upon his pleasant daydream. It traveled around the room and into his ears with an apologetic urgency.

He sat up and tried to identify the source. It came neither from the walls nor the door. But it definitely originated from *inside* the room . . . and, although muffled, as if underground, from somewhere close to him. Such a gentle sound—not loud enough to startle him, just this cautious, moderate *tap*, this minor key *rap*.

He listened carefully—and a smile lit his face. Why, it was coming from the table in front of him! Someone or something was *inside* the table, gently rapping. What a splendid disguise for the masquerade. Lake tapped back. Whatever was inside the table tapped back twice. Lake tapped twice, answered by three taps. Lake tapped thrice.

A frenzied rapping and *smashing* erupted from the table. Lake sucked in his breath and pulled his fist back abruptly. A frisson of dread traveled up his spine. It had just occurred to him that the playful game might not be a playful game after all. The black table, on which he had laid his invitation, was not actually a table but an unadorned coffin from which someone desperately wanted to get out!

Lake rose with an "Uh!" of horror—and at that moment, the Stork returned, accompanied by two other men.

The Stork's companions were both of considerable weight and height, and from a certain weakness underlying the ponderous nature of their movements, which he remembered from his days of sketching models, Lake realized both were of advancing years. Both wore dark suits identical to that worn by the Stork, but the resemblance ended there. The larger of the two men—not fat but merely broad—wore a resplendent raven's head over his own, the glossy black feathers plucked from a real raven (there was no mistaking the distinctive sheen). The eyes shone sharp and hard and heavy. The beak, made of a silvery metal, caught the subdued light and glimmered like a distant reflection in a pool of still water.

The third man wore a mask that replicated both the doorknocker and the seal on Lake's invitation: the owl, brown-gold feathers once again genuine, the curved beak a dull gray, the human eyes peering out from the shadow of the fabricated orbits. Unfortunately, the Owl's extreme girth extended to his neck and the owl mask was a tight fit, covering his chins, but constricting the flesh around the neck into a jowly collar. This last detail made him hideous beyond belief, for it looked as if he had been denuded of feathers, revealing the plucked skin beneath.

The three stood opposite Lake across the coffin—the top of which had begun to shudder upward as whatever was inside smashed itself against the lid.

"What . . . what is in there?" Lake asked. "Is this part of the masquerade? Is this a joke? Did Merrimount send you?"

The Owl said, "A very nice disguise," and still staring at Lake, rapped his fist so hard against the coffin lid that black paint rubbed off on his white glove. The thrashing inside the coffin subsided. "A good disguise for this masquerade. The frog, who is equally at home on land as in the water." The Owl's voice, like that of the Stork, came out distorted, as if the man had stuffed cotton or pebbles in his mouth.

"What," Lake said again, pointing a tremulous finger at the coffin, "is in there?"

The Owl laughed—a horrid coughing sound. "Our other guest will be released shortly, but first we must discuss your commission."

"My commission?" A thought flashed across his mind like heat lightning, leaving no impression behind: *Raffe was right. I am to paint their sex games for them.*

"It is an unusual commission and before I give you the details, you must resign yourself to it with all your heart. You have no choice. Now that you are here, you are our instrument."

Raffe had never suggested that he must *become* part of the pornography, and he rebelled against the notion: this was too far to take a commission, even for all the money in the world.

"Sirs," Lake said, standing, "I think there has been a misunderstanding. I am a painter and a painter only—"

"A painter," the Owl echoed, as if it were an irrelevant detail.

"—and I am going to leave now. Please forgive me. I mean no offense."

He began to sidle out from behind the coffin, but stopped when the Raven blocked his path, a long gutting knife held in one gloved hand. It shone like the twin to the Raven's beak. The sight of it paralyzed Lake. Slowly, he sidled back to the middle of the couch, the coffin between him and these predators. His hands shook. The frog mask was awash in sweat.

"What do you want?" Lake said, guarding unsuccessfully against the quaver in his voice.

The Owl rubbed his hands together and cocked his head to regard Lake with one steel-gray eye. "Simply put, your commission shall be its own reward. We shall not pay you, unless you consider allowing you to live payment. Once you have left this house, your life will be as before, except that you shall be a hero: the anonymous citizen of the city who righted a grievous wrong."

"What do you want?" Lake asked again, more terror-stricken than before.

"A murder," croaked the Raven.

"An execution," corrected the Stork.

"A beheading," specified the Owl.

"A *murder*?" Lake shouted. "A murder! Are you mad?"

The Owl ruffled its feathers, said, "Let me tell you what your response will be, and then perhaps you can move past it to your destiny all the quicker. First, you will moan. You will shriek. You will even try to escape. You will say 'No!' emphatically even after we subdue you. We will threaten you. You will weaken. Then you will say 'No' again, but this time we will be able to tell from the questioning tone of your voice that you are closer to the reality, closer to the deed. And then the cycle will repeat itself. And then, finally, whether it takes an hour or a week, you will find yourself carrying out your task, because even the most wretched dog wants to feel the sun on its face one more day.

"It would save us all some time if you just accepted the situation without all the attendant fuss."

"I will not."

"Open the coffin."

"No!"

Lake, his leg encumbering him, leapt over the coffin table. He made it as far as the bust of Trillian before the Stork and the Raven knocked him to the floor. He twisted and kicked in their grasp, but his leg was as supple as a wooden club and they were much too strong. They wrestled him back to the coffin. The Stork held him facedown on the couch, the frog mask cutting so painfully into his mouth that he could hardly draw breath. The Raven yanked his head up and held the knife to his throat. In such a position, his eyeholes askew, he could see only the interior of the mask and a portion of the maroon-gold leaf ceiling.

From somewhere above him, the Owl said, with almost sensual sloth, "Accept the commission, my dear frog, or we shall kill you and choose another citizen."

The Stork, sitting on Lake, jabbed his kidneys, then punched in the same spot—hard. Lake grunted with pain. The Raven bent Lake's left arm back behind him until it felt as if his bones would break.

He shrieked. Suddenly, they were both off of him. He flipped over on his back, adjusted his mask, and looked up—to find all three men staring down at him.

"What is your answer?" the Owl asked. "We must have your answer now."

Lake groaned and rolled over onto his side.

"Answer!"

What did a word mean? Did a single word really mean . . . anything? Could it exile whole worlds of action, of possibility?

"Yes," he said, and the word sounded like a death rattle in his throat.

"Good," said the Owl. "Now open the coffin."

They moved back so that he would have enough space. He sat up on the couch, his leg throbbing. He grappled with the locks on the side of the coffin, determined to speed up the nightmare, that it might end all the more swiftly.

Finally, the latches came free. With a grunt, he opened the lid . . . and stared down at familiar, unmistakably patrician features. The famous shock of gray hair disheveled, the sharp cheekbones bruised violet, the intelligent blue eyes bulging with fear, the fine mouth, the sensual lips, obstructed by a red cloth gag that cut into the face and left a line of blood. Blood trickled from his hairline where he had banged his head against the coffin lid. Strange symbols had been carved into his arms as if he were an offering to some cruel god.

Lake staggered backward, fell against the edge of the couch, unable to face this final, dislocating revelation—unable to comprehend that indeed the Greens were right: *Voss Bender was alive.* What game had he entered all unwitting?

For his part, Bender tried to get up as soon as he saw Lake, even bound as he was in coils of rope that must cruelly constrict his circulation, then thrashed about again when it became clear Lake would not help him.

The Raven stuck his head into Bender's field of vision and caw, caw, cawed like his namesake. The action sent Bender into a hysterical spasm of fear. The Raven dealt him a cracking blow across the face. Bender slumped back down into the coffin. His eyelids fluttered; the smell of urine came from the coffin. Lake couldn't tear his gaze away. This was Voss Bender, savior and destroyer of careers, politicians, theaters. Voss Bender, who had been dead for two days.

"Why? Why have you done this to him?"

The Stork sneered, said, "He did it to *himself*. He brought everything on himself."

"He's no good," the Raven said.

"He is," the Owl added, "the very epitome of Evil."

Voss Bender moved a little. The eyes under the imperious gray eyebrows opened wide. Bender wasn't deaf or stupid—Lake had never thought him stupid—and the man followed their conversation with an intense if weary interest. Those eyes demanded that Lake save him. Lake looked away.

"The Raven here will give you his knife," the Owl said, "but do not think that just because you have a weapon you can escape." As if to prove this, the Owl produced a *gun,* one of those sleek, dangerous-looking models newly invented by the Kalif's scientists.

The Raven held out his knife.

Lake glanced at Voss Bender, then at the knife. A thin line of light played over the metal and the grainy whorls of the hilt. He could read the words etched into the blade, the name of the knife's maker: *Hoegbotton & Sons.* That the knife should have a history, a pedigree, that he should know more about the knife than about the three men struck him as absurd, as horrible. As he stared at the blade, at the words engraved there, the full, terrible weight of the deed struck him. To take a life. To snuff out a life, and with it a vast network of love and admiration. To create a hole in the world. It was no small thing to take a life, no small thing at all. He saw his father smiling at him, palms opened up to reveal the shiny, sleek bodies of dead insects.

"For God's sake, don't make me kill him!"

The burst of laughter from the Owl, the Raven, the Stork, surprised him so much that he laughed with them. He shook with laughter, his jaw, his shoulders, relaxed in anticipation of the revelation that it was all a joke . . . before he understood that their laughter was throaty, fey, cruel. Slowly, his laughter turned to sobs.

The Raven's hilarity subsided before that of the Owl and the Stork. He said to

Lake, "He is already dead. The whole city *knows* he's dead. You cannot kill someone who is already dead."

Voss Bender began to moan, and redoubled his efforts to break free of his bonds. The three men ignored him.

"I won't do it. I won't do it." His words sounded weak, susceptible to influence. He knew that faced with his own extinction he would do *anything* to stay alive, even if it meant corrupting, perverting, destroying, everything that made him Martin Lake. And yet his father's face still hovered in his head, and with that image everything his father had ever said about the sanctity of life.

The Owl said, with remorseless precision, "Then we will flay your face until it is only strips of flesh hanging from your head. We will lop off your fingers, your toes, as if they were carrots for the pot. You, sir, will become a bloody red riddle for some dog to solve in an alley somewhere. And Bender will still be dead."

Lake stared at the Owl and the Owl stared back, the owl mask betraying not a hint of weakness.

The eyes were cold wrinkled stones, implacable and ancient.

When the Raven offered Lake the knife, he took it. The lacquered wooden hilt had a satisfying weight to it, a smoothness that spoke of practiced ease in the arts of killing.

"A swift stroke across the throat and it will be done," the Raven said, while the Stork took a white length of cloth and tucked it over Bender's body, leaving exposed only his head and neck. How many times had he drawn his brush across a painted throat, the model before him fatally disinterested? He wished he had not taken so many anatomy classes. He found himself counting and naming the muscles in Bender's neck, cataloging arteries and veins, bones and tendons.

The Raven and the Stork withdrew to beyond the coffin. The divide between them and Lake was enormous, the knife cold and heavy in his hand. Lake could see that tiny flakes of rust had infected the center of each engraved letter of *Hoegbotton & Sons*.

He looked down at Voss Bender. Bender's eyes bulged, bloodshot, watery. The man pleaded with Lake through his gag, words Lake could only half understand. *"Don't . . . Don't . . . what have I . . . Help . . ."* Lake admired Bender's strength and yet, as he stood over his intended victim, Lake found another, more unsettling feeling rise to the surface. To have such *control*. This was the man he had only the other day been cursing, the man who had so changed the city that his death had polarized it, splintered it.

Voss Bender began to thrash about and, as if the movement had broken a spell, Lake's sense of triumph turned to disgust, buttressed by nausea. He let out a broken little laugh.

"I can't do it. I *won't* do it."

Lake tried to drop the knife, but the Raven's hand covered his and, turning into a fist, forced his own hand into a fist that guided the knife down into the coffin, making Lake stoop as it turned toward Bender's throat. The Stork held Bender's head straight, caressing the doomed man's temples with an odd gentleness. The Owl stood aloof, watching as an owl will the passion play beneath its perch. Lake grunted, struggling against the Raven's inexorable downward pressure. Just when it seemed he must succumb, he went limp. The knife descended at a hopeless angle, aided by Bender's mighty flinch. The blade did only half the job—laying open a flap of skin to the left of the jugular. Blood welled up truculently.

As if the stroke had been a signal, the Raven and the Stork stood back, breathing heavily. Bender made a choking gurgle; he sounded as if he might suffocate in his own blood.

Lake rocked back and forth on his knees.

The Owl said to his companions, "You lost your heads. Do you want his blood on our hands?"

Lake stared at the knife and at Voss Bender's incompetently cut throat, and back at the knife.

Blood had obscured all but the "Hoeg" in "Hoegbotton." Blood had speckled his left hand. It looked nothing like paint: it was too bright. It itched where it had begun to dry.

He closed his eyes and felt the walls of the study rush away from him until he stood at the edge of an infinite darkness. From a great distance, the Owl said, "He will die now. But slowly. Very slowly. Weaker and weaker until, having suffered considerable pain, he will succumb some hours or days hence. And we will not lift a feather or finger to help him. We will just watch. *Your* choice remains the same—finish him and live; don't and die with him."

Lake looked up at the Owl. "Why me?"

"How do you know you are the first? How do you know you were chosen?"

"That is your answer?"

"That is the only answer I shall ever give you."

"What could he have done to you for you to be so merciless?"

The Owl looked to the Raven, the Raven to the Stork, and in the sudden quaver, the slight shiver, that passed between them, Lake thought he knew the answer. He had seen the same look pass between artists in the cafés along Albumuth Boulevard as they verbally dissected some new young genius.

Lake laughed bitterly. "You're afraid of him, aren't you? You're envious and you want his power, but most of all, you fear him. You're too afraid to kill him yourself."

The Owl said, "Make your choice."

"And the hilarious thing," Lake said. "The hilarious thing is, you see, that once he's dead, you'll have made him *immortal*." Was he weeping? His face was wet under the mask. Lake watched, in the silence, the blood seeping from the wound in Bender's throat. He watched Bender's hands trembling as if with palsy.

What did the genius composer see in those final moments? Lake wondered later. Did he see the knife, the arm that held it, descending, or did he see himself back in Morrow, by the river, walking through a green field and humming to himself? Did he see a lover's face contorted with passion? Did he see a moment from before the creation of the fame that had devoured him? Perhaps he saw nothing, awash in the crescendo of his most powerful symphony, still thundering across his brain in a wave of blood.

As Lake bent over Voss Bender, he saw reflected in the man's eyes the black mask of the Raven, who had stepped nearer to watch the killing.

"Back away!" Lake hissed, stabbing out with the knife. The Raven jumped back.

Lake remembered how the man in his nightmare had cut his hand apart so methodically, so completely. He remembered his father's hands opening to reveal bright treasures, Shriek's response to his painting of his father's hands. Ah, but Shriek knew nothing. Even Raffe knew nothing. None of them knew as much as he knew now.

Then, cursing and weeping, his lips pulled back in a terrible snarl, he drew the blade across the throat, pushed down with his full weight, and watched as the life drained out of the world's most famous composer. He had never seen so much blood before, but worse still there was a moment, a single instant he would carry with him forever, when Bender's eyes met his and the dullness of death crept in, extinguishing the brightness, the spark, that had once been a life.

❁

"Through His Eyes" has an attitude toward perspective unique among Lake's works, for it is painted from the vantage point of the dead Voss Bender in an open coffin (an apocryphal event—Bender was cremated), looking up at the people who are looking down, while perspective gradually becomes meaningless, so that beyond the people looking down, we see the River Moth superimposed against the sky and mourners lining its banks. Of the people who stare down at Bender, one is Lake, one is a hooded insect catcher, and three are wearing masks—in fact, a reprisal of the owl, raven, and stork from "The Burning House." Four other figures stare as well, but they are faceless. The scenes in the background of this monstrously huge canvas exist in a world which has curved back on itself, and the details conspire to convince us that we see the sky, green fields, a city of wood, and the river banks simultaneously.

As Venturi writes, "The colors deepen the mystery: evening is about to fall and the river is growing dim; reds are intense or sullen, yellows and greens are deep-dyed; the sinister greenish sky is a cosmetic reflection of earthly death." The entirety of the painting is ringed by a thin line of red that bleeds about a quarter of an inch inward. This unique frame suggests a freshness out of keeping with the coffin, while the background scenes are thought to depict Lake's ideal of Bender's youth, when he roamed the natural world of field and river. Why did Lake choose to show Bender in a coffin? Why did he choose to use montage? Why the red line? Some experts suggest that we ignore the coffin and focus on the red line and the swirl of images, but even then can offer no coherent explanation.

Even more daring, and certainly unique, "Aria for the Brittle Bones of Winter" creates an equivalence between sounds and colors: a musical scale based on the pictorial intensity of colors in which "color is taken to speak a mute language." The "hero" rides through a crumbling graveyard to a frozen lake. The sky is dark, but the reflection of the moon, which is also a reflection of Voss Bender's face, glides across the lake's surface. The reeds which line the lake's shore are composed of musical notes, so cleverly interwoven that their identity as notes is not at first evident. Snow is falling, and the flakes are also musical notes—fading notes against the blue-black sky, almost as if Bender's aria is disintegrating even as it is being performed.

In this most ambitious of all his paintings, Lake uses subtle gradations of white, gray, and blue to mimic the progression of the aria itself—indeed, his brush-strokes, short or long, rough or smooth, duplicate the aria's movement as if we were reading a sheet of music.

All of this motion in the midst of apparent motionlessness flows in the direction of the rider, who rides against the destiny of the aria as a counterpoint, a dissenting voice. The light of the moon shines upon the face of the rider, but, again, this is the light of the *reflection* so that the rider's features are illuminated from *below*, not above. The rider, haggard and sagging in the saddle, is unmistakably Lake. (Venturi describes the rider as "a rhythmic throb of inarticulate grief.") The rider's expression is abstract, fluid, especially in relation to the starkly realistic mode of the rest of the painting. Thus, he appears ambivalent, undecided, almost unfinished—and, certainly, at the time of the painting, and in relation to Voss Bender, Lake *was* unfinished.

If "Aria for the Brittle Bones of Winter" is not as popular as even the experimental "Through His Eyes," it may be because Lake has employed too personal an iconography, the painting meaningful only to him. Whereas in "Invitation" or "Burning House," the viewer feels empowered—welcomed—to share in the personal revelation, "Aria . . ." feels like a closed system, the artist's eye looking too far inward. Even the doubling of image and name, the weak pun implicit in the painting's lake and the painter Lake, cannot help us to understand the underpinnings of such a work. As Venturi wrote, "While Lake's canvases do not generally inflict a new language upon us, when they do, we have no guide to translate for us." The controversial art critic Bibble has gone so far as to write, in reference to "Aria," "[Lake's] paintings are so many tombstones, so many little deaths—on canvases too big for the wall in their barely suppressed violence."

Be this as it may, there are linked themes, linked resonances, between "Invitation," "Through His Eyes," and "Aria . . ." These are tenuous connections, even mysterious connections, but I cannot fail to make them.

Lake appears in all three paintings—and only these three paintings. Only in the second painting, "Through His Eyes," do the insect catcher and Bender appear together. The insect catcher does appear in "Invitation" but not in "Aria . . ." (where, admittedly, he would be a bizarre and unwelcome intrusion). Bender appears in "Aria" and is implied in "Through His Eyes," but does not appear, implied or otherwise, in "Invitation." The question becomes: Does the insect catcher inhabit "Aria" unbeknownst to the casual observer—perhaps even in the frozen graveyard? And, more importantly, does the spirit of Voss Bender in some way haunt the canvas that is "Invitation to a Beheading"?—From Janice Shriek's *A Short Overview of the Art of Martin Lake and His Invitation to a Beheading*, for *The Hoegbotton Guide to Ambergris*, 5th edition.

Afterward, Lake stumbled out into the night. The fog had dissipated and the stars hung like pale wounds in the sky. He flung off his frog mask, retched in the gutter, and staggered to a brackish public fountain, where he washed his hands and arms to no avail: the blood would not come off. When he looked up from his frantic efforts, he found the mushroom dwellers had abandoned their battle with the pigs to watch him with wide, knowing eyes.

"Go away!" he screamed. "Don't look at me!"

Farther on, headed at first without direction, then with the vague idea of reaching his apartment, he washed his hands in public restrooms. He sanded his hands with gravel. He gnawed at them. None of it helped: the stench of blood only grew thicker. He was being destroyed by something larger than himself that was still somehow trapped inside him.

He haunted the streets, alleys, and mews through the tail end of the bureaucratic district, and down a ways into the greenery of the valley, until a snarling whippet drove him back up and into the merchant districts. The shops were closed, the lanterns and lamps turned low. The streets, in the glimmering light, seemed slick, wet, but were dry as chalk. He saw no one except for once, when a group of Reds and Greens burst past him, fighting each other as they ran, their faces contorted in a righteous anger.

"It doesn't mean *anything*!" Lake shouted after them. "He's *dead*!"

But they ignored him and soon, like some chaotic beast battling itself, moved out of sight down the street.

Over everything, as he wept and burned, Lake saw the image of Voss Bender's face as the life left it: the eyes gazing heavenward as if seeking absolution, the body taking one last full breath, the hands suddenly clutching at the ropes that bound, the legs vibrating against the coffin floor . . . and then *stillness*. Ambergris, cruel, hard city, would not let him forget the deed, for on every street corner Voss Bender's face stared at him—on posters, on markers, on signs.

Eventually, his leg tense with a gnawing ache, Lake fell down on the scarlet doorstep of a bawdy house. There he slept under the indifferent canopy of the night, beneath the horrible emptiness of the stars, for an hour or two—until the Madame, brandishing curses and a broom, drove him off.

As the sun's wan light infiltrated the city, exposing Red and Green alike, Lake found himself in a place he no longer understood, the streets crowded with faces he did not want to see, for surely they all stared at him: from the sidewalk sandwich vendors in their pointy orange hats and orange-striped aprons, to the bankers with their dark tortoiseshell portfolios, their maroon suits; from the white-faced, well-fed nannies of the rich to the bravura youths encrusted in crimson makeup that had outgrown them.

With this awareness of others came once again an awareness of himself. He noticed the stubble on his cheek, the grit between his teeth, the sour smell of his dirty clothes. Looking around him at the secular traffic of the city, Lake discovered a great hunger in him for the Religious Quarter, all thoughts of a return to his apartment having long since left his head.

His steps began to have purpose and speed until, arrived at his destination, he walked among the devotees, the pilgrims, the priests—stared speechless at the endless permutations of devotional grottoes, spires, domes, arches of the cathedrals of the myriad faiths, as if he had never seen them before. The Reds and Greens made no trouble here, and so refugees from the fury of their convictions flooded the streets.

The Church of the Seven-Pointed Star had an actual confessional box for sinners. For a long time Lake stood outside the church's modest wooden doors (above which rose an equally modest dome), torn between the need to confess, the fear of reprisal should he confess, and the conviction that he should not be forgiven. Finally, he moved on, accompanied by the horrid, gnawing sensation in his stomach that would be his burden for years. There was no one he could tell. No one. Now the Religious Quarter, too, confounded him, for it provided no answers, no relief. He wandered it as aimlessly as he had the city proper the night before. He thirsted, he starved, his leg tremulous with fatigue.

At last, on the Religious Quarter's outskirts, where it kissed the feet of the Bureaucratic Quarter, Lake walked through a glade of trees and was confronted by the enormous marble head of Voss Bender. The head had been ravaged by fire and overgrown by vines, and yet the lines of the mouth, the nose, stood out more heroically than ever, the righteous eyes staring at him. Under the weight of such a gaze, Lake could walk no farther. He fell against the soft grass and lay there, motionless in the shadow of the marble head.

It was not until late in the afternoon that Raffe found him there and helped him home to his apartment.

She spoke words at him, but he did not understand them. She pleaded with him. She cried and hugged him. He found her concern so tragically funny that he could not stop laughing. But he refused to tell her anything and, after she had forced food and water on him, she left him to find Merrimount.

As soon as he was alone again, Lake tore apart his half-finished commissions. Their smug fatuousness infuriated him. He spared only the paintings of his father's hands and the oil painting he had started the day before. He found himself still entranced by the greens against which the head of the man from nightmare jutted threateningly. The painting seemed to contain the soul of the city in all its wretched depravity, for of course the man with the knife was himself, the smile a grimace. He could not let the painting go, just as he could not bring himself to finish it.

✦❀✦

Sometimes what the painter chooses *not* to paint can be as important as what he does paint. Sometimes an absence can leave an echo all its own. Does Bender cry out to us by his absence? Many art critics have supposed that Lake must have met Bender during his first three years in Ambergris, but no evidence for this meeting exists; certainly, if he did meet with Bender, he failed to inform any of his friends or colleagues, which seems highly unlikely. Circumstantial evidence points to the stork-like shadow in "Invitation . . . ," as Bender had a well-known pathological fear of birds, but since Lake *also* had a pathological fear of birds, I cannot agree. (Some also find it significant that it is Lake's apparent wish, upon his death, to be cremated in similar fashion to Bender, his ashes spread over the River Moth.)

In the absence of more complete biographical information about Lake following this period, one must rely on such scanty information as exists in the history books. As is common knowledge, Bender's death was followed by a period of civil strife between the Reds and the Greens, culminating in a siege of the Voss Bender Memorial Post Office, which the Reds took by force only to be bloodily expelled by the Greens a short time later.

Could this, then, as some critics believe, be the message of "Invitation"? The screaming face of the man, the knife blade through the palm, which is wielded by Death, who has just claimed Voss Bender's life? Perhaps. But I believe in a more personal interpretation. Given what I know about Lake's relationship with his father, this personal meaning is all too clear. For in these three paintings, beginning with "Invitation," we see the repudiation of Lake by his natural father (the insect catcher) and Lake's embrace of Bender as his real, artistic father.

What, then, does "Invitation" tell us? It shows Lake's father metaphorically leaving his son. It shows his son, distraught, with a letter sent by his father—a letter which contains written confirmation of that repudiation. The "beheading" in "Invitation to a Beheading" is the dethroning of the king—his father . . . and yet, when a king is beheaded, a new king always takes his place.

Within days of this spiritual rejection, Voss Bender dies and for Lake the two events—the rejection by his father, the death of a great artist—are forever linked, and the only recourse open to him is worship of the dead artist, a path made possible through his upbringing by a mystical, religious mother. Thus, "Through His Eyes" is about the death and life of Bender, and the metaphorical death of his real father. "Aria . . ." gives Bender a resurrected face, a resurrected life, as the force, the light, behind the success of the haggard rider, who is grief-stricken because he has buried his real father in the frozen graveyard—has allowed his natural father to be eclipsed by the myth, the potency, of his new father, the moon, the reflection of himself: Bender.

In the end, these paintings are about Lake's yearning for a father he never had. Bender makes a safe father because, being dead, he can never repudiate the son who has adopted him. If the paintings discussed become increasingly more inaccessible, it is because their meaning becomes ever more personal.—From Janice Shriek's *A Short Overview of the Art of Martin Lake and His Invitation to a Beheading*, for *The Hoegbotton Guide to Ambergris*, 5th edition.

∗ ✦ ∗

The days continued on at their normal pace, but Lake existed outside of their influence. Time could not touch him. He sat for long hours on his balcony, staring out at the clouds, at the sly swallows that cut the air like silver-blue scissors. The sun did not heat him. The breeze did not make him cold. He felt hollowed out inside, he told Raffe when she asked how he was doing. And yet, "felt" was the wrong word, because he couldn't feel anything. He was unreal. He had no soul— would never love again, never *connect* with anyone, he was sure, and because he did not experience these emotions, he did not miss their fulfillment. They were extraneous, unimportant. Much better that he simply *be* as if he were no better, no worse, than a dead twig, a clod of dirt, a lump of coal. (Raffe: "You don't mean that, Martin! You can't mean that . . .") So he didn't paint. He didn't do much of anything, and he realized later that if not for the twinned love of Raffe and Merrimount, a love that he need not return, he might have died within a month. While they were helping him, he detested their help. He didn't deserve help. They must *leave him alone.* But they ignored his stares of hatred, his tantrums. Worst of all, they demanded no explanations. Raffe provided him with food and paid his rent. Merrimount shared his bed and comforted him when his nights, in stark and terrifying contrast to the dull, dead, uneventful days, were full of nightmares, detailed and hideous: the white of exposed throat, the sheen of sweat across the shadow of the chin, the lithe hairs that parted before the knife's path . . .

The week after Raffe had found him, Lake forced himself to attend Bender's funeral, Raffe and Merrimount insistent on attending with him even though he wanted to go alone.

The funeral was a splendid affair that traveled down to the docks via Albumuth Boulevard, confetti raining all the way. The bulk of the procession formed a virtual advertisement for Hoegbotton & Sons, the import-export business that had, in recent years, grabbed the major share of Ambergris trade. Ostensibly held in honor of Bender's operas, the display centered around a springtime motif, and in addition to the twigs, stuffed birds, and oversized bumblebees attached to the participants like odd extra appendages, the music was being played by a ridiculous full orchestra pulled along on a platform drawn by draft horses.

This display was followed by the senior Hoegbotton, his eyes two shiny black tears in an immense pale face, waving from the back of a topless Manzikert and looking for all the world as if he were running for political office. Which he was: Hoegbotton, of all the city's inhabitants, stood the best chance of replacing Bender as unofficial ruler of the city . . .

In the back seat of Hoegbotton's Manzikert sat two rather reptilian-looking men, with slitted eyes and cruel, sensual mouths. Between them stood the urn with Bender's ashes: a pompous, gold-plated monstrosity. It was their number—three—and Hoegbotton's mannerisms that first roused Lake's suspicions, but suspicions they remained, for he had *no proof.* No telltale feathers ensnarled for a week to now slowly spin and drift down from the guilty parties to Lake's feet.

The rest of the ceremony was a blur for Lake. At the docks, community leaders including Kinsky, Hoegbotton conspicuously absent, mouthed comforting platitudes to memorialize the man, then took the urn from its platform, pried open the lid, and cast the ashes of the world's greatest composer into the blue-brown waters of the Moth.

Voss Bender was dead.

Is my interpretation correct? I would like to think so, but one of the great challenges, the great allures, of a true work of art is that it either defies analysis or provides multiple theories for its existence. Further, I cannot fully explain the presence of the three birds, nor certain aspects of "Through His Eyes" with regard to the ring of red and the montage format.

Whatever the origin of and the statement made by "Invitation to a Beheading," it marked the beginning of Lake's illustrious career. Before, he had been an obscure painter. After, he would be classed among the greatest artists of the southern cities, his popularity as a painter soon to rival that of Bender as a composer. Lake would design wildly inventive sets for Bender operas and thus be responsible for an interpretive revival of those operas. He would be commissioned, albeit disastrously, to do commemorative work for Henry Hoegbotton, de facto ruler of Ambergris after Bender's death. His illustrations for the Truffidians' famous *Journal of Samuel Tonsure* would be revered as minor miracles of the engraver's art. Exhibitions of his work would even grace the Court of the Kalif himself, while nearly every year publishers would release a new book of his popular prints and drawings. In a hundred ways, he would rejuvenate Ambergris's cultural life and make it the wonder of the south. (In spite of which, he always seemed oddly annoyed, even stricken, by his success.) These facts are beyond doubt.

What, finally, was the mystery behind the letter held in the screaming man's hand, the mystery of "Invitation to a Beheading," we may never know.—From Janice Shriek's *A Short Overview of the Art of Martin Lake and His Invitation to a Beheading*, for *The Hoegbotton Guide to Ambergris*, 5th edition.

A year passed, during which, as Raffe and many of his other friends remarked to Lake, he appeared to be doing penance for some esoteric crime. He spent long hours in the Religious Quarter, haunting back alleys and narrow streets, searching in the dirty, antique light for those scenes, and those scenes alone which best embodied his grief and the cruelty, the dispassionate passion, of the city he had adopted as his home. He heard the whispers behind his back, the rumors that he had gone mad, that he was no longer a painter but a priest of an as yet unnamed religion, that he had participated in some unspeakable mushroom dweller ritual, but he ignored such talk; or, rather, it did not register with him.

Six months after Bender's funeral, Lake visited 45 Archmont Lane, new cane trembling in his hand. He found it a burnt-out husk, the only recognizable object amidst the ruins the bust of Trillian, blackened but intact. At first he picked it up, meaning to salvage it for his apartment, but as he wandered the wreckage for some sign of what had occurred there, the idea became distasteful, and he left the head in the rubble, its laconic eyes staring up at the formless sky. Nothing remained but the faint smell of carrion and smoke, rubbing against his nostrils. It might as well have been a dream.

Later that month, Lake asked Merrimount—lovely Merrimount, precious Merrimount—to move in with him permanently. He did not know he was going to ask Merri, but as the words left his lips they felt like the right words and Merri, tears in his eyes, said yes, smiling for the first time since before Lake's ordeal. They celebrated at a café, Raffe giving her guarded approval, Sonter and Kinsky bringing gifts and good cheer.

Things went better for Lake after that. Although the nightmares still afflicted him, he found that Merrimount's very presence helped him to forget, or at least disremember. He went by Shriek's gallery and took all of his paintings back, burning them in a barrel behind his apartment building. He began to frequent the Ruby-Throated Calf again. His father even visited in late winter, a meeting which went better than expected, even after the guarded old man realized the nature of his son's relationship with Merrimount. He seemed genuinely touched when Lake presented him with the twin paintings of his own hands covered with insects, and with that approval Lake felt himself awakening even more. There were cracks in the ice. A light amid the shadows.

Yet Ambergris—city of versions and virgins both—did its best to remind him of the darkness. Everywhere, new tributes to Bender sprang up, for Bender's popularity had never been so high. It could be said with confidence that the man might never fade from memory. Under the vengeful eyes of Bender statues, posters, and memorial buildings, the Reds and Greens gradually lost their focus and exhausted themselves. Some merged with traditional political factions, but many died in a final confrontation at the Voss Bender Memorial Post Office. By spring, Ambergris seemed much as it had before Bender's death.

It was in the spring, one chilly morning, that Lake sat down in front of the unfinished painting of the man from his nightmare. The man smiled with his broken teeth, as if in warning, but he wasn't fearsome anymore. He was lonely and sad, trapped by the green paint surrounding his face.

Lake had snuck out of bed, so as not to disturb his still-sleeping lover, but now he felt Merri's eyes upon his back. Gingerly, he picked up a brush and a new tube of moss-green paint. The brush handle felt rough, grainy, the paint bottle smooth and sleek. His grasp on the brush was tentative but strong. The paint smelled good to him and he could feel his senses awakening to its promise. The sun from the balcony embraced him with its warmth.

"What are you doing?" Merrimount mumbled.

Lake turned, the light streaming from the window almost unbearable, and said, with a wry, haunted grin, "I'm painting."

the

Strange

Case

of

X

The objects that are being summoned assemble, draw near from different spots; in doing so, some of them have to overcome not only the distance of space but that of time: which named, you may wonder, is more bothersome to cope with, this one or that, the young poplar, say, that once grew in the vicinity but was cut down long ago, or the singled-out courtyard which still exists today but is situated far away from here?

—Vladimir Nabokov, "The Leonardo"

t was damp and unpleasant that morning, a methodical drizzle drifting down out of a dull gray sky. An ephemeral rain he might have thought, and yet the buildings, discolored and blackened in their sooty ranks, steeped in the smell of gasoline and hay mixed with dung, seemed to have been contoured and worn down by it, or at least *resigned* to it. The few passersby on the street, shivering against the cold, were subdued, anonymous, sickly; their shoes made wet *splacking* noises in the puddles. The sound, startling in the silence, depressed him and he was glad to reach his destination, glad when the glass doors closed behind him, shutting out the smell of the rain.

Inside, the ironic smell of mold and a sickly sweet sterility. He sneezed and put down his briefcase. He took off his galoshes, placed them by the door. Removed his raincoat, which looked as if the rain had worn grooves into it, and hooked it on the absurdly sinister coat rack with its seething gargoyle heads. He shook himself, stray water drops spraying in all directions, straightened his tie, and smoothed back his hair. Bemoaned the lack of coffee. Took a slip of paper from his jacket pocket. Room 54. Downstairs. Down many stairs.

He stared across the empty hall. White and gray tile. Anonymous doors. Sheets of dull lighting from above most of it aflicker with abnormalities. And clocks—clocks created for bureaucrats so that they formed innocuous gray circles every few yards, their dull hands clucking quietly. He could only hear them because most of the staff was away for the holidays. The emptiness lent a certain ease to his task. He meant to take his time.

He picked up his briefcase and walked up the hall, shoes squeaking against the shiny tile floor; amazingly enough, the janitorial staff had recently waxed it.

He passed a trio of coat racks, all three banal in their repetition of gargoyles, and not at all in keeping with the dream of a modern facility dreamt by his superiors. Ahead, a lone security guard stood at attention in a doorway. The man, gaunt to the point of starvation, looked neither right nor left. He nodded as he passed but the guard did not even blink. Was the guard dead? The man smelled of old leather and tar. Would he smell of old leather and tar if he was dead? Somehow the thought amused him.

He turned left onto another colorless, musty corridor, this time lit reluctantly by oval lightbulbs in ancient fixtures that might once have been brass-colored but were now a gunky black.

As he walked, he made a note of the water dripping from the ceiling; better that the janitors fix leaks than wax floors. Before you knew it, mold would be clotting the walls and mushrooms sprouting from the most unexpected places.

He approached a length of corridor where so much mud had been tracked in by way of footprints that a detective (which, strictly speaking, he was not) would have assumed a scuffle had broken out among a large group of untidy, rather frenzied and determined, individuals. Perhaps it had; patients often did not like being labeled patients.

The mud smell thickened the air, but entwined around it, rooted within it, another smell called to him: a fragrance both fresh and unexpected. He stopped, frowned, and sniffed once, twice. He turned to his left and looked down. In the crack between the wall and the floor, amid a patch of what could only be dirt, a tiny rose blossomed, defiantly blood-red.

He bent over the flower. How rare. How lovely. He blinked, took a quick look down the corridor to his right and left. No one.

Deftly, he plucked the rose, avoiding the thorns on the stem. Straightening up, he stuck the flower through the second buttonhole of his jacket, patted his jacket back into place, and continued down the corridor.

Soon he came to a junction, with three corridors radiating out to left, right, and center. Without hesitation, he chose the left, which slanted downward. The air quickly became colder, mustier, and overlaid with the faint scent of . . . *trout?* (Were cats hoarding fish down here?) The light grew correspondingly dimmer. He had hoped to review the files on "X" before reaching Room 54, but found it an impossible task in the gloom. (Another note to the janitors? Perhaps not. They were an unruly lot, unaccustomed to reprimand, and they might make it difficult for him. No matter: the words of his colleagues still reverberated in his head: "X is trapped between the hemispheres of his own brain"; "X is a tough nut to crack"; "X will make an excellent thesis on guilt.")

No matter. And although he appreciated the position of those who believed the building should be renovated to modern standards, he did enjoy the walk, for it created a sense of mystery, an atmosphere conducive to exploration and discovery. He had always thought that, in a sense, he shed irrelevant parts of himself on the long walk, that he became very much *functional* in his splendid efficiency.

He turned left, then right, always descending. He had the sensation of *things flitting* through the air, just on the verge of brushing his skin. A coppery taste suffused the air, as if he were licking doorknobs or bedposts. The bulbs became irregular, three burnt out for each buttery round glow. His shoes scraped against unlikely things in the darkness that lay beneath his feet.

Finally, he reached the black spiral staircase that led to Room 54. A true baroque monstrosity, in the spirit of the gargoyle coat racks, it twisted and turned crankily, almost spitefully, into a well of darkness dispelled only by the occasional glimmer of railing as it caught the light of the single, dull bulb hanging above it. Of all the building's eccentricities, he found the staircase the most delightful. He descended slowly, savoring the feel of the wrought-iron railings, the roughness of the black paint where it had chipped and weathered to form lichen-shaped patterns. The staircase smelled of history, of ancestors, of another world.

By the time he had reached the bottom, he had shed the last of his delight, his self-interest, his selfishness, his petty irritations, his past. All that remained were curiosity, compassion, instinct, and the rose: a bit of color; a bit of misdirection.

He fumbled for the light switch, found it, and flooded the small space beneath the stairs with stale yellow. He took out his keys. Opened the door. Entered. Closed it behind him.

Inside, he blinked and shaded his eyes against the brightness of superior lighting. Smell of sour clothes. Faint musk of urine. Had X been marking his territory?

When his eyes adjusted, he saw a desk, a typewriter, a bed, a small provision of canned goods, and a separate room for the toilet. Windows—square, of a thick, syrupy glass—lined the walls at eye level, but all that lay beyond them was the blankness of dirt, of mortar, of cement.

The writer sat behind the desk, on a rickety chair. But he wasn't writing. He was staring at me.

I smiled, put down my briefcase. I took off my jacket, careful not to disturb the rose, and laid it over the arm of the nearest chair.

"Good morning," I said, still smiling.

He continued to observe me. Very well, then, I would observe him back. We circled each other with our eyes.

From the looseness of his skin, I deduced that he had once been fat, but no longer; he had attained the only thinness possible for him: a condition which suggests thinness, which *alludes to* thinness, but is only a pale facsimile at best. He had too much skin, and broad shoulders with a barrel chest. His mouth had fixed itself halfway between a laconic grin and a melancholy frown. A new beard had sprouted upon his chin (it was not unkind to him) while above a slight, almost feminine, nose, his blue eyes pierced the light from behind the golden frames of his glasses. He wore what we had given him: a nondescript pair of slacks, a white shirt, and a brown sweater over the shirt.

What did he smell of? A strangeness I could not identify. A hint of lilacs in the spring. The waft of rain-soaked air on a fishing boat, out on the river. The draft from a door opening onto a room full of old books.

Finally, he spoke: "You are here to question me. Again. I've already answered all the questions. Numerous times." A quaver in the voice. Frustration barely held in check.

"You must answer them one more time," I said. Briefcase again in hand, I walked forward until I stood in front of his desk.

He leaned back in his chair, put his hands behind his head. "What will that accomplish?"

I did not like his ease. I did not like his comfort. I decided to break him of it.

"I'll not mislead you: I am here to decide your final disposition. Should we lock you away for five or ten years, or should we find some other solution? But do not think you can lie your way into my good graces. You have, after all, answered these questions several times. We must reach an understanding, you and I, based solely on your current state of mind. I can smell lies, you know. They may look like treacle, but they smell like poison."

I had given this speech, or a variant of it, so many times that it came all too easily to me.

"Let me not mislead you," he replied, no longer leaning back in his chair, "I am now firmly of the belief that Ambergris, and all that is associated with Ambergris, is a figment of my imagination. I no longer believe it exists."

"I see. This information does not in any way mean I will now pack up my briefcase and set you free. I must question you."

He looked as if he were about to argue with me. Instead, he said, "Then let me clear the desk. Would you like me to give you a statement first?"

"No. My questions shall provide you with the means to make a statement." I smiled as I said it, for although he need not hope too much, neither did I wish to drive him to despair.

X was not a strong man and I had to help him lift the typewriter off the desk;

it was an old, clunky model and its keys made a metallic protest when we set it on the floor.

When we had sat down, I took out a pen and pad of paper. "Now, then, do you know where you are and why?"

"I am in a Chicago psychiatric ward because I have been hallucinating that a world of my creation is actually real."

"When and where were you born?"

"Belfont, Pennsylvania. In 1968."

"Where did you grow up?"

"My parents were in the Peace Corps—are you going to write all of this down again? The scribbling irritates me. It sounds like cockroaches scuttling."

"You don't like cockroaches?"

He scowled at me.

"As you like."

I pulled his file out of my briefcase. I arranged the transcripts in front of me. A few words flashed out at me: *fire . . . Trial . . . of course I loved her . . . control . . . the reality . . . It was in the room with me . . .*

"I shall simply check off on these previous interrogatories duplications of answers. I shall only write down your answers when they are new or stray from the previous truths you have been so kind as to provide us with. Now: Where did you grow up?"

"In the Fiji Islands."

"Where is that?"

"In the South Pacific."

"Ah . . . What was your family like? Any brothers or sisters?"

"Extremely dysfunctional. My parents fought a lot. One sister—Vanessa."

"Did you get along with your sister? How dysfunctional?"

"I got along with my sister better than Mom and Dad. Very dysfunctional. I'd rather not talk about that—it's all in the transcripts. Besides, it only helps explain why I write, not why I'm delusional."

In the transcripts he'd called it the "ten-year divorce." Constant fighting. Verbal and some physical abuse. Nasty, but not all that unusual. It is popular to analyze a patient's childhood these days to discover that one trauma, that one unforgivable incident, which has shaped or ruined the life. But I did not care if his childhood had been a bedsore of misery, a canker of sadness. I was here to determine what he believed *now*, at this moment. I would ask him the requisite questions about that past, for such inquiries seemed to calm most patients, but let him tell or not tell. It was all the same to me.

"Any visions or hallucinations as a child?"

"No."

"None?"

"None."

"In the transcripts, you mention a hallucination you had, when you thought you saw two hummingbirds mating on the wing from a hotel room window. You were sick, and you said, rather melodramatically, 'I thought if I could only hold them, suspended, with my stare, I could forever feast upon their beauty. But finally I had to call to my sister and parents, took my eyes from the window, and even as I turned back, the light had changed again, the world had changed, and I knew they were gone. There I lay, at altitude, on oxygen—'"

"—But that's not a hallucination—"

"—Please don't interrupt. I'm not finished: 'on oxygen and, suddenly, at my most vulnerable, the world had revealed the very extremity of its grace. For me, the moment had been Divine, as fantastical as if those hummingbirds had flown out of my mouth, my eyes, my thoughts.' That is not a hallucination?"

"No. It's a statement on beauty. I really did see them—the hummingbirds."

"Is beauty important to you?"

"Yes. Very important."

"Do you think you entered another world when you saw those hummingbirds?"

"Only figuratively. I'm very balanced, you know, between my logical father and my illogical mother. I know what's real and what's not."

"That is not for you to determine. And what do your parents do? No one seems to have asked that question."

"My dad's an entomologist—studies bugs, not words. My mom's an artist. And an author. She's done a book on graveyard art."

"Ah!" I took out two items that had been on his person when he had been brought here: a book entitled *City of Saints and Madmen* and a page of cartoon images. "So you are a writer. You take after your mother."

"No. Yes. Maybe."

"I guess that would explain why we gave you a typewriter: you're a writer. I'm being funny. Have the decency to laugh. Now, what have you been writing?"

"'I will not believe in hallucinations' one thousand times."

"It's my turn to be rude and not laugh." I held up *City of Saints and Madmen.* "You wrote this book."

"Yes. It's sold over one million copies worldwide."

"Funny. I'd never heard of it until I saw this copy."

"Lucky you. I wish *I'd* never heard of it."

"But then, I rarely read modern authors, and when I do it is always thrillers. A straight diet of thrillers. None of the poetics for me, although I do dabble in writing myself . . . I did read this one, though, when I was assigned to your case. Don't you want to hear what I thought about it?"

X snorted. "No. I get—got—over a hundred fan letters a day. After a while, you just want to retire to a deserted island."

"Which is exactly what you have done, I suppose. Metaphorically." Only the island had turned out to be inhabited. All the worse for him.

He ignored my probing, said, "Do you think I *wanted* to write that stuff? When the book came out, all anyone wanted were more Ambergris stories. I couldn't *sell* anything *not* set in Ambergris. And then, after the initial clamor died down, I *couldn't* write anything else. It was horrible. I'd spend ten hours a day at the typewriter just making this world I'd created more and more real in this world. I felt like a sorcerer summoning up a demon."

"And this? What is this?" I held up the sheet of cartoons:

"Sample drawings from Disney—no doubt destined to become a collector's item—for the animated movie of my novella 'Dradin, In Love.' It should be coming out next month. Surely you've heard of it?"

"I don't go to the movies."

"What do you do then?"

"Question sick people about their sicknesses. It would be good to think of me as a blank slate, that I know nothing. This will make it easier for you to avoid leaving out important elements in your answers . . . I take it your books are grossly popular then?"

"Yes," he said, with obvious pride. "There are Dwarf & Missionary role-playing games, Giant Squid screen savers, a 'greatest hits' CD of Voss Bender arias sung by the three Tenors, plastic action figures of the mushroom dwellers, even Ambergris conventions. All pretty silly."

"You made a lot of money in a relatively condensed period of time."

"I went from an income of $15,000 a year to something close to $500,000 a year, after taxes."

"And you were continually surrounded by the products of your imagination, often given physical form by other people?"

"Yes."

Razor-sharp interrogator's talons at the ready, I zeroed in, no longer anything but a series of questions in human guise, as elegant as a logarithm. I'd tear the truth right out of him, be it bright or bloody.

INTERROGATOR: When did you begin to sense something was amiss?

X: The day I was born. A bit of fetal tissue didn't form right and, presto!, a cyst, which I had to have removed from the base of my spine twenty-four years later.

I: Let me remind you that if I leave this room prematurely, *you* may never leave this room.

X: Don't threaten me. I don't respond well to threats.

I: Who does? Begin again, but please leave out the sarcasm.

X: . . . It started on a day when I was thinking out a plotline—the story for what would become "The Transformation of Martin Lake." I was walking in downtown Tallahassee, where I used to live, past some old brick buildings. The streets are all narrow and claustrophobic, and I was trying to imagine what it might be like to *live* in Ambergris. This was a year after the U.S. publication of *City of Saints and Madmen*, and they wanted more stories to flesh out a second book. I was pretty deep into my own thoughts. So I turn a corner and I look up, and there, for about six seconds—too long for a mirage, too short for me to be certain—I saw, clotted with passersby— the Borges Bookstore, the Aqueduct, and, in the distance, the masts of ships at the docks: all elements from my book. I could smell the briny silt of the river and the people were so close I could have reached out and touched them. But when I started to walk forward, it all snapped back into reality. It just snapped . . .

I: So you thought it was real.

X: I could smell the street—piss and spice and horse. I could smell the savory aroma of chicken cooking in the outdoor stoves of the sidewalk vendors. I could feel the breeze off the river against my face. The light— the light was *different*.

I: How so?

X: Just different. Better. Cleaner. *Different.* I found myself saying, "I cannot capture the quality of this light in paint," and I knew I had the central problem, the central question, of my character's—Martin Lake's— life.

I: Your character, you will pardon me, does not interest me. I want to know why you started to walk forward. In at least three transcripts, you say you walked forward.

X: I don't know why.

I: How did you feel after you saw this . . . image?

X: Confused, obviously. And then horrified because I realized I must have some kind of illness—a brain tumor or something.

I stared at him and frowned until he could not meet my gaze.

"You know where we are headed," I said. "You know where we are going. You may not like it, but you must face it." I gestured to the transcripts. "There are things you have not said here. I will indulge you by teasing around the edges for a while longer, but you must prepare yourself for a more blunt approach."

X picked up my copy of *City of Saints and Madmen*, began to flip through it. "You know," he said, "I am so thoroughly sick of this book. I kept waiting for the inevitable backlash from the critics, the trickling off of interest from readers. I really wanted that. I didn't see how such success could come so . . . effortlessly. Imagine my distress to find this world I had grown sick of, waiting for me around the corner."

"Liar!" I shouted, rising and bending forward, so my face was inches from his face. "Liar! You walked toward that vision because it fascinated you! Because you found it irresistible. Because you saw something of the real world there! And afterward, you weren't sorry. You weren't sorry you'd taken those steps. Those steps seemed like the only sane thing to do. You didn't even tell your wife . . . your wife"—he looked at me like I'd become a living embodiment of the coat rack gargoyles while I rummaged through the papers—"your wife, Hannah, that you had had a vision, that you were worried about having a brain tumor. You *told* us that already. Didn't I tell you *not* to lie to me?"

This speech, too, I had given many times, in many different forms. X looked shaken to the core by it.

X: Haven't you ever . . . Wouldn't you like to live in a place with more mystery, with more color, with more life? *Here* we know everything, we can do everything. Me, I worked for five years as a technical editor putting together city ordinances in book form. I didn't even have a window in my office. Sometimes, as I was codifying my fiftieth, my seventy-fifth, my one hundredth wastewater ordinance, I just wanted to get up, smash my computer, set my office on fire, and burn the whole rotten, horrible place down . . . The world is so small. Don't you ever want—need—more mystery in your life?

I: Not at the expense of my sanity. When did you begin to realize that, as you put it, "I had not created Ambergris, but was merely describing a place that already existed, that was real"?

X: You're a bastard, you know that?

I: It's my function. Tell me what happened next.

X: For six months, everything was normal. The second book came out and was a bigger success than the first. I was flying high. I'd almost forgotten those six seconds in Tallahassee . . . Then we took a vacation to New Orleans, my wife and me—partly to visit our friend and writer Nathan Rogers, and partly for a writers' convention. We usually go to as many bookstores as we can when we visit other cities—there are so many out-of-print books I want to get hold of, and Hannah, of course, likes to see how many of the new bookstores carry her magazine, and if they don't, get them to carry it. So I was in an old bookstore with Hannah—in the French Quarter, a real maze to get there. A real maze, which is half the fun. And once there, I was anxious to buy something, to make the effort worthwhile. But I couldn't find anything to buy, which was killing me, because sometimes I just have a compulsion to buy books. I guess it's a security blanket of sorts. But when I rummaged through the guy's discard cart—the owner was a timid old man without any eyebrows—I found a paperback of Frederick Prokosch's *The Seven Who Fled* so I bought that.

I: And it included a description of Ambergris?

X: No, but the newspaper he had wrapped it in was a weathered broadsheet published by Hoegbotton & Sons, the exporter-importer in my novel.

I: They do travel guides, too?

X: Yes. You have a good memory . . . We didn't even notice the broadsheet until we got back to the hotel. Hannah was the one who noticed it.

I: Hannah noticed it.

X: Yeah. She thought it was a prank I was playing on her, that I'd put it together for her. I'll admit I've done that sort of thing before, but not this time.

I: You must have been ecstatic that she found it.

X: Wildly so. It meant I had physical proof, and an independent witness. It meant I wasn't crazy.

I: Alas, you never found that particular bookstore again.

X: More accurately, it never found us.

I: But Hannah believed you.

X: She at least knew something odd had happened.

I: You no longer possess the broadsheet, however.

X: It burned up with the house later on.

I: Yes, the much alluded to fire, which also conveniently devoured all of the other evidence. What was the other evidence?

X: Useless to discuss it—it doesn't exist anymore.

I: Discuss it briefly anyway—for my sake.

X: Okay. For example, later we visited the British Museum in London. There was an ancient, very small, almost miniature altar in a glass case in a forgotten corner of the Egyptian exhibits. Behind a sarcophagus. The piece wasn't labeled, but it certainly didn't look Egyptian. Mushroom designs were carved into it. I saw a symbol that I'd written about in a story. In short, I thought it was a mushroom dweller religious object. You remember the mushroom dwellers from *City of Saints and Madmen*?

I: I am familiar with them.

X: There were two tiny red flags rising from what would normally be considered incense holders. It was encrusted with gems showing a scene that could only be a mushroom dweller blood sacrifice. I took pictures. I asked an attendant what it was. He didn't know. And when we came back the next day, it was gone. Couldn't find the attendant, either. That's a pretty typical example.

I: You *wanted* to believe in Ambergris.

X: Perhaps. At the time.

I: Let us return to the question of the broadsheet. Did you believe it was real?

X: Yes.

I: What was the subject of the broadsheet?

X: Purportedly, it was put out by Hoegbotton on behalf of a group called the "Greens," denouncing the "Reds" for having somehow caused the death of the composer Voss Bender.

I: You had already written about Voss Bender in your book, correct?

X: Yes, but I'd never heard of the Greens and the Reds. That was the lucky thing—I'd put my story "The Transformation of Martin Lake" aside because I was stuck, and that broadsheet unstuck me. The Reds and Greens became an integral part of the story.

I: Nothing about the broadsheet, on first glance, struck you as familiar?

X: I'm not sure I follow you. What do you mean by "familiar"?

I: Nothing inside you, a voice perhaps, told you that you had seen it before?

X: You think I created the broadsheet and then blocked the memory of having done so? That I somehow then planted it in that bookstore?

I: No. I mean simply that sometimes one part of the brain will send a message to another part of the brain—a warning, a sign, a symbol. Sometimes there is a . . . division.

X: I don't even know how to respond to such a suggestion.

I sighed, got up from my chair, walked to the opposite end of the room, and stared back at the writer. He had his head in his hands. His breathing made his head bob slowly up and down. Was he weeping?

"Of course this process is stressful," I said, "but I must have definitive answers to reach the correct decision. I cannot spare your feelings."

"I haven't seen my wife in over a week, you know," he said in a small voice. "Isn't it against the law to deny me visitors?"

"You'll see whoever chooses to see you after we finish, no matter the outcome. *That* I can promise you."

"I want to see Hannah."

"Yes, you talk a great deal about Hannah in the transcripts. It seems to reassure you to think of her."

"If she's not real, I'm not real," he muttered. "And I know she's real."

"You loved her, didn't you?"

"I *still* love my wife."

"And yet you persisted in following your delusions?"

"Do you think I wanted it to be real?" he said, looking up at me. His eyes were red. I could smell the salt of his tears. "I thought I'd dug it all out of my imagination, and so I have, but at the time . . . I've lost the thread of what I wanted to say . . ."

Somehow, his confusion, his distress, touched me. I could tell that a part of him *was* sane, that he truly struggled with two separate versions of reality, but just as I could see this, I could also see that he would probably always remain in this limbo where, in someone else, the madness would have won out long ago . . . or the sanity.

But, unfortunately, it is the nature of the writer to question the validity of his world and yet to rely on his senses to describe it. From what other tension can great literature be born? And thus, he was trapped, condemned by his nature, those gifts and talents he had honed and perfected in pursuit of his craft. Was he a good writer? The answer meant nothing: even the worst writer sometimes sees the world in this light.

"Do you need an intermission?" I asked him. "Do you want me to come back in half an hour?"

"No," he said, suddenly stubborn and composed. "No break."

I: After the broadsheet incident, you began to see Ambergris quite often.

X: Yes. I was in New York City three weeks after New Orleans, on business—this is before we actually moved north—and I stayed at my agent's house. I took a shower one morning and as I was washing my hair, I closed my eyes. When I opened them, rain was coming down and I was naked in a dirty side alley in the Religious Quarter.

I: Of New York?

X: No—of Ambergris, of course. The rain was fresh and cold on my skin. A group of boys stared at me and giggled. The cobblestones were rough against my feet. My hair was still thick with shampoo . . . I spent five minutes huddled in that alley while the boys called to passersby beyond the alley mouth. I was an exhibit. A curiosity. They thought I was a Living Saint, you see, who had escaped from a church, and they kept asking me which church I belonged to. They threw coins and books—books!—at me as payment for my blessings while I shouted at them to go away. Finally, I ran out of the alley and hid at a public altar. I was crowded together with a thousand mendicants, many wearing only a loincloth, who were all chanting what sounded like obscure obscenities as loudly as they could. At some point, I closed my eyes again, wondering if I could possibly be dreaming, and when I opened them, I was back in the shower.

I: Was there any evidence that you'd been "away," as it were?

X: My feet were muddy. I could swear my feet were muddy.

I: You took something with you out of Ambergris?

X: Not that I knew of at the time. Later, I realized something had come with me . . .

I: You sound as if you were terrified.

X: I *was* terrified! It was one thing to see Ambergris from afar, to glean information from book wrappings, totally different to be deposited naked into that world.

I: You found it more frightening than New York?

X: What do you mean by that?

I: A joke, I guess. Tell me more about New York. I've never been there.

X: What's to tell? It's dirty and gray and yet more alive than any city except—

I: Ambergris?

X: I didn't say that. I may have thought it, but then a city out of one's imagination would have to be more alive, wouldn't it?

I: Not necessarily. I would have liked to have heard more about New York from your unique perspective, but you seem agitated and—

X: And it's completely irrelevant.

I: No doubt. What did you do after the incident in New York?

X: I flew back to Tallahassee without finishing my business . . . what did I say? You look startled.

I: Nothing. It's nothing. Continue. You flew back without finishing your business.

X: And I told Hannah we were going on vacation *right now* for two weeks. We flew to Corfu and had a great time with my Greek publisher—no one recognized me there, see? Hannah's daughter, Sarah, loved the snorkeling. The water was incredible. This clear blue. You could see to the bottom.

I: What did Sarah think of Ambergris?

X: She never read the books. She was really too young, and she always made a great show of being unimpressed by my success. I can't blame her for that—she did the same thing to Hannah with her magazine.

I: Did the vacation make a difference?

X: It seemed to. No more visions for a long time. Besides, I'd reached a decision—I wasn't going to write about Ambergris ever again.

I: Did Hannah agree with your decision?

X: Without a doubt. She saw how shaken I'd been after getting back from New York. She just wanted whatever I thought was best.

I: Did it work out?

X: Obviously not. I'm sitting here talking to you, aren't I? But at first, it did work. I really thought that Ambergris would cease to exist if I just stopped writing about it. But my sickness went deeper than that.

I: I'm afraid we have reached a point where I must probe deeper. Tell me about the fire.

X: I don't want to.

I: Then tell me about the thing in your work room first.

X: Can't it wait? For a little while?

The dripping of water had become a constant irritation for me. If it had become an irritation, then I had failed to concentrate hard enough. I had not left enough of myself outside the room. I wondered how long the session would last—more specifically, how long my patience would last. If we are to be honest, the members of my profession, then we must recognize that our judgments are based on our own endurance. How long can we go on before we simply cannot stand to hear more and leave the room? Often the subject, the patient, has nothing to do with the decision.

"I hear music down here sometimes," X said, staring at the ceiling. "It comes from above. It sounds like some infernal opera. Is there an opera house nearby, or does someone in this building play opera?"

I stared at him. This part was always difficult. How could it fail to be?

"You are avoiding the matter at hand."

"What did you think of my book?" X asked. "One writer to another," he added, not quite able to banish the condescension from his voice.

Oddly enough, the first novella in the book, "Dradin, In Love," had struck me, on a very primitive level, as evidence of an underlying sanity, for X clearly had conceptualized Dradin as a madman. No delusions there, for Dradin *was* a madman. I had even theorized that X saw Dradin as his alter ego, but dismissed the idea on the basis that it is unwise to match events in a work of fiction with events in the writer's life.

Of course, I did not think it useful to share any of these thoughts with X, so I shrugged and said, "It was fanciful in its way and yet some of its aspects were as realistic as any hardboiled thriller. I thought 'Dradin, In Love' moved slowly. You devote an entire chapter to Dradin's walk back to his hostel."

"No, no, no! That's foreshadowing. That's symbolism. That's showing you the beginning of the carnage, in the form of the sleeping mushroom dwellers."

"Well, perhaps it did not speak to me as forcefully as you wanted it to. But you must remember, I was reading it for clues."

"As to my mental state? Isn't that dangerous?"

"Of course. To both questions. And I must also determine whether you most identify with Dradin, or the dwarf Dvorak, or the priest Cadimon, or even the Living Saint."

"A dead end. I identify with none of them. And all of them contain a part of me."

I shrugged. "I must gather clues where I can."

"You mean if I don't give you enough information."

"Some give me information without meaning to."

"I am not sure I can give you what you want."

"Actually," I said, picking up *City of Saints and Madmen*, "there was a passage in here that I found quite interesting. Not from 'Dradin, In Love,' but from this other story, 'Learning to Leave the Flesh.' You make a distinction in the introduction to that tale—you call it a forerunner to the Ambergris stories, and yet in your response to the other interrogatories, you say the story was written quite recently."

"Surely you know that a writer can create a precursor tale after he has written the tales which come after, just as he can write the final tale in a series before he has finished writing the others."

The agitation had returned to X's features, almost as if he knew I was steering the conversation back toward my original objective.

"True, true," I said as I turned pages, "but there is one passage—about the dwarf, Davy Jones, that interests me most. Ah, here it is—where Jones haunts the main character. Why don't you read it for me?" I handed it to him and he took it with a certain eagerness. He had a good reading voice, neither too shrill nor too professional.

"Then he stands at the foot of my bed, staring at me. A cold blue tint dyes his flesh, as if the TV's glow has burnt him. The marble cast of his face is as perfect as the most perfect sentence I have ever written. His eyes are so sad that I cannot meet his gaze. He speaks to me and although I cannot hear him, I know what he is saying. I am crying again, but softly, softly. The voices on the street are louder and the tinkling of bells so very light."

I: A very nice passage from a rather eccentric story. Whence came the dwarf? Did he walk out of your imagination or out of your life?

X: From life, at first. When I was going to college at the University of Florida, I had a classmate named David Wilson who was a dwarf. We took statistics together. He tutored me past the rough bits. He was poor but couldn't get enough financial aid and his overall grades weren't good enough for scholarships, so he rented himself out for dwarf-tossing contests at local bars. He had a talent for math, but here he was renting himself out to bars, and sometimes to the county fair when it came by. One day, he stopped coming to class and the next week I learned from a rather lurid article in the local paper that he had drunk himself to death.

I: Did he visit *you* at the foot of your bed?

X: You will remember I had resolved not to write about Ambergris ever again, but at first I resolved not to write at all. So I didn't. For five months I quit writing. It was hell. I had to turn a part of myself off. It was like a relentless itching in my brain. I had to unlearn taking notes on little pieces of paper. I had to unlearn making observations. Or, rather, I had to ignore these urges. And I was thinking about David Wilson because I had always wanted to write about him and couldn't. I guess I figured that if I thought about a story I couldn't write, I'd scratch the itch in a harmless way . . . And it was then that the dwarf—or what I thought was the dwarf—began to haunt me. He'd stand at the foot of the bed and . . . well, you read the story. To stop him from haunting me, I relented and sat down to write what became "Learning to Leave the Flesh."

I: But he was already Dvorak.

X: No. Dvorak was just a dwarf. He had nothing of David Wilson in him. David Wilson was a kind and gentle soul.

I: The story mentions Albumuth Boulevard.

X: Yes, it does. I had not only broken my vow not to write, but Ambergris had, in somewhat distorted form, crept back into my work.

I: Did you see the dwarf again?

X: One last time. When he became the manta ray. That was when I realized that I had brought something back from Ambergris with me. It scared the shit out of me.

I: The manta ray is mentioned in the transcripts, but never described. What is a manta ray?

X: You've never heard of a manta ray?

I: Perhaps under another name. What is it, please?

X: A big, black, saltwater . . . fish, I guess, but wide, with flaps like huge, graceful wings. Sleek. Smooth. Like a very large skate or flounder.

I: Ah! A flounder! You'll forgive my ignorance.

X: Clearly you devote too much time to your job.

I: You may be right, but to return to our topic: you were given *this fish* by the apparition of the dwarf. It is important that we get the symbolism correct.

X: No. The "fish" was the dwarf all along, leading me astray. The dwarf *became* the manta ray.

I: How did this happen?

X: I wish I could say Hannah saw it too, but she had fallen asleep. It was a cold night and I was wide awake, every muscle in my body tense. Suddenly, as before, Wilson stood at the foot of my bed. He just watched me for a long time, a smile upon his face . . . and then, as I watched him, he became like a pen-and-ink drawing of himself—only lines, with the rest of him translucent. And then this drawing began to fill up with cloudy black ink—like from a squid; do you know what a squid is?

I: Yes.

X: And when he was completely black with ink, the blackness oozed out from his body, until his body was eclipsed by the creature that looked exactly like a manta ray. It had tiny red eyes and it swam through the air. It terrified me. It horrified me. For the creature *was* Ambergris, come to reclaim me. The blackness of it was diffused by flashes of light through which I could see scenes of the city, of Ambergris, tattooed into its flesh—and they were *moving*. I hid under the covers, and when I looked again, in the morning, it was gone.

I: Did you tell your wife?

X: No! I should have, but I didn't. I felt as if I were going mad. I couldn't sleep. I could hardly eat.

I: This is when you lost all the weight?

X: Yes.

I: What, specifically, did you think this black creature was? Surely not "Ambergris," as you say?

X: I thought I'd brought it back with me from Ambergris—that it was a physical manifestation of my psychosis.

I: You thought it was a part of you. I know you were terrified by it, but did you ever, for a moment, consider that it might have been benevolent?

X: No!

I: I see. It has been my experience—and my experience is substantial—that some men learn to master their madness, so that even if all manner of horrific hallucinations surround them, they do not react. They live in a world where they cannot trust their senses, and yet no one would guess this from their outward composure.

X: I am not one of those men. It terrified me to my soul.

I: And yet such men find such hallucinations a blessing, for they give warning of a skewed reality. How much worse to slip—to just *slip*, as if slouching in your chair, as if blinking—into madness with no immediate sign that you had done so. So I call your visitation a helper, not a destroyer.

X: You may call it what you will. I did not think to call it anything.

I: What did you do to reestablish your equilibrium after this incident?

X: I began to write again. I spent eight to ten hours in my work room, scribbling away. Now I felt my only salvation *was* to write—and I wrote children's stories. "Sarah and the Land of Sighs" was the first one, and it went well. My agent liked it. It sold. Eventually, it won an honorable mention for the Caldecott. So I wrote more stories, except that at some point—and I still can't recall when exactly—the manta ray reappeared.

I: What was your reaction?

X: Fear. Pure, unadulterated fear.

I: Tell me what happened.

X: I will not discuss what happened. But I have written about it—a story fragment you could call it.

X reached under the desk and handed me a thin sheaf of papers. I took them with barely disguised reluctance.

"Fiction lies."

X snorted. "So do people."

"I will read with reservations."

"Yes, and if you'll excuse me . . ." He trotted off to use the bathroom.

Leaving me with the manuscript. The title was "The Strange Case of X."

I began to read.

The man sat in the room and wrote on a legal sheet. The room was small, with insufficient light, but the man had good pens so he did not care. The man was a writer. This is why he wrote. Because he was a writer. He sat alone in the room which had no windows and he wrote a story. Sometimes he listened to music while he wrote because music inspired him to write. The story he wrote was called "Sarah and the Land of Sighs" and it was his attempt to befriend the daughter of his wife, who was not his own daughter. His children were his stories, and they were not always particularly well-behaved. "Sarah and the Land of Sighs" was not particularly well-behaved. It had nothing at all to do with the world of Ambergris, which was the world he wrote about for adults (all writers have separate worlds they write about, even those writers who think they do not have separate worlds they write about). And yet, when he had finished writing for the day and reread what he had written, he found that bits and pieces of Ambergris were in his story. He did not know how they had gotten into his story but because he was a writer and therefore a god—a tiny god, a tiny, insignificant god, but a god nonetheless—he took his pen and he slew the bits and pieces of Ambergris he found in his children's story. By this time, it was dusk. He knew it was dusk because he could feel the dusk inside of him, choking his lungs, moving across that part of him which housed his imagination. He coughed up a little darkness, but thought nothing of it. There is a little darkness in every writer. And so he sat down to dinner with his wife and her daughter and they asked him how the writing had gone that day and he said, "Rotten! Horrible! I am not a writer. I am a baker. A carpenter. A truck driver. I am not a writer." And they laughed because they knew he was a writer, and writers lie. And when he coughed up a little more darkness, they ignored it because they knew that there is a little more darkness in a writer than in other souls.

All night the writer coughed up bits of darkness—shiny darkness, rough darkness, slick darkness, dull darkness—so that by dawn all of the darkness had left him. He awoke refreshed. He smiled. He yawned. He ate breakfast and brushed his teeth. He kissed his wife and his wife's daughter as they left for work and for school. He had forgotten the darkness. Only when he entered his work room did he remember the darkness, and how much of it had left him. For his darkness had taken shape and taken wing, and had flown up to a corner of the wall where it met the ceiling and flattened itself against the stone, the tips of its wings fluttering slightly. The writer considered the creature for a moment before he sat down to write. It was dark. It was beautiful. It looked like a sleek, black manta ray with catlike amber-red eyes. It looked like a stealth bomber given flesh. It looked like the most elegant, the wisest creature in the world. And it had come out of him, out of his darkness. The writer had been fearful, but now he decided to be flattered, to be glad, that he had helped to create such a gorgeous apparition. Besides, he no longer coughed. His lungs were free of darkness. He was a writer. He would write. And so he did—all day.

Weeks passed. He finished "Sarah and the Land of Sighs" and moved on to other stories. The writer kept the lights ever dimmer so that when his wife entered his work room she would not see the vast shadow clinging to the part of the wall where it met the ceiling. But she never saw it, no matter how bright the room was, so the writer stopped dimming the room. It did not matter. She could not see the gorgeous darkness. It glowed black, pulsed black, while he wrote below it. And although the creature had done him no harm, and he found it fascinating, the writer began to end his evenings early and take the work he had done for the day out into the living room. There he would reread it. He was a writer. Writers write.

But writers also edit. And it was as he sat there one day, lips pursed, eyebrows knit, absorbed in the birth of his latest creation, that he noticed a very disturbing fact. Some of the lines were not his own. That one, for instance. The writer distinctly remembered writing, "Silly Sarah didn't question the weeping turtle, but, trusting its wise old eyes, followed it cheerfully into the unknown city." But what the writer read on the page was, "Silly Sarah didn't question the mushroom dweller, and when she had turned her back on it, it snatched her up cheerfully and took her back into Ambergris." There were others—a facet of character, a stray description, a place name or two. The story had been taken over by Ambergris. The story had been usurped by the city. How could this have happened? Writers work hard, sometimes too hard. Perhaps he had been working too hard. That must be it. The writer thought only fleetingly of the beautiful, sleek manta ray. All writers had a little darkness. And even though this darkness had become externalized, it was still a little darkness, and now it did not clot his lungs so. The writer thought of the calming silence of the creature, unmoving but for the slight rippling of its massive wings. The writer frowned as he sat in his chair and corrected the story. Could a thing his wife could not see impact upon the world? On him?

The next day, as the writer wrote, he felt the weight of the dark creature on his shoulder, but when he looked up, it still hugged the wall where it met the ceiling. He returned to his work, but found himself overcome by thoughts of Ambergris.

Surely, these thoughts said, he had abandoned Ambergris for too long. Surely, it was time to come home to the city. His pen, almost against his will, began to write of the city: the tendrils of vines against the sides of buildings in the burnt out bureaucratic district; the sad, lonely faces on the statues in Trillian Square; the rough lapping of water at the docks. The pen was a black pen. Writers write with black pens. He dropped the pen, picked up the blue pens he used for editing, but the best he could do when he tried to run a line through what he had written was to correct his poor spelling. Writers may write, writers may edit, but writers are lousy spellers. He looked up again at the manta ray. He looked up at the little darkness and he said, "You are dark, and all writers have a little darkness inside them, but not all writers have a little darkness outside them. What are you? Who are you?" But the darkness did not answer. The darkness could only write. And edit. As if it too were a writer.

Within a short time, the writer wrote only about Ambergris. He described every detail of its glistening spires as the morning light hit them. He described the inner workings of the Truffidian religion that so dominated the city's spiritual life.

He described houses and orphans, furniture and social customs. He wrote stories and he wrote essays. He wrote stories disguised as essays. A part of him delighted in the speed with which the pen sped effortlessly, like a talented figure skater, across the ice of his pages. A part of him pompously scorned the children's stories he had worked on before his transformation. A part of him was so frightened that it could not articulate its fear. A part of him screamed and gibbered and raged against the darkness. It seemed that Ambergris was intent on becoming real in the world that the writer knew as real, that it meant to seduce him, to trick him into believing it existed without him. But a writer writes, even when he doesn't want to write, and so he wrote, but not without pain. Not without fear. For days he ate nothing and fed the creature on the wall everything, hoping it would reveal more of Ambergris to him. His wife began to worry, but he impatiently told her everything was fine, was fine, was fine. He began to carry a notebook everywhere and write notes at embarrassing times during social events. Soon, he stopped attending social events. Soon, he slept in his work room, with the bright darkness above him as a night-light. Being a writer is addictive. Being a writer is an addiction. All those words, all those words. The act of writing is addictive. But the writer didn't feel like a writer anymore. He felt like a drug addict. He felt like a drug addict in constant need of a fix. Could he be fixed? His fingers and his wrist were constantly sore and arthritic from overuse. His mind was a soaring, wheeling roller coaster of exhilaration and fear. When the creature held back information or he was forced away from his desk by his wife, or even the need to perform bodily functions, he had the shakes, the sweats. He vomited. He was sick with Ambergris. It was a virus within him, attacking his red and white blood cells. It was a cancer, eating away at corpuscles. It was a great, black darkness in the corner of his mind. He was drunk on another world. And the thing on the wall, always growing larger, stared down at him and rippled its wings and mewled for more food, which, of course, consisted of pieces of the writer's soul. His whole life had become a quest for Ambergris, to make Ambergris more real. He would find notes on the city that he did not remember writing scattered around the house, even the manuscripts of librettos by Bender, stories by Sirin. His wife thought he had written them, but he knew better. He knew that the creature on the wall had written them, and then left them, like bread crumbs, for him to follow, to the gingerbread house, to the witch, to death.

Finally, one wan autumn day, when the leaves outside the house had turned golden brown and distributed themselves across the lawn, the writer knew he must destroy the creature or be destroyed by it. He was sad that he must destroy it, for he knew that he was destroying a part of himself. It had come out of him. He had created it. But he was a writer. All writers write. All writers edit. All writers, surely must, on occasion, destroy their creations before their creations turn stale and destroy them. The writer had no love for the creature anymore, only hatred, but he did love his wife and his wife's daughter, and he thought that such love was the greatest justification he could ever have for his actions. And so he entered his work room and attacked the darkness. His wife heard terrible sounds coming from the work room—a man crying, a man screaming, a man pounding on the walls; and was that the smell of fire?—but before she could come to his rescue, he stumbled out of the room, his features stricken with fear and failure. She asked what was wrong and held him tight. "All writers write," he whispered. "All writers edit," he muttered. "All writers have a little darkness in them," he sobbed. "All writers must sometimes destroy their creations," he shouted. But only one writer has a darkness that cannot be destroyed, he thought to himself as he clutched his wife to him and kissed her and sought comfort in her, for she was the most precious thing in his life and he was afraid—afraid of loss, afraid of the darkness, and, most of all, afraid of himself.

After I had finished reading, I turned to the writer and I said gently, "This is an interesting allegory in its way, although the ending seems a little . . . melodramatic? And a most valuable document as well. I can see how people would like your writing."

The writer again sat behind the desk. "It's not an allegory. It's my life." He seemed defeated, as if he had reread the tale over my shoulder.

"Don't you think it is time to discuss the fire?" I asked him. "Isn't this all leading to the fire?"

He turned his head to one side, as if he were a horse resisting a bit. "Maybe. Maybe it is. When can I see my wife?"

"Not until we're done," I said. Who knew when he would see his wife? It has been my experience that I must lie, or half-lie, in order to preserve a certain equilibrium in the patient. I do not enjoy it. I do not relish it. But I do it.

"You have to understand," X said, "that I don't fully understand what happened. I can only guess."

"I will gladly accept your best guess."

But, despite my control, a grim smile played across my lips. I could smell his desperation: it smelled like yellow grass, like stale biscuits, like sour milk.

X: Gradually, the manta ray grew in size until it covered more than ten feet of the wall. As it grew, it began to change the room. Not visual changes, at first, but I began to smell the jungle, and then auto exhaust, and then to hear noises as of a bustling but faraway city. Gradually, the manta ray fit itself into its corner and shaped itself to the wall like a second skin. It also began to smell—not a pleasant smell: like fruit rotting, I guess.

I: And this continued until . . . ?

X: Until one day I woke up early from a terrible nightmare: I was being stabbed in the palm by a man with no face, and I didn't even try to pull away while he was doing it . . . I walked into my work room and there was an intense light coming from the corner where the creature had been— just a creature-shaped hole through which Ambergris peeked. It was the Religious Quarter endless calls to prayer and lots of icons and pilgrims.

I: What did you feel?

X: Anger. I wanted to tear Ambergris apart stone by stone. I wanted to lead a great army and batter down its gates and kill its people and raze the city. Anger would be too weak a word.

I: And do you believe this was the manta ray's purpose when it gave you the gift of returning to Ambergris?

X: "Gift"? It was *not* a gift, unless you consider madness a gift.

I: Forgive me. I did not mean to upset you. Do you believe the curse visited upon you by the manta ray was given so you could destroy Ambergris?

X: No. I was always, deep down, at cross-purposes with the creature. It destroyed my life.

I: What did you do when confronted by the sight of Ambergris? Or what do you think you did?

X: I climbed up the wall and over into the other world.

I: And this, according to the transcripts, is where your memory grows uncertain. Would it still be accurate to say your memory is "hazy"?

X: Yes.

I: Then I will redirect my questioning and come back to that later. Tell me about Janice Shriek.

X: I've already—never mind. She was a fan of my work, and Hannah and I both liked her, so we had let her stay with us—she was on sabbatical. She painted, but made her living as an art historian. Her brother Duncan was a famous historian—had made his fortune writing about the Byzantine Empire. Duncan was in Istanbul doing research at the time, or he would have come to see us too. He didn't get to see his sister much.

I: And you wrote them into your stories?

X: Yes, I'd given them both "parts" in stories of mine, and they'd been delighted. Janice even helped me to smooth out the art history portions of "The Transformation of Martin Lake."

I: Did you feel any animosity toward Janice Shriek or her brother?

X: No. Why would I?

I: Describe Janice Shriek for me.

X: She was a small woman, not as small as, for example, the actress Linda Hunt, but getting there. She was a bit stooped. A comfortable weight. About fifty-four years old. Her forehead had many, many worry wrinkles. She liked to wear women's business suits and she smoked these horrible cigars she got from Syria. She had a presence about her, and a wit. She was a polyglot, too.

I: You said in an earlier interrogation that "sometimes I had the feeling she existed in two places at once, and I wondered if one of those worlds wasn't Ambergris." What did you mean?

X: I wondered if I hadn't so much written her into Ambergris as she'd already had a life in Ambergris. What it came down to was this: Were my stories verbatim truths about the city, including its inhabitants, or were only the settings true, and the characters out of my head?

I: I ask you again: Did you feel any animosity toward Janice Shriek?

X: No!

I: You did not resent her teasing you about the reality of Ambergris?

X: Yes, but that's no motive for . . .

I: You did not feel envy that, if she indeed existed in both worlds, she seemed so self-possessed, so in control. You wanted that kind of control, didn't you?

X: Envy is not animosity. And, again, not a motive for . . . for what you are suggesting.

I: Had you any empirical evidence—such as it might be—that she existed in both worlds?

X: She hinted at it through jokes—you're right about that. She'd read all of my books, of course, and she would make references to Ambergris as if it were real. She said to me once that the reason she'd wanted to meet me was because I'd written about the real world. And once she gave me a peculiar birthday gift.

I: Which was?

X: *The Hoegbotton Travel Guide to Ambergris.* She said it was real. That she'd just ducked into the Borges Bookstore in Ambergris and bought it, and here it was. I got quite pissed off, but she wouldn't say it was a lie. Hannah said the woman was a fanatic. That of course she had created it, and that I'd better either take it as a compliment or start asking lawyers about copyright infringement.

I: Why did you doubt your wife?

X: The guidebook was so *complete,* so perfect. So detailed. How could it be a fake?

I: Surely a polyglot art historian like Janice Shriek could create such a work?

X: I don't know. Maybe. Anyway, that's where I got the idea about her.

I: Let us return to your foray into Ambergris. The manta ray had become an opening to that world. I know your memory is confused, but what do you recall finding there?

X: I was walking down Albumuth Boulevard. It was very chilly. The street was crowded with pedestrians and motor vehicles. I wasn't nude this time, of course, for which I was very appreciative, and I just . . . I just lost myself in the crowds. I didn't think. I didn't analyze. I just walked. I walked down to the docks to see the ships. Took in a parade near Trillian Square. Then I explored the food markets and, after a while, I went into the Bureaucratic Quarter.

I: Where exactly did it happen?

X: I don't . . . I can't . . .

I: I'll spare you the recall. It's all down here in the transcripts anyway. You say you saw a woman crossing the street. A vehicle bore down on her at a great speed, and you say you pushed her out of harm's way. Would that be accurate?

X: Yes.

I: What did the woman look like?

X: I only saw her from behind. She was shortish. Older than middle-aged. Kind of shuffled as she walked. I *think* she was carrying a briefcase or portfolio or something . . .

I: What color was the vehicle?

X: Red.

I: And after you pushed the woman, what happened?

X: The van passed between me and the woman, and I was back in the real world. I felt a great heat on my face, searing my eyebrows. I had collapsed outside of my writing room, which I had set on fire. Soon the whole house would be on fire. Hannah had already taken Sarah outside and now she was trying to drag me away from it when I "woke up." She was screaming in my ear, "Why did you do it? Why did you do it?"

I: And what had you done?

X: I had pushed Janice Shriek into the flames of the fire I had set.

I: You had murdered her.

X: I had pushed her into the fire.

We faced each other across the desk in that small, barren room and I could see from his expression that he still did not understand the crux of the matter, that he did not understand what had truly happened to Janice Shriek. How much would I tell him? Very little. For his sake. Merciless, I continued with my questioning, aware that he now saw me as the darkness, as his betrayer.

I: How happy do you feel having saved the life of the woman in Ambergris in relation to the sadness you feel for having killed Janice Shriek?

X: It's not that simple.

I: But it is that simple. Do you feel guilt, remorse, for having murdered Janice Shriek?

X: Of course!

I: Did you feel responsible for your actions?

X: No, not at first.

I: But now?

X: Yes.

I: Did you feel responsible for saving the woman in Ambergris?

X: No. How could I? Ambergris isn't *real*.

I: And yet, you say in these transcripts that in the trial that resulted from Shriek's death, you claimed Ambergris was real! Which is it? Is Ambergris real or isn't it?

X: That was then.

I: You seem inordinately proud that, as you say, the first jury came back hung. That it took two juries to convict. Indecently proud, I'd say.

X: That's just a writer's pride at the beautiful trickery of my fabrication.

I: "That's just a writer's pride at the beautiful trickery of my fabrication." Listen to yourself. Your pride is ghastly. A human being had been murdered. You were on trial for that murder. Or did you think that Janice Shriek led a more real existence in Ambergris? That you had, in essence, killed only an echo of her true self?

X: No! I didn't think Ambergris was more real. *Nothing* was real to me at that point. The arrogance, the pride, was a wall—a way for me to cope. A way for me not to think.

I: How did you get certain members of the jury to believe in Ambergris?

X: It wasn't easy. It wasn't even easy to get my attorney to pursue the case in the rather insane way I suggested. He went along with it because he believed the jury would find me crazy and remand me to the psychiatric care I'm sure he thought I needed. There seemed no question that I would be convicted—my own wife was a witness.

I: But you convinced some of the jurors.

X: Perhaps. Maybe they just didn't like the prosecuting attorney. It helped that nearly everyone had read the books or heard about them. And, yes, it proves my imagination is magnificent. The world was so complete, so fully realized, that I'm sure it became as real to the jurors as that squalid, musty back room they did all their deliberations in.

I: So you convinced them by the totality of your vision. And by your sincerity—that *you* believed Ambergris was real.

X: Don't *do* that. As I told you before we began, I don't believe in Ambergris anymore.

I: Can you describe the jurors at the first trial for me?

X: What?

I: I said, describe the jurors. What did they look like? Use your famous imagination if you need to.

X: They were jurors. A group of my peers. They looked like . . . People.

I: So you cannot remember their faces.

X: No, not really.

I: If you made them believe in Ambergris so strongly that they would not convict you, why can't you believe in it?

X: Because it doesn't exist! It doesn't exist, Alice! I made it up. Or, more properly, *it* made *me* up. It does not exist.

X was breathing heavily. He had brought his left fist down hard on the desk.

"Let us sum up, for there are two crucial points that have been uncovered by this interrogation. At least two. The first concerns the manta ray. The second concerns the jury. I am going to ask you again: *Did you never think that the manta ray might be a positive influence, a saving impulse?*"

"Never."

"I see it as a manifestation of your sanity—perhaps a manifestation of your subconscious, come to lead you into the light."

"It led me into the darkness. It led me into never-never land."

"Second, there was no trial, except in your head as you ran from the scene of the crime. Your jurors who believed in Ambergris—they represented the part of you that still clung to the idea that Ambergris was real. No matter how you fought them, they—faceless, anonymous—continued to tell you Ambergris was real!"

"Now you are trying to trick me," X said. He was trembling. His right hand had closed around his left wrist in a viselike grip.

"Do you remember how you got here?" I asked.

"No. Probably through the front door, don't you think?"

"Don't you find it odd that you don't remember?"

"In comparison to what?" He laughed bitterly.

I stared at him. I said nothing. I think it was my silence, in which I hoped for some last minute redemption, that forced him to the conclusion my decision would not be favorable.

"I don't believe in Ambergris. How many times do I have to say it?" He was sweating now. He was shaking.

When I did not reply, he said, "Are there any more questions?"

I shook my head. I put the transcripts back in my briefcase and locked it. I pushed the chair back and got up.

"Then I am free to go. My wife is probably waiting in—"

"No," I said, putting on my jacket. "You are not free to go."

He rose quickly, again pounded his fist against the desk. "But I've told you, I've told you—I don't believe in my fantasy! I'm rational! I'm logical! *I'm over it!*"

"But you see," I said, with as much kindness as I could muster as I opened the door, "that's precisely the problem. This *is* Ambergris. You are *in* Ambergris."

The expression on X's face was quite indescribable.

As he locked the door behind him and ascended the staircase, he realized that it was all a horrible shame. Clearly, the writer had lost contact with reality, no matter how desperately that reality had struggled to get his attention. And that poor woman, still unidentified, that X had pushed into the path of a motored vehicle (he hadn't quite had it in him to tell X just how faulty his memory was)—she was proof enough of his illness. In the end, the fantasy had been too strong. And what a fantasy it was! A place where people flew and "made movies." Disney, tee-vee, New York City, New Orleans, Chicago. It was all very convincing and, within limits, it made sense—to X. But as he well knew, writers were a shifty lot—not to be trusted—and there were far too many lunatics on the streets already. How would X have coped with freedom anyhow? With his twin fantasy of literary success and a happy marriage revealed as a lie? (And there were X's last words as the door had closed: "All writers write. All writers edit. All writers have a little darkness in them.")

They had found no record of him in the city upon his arrest, so he had probably come from abroad—from the Southern Isles, perhaps—carrying his pathetic book, no doubt self-published by "Spectra," a vanity operation by the sound of it. He knew those sounds himself from his modest dabbling in the written arts. In fact, he reflected, the only real benefit of the session, between the previous transcripts and the conversation itself, had been to his fiction; he now had some very interesting elements with which to compose a fantasy of his own. Why, he could already see that the report on this session would be a kind of fiction itself, as he had long since concluded that no delusion could ever truly be understood. He might even tell the story in first *and* third person, to both personalize and distance the events.

When he reached the place where he had plucked the rose, he took it from his buttonhole and stuck its stem back in the crack. He regretted having picked it.

But even if he had not, it would have been doomed to a short, brutish life in the darkness.

Out on the street the rain had stopped, although the moist rain smell lingered, and the noontime calls to prayer from the Religious Quarter echoed through the narrow streets. He could almost taste the wonderful savoriness of the hot sausage sold by the sidewalk vendors. After lunch, he would take in some entertainment. The Manzikert Opera theater had decided to do a Voss Bender revival this season, and with any luck he could still catch the matinee and be home to the wife before dinner. With this thought uppermost in his mind, he stepped out onto the street and was soon lost to view among the lunchtime crowds.

AN AFTERWORD TO

THE EARLY HISTORY OF AMBERGRIS

BY JANICE SHRIEK

(And Duncan Shriek)

A NOTE FROM THE AUTHOR

The following is my account of the life of noted historian Duncan Shriek. This text was originally begun as a belated afterword to Duncan Shriek's *The Hoegbotton Guide to the Early History of Ambergris*, but circumstances have changed since I began the book.

Having begun this account as an afterword, ended it as a dirge, and made of it a fevered family chronicle in the middle, all I can say now, as the time to write comes to an end, is that I did the best I could, and am gone. Nothing in this city we call Ambergris lasts for long.

As for Mary Sabon, I leave this account for her as much as for anyone. Perhaps even now, as late as it has become, reading my words will change you.

Goodbye.

—Janice Shriek

(When I found this manuscript, I contemplated destroying the entire thing, but, in the end, I didn't have the will or the heart to do so. It is flawed and partisan and often crude, but it is, ultimately, honest. I hope Janice will forgive or forget my own efforts to correct the record.—Duncan)

PART I

[Upon the altar, the Cappan Aquelus's men found an] old weathered journal and two human eyeballs preserved by some unknown process in a solid square made of an unknown clear metal. Between journal and squared eyeballs blood had been used to draw a symbol . . .

More ominous still, the legendary entrance, once blocked up, boarded over, lay wide open, the same stairs that had enticed Manzikert I beckoning now to Aquelus.

The journal was, of course, the one that had disappeared with Samuel Tonsure 60 years before. The eyes, a fierce blue, could belong to no one but Manzikert I. Who the blood had come from, no one cared to guess.

—From Duncan Shriek's depiction of the Silence in
The Hoegbotton Guide to the Early History of Ambergris

1

 Sabon once said of my brother Duncan Shriek that "He is not a human being at all, but composed entirely of digressions and transgressions." I am not sure what she hoped to gain by making this comment, but she said it nonetheless. I know she said it, because I happened to overhear it three weeks ago at a party for Martin Lake. It was a party I had helped put together, to celebrate the artist's latest act of genius: a series of etchings that illustrated *The Journal of Samuel Tonsure*. (One of many parties I have missed over the years. Maybe if I'd been there, everything would have turned out differently. Maybe it even would have affected the past portrayed in Mary's books.)

Sabon arrived long after Lake, a reticent and not entirely undamaged man, had left for the Café of the Ruby-Throated Calf. I had not invited her, but the other guests must have taken her invitation for granted: they clustered around her like beads in a stunning but ultimately fake necklace. The couples on the dance floor displayed such ambition that Sabon's necklace seemed to move around her, although she and her admirers stood perfectly still.

Rain fell on the skylight above with a sound like lacquered fingernails tapping on a jewelry box. Through the open balcony doors came the fresh smell of rain, mingled—as always in Ambergris—with a green dankness. As I hobbled down the wide marble staircase, into their clutches, I could pick out each individual laugh, each flaw, each fault line, shining through their beaded faces. There were names in that flesh necklace—names that should someday be ticked off a list, names that deserve to be more public.

At ground level, I could no longer see anything but patches of Sabon—a glimpse of red hair, of sallow cheek, the pink allure clumping, a flash of eye, the eyelashes overweighed with liner. The absurd pout of a lip. The crushing smell of a perfume more common to a funeral parlor. She looked so different from the first time I had met her—lithe, fresh student—that I thought for a moment she had put on a disguise. Was she in hiding? From what?

"He is not a human being at all, but composed entirely of digressions and transgressions."

I admit I laughed at Sabon's comment, but I laughed out of affectionate recognition, not cruelty. Because Duncan did digress. He did transgress. He might well have dashed Sabon's living necklace to bead pieces with just as amusing a phrase to describe Sabon, had he not disappeared, possibly forever, a few days before the party. That was another thing—Duncan was always disappearing, even as a child.

Sabon's comment was amusing, but not, as one gentleman misidentified it, "the definitive statement." A shame, because my brother loved definitive statements. He used to leap up from his chair at definitive statements and prick the air out of them, deflate them with his barbed wit, his truculent genius for argument, his infinite appreciation of irony. (I think you both mock me here. Whatever I might have been in my youth—and I can't remember ever having been a witty conversationalist—I'm long past any such trickery. Let the spores be tricky. Let those who ignore them—from the Nativists on down—expend their energy in fanciful phrasings, for all the good it will do them.)

I really ought to start again, though. Begin afresh. Leave Sabon to her admirers for now. There will be time to return to her later.

Duncan often started over—he loved nothing better than to start again in the middle of a book, like a magician appearing to disappear—to leave the reader hanging precariously over an abyss while building up some other story line, only to bring it all back together seamlessly in the end, averting disaster. I would be a fool to promise to duplicate such a feat.

For a time, Duncan sat next to the desk in my apartment—in an old comfortable yellow chair our parents had bought in Stockton many years before. There he would sit, illumined by a single lamp in a twilight broken only by calls to prayer from the Religious Quarter, and chuckle as he read over the transcript of his latest chapter. He loved his own jokes as if they were his children, worthy of affection no matter how slack-jawed, limb-lacking, or broken-spined.

But I best remember Duncan at his favorite haunt, the Spore of the Gray Cap, a place as close as the tapping of these keys. (Favorite? Perhaps, but it was the only one that would have me, at times. At the more respectable establishments, I would walk in and be greeted with a silence more appropriate to the sudden appearance of some mythical beast.) Sober or drunk, Duncan found the Spore perfect for his work. Within its dark and smoky back chambers, sequestered from the outer world by myopic, seaweed-green glass, my brother felt invisible and invincible. Through a strange synchronicity of the establishment's passageways out of keeping with its usual labyrinthine aura, those who congregated at the altar of the bar could, glancing sideways down the glazed oak counter, see Duncan illuminated by a splinter of common space—at times scribbling inspired on his old-fashioned writing pad, at times staring with a lazy eye out of a window that revealed nothing of the outer world, but which may, reflecting back with a green wink, have revealed to him much of the inner world. (The outer world came to me—at various times I entertained Mary, Sirin, Sybel, and, yes, even Bonmot, pillar of the community, in that place.)

He had become a big man by then, with a graying beard, prone to wearing a gray jacket or overcoat that hid his ever-evolving physical peculiarities. Sometimes he would indulge in a cigar—a habit newly acquired from his association with the fringe historian James Lacond—and sit back in his chair and smoke, and I would find him there, gazing off into a memory I might or might not be able to share. His troubles, his disease, could not touch him in those moments.

I much prefer to remember my brother in that space, calm and at the center of himself. While he was there, many regular taverngoers referred to him as the God of the Green Light, looking as he did both timeless and timeworn. Now that he is gone, I imagine he has become the Ghost of the Green Light, and will enter the annals of the Spore as a quiet, luminescent legend. Duncan would have liked that idea: *let it be so.*

But I *do* choose to begin again—Duncan, after all, often did. Like the shaft of green light shooting down the maze of passageways at the Spore, each new shift of attention and each new perspective will provide only a fraction or fracture of the man I knew, in several senses, not at all.

If there is a starting point in Duncan's life, it would have to be the day that our father, Jonathan Shriek, a minor historian, died at our house in Stockton, a town some hundred miles south of Ambergris, on the other side of the River Moth. Unexpected reversal ripped through Dad and destroyed his heart when I was thirteen and Duncan only ten. I remember because I was seated at the kitchen table doing my homework when the mailman came to the door. Dad heard the bell and hopped up to answer it. "Hopped" is no exaggeration—Dad was a defiantly ugly man, built like a toad, with wattles and stocky legs.

I heard him in the hall, talking about the weather with the mailman. The door shut. The crinkle of paper as my father opened the envelope. A moment of silence, as of breath being sucked in. Then a horribly huge laugh, a cry of joy or triumph, or both. He came into the kitchen and barreled past me to the open hallway that led to the back door.

"Gale," he was shouting. "Gale," my mother's name. Out into the backyard he stumbled, me right behind him, my homework forgotten, beside myself with suspense. Something marvelous had happened and I wanted to know what it was.

At the far end of the lawn, Duncan, ten and still sandy-haired, was helping our mother with the small herb garden. My father ran toward them, into the heart of the summer day. The trees were lazy in the breeze. Bees clustered around yellow flowers. He was waving the letter over his head and yelling, "Gale! Duncan! Gale! Duncan!" His back to me. Me running after him, asking, "What, Dad? What is it?" (I remember this with the same kind of focused intensity as you, Janice. Dad was running toward us. I was smiling because I loved seeing Dad's enthusiasm. I loved seeing him so euphoric, so unselfconscious for once.)

He was almost there. He was going to make it. There is no doubt in my mind, even today, that he was going to make it. But he didn't. He stumbled. He fell into the sweet, strange grass. ("Mottled with shadows from the trees," I wrote in my journal later. It is those shadows I remember most from that day—the dappling and contrast of light and dark.) The hand with the letter the last to fall, his other hand clutching at his chest.

I stopped running when I saw him fall, thought he had tripped. Looked up across the lawn at my mother and brother. Mom was rolling her eyes at her husband's clumsiness, but Duncan's face was pale with horror. Duncan knew our father hadn't fallen, but had been *made* to fall. (I don't know how I knew, just remember the way Dad's smile flattened and his face took on a sudden pallor and sadness as he fell, and know he knew what was happening to him.) A moment later, Mom realized this, too, and all three of us ran-to-him converged-on-him held-him searched-for-a-pulse called-for-the-doctor, and sat there crying when he did not move, get up, say it had all been a joke or accident. (Even now, the smell of fresh grass is the smell of death to me. Was there, even then, a sentinel in the shadows, peering out at us?)

It was Duncan who took the letter from Dad's hand and, after the doctor had gone and the mortician had removed the body, sat down at the kitchen table to read it. First, he read it to himself. Then, he read it to us, Mom staring vacant-eyed from the living room couch, not hearing a word of it.

The letter confused Duncan in ways that did not occur to my mother, to me. It bent the surface of his world and let in a black vein of the irrational, the illogical, the nonsensical. To me, my father was dead, and it didn't matter how or why, because he was dead regardless. But to Duncan, it made all the difference. Safely anchored in place and family, he had been a madly fearless child—an explorer of tunnels and dank, dark places. He had never encountered the brutal dislocation of chance and irony. Until now. (Did it make a difference? I don't know. My resolve has always seemed something fiercely internal.)

For our father, Jonathan Shriek, minor historian, had died in the grasp of a great and terrible joy. The letter, which bore the seal of the Kalif himself, congratulated him "for having won that most Magnificent Award, the Laskian Historical Prize," for a paper published in the *Ambergrisian Historical Society Newsletter*. The letter asked my father to accept an all-expenses-paid trip to the Court of the Kalif, and there study books unread for five centuries, including the holiest-of-holies, *The Journal of Samuel Tonsure*.

The letter had become a weapon. It had rescued our father from obscurity, and then it had killed him, his blood cavorting through his arteries at a fatal speed. (I couldn't get it out of my head that he had died due to something in his research, as irrational as that might seem. It instilled in me a kind of paranoia. For a while, I even thought it possible that the letter had been poisoned in some way by the Kalif's men, that Dad had been too close to the solving of some historical mystery the Kalif would prefer remain unsolved.)

The funeral that followed was farce and tragedy. We attended the wrong casket and were shocked to be confronted by the visage of a young man, as if death had done my father good. Meanwhile, another family with a closed casket had buried our father.

"Death suited him." It didn't matter that it wasn't true—it seemed true. That he had gone into death old and come back young. And more comforting still—the idea that there had been a mistake and he was alive somewhere.

Of us all, Duncan stared the longest at that young man who was not our father, as if he sought the answer to a mystery for which there could be no solution.

Four years later, we moved from Stockton to Ambergris, there to live with our mother's side of the family in a rheumy old mansion with a flooded basement. Set against the banks of the River Moth, remote from much of Ambergris, the place could hardly be called an improvement over the house we had grown up in, but it was less expensive, and our mother had come to realize that with her husband dead nothing much remained to keep her in Stockton. Thus, we shared space with an ever-changing mob of aunts, uncles, cousins, nephews, nieces, and friends of the family. (Although, over the years, this cacophony of distant relations reduced itself to just our mother, which is probably how she would have preferred it from the beginning.)

We came to Ambergris across the thick sprawl of the muddy River Moth, by ferry. I remember that during the journey I noticed Duncan had a piece of paper in his shirt pocket. When I asked him what it was, he pulled it out and showed it to me. He had kept the letter from the Kalif to our father; as far as I know, he has it still, tattered and brittle. (I do have it—or the remains of it, anyhow. I don't dare open it anymore, for fear it will turn to dust.)

"I don't want to forget," he said, with a look that dared me to doubt his loyalty to our father.

I said nothing, but the thought occurred to me that although we might be traveling to a new place, we were still bringing the past with us.

Not that Ambergris didn't have a rich past of its own—just that we knew much less about it. We knew only that Ambergris played host to some of the world's greatest artists; that it was home to the mysterious gray caps; that a merchant clan, Hoegbotton & Sons, had wrested control of the city from a long line of kings; that the Kalif and his great Western Empire had thrice tried to invade Ambergris; that, once upon a time, some centuries ago, a catastrophe called the Silence had taken place there; and that the annual Festival of the Freshwater Squid often erupted into violence, an edgy lawlessness that some said was connected to the gray caps. The gray caps, we learned from helpful relatives seeking to reassure us, had long since retreated to the underground caverns and catacombs of Ambergris, first driven there by the founder of the city, a whaler despot named Manzikert I. Manzikert I had razed the gray caps' city of Cinsorium, massacred as many of them as he could, and built Ambergris on the smoldering ruins. (It all sounded incredibly exciting and exotic to us at that age, rather than horrifying.)

Of artists, we found ample evidence as soon as we arrived—huge murals painted onto the sides of storehouses—and also of the Hoegbotton clan, since we had to pay their tariffs to leave the docks and enter the city proper.

As for the gray caps, as our relatives had promised, we discovered scant initial trace of this "old, short, indigenous race," as the guidebooks called them. They were rarely seen aboveground during the day, although they could be glimpsed in back alleys and graveyards at dusk and during the night. We knew only what we had gleaned from Mom's rare but unsettling bedtime stories about the "mushroom dwellers of Ambergris," and a brief description from a book for children that had delighted and unnerved us simultaneously:

> Fifty mushroom dwellers now spilled out from the alcove gateway, macabre in their very peacefulness and the even hum-thrum of their breath: stunted in growth, wrapped in robes the pale gray-green of a frog's underbelly, their heads hidden by wide-brimmed gray felt hats that, like the hooded tops of their namesakes, covered them to the neck. Their necks were the only exposed part of them—incredibly long, pale necks; at rest, they did indeed resemble mushrooms.

Of the Silence, we had heard even less—a whisper among the adults, a sense that we should not ask about it. Even in Stockton, so far from what had happened— separated by both time and geography—there seemed to be a fear that, some-how, the event might be resurrected by the most casual of comments. No, I discovered the Silence much later—only learned during my brief attendance at the Hoegbotton School for Advanced Studies, for example, that the annotations in Ambergrisian history books (A.S. and B.S.) stood for After Silence and Before Silence. Of Samuel Tonsure's journal, so inextricably linked to the Silence, I heard not even a whisper until Duncan educated me. (I may have given you the most personalized and eccentric education on the Silence in the history of Ambergris!)

We did not learn much about any of this from Mom. For a good portion of our youth in Ambergris, rare was the day that she rose before noon. Sometimes we barely saw her. She had so many rooms to hide in in that house. Her internal clock, her rhythms, became nocturnal and erratic. She continued to paint, but sometimes we would return home to find that instead of a canvas she had painted the wall of an unused room in a welter of dissonant colors. Until the basement began to flood with river water every time it rained, she loved to sit down there in the damp and read by an old oil lamp we'd brought with us from Stockton, an heirloom dating back to the time of the pirate whalers. (When she was there, Janice and I would sometimes join her. We'd pull up chairs and listen to the whispering gasp of the river water as it tried to get in through the floorboards, and we'd read our books or do our homework. Mom rarely said anything, but there was something about being together in the same room that felt comfortable. I think she enjoyed it, too, but I don't know for sure.)

I do remember that in our mother's absence one of my aunts tried to help orient us to the city, telling us, "There's a Religious Quarter, a Merchant Quarter, and an old Bureaucratic Quarter, and then there are places you don't go no matter what. Stay out of them." Faced with such vague warnings, we had to discover Ambergris in those early days by exploring for ourselves or asking our classmates.

The move to Ambergris changed my relationship with Duncan. Before the move, Duncan had been the annoying shadow, the imitator who always had to do what I was already doing. When I started a rock collection at the age of eight, inspired by the exposed granite on the hillside near our house in Stockton, Duncan started one, too, even though he didn't understand why. No matter how I shooed him away, Duncan had to follow me up the hill. A cautious distance away from my irritated mumblings, he would squat in his wobbly way and run his hand through the pebbles, looking for the shiniest ones. Over time, he would squinch closer and closer, waddling like a duck, until before I knew it we were looking for stones together and my collection became our collection.

When I became entranced by the children's stories of mammalogist Roger Mandible, Duncan not only stole the books from my room but colored in them and scrawled his name, handwriting as neat as a drunken sailor's, across many of the pages.

By the time I'd reached the age of fourteen or fifteen, I'd realized he copied me because he loved me and looked up to me. (I didn't look up to you for long— you stopped growing after you turned fourteen, I believe.)

But by then the death of our father and the move to Ambergris had transformed me into something more than Duncan's sister. There was something in the connection Dad and Mom had that had energized them both—that had made them both more than they had been alone. Because without Dad, Mom lost, or forgot, how to take care of us. I'm certain if Mom had died instead that Dad would have behaved the same way. He was no more practical than our mother. He was as apt to fall over and stub a toe putting on his pajamas as she was to cut herself chopping up carrots. They shared a general absentmindedness that Duncan and

I, looking back on those years as adults, found endearing. Dad searching for the newspaper he held in the crook of his arm. Mom looking for the earrings she'd just put back in the jewelry case. Somehow, together, though, they muddled through and managed to disguise their individual incompetence at the job of parenting.

With Dad dead and the move to Ambergris having unmoored Mom from any last vestiges of parental regard, I became Duncan's mother in many ways. I made sure he got up in time for school. I made him breakfast. I helped him with his homework. I made sure he got to bed on time. He stopped copying me and started obeying me. (. . . Although with a smoldering disrespect for authority as embodied by my suddenly strict sister. But I'm lying. I welcomed it. I needed some structure. I needed someone to tell me what to do back then. I was still just a child. And a frequently scared one, despite all of my explorations. To take the lead while exploring seemed natural; to take the lead in everyday life was monstrously difficult.) Gone was the admiration, perhaps, but so too the corrosive disease of competition. At least, back then.

Somehow, despite our rough knowledge and this change in our roles, we managed to fit in, to get along, to come to feel part of Ambergris with greater ease than might have been expected. Much of it had to do with our attitude, I think. Duncan and I should have been upset about leaving our old school and friends behind, but we weren't. Not really. In a sense, it came as a great relief to escape the pity and concern others showed us, which trapped us in an image of ourselves as victims. Freedom from that meant, in a way, freedom from the moment of our father's death. This made up for the other dislocations.

(Dare I deprive the reader of that first glimpse of Ambergris? That first teasing glimpse during the carriage ride from the docks? That glimpse, and then the sprawl of Albumuth Boulevard, half staid brick, half lacquered timber? The dirt of it, the stench of it, half perfume, half ribald rot. And another smell underneath it—the tantalizing scent of fungi, of fruiting bodies, of spores entangled with dust and air, spiraling down like snow. The cries of vendors, the cries of the newly robbed, or the newly robed. The first contact of shoe on street out of the carriage— the resounding solidity of that ground, and the humming vibration of coiled energy beneath the pavement, conveyed up through shoe into foot, and through foot into the rest of a body suddenly energized and woken up. The sudden hint of heat to the air—the possibilities!—and, peeking from the storm drains, from the alleyways, the enticing, lingering darkness that spoke of tunnels and sudden exploration. One cannot mention our move to Ambergris without setting that scene, surely! That boulevard became our touchstone, in those early years, as it had to countless people before us. It was how you traveled into Ambergris, and it was how they carried you out when you finally left.)

But as fascinated as Duncan would become with Ambergris, he went elsewhere for his education. At our mother's insistence, in one of her few direct acts of parenting, Duncan received his advanced degrees in history from the Institute of Religiosity in Morrow (or as historians often call it, "that other city by the River Moth," a good hundred miles from Ambergris), his emphasis on the many masters of the arts who had been born or made their fortune in Ambergris, as well as on the Court of the Kalif—for he saw in these two geographical extremes a way to let his interests sprawl across both poles of the world. He could not study the artists of Ambergris without studying the very anatomy of the city—from culture to politics, from economics to mammalogy. And because Ambergris spread tentacles as long and wide as those of the oldest of the giant freshwater squid, this meant he must study Morrow, the Aan, and all of the South. Study of the Kalif, which I always felt was a secondary concern for him, meant mapping out all of the West, the North. (Early on, I had no idea what constituted a "secondary concern." Anything and everything could have been useful. The important thing was to accumulate information, to let it all but overwhelm me.)

In that Duncan was never what I would call religious, I believe that this monumental scope represented his attempt to re-place himself within the world, to discover his center, lost when our father died, or to build himself a new center through accumulation of knowledge. In a sense, History was *always* personal to Duncan, even if he could not always express that fact.

To say Duncan studied hard would be to understate the ardor of his quest for knowledge. He devoured texts as he devoured food, to savor after it had been swallowed whole. He memorized his favorite books: *The Refraction of Light in a Prison*, *The Journal of Samuel Tonsure*, *The Hoegbotton Chronicles*, *Aria: The Biography of Voss Bender*. Years later, he would delight me, no matter how odd the circumstances of our meetings, with dramatic readings, in the imagined pitch and tone of the authors, him still so passionate in his love of the words that I would forever find my own enthusiasm inadequate.

In short, Duncan became overzealous. Obsessed. Driven. All of those (double-edged) (s)words. He did not allow for his own human weakness, or his need to feel connected to the world through his flesh, through interactions with other human beings. Better, I am sure he felt, to become the dead hand of the past, to become its instrument.

Duncan did not make friends. He did not have a woman friend. When I visited him, during breaks in my own art studies at the Trillian Academy, at his rooms at the Institute, he could not introduce me to a single soul other than his instructors. Duncan must have appeared to be among the most pious of all the pious monks created by History. (I had friends. Your infrequent trips to visit meant your idea of my life in that place was as narrow as that sliver of emerald light in the Spore that you keep going on about. I needed to converse with people to test out my theories, to gauge dissent and to begin to realize what ideas, when expressed to others in the light of day, evaporated into the air.)

Recognizing both his genius and his desire for lack of contact, the Institute, its generosity heightened by the small scholarship our father had endowed it with as well as the memory of him walking its hollowed halls, had, by the second semester, isolated Duncan in rooms that expanded with his loneliness. My brother's only window looked out at the solid, unimaginative brick of the Philosophy Building, giving him no alternative to his vibrant inner life. (This was, after all, the point of the Institute—to focus on the unexamined life. Nothing wrong with that.)

As if to embody the complexity and brittle joy of his inner life in the outer world, Duncan slowly covered the walls of his rooms with maps, pictures, diagrams, even pages torn from books. Ambergrisian leaders stared down impishly, slightly crooked, half-smothered by maps of the Kalif's epic last battle against the infidel Stretcher Jones. Bark etchings by the local Aan tribespeople shared space with stiff edicts handed down by even stiffer Truffidian priests. James Alberon's famous acrylic painting of Albumuth Boulevard formed the backdrop for a hundred tiny portraits of the original Skamoo synod. The bewildering greens and purples of Darcimbaldo's "The Kiosks of Trillian Square" competed with the withered yellows of ancient explorers' maps, with the red arrows that indicated skirmishes on military schemata.

Duncan devoted one dark, ripe little corner to the "changing facade of Ambergris," as he called it. At first, this corner consisted only of overlapping street plans, as if he were building an image of the city from its bones. The stark white paper, the midnight-black veins of ink, contrasted sharply with everything else in his rooms. The maps were so densely clustered and layered that the overall effect reminded me of a diagram of the human body. Or, perhaps more metaphorically accurate, like a concentrated forest of intertwining vines (recalling the forests of my youth in Stockton), through which no one could possibly travel, even armed with a machete. (My first great accomplishment—a way of cross-referencing dozens and dozens of seemingly unrelated phenomena so that, in a certain light, in a certain darkness, I could begin to see the patterns, the connections. Later, I would use this same technique, on a vastly different scale, at the Blythe Academy.)

With each visit, I noticed that the forest had grown—from a dark stain, to a presence that variously resembled in shape a mushroom, a manta ray, and then some horribly exotic insect that might kill you with a single sting. Gradually, in an inexorable invasion through both time and space, Ambergris came to dominate his rooms, and then layer itself to a thickness greater than the walls, or so it often seemed, sitting in my chair, looking over a manuscript.

The stain had become the wallpaper, and the last remnants of non-Ambergris materials had become the stain. Looking back on those earliest diagrams and montages on his walls, could he have guessed how far they would lead him? How far he would travel, and at what price? (Underneath, any astute observer could have found a wealth, a riot, of new information. You had only to peel away a corner and there, revealed, the secret obsession: the ghosts of the Silence, the gray caps, and much else. "I'm going underground," it all said. For those who could read it.)

"Your wall has changed. Has it changed your focus?" I asked him once.

"Perhaps," he replied, "but it still doesn't make sense."

"What doesn't make sense?" I asked.

"They're the only ones who could have done it. But why? And how?"

I looked at him in confusion.

"The Silence," Duncan said, and a shiver, a resonance, passed through me. *The Silence and the gray caps.*

More than two hundred years before, twenty-five thousand people had disappeared from the city, almost the entire population, while many thousands had been away, sailing down the River Moth to join in the annual hunt for fish and freshwater squid. The fishermen, including the city's ruler, had returned to find Ambergris deserted. To this day, no one knows what happened to those twenty-five thousand souls, but for any inhabitant of Ambergris, the rumor soon seeps through—in the mottling of fungi on a window, in the dripping of green water, in the little red flags they use as their calling cards—that the gray caps were responsible. Because, after all, we had slaughtered so many of them and driven the rest underground. Surely this was their revenge?

I had only learned about the Silence the semester before; it was frightening how adults could keep the details of certain events from their children. It came as a revelation to me and my classmates, although it is hard to describe how deeply it affected us.

"It keeps coming back to the Silence," Duncan said. "My studies, Dad's studies. And Samuel Tonsure's journal."

Tonsure, Duncan had told me, was one of those who pursued the gray caps underground during the massacre that had preceded the founding of Ambergris. He had never returned to the surface, but his journal, a curious piece of work that purported to describe the gray caps' underground kingdoms, had been found some seventy-five years later, and subsequently pored over by historians for any information it might impart on the Silence or any other topic related to the gray caps. They were studying it still, Duncan included.

"You're not Dad, Duncan," I said. "You could study something else."

Even then, before he was employed by James Lacond, before he met Mary, I sensed the danger there for Duncan. Even then, I knew somehow that Duncan was in peril. (We're all in peril from something. I count myself lucky not to have succumbed to the usual perils, like addiction to mushrooms or alcohol.)

But Duncan just stared at me as if I were stupid and said, "There's nothing else to study, Janice. Nothing important."

I remember the inevitable progression of the images on his walls with the clarity of dream. However, beyond the few words reproduced above, our conversations have faded into the oblivion of memory.

Duncan emerged from those rooms with a degree and good prospects (an exaggeration; I perhaps had the prospect of a brief flash of fame, followed by an urgent need to make a living in a profession other than the one I had chosen as my passion), but even then he was different from the other students. I watched his professors circle him at the various graduation parties. They treated him with a certain worried detachment, perhaps even fearfully, as if he had grown into something they could no longer easily define. As if they dared not develop any emotional attachment to this particular student. (Mom, who had continued to recede into her memories, did not come up for the ceremony—and we rarely went to see her, now that we were grown.)

Later, Duncan told me that he had never known solitude, never known loneliness, as he did in those few hours after graduation when he walked like a leper through gilded rooms tabled with appetizers and peppered with conversations meant for everyone but him. The tall towers of senior professors glided silent and watchful, the antithesis of Mary Sabon and her quivering, eager necklace of flesh. (Everyone feels isolated at those types of events, no matter how good the party, or how scintillating the conversation, because you're about to be expelled into the world, out from your own little piece of it.)

Yet out of his zeal, his loneliness, his passion that had literally crawled up the walls of his rooms, Duncan had already created something that might take the place of the silence or at least provide an answer to it. He had written a book entitled *On the Refraction of Light in a Prison.*

Despite countless exams, essays, and oral presentations, Duncan had found the time to write a groundbreaking tome that analyzed the mystical text *The Refraction of Light in a Prison* (written by the imprisoned Monks of Truff from their high tower in the Court of the Kalif). It will not surprise anyone that this was one of the subjects our father had meant to tackle prior to his sudden death. (How could I not tackle it before going on? It was like completing my father's life in some small part. I remember looking at the finished book, with the inscription, "To my father, Jonathan Shriek," and thinking that I had resurrected him for a time, that he was alive again in my book. When I sent the book to our mother, she broke from her usual stoic silence to write me a long letter relating stories about Dad she had never felt comfortable telling me before.)

I had the privilege of reading the book (and helping to edit it, in your incendiary way) in manuscript form on one of my trips to Morrow. By then, my own education in Stockton and Ambergris had reached its somewhat disappointing end, and I was torn between pursuing a career in art or diving into art history. I had done much advanced research and encountered much in the way of genius, but I remember even then being astounded by the brilliant audacity of my brother's conclusions. At the same time, I was concerned that the book might be too good for its intended audience. Perhaps my brother was destined for obscurity. I admit to a sting of satisfaction in the thought, for nothing is more savage than sibling rivalry.

In any event, Duncan found a publisher in Morrow after only three months: Frankwrithe & Lewden, specialists in reference books, odd fictions, and histories.

Frankwrithe & Lewden was an ancient publisher, rumored to have been established under the moniker "Writhelewd" during the last century of the Saphant Empire. Then, as the Empire collapsed into fragments not long after "Cinsorium" became "Ambergris," they transplanted their operations to Morrow, their name mangled and transformed during the long trek upriver in flat-bottomed boats. Who better to publish Duncan's esoteric work?

Frankwrithe & Lewden published fifteen thousand copies of *On the Refraction of Light in a Prison*. By barge, cart, and motored vehicle, the book infiltrated the southern half of the continent. Bookstores large and small stocked it. Traveling book dealers purchased copies for resale. Review copies were sent out with colorful advance blurbs from the dean of the Institute and the common man on the street (a badly conceived F&L publicity stunt, soliciting random opinions from laypeople that resulted in blurbs like, "'Not as good as a bottle of mead, but me and the missus quite enjoyed the bit about monk sex.'—John Tennant, plumber").

At first, nothing happened. A lull, a doldrums of no response, "as if," Duncan told me later, "I had never written a book, never spent four years on the subject. In fact, it felt as if I, personally, had never existed at all." Then, slowly, the book began to sell. It did not sell well, but it sold well enough: a steady drip from a faucet.

The critical response, although limited, did give Duncan hope, for it was, when and where it appeared, enthusiastic: "After an initial grounding in cold, hard fact, Shriek's volume lofts itself into that rarefied air of unique scholarly discourse that distinguishes a good book from a bad book" (Edgar Rybern, *Arts & History Review*). Or, this delicious morsel: "I never knew monks had such a difficult life. The overall sentiment expressed by this astonishing book is that monks, whether imprisoned or not, lead lives of quiet contemplation broken by transcendental bursts of epiphany" (the aforementioned James Lacond, Truff love him, with a rare appearance in the respectable *Ambergris Today*).

The steady drip became stronger as the coffers of the various public and private libraries in the South, synchronized to the opinions of men and women remote from them (who might well have been penning their reviews from a lunatic asylum or between assignations at a brothel), released a trickle of coins to reward words like "rarefied air," "good," and "astonishing."

However, even the critics could not turn the trickle into a torrent. This task fell to the reigning head of the Truffidian religion, the Ambergris Antechamber himself, the truculent (and yet sublime) Henry Bonmot. How dear old Bonmot happened to peruse a copy of *On the Refraction of Light in a Prison* has never been determined to my satisfaction (but it makes me laugh to think of how he became introduced to us). The rumor that Bonmot sought out blasphemous texts to create publicity for Truffidianism (because the rate of conversions had slowed) came from the schismatic Manziists, it was later proved. That Duncan sent Bonmot a copy to foment controversy demonstrates a lack of understanding about my brother's character so profound I prefer not to comment on it.

The one remaining theory appears the most probable: Frankwrithe & Lewden conspired to place a copy on the priest's nightstand, having first thoughtfully dog-eared those pages most likely to rescue him from his impending slumber. Ridiculous? Perhaps, but we must remember how sinister F&L has become in recent years. (Once upon a time, in a still-distant courtyard, I did ask Bonmot about it, but he couldn't recall the particulars.)

Regardless, Bonmot read Duncan's book—I imagine him sitting bolt upright in bed, ear hairs singed to a crisp by the words on the page—and immediately proclaimed it "to contain uncanny and certain blaspheme." He banned it in such vehement language that his superiors later censured him for it, in part because "there now exists no greater invective to be used against such literature or arts as may sore deserve it." (It was my good fortune that he turned to my explication of Chapter One of *The Refraction of Light in a Prison*, "The Mystical Passions," which in its protestations of purity manages to list every depraved sexual act concocted by human beings over the past five thousand years. It was my theory, and Dad's, that this was the monks' method of having it both ways. It didn't help that I included Dad's mischievous footnote about the curious similarity between the form of certain Truff rituals and the acts depicted in the chapter.)

Luckily for Duncan, the darling (and daring!) Antechamber's excellent imitation of a froth-mouthed dog during his proclamation so embarrassed the more practical administrative branch of the Truffidian Church—"them what pay the bills," as an artist friend of mine once put it—that they neglected to impose a sentence or a penalty. Neither did the Truffidian Church exhort its members to "stone, pummel, or otherwise physically assault" Duncan, as occurred some years later to our soon-to-be editor Sirin, who had decided to champion a book on the "cleansing merits of interreligious romantic love." (Sirin, alerted by a sympathetic typesetter, managed to change both the decree and the flyers created by it, causing the designated Truffidian Voice, the Antechamber standing by his side, to read a decree in front of the famous porcelain representation of the God Truff and all others in the Truffidian Cathedral that called for the Antechamber's stoning, pummeling, and much worse. I teased Bonmot about this event many times.)

The ban led to the predictable upswing in sales, lofting the book into the "rarefied air" that distinguishes an almost-bestseller from a mediocre seller. (F&L took advantage of the ban to an uncanny degree, I must say, but it is not true that they had ten thousand copies of a new edition printed two nights before the announcement with "Banned by the Antechamber!" blaring across the cover in seventy-two-point bold Nicean Monk Face.)

Suddenly, Duncan had something of a reputation. Newspapers and broadsheets, historians and philosophers, decried and debated, lauded and vilified both the book and Duncan—on unusually obscure elements of Duncan's argument (for example, whether or not the Water People of the Lower Moth Delta had ever been exposed to the teachings of Truff). Meanwhile, the Court of the Kalif denied it still held the monks who had written the original *The Refraction of Light in a Prison* and declared the new book to consist of a vast, sprawling fiction built on the foundation of another vast, sprawling fiction. (The Kalif also revoked Father's prize, an action I never forgave.)

But no matter what position a particular commentator took, it was always with the underlying assumption that *On the Refraction of Light in a Prison* contained ideas of substance and scholarship. Duncan was asked to contribute articles to several major and minor historical journals. Inasmuch as the fate of the monks had become a political issue, and thus one of interest to many people, he was invited to more parties peopled by the Important than he could have stomached on his most extroverted day . . . and yet did not reply to a single invitation.

What made him reluctant to savor his newfound notoriety? The fear of the consequences of the ban did not make him a recluse, nor did his innate distress in social situations. The true answer is hinted at in his journal, which I have beside me now for verification purposes. Scrawled in the margin of an entry from this era, we find the words "Is this how Dad felt?" Remembering the fate of our father, dead at the zenith of his happiness, Duncan truly believed he too would die if he partook of too much joy—if not by heart attack, then by some other means. (Your theory may be correct on a subconscious level, but on the conscious level, I was merely obsessed and somewhat paranoid. Obsessed with the possibilities of the next book. Paranoid about how people would continue to receive my studies. Worried about how I would do on my own, so to speak, without Dad's research notes to prop me up.)

Of course, I did not understand this until much later. At the time, I believed his shyness had led him to squander perhaps his only opportunity to take up a permanent place in the public imagination. On this, I turned out to be wrong. Debate raged on for a while regardless, perhaps fed by Duncan's very absence.

Then, to compound the communal mystification, Duncan disappeared from sight—much as he would several decades later in the week before Martin Lake's party. His rooms in Morrow (which the Institute had let me keep for a year following graduation) were untouched—not a sock taken, not a diagram removed from the walls . . . Duncan simply wasn't there.

I walked around those rooms with the school's dean, and it struck me as I stared at the crowded walls that Duncan's physical presence or absence meant nothing. Everything that comprised his being had been tacked or glued or stabbed to those walls, an elaborate mosaic of obsession.

Clearly, the school understood this aspect of Duncan, for they made a museum out of the rooms, which then became the physical location for discussions of Duncan's work. Much later, the "museum" became a storehouse, crumbled over time into a boarded-up mess, and then a broken-down safety hazard; such is the staying power of fame. (I never expected it would last as long as it did, to be honest.)

As we walked together, the Dean made sympathetic sounds, expressed the hope that Duncan would "soon return to his home." But I knew better. Duncan had emerged from his cocoon. The wallpaper of plans, photographs, diagrams was just the husk of his leaving, the remains of his other self. Duncan had begun to metamorphose into something else entirely.

That is, assuming he was still alive—and without the evidence of a dead body, I preferred to believe he was. (I was. As you know. Such melodrama!)

<hr>

Now I should start again. Now I should skip six months of worry. Now I should tell you how I came to see Duncan again. This is such a difficult Afterword to write. Sometimes I am at a loss as to what to put in and what to leave out. Sometimes I do not know what is appropriate for an Afterword, and what is not. Is this an Afterword or an afterward? Should I massage the truth? Should I maintain an even tone? Should I divide it all into neat, easily digestible chapters? Should I lie? (Dad, in his notes on writing: "A historian is half confidence artist and half stolid purveyor of dates and dramatic re-creations.")

Duncan reintroduced himself to me six months later with a knock on my door late one night in the spring. The prudent Ambergrisian does not eagerly open doors at night.

I called out, "Who is it?" and received, in such a jubilant tone that I could not at first place the voice, the response, "Your brother, Duncan!" Shocked, relieved, perplexed, I opened the door to a pale, worn, yet strangely bulky brother wrapped in an old gray overcoat that he held closed with both hands. Comically enough, a sailor's hat covered his head. His face was flushed, his eyes too bright as he staggered past me, pieces of debris falling from him onto the floor of my living room.

I locked the door behind him and turned to greet him, but any words I might have spoken died in my throat. For he held his overcoat open like the wings of some great bird, and what I saw I could not at first believe. Just brightly colored vest and pants, I thought, but protruding, like barnacles on a ship's hull. How unlike my brother to wear anything that outlandish. I took a step closer . . .

"That's right," Duncan said, "step closer and really *see*."

He tossed his hat onto a chair. He had shaved off his hair, and his scalp was stippled and layered in a hundred shades of blue, yellow, green, orange.

"Mushrooms. Hundreds of mushrooms. I had to wear the overcoat and hat or every casual tourist on Albumuth Boulevard would have stared at me." He looked down at his body. "Look how they glow. What a shame to be rid of them." He saw me staring unabashedly. "Stare all you like, Janice. I'm a dazzling butterfly, not a moth . . . well, for another hour or two." (A butterfly could not compare. I was magnificent. Every part of my body was *receiving*. I could "hear" things through my body, feel them, that no human short of Samuel Tonsure could understand.)

He did not lie. From the collar of his shirt to the tips of his shoes, Duncan was covered in mushrooms and other fungi, in such a riot and welter and rash of colors that I was speechless. I walked up to him to examine him more closely. His eyelashes and eyebrows were lightly dusted with purple spores. The fungi had needled his head, burrowed into the skin, forming whorls of brightness that hummed with fecundity. I took his right hand in mine, examined the palm, the fingers. The palms had a vaguely greenish hue to them. The half-moons of his fingernails had turned a luminous purple. His skin was rubbery, as if unreal. Looking up into his eyes, I saw that the spark there came from pale red ringing the pupil. Suddenly,

I was afraid. (To be honest, to dull the pain a bit, I'd had a few drinks at a tavern before stumbling to your door. That might have contributed to the condition of my eyes.)

"Don't be," he said. "Don't be afraid," scaring me even more. "It's a function of diet. It's a function of disguise. I haven't changed. I'm still your brother. You are still my sister. All of this will wash away. It's just the layers added to me the past three months. I need help scraping them off."

I laughed. "You look like some kind of clown . . . some kind of mushroom clown."

He took off his overcoat, let it fall to the floor. "I agree—I look ridiculous."

"But where have you been? How did this happen?" I asked.

He put a finger to his lips. "I'll answer your questions if you'll help me get rid of this second skin. It itches. And it's dying."

※

So I helped him. It was not as simple as having him step out of his clothes, because the mushrooms had eaten through his clothes and attached themselves to his poor pale skin. A madness of mushrooms, mottling his skin—no uniform shape or variety or size. Some pulsed a strobing pink-blue. Others radiated a dull, deep burgundy. A few hung from his waist like upside-down wineglasses, translucent and hollow, the space inside filled with clusters of tiny button-shaped green-gold nodules that disintegrated at the slightest touch. Textures from rough to smooth to rippled to grainy to slick. Smells—the smells all ran together into an earthy but not unpleasant tang, punctuated by a hint of mint. The mushrooms even made noises if you listened carefully enough—a soft *pough* as they released spores, an intermittent whine when left alone, a *pop* as they became ghosts through my rough relocations.

"Remember BDD when you three had to wash all that mud and filth off of me?" he asked, as we worked with scrubbing implements and towels in the bathroom.

"Of course I do," I said.

Before Dad Died, BDD, a grim little acronym meant to help us remember when we had been a happy family. If we had arguments or bouts of depression that threatened to get out of control, one of us would remind the others that we had all behaved differently before Dad died. We held BDD time in our heads as a sanctuary whenever our anger, our loss, became too great.

Once, Duncan, his usual mad, exploring, BDD self, had managed to get stuck in a sewer pipe under our block and we had had to pull him out after a frantic half hour searching for the source of his pathetic, echoing voice. Then Mom, Dad, and I spent another three hours forcing the black-gray sludge off of him, finally standing back to observe the miracle we had wrought: a perfectly white Duncan, "probably as clean as he's ever been," as Dad observed.

I wonder, Mary, if Duncan ever shared memories like this with you, while the lights flickered outside his apartment windows?

"Remember BDD . . ."

Duncan's remark made me laugh, and the task at hand no longer seemed so strange. I was just helping clean up Duncan after another BDD exploration mishap, while Duncan looked on half in relief, half in dismay, as the badges of his newly gained experience fell away, revealed as transitory. (I was losing sensation with each new layer peeled off—reduced to relying on old senses. I knew it had to be done, but I felt as if I were going blind, becoming deaf, losing my sense of smell.)

Me, I felt as if I were destroying a vast city, a community of souls. On one level, I lived with the vague sense of guilt every Ambergrisian feels who can trace their family's history back to the founding of the city. Even for me, even come late to Ambergris, a mushroom signifies the genocide practiced by our forefathers against the gray caps, but also the Silence and our own corresponding loss. Can anyone not from Ambergris, not living here, understand the fear, loss, guilt, each of us feels when we eradicate mushrooms from the outside of our apartments, houses, public buildings? *The exact amount of each emotion in the pressure of my finger and thumb as I pulled them from their suction cup grip on Duncan's skin.*

It took five hours, until my fingertips were red and my back ached. Duncan looked not only exhausted but diminished by the ordeal. We had moved back into the living room, and there we sat, surrounded by the remains of a thousand mushrooms. It could have been a typical family scene—the aftermath of a haircut—except that Duncan had left behind something more profound than his hair. Already the red brightness had begun to fade from his eyes, his hands less rubbery, the half-moons of his fingernails light purple.

I had opened a window to get the smell of mushrooms out and now, by the wet, glistening outdoor lamps, I could see the beginning of a vast, almost invisible spore migration from the broken remains at our feet, from the burgundy bell-shaped fungi, from the inverted wineglasses, from the yellow-green nodules. Like ghosts, like spirits, a million tiny bodies in a thousand intricate shapes, like terrestrial jellyfish—oh what am I trying to say so badly except that they were gorgeous, as they fled out the window to be taken by the wind. In the faint light. Soundlessly. Like souls.

In that moment, almost in tears from the combination of beauty, exhaustion, and fear of the unknown, I think I caught a glimpse of what Duncan saw; of what had created the ecstasy I had seen in him when he had stumbled into my apartment five hours before. A hundred, a thousand years before. (I tried so hard to capture this for Mary, and yet I couldn't make her see it. Maybe *that* is where the failure occurred, and maybe it is *my* failure. Not all experiences are universal, even if you're in the same room when something miraculous occurs. I suppose it was too much to ask that she take it on faith?)

"Look," I said, pointing to the spores.

"I know," my brother said. "I know, Janice."

Such regret in that voice, mixed with a last, lingering joy.

"I'm less than I was, but I've captured it all here." He tapped his head, which still bore the scars of its invaders in the vague echo of color, in the scrubbed redness of it. "The spores are part of the record. They will float back to where I've been, navigating by wind and rain and by ways we cannot imagine, and they will report to the gray caps. Who I was. Where I was. What I did. It will make it all the more dangerous next time."

I sat upright in my chair. Next time? He stood there, across the room from me, dressed in the rags of his picked-apart clothes, surrounded by the wreckage of fungal life, and he might as well have been halfway across the city. I didn't understand him. I probably never would. (I didn't need you to understand what I myself saw but dimly. I wanted you to *see*—and you saw more than most, even then. Mary saw it all, by the end, and she stitched her eyes shut, stopped up her ears, taped her mouth.)

"Yes, well, Duncan, it's been a long night," I started to say, but then his eyes rolled up in their sockets and he fell to the soft floor, dead asleep. I had to drag him to the couch.

There he remained for two days. I took time off from my job at an art gallery to watch over him. I went out only for food and to buy him new clothes. He slept peacefully, except for five or six times when he slipped into a nightmare that made him twitch, convulse, cry out in a strange language that sounded like birdsong. I remember staring down at his pale face and thinking that he resembled in texture and in color nothing more or less than a mushroom.

Duncan had no believable explanation for his enfeebled state when he finally awoke on the third morning. As I fed him toast and marmalade at the kitchen table, I tried to get some sense of what he might have endured in the six months since I had last seen him. Although I had swept away the remains of the mushrooms, their presence haunted us.

Elusiveness, vagueness, as if a counterpoint to the terrible precision of his writing, had apparently become Duncan's watchwords. I had never known him to be talkative, but after that morning, his terseness began to take on the inventiveness of an art form. I had to pull information out of him. (I was trying to protect you. Clearly, you still don't believe that, but I will give you this: you're right that I should have found a way to tell you.)

"Where have you been?" I asked him.

He shrugged, pulled the blanket closer around him. "Here and there. Mostly *there*," and he giggled, only trailing off when he realized he had lapsed into hysteria.

"Was it because of the Truffidian ban?" I asked.

He shook his head. "No, no, no. That silliness?" He raised his head to stare at me. His gaze was dark and humorless. "No. Not because of the ban. They never published my picture in the newspapers and broadsheets. No Truffidian outside of Morrow knows what I look like. No, not the ban. I was doing research for my next few books." He rolled his eyes. "This will probably all go to waste."

"Did you only go out at night?" I asked. "You're as pale as I've ever seen you."

He would not meet my gaze. He wrenched himself out of the chair and walked to the window, hands in his pockets. "It was a *kind* of night," he said.

"Why can't you just tell me?"

He grinned. "If you must know, I've been with Red Martigan and Aquelus, Manzikert and Samuel Tonsure." A thin smile, staring out the window at some unnameable something.

A string of names almost as impenetrable as Sabon's necklace of human beads, but I did recognize the names Manzikert I and Tonsure. I knew Duncan had continued to study Tonsure's journal.

"I found," Duncan said in a monotone, as if in a trance, "something in Tonsure's journal that others did not, because they were not looking for it . . ."

Here I mix my memories of the conversation with a transcript of the account found in my brother's journal, which I am lucky enough to have in a trunk by my side along with several other things of Duncan's. (It's something of a shock to find you rifling through my papers and notebooks. Usually, it takes a person years to develop the nerve to attempt outright theft. For a moment, I was upset, even outraged. But, really, Janice, I'd rather you quote me than paraphrase, since the meaning becomes distorted otherwise.)

I found something in Tonsure's journal that others did not, because they were not looking for it. Everyone else—historians, scholars, amateurs—read it as a historical account, as a primary source to a time long past, or as the journal of a man passing over into madness. They wanted insight into the life of Tonsure's captor, Manzikert I. They wanted insight into the underground land of the gray caps. But although the journal can provide that insight, it is also another thing entirely. I only noticed what was hidden because I had become so accustomed to staring for hours at the maps and diagrams on the walls of my rooms at the Institute. I fell asleep to their patterns. I dreamt about their patterns. I woke up to their patterns.

When I finally began to read Tonsure's journal, I was alive with patterns and destinations. As I read, I began to feel restless, irritable. I began to feel that the book contained another level, another purpose. Something that I could catch only flashes of from a copy of the journal, but which might be as clear as glass or a reflecting mirror in the original.

As I reached the end of the journal—the pages and pages of Truffidian religious ritual that seem intended to cover a rising despair at being trapped belowground—I became convinced that the journal formed a puzzle, written in a kind of code, the code weakened, diluted, only hinted at, by the uniform color of the ink in the copies, the dull sterility of set type.

The mystery ate at me, even as I worked on *On the Refraction of Light in a Prison*, especially because one of the footnotes added to *The Refraction of Light in a Prison* by the editor of my edition contains a sentence I long ago memorized: "Where the eastern approaches of the Kalif's empire fade into the mountains no man can conquer, the ruined fortress of Zamilon keeps watch over time and the stars. Within the fortress, humbled by the holes in its ancient walls, Truffidian monks guard the last true page of Tonsure's famous journal."

That the love of a woman might one day become as mysterious to Duncan as a ruined fortress, that he could one day find the flesh more inexplicable than stone, must have come as a shock.

After the discovery, my curiosity became unbearable. I could not fight against it. As soon as I graduated, I began to make plans to visit Zamilon. These plans, in hindsight, were pathetically incomplete and childish, but, worse, I didn't even follow the plans when I finally made the journey.

One night, as I stared at the maps on my walls, the pressure grew too great—I leapt out of bed, put on my clothes, took my advance money from Frankwrithe & Lewden from the dresser, peeled a map of the eastern edge of the Kalif's empire from the wall, and dashed out into the night.

Without a thought for my peace of mind, or our mother's. Typical. How many times should we have to forgive Duncan just because he was always the eccentric genius in the family? (Surely this doesn't reflect your feelings now, but only your emotions at the time? Not with everything you've seen since? I refuse to defend myself on this count, especially since we would have need to forgive you many times over in the years to come.)

The wanderings and mishaps of the next two months are too strangely humorous for me to bother relating, but suffice it to say that my map was faulty, my funds inadequate. I spent as many days earning money as traveling to my destination. I became acquainted with a dozen different forms of transportation, each with its own drawbacks: mule, mule-drawn cart, mule-powered rolling barge, leaky canoe, the rare smoke-spitting, back-farting motored vehicle, and my own two slogging feet. I starved. I almost died from lack of water. Once, when I had had the good fortune to earn some money as a scribe for an illiterate local judge, I was robbed within minutes of leaving the accursed town. I survived a mudslide and a hail-storm. My feet became thick, insensate slabs. My senses sharpened, until I could hear the stirrings of a fly on a branch a hundred feet away. In short, in every way I became more attuned to the details of my own survival.

Nor were the monks of Zamilon more understanding than the elements of nature or the vagaries of village dwellers. It took an entire week to convince the monks that the rag-clad, unshaven, stinking stranger before them was a serious scholar. I stood in front of Zamilon's hundred-foot gates, upon the huge path cut out of the side of the mountain, the massive stone sculptures from some forgotten demonology leering at me from either side, and listened while the monks dumped down upon me, like boiling oil, the most obscure religious questions ever shouted from atop a battlement.

However, eventually they relented—whether because of my seriousness or the seriousness of my stench, which was off-putting to other pilgrims, I do not know. But when I was finally allowed to examine the page from Tonsure's journal, all my suffering seemed distant and unimportant. It was as I had suspected: the original pages, the supposed idiosyncrasies found upon them, created a pattern intended as a map for anyone lucky enough to decipher it. I only had access to one page—and would never see the rest, imprisoned as it was by the Kalif along with the authors of *The Refraction of Light in a Prison*—but that was enough to parse a fragmented meaning of the whole.

I wrote down my findings—and, indeed, a first account of my journey—on a dozen sheets of paper, forced myself to memorize the evidence before I left Zamilon, and then burned my original scribblings. The knowledge seemed too precious and too personal to commit permanently to paper. It frightened me. With what I had learned, I could now, if I dared, if I desired, access the gray caps' underground kingdom . . . and survive.

I thought about at least two things on my long journey to Ambergris from Zamilon. (I had no intention of returning to Morrow.) First, to what extent had Tonsure corrupted his own journal in order to transmit this secret code—or had he corrupted it at all? In other words, did the coherent elements of the journal accurately reflect events and Tonsure's opinions of those events, or had he, to create a book that was also a map, sacrificed reality on the altar of symbolism?

Further, I was now convinced that Tonsure had written the entire journal *after* he followed Manzikert I belowground. He had encrypted it in the hope that even if he never made it back to the surface, the gray caps might preserve the journal, not realizing it posed a threat to their secrets. This revelation, if supportable, would change the entire nature of discourse surrounding the journal, render obsolete a hundred scholarly essays, and not a few whole books besides. The battered journal returned to the surface by the gray caps had not been the half-coherent ramblings of a mind slowly going insane, but a calculated risk taken by a man all too aware of his predicament.

What followed from this conclusion is simply this: Another, earlier version of the journal must have, at one point, existed, whether a polished product or a loose collection of notes. And from this earlier version, Tonsure had created a facsimile that contained the map, the schematic, for navigation of the gray caps' underground strongholds. Something even the gray caps had not been able to decipher. Something that would be Tonsure's secret and his alone.

Second, and most important, my head was filled with the grandeur of Tonsure's design, the genius of it, which I had seen but a fragment of and which our father had glimpsed only in the potential for research revealed by the letter that had killed him.

When I finally made my way back to Ambergris and strode down Albumuth Boulevard, I had only one thought. It ran through my mind over and over, like a challenge, like a curse: Did I have the courage to act on what Tonsure had given me? Could I live with *not* acting on that knowledge?

I found out that my courage outweighed my fear. Perhaps because I could not let Tonsure's supreme act of communication go to waste. The thought of him reaching out from beyond his own death only to be thwarted by my cowardice . . . it was too much to bear. More's the pity.

So I found my way down among them and back again without being disfigured or murdered. It was easy in a way. With Tonsure as my guide, I could not miss this sign here, that symbol there, until even the vaguest scratch in muddied rock, the slightest change in temperature or fruiting bodies alerted me to the next section of the path. It was a strange, dark place, and I was afraid, but I was not alone. I had Tonsure with me.

Do I understand most of what I saw down there? No. Does the memory of seeing things I do not understand help me, do me any good at all? No. For one thing, who would believe me? They would say I am having visions. I'm not sure I believe it all myself. Thus, I have become no better off than Samuel Tonsure, except that I may move above- and belowground at will.

When Duncan related portions of this to me in person, he ended with the lines, "And now you will have to believe me when I say that I cannot tell you anything else, and that it will do no good to press me for information or ask more questions. This is for your own protection as much as anything else. Please trust me on this, Janice."

Such a sense of finality informed his words that it never occurred to me to probe further. I just nodded, thinking about the mushroom spores floating out the window three nights before, from a room that now seemed so gray and empty. I was still trying to absorb that image. Unhappily, Duncan's journal entries are no more revealing than our conversations (You didn't think I'd leave *both* of my journals aboveground, did you?), but at the time, I was secretly glad he didn't tell me more—his experience was so remote from mine that the simplest word sounded as if spoken in another language.

"I'm just glad you're safe again, and home," I said.

"Safe?" he said with a bitter little laugh. "Safe? Look at my hands." He held them out for my inspection. The half-moons of his fingernails shone a faint green. Along the outer edge of both hands a trail of thin, fernlike fungi followed a rough line down to the wrists. Perhaps, in certain types of light, it might be mistaken for hair.

"That will go away in time," I told him.

"No," he said. "I don't think so. I think I've been branded. I think I will always have these marks, no matter how they manifest themselves."

Duncan was right, although the manifestations would not always be fungal: for decades, he would carry everywhere a reproduction of Tonsure's journal, the pages more worn with each passing year, until finally I began to feel that the diary of the madman had become Duncan's own. And he would add more marks to the book, nearly silent scars that would leave their own strange language on his skin. Unspoken. Unwritten. But there.

Until only in the dim green light of the Spore would he feel truly comfortable aboveground.

2

Can I start again? Will you let me start again? Do you trust me to? Perhaps not. Perhaps all I can do is *soar* over. Perhaps we'll fly as the crow flies—on night wings, wind rattling the delicate bones of the rib cage, cold singeing feathers, gaze scouring the ground below us. The landscape will seem clear but distant, remote yet comprehensible. We will fly for ten years straight, through cold and rain and the occasional indignant sparrow certain we've come to raid the nest. Ten years shall we fly across before we begin our slow, circling descent to the cause of Duncan's calamity. Those ten years brought five black books flapping their pages. Five reluctant tombstones. Five millstones round my brother's neck. Five brilliant bursts of quicksilver communication. Five leather-clad companions for Duncan that no one can ever take away. (Five progressively grandiose statements that stick in my craw.)

We fly this way because we must fly this way. I did not see much of Duncan during those ten years. The morning after my conversation with him, he borrowed money from me against expected book royalties and left my apartment. He rented a small one-bedroom at the east end of Albumuth Boulevard in one of the several buildings owned by the legendary Dame Truff. Did he delight in living so close to the Religious Quarter, to know that he, the blasphemer, slept within a few blocks of the Antechamber's quarters in the Truffidian Cathedral? I don't know. I never asked him. (I delighted in the dual sensations of normalcy and danger, something you, Janice, always craved, but was new for me. To wake up every morning and make eggs and bacon with the full knowledge that my dull routine might be swiftly shattered by the appearance of the Antechamber's goons.)

While Duncan published, I perished half a dozen times. I shed careers like snakeskins, molting toward a future I always insisted was the goal, not merely an inevitable destination. Painter, sculptor, teacher, gallery assistant, gallery owner, journalist, tour guide, always seeking a necklace quite as bright, quite as fake, as Mary Sabon's. I never finished anything, from the great sprawling canvases I filled with images of a city I didn't understand, to filling the great sprawling spaces in my gallery. I've never lacked energy or drive, only that fundamental secret all good art has and all bad art lacks: a healthy imagination. Which, as I look back, is intensely ironic, considering how much imagination it took to get to this moment with my sanity intact, typing up an afterword that, no matter how sincere, will no doubt be as prone to accusations of pretense and bombast as any of my prior works.

I did my best to keep in contact with Duncan, although without much enthusiasm or vigor. The long trek to his loft apartment from mine often ended in disappointment; he was rarely home. Sometimes, curious, I would sneak up to the door and listen carefully before knocking; I would look through the keyhole, but it revealed only darkness.

My reward for spying usually took the form of a rather echoing silence. But more than once I imagined I heard someone or something scuttling across the floor, accompanied by a dull hiss and moan that made me stand up abruptly, the hairs rising on my arms. My tremulous knock upon the door in such circumstances—whether Duncan Transformed or Duncan with Familiars, I wanted no part of that sound—was usually enough to reestablish silence on the other side. And if it wasn't, my retreat back into the street usually changed from walk to run. (I heard you sometimes, although I was usually engrossed in my work and thought it best that you not enter. Ironically enough, a couple of times, I thought you were *them*, gray-capped sister.)

I imagine I looked rather pathetic in front of his apartment—this thin, small woman crouched against a splintery door, eagerly straining for any aural news of the interior. I remember the accursed doorknob well—I hit my head on it at least a dozen times.

Thwarted, I gained any news of Duncan from rare interviews in the newspapers, which usually focused on writing technique or opinions on current events. For some reason, people are under the deluded impression that a historian—blessed with hindsight—can somehow illuminate the present and the future. Duncan knew nothing about the present and the future. (I knew nothing about the present and the immediate past. I would argue, however, that I began to glean an inkling of the future.)

The biographical notes on the dust jackets of his books were no help—they crackled with a terseness akin to fear: "Duncan Shriek lives in Ambergris. He is working on another book." Even by investigating the spaces between the words, those areas where silence might reveal a clue, could anyone ever "get to know" the author from such a truncated paragraph? More importantly, no one would ever want to know the author from such a paragraph.

Only in the fifth book did more information leak through, almost by accident, like a water stain on a ceiling: "Shriek intends to write a sequel to his bestselling tome, *Cinsorium*."

By then, Duncan's luck had run out, and all because of a single book we must circle back to, a delighted Sabon as raptor swooping down to observe over our feathered shoulder—Mary's presence doubling, trebling, the scope of the disaster, because it was she who turned Duncan into fodder for her own . . . what shall we call it? Words fail/cannot express/are not nearly enough. (Triumph. Unqualified. You must give her that. Bewitching eyes and the pen of a poet.)

Gliding, wheeling, we circle back through the wind stream and let the titles fall in reverse order so that we might approach the source by a series of echoes or ripples: *Vagaries of Circumstance and Fate Amongst the Clans of the Aan; Mapping the Beast: Interrogatories Between the Moth and Those Who Travel Its Waters;*

Stretcher Jones: Last Hope of the West; *Language Barriers Between the Aan and the Saphant Empire*. And the first book, sprawling out below us in all of its baroque immensity: *Cinsorium: Dispelling the Myth of the Gray Caps*. This maddening book, composed of lies and half-truths, glitters beneath us in all of its slivers and broken pieces, baubles fit for our true crow-self.

What is it about even half of the truth that can tear at the fabric of the world? Was it fear? Guilt? The same combination of emotions that flickered through my thoughts as I extinguished the welter of mushrooms from Duncan's poor pale body?

I don't mean to speak in riddles. I don't mean to fly too high above the subject, but sometimes you have no choice. Still, let me land our weary crow and just tell the story . . .

Perhaps Duncan should have realized what he had done after Frankwrithe & Lewden's reaction to the manuscript. (I realized it when I read over the first draft and saw the thousand red wounds of revision marks left by my second editor—lacerations explaining in their cruel tongue that this book would either behave itself or not be a book at all.)

A month after submission of the book, Duncan's editor, John Lewden, summoned Duncan to F&L's offices in downtown Morrow. The journey from Ambergris took Duncan two grueling days upriver by barge, into the heart of what proved to be a glacial Morrow winter. Once there, Duncan found that his editor was "on vacation" and that F&L's president, Mr. L. Gaudy, would talk to him instead.

A secretary quickly escorted Duncan into Gaudy's office, and left immediately. (I remember the office quite well. It was "resplendent," with a rosewood desk, a dozen portraits of famous F&L authors, and an angry, spitting fireplace in the corner opposite the desk.)

Gaudy, according to Duncan's journal, was "a bearded man of indeterminate age, his gaunt flesh wrapped across sharp cheekbones." He sat behind his desk, staring at the room's fireplace. (His eyes were like blue ice, and in his presence I smelled a certain cloying mustiness, as if he spent most of his time underground, or surrounded by hundred-year-old books.)

Duncan moved to sit, but Gaudy raised one hand, palm out, in abeyance. The calm behind the gesture, almost trancelike, made Duncan reluctant to disobey the man, but "also irritated me intensely; I had the feeling he knew something I did not, something I wanted to know."

They remained in those positions, respectively sitting and standing, for over five minutes. Duncan somehow sensed that just as he should not sit down, he also should not speak. "I began to think this man held some power over me, and it was only later that I realized something in his eyes reminded me of Dad."

When Gaudy finally lifted his bespectacled face to stare at Duncan, the flames reflected in the glass, Duncan saw an expression of absolute peace on the man's face. Relieved, he again moved to sit down, only to again be told, through a gesture, to remain standing.

Duncan began to wonder if his publisher had gone insane. "At the very least, I wondered if he had mistaken me for someone else."

As the fire behind them began to die, Gaudy smiled and broke the silence. He spoke in a "perfectly calm voice, level and smooth. He stared at the fireplace as he spoke, and steepled his fingers, elbows on the desk. He appeared not to draw a single extra breath."

He said:

"You need not sit and thus defile my perfectly good chair because it will take no time at all to say what needs to be said to you. Once I have said what I am going to say to you, I would like you to leave immediately and never return. You are no longer welcome here and never will be welcome again. Your manuscript has performed the useful function of warming us, a function a thousand times more beneficial than anything it might have hoped to accomplish as a series of letters strung together into words, phrases, sentences, paragraphs, and chapters. The fire has purified it, in much the same manner as I would like at this moment—and will desire at all moments in the future—to purify *you*, were it not outside of the legal, if not moral, boundaries placed upon us by the law and society in general. By this time it ought to be clear to you, Mr. Shriek, that we do not intend to buy the rights to your 'book'—and I use the word 'book' in its loosest possible sense—nor to its ashes, although I would sooner buy the rights to its ashes than to its unblemished pages. However, on the off chance that you still do not comprehend what I am saying to you, and allowing for the possibility that you may have entered a state of shock, I shall continue to talk until you leave this room, which happy event I hope will take place before very much longer, as the sight of you makes me ill. Mr. Shriek, as you must be aware, Frankwrithe & Lewden has a history that goes back more than five hundred years, and in that time we have published our share of controversial books. Your first book—which, by the way, you may be fascinated to know is as of this moment out of print—was the forty-first book to be banned by the various Antechambers of Ambergris over the years. We certainly have no qualms in that regard. Nor have we neglected to publish books on the most arcane and obscure topics dreamt of by the human brain. As you are no doubt aware, despite the fact that many titles no longer have even a nostalgic relevance, we keep our entire, and considerable, backlist in print—*Pelagic Snail Rituals of the Lower Archipelago* comes to mind, there being no such snail still extant, nor such an archipelago; still, we keep it in print—but we will make an exception for your first book, which shall be banished from all of our catalogs as well. As I would have hoped you had guessed by now, although you have not yet left this office never to return, we do not like your new book very much. In fact, to say I do not like your book would be like calling a mighty tree a seedling. I loathe your book, Mr. Shriek, and yet the word 'loathe' cannot convey in even a thousandth part the full depths of my hatred for this book, and by extension, you. But perhaps I should be more specific. Maybe specifics will allow you to overcome this current, potentially fatal, inertia—tied no doubt to the aforementioned shock—that stops you from leaving this office. Look—the last scrap of your manuscript has become a flake of ash floating above the fireplace. What a shame. Perhaps you would like an urn to collect the ashes of your dead newborn? Well, you can't have one, because not only do we not have an urn, but even if we did, we would not allow you to use it for the transport of the ashes, if only from the fear that you might find some way to reconstruct the book from them—and yes, we do know it is likely you have a copy of the manuscript, but we will feel a certain warmth in our hearts if by burning this copy we can at least slow down your reckless and obstinate attempt to publish this cretinous piece of excrement. Returning to the specifics of our argument against this document: your insipid stupidity is evident from the first word of the first sentence of the first paragraph of your acknowledgments page, 'The,' and from there the sense of simple-minded, pitiable absence of thought pervades all of the first paragraph until, by the roaring crescendo of imbecility leading up to the last word of the first paragraph, 'again,' any possible authority the reader might have granted the author has been completely undermined by your inability to in any way convey even an unoriginal thought. And yet in comparison to the dull-witted pedantry of the second paragraph, the first paragraph positively shines with genius and degenerate brilliance. Perhaps at this point in our little chat, I should repeat that I don't very much like this book."

Gaudy then rose and shouted, "YOU HAVE BEEN MEDDLING IN THINGS YOU KNOW NOTHING ABOUT! DO YOU THINK YOU CAN POKE AROUND *DOWN THERE* TO YOUR HEART'S CONTENT AND NOT SUFFER THE CONSEQUENCES?! YOU ARE A COMPLETE AND UTTER MORON! IF YOU EVER COME BACK TO MORROW, I'LL HAVE YOU GUTTED AND YOUR ORGANS THROWN TO THE DOGS! DO. YOU. UNDERSTAND. ME??!"

What other rhetorical gems might have escaped Gaudy's lips, we will never know, for Duncan chose that moment to overcome his inertia and leave Frankwrithe & Lewden's offices—forever.

"It's not so much that he frightened me," Duncan told me later. "Because after going belowground, really, what could scare me? It was the monotone of his delivery until that last spit-tinged frothing." (I was terrified, Janice. This man was the head of an institution that had been extant more than five hundred years ago. And he was telling me my work was worthless! It took a month before I even had the nerve to leave my apartment in Ambergris. I rarely visited Morrow again, and kept a low profile whenever I did.)

Later, during the War of the Houses (as it came to be called), we realized that Gaudy, for political reasons, could hardly have reacted any other way to Duncan's manuscript. But how could Duncan know that at the time? He must have been shaken, at least a little bit. (Yes. A bit.)

Undaunted, Duncan found a new publisher within six months of Gaudy's strange rejection. Hoegbotton Publishing, a newly created and overeager division of the Hoegbotton & Sons trading empire, gave Duncan a contract. In every way, the book struck Duncan's new editor, Samuel Hoegbotton—an overbearing and inconsequential young man with hulking shoulders, a voice like a cacophony of monkeys, and severe bad breath (who would never find favor in the eyes of his tyrannical father, Henry Hoegbotton)—as "A WORK OF GENIUS!" Duncan was happy to agree, bewildered as he might have been, unaware at the time that Samuel had transferred from the Hoegbotton Marketing Division. Samuel had not set foot in a bookstore since his twelfth birthday, when his mother had presented him with a gift certificate to the Borges Bookstore. ("Promptly traded in for its monetary value," Sirin, our subsequent editor, mused disbelievingly some years later.) That Samuel died of a heart attack soon after publishing Duncan's fifth book surprised no one. (Except me!)

The book, published with the full (perhaps crushing) weight of the Hoegbotton empire behind it, was called *Cinsorium: Dispelling the Myth of the Gray Caps.* It became an instant bestseller.

Despite this success, *Cinsorium* signaled the beginning of Duncan's slide into the obscurity I had previously wished upon him. If he had dreamt of a career as a serious historian—the sort of career our father would have died for—he should have suppressed the book and moved on to a new project. Samuel Hoegbotton, contributing to the disaster, ordered the printing of a banner across the top of the book (almost, but not quite, obscuring my name) that proclaimed: "At Last! The Truth! About the Gray Caps! All Secrets! Revealed!"

I bought the book as soon as it came out, not trusting Duncan to send me a copy. (I would have, if you'd asked.) It disappointed me for contradictory reasons: because it showed little of the scholarly care displayed by *On the Refraction of Light in a Prison*, and because it never mentioned, even once, Duncan's underground journey. I had already accepted the irritation of waiting to read about the trip along with everyone else. This I could have tolerated, even though it indicated a lack of trust. But not to mention it at all? It was too much. (I did mention Zamilon, though. Wasn't that enough? To start with?)

The book did not "reveal" all secrets. It obscured them. Duncan tantalized readers with incredible images he claimed had come from ancient books, the existence of which most scholars discounted. Mile-high caverns. Draperies of fungi that "undulated in time to a music conveyed at too high a pitch for the human ear." Mushrooms that bleated and whined and "talked after a fashion, in the language of spores." (Yes, perhaps I obscured some deeper truths, but nothing was made up.)

In typical Duncanesque prose, it tried with almost superhuman effort to hide the paucity of its insight:

> Although the inquisitive reader may wish for further extrapolation regarding this aspect of Tonsure's journal, such extrapolation would be so speculative as to provide a poor gruel of a meal indeed, even for the layperson. Some mysteries are unsolvable.
>
> (One part fear, I suppose. One part truth. Some mysteries *are* unsolvable. Just when you unearth the answer, you discover another question.)

A beautiful sword, but blunt, the book relied on quotations from "unnamed sources" for the bulk of its more exotic findings. Although claiming to know the truth about the gray caps, Duncan instead spent most of the book combining a history of fungi with historical suppositions that made me laugh:

> Could it be that the rash of suicides and murders in the Kalif's Court fifty years before the Silence were the result of emanations from a huge fungus that lay under the earth in those parts? Might much of the supposed "courtly intrigues" of the period actually have more to do with fruiting bodies? Might this also reveal the source of the aggression behind so-called bad Festivals in Ambergris?

The book, in short, violated most rules of historical accuracy and objective evidence. Duncan mentioned that he had journeyed to examine the page of Tonsure's journal, but he gave no specifics of location or content. Certainly nothing like the detail and "local color" provided by his own journal. (I admit *Cinsorium* was hardly my finest hour, although I had my reasons for writing it at the time. My thoughts turned to Tonsure and his encryptions. My need for encryption was not as urgent as his, or as profoundly solitary, but I still felt a certain danger. Not just from the gray caps, but from those who might read the unexpurgated truth and . . . reject it. And reject it violently. Couldn't I, I reasoned—falsely—allude to and suggest that truth so that, perhaps, even if in just a thousand minds, my suspicions might harden into certainty? It is a question I wrestled with even later, working with James Lacond, although by then I had come to realize that the best I could hope for was a hardening certainty in a mere handful of souls.)

The most daring idea in *Cinsorium* was the theory that Tonsure had rewritten the journal after completing it, which alienated dozens of influential scholars (and their followers, don't forget) who had based hundreds of books and papers on the conventionally accepted chronology. (I don't think it alienated them—most of them lacked the resources or the knowledge to verify or deny the discovery. I didn't feel like an outcast, at first. Besides, is it fair to chastise me for both poor scholarship and unique ideas?)

As I read, I became struck by the way that half-truths wounded Duncan's cause more seriously than outright lies. He stumbled, he faltered throughout the book, but continued on anyway—persevering past the point where any reasonable person might have given up on such a hopeless trek.

Oddly, it made me love him for being brave, and it almost made me cry as well. I knew that he held our father in his head as he wrote, running toward him across the summer grass. That, I could respect. But by not revealing all, he became lost in the *land between*, where lies always sound like lies, and so does the truth. He could not protect the gray caps *and* satisfy serious readers without betraying both groups. (The gray caps needed no protection, only the readers. Janice, you may now be beyond protection, but there are still things that can be done for those aboveground.)

In part due to these defects, *Cinsorium* had a peculiar publication history. It became an instant bestseller when the Kalif's Minister of Literature, rather than ban the book, had his operatives buy all available copies and ship them off to the Court. Readers in the South bought most of the second printing, the Kalif distracted by warfare with the Skamoo on his northern border. However, despite the sale of more than fifty thousand copies, Hoegbotton refused to go to a third printing.

Certainly the strange and curious silence created by the book must be seen as a reason for Hoegbotton's reluctance to reprint *Cinsorium*. This silence occurred among those most raucous of vultures, critics. In the superheated atmosphere that is the Southern book culture, such omissions rarely occur. Even the most modest self-published pulp writer can find space in local book review columns. (Fear. It was fear.) This lack of attention proved fatal, for although many journals noted the book's publication in passing, only two actual reviews ever appeared, both in a fringe publication edited by James Lacond. Lacond, a passing acquaintance of Duncan's even in those days before the war, wrote that "Subtle subjects require subtle treatments. For every two steps back, Shriek takes three steps forward, so that in the circular but progressive nature of his arguments one begins to see this pattern, but also a certain truth emerging." Perhaps. Perhaps not. (At least someone was prepared to accept it!)

But none of these events concerned me, not in light of what I thought the book told me about Duncan. The book, I felt, was an argument between Duncan and Duncan, and not about any of the surface topics in the book. Duncan did not know what, exactly, he had seen while underground. He had only a rudimentary understanding of the gray caps. (This is true—I didn't know what I'd seen. But I couldn't keep what I didn't know to myself. How could I? I saw too many things that might shake someone's worldview.) This kept alive Duncan's compulsion to do what I most feared: return to the underground until he felt he understood . . . everything.

Perhaps it should not have surprised me that Duncan's next four books settled back into the realm of acceptable accomplishment. Duncan reverted to the scholarship that had been his trademark. It was too late, of course. It didn't, and couldn't, matter, because the cowardly critics who had refused to review *Cinsorium had* read it. And so Duncan's scholarly style steadily lost readers seeking further crass sensationalism, while critics savaged later books, most of them omitting any reference to *Cinsorium*. It hung over Duncan's work like a ghost, an echo. The reviews that did appear dismissed Duncan's work in ways that made him appear a crank, a misfit, even a heretic. (I've always blamed Gaudy for this, although for a long time I had no proof, or even a coherent theory. But I now believe Gaudy used his connections to blacklist me in typical F&L fashion—with the underhanded compliment, the innuendo, the insinuation. Did Gaudy do more than meet with a few influential journal editors? Perhaps not, but that might have been enough.) They appended the story of his banning by Bonmot in harmful ways: "This, the latest offering from the author who blasphemed against the Truffidian Church, concerns . . ." It did not matter what it concerned.

Shortly after the publication of *Vagaries of Circumstance and Fate Amongst the Clans of the Aan*, Hoegbotton announced that Duncan had been dropped from their stable of writers. Gaudy must have been laughing from behind his rosewood desk in Morrow. No other publisher of note would prove interested in Duncan's sixth book. None of his books would long remain in print. For all practical purposes, Duncan's career as a writer of historical books had come to an end, along with any hopes of serious consideration as a historian. At the age of thirty-three.

It would only get worse after he met Sabon, who would spend much of her time chipping away at Duncan's respectability, so that his books no longer contained anything but metaphorically shredded pages.

Odd. It strikes me for the first time that Duncan has been preparing me for this moment all of my life. There's a green light shining upon the typewriter keys, and maybe it's the light that allows me to see so clearly. Must we always be blind to those we are close to? Must we always fumble for understanding? Duncan never mistrusted me. He just didn't want me to implode from the information he had—he wanted to dole it out in pieces, so that it would not be such a shock to my system. And yet it would have been a shock, no matter how gradual. I don't see how it could be otherwise.

If Duncan feared losing me, he must have also feared losing his audience.

Which reminds me. I should ask: Am I losing you? Have I lost you already? I hope not. There's still a war to come, for Truff's sake.

Maybe the only solution is to start over.

Should I? Perhaps I should.

3

We don't see many things ahead of time. We usually only avoid disaster at the last second, pull back from the abyss by luck or fate or blind stupid chance. Exactly nine years before Mary Sabon began to destroy my brother like an old house torn down brick by brick, Duncan sought me out at my new Gallery of Hidden Fascinations. How he found me there, I still don't know (a mundane story, involving broadsheet adverts and luck). I had just bought the gallery—a narrow place off Albumuth Boulevard (I remember when it was a sweets shop that also sold mood-altering mushrooms—a much more honest trade)—with the help of a merchant loan against our mother's property along the River Moth. (*That* took some persuading!)

Outside, the sky was a blue streaked with gold, the trees once again threatening to release their leaves, turning yellower and yellowest. The smell of burning leaves singed nostrils, but the relief of slightly lower temperatures added a certain spring to the steps of passersby.

Half the proposed gallery lay in boxes around my feet. Paintings were stacked in corners, splashes of color wincing out from the edges of frames. Piles and piles of papers had swallowed my desk.

I was happy. After years of unhappiness. (It's easy to think you'd been unhappy for years, but I remember many times you were invigorated, excited, by your art, by your studies. The past isn't a slab of stone; it's fragmented and porous.) By now I had given up my dream of a career as a painter. Rejection, rejection, rejection. It had made the part of me that wanted to paint wither away, leaving a more streamlined Janice, a smoother Janice, a less creative Janice. I had decided I would do better as a gallery owner, had not yet realized I was still traveling toward remote regions marked on maps only by terms such as "Art Critic" and "Historian." (You were traveling toward me, Janice. That's not such a bad thing.) Only later did I come to see my initial investment in the gallery as a form of self-torture: by promoting the works of others I could denigrate my own efforts.

❧❦❧

This time, Duncan had a haunted look about him, the joy of his previous underground adventures stripped away, leaving behind only a gauntness akin to death. The paleness that had taken over his features had blanched away any expression, any life, in his limbs, in his movements. He:

Beard like the tendrils of finely threaded spores.

Swayed in the doorway like a tall, ensanguinated ghost, holding the door open with one shaking, febrile arm.

Shoes tattered and torn, as if savaged by a dog.

Muttered my name as if in the middle of a dream.

Clothes stained everywhere with spores, reduced to a fine, metallic dust that glittered blackly all around him.

Trailed tiny obsidian mushrooms, trembling off him at every turn.

Eyes embedded with black flecks, staring at some nameless vision just beyond me.

Clutched something tightly in his left hand, knuckles pale against the dark coating of spore dust.

❧❦❧

He staggered inside, fell to the floor amid the paintings, the curled canvases, the naked frames vainglorious with the vision of the wall behind them. The gallery smelled of turpentine, of freshly cut wood, of drying paint. But as Duncan met the floor, or the floor met Duncan, the smells became one smell: the smell of Duncan. A dark green smell brought from deep underground. A subtle interweaving of minerals and flesh and fungus. The smell of old water trickling through stones and earth. The smell of lichen and moss. (Flesh penetrated by fungus, you mean—every pore cross-pollinated, supersaturated. Nothing very subtle about it. The flesh alive and prickly.) The smell, now, of my brother.

I locked the door behind him. I slapped his face until his gaze cleared, and he saw me. With my help, he got to his feet and I took him into the back room. He was so light. He might as well have been a skeleton draped with canvas. I began to cry. His ribs bent against my encircling arm as I gently laid him down against a wall. His clothes were so filthy that I made him take them off and put on a painter's smock.

I forced bread and cheese on him. He didn't want it at first. I had to tear the bread into small pieces and hold his mouth open. I had to make him close his mouth. "Swallow." He had no choice. He couldn't fight me—he was too weak. Or I was, for once, too strong.

Eventually, he took the bread from my hands, began to eat on his own. Still he said nothing, staring at me with eyes white against the dust-stippled darkness of his forehead and jutting cheekbones.

"When you are ready, speak," I said. "You are not leaving here until you tell me exactly what happened. You are not leaving here until I know why. Why, Duncan? What happened to you?" I couldn't keep the anguish from my voice.

Duncan smiled up at me. A drunkard's smile. A skeleton's smile. My brother's smile, as laconic as ever.

"Same old sister," he said. "I knew I could count on you. To half kill me trying to feed me." (To help me. Who else would help me back then?)

"I mean it. I won't let you leave without telling me what happened."

He smiled again, but he wouldn't look at me. For a long time, he said nothing as I watched him.

Then the flood. He spoke and spoke and spoke—rambling, coherent, fragmented, clever. I began to grow afraid for him. All these words. There was already less than nothing inside of him. I could see that. When the last words had left his mouth, would even the canvas of his skin flap away free, the filigree of his bones disintegrate into dust? Slowly, I managed to hear the words and forget the condition of the one who spoke them. Forget that he was my brother.

He had gone deeper into the underground this time, but the research had gone badly. He kept interspersing his account with mutterings that he would "never do it again." And, "If I stay on the surface, I'm safe. I should be safe." At the time, I thought he meant staying physically aboveground, but now I'm not so sure. (Be sure.) I wonder if he also meant the surface of his mind. That if he could simply restrain himself from the divergent thinking, the untoward analysis, that had marked some of his previous books, he might once again be a published writer. (Who knows? I might have given up on myself if forced to listen to my own ravings. I might have even become a respectable citizen.)

As he spoke, I realized I wasn't ready for his revelations. I had made a mistake—I didn't want to hear what he had to say. I needed distance from this shivering, shuddering wreck of a man. He clung to the edges of the smock I had given him like a corpse curling fingers around a coffin's lining. The look on his face made me think of our father dying in the summer grass. It frightened me. I tried to put boundaries on the conversation.

"What happened to the book you were working on?" I asked him.

He grimaced, but the expression made him look more human, and his gaze turned inward, the horrors reflected there no longer trying to get out.

"Stillborn," he gasped, as if breaking to the surface after being held down in black water. He lurched to his feet, fell back down again. Every surface he touched became covered in fine black powder. "Stillborn," he repeated. "Or I killed it. I don't know which. Maybe I'm a murderer. I was . . . I was halfway through. On fire with ancient texts. Bloated with the knowledge in them. Didn't think I needed firsthand experience to write the book. Such a web of words, Janice. I have never used so many words. I used so many there weren't any left to write with. And yet, I still had this fear deep in my skull. I couldn't get it out." (I still can't get it out of my head, sometimes. Writing a book and going underground are so similar. That fear of the unknown never really goes away. But, after a while, it becomes a perverse comfort.)

He relinquished his grasp on the object in his hand, which I had almost forgotten.

It rolled across the floor. We both stared at it, he as astonished as I. A honey-and-parchment-colored ball. Of flesh? Of tissue? Of stone?

He looked up at me. "I remember now. It needs moisture. If it dries, it dies. Cracks form in its skin. It's curled into a ball to preserve a pearl of moisture between its cilia."

"What is it?" I said, unable to keep the fear from my voice.

He grinned in recognition of my tone. "Before Dad died," he said, "you would have found this creature a wonderful mystery. You would have followed me out into the woods and we would have dug up fire-red salamanders just to see their eyes glow in the dark."

"No," I said. "No. There was no time when I would have found this *thing* a wonderful mystery. Where did you find it?"

His smirk, the way it ate up his face, the way it accentuated the suddenly taut bones in his neck, made the flesh around his mouth a vassal to his mirth, sickened me.

"Where do *you* think it came from?"

I ignored the question, turned away, said, "I have a canteen of water in the front, near my desk. But keep talking. Keep telling me about your book."

He frowned as I walked past him into the main room of the gallery. From behind me, his disembodied voice rose up, quavered, continued. A thrush caught in a hunter's snare, flapping this way and that, ever more entangled and near its death. His smell had coated the entire gallery. In a sense, I was as close to him searching for the canteen as if I stood beside him. Beyond the gallery windows lay the real world, composed of unnaturally bright colors and shoppers walking briskly by.

"So I never finished it, Janice. What do you think of that? I couldn't. Wouldn't. I wrote and wrote. I wrote with the energy of ten men each evening. All texts I consulted interlocked under my dexterous manipulations. It all made such perfect sense . . . and then I began to panic. Each word, I realized, had been leading me further and further away from the central mystery. Every sentence left a false trail. Every paragraph formed another wall between me and my thesis. Soon, I stopped writing. It had all been going so well. How could it get so bad so quickly?

"I soon found out. I backtracked through the abyss of words, searching for a flaw, a fissure, a crack in the foundation. Perhaps some paragraph had turned traitor and would reveal itself. Only it wasn't a paragraph. It was a single word, five pages from the end of my silly scribblings, in a sentence of no particular importance. Just a single word. I know the sentence by heart, because I've repeated it to myself over and over again. It's all that's left of my book. Do you want to hear it?"

"Yes," I said, although I wasn't sure. I was still searching for the canteen under all the canvases.

"Here it is: 'But surely, if Tonsure had not known the truth then, he knew it after traveling underground.' The word was 'truth,' and I could not get past the truth. The truth stank of the underground, buried under dead leaves and hidden in cold, dry, dark caverns. The truth had little to do with the surface of things.

"From that word, in that context, on that page, written in my nearly illegible hand, my masterwork, my beautiful, marvelous book unraveled syllable by syllable. I began by crossing out words that did not belong in the sentence. Then I began to delete words by rules as illegitimate and illogical as the gray caps themselves.

Until after a week, I woke up one morning, determined to continue my surgical editing of the manuscript—only to find that not even the original sentence had been spared: all that remained of my once-proud manuscript was that single word: 'truth.' And, truth, my dear sister, was not a big enough word to constitute an entire book—at least not to me." (Or my publishers, come to think of it. If there had been any publishers.)

I had found the canteen. I came back into the room and handed it to him. "You should drink some. Rinse out the lie you've just told."

He snorted, took the canteen, raised it to his lips, and, drinking from it, kissed it as seriously as he would a lover.

"Perhaps it is in part a metaphor," he said, "but it is still, ironically enough, the truth."

"Don't speak in metaphors, then. How do you tell truth from lies otherwise?"

"I want to be taken literally."

"You mean literarily, Duncan. Except you've already been taken literarily—they've all ravished you and gone on to the next victim."

"Literally."

"Is that why you brought this horrible rolled up ball of an animal with you?"

"No. I forgot I had it. Now that I've brought it here, I can't let it die." (Actually, Janice, I did bring it with me on purpose. I had just forgotten the purpose.)

He sidled over to the golden ball of flesh, poured water into his hand.

He looked up at me, the expression on his face taking me back to all of his foolish explorations as a child. "Watch now! Watch carefully!"

Slowly, he poured water over the golden ball. After a moment the gold color blushed into a haze of purple-yellow-blue-green, which then returned to gold, but a more vibrant shade of gold that flashed in the dim light. Duncan poured more water over the creature. It seemed to crack apart, fissures erupting across its skin at regular intervals. But no—it was merely opening up, each of its four legs unfurling from the top of the ball, to settle upside down on the floor. Immediately, it leapt up, spun, and landed, cilia down, revealed as a kind of phosphorescent starfish.

Duncan dribbled still more water over it. Each of its four arms shone a different glittering shade—green-blue-yellow-purple—the edges of the blue arm tinged green on one side, yellow on the other.

"A starfish," I said.

"A compass," he said. "Just one of the many wonders to be found belowground. A living compass. North is blue, so if you turn it like so," and he reached over and carefully turned the starfish, "the arm shines perfectly blue, facing as it does due north."

Indeed, the blue had been cleansed of any green or yellow taint.

"This compass saved me more than once when I was lost," he said.

I stared at my ungainly, stacked frames. "I'm sick of wonders, Duncan. This is just a color to me, just a trick. The true wonder is that you're still alive. No one could have expected that. You suffer what may have been a mental breakdown, go down below, return with a living compass, and expect me to say . . . what? How *wonderful* that is? How *awed* I am by it all? No. I'm appalled. I'm horrified. I'm angry. I've failed at one career after another. I'm about to open my own gallery. I haven't seen you in almost ten years, and you shamble in here, a talking skeleton— and you expect me to be impressed by a magic show? Have you seen yourself lately?"

I can't remember ever being so furious—and out of nowhere, out of almost nothing. My hands shook. My shoulders had become rigid blocks of stone. My throat ached. And I'm not even sure why. (Because you were scared, and because you were my sister, and you loved me. Even when you were mad at me, I was your family.) I almost want to laugh, typing this now. Having seen so many strange things since, having been at peace lying on a floor littered with corpses, having accepted so much strangeness from Duncan, that starfish seems almost mundane in retrospect, and my anger at Duncan self-indulgent.

He scooped up the starfish, held it in his hands. It lay there as contentedly as if in a tidal pool. "I don't expect anything, Janice," he said, each word carefully weighed, wrapped, tied with string before leaving his mouth. "I have no one else to tell. No one else who saw me the last time. No one else who might possibly believe anything I saw. Starfish or no starfish."

"Tell Mom then. Mom would listen. If you speak softly enough, Dad might even pick up a whisper of it. Did you meet him down there?"

He winced, sat back against the wall, next to a leering portrait by a painter named Sonter. The shadows and the sheen of black dust on his skin rendered him almost invisible.

Coated by the darkness, he said, "I'm sorry. I didn't mean to—I didn't realize . . . But you know, Janice, you *are* the only one who won't think me crazy."

The starfish had begun to explore the crook of Duncan's arm. Its rejuvenated cilia shone wetly, a thousand minute moving jewels among the windless reeds of his arm hairs.

"It's so hard," he said. "Half of what you see seems like a hallucination, or a dream, even while you're living it. You are so unsure about what's real that you take all kinds of stupid risks. As if it can't hurt you. You float along, like a spore. You sit for days in caverns as large as cities, let the fungi creep up and devour you. The stars that can't be stars fall in on you in waves. And you sit there. An afternoon in the park. A picnic for one.

"*Things* walk by you. Some stop and stare. Some poke you or hit you, and then you have to pretend you're in a dream, because otherwise you would be so afraid that nothing would stop you from screaming, and you'd keep screaming until they put a stop to you."

He shivered and rolled over on his side. "Sorry, sorry, sorry," he whined, the starfish on his shoulder a golden glimmer.

"Was it worth it?" I asked him, not unkindly. "Was it?"

"Ask me in fifty years, Janice. A hundred years. A thousand." (It didn't take that long. Within five years, I began to recognize that my sojourn underground was akin to one more addict's hit of mushrooms. It took ten years of these adventures for me to realize that I could only *react* to such journeys, never *predict*. Always *absorbing*, but mostly in the physical sense.)

He twisted from side to side, holding his stomach.

"I thought I could get it out of me if I talked about it," he said. "Flush it from my brain, my body. But it's still in there. It's still in me."

Again, he was talking about two things at once, but I could only bear to talk about what I might be able to help him with right then.

"Duncan," I said, "we can't wash it off of you this time. I think it's inside of you, like some kind of poison. Your pores are clogged with black spores. Your skin is . . . different."

He gasped. Was he crying? "I know. I can feel it inside of me. It's trying to change me."

"Talk about it, then. Talk about it until you talk it all out."

He laughed without any hint of humor. "Are you mad? I can't talk it out of my skin. I can't do that."

I joined him along the wall, moving Sonter's portrait to the side. The starfish had splayed itself across the side of his neck like an exotic scar.

"You're due north," I said. "Its arm is blue. And you're right, Duncan. It's beautiful. It's one of the most beautiful things I've ever seen."

He moved to pull it off, but I caught his arm. "No. Don't. I think it's feeding on the spores embedded in your skin." It left a trail of almost-white skin behind it.

"You think so?" His eyes searched mine for something I'm not sure I've ever been able to give.

In that moment before he began to really tell me his story, to which all of this had been foolish, prattling preamble—in that moment, I think I loved my brother as much as I ever had in all the years since his birth. His face shone darkly in my doomed gallery, more precious than any painting.

✻

We lay side by side, silent in the semi-darkness of the back room, surrounded by dead paint. The now-reluctant glare from the main room meant the sun had begun to fade from the sky. The starfish flinched, as if touched by the memory of light, as it continued its slow migration toward the top of Duncan's head.

I could remember afternoons when Duncan and I would sit against the side of the house in Stockton, out of the sun, eating cookies we'd stolen from the kitchen while we talked about school or the nasty neighbor down the street. The quality of light was the same, the way it almost bent around the corner even as it evaporated into dust motes. As if to tell us we were never alone—that even in the stillness, with no wind, our fingers stained by the grass, we are never really outside of time.

Duncan began to talk while I listened without asking questions or making comments. I stared at nothing at all, a great peace come over me. It was cool and dark in that room. The shadows loved us.

But memory is imperfect, incomplete, fickle. It tells us the exact shade of our mother's blouse the day our father died, but it cannot accurately recall a conversation between siblings decades after that. Thus, I resort, as I already have through most of this afterword, to a much later journal entry by Duncan—clearly later because it is polluted by the presence of Mary Sabon; so polluted that I could not easily edit her out of it. (You can't erase the past just because you wish it hadn't happened.)

Does it make any difference now to Duncan who sees it? None. So why not steal his diary entry and spill his innermost thoughts like blood across the page, fling them across the faces of Sabon's flesh necklace in a fine spackle of retreating life. I'll let Duncan tell us about his journeys underground. (Do I have a choice?

But you're right—it doesn't matter anymore. I will not edit it, or anything else, out, although I may protest from time to time. I haven't decided yet if you're a true historian or one step removed from a gossip columnist.)

Tonsure got parts of it right—the contractions of spaces, small to large, and how mysterious perspective becomes after long periods underground. The way the blackness picks up different hues and textures, transformed into anti-color, an anti-spectrum. The fetid closeness and vastness, the multitude of smells, from the soothing scent of something like mint to the putrid stench of rotting fungi, like a dead animal . . . and yet all my words make of me a liar. I struggle to express myself, and only feel myself moving further from the truth. No wonder Mary thinks me a fool. No wonder she looks at me as if I am much stranger than the strangest thing she has ever seen. I caught a glimpse of her soft white breast when she leaned down to pick up a book. I'd be rougher than nails to her skin. The thought of being close tantalizes and yet makes me sick with my own clumsiness.

That is one thing I prefer about the underground: the loss of self to your environment is almost as profound as orgasm or epiphany, your senses shattered, rippled, as fragmented and wide as the sky. Time releases its meaning. Space is just a subset of time. You cease to become mortal. Your heartbeat is no longer a motion or a moment, but a possibility that may someday arrive, and then pass, only to arrive again. It's the most frightening loss of control imaginable.

For me it was still different than for Tonsure. He had no real protection, no real defenses, until he adapted. At least I had the clues Tonsure left behind. At least I knew how to make myself invisible to them, to lose myself but not become lost. To become as still as death but not dead. Sometimes this meant standing in one place for days. Sometimes it meant constant, manic movement, to emulate the frantic writhing of the *cheraticaticals* [no known translation].

I found the standing still worse than the walking and running. I could disguise myself from the gray caps, but not from their servants—the spores, the parasites, the tiny mushroom caps, fungi, and lichen. They found me and infiltrated me—I could feel their tendrils, their fleshy-dry-cold-warm pseudopods and cilia and strands slowly sliding up my skin, like a hundred tiny hands. They tried to remake me in their image. If it had been you, Mary, I would not have minded. If you had found me, I would have given up my identity as easily as a wisp of cloud.

I drifted and drifted, often so in trance that I did not have a single conscious thought for hours. I was a pair of eyes reporting to a brain that had ceased to police, to analyze, the incoming images. It all went through me and past, to some place other. In a way, it was a kind of release. Now, it makes me wonder if I had learned what it feels like to be a tree, or even, strike me dead, a gray cap. But, that cannot be so—the gray caps are always in motion, always thinking. You can see it in their eyes.

Once, as I stood in one of my motionless trances, a gray cap approached me. What did he do? Nothing. He sat in front of me and stared up at me for hours, for days. His eyes reflected the darkness. His eyes had a quality that held all of me entirely, held me against my will. Mary holds me, but not against my will—her eyes and my will are in accord. Her eyes: green, green, green. Greener than Ambergris. Greener than the greenest moss by a trickling stream.

After a time, I realized the gray cap had gone, but it took me weeks to return to the surface of my thoughts, and months to find the real surface, and with it the light. The light! A weak trickle of late afternoon gloom, presage of sunset, and yet it pierced my vision. I could not open my eyes until after dusk, fumbling my way along the Moth riverbank like some pathetic mole. The light burned into my closed eyelids. It seemed to crack my skin. It tried to kill me and birth me simultaneously. I lay gasping in the mud, writhing, afraid I would burn up.

I took a long sip from the canteen at this point, if only to assuage Duncan's remembered heat. The starfish now served as an exotic, glowing ear, eclipsing flesh and blood. It hummed a little as it worked. A smell like fresh-cut orange surrounded it.

I offered Duncan the canteen. He used the opportunity to pour more water on his pet. I was about to prod him to continue when he pulled the starfish from his ear, sat up, and said, looking down at the compass as it sucked on his fingers, "Do you know the first sentences of the Truffidian Bible?"

"No," I said. "Do you?" Our parents had treated religion like a door behind which stood an endless abyss: better not to believe at all, the abyss revealed, than have it be closed over, falsified, prettied up. (And yet, there is something in my skin now, after all these years, that hums of the world in a way that predicts the infinite.)

"Yes, I do know them. Would you like to hear them?"

"Do I have a choice?"

"No. Those words are 'The world is broken. God is in exile.' Followed shortly thereafter by 'In the first part of creation, God made light and made vessels for the light. The vessels were too fragile: they broke, and from the broken vessels of the supernal lights, the material world was created.'"

Something very much like a void opened up inside me. A chill brought goose-flesh to my skin. Each word from my mouth sounded heavier than it should have: "And what does the creation of the world have to do with the gray caps?"

He put a finger to his lips. His face in the sour light gave off a faint glow, pale relative to the illumination of the starfish. His skin winked from behind the mushroom dust. He looked so old. Why should he look so old? What did he know?

He said: "A machine. A glass. A mirror. A broken machine. A cracked glass. A shattered mirror."

I remember now the way he used the phrases at his disposal. Clean, fine cuts. Great, slashing cuts. Fractures in the word and the world.

"Some things should not be articulated. Some words should never be used in exact combination with other words." My father said that once, while reading a scathing negative review of one of his essays. He said it with a tired little sigh, a joke at his expense. His whole body slumped from the words. Weighed down with words, like stones in his pocket.

A machine. A glass. A mirror. Duncan's journal, with the advantage of distance, described his discovery much more gracefully . . .

But it doesn't work right. It hasn't worked right since they built it. A part, a mechanism, a balance—something they don't quite understand. How can I call it strictly a machine? It is as much organic as metallic, housed in a cavern larger than three Truffidian Cathedrals. You feel it and hear it before you see it: a throbbly hum, a grindful pulse, a sorrowful bellow. The passageways rumble and crackle with the force of it. A hot wind flares out before it. The only entrance leads, after much hard work, to the back of the machine, where you can see its inner workings. You are struck by the fact of its awful carnality, for they feed it lives as well as fuel. Flesh and metal bond, married by spores, joined by a latticework of polyps and filaments and lazy strands. Wisps and converted moonlight. Sparks and gears. The whole is at first obscured by its own detail, by those elements at eye level: a row of white sluglike bodies curled within the cogs and gears, eyes shut, apparently asleep. Wrinkled and luminous. Lacking all but the most rudimentary stubs of limbs. But with faces identical to those of the gray caps.

You cannot help but look closer. You cannot help but notice two things: that they dream, twitching reflexively in their repose, eyelids flickering with subconscious thought, and that they are not truly curled within the machine—they are curled *into* the machine, meshed with it at a hundred points of contact. The blue-red veins in their arms flow into milk-white fingers, and at the border between skin and air, transformed from vein into silvery wire. Tendrils of wire meet tendrils of flesh, broken up by sections of sharp wheels, clotted with scraps of flesh, and whining almost soundlessly as they whir in the darkness.

As you stare at the nearest white wrinkled body, you begin to smell the thickness of oil and blood mixed together. As the taste bites into your mouth, you take a step back, and suddenly you feel as if you are falling, the sense of vertigo so intense your arms flail out though you stand on solid ground. Because you realize it isn't one pale dreamer, or even a row of them, or even five rows of five hundred, but more than five thousand rows of five thousand milk-white dreamers, running on into the distance—as far as you care to see—millions of them, caught and transfixed in the back of the machine. And they are all dreaming and all their eyelids flicker in unison, and all their blood flows into all the wires while a hundred thousand sharpened wheels spin soundlessly.

The hum you hear, that low hum you hear, does not come from the machinery. It does not come from the wheels, the cogs, the wires. The hum emanates from the white bodies. They are humming in their sleep, a slow, even hum as peaceful as they are not—how can I write this, how? except to keep writing and when I've stopped never look at this again—while the machine itself is silent.

The rows blur as you tilt your head to look up, not because the rows are too far away, but because your eyes and your brain have decided that this is too much, this is too much to take in without going mad, that you do not want to comprehend this crushing immensity of vision, that if comprehended completely, it will haunt not just your nightmares for the rest of your life—it will form a permanent overlay upon your waking sight, and you will stumble through your days like a blind man, the ghost-vision in your head stronger than reality.

So you return to details—the details right in front of you. The latticework of wires and tubes, where you see a thrush has been placed, intertwined, its broken wings flapping painfully. There, a dragonfly, already dead, brittle and glassy. Bits and pieces of flesh still writhing with the memory of interconnection. Skulls. Yellowing bones. Glossy black vines. Pieces of earth. And holding it all together, like glue, dull red fungus.

But now the detail becomes too detailed, and again your eyes blur, and you decide maybe movement will save you—that perhaps if you move to the other side of the machine, you will find something different, something that does not call out remorselessly for your surrender. Because if you stand there for another minute, you will enmesh yourself in the machine. You will climb up into the flesh and metal. You will curl up to something pale and sticky and embrace it. You will relax your body into the space allowed it, your legs released from you in a spray of blood and wire, you smiling as it happens, your eyes already dulled, and dreaming some communal dream, your tongue the tongue of the machine, your mouth humming in another language, your arms weighed down with tendrils of metal, your torso split in half to let out the things that must be let out.

For a long time, you stand on the fissure between sweet acceptance of dissolution and the responsibility of movement, the enticing smell of decay, the ultimate inertia, reaching out to you . . . but, eventually, you move away, with an audible shudder that shakes your bones, almost pulls you apart.

As you hobble around to the side of the machine, you feel the million eyes of the crumpled, huddled white shapes snap open, for a single second drawn out of their dreams of you.

✻✻✻

There is no history, no present. There are only the sides of the machine. Slick memory of metal, mad with its own brightness, mad with the memory of what it contains. You cling to those sides for support, but make your way past them as quickly as possible. The sides are like the middle of a book—necessary, but quickly read through to get to the end. Already, you try in vain to forget the beginning.

✻✻✻

The front of the machine has a comforting translucent or reflective quality. You will never be able to decide which quality it possesses, although you stand there staring at it for days, ensnared by your own foolish hope for something to negate the horrible negation of the machine's innards. Ghosts of images cloud the surface of the machine and are wiped clean as if by a careless, a meticulous, an impatient painter. A great windswept desert, sluggish with the weight of its own dunes. An ocean, waveless, the tension of its surface broken only by the shadow of clouds above, the water such a perfect blue-green that it hurts your eyes. A mountain range at sunset, distant, ruined towers propped up by the foothills at its flanks.

Always flickering into perfection and back into oblivion. Places that if they exist in this world you have never seen, or heard mention of their existence. Ever.

You slide into the calm of these scenes, although you cannot forget the white shapes behind the machine, the eyelids that flicker as these images flicker. Only the machine knows, and the machine is damaged. Its thoughts are damaged. Your thoughts are damaged: they run liquid-slow through your brain, even though you wish they would stop.

※❀※

After several days, your vision strays and unfocuses and you blink slowly, attention drawn to a door at the very bottom of the mirror. The door is as big as the machine. The door is as small as your fingernail. The distance between you and the door is infinite. The distance between you and the door is so minute you could reach out and touch it. The door is translucent—the images that flow across the screen sweep across the door as well, so that it is only by the barely perceived hairline fracture of its outline that it can be distinguished beneath the desert, ocean, mountains, that glide across its surface. The door is a mirror, too, you realize, and after so long of not focusing on anything, letting images run through you, you find yourself concentrating on the door and the door alone. In many ways, it is an ordinary door, almost a nonexistent door. And yet, staring at it, a wave of fear passes over you. A fear so blinding it paralyzes you. It holds you in place. You can feel the pressure of all that meat, all that flesh, all the metal inside the machine amassed behind that door. It is an unbearable weight at your throat. You are buried in it, in a small box, under an eternity of rock and earth. The worms are singing to you through the rubble. The worms know your name. You cannot think. Your head is full of blood. You dare not breathe.

There is something behind the door.

There is something behind the door.

There is something behind the door.

The door begins to open inward, and *something* fluid and slow, no longer dreaming, begins to come out from inside, lurching around the edge of the door. You begin to run—to run as far from that place as you possibly can, screaming until your throat fills with the blood in your head, your head now an empty globe while the rest of you drowns in blood. And still it makes no difference, because you are back in that place with the slugs and the skulls and the pale dreamers and the machine that doesn't work that doesn't work that doesn't work thatdoesn'twork hat doesnwor atdoeswor doeswor doewor dowor door . . .

This entry about a defective "machine" built by the gray caps is the strangest part of my brother's journal. By far. In its pure physicality I sense a level of discomfort rare for Duncan. As if, from fretful tossing and turning, he woke, reached for pen and notepad from the nightstand, and wrote down his first impressions of a fading nightmare. He appears at first anxious to record the experience, and then less so, the use of second person intended to place the burden of memory on the reader, to purge the images from his head. (It is more that I could not find words to accurately convey what I saw, and so I tried to describe how I *felt* instead—in a sense presaging Ambergrisians' reaction to the recent Shift.)

If Duncan had, in the gallery that afternoon, told me about the machine with the calm madness of that journal entry, a silence would have settled over us. Our conversation would have faded away into a nothingness made alive and aware by his words. Thankfully, Duncan told his story with less than brutal lucidity. He used stilted words in rows of sentences crippled by fits and starts—a vagabond, poorly rehearsed circus of words that could not be taken seriously. He focused on the front of the machine with its marvelous visions of far-distant places. He dismissed the back of the machine with a single sentence. Somehow, I could not reconcile his vision with my memory of the spores floating out of my apartment window.

Even so, an element of unreality entered the gallery following his revelation. I remember staring at him and thinking that his face could not be composed of flesh and blood, not with those words coming from his mouth. The light now hid his features, but his hands, lit by the starfish, glowed white.

"The door in the machine never fully opens," Duncan said in a distant tone.

"What would happen if it did?"

"They would be free . . ."

"Who?" I asked, although I knew the answer.

"The gray caps."

"Free of what?"

Pale hands, darkened face, gray speech. "I think they care nothing for us one way or the other, Janice. They have only one purpose now. The same purpose they've had for centuries."

"In your unconfirmed opinion, brother," I said, and shivered at the way the mushroom dust on his face still glittered darkly.

"What do you know about the Silence?"

"The gray caps killed everyone in the city," I said.

He shook his head. Forgetting the starfish in his hands, he stood abruptly. The starfish fell to the floor and began to curl and uncurl in a reflexive imitation of pain. Now Duncan was stooped over me. Now he was crouched beside me. If there were ever a secret he truly wanted to tell me, this was the secret. This was the cause of it. We had returned to the last survivor of his sixth book, alive amid all of the suicides: the truth. As my brother saw it.

"You learned it wrong," he told me. "That's not what happened. It didn't happen like that. I've seen so many things, and I've thought a lot about what I've seen. They disappeared without a single drop of blood left behind. Not a fragment of bone. No. They weren't killed. At least not directly. Try to imagine a different answer: a sudden miscalculation, a botched experiment, a flaw in the machine. All of those people. All twenty-five thousand of them. The men, the women, the children—they didn't die. They were *moved*. The door opened in a way the gray caps didn't expect, couldn't expect, and all those people—they were *moved* by mistake. The machine took them to someplace else. And, yes, maybe they died, and maybe they died horribly—but my point is, it was all an *accident*. A mistake. A *terrible, pointless blunder*."

He was breathing heavily. Sweat glistened on his arms, where before the black dust had suppressed it.

"That's crazy," I said. "That's the craziest thing I have ever heard in my life. They've killed thousands of people. They've done terrible things. And you have the nerve to make apologies for them?!"

"Would it be easier to accept that they don't give a damn about us one way or the other if we hadn't massacred them to build this city? What I think is crazy is that we try to pretend they are just like us. If we had massacred most of the citizens of Morrow, we would expect them to seek revenge. That would be natural, understandable, even acceptable. But what about a people that, when you slaughter hundreds of them, doesn't even really notice? That doesn't acknowledge the event? We can't accept that reaction. That would be incomprehensible. So we tack the idea of 'revenge' onto the Silence so we can sleep better at night—because we think, we actually have the nerve to think, that we understand these creatures that live beneath us. And if we think we understand them, if we believe they are like us in their motivations, then we don't fear them quite as much. If we meet one in an alley, we believe we can talk to it, reason with it, communicate with it. Or if we see one dozing beneath a red flag on the street during the day, we overlook it, we make it part of the scenery, no less colorful or benign than a newly ordained Truffidian priest prancing down Albumuth Boulevard in full regalia."

"You're crazy, Duncan. You're unwell." Anger again burned inside of me. The idea of the Silence reduced to a pathetic mistake enraged me. The idea that my own brother might utter the words that made it so seemed a betrayal of an unspoken understanding between us. Before this moment, we could always count on sharing the same worldview no matter what happened, even when we saw each other at wider and wider intervals.

"It's more complicated than you think," he said. "They are on a journey as much as we are on a journey. They are trying to get somewhere else—but they can't. It doesn't work. With all they can do, with all they are, they still cannot make their mirror, their glass, work properly. Isn't that sad? Isn't that kind of sad?"

I slapped him across the face. My hand came away black with spores. He did not move an inch.

"Sad?" I said. "Sad? Sad is twenty-five thousand lives snuffed out, not a broken machine. Not a broken machine! What is happening to you that you cannot see that? Regardless of what happened. Not that I believe you. Frankly, I don't believe you. Why should I? For all I know, you've been in the sewers for the past few weeks, living off of rats and whatever garbage you could get your hands on. And all you've seen is the reflection of your own filthy face in a pool of scummy water!"

Duncan smiled and pointed at the starfish. "How do you explain that?"

"Ha!" I said. "It was probably groveling for garbage along with you. It definitely isn't proof of anything, if that's what you mean. Why didn't you bring something substantive, like a gray cap willing to corroborate your statement?"

"I did bring a gray cap," he said. "Several, in fact. Although not by choice. Take a good look through the doorway, out the front window, to the left. I doubt they would corroborate anything, though. I think they'd like to see me dead."

"Don't joke."

"I'm not. Take a look."

Reluctantly, I raised myself, my left leg asleep—even less impressed by Duncan's story, apparently, than I was. I peered around the doorway. Sheathed like swords by the fading light, more sharp shadow than dream, three gray caps stood staring in through the window. They stood so still the cobblestones of the street behind them seemed more alive. The whites of their eyes gleamed like wet paint. They stared at and through me. As if I meant nothing to them. The sight of them sent a convulsive shudder through me. I ducked back, beside Duncan.

"Maybe we should leave by the back door," I said.

A low, humorless laugh from Duncan. "Maybe they came for your gallery opening."

"Very funny. Follow me . . ."

In a pinch, I still trusted my brother more than anyone else in the world.

✵✵✵

Every human being is a puppet on strings, but the puppet half controls the strings, and the strings do not ascend to some anonymous Maker, but are glistening golden strands that connect one puppet to another. Each strand is sensitive to the vibrations of every other strand. Every vibration sings in not only the puppet's heart, but in the hearts of many other puppets, so that if you listen carefully, you can hear a low hum as of many hearts singing together . . . When a strand snaps, when it breaks for love, or lack of love, or from hatred, or from pain . . . every other connected strand feels it, and every other connected heart feels it—and since every strand and every heart are, in theory, connected, even if at their most distant limits, this means the effect is universal. All through the darkness where shining strings are the only light, a woundedness occurs. And this hurt affects each strand and each puppet in a different way, because we are all puppets on strings and we all hurt and are hurt. And all the strings shimmer on regardless, and all of our actions, no matter how small, have consequences to other puppets . . . After we are dead, gone to join the darkness between the lines of light, the strands we leave behind still quiver their lost messages into the hearts of those other puppets we met along the way, on our journey from light into not-light. These lost strands are the memories we leave behind . . . Magnify this effect by 25,000 souls and perhaps you can see why I cannot so lightly dismiss what you call a mistake. Each extinguished life leaves a hole in many other lives—a series of small extinguishments that can never be completely forgotten or survived. Each survivor carries a little of that void within them.

This is part of a letter I wrote to Duncan—the only attempt following our conversation to express my feelings about the Silence to him. One day I came home to my apartment early to find Duncan gone on some errand. For some reason I had been thinking about the Silence that day, perhaps because two or three new acquisitions had featured, in the background, the shadowy form of a gray cap. I sat down at my desk and wrote Duncan a letter, which I then placed in his brief-case full of papers, expecting he'd come across it in a week or a month. But he never mentioned it to me. I never knew whether he had read it or not until, going through his things after this final disappearance, I found it in a folder labeled simply "Janice." (I did read it, and I cried. At the time, it made me feel more alone than I had ever felt before. Only later did I find it a comfort.)

Duncan stayed at my apartment for nearly six months. By the fifth month, he appeared to have made a full recovery. We did not often speak of that afternoon when he had told me his theory about the Silence. In a sense, we decided to forget about it, so that it took on the hazy lack of detail specific only to memory. We were allowed that luxury back then. We did not have Sabon's glittering necklace of flesh to set us straight.

The starfish lasted four months and then died in a strobe of violent light, per-haps deprived of some precious nutrient, or perhaps having attained the end of its natural life cycle. Its bleached skeleton on the mantel carried hardly more signifi-cance than a snail's shell found by the riverbank.

4

Time to start over. Another dead white page to fill with dead black type, so I'll fill it. Why not? I've nothing better to do, for now anyway. Mary's still holding court at the bottom of that marble staircase at Lake's party, but I think I'll make her wait a little longer.

Especially since it strikes me that at this point in the narrative, or somewhere around here, Duncan would have paused to catch his breath, to regroup and place events in historical context. (If it were me, I would have skipped "historical con-text" and returned to that marble staircase, since that's really the only part of this story I don't know already.) *Years passed. They seem now like pale leaves pressed between the pages of an obscure book.*

Oddly enough, I don't give a damn about historical context at the moment. I can see the sliver of green light becoming dull, indifferent—which means the sun is going down outside. And we all know what happens, or can happen, when the sun goes down, don't we? Don't answer that question—read this instead:

The death of composer/politician Voss Bender and the rise of the Reds and Greens, who debate his legacy with knives: a civil war in the streets, which the trader Hoegbotton uses to solidify control of the city. I witness a man die right outside my gallery, hit in the head with a rock until his skull resembles a collection of broken eggshells dripping with red-gray mush. No art to it that I could see. No reason, either. Followed by: defeat of the Reds, disbanding of the Greens, the tossing of Bender's ashes in the River Moth—only, the wise old river doesn't want them, according to legend, and blows them back in the faces of the assembled mourners; thus dispersing Bender all across the city when the mourners go home. Scandal in the Truffidian Church—boring as only a Truffidian scandal can be: oh my goodness, the Antechamber Henry Bonmot, whom I still miss terribly, has been caught taking money from the collection plates! At the same time, the River Moth overflows its banks for a season and takes a sizable portion of our mother's property with it, making us officially heirs of Nothing but an old, rotting mansion. The Kalif of the Western Empire chokes on a plum pit, replaced by another faceless bureaucrat. Meanwhile, infant mortality continues to decline, along with the birth rate, while old people die in droves from a heat stroke that withers even the hardiest southern trees. A slight upswing in the fortunes of motored vehicles due to an influx of oil from the Southern Islands is offset by a plummet in the availability of spare parts. Voss Bender's posthumously produced opera, *Trillian*, reaches the two-year mark of its first run, its full houses unscathed by the dwindling tourist trade (no one likes to die while on holiday, whether by heat stroke or by gray cap). Other composers and playwrights, who could really use the Bender Memorial Theater as a venue for their own drivel, gnash their teeth and whine in the back rooms of bars and taverns: Bender, dead, still lives on! Three Festivals of the Freshwater Squid pass by without so much as a pantomime of real violence— what is wrong with us as a people, I ask you, that we have become so passive? Are we not animals? Perhaps this squalid, shameful peace has something to do with the introduction of the telephone, at least for the well-off, which allows Ambergrisians to call up total strangers and breathe at them, make funny noises, or vent our rage at the string of flat, bloodless festivals. The telephone: come to us from the Kalif, his empire, a domesticated beast, taken to colonizing through commerce rather than warfare; the ghost of the rebel Stretcher Jones, as Duncan might have put it, would never have recognized this temporarily toothless Empire, slumped back on its haunches. Inexplicably, guns arrive with the telephone. Lots of guns. In all types and sizes, mostly imported through Hoegbotton & Sons. Hoegbotton's armed importer-exporters, now doing a brisk trade in bandages, tourniquets, and bolted locks, are respected and feared the length and breadth of the River Moth—except by the operatives of Frankwrithe & Lewden, who continue their quiet infiltrations of Hoegbotton territory. More festivals, replete with the sound of gunplay. More years of *Trillian* and its vainglorious blather; will Voss Bender *never* die? Yes, this really is a historical summary of which my brother would be proud. (Not really, but think anything you like.)

Meanwhile, everything Duncan had told me about his underground adventures began to recede into the distance as "real life" took over again, for both of us. A retreat of sorts, you could call it—me from what Duncan had said, Duncan from what he had done. Perhaps he needed time to absorb what had happened to him. Perhaps he had been exhausted by what he had seen, and he couldn't physically undertake another journey so soon. Whatever the reason, he would become, in a sense, a religious man, while I would take a different path entirely. (I never became any more or less religious than I'd always been, or do you mean this as a joke? What I became was more aware of the world, the texture and feel of it, the way it changed from day to day, minute to minute, and me with it. And I did continue with my work, although I don't blame you for not noticing.)

If I gave Duncan's life less attention in those years after the starfish, it was because my fortunes waxed unexpectedly. Martin Lake—an arrogant, distant prick of a man—rose to prominence through my gallery, his haunted haunting paintings soon a fixture next to the telephones in the living rooms of the city's wealthiest patrons of the arts. (And who can say, in the long run, which was the worthier work—Lake's bizarre melancholia or the telephone's febrile ring.)

My gallery sparked a nameless, shapeless, and unique art revolution that soon became labeled (pinned like one of Sirin's butterflies) "the New Art." The New Art emphasized the mystical and transformative through unconventional perspective, hidden figures, strange juxtapositions of color. (It would be most accurate to say that the New Art *opened up* to include Martin within its ranks, and that he devoured it whole.)

As soon as I saw the change in Lake's art—he had been, at best, uninspired before whatever sparked his metamorphosis—I sought out anything similar, including the work of several of Lake's friends. Within months, I had a monopoly on the New Art. Raffe, Mandible, Smart, Davidson—they all displayed their art with me. Eventually, I had to buy the shop next door as an annex, just to have enough space for everyone to come see my art openings.

I had begun to experience what Duncan had known briefly after the publication of his first book: fame. And I hadn't even had to create anything—all I had had to do was exploit Lake's success, and build on it. (You're too modest. You made some brilliant decisions during that time. You were like one of the Kalif's generals, only on the battlefield of art. Nothing escaped your attention, until much later. I admired that.)

Suddenly, the local papers asked for my opinion on a variety of topics, only a few of which I knew anything about, although this did not stop me from commenting.

I have some of the clippings right here. In the *Ambergris Weekly*, they wrote, "The Gallery of Hidden Fascinations lives up to its name. Janice Shriek has assembled a group of top-notch new artists, any one of whom might be the next Lake." *The Ambergris Daily Broadsheet*, which Duncan and I would one day work for, noted, "Janice Shriek continues to build a dynasty of artists who are determining the direction of the New Art in Ambergris." The clippings are a bit faded, but still readable, still a source of pleasure. (As well they should be—you worked hard for your success.) I can remember a time when I kept such clippings in a jacket pocket. I'd pull them out and make sure they still said what I thought they had said, that I hadn't imagined it.

However, the New Art soon became about something other than artistic expression. A kind of tunnel vision set in whereby a painting was either New Art or Not New Art. Those works identified as Not New Art were dismissed as unimportant or somehow of lesser ambition. I admit to participating in this mindset, although for the ethically pure reason that I wanted my gallery to make money. So I would do my best to label whatever I had hanging there as "New Art," from the most experimental mixing of media to the most hackneyed scene of houseboats floating idyllically down the River Moth.

"That's an ironic New Art statement," I would say of the hackneyed houseboats, mentally genuflecting before the latest potential customer. "In the context of New Art, this painting serves as a condemnation of itself in the strongest possible terms."

I have to say, I loved the sheer randomness of it all—there is nothing more liberating than playing an illogical game where only you understand all of the rules.

My gallery grew fat on Lake's leavings, even after he left me, while Ambergris continued to prosper even as it headed ever deeper into complete moral and physical collapse or exhaustion. As the city's fate, so my own—and it took so little time. This is what, looking back, I marvel at—that I could discover so many new appetites, vices, and affectations in so short a time. Four years? Maybe five? Before beginning the inevitable plummet. These things never last—you ride them, you live inside of them, and then, almost without warning, you are flung to the side, spent, used up. (Although you must admit that, in this case, you flung yourself to the side.)

Most nights, I would be at a party until close to dawn. If not a party, then permanent residency at the Café of the Ruby-Throated Calf, drinking. I wore the same clothes for three or four days, no longer able to distinguish between dawn and dusk. It was one continuous swirling spangle of people and places in which to revel in my fame ever more religiously.

I met many influential or soon-to-be-influential people during that time (unsurprising, as you *were* one of those people, Janice), Sirin being a prime example.

My first memory of Sirin, our enigmatic future editor, has me slouched in a chair at the café and feeling someone slide into the chair next to me. When I opened my eyes, a slender, dark-haired man sat there. He held his head at a slight angle. He smelled of a musky cologne. His mouth formed a perpetual half smile, his eyes bright, penetrating, and reflectionless. The man I saw reminded me of old tales about people who could shape-change into cats. He looked like a rather smug, perhaps mischievous, feline. (He was the most exasperating, talented, maddening genius I've ever met. My initial reaction to meeting him was to want to simultaneously punch him, hug him, shake his hand, and throw him down a dark well. Instead, I generally stayed clear of him and let Janice serve as my intermediary, as she saw mostly his charming side.)

"Janice Shriek," he said. It was not a question.

"Yes?"

"Sirin," he said. He handed me a card.

Still struggling with context (with alcohol, you mean), I looked down. The card gave his address at Hoegbotton & Sons, on Albumuth Boulevard.

"I like what you do," he said. "Come find me. I may have a use for you."

Then he was gone. At the time, Sirin was a great womanizer, attending parties and cafés just to identify his next victims. I wasn't sure what "use" he might have for me, and I was skeptical.

Sirin's fame as an editor and writer had begun to spread by that time. He had, like the mythical beast he took his name from, generic yet universal qualities. He brought to his editing the same sensibilities found in his writing. He could mimic any style, high or low, serious or comedic, realistic or fabulist. It sometimes seemed he had created the city from his pen. Or, at least, made its inhabitants see Ambergris in a different light. That he thought too much of himself was made tolerable by the depth and breadth of his talent. It never occurred to me that he would want me to write for him.

People like Sirin would come out of the haze of lights and nights, and I would receive them with a gracious smile, an arm outstretched, to indicate, "Sit. Sit and talk awhile!" I was very trusting and open back then. (Trusting? Perhaps. But can you be trusting or suspicious when you are not yourself? I came to some of those all-night sessions at the café, Janice, but most of the time you were in such an altered state that you didn't recognize me. And that conversation you recall so fondly? Your end of it was often, I hate to say it, a garbled warble of slurred speech and mumbled innuendo. Although it probably didn't matter, because only rarely were the people you spoke to any better off. I don't mean to reproach, but I must bring a sense of reality to this glorious, decadent age you write of with such wistful fondness. I became so bored that I stopped coming to the café. It wasn't worth my time. I'd rather be underground, off on the scent of some new mystery.)

Sybel—luminous, short, sweet Sybel—was one of those people I met during this time. He had a thick rush of dirty blond hair exploding off the top of his head like waves of pale flame, clear blue eyes, a grin that at times appeared to be half grimace, and he wore outrageous clothes in the most impossible shades of purple, red, green, and blue. He rarely sat still for very long. In those early years, he had the metabolism of a hummingbird. A coiled spring. A hummingbird. A marvel.

The first thing Sybel said to me was, "You need me. New Art will soon be dead. The newest art will be whatever Janice Shriek decides it is. But you still need me." Which made me laugh.

But I did need him. Sybel had explored every crooked mews in Ambergris. A courier for Hoegbotton, he also knew everyone. A member of the Nimblytod Tribes, he had an affinity for tree climbing that no one could match, and a cut-bark scent that clung to him as if it was his birthright. His only pride revolved around his knowledge of the streets, and his well-tended, lightweight boots, which had been given to him by his tribe when he had left for the city. He couldn't have been more than eighteen years old when I met him for the first time.

"I'm quick and good," he said, but did not specify good at what. "I'm eyes and ears and feet, but I'm not cheap," he told me, and then named a large monthly fee.

I suggested a smaller amount, but added, "And you can stay at my apartment whenever you like." After all, I was rarely there, except to catch up on three or four hours of sleep.

So it was that I acquired a roommate I rarely saw. I know he welcomed the refuge, though: his tumultuous love life meant he was continually getting kicked out of some woman's bed.

I soon found I had chosen well. From careful observation at Hoegbotton—when he was not out all night cavorting with painters and novelists, sculptors and art critics—Sybel had learned how to run a business, something I never did well. Over time, he became my gallery assistant—on and off, because he had a habit of disappearing for several days at a time. But I was hardly punctual myself, and I loved his energy, so I always forgave him, no matter what his transgressions. I used to imagine that every once in a while, Sybel got the urge to return to his native forests, that he would fling off his clothes and climb into the welter of trees near the River Moth, soon happily singing as he leapt from tree to tree. But I'm sure his absences had more to do with women. (Actually, Sybel's absences had a myriad of causes, because he led a myriad of lives, some of which he did not tell you about. I cannot remember exactly when I entered into one of those lives, but I do remember many a morning when, having emerged from yet another dank hole in the ground, grimy with dirt and sweat, I would stand exhausted by the banks of the River Moth beside a particular tree chosen in advance, inhabited by a certain member of the Nimblytod Tribe.

(Sybel always smiled down at me from that tree. I don't know if he liked the dawn or liked the tree or liked me, but it always made me smile back, no matter how grim the context of my emergence.

(Our meetings had a practical purpose, though. The Nimblytod were renowned for their natural cures, using roots, bark, and berries. Sybel made a considerable amount of money on the side selling various remedies. You had to go to him, though, and that meant appearing at a particular tree by the riverbank at a particular time.

(For me, he did two things—sold me a tincture of ground bark and leaves for fatigue and, if I thought it was warranted, snuck a rejuvenating powder into your tea, Janice, to balance the effects of your debauchery.

("If she ever found out, she'd be furious," Sybel told me once.

("Better that than dead," I said.

("She's much stronger than you think," Sybel said. "She can go on this way for a long time. So can I." He was looking at me with some measure of amusement—me in my fungal shroud, giving every appearance of being on my last legs. Who was I to lecture anyone about these things?

(I just stared back at him and said, "I want my tincture. Where's my tincture, tree man?"

(He never left that damned tree during any of my meetings with him there. Not once. Just tossed my cure down to me.)

Sirin and Sybel were the only men I didn't sleep with during that time—for, suddenly, I had dozens of lovers. I slept with more men than there were paintings on the walls of my gallery, my nights a blurred fantasy of probing tongues, stroking hands, and hard cocks. I slept, quite a few times under the stars, with Lawrence, with John, with James, with Robert, with Luke, with Michael, with George . . . and the list goes on without me, intertwined with the sound of drums and a line of dancers. About as interesting, in retrospect, as Sabon's necklace. I'm sure Duncan rolled his eyes behind my back whenever I mentioned a new "boyfriend," since the longevity of my boyfriends was akin to that of a mayfly. I can hardly remember their names. (Since I was actually paying attention during that period, I remember them. There was the painter James Mallock, whom you called "old hairy back"; and the sculptor Peter Greelin—too clutchy, you said; and the theater owner Thomas Strangell, who had trouble getting it up on opening nights; and so many more—"an endless parade of erotic follies," as you used to typify it. In an odd sense, it didn't bother me, Janice. At least you were enjoying yourself. I don't know if you ever realized this, but before that you rarely seemed to enjoy yourself.)

I became addicted to anonymous sex, sex without love, sex as an act. I loved the feel of a man's chest against my breasts, the quickening of his breath while inside me, the utterly sublime slide of skin against skin. Each encounter faded from memory more quickly than the last, so that I only became more ravenous. Before, I had been starving; now, I felt as if I could never be satiated.

In other words, I began, under the steady, orgasmic pressure of fame, to become someone totally different than I had been. Can I blame me? It felt marvelous. It felt so good I thought I would die from ecstasy. I was successful for the first time ever.

For the first time ever, it was me, not Duncan, who commanded respect. If our father had been alive, he wouldn't have ignored me—he couldn't possibly have ignored me. (He never ignored you, Janice. No one ignored you. You just couldn't see them looking at you, for some reason.)

And still I consumed and consumed and consumed. I could not stop. Even in the midst of such carnality, a part of me remained distant, as if I were pulling the strings of my own puppet. I used to walk through a crowd of people, most of whom I knew intimately, and feel utterly alone. I had written that letter to Duncan about the golden threads and yet forgotten everything it meant.

Even Sybel had his doubts about my philosophy of life, despite how perfectly it fit in with the New Art ideal. We'd sit on the steps leading into the courtyard at Trillian Square, eating fruit that Sybel had plucked from some trees near the River Moth.

"How do you think everything is going?" Sybel would ask, a typical way for him to start a conversation if concerned about me.

I'd reply, "Great! Wonderful! Spectacular! Did you see that new painting? The one by Sarah Sharp? And it only cost us half of what it should have. If I can sell it, there are twenty more where that one came from. And after that there will be twenty more from somewhere else and then before you know it another gallery and after that, who knows. And that reminds me, did you see the mention in the *Broadsheet*? You need to make sure the theater owners see that—free advertising for us both. We have to maximize any leverage we get."

And I couldn't. Stop. Talking. And Sybel would eat his fruit and sometimes he'd put his hand on my shoulder and he'd feel that I was trembling and that I couldn't control it, and that touch would become a firmer grip, as if he were steadying me. Righting me.

Despite this, I didn't stop. I refused to stop—I wanted to eat, drink, and screw the world. Each new party, each new artist, each new day, started the process anew. With what glittering light shall we drape the new morning? Starved for so long, I now became the Princess of Yes. I. Simply. Could. Not. Say. No.

✾

It is because I could not say no, ironically enough, that I became involved in so many projects for Sirin at Hoegbotton Publishing—and inadvertently provided the catalyst for the clandestine (and erratic) second career of Duncan, my by then thirty-six-year-old brother.

This new secret history he would carry with him was only one of many. He already brought with him the labyrinth beneath the city. He already brought with him a secret understanding of his own books—and a personal history increasingly intertwined with Ambergris's. For Duncan had discarded his public self; he had returned to the facelessness from which he had come. (What freedom there can be in this! Unfettered from all of the distractions, finally and forever. Yes, I would long for, pine for, legitimate publication many times—but then I felt that first rush of anonymity after the last book went out of print, and with it fled any obligation to anything other than tracking the mystery of the gray caps.)

To become . . . someone else. I was learning that lesson every day as *Janice Shriek* remade herself into a hundred different images reflected from store windows and mirrors and the approving or disapproving expressions on other people's faces. No longer jailed by expectations—of himself or anyone else. No longer anything but himself.

And yet, even then, he was beginning a slow slog back toward the printed page, from a different angle—a forced march with no true destination, just a series of way stations. At first, it must have seemed more of a trap than an opportunity . . .

Duncan could publish nothing with Hoegbotton, at least directly. The last meeting with his editor had ended with a violent shouting match and an overturned desk. (For the record, I had nothing against either my editor or the desk—especially the desk. My reaction to the rejection of what would have been my sixth book for Hoegbotton was a delayed reaction to L. Gaudy's calm diatribe several years earlier in the offices of Frankwrithe & Lewden. All my editor at Hoegbotton said was, "I'm very sorry, Duncan, but we cannot take your latest book." Yet I found myself doing what I should have done to Gaudy—trying to beat his silly, know-nothing head against a desk. I'm lucky he didn't have me detained by Hoegbotton's thugs.)

But as I have written, Hoegbotton offered me more opportunities than I could possibly accept, and I did not turn them down. With the result that I had no choice but to enlist Duncan's help. Duncan took to it easily enough. (What choice did I have?) He was even eager for it. In fact, I can now reveal that the entire series of seventy-five travel pamphlets Hoegbotton published, one for each of the Southern Islands, was written by Duncan, not me. He would take my feverish, indifferent research, fortify it with his less-frenzied studies, and try to mimic my prose style, codified in many an art catalog:

> *Archibald with Earwig*, by Ludwig Poncer, Trillian Era, oils on canvas. This titular crenellation of high and low styles, by virtue of its unerring instinct for the foibles of both the human thumb and the inhuman earwig, has delighted generations of art lovers who pine for the shiver of dread up the spine even as their lips part to offer the sinister white of a smile.

Blah blah mumble mumble and so forth and so on yawn yawn.

Duncan also wrote, under the pseudonym "Darren Nysland," the three-hundred-page *Hoegbotton Study of Native Birds* (which included my lovely, poetic entry on the plumed thrush hen), still in print and often referenced by serious ornithologists. (As well it should be. It came into existence with excruciating slowness over many months. I soon wished a pox upon the entire avian clan. I never want to see another bird, unless eggwise, sunny-side up on my breakfast plate, or simmering in some sort of mint sauce.)

When, much later, I could not complete an essay on Martin Lake for the *Hoegbotton Guide to Ambergris*, Duncan did an admirable job of presenting my (crackpot, or at least unsupportable) ideas in good, solid prose. (And doing what you would not—protecting the identity of Lake's real lover. I wonder if you noticed. That and the peculiar "messages" I embedded in the text.) As if this was not confused enough, my work sometimes appeared under pen names, and thus when this work was actually written by Duncan, he appeared in print twice removed from his words.

I loved helping Duncan in this way. I loved that his style and my style became entangled so that we could not between us tell where a Janice sentence began and a Duncan sentence ended. For this meant I was very nearly his equal. (No comment.)

It was during this period that the Spore of the Gray Cap first became his favorite haunt. He had begun to put on a little weight, to grow a mustache and beard, which suited him. He even began to smoke a pipe. Thus outfitted, he would spend a few hours a day at the Spore, sitting in the (this very) back room, where he could keep a friendly eye on the bar's regulars and yet not have to speak to them. The bartenders loved him. Duncan never made a fuss, tipped well when he could, and added a sense of authentic eccentricity that the Spore needed. (These were not the only or even the primary reasons I spent so much time here. At some point, Janice, you will have to abandon suspense for a fully dissected chronology, will you not? Or perhaps I can help. It just so happens that below the back room of the Spore lies the easiest portal to the gray caps' underground kingdom.)

This deception continued for over three years, to the continued glorification of Janice Shriek, with rarely even the warmth of reflected light for poor Duncan. Hoegbotton did pay very well, and I dutifully gave Duncan sometimes as much as three-fourths of our earnings. (H&S could afford to pay well—not only were its trading activities booming, but it had managed to make inroads into the Southern jungles, and to consolidate control of almost all trade entering Ambergris. This was no benevolent organization, but perhaps being an anonymous thrall was better than the alternative.)

I suppose for this reason alone Duncan would have continued to supply his work for my byline. But we eventually put a stop to it anyway. I believe it was because my own instability made him yearn for stability of his own. When your sister continually looks pale as death, throws up on a regular basis, introduces you to a new boyfriend every other week, and is given to uncontrollable shaking, you begin to wonder how long it will be before people stop assigning her freelance work. (Not true—you flatter yourself. There were two reasons. First, I was sick of writing fluff. You try writing seventy-five articles on vacation opportunities in the Southern Islands and you will have written a new definition of boredom. Vomiting would be the least of your worries. Second, freelancing did not appeal because there was no set schedule, and I could never know when you might have work for me. Third, I began to see that this facile copy writing was taking a lot of energy away from my underground inquiries, which became more urgent the more it seemed that the symptoms I'd manifested after coming aboveground were not going away.)

Besides, Sirin, now my editor at Hoegbotton, had published all manner of pamphlets early in his career, passing off fiction as nonfiction and nonfiction as fiction; when his readers could not tell the difference between the two, it filled him with a nonsensical glee. Several times, he wrote an essay in a periodical, a scathing review of it under a pen name, then a letter to the editor under yet another pen name, this alter-alter ego defending Sirin's original point. In short, Sirin was as apt to ape a novel in his essays as to mummify a treatise in his fancies. He was also a scrupulous rewriter of other writers' work, always sensitive to a change in tone or style, and drove Duncan to near insanity with his relentless line edits.

With such an editor, it would not have been long before Sirin sniffed out the hoax. (I'm sure he sniffed out the hoax from nearly the beginning but chose not to say anything. What did it matter to him who wrote what so long as someone wrote it?)

For these reasons (and more, too tedious to, etc., etc.), the arrangement did not last. One day I came to Duncan with an assignment (the abysmal task of creating an "upbeat" listing and description of funeral homes and cemeteries in Morrow; it made me suspicious—had Sirin come up with that to torment me?) and Duncan told me he couldn't do it. No, Duncan had taken a "regular" job.

My brother, Duncan Shriek, the fearless explorer, had finally accepted everyday reality as his own—just as I had begun to reject it. Joined the humdrum, wash-the-dishes, take-out-the-garbage, go-to-bed-early, get-up-and-go-to-work life shared by millions of people from Stockton to Morrow, Nicea to Ambergris. My shock only amused him. (Actually, dear sister, it was your squinty-eyed, sallow face, the way your pupils seemed ready to rise up into your head as your jaw, as if in balance, dropped. You looked, in short, as if we had traded places, sunshine for the subterranean. At least one of us was taking out the garbage.)

What job had Duncan taken? A teaching job at Blythe Academy, a minor Truffidian religious school. Blythe might have been best known for its longevity—it had been established some years before the Silence, although it had wandered from place to place, finally coming to rest a few blocks from the Truffidian Cathedral. In a bit of irony I'm sure they had thought made good sense, Blythe's library had been superimposed on the ruins of an old gray cap library. (It wasn't ever a library. It was more of a marker for the Machine.) In the center of their main reading room, the circular nubs of that former structure remained, looking cold, remote, and threatening.

Blythe had a pointed history of accepting as many students from "artistic" or "creative" parents as possible, especially those of a certain social status—regardless of whether they believed in Truffidianism. I suppose the founders believed that the rote, compulsory weekly religious services in the small chapel behind the school might eventually permeate the brains of their charges—or at the very least instill the kind of guilt that in later years results in large sums of money being sent in to support new buildings, philosophies, or styles of teaching.

Blythe had also had famous teachers from time to time—Cadimon Signal for a few years, and even some of the Gorts who had gained such fame from the statistician Marmy Gort's controversial findings. Certainly, there was no shame in attending as a student or teaching at the school. However, as Duncan soon found out, greater shame could be found in those serving as headmaster, or Royal, to the school.

Imagine Duncan's shock the first day, arriving in starched collar and suffocating tie, to find his interviewer, the Vice Royal of Blythe Academy, joined by the Royal himself, who turned out to be none other than the former Antechamber, Bonmot. His features, already naturally condensed into a look of continual bemusement by the circumstances of his fall from grace, had attained a sublime parody of surprise (did anything really surprise him anymore?) as he looked up at Duncan and slowly realized who he was.

"Ironic, isn't it?" Duncan said with a toothy grin, as Bonmot nodded like a man in dream.

⁂

For a short while, Duncan once again disappeared from my life, although this was a much gentler disappearance: his ghost remained behind. Postcards fluttered into my mailbox with alarming regularity, for him—at least one every two weeks. Duncan wrote in tiny letters, fitting long-winded, philosophical diatribes on them. (Not long-winded. Just, perhaps, impractical for the allotted space.) I would respond with postcards that teased him in the language of fashions and gossip—although, truth be told, sometimes I had Sybel write them when I was too busy. (It was no secret. Sybel told me, and his handwriting was markedly different from yours. He used to apologize to me for you when I collected my remedies from him. It was no secret, but also no sin. Still, I must admit to exasperation at the few times Sybel asked for advice on what he should write to me about!) From the evidence of the postcards alone, we might have been the two most uniquely different people in the world.

But the postcards were a way to remind each other of our existence, and those things most important to us at the time. Could I help it that my mind concerned itself with the ephemeral, the weightless, the surface, while Duncan continued to plunge into the depths?

On the corporeal level, the postcards meant nothing. What is a scrawl of letters next to that infinity of physical details that makes up a face? So I dropped by the Blythe Academy for lunch whenever I could find the time—at least once a month, depending on what demands Sybel and my ever-expanding gullet of a gallery made on me.

I shared the ghost of Duncan, this Serious Man seemingly more concerned about his students than his life's work (so it might have seemed, I'll admit) with Bonmot, for the Antechamber and my brother had become friends. (Good friends? Great friends? I honestly don't know. The dynamic of our relationship was transformed day by day. On some level, despite our affection for one another, I think there was a certain caution, a certain wariness. He may have felt my obsession with the gray caps would lead me to discoveries that might bring dishonor to his faith in God. I know I was afraid that his religion might somehow infect my studies, change me in a way that I did not want to be changed.)

Without question, these lunches became the high point of my days. Whether in the sleepy cool heat of spring, the hot white light of summer, or the dry burnt chill of fall and winter. By the carp-filled fountain. They laughed so much!

I'd never seen Duncan laugh without bitterness or sarcasm since Before Dad Died. It almost felt like we were huddled around the dinner table in the old house in Stockton again, with Dad telling us some obscure fact he'd dug up in his research. Usually, he would mix in some lie, and the unspoken assumption was that we'd try to ferret it out with our questions. Sometimes, the truth was so outrageous that finding the lie took a while. He would sit back in his chair, eyebrows raised in a look of innocence—something that always made Mom laugh—and answer us with a straight face. (I always knew when Dad wasn't telling the truth, because the faintest lilt or musical quality would enter his voice—as if the joy of constructing the story was too much for him to contain.)

These lunches with Bonmot formed pockets of time and space separate from the stress and rigor of my responsibilities (or lack thereof). Where everything else blended together in a blur of faces and cafés and alcohol, that sun-filled courtyard with its rustling willows, light-soaked dark wooden benches, and aged gray stone tables riven with fissures still remains with me, even in this place. And Bonmot was one with the benches and tables: weathered but comfortable, solid and stolid both. His hands felt like stone hands, his two-fisted greeting like having your skin encased in granite. He had been a farmer's son before he found his calling, and his hulking physique remained intact, along with a startling openness and honesty in his light brown eyes. Nothing in him indicated a propensity for clerical crimes. (The honesty didn't come easily to him. He had earned his reform, and it had transformed him.) His speech rippled out like liquid marble, strong and smooth. He was, in all ways, a comfort.

As for Bonmot and Duncan, they pulled back far enough from the rift that was Duncan's long-ago banned book to find they shared many interests, from explorations of history and religion to a taste for the same music and art. More than once, I would walk into that blissful place carrying sandwiches bought from a sidewalk vendor to find the two men deep in conversation, Bonmot's wrinkled face further creased with laugh lines, his melon-bald head bowed and nodding as Duncan hammered home some obscure point, Duncan's hands heavy with the weight of knowledge being expressed through them. Two veterans of exile, reborn in the pleasure of each other's company. (Which isn't to say we didn't argue—we argued, sometimes viciously. We knew where we stood with one another.)

Early on, Duncan dispensed with politeness and pressed Bonmot about his faith. Duncan's journal relates one such discussion, over an early lunch I wasn't at:

Bonmot irritates me with his faith sometimes, because it seems based on nothing that is not ephemeral. And yet my own faith, misdiagnosed as "obsession," cannot incite such blind obedience or trust.

"What I don't understand," I said to Bonmot today, "is how you went from corrupt Truffidian Antechamber to beatific Blythe Academy Royal."

I supposed I was interested because of my own "scandal," even if it was just the ignominious fate of being out of print. Perhaps I could re-create Bonmot's path.

But Bonmot laughed and dispelled any hope of true explanation by saying, "Better to ask how I became corrupt in the first place. But, really, to answer your question, I had no choice. It just happened. When you are inside a situation like that, you see the world in a way that allows you to rationalize what you are doing. When you lose that perspective, you wake up."

"Are you saying that no trigger, no incident, brought you to the realization?"

"No," Bonmot said. "I literally woke up one day and had the distance to realize that I had gotten onto the wrong path and I had to change."

"Very convenient," I said, which made Bonmot emit one of his rare belly laughs, doubled over for a moment or two.

(Did the disappointed look on my face amuse him? No, he was too kind for that. Was he laughing at something else entirely—some cosmic personal or religious joke? I couldn't tell at the time, but I thought about it often, because it confused me. Now, if I had to guess, I would say that Bonmot was laughing at the memory of his own foolishness, laughing too at the sheer luck of having escaped it.)

"Ah, Duncan," he said, wiping a tear from his cheek. "I admit it is convenient. That I should have been redeemed so easily. Such a pat revelation. But the good news is, the same may happen for you one day, if you have need of it."

"I do need a few revelations," I said.

"Maybe you need God," Bonmot said, though with a lilt to his voice that let me know he might be teasing. "Do you think maybe that's why you've come to me?" His tone made it so. I hadn't come to him for that reason, and yet I was almost open to it in a strange way.

"You have faith in something you cannot see," I said. "I can understand that, but I can't believe in it."

He shrugged. "'There is no speech, there are no words; the song of the heavens is beyond expression.' Not just some*thing*, but some*one*."

"Someone, then," I said. "So tell me—why are we so different? I also believe in something or someone I cannot see. It just happens to live underground." I said it casually, and it came out like a joke, but my breath quickened, and I think that on some level, I really wanted a profound answer. I wanted an answer of some kind, at least—one that would help me understand why I could not stop pursuing *my* mystery.

"There's a difference," Bonmot said, although I've wondered ever since how he could know such a thing, without having seen what I've seen, down there.

"What is the difference?"

"Your unseen world only exists inside your head," he said, in as gentle a way as he could—he even reached out across the table with his huge hands, as if, for a second, he meant to console me. "My unseen world, however, *is* the truth. It is truth that convinces and the divine that gives the gift of true faith."

I've always had a problem with Truth and those who espouse Truth, no matter how much I might love and respect them. Faith, on the other hand, has never been an issue for me. But, I said, because I could: "I thought it might be a question of *scale*. Of the *number* of souls infected with the delusion."

Bonmot wasn't smiling anymore. "No, it's not a matter of scale."

(But *of course* it was a question of scale. That's why I failed. You must infect the minds of hundreds of thousands to get anything done, to make an impact. You can't live out your days presenting your theories to a hundred souls at a meeting of a discredited historical society. It doesn't make a difference.)

"What, then?"

Bonmot said, "I told you already. But you aren't ready to listen. You have to know the truth—have something worth believing in. Over time. Over centuries. Something so important people are willing to form their whole lives around it. To live, and, yes, die for it. And that means it must be much bigger than anything imaginable. 'Silence with regard to You is praise,'" he quoted. "'The sum total of what we know of You is that we do not know You.'"

I leaned closer, across the table. "What if you *could* know, though? Would that diminish it? If you could see what I have seen. I think it might change your mind." (And, toward the end, didn't he change? And didn't I wish then that I'd never tried to see him uncertain.)

"'The angels of darkness, whose names I do not know,'" Bonmot said. "You must take care to resist the false light."

"*The false light.*" I shivered. Samuel Tonsure had written that once in his journal. But Tonsure hadn't known about the Machine, about the door. There was, I had become convinced, a *real* door, not just an illusion or a delusion or a mirror. A door. And here Bonmot was talking about not letting in a false light. For a moment, just a moment, I asked myself if he might have some insight into the same truth I sought. (After all, Bonmot often professed to be an expert on Zamilon, a place I had become convinced held, in some time period, the answer to the mystery of the Machine. But the tough old bastard never imparted what he knew, no matter how I tried to pry that knowledge from him. And then it was too late.)

I pulled away, sat up straight on the bench, felt the lacquered rough-smoothness of its grain against my palms. Felt the sun against my face. Felt the breeze. Wondered at how I could get so lost in a conversation that I forgot the world around me.

I started again. I don't know why I tried. Bonmot couldn't convince me and I couldn't convince him. "It *is* that important to me, Bonmot. It's a religion to me."

"I've no doubt of your sincerity," Bonmot said. "I'm just not sure what you want from me."

"To say my theories are not incompatible with your beliefs," I said.

"But your theories are impossible. Nor are they truly relevant to the larger world."

This made me angry for an instant. "Relevant? Relevant. How about this—our future survival in Ambergris. A second Silence. Is that relevant enough for you?"

Bonmot sighed. It was like stone or solid earth sighing. "That's what Truffidianism is all about, my friend. Exactly that—you should read our texts more closely in future. 'The same fate is in store for everyone, pure and impure, righteous and wicked, the good and the sinners.'"

"'No one makes it out,' as Tonsure once wrote," I said. "But what if that fate is coming sooner to all of us than it should?"

Bonmot shrugged. "I don't believe in what you believe."

But I knew that, faced with the reality of it, he would not be so calm or accepting. I knew that the reality of what might one day happen would trump the imaginations of even those who had the capacity to believe in an all-powerful being that had never once manifested in the flesh to Bonmot or, to the best of my knowledge, anyone else.

(I once had a conversation about Faith and Truth with Sybel while waiting for him to relinquish a tincture. "What's the attraction of Truffidianism? Of a *single* Truth, Sybel?" I asked. "It's simple," he replied. "You don't have to *search* anymore. You can just *be*." "So can a tree, Sybel," I said, which was probably the wrong thing to say.)

Conversations like this one usually ended amicably on both sides—for Duncan because he found much about Truffidianism compelling (that may be wish fulfillment on your part, Janice) and for Bonmot because he had been too flawed in his past to judge the disbelief of others too harshly. And still they went back and forth, sometimes comically.

Duncan: "I've seen a kind of a god. It lives underground."
Bonmot: "The Silence was more about sin than mushrooms."
Duncan: "But rats, Bonmot? Why do you have to worship rats?"
Bonmot: "The ways of God are mysterious, Duncan. And, besides, you are coming perilously close to blasphemy . . . only some of us worship rats. I do not worship rats."
Duncan: "Rats, Bonmot? Rats?"

We talked about serious subjects, yes, but we also told dirty jokes and teased each other mercilessly. I shared wicked stories about the outrageous behavior of my artists, while Bonmot shared tales from his days at the religious academy in Morrow. (My personal favorites concerned the exploits of the head instructor, Cadimon Signal.) Rarely were our conversations revelatory. That's not the point. These were people I loved and came to love. For me, some months, it saved me to be in such company. It took me out of the self-destructive spiral of my own thoughts in a way that even Sybel couldn't. For Bonmot, I think our lunches allowed him to relax in a way he had not relaxed since he entered the priesthood. (And I had fun, too. But, really, Janice, you make it all sound so perfect. It was fun, but it wasn't perfect.)

I should have been envious of the way Duncan and Bonmot talked, but the truth is, it made me happy for them both: the hulking giant and my relatively "dainty" brother. When I approached them with my sandwiches, I often felt guilty for taking them from their collective world of words and ideas, twinned heads turning to look up at me, bewildered—who was this intruder?—followed by recognition and a gracious acceptance into their company. (This is a subtle piece of misdirection that allows you to keep your own emotional intimacy with Bonmot secret, I think. As I had Lacond later, so you had Bonmot, in a way I didn't. *I* was often the intruder, Janice. You two took so easily to one another it was remarkable. But if you don't want to share such details here, I won't make you.)

I still remember how Bonmot's generous drum of a laugh, deep and clear, often drew disapproving looks from the students studying nearby. And yet even then, during what I considered retreats from the exhausting carnality of my "normal" life, Mary Sabon was with us, folded into the pages of the grade book Duncan kept with him. There never really is a finite beginning, is there? No real starting point to anything. Beginnings are continually beginning. Time is just a joke played by watchmakers to turn a profit. Through memory, Time becomes conjoined so that I see Mary as a physical presence at those lunches, leaning against Duncan, trying to get his attention.

She is everywhere now. I am, almost literally, nowhere.

5

Can a childhood memory be misconstrued as starting over? I don't think so. Not if I tell it this way:

The forests outside Stockton remain as real to me as the humid, fungi-laden streets of Ambergris, maybe more so. The dark leaves, the mottled trunks, the deep green shadows reflected on the windows of our house, as of some preternatural presence. All sorts of trees grew in Stockton, but the difference between the staid oaks that lined our street and the misshapen, twisted, coiled welter of tree limbs in the forest seemed profound. It both reassured us and menaced us in our youth: limitless adventure, fear of the unknown.

Our house lay on the forest's edge. The trees stretched on for hundreds of miles, over hills and curving down through valleys. Various were the forest's names, from the Western Forest to the Forest of Owls to Farely's Forest, after the man who had first explored the area. Stockton had been nestled comfortably on its eastern flank for centuries, feeding off the timber, the sap, the animals that took shelter there.

By the time I had turned thirteen and Duncan was nine, we had made the forest our own. We had colonized our tiny corner of it—cleared paths through it, made shelters from fallen branches, even started a tree house. Dad never enjoyed the outdoors, but sometimes we could persuade him to enter the forest to see our latest building project. Mom had a real fear of the forest—of any dark place, which may have come from growing up in Ambergris. (I never had the sense that growing up in Ambergris had been a trauma for her—she lived there during very calm times—but it is true she never talked about it.)

One day, Duncan decided we should be more ambitious. We had made a crude map of what we knew of the forest, and the great expanse labeled "Unknown" irked him. The forest was one thing that could genuinely be thought of as his, the one area where he did not mimic me, where I followed his lead.

We stood at the end of our most ambitious path. It petered out into bushes and pine needles and the thick trunks of trees, the bark scaly and dark. I breathed in the fresh-stale air, listened to the distant cry of a hawk, and tried to hear the rustlings of mice and rabbits in the underbrush. We were already more than half a mile from our house.

Duncan peered into the forest's depths.

"We need to go farther," he said.

Back then, he was a mischievous sprout, small for his age, with bright green eyes that sometimes seemed too large for his face. And yet he could effortlessly transform into a little thug just by crossing his arms and giving you an exasperated look. Sometimes he'd even sigh melodramatically, as if fed up with the unfairness of the world. His shocking blond hair had begun to turn brown. He liked to wear long green shirts with brown shorts and sandals. He said it served as a kind of camouflage. (Camouflage or comfort—I don't remember.) I used to wear the same thing, although, oddly enough, it scandalized Mom when I did it. Dad couldn't have cared less.

"How *much* farther?" I asked.

I had become increasingly aware that our parents counted on me to keep watch over Duncan. Ever since he'd gotten trapped in a tunnel the year before, we'd all become more conscious of Duncan's reckless curiosity.

"I don't know," he said. "If I did, it wouldn't be much of an adventure. But there's something out there, something we need to find."

His expression was mischievous, yes, but also, somehow, *otherworldly*. (Otherworldly? I was nine. There was nothing "otherworldly" about me. I liked to belch at the dinner table. I liked to blow bubbles and play with metal soldiers and read books about pirates and talking bears.)

"But there's all that bramble," I said. "It will take ages to clear it."

"No," he said, with a sudden sternness I found endearing, and a little ridiculous, coming from such a gangly frame. "No. We need to go out exploring. No more paths. We don't need paths."

"Well . . . ," I said, about to give Duncan my next objection.

But he was already off, tramping through the bramble like some miniature version of the Kalif, determined to claim everything he saw for the Empire. He had always been fast, the kind to set out obstinately for whatever goal beckoned, whatever bright and shiny thing caught his eye. Usually, I had control over him. Usually, he wanted to stay on my good side. But when it came to the forest, our relationship always changed, and he led the way.

So off he dashed into the forest, and I followed, of course. What choice did I have? Not that I hated following him. Sometimes, because of Duncan, I was able to do things I wouldn't have done otherwise. And, such a relief, when I followed him, the weight of being the eldest lifted from me—that was a rare thing, even BDD.

The forest in that place had a concentrated darkness to it because of the thick underbrush and the way the leaves and needles of the trees diluted the sun's impact. To find a patch of light in the gloom was like finding gold, but those patches only accentuated the surrounding darkness. The smell of rot caused by shadow was a healthy smell—I didn't mind it; it meant that all of the forest still worked to fulfill its cycle, even down to the smallest insect tunneling through dead wood. It did not mean what it would come to mean in Ambergris.

Duncan and I fought our way through stickery vines and close-clumped bushes. We felt our way over fallen trees, stopping in places to investigate nests of flame-colored salamanders and stipplings of rust-red mushrooms. The forest fit us snugly; we were neither claustrophobic nor free of its influence. The calls of birds grew strange, shrill, and then died away altogether. (As if we had gone through a door to a different place, a different time, Janice. I could not believe, sometimes, while in the forest, that it existed in the same world as our house.)

At times, the ground rose to an incline and we would be trudging, legs lifting for the next step with a grinding effort. The few clearings became less frequent, and then for a long time we walked through a dusk of dark-green vegetation under a canopy of trees like black marble columns, illuminated only by the stuttering glimmer of a firefly and the repetitive clicking of some insect. A smell like ashes mixed with hay surrounded us. We had both begun to sweat, despite the coolness of the season, and I could hear even undaunted Duncan breathing heavily. We had come a long way, and I wasn't sure I could find the route back to our familiar paths. Yet something about this quest, this foolhardy plunge forward, became hypnotic. A part of me could have kept on going hour after hour, with no end in sight, and been satisfied with that uncertainty. (Then you know how I have felt my entire adult life—except that we're told there is no uncertainty. *No one makes it out*, we're told, from birth until our deathbed, in a thousand spoken and unspoken ways. It is just a matter of when and where—and if I could discover the truth in the meantime.)

The sting, the burn, of hard exercise, the doubled excitement and fear of the unknown, kept me going for a long time. But, finally, I reached a point where fear overcame excitement. (You mean common sense overcame excitement.)

"Duncan!" I said finally, to his back. "We have to stop. We need to find our way home."

He turned then, his hand on a tree trunk for support—a shadow framed by a greater gloom—and I'll never forget what he said. He said, "There is no way to go but forward, Janice. If we go forward, we will find our way back."

It sounded like something Dad would have said, not a nine-year-old kid.

"We're already lost, Duncan. We have to go back."

Duncan shook his head. "I'm not lost. I know where we are. We're not *there* yet. I know something important lies ahead of us. I know it."

"Duncan," I said, "you're wearing *sandals*. Your feet must be pretty badly cut up by now."

"No," he said, "I'm fine." (I wasn't fine. The brambles had lacerated my feet, but I'd decided to block out that discomfort because it was unimportant.)

"There's something ahead of us," he repeated.

"Yes, more forest," I said. "It goes on for hundreds of miles." I thought about whether I had the strength to carry a kicking, struggling Duncan all the way back to the house. Probably not.

I looked up, the long trunks of trees reaching toward a kaleidoscope of wheeling, dimly light-spackled upper branches, amid a welter of leaves. In those few places where the light was right, I could see, floating, spore and dust and strands of cobweb. Even the air between the trees was thick with the decay of life.

"Trust me," Duncan said, and grinned. He headed off again, at such a speed that I had no choice but to follow him. In the shadows, my brother's thin, wiry frame resembled more the thick, muscular body of a man. Was there any point at which I could convince him to stop, or would he stop on his own?

Another half hour or so—just as I could no longer identify our direction, so too I had begun to lose my sense of time—and a thick, suffocating panic had begun to overcome me. We were lost. We would never make it home. (You should have trusted me. You will need to trust me.)

But Duncan kept walking forward, into the unknown, the thick loam of the forest floor rising at times to his ankles.

Then, to my relief, the undergrowth thinned, the trees became larger but spread farther apart. Soon, we could walk unimpeded, over a velvety compost of earth covered with moist leaves and pine needles. A smell arose from the ground, a rich smell, almost like coffee or muted mint. I heard again the hawk that had been wheeling overhead earlier, and an owl in the murk above us.

Duncan stopped for me then. He must have known how tired and thirsty I was, because he took my hand in his, and smiled as he said, "I think we are almost there. I think we almost are."

We had reached the heart—or a heart—of the forest. We had reached a place that in a storm would be called the eye. The light that shone through from above did so in shafts as thin as the green fractures of light I can see from the corner of my eye as I type up this account. And in those shafts, the dust motes floated yet remained perfectly still. Now I heard no sound but the pad of our feet against the earth.

Duncan stopped. I was so used to hurrying to keep up that I almost bumped into him.

"There," he said, pointing, a smile creasing his face.

And I gasped, for there, ahead of us, stood a statue.

Made of solid gray stone, fissured, splashed with light, overgrown with an emerald-and-crimson lichen, the idol had a face with large, wide eyes, a tiny nose, and a solemn mouth. The statue could not have been taller than three or four feet.

We walked closer, in an effortless glide, so enraptured by this vision that we forgot the ache in our legs.

Iridescent beetles had woven themselves into the lichen beads of its smile, some flying around the object, heavy bodies drooping below their tiny wings. Other insects had hidden in the fissures of the stone. What looked like a wren's nest decorated part of the top of the head. A whole miniature world had grown up around it. It was clearly the work of one of the native tribes that had fled into the interior when our ancestors had built Stockton and claimed the land around it. This much I knew from school.

"How?" I asked in amazement. "How did you know this was here, Duncan?"

Duncan smiled as he turned to me. "I didn't. I just knew there had to be something, and if we kept looking long enough, we'd find it."

At the time, while we stood there and drank in the odd beauty of the statue, and even as Duncan unerringly found our way home, and even after Mom and Dad, waiting in the backyard as the sun disappeared over the tree line, expressed their anger and disappointment at our "irresponsibility"—especially mine—I never once thought about whether Duncan might be crazy rather than lucky, touched rather than decisive. I just followed him. (Janice, I lied to you, just a little. It's true I didn't know exactly where to find the statue, but I had already heard about it from one of the older students at our school. He'd given me enough information that I had a fairly good idea of where to go. So it wasn't preternatural on my part—it was based on a shred, a scrap, of information, as are all of my wanderings.)

✴✴✴

Just as Duncan pushed me and himself farther than was sane that day, so too Duncan pushed Blythe Academy. It was not only the impending matter of Mary Sabon—it was the clandestine way in which Duncan used the Academy to further his primary lifelong interest: the gray caps and their plans.

I've no inkling about Duncan's ability to teach (thanks a lot). I never sat in on his classes. I never even asked him much about the teaching. I was too busy. But I do know he discovered that he enjoyed "drawing back the veil of incomprehension" as he once put it (jokingly). The act of lecturing exercised intellectual muscles long dormant, and also exorcised the demons of self-censorship by letting

Duncan speak, his words no longer filtered through his fear of the reading public. (Not to worry—I never had a real reading public, or I'd have continued to find publication somewhere. But, yes, I was fearful that I might one day develop one. Just imagine—someone actually reading those thick slabs of paper I spent years putting together.) He could entertain and educate while introducing his charges to elements of the mysterious he hoped might one day blossom into a questioning nature and a thirst for knowledge.

But was it all innocent education? Was there, perhaps, something else beneath it?

An examination of his lesson plans reveals a pattern not unlike the pattern formed by the poly-glut documents, maps, illustrations, and portraits that had once lined Duncan's room at the Institute of Religiosity. (I never told you, but I received word only a year ago that, at Cadimon Signal's request, the entire display had been lovingly preserved under glass, framed, and spirited away to some dark, vile basement in Zamilon for a prolonged period of zealot-driven dissection. What they hope to find among my droppings, I don't know, but the thought of their clammy hands and ratty eyes pawing through my former wall adornments is a bit much.)

While Duncan could not, and would not, divulge the essence of his underground journeys, he taught a stunningly diverse series of social, economic, religious, cultural, psychological, geographic, and confessional texts intended to re-create a complete context for the formation of the early Truffidian Church. The course centered around *The Journal of Samuel Tonsure*—ostensibly to give them a feel for Truffidian twaffle, pamp, and circumglance—and included a number of supporting elements, such as Truffidian folklore, study of the mushroom dwellers, and scrutiny of transcripts of conversations between Truffidian priests around the time of Tonsure's adventures.

I have, in this trunk of Duncan's papers that I have half dragged, half had dragged here, some of his lesson plans. For example:

Spring Semester
Primary Texts
- *Cinsorium*: teacher's copy; to be loaned, three days each student
- *The Journal of Samuel Tonsure* by Samuel Tonsure
- *Red Martigan: A Life* by Sarah Carsine
- *The Relationship Between the Native Tribes of Stockton & the Gray Caps* by Jonathan Shriek: thesis paper; copies to be distributed

- *The Refraction of Light in a Prison* by the Imprisoned Truffidian Monks
- *Zamilon for Beginners* by Cadimon Signal: in preparation for next semester

Areas of Study
- *Samuel Tonsure's Journal*: The Apparently Impossible Spatial Perspective Expressed in the Sections on the Underground. (I've since come to understand that the problem lies with the limitations of human senses, not Tonsure's account.)
- *Evidence of the Gray Caps in Morrow*: A Selection of Texts, including a cavalryman's diary from the period of the Silence. (Alas, this now appears to have been at worst a hoax, at best bad research.)
- *An Examination of Fungi Found on Religious Structures*: Field trip.
- *Guest Lecture by James Lacond*. (Oddly, Lacond and I did not converse much during that first face-to-face meeting. He was polite but not inquisitive, gave his lecture on his own theories about the gray caps, and left. This was the first and only time Bonmot met Lacond. They circled each other warily, looking at each other as if two creatures from vastly different worlds. A muttered pleasantry or two, and they set off in opposite directions, literally and figuratively, Bonmot not staying for the lecture. Yet, how similar they were in many ways.)

Alas, Duncan either did not preserve his accompanying private notes or did not include them with these plans. However, after a careful review of all of the lesson plans—most too tedious to replicate here—I believe Duncan had more on his mind than teaching students. I believe he sought independent verification of his own findings. He thought that, subjected to the same stimuli, his students— maybe only one or two, but that would be enough—would one day vindicate him of historical heresy. How ironic, then, that his efforts would instead lead one of his students to *convict* him of historical heresy.

(Janice, enough! You had ample opportunity to *ask* me about any and all of this, and would have received a more honest answer than the one generated by your suppositions. We may be siblings, but you cannot see into or through my mind. You have gotten it half right—which means you have gotten it all wrong. I did seek to educate my students first and foremost. This did require a varied and wide approach, primarily because few existing texts interwove the complexity of historical issues with a thorough cross-disciplinary approach. Why do you think I had to create that "document" on my wall back at the Institute in the first place? So I taught them, and taught them well. The subtext of my teaching—yes, there was a subtext, I admit it—had nothing to do with hoping my students would replicate my work. The only true way any of them could replicate my work would be to follow me underground, and, as you well know, I made that mistake only once.

(No. What you fail to see are the truly diabolical intentions behind my approach. You underestimate me. Validation? Hardly. *Three hundred* students could validate my findings and still not a soul would believe them, or me. No, my plan concerned *additional* research. With plucking the half-formed thoughts like plums. With growing another thirty or forty brains and limbs each semester, to become this multi-spined creature that might, in its flailing, lurching way, accomplish more than a single, if singular, scholar, ever could. Each text I made them read, every essay question answered, every research paper written, corresponded to a section of the grid in the incomplete map of my knowledge. *They* taught *me* in many cases. They didn't have the scars I had, or the foreknowledge; they were unblinkered, unfettered by my peculiar brand of orthodoxy. I used to watch them, heads bowed, heavy with knowledge, working on the latest test, each swirling loop of letter from their pens on paper signifying a kind of progress—this permutation, that permutation, forever tried, discarded, yielding nothing, and yet valuable for that fact alone. Discount *this,* and you can begin testing *that.* Sabon was part of it at first, certainly—she bought into it, and may even have understood what I was doing.

(When one puzzle piece—and a semester of thirty students might fill in a single puzzle piece, at best—had been locked into position, we would move on to the next. A careful observer might have noticed that my curriculum began to resemble cheesecloth. Much of it was useless, much of it redundant, much of it insanely boring and obscured by lazy or talentless students. But they did receive a relatively full education from me. And keep in mind that I was not their only teacher.

(In time, the game did outgrow its original boundaries. At every opportunity, I would murmur in the ears of my fellow instructors, like an echo of their own desires, hints of scholarship and glory if they only turned their attention to this or that ignored corner of history. "I wonder if anyone has ever compared the version of Nysman's report on the Silence stored at Nicea with the version stored at Zamilon. I am told they diverge in ways that speak to issues of authenticity in Samuel Tonsure's journal." Casually, off-the-cuff, as if it fell outside my area of expertise, but should be pursued by someone, with great rewards for any enterprising scholar. In all of this, Bonmot was an interesting factor. He guessed what I was up to rather early on, I think, but never did anything to stop me. Raised an eyebrow, gave me a penetrating stare, but that was it.

(And so, by the fourth year of my employment at Blythe Academy, I had built my own machine, fully as terrible and far-reaching as the Machine I had encountered underground. You understand now, I hope? I had managed to subvert and divert the resources of an entire institution of higher learning to the contemplation of a single question with many branches. The diagram I drew to exemplify this question was based on Tonsure's account and deliberately resembled the gray caps' most recurrent symbol, which had been drawn on walls, on cobblestones, but never explicated.

(Intentionally incomprehensible to outsiders, the diagram helped me see the relationships between various people and concepts in a new way. Manzikert I had triggered the Silence, I felt certain, with his actions in founding Ambergris. Samuel Tonsure had somehow cataloged and explained the gray caps during his captivity underground. Aquelus, a later ruler of Ambergris, had suffered Manzikert's same fate, but survived to return aboveground. As Zamilon held some answer, so too did Alfar, the ruined tower to which Aquelus's wife had retired prior to the Silence, thus ensuring her survival. And then there were the Silence and the Machine. How did they connect? And how did it all tie back in to the gray caps? These were the perhaps unanswerable questions I struggled with, and the structure through which I examined them.

(Although this is perhaps the least of what I unearthed during that time, it still represents an impressive experiment in collective unconsciousness, in beehive mentality. Did more than a few of those brains set diligently upon the course plotted for them ever suffer a tremor, a tickle of an inkling of my manipulation? I doubt it. I'm too proud of my work, perhaps, but I did little harm and much good. Several instructors published papers in prominent journals without ever knowing I had color-coded their innocent discoveries into a vast pattern of conspiracy and misdirection. They stood in their sunlit lecture halls turning their ideas over and over in their hands—brightly colored baubles for their students to applaud, confident they had solved a complete puzzle rather than assembled a single piece. The students, meanwhile, became specialists sensitive to the rhythms of synergy, analysis, and synthesis. Tuning forks for knowledge, they vibrated prettily, their shiny surfaces one by one catching the light. I admit, I derived great satisfaction from all of this. To have such a measure of control made me nearly ecstatic at times, fool that I was. And still, I wasn't gathering enough knowledge fast enough. I felt frustrated, twice-removed from where I needed to be: underground. Ironic that, aboveground, I felt much as James Lacond once described Tonsure underground:

> Most of the time [Tonsure] walks in the darkest night. Now and again, a wavering finger of light flutters across the darkness, teasing him with the outline of a path. Hopeful, he runs toward it, only to find himself in another maze. The hope that night must give way to day allows him to continue, and he tries to guess where a more permanent light might break through—a crack, a crevice, a hole—but the end of night never comes.)

Early on, I met these students, Duncan's unwitting accomplices in esoteric, possibly meaningless, research. They made no particular impression on me: a formless row of fresh-scrubbed faces attached to identical dark blue uniforms. The eyes that populated those ruddy faces sparkled or flared or reflected light according to the intensity of their ambition. Some students stared defiantly at you. Some let you stare *through* them. Still others looked away, or down at their feet—every foot hidden by proper white socks, sheathed in black, brightly polished shoes. They smelled like soap and sweat. Their voices cracked and buzzed and sang out with equal innocence and brashness. In their uniformed rows, I could not tell the poor from the rich, the smart from the stupid. Thus did Blythe Academy serve as an equalizer of souls.

Never once did I think to challenge that semblance of equality, to search for that one variant, that one mimic cleverly made up to resemble the others, but actually of a different species altogether. (She was just another student in so many ways. You shouldn't think that she was other, or different. I was the mimic, if anyone was. I threw off the balance in that place.)

Mary's presence, when I look back, first resonated as a faint music vibrating through the strings of my golden metaphor: a resonance neither sinister nor angelic. In that respect, she reminds me of a character in a novel by Sirin. She exists on the edges of the pages, in the spaces between the words, her name unwritten except in riddles: a woman's green-and-gold scarf on Duncan's apartment desk, sudden honeysuckle in a glass in his school office, a puzzling hint of cologne during lunch. A half-dozen passive yet sensual details a jealous wife might hoard—or that a sibling might half-remember with amusement, but later revisit harshly.

Duncan never mentioned Mary during that time. (She was my student, for Truff's sake! Why would I mention her? You make this all sound so tawdry yet ethereal. Is it possible she just escaped your myopic powers of observation? Is it possible you were so continually drugged and drunk that you noticed no one? You should strike all of this from the record. There's no reason for it and no one cares. I don't even care anymore, except the now-dulled sting that you tried to undermine my relationships rather than support them.) Curiously, though, Duncan's postcards began to contain more personal information than our lunchtime conversations, possibly because of Bonmot's presence.

Sometimes the postcards consisted of odd lines that told me he had reopened his investigations well beyond Blythe Academy:

Even the flies have eyes, Janice. Eyes for them. There is no corner of this city they cannot see in some form. But it's too much information. They cannot review it all at once. I imagine them down there, in the fungal light, reviewing intelligence gathered a decade ago—awash in information, none of it useful to them because it overwhelms them. And yet—why? Why attempt to gather it?

If Dad had actually studied Tonsure's journal, I wonder if he would have found what I found. Even more important—what would he have done with the knowledge?

Sometimes they gather around my door. Sometimes they burrow up from below. When they get in—which isn't often; I've learned some of their tricks—they watch me. Observe. It is more unnerving than if they were to hurt me.

Either he, in a sense, hoped to distance himself from such knowledge by physically sending it away from him on postcards or, intensely involved in his studies, cast off these postcards in the fever of scholarship, like heat lightning. Anyone other than his sister would have thought these notes the ramblings of a madman. (Actually, Bonmot and I discussed "personal information," as you call it, quite often, and he never thought I was mad. I admit to writing most of the postcards during bouts of considerable pain caused by my diseases. Sometimes they reflected my research. Sometimes they simply reflected my agony. Even the starfish had been unable to remove the source of the infection. I was changing, and I was changing my mind to come to terms with that fact.)

More alarmingly, Duncan changed his living quarters with insane frequency, sending dozens of change-of-address postcards to the (newly renamed but still comfortingly inept) Voss Bender Memorial Post Office before finally giving up and listing the Academy as his mailing address. He refused to live at the Academy, although he would sleep in a guest room on nights when he worked late. Even after he met Sabon, Duncan moved from apartment to apartment. He never signed a lease of more than six months. He never took a ground-floor apartment. He always moved up—from the second floor, to the third, to the fourth, as if fleeing some implacable force that came up through the ground. (Yes—bad plumbing. Not to mention gray caps.)

Clearly he was hiding from something, but why should his plight affect me? After all, he had been stumbling into danger even BDD. Yes, I had written him the note about golden threads, the way our lives touch each other, but do you know how hard it is to keep that in mind from day to day? You'd have to be a priest or a martyr. So I let him go his separate way, confident that, like the time we had gotten lost in the forest, he would find his way out again.

Besides, I was distracted. By then, I had ascended to the very height of my powers. I led a council of gallery owners. I wrote withering and self-important reviews for *Art of the Southern Cities*. I had lunch with Important People like Sirin and Henry Hoegbotton at such upscale restaurants as the Drunken Boat.

For two years running, my stable of artists had received more critical attention and created more sales than the rest of the city's galleries combined. A word from me could now cripple an artist or redeem him. Utterance of such words became almost sexual, each syllable an arching of the back, a shudder of pleasure. Even when Martin Lake moved his best paintings to his own gallery, leaving me only his dregs, I told Sybel not to worry, for surely a thousand Lakes waited to replace him.

"Are you sure?" he asked me. "I expected the world to leave Lake behind, which hasn't happened. That we could deal with. But his leaving you behind could cause you damage."

I dismissed his concerns with a wave of my hand. "There are more where he came from."

I should have taken heed of his astonished look. I had yet to realize that my power had limits—that it could recede like the River Moth during drought.

The sheer opulence of my life disguised the truth from me. Not content with attending parties, I had begun to host parties. I entertained like one of Trillian's Banker-Warriors from the old days, my parties soon so legendary that some guests were afraid to attend. Legendary not just for the food or music or orgies, but how all three elements could be artfully combined in new and inventive ways. Outside of the incessant, unceasing rumors that they were "squid clubs" (a euphemism for the more sadomasochistic sex parlors, so named for the old squid-hunter habit of tying up their catch and delivering it alive to the buyer), nothing could diminish the allure of my parties.

Sybel was a great help in this arena—he took to party planning as if he had found his true calling. Under his artful administration, we staged many delightful debacles of alcohol and drugs. Each weekend, we would move to some new, more exotic, location—the priests of the Religious Quarter, in their greed, would rent to me their very cathedrals. Or Sybel would hire "party consultants" to scout the burnt-out Bureaucratic Quarter for suitable locations. Then, to the surprise of the homeless and the criminal element, some blackened horror of a building—say, the former Ministry of Foreign Affairs—would, well after midnight, erupt with light and mirth and the loud confusion of alcohol-aided conversations. The artists so *elsewhere* that they stood in corners talking to statues, coat racks, and desks. Morning revealed as grainy light touching pale bodies that in turn touched each other casually among the random abandoned divans and couches and makeshift beds crusted with cake and cum.

I remember waking up once, in the middle of the night, my cold sweat moistening the bedsheets, my skin crawling with a nameless dread. Sybel sat in a chair beside my bed, snoring.

I woke him up in a complete panic, chest tight, lungs heavy. I couldn't bear to be alone with my thoughts. "How long can we keep this up? How long can we keep going like this?"

Poor, beautiful, sly Sybel rubbed his eyes, looked up at me, smiled a sleepy smile, and said, "As long as you tell me to."

I hit him in the shoulder. The smile never left his face. "What does that mean?" I asked.

Sybel's gaze sharpened and he sat up in the chair. "Forever, Janice. Or close enough. This is just the beginning."

Poor stupid me. I believed him.

This is just the beginning. And so it was. But the beginning of what? The beginning of the end, really. The one time Janice Shriek's life significantly impacted Duncan Shriek's life. I became addicted to hallucinogenic mushrooms. Little purple mushrooms with red-tinged gills. So tiny. So cute. They magnified the minute and humbled the magnificent, and I couldn't get enough of them. I'd have a meeting with Sirin while on them and watch as his head became bigger and bigger, eclipsing his body. I would eat one while in the middle of another all-night drunken escapade and suddenly the noise and confusion around me would: stop. I would see the glittering detail of a streetlamp light shining off of the water in the gutter, and that sudden moment would become as large as the world. A comfort, really. A solace. (A plague. A way for you to escape the world.)

Sybel called them Tonsure's Folly, and I can't really complain, because I asked him to get them for me. And I can't even blame the mushrooms for everything that happened next. I was wandering further and further from the golden threads of my note to Duncan. I was becoming more and more unhappy, even though I was filling myself with so many substances and preying off enough new people, new experiences, that my distress was for the longest time just an echo of an ache in my belly. (No, you can't blame the mushrooms. But those mushrooms, over time, make the user more and more depressed. And you were already in a fragile state. I'm afraid I'd lost the thread of your life, caught up in my own problems, or I would have insisted that Sybel intervene.)

The parties I still remember with fondness, although the only one I've really come close to describing happened ages afterward—the Martin Lake party I was asked to help organize recently. The first party I'd been to for years, and haunted by the ghosts of other, grander parties. These ghosts lingered long enough to laugh at the staid properness of Janice Shriek in her old (c)age. No guests rolling naked over the carpet. No fruit served from the delicious concavities of the lithe bodies of young men and women. Not even the simple pleasures to be found in bowls of mushroom drugs. Just guests, music, light dancing, and lighter punch, not even spiked. Oh, what humiliation!

"Do you think she can see us from in there?"

"Naw—she's busy."

"She's deep in thought, she is—but what could she be thinking *about*, do you think?"

"About the next word she puts her hard finger to."

Distractions abound. Sometimes they become part of the story. Anyway:

The careful reader will remember that when I last left off the story of my final confrontation with Mary Sabon and her necklace of flesh—which, if you will remember, consisted, before the metaphor came to life and lurched forward, of two dozen of those social climbers who had become convinced she was the best historian since my brother—I was walking down the marble stairs in their direction.

I descended to the foot of the stairs. The marble shone like glass; my face and those of the others reflected back at me. The assembled guests slowly fell apart into their separate bead selves. Blank-eyed beads wink-winking at me as they formed a corridor to Sabon. Smelling of too little or too much perfume. Shedding light by embracing shadows. A series of stick-figures in a comedy play.

"What can she be typing so furiously?"

"How long's she been in there?"

"At least five days. I bring her food and drink. I take it out again. She's enough paper in there to last another week."

"Do *they* mind?"

"What? *They*? Haven't seen them here for weeks. They'll not be around again."

Mary Sabon. We are approaching Sabon now. Or I am, now that I've made it down the marble staircase. I suppose I must conjure her into existence before I can banish her . . . Red hair. Massive long locks of red hair, forest-thick and as uncivilized. Emerald eyes—or, perhaps, paste pretending to be jewel. A figure that. A voice which. A smile of.

I'm afraid I cannot do her the justice Duncan did in his journal entries, so I will stand aside to let him speak, even if he does stutter, enraptured by a schoolgirl-smell, white-socks fantasy with as much reality to it as a paper chandelier.

Mary Sabon. Sabon, Mary. Sabon. Mary. Mary. Mary Sabon. Sabon. Sabon. Sabon. The name burns like a flame in my head like her hair burns like her name burns like a flame in my head. She burns in my head. She burns in my head. I am delirious with her. I am sick with her. Blessed infection. I think of nothing but her. Walking home today, I could sense that the trees lining the boulevard contained her. I see her features when I stare down at the pavement upon which I tread. She is half-formed in the air. The faint smell of Stockton pine needles and incense. As of her. As of an echo of her. Her form a flame in the world that burns through everything, and there is nothing in the world but her—the world revealed as paper that burns away at the first hint of her. Above and below, a flame in my head. I cannot get her out. I am not sure I want to get her out. Rather banish myself from myself than to banish her from me.

✸✦✸

"Does she tip well?"

"Well enough. I don't mind her. She's no trouble. Not like you lot."

"That's a rough thing to say."

They are beginning to annoy me. I cannot keep them out of the text. Everything around me is going into the text—every dust mote, every scuff upon the floor, the unevenness of this desk, the clouded quality of the windows. I cannot keep it out right now.

Flame or not, at my party, Mary Sabon wore dark green. She almost always wore dark green. She might as well have been a shrub or a tree or a tree trunk.

Ignoring my presence—something she would have done at her peril in the old days—she said, "Duncan Shriek? Why, Duncan is not a human being at all, but composed entirely of digressions and transgressions. Assuming he is still alive, that is."

As she said this, she turned and looked right at me.

I stared at her for a moment. I let her receive the venom in my eyes. Then I walked up to her and slapped her hard across the face. The impact shone as red as her hair, as flushed as the gasp from the necklace of flesh. It lit up her face in a way that made her look honest again. It spread across her cheek, down her neck, swirled between the tops of her breasts, and disappeared beneath her gown.

If the world is a just place, that mark will never leave her skin, but remain as a pulsing reminder that, at some point in the past, she hurt someone so badly that she hurt herself as well.

But I was not done. Not by half. I had just begun.

What did I do? You'll find out soon enough. Jump pages. Jump time. Skip through the rest as if it were a park pathway on a Sunday afternoon, and you eager to feed the ducks at the far end, in Voss Bender Memorial Square. But I haven't written the path yet, and you'd get lost without it—and, paper cuts aside, I'll find ways to make you wait. Waiting is good. I've been waiting for over five days now. I know something about waiting. And afterwords.

"I say again: What's she typing in there? Clack-clack-clack—it's disturbing my peace of mind."

"Wasn't her brother the writer?"

"Obviously not the only one in the family."

"You must be new to this conversation."

"What's she writing, do you think?"

"The story of your life, Steen. A history of the Cappans. How should I know?"

"Whatever it is, it must be important. To her."

Pickled eyes in pickled light. A glimpse of cheddar-wedge nose.

"Funny. It's like an echo. It falls away when we stop talking."

. . .

"See. No typing. Do you think she's . . . ?"

She's what? Typing your inane speech, perhaps? Why not? You've become my companions after a fashion. Although I've never talked to them, I've shared this place with them for days now. I ought to feel grateful for their interest. I ought to get out of this dank back room and go over and suggest a game of darts.

"Naw—she's not typing us. Hasn't got anything to do with us."

I think I'll go for a walk. I'm going to go for a walk. My hands are cramping. My stomach growls. The clock on the wall tells me I've been here much longer than I thought.

Even ghosts can take a walk, so why not me?

6

I was beginning to sound like a character in a book. I had to escape the relentless pressure of the words. I had to get away. From the typewriter keys. From my wrinkled hands, which prove my brain lies to me about my age. From the faces staring through the green crack where the corridors synchronize into a fracture of seeing. From the feeling that I had begun to *parrot* on these pages, blandly resuscitating facts. (Janice, once you start a project like this, it's impossible to tell what is truly important or who will find what the most interesting, so it's no use second-guessing your decisions, no matter how I may have protested against some of them.)

I went for a hobbling walk, leaning heavily on my cane every step of the way. But when you've lived in a place this long, no walk can occur solely in the present. Every street, every building, appears to you encrusted with memories, with perspectives that betray your age, your cynicism, your sentimentality, or your lack of feeling where you *should* feel something. Here, the site of a quick fuck, a fumbling moment of ecstasy. ("Lover's tryst," Janice, is, I believe, the preferred term; once again your style slips from Duncanisms to gutterisms.) There, a farewell to a departing friend. A fabled lunch with an important artist. The dust-smudged window of a rival gallery, still floundering along while you are forever out of business. A community square, where once you held an outdoor party, strung with paper lanterns. And if this were not enough—not relentless enough, not humbling enough—that unspeakable vision overlaying all of it, had you only the glasses to see: the mark of the gray caps on the city in a thousand secret signs and symbols.

It is not an easy thing for me to walk through Ambergris these days, but there is also comfort: why, she said, her heart breaking a little, there are so many friends to visit, even if they are all in the ground.

But at first I just hobbled down Albumuth Boulevard in the late afternoon light, letting my path be decided by the gaps between supplicants and pilgrims. Happy that everything appeared normal, that evidence of the Shift was hidden, or so minute that I didn't notice it. (Or maybe you didn't notice it because you had become so used to it.)

I took deep breaths, to catch all the smells in this most beautiful and cruel of all cities: passionflower and incense, lemon trees and horse flop, rotting meat and coffee grounds. For a few minutes I tried to pretend to be a tourist, a passerby, an incidental part of the city. It didn't work. How could it? I am Janice Shriek.

※

My leg was already beginning to ache, but I thought I might feel more optimistic if I headed for the site of my greatest triumphs. I hadn't visited it in ages, so I went despite the discomfort. After a good half hour, I finally stood in front of what had once been the Gallery of Hidden Fascinations. A flower shop and a bakery stood to either side, but the part of the building that had housed the gallery lay empty as if cursed. The shadow where the hand-painted sign had once hung had been branded into the wall by years of hard weather. Beyond the cracked windows lay dust, moldy frames, and darkness. No paintings. No paint not peeling. Just seasons and seasons of neglect. The smell of stale bread, rotting wood. Layers of purple fungus had taken root in the closest wall. Passersby hardly spared the place a second glance. It should have been a monument, or at least a memorial. It had housed dozens of famous paintings and painters. Conversations that shaped all aspects of the art world had taken place there. Much of the art mentioned in the Hoegbotton tourist guides, the descriptions of the New Art movement, had started with my gallery. *I* had started there. Everything I have been since came from my gallery. This dump. This husk of broken timbers. Even my memories of it—saturated in the marinade of all five senses and as sharp as yesterday—could not bring it to sudden life. I might as well have never left the typewriter. I was still trapped in an afterword.

I headed into the Religious Quarter, immediately calmed by the sound of bells—bells from steeples and cathedrals, from alcoves and altars, which I could never quite find the source of, which lingered at the edge of hearing.

I disturbed a boy in the act of lighting a candle in the recess that marked the northernmost corner of the Church of the Seven-Edged Star. He looked up at me, his face whiter even than his white robes against the tousle of black hair, his eyes a glistening green, his mouth forming a half-conscious "O," the long match held with divine grace in his slightly upturned right hand. The white of his revealed wrist sent a shudder through me, but he smiled and the image of grace returned.

He was right to light the candle, for the Quarter at that hour had not only distant bells but distant light, the dusk so strong it might as well have been a smell, a musk, that slid over the unprotected surfaces of cobblestones, windows, and walls, leaving behind the chaos of rippling illuminations that remain in the Quarter after dark. Priests shuffled past, murmuring mouths and bare feet. Truffidians, Manziists, Menites, Cultists? Doubtless Duncan the historian would have known. No matter how Ambergris Shifted, we could count on the rituals of the Quarter remaining the same.

Moving on, I walked to the edge of the Religious Quarter—by now an act of will, as my leg really hurt—past the stern-looking Truffidian Cathedral, and by way of a flurry of alleys soon found myself in front of Blythe Academy. The dark covered the Academy comfortably, content to linger at the outskirts of lamps and torches.

Even from the street I could see directly into the courtyard, and beyond the courtyard into the student apartments, here and there a window illuminated with golden light. In the foreground, the pale willow trees rustled in the breeze. (As pale willow trees are wont to do.) The stone benches and tables were solid, dark, strangely comforting masses. A monk strode across the courtyard. Another followed, cowl hiding his face. The sweet, pungent scent of honeysuckle wound itself around me.

I do not know how long I stood there, remembering those long-ago conversations, but as I did, an unbearable sadness came over me. Nothing I can type on these pages can convey—truly—what I felt as I looked into the darkened courtyard where Duncan, Bonmot, and I had sat and talked. And, if I am truthful, that place I stood in front of, which meant so much to me, no longer had any more to do with me than the Borges Bookstore. The moment, the spirit, had passed out of it and it was just a place once more. Duncan no longer taught there. Bonmot no longer sat behind the desk in his office, listening to the imagined miseries of yet another homesick student. Duncan had disappeared. Bonmot had died more than twelve years ago.

What strange creatures we are, I thought as I stood there. We live, we love, we die with such random joy and grief, excitement and boredom, each mind as individual as a fingerprint, and just as enigmatic. We make up stories to understand ourselves and tell ourselves that they are true, when in fact they only represent an individual impression of one individual fingerprint, no matter how universal we attempt to make them.

I stood there, mourning the death of that place, even though it had not really died, even though it had since spawned a thousand stories to join the millions of stories that comprised the city, and then I walked back here, to the typewriter, to continue my epic, my afterword, so consumed by what? By emotion. That my hands are shaking. They are shaking right now. What shall stop them? Perhaps a dose of the dead past.

At Bonmot's funeral, some twelve years ago, men and women who would not have dared visit him while he was alive circled around the polished oak coffin like impatient iridescent flies. The day held a hint of rain in the gravel sky, the air moist and cool. The smell of mold was everywhere.

Outside the Truffidian Cathedral, Martin Lake dourly limped about on his polished cane, stopping to mutter grim Lakeisms to friends such as Merrimount and Raffe, all of whom avoided me as if I embodied a disease they might one day become. That's how far I had fallen. I limped like Lake by then. I had a cane like him. But I was not enough like him, especially now that he had passed from "successful" to that ethereal realm where one's fame will always outlive the fading mortal body.

The Morrow ambassador to the House of Hoegbotton—newly renamed to reflect the aftermath of war—presented a dapper sight in slick black tuxedo and tails, at least until he managed to slide in a patch of mud created by overzealous gravediggers and groundskeepers. A general from the Kalif's army, a supposed friend of Bonmot's in his youth, looked out of place in turban and gold-and-red glittery uniform, his presence barely tolerated by a city that so frequently had been bombarded by his masters.

Dozens of priests arrived from the Religious Quarter, from orders as diverse as the Cult of the Seven-Edged Star and Manziism. They all wore variations of black-on-white and somber stares. They all had guards with them. Ever since the War of the Houses, no one trusted anyone else. Hoegbotton's men were out in force as well, armed with guns and with knives. Some of them stood in motored vehicles, in well-heeled clumps, staring.

Business leaders also arrived to pay their bemused respects. The newly ascendant Andrew Hoegbotton, a weasely stick figure of a man with large, liquid eyes, shared uneasy space with Lionel Frankwrithe, a smug middle-aged man who kept snapping out his pocket watch in sudden motions that kept wretched Andrew flinching. Truces between House F&L and House H&S rarely lasted very long anymore.

At the edges, surrounding these dim luminaries, stood beggars, prostitutes, and the working poor, all of whom Bonmot had helped at some period in his life, whether as Antechamber or as the Royal of Blythe Academy. As *The Ambergris Daily Broadsheet* noted:

> Every element of Ambergrisian society turned out yesterday to grieve the death of a man most had abandoned in his exile and which, happy coincidence, they now remembered as the hour of heartfelt high-profile memorial speeches grew near. (Janice, you know I wrote this.)

The procession from the Cathedral to Bonmot's final resting place was silent. The flags of the Religious Quarter lay limp against the breezeless sky. As we walked, our procession grew larger and more diverse. More and more people left their homes or temples to join us. I remember thinking that this wasn't just a funeral for Bonmot—it was a funeral for the city. So much uncertainty faced us now. We'd been shaken out of our preconceptions by the war and its aftermath. We'd been roused from our blindness—or so we hoped.

The procession ended with an interminable parade into and through Trillian's cemetery. They say Trillian populated the cemetery with the victims of his bloody merchant wars. But within its walls, I have always felt a theme of renewal and peace rather than death. Its massive oak trees, its giant, curling green ferns, its elegant stone houses for the departed—they all conspired to make the visitor think of woodland walks and primordial forests rather than decay. That day, the graveyard seemed more alive than the insensate, gangrenous city surrounding it.

The trio of violinists abruptly stopped playing. The coffin was lowered into its final resting place, a headstone to be added later. The gravediggers who would fill in the dirt stood leaning on their shovels next to the mound of earth, their stares flat and steady. In front of them, the current Antechamber began to give the final speech of the afternoon, a few hollow words about his predecessor, couched in platitudes and numbing repetition.

"Give back to this earth this good man, O Lord," he said, much to the grumbling dismay of several Manziists present, who missed their traditional rat-festooned funeral ceremony. "Give back to this good man the earth, O Lord," he said again, like a man who, having missed his memorized mark, has to start over in the correct order. "And let you, O Lord, serve as a light to him, for we are imperfect vessels and we platitude simile extended metaphor with barely any pauses followed by more repetition. Period. Comma. Stop. Start. Here I go again about God and the dirt and wait: another platitude, quote from the Truffidian Bible everyone's heard a thousand times before, and even though I once actually knew Bonmot when I was a junior priest, not a single personal anecdote about the man because the scandal of his long-ago departure as Antechamber might somehow still cling to me like a fetid stench. Amen."

While they buried our friend, I watched a glossy emerald beetle, carapace age-pocked and mossy, fend off an attack by a dozen fuzzy ants, their red thorax glands releasing tiny jets of bubbly white poison. This drama took place in a leafy alcove while storks flew against the rapidly darkening sky and moth wings muttered on mottled tree trunks, the world in constant rebellious motion against the stark silence within the coffin.

Duncan came, of course, his face ever more deeply lined with the weight of secret knowledge (or maybe I had just stayed out too late the night before), his gaze settling upon the assembled rabble in search of one perfect, elusive face . . . but Mary did not come. Parties, lecture series, concerts, readings, she attended, even during wartime. Funerals, however, never made Mary's agenda. She did not like funerals. People, for her, did not die, and places never became disenfranchised from those moments that made them important. Both became entombed in her books and, until placed there, never failed to behave as less than caricature or puppetry.

"Duncan," I said. "She's not coming. She never was going to come. Not for you. Not for Bonmot." She would be writing, or doing something equally destructive to Duncan's (lack of a) career.

He would not answer me. He would not look at me. As the Antechamber tossed a clot of earth on Bonmot's coffin, Duncan stared at it, too downcast at Sabon's absence to utter a word.

Time had made no difference. Whether minutes after the dissolution of their relationship or years after, Duncan was the same. Even when increasingly attacked and hounded by the words like knives from her various books, he allowed her to control his heart.

As we left the funeral, Duncan was still searching the crowd for any sign of Mary.

(Janice, I accepted your dressing down, which you conveniently dilute and misremember, because I knew you hurt from Bonmot's death as much as I did. But please do not mistake my silence for agreement with your reading of my thoughts. If I surveyed the crowd, it wasn't to search for Mary. I knew she wasn't coming. My gaze was blind—I saw nothing, but always looked inward to my memories of Bonmot. While the procession lurched toward the cemetery, while the Antechamber gave his depressing speech, even while you lashed out at me, I was nowhere near that place. I was where you should have been—in the courtyard, sitting on a bench beside Bonmot and talking. Besides you, our mother, and Lacond, Bonmot was one of the only people keeping me aboveground. I never really bought into religion, but I believed in Bonmot, and because he had faith, I had faith through him. And I was heartbroken for missed opportunities, because it had been so many years since I'd had a personal conversation with him.

(You congratulate yourself on being sensitive to my thoughts, but you barely knew them at times. It stung that you saw what no one else could—that the fungus had continued to colonize my skin, that even as I stood there and watched them pour dirt over Bonmot's coffin my body fought a thousand battles more vigorous than those between beetle and ants—and yet you could not understand why I might be distracted. That my mind was consumed by another attempt to stand firm against the invasion of my own body on the most basic levels, like pissing black blood or sweating out green liquid fungus.)

Duncan and Mary. For a time, long before that horrible day in the graveyard, they were inseparable. And yet: Never a more unlikely couple, a pair less paired, less suited for suitability. Would that I could provide a complete chronicle of the misshapen event. Alas, I cannot tell this part of the story through Duncan's journal. I am embarrassed to report that Duncan's journal entries on these matters prove nearly incomprehensible in their extremes of love, despair, lust, and, yes, love again, repetitious and maudlin. I will spare the reader the full scope of their sexual senility by only providing excerpts. I suggest you fill in any blanks with applicable entries from your own diary . . .

It was, as they say, a beautiful spring day when Duncan first recorded his utter surrender. Outside, the willow trees breathed gently from side to side under a merciful sun, and street vendors danced joyously in anticipation of Duncan's ardor, and the birds stopped in midair to witness the innocence that was Duncan's lust, and the gray caps came aboveground to gift all citizens of the city with garlands of sweet-smelling fungus, and I must stop before I make myself sick. (I'm already sick. This whole section will make me sick, I think.)

Inside the Academy, Duncan breathed gently on the neck of the woman child (she was already twenty-one!) he had kept after class for "further instruction":

Today Mary wore a white blouse, and as I pointed out a relevant passage in Tonsure's journal, she stood next to me, our clothes just touching. I felt a pressure between us, as if she held me up or I held her up, and if the tension was broken, one of us would fall. I turned my head into the blindness of that endless white as she stood beside me, and every inch of my body knew the certainty of her generous hips where the blouse disappeared into her skirt and the reckless knowledge of her soft neck above the blouse, the face shining above the neck. All of these elements destroyed me more than what I saw, which was just the blouse, filled with her. The stitching on the blouse. The texture of the fabric itself. The soft curving caress of her breast beneath. So near. The nearness of her made me tremble. The smell of her, the smell of clean, firm skin. All I would have had to do was incline my head forward a fraction of an inch and my lips would have kissed her through the fabric. Time was extinguished by the tension between giving in, feeling her breast against my mouth for what might be only a second before her mutiny, and staying in position, forever teased by the possibility. Teetering on the edge of an abyss, where to fall was to fall was to fall into bliss, bliss, bliss; but torment, too . . . And yet what if the action met not with outrage or rejection, but with a sigh of acceptance? Would that not be worth the risk? Would it not be worth the cost to remove the torment by attempting to consume it? To extinguish the flame by joining it?

For all of his wretched fumbling for words—I hope he didn't fumble that way with her bra strap!—I could have defined his condition for him with one word: lust. Why, I had become a world-renowned expert on lust by then, seeing the problem firsthand from several dozen different positions. I could have helped Duncan, except he didn't ask my advice; instead, he wrote it all down in his journal. (Not fair. I knew you would have advised me against it, and this I could not bear the thought of. I must say—I do appreciate you baring *my* soul in *your* afterword.)

I was destroyed by this. Destroyed. How can I describe the heaviness of her body next to me? The rich physicality of her, the smell of her skin, the way her body eclipsed my senses. She annihilated my dream of her—even flame too light a metaphor. Confronted by the reality of her, I was tormented by the urgency of a choice I could not make. I shuddered and drew back, so overcome with desire that I shivered and said nothing, even though an awkward pause had descended over our conversation, her gaze upon me.

Had Duncan taken lovers before Sabon? Rarely. He had no time for love with so much mucking about in underground tunnels ahead of him. I'll tell you the distasteful truth: he lost his virginity to a prostitute the night he graduated from the Religious Institute in Morrow. (One begins to wonder if you really have my best interests in mind.)

I remember it quite well. She arrived at the Institute much earlier than Duncan intended, before I had left for my own quarters. He made her wait in the cloakroom while he finished getting dressed; I felt like asking him why he bothered.

She and I had nothing to talk about, although I looked her over as thoroughly as if she had been meant for me. She seemed as respectable as anyone from Sabon's necklace of flesh, which is to say: not at all. Her blond hair had streaks of brown in it, and her face was too pale. Her hastily applied makeup encircled her eyes with too much blue. She looked ghostlike, waiflike, her dress a size too big. She wore it bravely nonetheless, struggling not to be lost in the greens of it.

Duncan came out then, his entrance accompanied by an expression of such utterly pathetic excitement that I found myself forgiving him, almost envying him. How could I pass judgment knowing how alone he had been? . . . But that wasn't all: as I closed the door, I saw them standing there in front of his wall of oddities, and the stare of recognition that passed between them, the alone meeting the lonely, carried with it a level of comprehension much deeper than anything I ever saw between Duncan and Mary; as deep as if they had been lovers for twenty years (the truth was, you spent about as much time with that prostitute as you did with Mary over the years, so how could you know?).

> The deliciousness of that moment, my intent almost exposed to Mary by my silence, lingers with me still, and I wonder if the consummation of this feeling could ever compare to the sheer, excruciating sweetness of this tension that binds me to her and her to me in this enclosed space of memory—my mouth so close to her blouse, which I must either kiss or tell her how I burn, and yet can do neither. There is no time in such a place, only thoughts and flesh transposed. The white of her blouse. The white of her beneath the white. And in my thoughts, where I can enslave everyone and everything, I cross the space between our bodies. I place my mouth upon her breast. She expresses neither surprise nor shock, but only sucks in her breath, moans, and slowly places her soft hands behind my head, drawing me into her, her hands so cool on my hair, her body soft soft soft.
>
> I think I am going mad.

Mad? What did my poor, deluded brother know about going mad? I find it somewhat pathetic that my brother, the great historian, could not tell the difference between going mad and falling in love. The difference, as I know from bitter experience, is that when you go mad, you go mad utterly alone. Quite perfectly alone. That is the only difference.

How do I know this? I know this because one afternoon, while Duncan wrestled with an entirely different sort of madness, I entered my apartment, turned on the lights, and went into the bathroom, never intending to come back out again . . .

7

Start again. Start over. How am I supposed to get through this part? I could ignore it, I suppose, but it wouldn't go away—it would be a huge, gaping hole in this afterword. A few snapped golden threads. An unrealized opportunity. Did I become more of Duncan's life then, or did I become a shadow to him?

Release my breath. Breathe in again. Imagine a courtyard with stone benches and willows and the scent of honeysuckle and sweet, good conversation.

I remember Bonmot asked me about death once when Duncan was off grading papers. I don't recall the context, or who had broached the subject.

"Are you afraid of death?" he asked me.

"I'm afraid of not knowing," I said. "I would like to know. I would like to know when I am going to die."

Bonmot laughed. "If you knew, you might relax too much. You might think, 'I've got twenty years. Today, I don't need to do a thing.' Or you might not. I don't know." He took a bite of his sandwich.

"Duncan's not afraid of death," I said.

Bonmot looked at me sharply. "What makes you think that?"

"The way he courts it. The way he puts himself in the path of death."

Suddenly, I felt as if Bonmot was angry with me.

"Duncan is afraid of death, trust me. Sometimes, I think he is more afraid of death than anyone I've ever met. Do you understand why I say that?" (I'm not afraid of death—I'm afraid of dying too soon.)

At the time, I didn't. I didn't understand at all. Now, I do understand. It is all too clear now.

A courtyard. Stone benches. Willow trees. Honeysuckle.

Bonmot: "You needn't be afraid of death. If you believe, you will come back."

Me: "Believe in what?"

Bonmot: "Anything. It doesn't matter what."

But I'm not there. I am here, and I know that we die. We die and we don't come back. Ever. Why should it matter that I tried to hasten the process—to go further than Duncan, to beat him to the beginning of the race, to fall between the glistening strands and keep on falling through the darkness? (I had my watchers on you by then. I would never let you fall between the strings—me, yes, but not you.)

I'm sorry. I've tried so hard to stick to a *sophisticated* style, something I thought Duncan would recognize and appreciate, even if he is gone forever. But the truth is, I can't keep on this way. Not all the time. The green glass glares at me. The hole in the floor is opening. I defy anyone under these circumstances to smile and dance and prattle on as if nothing had gone wrong.

We die. We die. It shrieks at me from an empty cage. Let my future editor, strange beast that he is, earn his wages and edit me. Edit all of me. Edit me out if necessary. By then I won't care. The flesh necklace can glitter with its scornful laughter and, laughing, shiver to pieces.

But where was I? It feels strange to type the words "But where was I?" but it helps orient me when I am truly lost. There's a loud gaggle of musicians—some might call them a "band," but I wouldn't—out there now, and although I glimpse only frenetic slices of them, the sound distracts me. Sometimes, I wonder if the lyrics infiltrate my own words, change them or their meaning. Sometimes, I wonder if my words fly off the page and into their mouths, to infiltrate their lyrics, change them as they are changing me. Surely this is how Duncan became misunderstood. (No, my dear sister—I became misunderstood because everyone was terrified of understanding me.)

So if you can hear me through all of this noise, lean close, listen, and I will tell you a kind of truth that once made sense to me and may again, in time, undergo that startling transformation from madness to the purest form of sanity: If you are feeling low. If you are so full of poison that you can find no light within you. If everywhere you look you see only bitterness or despair. If all of these conditions and situations apply to you, I recommend a refreshing suicide attempt. No matter what the so-called experts might say, a suicide attempt will clean you right out. True, it will also squeeze from your body the last remnants of the last smile, the last laugh, the last scrap of hope, of any small, shy, but still-bright part of you that ever cared about *anything*. Nothing will remain. Not religion. Not friends. Not family. Not even love. A carcass picked clean and lying forgotten by the side of Albumuth Boulevard. A hollowed-out statue. A wisp of mist off the River Moth.

But that doesn't last—how could it?—and at least it drains the poison so that even in your isolation from yourself, you feel . . . gratitude. Which fades in turn because at the end you don't even feel numb, because to feel numb implies that at some point you were not numb, and so you feel like you don't really exist anymore—which is the truest sort of truth: after a suicide attempt, you *don't* really exist anymore, just the images of you in other people's eyes.

Later, as I stared at the blood welling up from an accidental pen puncture (how could they let you have a pen, with all the money I was paying them?!), absentminded and remote from the pain, I was amused at how concerned doctors get about such things; one would have thought a gardening convention had blossomed around the fertile flower bed of my body for all the quick consternation they displayed at this pinprick.

Which belonged to a different world than my poor wrist, sliced to the bone. I could see the bone wink through at me the night I did it, as if it shared the joke in a way the blood could not. The blood wanted only to escape, but the good, solid bone—it ground against the knife, made me reconsider, if only for a moment, the bravery, the honesty, of pain. Craven, quivering flesh. Foolish blood. And the bone winking through. I wish I could remember what it said to me. I remember only fragments: the roar of blood as it raced away, drowned out the murmur of the bones. Besides, I was preoccupied: I was laughing because my hand flopped off the end of my wrist in a way I found hilarious. I was shaking so hard that I could not hold the knife to cut my other wrist. This was simply the most stunning miscalculation I had ever made! I flopped around like a half-dead fish, unable to finish what I had started, but had no one to help me out. Even funnier—and I almost tore myself apart with laughter over this one—I was not enveloped in a warm hum of numbness. Not so lucky, no. The pain blazed through me as intensely as if my blood were boiling as it left me. So intense my laugh became a scream, my scream something beyond even the vocal cords of an animal. Death, it seemed, wasn't all that much fun after all, especially when I became vaguely aware that someone had smashed in the door and was carrying me out of the apartment, and he was weeping louder than I was . . . (That was me, Janice. When I saw you like that, your eyes so blank, blood everywhere, I couldn't take it. Nothing affected me like that. Not the underground. Not the disease taking over my body. But you, crumpled in the bathtub, half-dead. You looked as though, without ever going underground, you had suffered all the terrors to be found there.)

So you can imagine my amusement over the doctor's concern about my thumb prick. The pricks should have been more concerned about where I found the pen—and where they had made me stay, and whose company I'd been keeping.

For you see, the Voss Bender Memorial Mental Hospital is not what I would call the most hospitable of accommodations. I will not be recommending it to my friends and family. I will not be tipping generously. Indeed, I will not even be stealing the bath towels or the little soaps from the shower. (I did think about putting you in Sybel's care—having him take you to live with the Nimblytod Tribes amid the thick foliage of tall trees. You would drink rainwater from the cups of lilies and feast on the roasted carcasses of songbirds. But then I remembered the casual nonchalance with which Sybel provided anyone who asked with the tinctures/powders/substances of their choice, and knowing of your addictions, I could not take the chance. Thus, you wound up in the Voss Bender Memorial Mental Hospital instead.)

Strange light, strange life, to end up in a place like that: an ivy-shrouded fortress of cruel stone and sharp angles, and gray like the inside of a dead squid, gray like a gray cap, gray like a thunderstorm, but not as interesting. Little windows like crow-pecked eyes, not even round or square sometimes, but misshapen. Had former inmates chiseled at them, attempting to escape? If you looked at the gray stone up close, you could see that it wasn't just stone—a type of gray fungus had coated those walls. It fit over the stone like skin; you could almost see the walls breathing through their fungal pores.

Smells? Did I mention smells? The smell of sour porridge. The smell of rotting cheese. The smell of unwashed *others*. Stench of garbage, sometimes, wafting up from the lower levels. Oil, piss, shit. All of it covered by the clean smell of soap and wax, but not covered well enough.

Intertwined with the echo of smells came the echo of sounds—screams so distant behind padded walls that I sometimes thought they came from inside my own head. The panting of inmates like animals in distress. A low screeching warble for which I could never find a source.

The hallways were like corridors to bad dreams. They rambled this way and that with no order, no coherence. You might find your destination, or you might not. It all depended on luck. I remember that once I turned a corner, and there was a dandelion growing out of a clump of dirt on the floor. After that, I wouldn't have been surprised if the lower levels were vast swamps or brambles, through which inmates thrashed their way to open space. Once, I swear I even saw a gray cap in the distance, running away from me, toward a doorway. But I was not particularly stable; who knows what I really saw. (You're exaggerating. It wasn't *that* bad. I wouldn't have sent you there if it was a torture chamber.)

All of this—this grand design, this palace—was run by a man they called only Dr. V, as if his last name were so hideous or so forbidden that even saying "Dr. V" aloud might lead to some arcane punishment. I had the impression that the man's name was very long. All I know is, I never saw him, not once, during my stay in those glorious apartments, those rooms fit for a king, or at least a rat king.

But as bad as the facilities might have been, I found my fellow inmates more disturbing. My new best friends were, predictably, all depressed, suicidal people. If you want to make a suicidal person even more depressed, keep them cooped up with several other suicidal people, that's what I always say.

My friends included Martha of the Order of Eating Disorders, who looked like a couple of wet matchsticks sewn together with skin; a writer who would not give his name and thought he had created all of us; Sandra, who suffered through experimental treatments, involving streetlamps and an engine from a motored vehicle, that could have cooked a couple of hundred dinners; Daniel, who had reason to be devoid of hope—his deformity had fused his two legs into one stump that fed into his head, which had stuck to his shoulder in an unattractive way—and, of course, Edward.

Edward was different from the rest, and he stayed away from us. I would see him in the mornings, hunched in a corner. Short, dressed all in gray, with a large felt hat. Bright, dark eyes that peered from a pale, slack face. His hands had long dirty nails that looked as if they might snap off at the slightest suggestion of a breeze. A stale, dull, rotting smell came from his general direction, which I later discovered was due to the mushrooms he kept about his person. Sometimes, he made little chirping sounds, kin to the cricket that sang to me from outside my cell when the moon was full.

Edward, according to the experts, thought he was a gray cap. His misfortunes included losing his job as a bookbinder for Frankwrithe & Lewden; falling in love with a woman who could not love him back; the recent death of his grandfather, his only living relative; and not being taken seriously. (This last the fate of many of us.) He'd swallowed whole handfuls of poisonous mushrooms. The landlady had found him in time, but only because she stopped by to inquire about the lateness of the rent. He should have been grateful, but he was not.

In Edward, I seemed to have found someone who was distant cousins with Duncan. (I'd have been much like Edward if I'd let my obsession eat me. But I didn't want to *be* a gray cap, Janice—I wanted to *learn* about them.) I told Edward—with dull sunlight seeping through the dusty fungal filigree of the dull windows, in that dull common room with dull faded carpets and dull faded paint covered with lichen, while we and the other dull inmates sat in our stupid dull deck chairs—pulled off a Southern Isles vacation ship? or a Moth River ferry?—waiting to start another dull hopeless session of rehabilitation with a woman so cheerless and uninteresting that I cannot even conjure up a shadow of her name—I told him about the singing of the blood, the murmuring of the bone, and he agreed it sounded like a much superior method for a suicide attempt. The mushrooms he had taken had just made his body fall asleep. A knife wound, on the other hand, spoke to you in a myriad of voices. It told you how you really felt. He nodded like he understood. I nodded back as if *I* knew what I was talking about.

Edward only spoke to me using his chirps and whistles, and the occasional drawing. He always drew tunnels—crisscrossing tunnels, honeycombing tunnels, tunnels without end. He used black chalk or charcoal on butcher's paper. That was all we had in there to chart our creativity.

"I know," I told him. "I know. You want to go underground. Like my brother. My brother's been underground. Trust me. You don't want to go there."

Chirp, chirp, whistle. Huge eyes glistening from beneath his hat and his cowl.

"No, no—trust me, Edward. The world aboveground holds more than enough for you, if you give it a chance," I replied, even though I didn't believe a word of it.

Some days I made fun of Edward. Some days I thought he was more in love with the whole idea of the gray caps than my brother. Some days I thought he was my brother. (I was never crazy, just committed.)

One day, on an impulse, I silenced his chirping with a hug. I held him tight, and I could feel his body shudder, relax, and melt into that embrace. I heard him whisper a word or two. I could not understand the words, but they were human. He did not want to let go. Something inside of him didn't believe in his own insanity. And suddenly, I found myself holding him tighter, and crying, and not believing in my insanity, either.

Soon enough, though, the guards pulled us apart, and we each returned to our separate madness.

Over time, the days took on a sameness in that place. A crushing gray sameness. The only relief came in the form of Sybel, who visited two or three times. He let me know how my reputation fared in the outside world—not well—and brought with him "sympathy" cards from Sirin, Lake, and several others. Sirin had written his using letters cut from the wings of dead butterflies, while Lake had scrawled a sketch and an indecipherable message that appeared to be an attempt at a pun that had gone horribly wrong.

Startling proof of my former life running a gallery for unstable artist types, and yet that whole life seemed unreal, as if I had never lived it. I felt as if I were receiving messages from foreign lunatics.

"When are you coming back?" Sybel asked as he held my hand. I could see real sympathy in his eyes, not just pity.

I shrugged. "It depends."

"On what?" he asked.

"On when Duncan's money runs out. Where is Duncan anyway?"

"I don't know. I think he's gone underground."

The truth was, Duncan never visited me. I never asked him why. I didn't want to know. (I was too angry at you. And I had pressing matters to attend to underground.)

"How's the gallery?" I asked Sybel.

"As well as can be expected with Lake gone and you . . . recovering."

"Recovering. A nice word for it."

"What word would you like me to use?" Sybel asked. A glint of anger showed in his expression. It was the only time I angered him, or the only time I saw his anger.

"Any other word, Sybel," I said. "Any word that conveys just how fucked up I am."

Sybel laughed. "Just look at your sympathy cards. You're not the first and you won't be the last."

I stayed in that place for five months, until it became clear that I needed additional help, the kind that could not be provided at the hospital. At least they realized I would not try again. That madness was over with, although I had nightmares: *Their hunger was savage. They ate like wild animals, ate mushrooms and*

worse, drank and drank, fornicated in front of me, all against the backdrop of a city mad with fire.

Two days before I left that place for a succession of other places, Edward told me he loved me as we played another ludicrous game of lawn bowling in the tiny interior courtyard around which the building curled like a half-open fist—me unable to hold the ball because of my traitorous wrist, him short-sighted and un-coordinated. Our legendary games lasted for brutal hours of incompetence while Martha, Daniel, the Nameless Writer, and Sandra watched with a kind of disin-terested interest. This was the first time Edward had used recognizable human speech.

Applying the doctor's advice like a universal salve for any ill, I told Edward the truth: at the moment, I had no capacity for any kind of love. I did not love him back. I didn't love anyone back. I wouldn't have loved myself back if I'd walked past myself on a deserted street . . .

The day before I left, Edward used a variation on the Janice Shriek Method to try to kill himself. He stood in his corner as usual, his hands hidden as he cut at his wrists with a piece of metal he'd loosened from the underside of one of the deck chairs. He slowly rubbed the skin and flesh off his wrists until the blood came and his body trembled with the anticipation of stillness.

He stood there for at least half an hour, propped up by the wall, the blood hidden by his gray robes. He must have been very determined. I imagine the blood sang softly to him, comforting him. So I imagine. The truth must have a harder, sharper edge. It certainly did for those of us who had not noticed him in his corner, killing himself.

Luckily, or unluckily, an attendant discovered Edward's sin before it could claim him.

I swear I felt no guilt over the incident. It hurt terribly. No, it didn't. I cried for hours. No, I couldn't. He had bright, wide eyes, and he had a mind inside his body, a mind that could feel. I didn't have anything inside of me. My troubles looked so trivial next to his. Would it have hurt so much to say I loved him when I didn't? I couldn't even feel anger. Or despair. No despair for me today, thank you. Just an endless cool desert inside, and a breeze blowing and the sun going down, and this sense of calm eating at me. I only knew him for a few months and yet it hurt me terribly that memories of me would most likely be triggered every time he saw the scars on his wrists. (Do you get away with it that easily, Janice? Don't I have to forgive you, too? I was mad at you for a long time after that. There I was, lost in the tunnels under the city for days at a time, risking my life, and yet I never gave up the hope you abandoned all too easily.)

As it was, I never saw Edward again, or learned what happened to him or any of the other patients in that place. I had just been passing through.

So I left the hospital, but not for home—oh no. Duncan seemed to feel mental illness could only be cured by a great deal of travel at the disembarkation from which various "experts" poked and prodded various parts of your brain, only to prescribe more travel for the cure. From one end of Ambergris to the other, with Sybel my unwilling steward (you have no idea how much I was paying him—he *should* have been willing), I spun like some poor gristle-and-yarn shuttlecock in a lawn tennis game.

Let me try to remember them all. Dr. Grimshaw tried some gentle water shock treatment that left me with a nervous tic in my left eye. Dr. Priott hypnotized me, which only made my tongue feel dry. Dr. Taniger tried night aversion therapy, but this only made me sleepy. Dr. Strandelson tried to make me believe that a life of severe and perfect nudity held the answer to my problems. Some tried religion, some science. None of them convinced me for even a moment. I rarely said anything. When I did, it was just to talk about Edward, the pretend gray cap.

When my brother had exhausted the restorative talents of over two dozen Ambergrisian quacks, he and Sybel contrived to transport my morbidly bored carcass to Morrow by the reincarnation of the locomotive engine: Hoegbotton Railways.

Hoegbotton & Sons, with their customary twinned avarice and industry, had unearthed vast coal deposits in the mountainous western reaches of the Kalif's empire, waged a private war to wrest the disputed area from the control of the Kalif's generals, and then, through a crippling act of sheer will, ripped the old steam engines from their deathlike slumber in Ambergris's metal graveyards, refurbished them, straightened and derusted by various unarcane means, and set them back on track. Like me, they had been resurrected. Like me, they resented it.

The view from the pretty paneled windows reminded me of a thousand respectable landscape paintings laid side by side and brought to sudden life. I amused myself by rating each landscape against the next until my vision blurred—sobbing uncontrollably and staring down at the rewelded floors of the compartment while wondering what rats and hobos had lived there before the exhumation, what myriad battles over bread or scraps of clothing or glints of loose change had taken place, and how much dried blood had been painted over, and was that a scar the workmen had been unable to remove in the shape of the gray caps' favorite symbol, and what was that stain/vein of green along the lower right side of the seats opposite—some fungus, some mold, some rot—and so just generally composing a long sentence in my head to keep out the emptiness, the sadness, and the plain old ordinary human embarrassment of what had occurred: waking up from my attempt to find Duncan and Sybel looking down at me with a mixture of pity and sorrow. (My look was not pitying—I was furious with you. Perhaps that is why I sent you to so many specialists. Here we had helped save you, and all you could do was scowl and scream at us. Do you wonder why we didn't visit much?)

In Morrow I nearly died of boredom and the cold. Morrow is such a dry, dead town, a city of wooden corpses that talk and move about, but quietly, quietly. Morrow could never kill a soul with casual flair, as could Ambergris. Not instantly, snuffed out with a cruelty akin to the divine. No, Morrow would grind you down between its implacable wooden molars and create out of the resulting human-colored paste an acceptable, placid citizen who would marry, settle down, have children, retire, and die without a flicker of a flame of passion to warm/warn you on a cold winter night. In Morrow, a noise among the sewer pipes could never inspire fear, only conjure up a plumber. In Morrow, Duncan would have had to build tunnels or go mad and, sent to Ambergris to recuperate, have fallen in love with Her. No wonder Morrow was one of Mary's favorite cities; you're more than welcome to it, Mary—it deserves you.

Menite Morrow had always been—eternal heretics in the eyes of the Truffidians—and I soon discovered that the goal of the great, frozen Menite soul was to trudge on toward some ill-defined transition from unaccountable boredom to the responsible boredom of a transcendental bliss that would be enjoyed in the next life. Every doctor there was sensible to a fault, and not a one could help me because none of them had ever been where I had been. Relief came only in small doses; the bracing sense of embarrassment when Cadimon Signal, one of Duncan's more ancient former instructors, visited me: I could feel real warmth flood my face.

"Good," Cadimon said. "Shame is a good thing. It means you are alive, and you care what other people think."

Funny, I thought it was an involuntary reaction.

Another thaw quickly followed my bout of embarrassment: my curiosity returned as well, mostly due to frequent glimpses of the minions of Frankwrithe & Lewden from the window of my guarded room in an ice block of a hotel. With their sinister red-and-black garb, their aggressive sales tactics, their posters pounded into posts with straight nails, proclaiming forbidden books for sale—and their practiced street fights, their marching in closed ranks—they seemed better suited for Ambergris. As indeed they were destined, in time. They were preparing for the war—first with the ruler of Morrow and then anyone farther south who might get in their way.

One time, I even imagined I saw L. Gaudy watching his underlings from the shadow of an awning, smoking a pipe, nodding wisely. I wondered as I watched them at work if the town irritated them in the same way it irritated me. It made sense that they had to acquire Ambergris, if for no other reason than to escape Morrow. (Even then, I am sure, the emissaries of Hoegbotton & Sons haunted the streets, gliding through anonymously, eager for details, gossip, and trade.)

After two weeks of this foolishness, Duncan's attention wandered, no doubt due to Sabon's soft charms. The details of his well-intentioned plans for my imprisonment and rejuvenation became fuzzy and indistinct—as blurry as windows weighed down with sleet. I escaped from between the bars of a logic suddenly lost or nonexistent: doctor's bills unpaid, a nurse given no follow-up orders, a forgotten key languishing in a ready lock . . .

. . . and stepped out into the miserly heat of Morrow's sunrise, savoring and favoring my freedom. I had a sharp ache in the right wrist to remind me of my iniquities, and not a sign of a ticket home from my dear darling brother. (The nurse stole it, as I've told you dozens of times since.)

As I was lost, so too the light that lingered seemed lost as it stole gingerly across the snow in tones of dappled gold. It crept up my legs, purred its warmth across my face. Revealed: fir trees, two-story wooden houses, belching factories, thoroughfares full of hardworking hard-living quack psychologists. Morrow. I tried to love her in that last glance before I set off for the docks, a pathetic suitcase in hand. But failed. The light had revealed two truths: I was free, and rather than return directly to my former life, I had decided to visit my mother . . .

Here's a tale for you . . .

Once upon a time, a woman decided to tell a story about how she tried to kill herself. Her brother saved her at the last second—and then sent her north to be dissected by various disciples of empirical religions. Until one day, when her brother's attention wandered, she escaped, and made her way south, back to her mother's home in the fabled city of Ambergris. She felt so hollow inside that she could no longer bear to think of herself as "I."

The bitter cold of the north followed her south to Ambergris. She could see her breath. The drone of insects faltered to an intermittent click of surprise, a sleep-drenched distress signal.

She first saw her mother's house again through a flurry of snow, flakes sticking to the windshield of the hired motored vehicle. As they lurched down the failed road that led to the River Moth and her mother, the driver cursing in a thick Southern accent scattered with Northern cold, the dark blue muscles of the river came into view, and then three frail mansions hunched along the riverbank among the tall trees. The river was silent with cold and snow.

The mansions were silent, too: Three weary debutantes at a centuries-long ball. Three refugees of a bygone era. Three memories.

The force and pull of the past glittered from the wrought-iron balconies, from the hedge gardens sprinkled with snow. The faded appeal of the weathered white roofs that disappeared as the vehicle drove nearer, even the slender, hesitant windows reminding her of the tired places she had just left, with their incurable patients, their incurable boredom . . . the same lived-in appeal as the unstarched dress shirts her father used to wear, the white fabric coarse and yellow with age.

They drove through the remnants of fairyland—the frozen fountains in the brittle front yards, the pale statuary popular decades ago, the ornately carved doors with their tarnished bronze door knockers—until the vehicle came to a rest half-mired in snow, and for a heartbeat they watched the quiet snow together, she and the driver, content to marvel at this intruder: a strange incarnation of the invasion the Menites had long promised the lascivious followers of Truff.

Then, the moment over, the woman who had undergone a reluctant resurrection, exhumed while still living, paid the driver, picked up her suitcase, opened the door to the sudden frost, and trudged up the front steps of her mother's house. The driver drove away but she did not look back; she had no inclination to make him wait. She had resolved to stay in that place, and in her present state of mind she could not hold alternatives in her head without her skull breaking loose and rising, a bony balloon without a string, into the fissures of the cold-cracked sky. *What if?* had frozen along with the rosebushes.

Her mother's house. What made the middle mansion different from the other two aside from the fact that her mother lived there? It was the only inhabited mansion. It was the only mansion with the front door ajar. Icicled leaves from the nearby trees had swept inside as if seeking warmth, writing an indecipherable message of cold across the front hallway.

An open door, the woman thought as she stood there, suited her mother as surely as a mirror.

She stepped inside, only to be confronted by a welter of staircases. Had she caught the house in the midst of some great escape? Everywhere, like massive, half-submerged saurians, they curled and twisted their spines up and down, shadowed and lit by the satirical chandelier that, hanging from the domed ceiling, mimicked the ice crystals outside as it shed light that mingled in a delicate counterbalance with the frozen leaves.

Even there, in the foyer, the woman could tell the mansion's foundations were rotting—the waters of the Moth gurgled and crunched in the basement, the river ceaselessly plotting to steal up the basement steps, seeping under the basement door to surprise her mother with an icy cocktail of silt, gasping fish, and matted vegetation.

Having deciphered the hollow, grainy language of the staircases, the woman strode down the main hallway, suitcase in her hand. The hallway she knew well, had seen its doppelganger wherever her mother had lived. Her mother had lined both sides with photographs of the woman's father, father and mother together, grandparents, uncles, aunts, nieces, nephews, cousins, friends of the family, followed by paintings in gaudy frames of ancestors who had not had the benefit—or curse—of the more modern innovations. Most relatives were dead, and the others the woman hadn't seen for years.

She could feel herself progressing into a past in which every conceivable human emotion had been captured along those walls, frozen into a false moment. (The predominant expression, her brother would later point out, whatever the emotion behind it, was a staged smile, the only variation being "with teeth" or "without teeth." Perhaps, he would say to her later, parenthetically, outside the boundaries of frozen fairytale-isms, that she should understand the main reason he didn't like to visit their mother: he had no wish to draw back the veil, to exhume their father's corpse for purposes of reanimation; wasn't it bad enough that he died once?) Soon, it was difficult not to think of herself as a photograph on a wall.

The woman found her mother on the glassed-in porch that overlooked the river, her back to the fireplace as she sat in one of the three plush velvet chairs she had rescued from the old house in Stockton. The view through the window: the startling image of a River Moth swollen blue with ice, flurried snowflakes attacking the thick, rise-falling surface of the water, each speck breaking the tension between air and fluid long enough to drift a moment and then disintegrate against the pressure from the greater force. Disintegrate into the blue shadows of the overhanging trees, leaves so frozen the wind could not stir them.

Her mother watched the river as it sped-lurched and tumbled past her window, and now, from the open doorway, her daughter watched her watching the river as the flames crackled and shadowed against the back of her chair.

The daughter remembered a far-ago courtyard of conversation, a question posed by a gravelly voiced friend of her brother: "And how is your mother? I know all about your father. But what about your mother?" The glint of his eye—through the summer sun, the crushed-mint scent from the garden beyond, and she, with eyes half closed, listening to his voice but not hearing the question.

Her mother. A woman who had collapsed in on herself when her husband died, and was never the same happy, self-assured person again. Except. Except: She *had* provided for them. She just hadn't *cared* for either of them.

The woman had not seen her mother for five years, and at first she thought she saw a ghost, a figure that blurred the more she focused on it. Wearing a white dress with a gray shawl, her mother sat in half profile, her thin white hands like twin bundles of twigs in her lap. Smoke rose from her scalp: white wisps of hair surrounding her head. The bones of her face looked as delicate as blown glass.

The daughter could see all of this because she was not actually in that room in the past, but in another room altogether, and as she typed she could see her own reflection in the green glass of the window to her left, since she had always been the mirror of her mother, and now looked much as her mother had looked, sitting in a chair, watching the river tumble past her window.

The daughter stood there, staring at her mother, clearly visible, *and her mother did not see her . . .*

Dread trickled down the woman's spine like sweat. Was she truly dead, then? Had she succeeded and all else been a bright-dull afterlife dream? Perhaps she still lay on the floor of her bathroom, a silly grinning mask hiding her face and a bright red ribbon tied to her right wrist.

She shuddered, took a step forward, and the simple touch of the wooden door frame against her palm saved her. She was alive, and her mother sat in front of her, with delicate crow's-feet at the corners of her wise pale blue eyes—the mother she had known her whole life, who had tended to her ills, made her meals, put up with youthful mistakes, helped her with her homework, given her advice about boys and men. Somehow, the sudden normalcy of that revelation struck her as unreal, as from a land more distant than Morrow or the underground of Ambergris.

The woman dropped to her knees, facing her mother, saw that flat glaze flicker from the river to her and back again.

"Mother?" she said. "Mother?" She placed her hands on her mother's shoulders and stared at her. As if a thaw to spring, as if a mind brought back from contemplation of time and distance, her mother's eyes blinked back into focus, a slight smile visited her lips, her hands stirred, and she wrapped her arms around her daughter. Her light breath misted my cold ear.

"Janice. My daughter. My only daughter."

At my mother's words, a great weight dropped from me. A madness melted out of me. I was myself again as much as I ever could be. I hugged her and began to sob, my body shuddering as surely as the River Moth shuddered and fought the ice outside the window.

(What is it about distance—physical distance—that allows us to create such false portraits, such disguises, for those we love, that we can so easily discard them in memory, make for them a mask that allows us to keep them at a distance even when so close?)

It would be nice to report that my mother and I understood each other with perfect clarity after that first moment of affection, but it wasn't like that at all. The first moment proved the best and most intimate.

We talked many times over the next two weeks, as she led me up and down the rotting staircases in search of this or that memory, now antique, in the form of a faded photograph, a tarnished jewelry case, a brooch made from an oliphaunt tusk. But while some words brought us closer, other words betrayed us and drew us apart. Some sentences stretched and contracted our solitude simultaneously, so that at the end of a conversation, we would stand there, staring at each other, unsure of whether we had actually spoken.

I fell into rituals I thought I had abandoned years before, arcs of conversations in which I chided her for not pursuing a career—she had rooms full of manuscripts and paintings, but had never tried to sell them. For me, to whom creativity came so hard—each painting, each sculpture, each essay a struggle, a forced march—the easy way in which our mother created and then discarded what she created seemed like a waste. (Which begs the question, Janice: why didn't you sell her paintings in your gallery? It wasn't just because she didn't want you to have them; they also weren't very good.) She, meanwhile—and who could blame her?—chastised me for my lifestyle, for abusing my body. She had not missed the blue mottlings on my neck and palms that indicated mushroom addiction, although I had inadvertently kicked the habit in the aftermath of my attempt.

And so I slowly worked my way toward talking about the suicide attempt, through a morass of words that could not be controlled, could not be stifled, that meant, for the most part, nothing, and stood for nothing.

One day, as we watched the River Moth fight the blocks of ice that threatened to slow it to grimy sludge, we talked about the weather. About the snow. She had seen snow in the far south before, but not for many years. She sang a lullaby for the snow in the form of a soliloquy. At that moment, it would not have mattered if I were five hundred miles away, knocking on the doors of Zamilon. Her gaze had focused on some point out in the snow, where the river thrashed against the ice. The ice began to form around my neck again. I could not breathe. I had to break free.

"I tried to kill myself," I told her. "I took out a knife and cut my wrist." I was shaking.

"I know," she said, as casually as she had commented about the weather. Her gaze did not waver from the winter landscape. "I saw the marks. It is unmistakable. You try to hide it, but I knew immediately. Because I tried it once myself."

"What?"

She turned to stare at me. "After your father died, about six months after. You and Duncan were at school. I was standing in the kitchen chopping onions and crying. Suddenly I realized I wasn't crying from the onions. I stared at the knife for a few minutes, and then I did it. I slid down to the floor and watched the blood. Susan, our neighbor—you may remember her?—found me. I was in the hospital for three days. You both stayed with a friend for a week. You were told it was to give me some rest. When I came back, I wore long-sleeved shirts and blouses until the marks had faded into scars. Then I wore bracelets to cover the scars."

I was shocked. My mother had been mad—mad like me. (Neither of you were mad—you were both sad, sad, sad, like me. I didn't know Mom tried to take her own life, but thinking back, it doesn't surprise me. It just makes me weary, somehow.)

"Anyway," she said, "it isn't really that important. One day you feel like dying. The next day you want to live. It was someone else who wanted to die, someone you don't know very well and you don't ever want to see again."

She stood, patted me on the shoulder. "There's nothing wrong with you. You'll be fine." And left the room.

I didn't know whether to laugh or cry, so I did both.

Did I believe her? Was it true that you could leave your old self behind so easily? There was an unease building in me that said it wasn't true, that I would have to be on my guard against it, as much as Duncan was on guard against the underground. (You misunderstand me—I *embraced* the underground. It fascinated me. There was no dread, only *situational dread*—the fear that came over me when I clearly *did not* fit in underground, when I thought the gray caps might no longer suffer my presence.)

✳

After that, we avoided the subject. I never discussed my suicide attempt with my mother again. But we did continue to talk—mostly about Duncan. Duncan's books. Duncan's adventures. Duncan's early attempts at writing history papers.

We shared memories we both had of Duncan. Back in Stockton, sometimes, after breakfast, Duncan would sit by Dad's side and scribble intensely, a stern look on his face, while Dad, equally stern, wrote the first draft of some paper destined for publication in *The Obscure History Journal Quarterly*. Mother and I would laugh at the two of them, for Dad could not contain the light in his eyes that told us he knew very well his son was trying to imitate him. To become him.

It seemed safe, to talk about Duncan in such a way. Or at least it did, until I discovered my mother had one memory of him I did not share with her.

Something "your father would have been able to tell better," she said. We were in the kitchen preparing dinner—boiling water for rice and preparing green beans taken from the deep freezer in the basement. Outside, the river stared glassily with its limitless blue gaze.

"You know," she said. "Duncan saw one when he was a child—in Ambergris. Your father went there for research and he took Duncan while I took you to Aunt Ellis's house for the holidays. You can't have been more than nine, so Duncan was four or five." (Yet I remember this trip as if it had happened this morning.)

"What do you mean he 'saw one'?" I asked.

"A gray cap," she said, snapping a bean as she said it.

The hairs on my neck rose. A sudden warm-cold feeling came over me.

"A gray cap," I said.

"Yes. Jonathan told me after he and Duncan came back. He definitely saw one. Your father thought it might be fun to go on an Underground Ambergris tour while in the city. They still offered them back then. Before the problems started."

"Problems." My mother had a gift for understatement. The tours to the tunnels beneath the surface stopped abruptly when the ticket seller to one such event popped downstairs for a second, only to run screaming back to the surface. The room below contained no sign of the tour guide or the tourists—just a blood-drenched room lit by a strange green light, the source of which no one could identify. Much like the light I write by at this very moment. (Apocryphal. Most likely, they closed up shop because they were losing money due to their poor reputation. The gray caps have often been bad for certain types of business.)

"They bought their tickets," my mother continued, "and walked down the stairs with the other tourists. Your father swears Duncan held on to his hand very tightly as they went down into a room cluttered with old Ambergris artifacts. They went from room to musty old room while the tour guide went on and on about the Silence and Truff knows what else . . . when suddenly Jonathan realizes he's not holding Duncan's hand anymore—he's holding a fleshy white mushroom instead."

Our dad stood there, staring at the mushroom, paralyzed with fear. Then he dropped it and began to run from room to room. He was shaking. He had never been so scared in his entire life, he told my mother later. (Where was I? One minute I was holding my father's hand. The next . . .)

He started to shout Duncan's name, but then he caught a blur of white from the next room over. He ran into the room, and there was Duncan, in a corner, staring at a gray cap that stood right in front of him, staring right back. (. . . I was staring at a gray cap. Just as my mother said. I wish I knew what happened between those two points in time.)

"It was small," my mother said. "Small and gray and wearing some sort of shimmery green clothing. There was a smell, Jonathan said—a smell like deep river water trickling through lichen and water weeds." (It smelled like mint to me. It opened its mouth and spores came out. Its eyes were large. I felt a feeling of unbelievable peace staring at it. It immobilized me.)

Our father screamed when he saw the gray cap—and he knows he screamed, because the other tourists came running into the room.

But it was as if Duncan and the gray cap were deaf. They continued to stare at each other. Duncan was smiling. The look on the gray cap's face could not be read. (Later, I became aware that we had stood there, watching each other, for a long time. At that moment, in that moment, it seemed like seconds. I felt as if the gray cap was trying to tell me something, but I couldn't understand what it was saying. I don't know why I thought that—it never made a sound. And yet that's the way I felt. I also felt as if I had been somewhere else part of the time, even if I could not remember it. Somewhere underground. I had a taste of dirt and mud in my mouth. I felt dirt under my fingernails as if I'd been digging, frantically digging for hours. But, later, when I checked them, my fingernails were clean.)

Then, as the other tourists entered the room, two things happened.

"First, the gray cap pulled a mushroom out of its pocket. Then it blew on the mushroom, softly."

A thousand snow-white spores rose up into Duncan's face, "and then the gray cap disappeared."

The gray cap, my father said, melted into, blended in with, the wall and *wasn't there anymore*. Although he knew this couldn't have happened, although he knew there must be something—a secret passageway, a trapdoor in the floor—to explain it . . .

Duncan, awash in the milk-white spores, turned at the sound of his father's voice—which he could finally hear—and smiled so broadly, with such delight, that our father, for a moment, smiled back. (It's true. When the gray cap disappeared, a feeling of utter well-being came over me, and of wonder. Again, I can't say why. I don't know why. I was too young to know why. The gray caps and the underground have rarely since provided me with anything approaching a sense of calm.)

"Jonathan took Duncan to the doctors right away, but they couldn't find anything wrong with him. Duncan was the same as he ever had been, even if Jonathan wasn't. Jonathan was shaken by what had happened. It even changed the nature of his research. Suddenly, he became interested in *The Refraction of Light in a Prison* instead of the rebellion of Stretcher Jones against the Kalif. *The Refraction of Light* led him to the monks of Zamilon, and from there to the Silence. (Much as it led me there. The key may still be in Zamilon, but not at this time.)

"I never told you because I didn't know how to explain it. It sounded absurd. It sounded dangerous."

They never found anything wrong with Duncan, although they took him to doctors frequently over the next year. Gradually, they forgot about it, buried the memory alongside other memories because, in their hearts, it terrified them. (There were several times I thought about telling you, Janice. I would open my mouth to tell you and the image of the gray cap standing silent in front of me would come to me, and somehow I couldn't say anything. After a while, it was no longer possible to tell you without it being clear I'd kept it from you. I still don't know why I felt such a compulsion against telling you. Was I protecting you? Was I protecting myself? I was so young, perhaps I just couldn't express what I'd seen.)

"What terrified Jonathan the most," my mother said, "was not the gray cap, or the spores, but the happy smile on your brother's face."

The beans were in the pot. The rice was on the boil.

I asked, "So Duncan wasn't changed by the event? No nightmares? No insomnia?"

My mother shook her head. "Nothing like that."

She paused, put her hand to her throat, her gaze distant. "There was one change, although I'm sure it's just that he was growing up. A year after he came back, he began to explore the drain tunnels near the house. Before that, I remember he hated dark places. But then he just . . . lost the fear." (Is it possible my encounter had been an invitation? That the point had been to invite me to explore?)

Old mysteries, brought home to me in a new way. I kept thinking back, trying to remember my impressions of Duncan at the age of four or five. There was precious little. I remembered him smiling. I remembered him blowing out the candles on a birthday cake, and the time I made him cry by pinching him because he'd pulled apart one of my dolls.

My mother's story gnawed and gnawed at me, even though I could not see the greater significance of it. (What were you meant to see, do you think? That I've been an agent of the gray caps my entire life? What, exactly, are you trying to say, Janice?)

Suddenly, it no longer seemed so safe to talk about Duncan. For the first time, I felt the urge to return to Ambergris, to my gallery, to my life. So I left the very next day, surprising myself as much as I surprised my mother. Even by then, though, we had slowly grown apart, so that I am sure that she, like me, in that awkward moment by the front door, with the motored vehicle waiting, thought that five years until my next visit might be no great hardship.

8

Nothing was the same when I came back.

It's night here, as I type, and hot, and I don't know if it's a normal kind of heat or something related to the Shift. Something is gnawing away at the wood between the ceiling of this place and the roof. I find it almost relaxing to listen to the chewing—at least, I'd rather listen to that than to the sounds I sometimes hear coming from below me. It does not bear thinking about, what may be going on below me. Really, this afterword has been the only thing saving me from too many thoughts about the present. The green light is ever-present, but the clientele is not. It's late. They've gone home. It's just me and the lamp and the typewriter . . . and whatever is chewing above me and whatever is moving below me. And I feel feverish. I feel like I should lie down on the cot I had them bring in here. I feel like I should take a rest. But I can't. I have to keep going on. Despite the heat. Despite the fact that I'm burning up. I have some mushrooms Duncan left behind, but I'm not sure I should eat them, so I won't. They might help, but they might not. (Good decision! Those are weapons. If you'd eaten them, it would've been like eating gunpowder.)

So, instead, to stave off burning up, I'll write about the snow. I'll write about all of that wonderful, miraculous snow that awaited me on my return to Ambergris. Maybe the gnawing will stop in the meantime. Unless it's in my mind, in which case it may never stop.

I returned to an Ambergris transformed by snow from semitropical city to a body covered by a white shroud. Every street, alley, courtyard, building, storefront, and motored vehicle had succumbed to the mysteries of the snow. Ambergris was not suited to white. White is the color of surrender, and Ambergris is unaccustomed to surrender. Surrender is not part of our character.

At first, the city appeared similar to dull, staid Morrow, but underneath the anonymous white coating lay the same old city, cunning and cruel as ever. Merchants sold firewood at ten times the normal price. Frankwrithe & Lewden, in a hint of the strife to come, raided a warehouse of Hoegbotton books and distributed the torn pages as tinder. Beggars contrived to look as pathetic as possible, continuing a trend that had been refined since before the advent of Trillian the Great Banker. Thieves took advantage of the icy conditions to make daring daylight purse-pinchings on homemade ice skates. Priests in the Religious Quarter preached end-of-the-world hysteria to boost dwindling congregations. Theaters rushed a number of "jungle comedies" and other warm-weather fare into production, finally dethroning Voss Bender's *Trillian*, that play's six acts too long for most theater admirers, frozen bottoms stuck to icy seats. Swans died shrieking in ice that trapped their legs. Lizards shrugged philosophically and grew fur. Sounds once dulled by a species of heat intense enough to corrode even hearing were now bright and brassy.

But I remember most the smell, or lack of it. Suddenly, the ever-present rot-mold-rain scent was missing from the air, replaced by the clean, boring smell of Morrow. It was as if Morrow had colonized a vital element of the city, presaging the war.

(Not to mention the fungi, which adapted almost as if the gray caps had planned the change in the weather. There was something unreal about seeing mushroom caps in jaunty bright colors rise through the snow cover, unaffected by the cold.)

Sybel forced me to go back to the gallery. I would have stayed in my apartment for weeks, if I'd had the choice, conveniently ignoring a few bloodstains my brother had missed when cleaning up. I no longer felt hollow, but I did feel weak, sluggish, indecisive. I didn't have any of the normal props that used to stop me from thinking about . . . everything.

Sybel looked like he always looked—a faint half smile on his face, eyes that stared through you to something or somewhere else, presumably his future.

On the way to the gallery, walking through the frozen streets, Sybel turned to me, and said, "You don't know who your friends are, do you?"

I stared at him for a second. "What are you trying to tell me?"

We were only a few minutes from the gallery at that point.

"You gave keys out to people," he said.

"Gallery keys."

"Yes."

"And I shouldn't have."

"No. How could I stop them when they had keys of their own?"

I sighed. "Let me guess."

Inside the gallery, the only element that remained the same was my desk, with its two dozen bills, five or six contracts, and a litter of pens obscuring its surface. The rest had been stripped bare. Those paintings least popular, hung for several months, had left the beige shadow of their passing, but otherwise, I might as well have been starting up a gallery, not losing control of one. Everyone had abandoned me, as if I were whirling so fast toward oblivion that, at some point, they were simply flung clear by my momentum.

"When did this happen?"

"Gradually, over months," Sybel said, throwing the gallery keys on the desk and sitting in a chair. "They were pretty thorough, weren't they?"

"They?"

"The artists. I'm fairly certain it was the artists."

I looked around. The gallery had, in its emptiness, taken on aspects of my life. What was I to do?

"I couldn't be here day and night," Sybel said. Unspoken: *I had parties to plan. I had a suicidal boss to worry about.*

A sudden anger rose up inside of me, though I had no reason to be angry at Sybel. What could he have done?

"You just let them take all of their art?"

He shook his head. "David let them in. David's the one who started it . . ."

David. Former boyfriend. A not-unpleasant memory of David and me escaping into the gallery's back room to make love.

"Oh." The anger left me.

Sybel stared up at me. "There's nothing left to manage, Janice. There's no gallery. I wish there were. But," and he stood, "there's nothing here for me to do. I'm not a rebuilder, I'm a manager. If you need help in the future, let me know."

I would need help in the future. A lot of help, but he couldn't know that now. He couldn't know how quickly everyone's fortunes would change.

"What will you do now, Sybel?"

Sybel shrugged. "I'll take some time off. I'll climb trees. I will enjoy the feel of the sun on my face in the morning. I will swim in the River Moth." (Right. And after about thirty minutes, when he was done gamboling about in the sunlight, Sybel would go on providing people with whatever they most desired. Specifically, providing me with what I most desired—whatever could get me through the night.)

I smiled and put a hand on his shoulder. "Take me with you."

"You wouldn't like it," Sybel said, somewhat wistfully, I thought. "You would be bored."

I nodded. "You're probably right."

At the door, Sybel turned to me one last time and said, "I'm glad you made it back. I really am. But you'll find it's changed out there. It's no longer the same place."

"What do you mean, it's changed?"

"There is no New Art anymore."

Later, a short investigation would prove Sybel right. While everyone's attention had been on the New Art, real innovation had been occurring outside of our inbred, self-congratulatory little circle. Real imagination meshed with real genius of technique had been bypassing and surpassing the New Art, sometimes with a chuckle and a condescending nod. This was the era during which Hale Jargin first displayed his huge "living canvases," complete with cages for small creatures to peep out from shyly. Sarah Frayden began to create her shadow sculptures, too. But neither of these qualified as New Art, in part because the galleries they showed in had no connection to the New Art.

By the time those of us associated with the New Art realized New Art was Old Art—my only excuse being my forced absence from the scene—the only one who had the option of escaping the death of the term was the only one who had never uttered the words in the first place: Martin Lake.

If they hadn't fled my gallery, I would have been stuck with a long line of has-beens who, squinting, had emerged from their corridor of tunnel vision to realize that, far from being on the frontier, they'd been in a backwater, as obsolete as the first generation of Manzikert motored vehicles the factories had trundled out over a hundred years ago.

"*There is no New Art anymore,*" Sybel said, and then was gone, leaving me in my empty gallery, wondering what to do.

❋

What could I do? I needed to find my brother—and find him I did, amid the tinkling rustle of the frozen willow trees outside of Blythe Academy. I think he knew I was coming. I think he knew I was looking for him. There he was in a long coat, sitting at a stone table and smiling at me. (Grimacing, actually. I experienced a lot of pain during the early days of my transformation. I was still changing.) He had regained his customary thinness.

"Hello, helpless helping brother," I said, smiling back as I sat down across from him. Behind him, the Academy was just waking up. It was a beatific morning—the sun lit the snow and ice into a fractured orange blaze.

"Hello, suicidal sister," he said, his gaze clear, focused on the present, on me.

"You should use more careful language," I told him. "I could do it all over again, and you'd have to send me on another tour of the world."

Duncan grinned. His teeth revealed an underlying rot, despite his apparent health: they were stained a gray-black along the gums.

"Not likely," he said. "I've already sent you to every head doctor within three hundred miles. If you were going to do it again, you would have done it while listening to the seventh or eighth as he droned on about your disturbed dream life."

"But I am fragile," I insisted. "I've been without drugs for weeks. I've been getting lots of sleep. I've been eating well. I could suffer a mental collapse at any moment."

(To see you that way, tired but whole, made me happy. A few months before I had had no idea if you would survive, or if you'd be the same person afterward. It didn't matter that you were thin or drawn, just that you seemed sane once more.)

"The city is falling apart, not you. The snow. Look—it's snowing again."

He was right—thin, small flakes had begun to drop out of the sky.

"It hasn't really stopped snowing," I reminded him.

"I think the gray caps . . ."

I rolled my eyes to cut him off. "You think they're responsible for everything." (Because they are, Janice!)

He shrugged. "Aren't they?"

"Actually, no," I replied. "I brought the snow with me from Morrow—the most heartless, boring, terrible place you could possibly have sent me to."

Anger, rising up. It felt good. It felt right. It was the only thing I'd felt besides pain and sorrow in a long time.

"I saved your life," he said. "You'd be dead otherwise."

"Maybe I wanted to be dead," I replied. "Did you ever think of that?"

"No," Duncan said, shivering, "I don't think you wanted to be dead. I think you didn't want to feel. There's a difference. And I know all about not wanting to feel."

All the air went out of me with a single sigh. The truth was, it took too much energy to talk about such things.

A thought occurred to me. "How did you know I'd be here?"

Duncan grimaced, as if from some physical pain. (As *if*? Every time I moved, I could feel them all over me, burrowing into my skin.)

He looked away. "I have . . . friends . . . who tell me things. That's all. It's the same reason I found you in time."

I laughed, said, "Friends! I can only guess what kinds of friends. Do they have legs or spores? Do they walk or do they float?"

Duncan stared down at the snow. Now I could see, where the light caught his cheek, the side of his neck, that a faint black residue, insubstantial as smoke, had attached itself to his skin.

"Why did you do it?" he asked me.

I stared at him, the anger boiling over. What could I say to him? Why should I say anything to him?

"What kind of answer would you like?" I asked him. "Would you like me to say the pressure was too much? That I couldn't handle it? Do you want me to say I was under the influence of drugs? Do you want me to say my relationships all failed and I was lonely?"

My voice had risen with each new question until I was shouting. I stopped. Abruptly. While Duncan stared at me, concerned.

I realized I didn't know why I had done it. Not really. Every reason I could dredge up seemed ridiculous. I had written lots of notes about it, true. All the doctors wanted me to write things down, as if they could pull it out of me through ink applied to paper. I wrote nonsensical sentences, pompous things like:

> I have finally figured it out. We are redeemed, if at all, by love and by imagination. I had imagination enough to realize I was not receiving enough love, and so I allowed myself to be seduced by those who did not love me, and whom I did not love. And then convinced myself, in my imagination, that I did love them, and that they did love me.

Or, on another scrap of paper I saved as a testament to my foolishness:

> I spent my youth gripped in the fear of a sudden exit—like that of my father. I too might run across the sweet, strange grass only to fall prematurely inert at someone's feet. ("Sudden exit"? "prematurely inert"? For someone who wanted to die you have a real aversion to the word death.) And yet as an adult I have tried my best to run to meet that exit anyway, despite all of those careful steps. Driving my gallery into ruin. Driving my relationships into ruin with excess and promiscuity. Overindulging in drugs and sex.

And, finally, dredging up the distant past:

> My dad was a hard man to love. He lived for his work, and anyone who did not live for that work would receive very little love. Not a bad man, or a man who could be intentionally cruel. Not a man like that, no, but a man who could ignore you with an imperiousness that could burn into your soul. Duncan rarely saw that side of our father. Duncan was protected by his interest in the mysteries of history. Me, I couldn't have cared less about history growing up. I was interested in many things—painting, reading, singing lessons, boys; in that order—but not history. I never could see the personal side to history until I started living it. Until Mary and Duncan showed me what history could mean. And by then it was too late: Dad was dead, and nearly me as well.

The doctors had made me do it—had made me feel like a political prisoner of the Kalif, forced to recant my beliefs and spout pseudo-personal parody to regain my freedom. (And yet, Janice, some of it rings true. I wish I could say it didn't.)

"I don't need an answer," Duncan said quietly. "I just thought I'd ask."

But I needed an answer, so I could stop it from happening again. Why had I done it?

I don't recall what I said to Duncan next, sitting in the freezing cold outside of Blythe Academy, students beginning their groggy paths across the courtyard to their classes. I don't remember any of the rest of our conversation. (We talked about the past, Janice. We talked about what Bonmot had been up to at the Academy. You told me about Mom and the condition of that old mansion. I told you about the research I had my students doing on Zamilon. Nothing you needed to remember.) I'm sure it didn't satisfy him. It didn't satisfy me.

I could remember, however, the night of the attempt—a night that seemed to epitomize the parties, the drugs, the lack of direction, the stretched, unreal quality of my existence. The late, late nights merging into days, the black of the sky, the hunt for yet another bar.

I had blown half of my remaining money on what I now realize was a suicide banquet—so much food, so many bodies, so little restraint. The pale white of people in a corner of the room, in a writhing orgy of legs and arms and torsos. The leering smiles of the onlookers. The smell of wine, of rot, of decay, of sex. But it wasn't enough for me, even then. We kept going *elsewhere.*

We were in a café. We were inside a burned-out building. We were on the street, giggling under a streetlamp. It was all merging together into one place, one time. I didn't know where I was. Sybel was there, then he wasn't there, then he was.

Finally, we came to the steps of an abandoned church. Sybel stood on one side and David, the cipher I was sleeping with at the time, stood on the other. I floated between them, staring at the huge double doors of the church, the old oak bound in iron and carved with flourishes. I could hear people talking loudly inside.

"Did I pay for this?" I asked. It had become my standard question over the past few months.

"No," Sybel said. "You didn't pay for this. You didn't like your own party."

"You wanted us to take you somewhere else," David said, an arm around my shoulders.

"From what I paid for?" I said.

Sybel laughed. "Yes, to something you didn't pay for. And you definitely didn't pay for this—this is a party sponsored by one of the new galleries."

"And somewhere else is something I paid for?"

"We thought it might be fun to spy," David added, ignoring me.

"In a church?" I said, incredulous, forgetting all of the blasphemous functions I'd sponsored inside even holier buildings.

David said, "It used to be for the Church of the Five-Pointed Star, but they don't really exist anymore."

Obviously. The grass was high and the steps cracked with vines. The door was beginning to rot on its hinges.

"Lead the way," I said, giving up.

Sybel pushed open the door and we walked inside, the two of them practically carrying me—into the cacophony of music, the swirl of lights. We blended in perfectly. Same clothes. Same attitude. Within minutes, while Sybel and David looked on, I was carrying on a conversation with a young male artist who had the kind of pale waif look I find irresistible. It was crowded. I had to shout. I didn't know what I was shouting. I didn't know who I was rubbing up against. Sybel and David tried to act as my bodyguards; I ignored them. I was babbling.

At some point, I lost focus and stopped talking, trying unsuccessfully to nod as the young artist who I really didn't give a damn about rambled on about "the inspiration for my art." I was standing on a stool by then. I don't know who had provided the stool, but it gave me enough height to survey the crowd.

Off to the side, I could see the rival gallery owner, John Franghe, chatting up a couple of my clients, oblivious to my presence. I recognized darling Franghe's hand gestures. I recognized his body language. The odd combination of fawning flattery and absolute authority. He had a glass in his hand and was obviously drunk. He kept putting his hand on the arm of the prettier of the two artists and squeezing it, giving her a quick glance to catch her eye. There was nothing artful about it.

At some point while watching, I fell off my stool. My head was full of nails. My thoughts were coiled and frightened. David and Sybel came to my aid, set me down at a chair beside a table, beside two old veterans of the art movement. Bodies were swirling around me. The texture of the table even seemed to swirl, to become a whirlpool of wooden grain. I could smell the beer, the drugs, the sweat of all of those bodies in such an enclosed space.

At some point, I realized that none of it mattered, that none of it meant anything. I hated what I saw—the corrosion of fame, the accretion of falseness, the misuse of sex and desire. A strange dread came over me. I was alone in that church. I did not know who I was, or how I had come to this. I had become an observer in my own life.

I sent David and Sybel off on a mission to ask the hosts to find more of my favorite mushrooms. As soon as they had been swallowed up by the crowd, I stood up and snuck out of the church, through those rotting oak doors.

Stumbling, drunk out of my mind, I made my way down to a dirty little club at the dock-end of Albumuth Boulevard. Through the murmurous sounds of the River Moth, right outside, I listened to an old singer that someone said had once been famous.

As one will, I quickly became close friends with everyone at the bar, but even as I sat there joking and drinking with them, in the dark, I knew I was all alone. I knew the singer realized this, too. He seemed to sing for me and me only. No one else paid attention to him. It was horrible and wonderful at the same time. He would never reach the heights he had once known. One day, the people in the bar might not even recognize his best-known songs. But he sang them with a kind of terrible defiance. It wore me out to watch him. The empty laughter of the bar wore me out. All of it wore me out.

I sat there smoking a mushroom someone had given me and looking at the singer, but really staring past him into the distance, the foreground a blur, with not a thought in my head other than the melody of the song, the voice of the singer.

You become what you pretend to be. I could pretend that I was pretending when it came to the New Art, but eventually I had begun to believe the lies that justified the excesses.

Slowly, over time, a thought snuck past the music and the voice: that I could never be as brave as that singer, that I could never sing old songs to people who didn't care. (Though, ironically enough, some would say that is what you've wound up doing with this account.)

Is that a good reason? Would that have satisfied the doctors?

Because nothing else did.

I lied earlier, though. I do remember something else from my conversation with Duncan in the frozen courtyard. I remember that I smelled perfume on him. It brought me up short, changed the subject forever.

"What's her name?" I asked.

He smirked and said, "Mary Sabon."

Mary Sabon. Sabon and her necklace of liars. Where to start?

Sybel was right—the New Art was dead. But it wasn't just the New Art that had died.

Before my "accident," I had lived almost exclusively within the secret history of the city—a history of moments, not events, a history that vanished as it came and lived on only in the shudder of remembered ecstasy. This secret history descends (transcends) through the bedrooms of a hundred thousand houses, in the dark, through the tips of our fingers as we learn that our bodies have a thousand eyes to feel with, a thousand ways to learn the true meaning of *touch*. From foreplay to orgasm, from first touch to last, everything we know is in our skins—this secret history that so few people will be part of. We don't talk about this history, although it made us and will make us and is the only way to get as close as we can to each other: an urgent coupling to close the space, to experience a pleasure that—excuse me as I stumble into this rapturous gutter (can we stop you?)—is on one level being filled or filling, but is also so much more. This is where I was and what I lived for before the accident. Afterward, I gave it all up, even though it wasn't the problem.

I traded my secret history for another type of history altogether. I saw the backs of a lot of heads, sang a lot of songs, and had my fundament put to sleep by the hard wood I was sitting on on more than one occasion. Chanting, reading ancient books, fingering beads on a necklace much more humble than Sabon's. Always worried that this new dependency might end as the old one had, but willing to take the chance anyway.

But, in some great confluence of chance and destiny, as my erotic star fell, Duncan's rose, and shone all the more passionately, as his ardor—unlike mine—was directed toward one person: Mary Sabon.

I already knew Mary, although I did not realize it at the time. Duncan had talked about her for several months before the details of his attraction to her became clear. There was a potentially brilliant student in his class, he told me at lunch one day while Bonmot stared at both of us from beneath his bushy eyebrows. A student who absorbed theory like a sponge and immediately applied it to her own interests. A student who could, moreover, write, and write well. It was so obvious that this student should be in a more advanced class that at first he was undecided as to whether to let her go to some other school, but, finally, could not bring himself to suggest it.

"She does not have the necessary social maturity," I remember him saying. "She's still young. To go to the Religious Academy in Morrow, with much older students," he said, shaking his head. "She needs more time. Extraordinary student."

Bonmot frowned at that, gave Duncan a look that I didn't understand.

"Sometimes," he said to Duncan pointedly, "it's better to let them go. Better for the student and better for the teacher."

Duncan shook his head again. "No. She needs more time."

I should have known from the way he refused to use her name. Thank God I missed the courtship. Thank God I was trying to die.

For Duncan had, while hounding me from hospital to ward, ward to doctor's office, been displaying all the conjoined lust and random stupidity of a rabbit. He "succumbed to temptation," as he put it in his journal, when, one afternoon while tutoring Mary privately after class, his hand crossed that space between how-it-is and how-it-might-be . . . and found purchase on the other side.

"Tell me you don't love me and I will be glad to escape this fever, this vision," he wrote in his journal, and much else I cannot tell from the torn pages. "I've never been more naked," he tells her, apparently forgetting the night I scraped the fungus from his body, surely his most naked moment.

She did not leave him alone in his nakedness, for as he succumbed, and kept succumbing, without thought of the link between bliss and torment, she reciprocated, and continued to reciprocate. (Truly the driest account of making love I've ever read.) What promises they made to each other in those first few sweet, fumbling hours, I cannot tell you. Duncan has ripped those pages from his journal in such brutal fashion that even the pages surrounding that night are shredded—mangled words, mutilated phrases, quartered sentences. No one can read between lines that no longer exist.

Did he tear them out from anger later, or love before? (I'm not telling.) Did he premeditate their slaughter, or was it a crime of passion? For that matter, why would he rip out *those* pages as opposed to—for example—the pages about the gray caps' infernal machine? With the pages lost, and Duncan with them, we can only guess. (And yet, dear sister, here I am, editing your work, even after "death." Some things never change.)

All I have left as proof are a few short, unintentionally humorous letters from

Sabon to Duncan, and from Duncan to Sabon—shaken out of Duncan's journal like dead moths.

> *Sabon*: My love, last night was wonderful. I've never talked to anyone the way I've talked to you. You teach me so much. You make me understand things so well. You make me feel like I'm floating on a cloud, on a star, so light do you make me feel. Until next time, I am sorrowful and sick. I will not sign this letter, in case it is discovered, but you know who I am.
>
> *Duncan*: Your skin is so smooth I want to lick it all day long. Your body makes my body hum with pleasure. Your hair, your breasts, your small hands, your ears, as delicate as the most delicate of fungi, your strong thighs, your elbows, your eyes, your kneecaps, even! I want all of you, again and again.
>
> *Sabon*: My beautiful love—last night I felt I knew you better than before, if that is possible. In the dark where we could not see each other, I still felt I *could* somehow see you. (Humorously enough, there was, thinking back, a certain glow to me back then, due to the colonization by the fungi.) The way you talk to me—I don't know if I'm worthy of the love I hear in your voice. But I will try.
>
> *Duncan*: It is truly amazing, the way our bodies fit together like some kind of perfect jigsaw puzzle. Yours makes mine feel so good. I hope I make yours feel half as good. Every night I cannot come to you is agony. I can't think of anything else—even in the classroom when I'm supposed to be teaching. And when you are near me then, I tremble. My hands, my legs, shake, and I cannot hear anyone but you, and I want you there, then. This is a craving I cannot satisfy.

Standard nattering romantic fare, uttered from the lips and pens of a thousand lovers a year, although usually not in such a staccato point-counterpoint of romance/lust, romance/lust. (Not fair! That was early on, Janice! When I remained acutely aware that I was older and she was younger, and she worried that she was too young and I was too mature. So we each tried to shed our age, to reverse the expected. It might have been foolish, but it reflected concern, affection, care, for the other. Besides, we used to hide these letters in dozens of places inside Blythe and on the grounds. Some never reached the intended recipient. Of those that did, I only kept a few of hers, and not all of mine were returned. Sometimes she was lustful and I was loving. Sometimes I would look out across the Academy from my office and see nothing but a world of potentially hidden love letters, all for me or by me.)

Following that first contact and conquest, Duncan offered up a marvelous spectacle to an unsuspecting potential audience of students, teachers, administrators, and five different orders of monks, none of whom would have sanctioned the holiness of lust between teacher and student if they'd been awake to see it. For more than two years, Duncan slunk, sneaked, crept, crawled, climbed, and slithered past various obstacles to be with his beloved. The logistics of these lust-driven maneuvers were perhaps as complex as Duncan's perilous wanderings belowground, and almost as dangerous. If caught, Duncan would be fired and barred from teaching elsewhere in the city.

Having already exhausted the careers of respectable historian and pseudonymous writer-for-hire, I would have thought Duncan would be wary of ruining a third. And in a way, I guess he was—he took great care to be precise. His meticulousness took the form of a map to guide him in his strategic penetrations of Sabon's room. Each method of penetration had elements to recommend it. Some involved the excitement of speed, while others, in their lengthy explorations, yielded pleasures of a different kind. All, however, flirted with discovery; there would never be any safe way to enter Sabon's room. "Neither in the morning nor the night," Duncan wrote with a kind of unintentional poetry, "neither at noon nor at sunset." (Bonmot thought it showed a new level of devotion to the Academy, the way I would often trade the comforts of my apartment for a sad barren room on the premises.)

Complicating matters, Academy rules dictated that all students change rooms every semester, presumably to make trysts more difficult, although two or three girls got pregnant every year anyway. Therefore, Duncan had to readjust his perambulations every six months or so.

Duncan used three routes to Sabon's room during her sixth semester at the school. These routes constitute "love letters" in the purest sense of the term. Indeed, in his madness, in his missives to Sabon he even gave them names:

Route A: The Path of Remembering You. This path, this love, can never lead me to you fast enough and yet, cruelly, reminds me of you in every way—from the rough rooftops where we sat and watched the sky turn to amber ash, to the gardens where your walking silhouette would confuse my mind with your scent, with the sight of pale perfect legs sheathed in clean white socks. This path requires that I slip past all the male students who cannot have you as I have had you and, at the center of their snoring rooms, ascend the stairs to the roof. On the roof, I gaze out upon the line between the dormitory and the classrooms where I teach you things that no longer seem important. Then into the sometimes moonlit gardens, rushing through shrubbery as I throb for you—using the blind shoulder of the storage room to hide me from the night watchmen, only to arrive below your window, your outline ablaze against the curtain.

Route B: The Path of Naked Necessity. When I burn for you and I do not care for anything but you, I use this path, for it is as direct as my desire—past the Royal's sleeping quarters, past all teachers' rooms, on to the border, there to creep over unforgiving gravel below every student's dormitory window, not caring that an errant head might poke out between curtains after curfew and recognize me—and so once again, in the urgency of my need, I come to your window and you.

Route C: The Path of Careless Ecstasy. When my love for you quivers between caution and bravery, when I am too full of joy to be either brief or circumspect, this is when I glide through the alley that separates dormitory from classroom and brazenly stride down the path past the cafeteria in time to dance with the night watchman at the front gate—zigzagging between entrances, climbing up the fence and back again, waiting in shadow as he walks by oblivious. And then down the wall that separates gardens and the second wing of classrooms—until, once again, breathless but happy, I am outside your window.

He alluded to them at the time, even seemed proud of himself, but I didn't discover the full sad weight of his obsession until I read those descriptions in his journal. My favorite phrase is "rushing through shrubbery as I throb for you" (allow a love-besotted fool *some* latitude). As Sabon wrote in her response to this letter, "I throb for you, too, dear-heart, especially rushing through the shrubbery." Sarcasm? Or gentle mockery? When, exactly, did Sabon's intent become treacherous? (Never, really. It was an incidental treachery.)

All rushing throbbery aside, this was dangerous work for Duncan. He used the paths not according to his mood, but according to the by now well-known and ritualistic bumblings of Simon and Jonathan Balfours, the two sixty-year-old night watchmen, twins of (in) habit(s). He would also factor in the arrival of guests who might conceivably tour the academy at night and the random nocturnal walks of Bonmot. (However, by far the most dangerous person in all of Blythe Academy was Ralstaff Bittern, the gardener. What a tough old buzzard! Stringy as a dead cat, and twice as ugly. He had it in for me from the day I accidentally stepped on one of his precious rosebushes. He'd lie in wait for me at night, positioned strategically behind a willow tree, where he could see the entire courtyard. Many a night, I dared not brave his gaze.)

Indeed, Duncan came close to discovery every few weeks. The first time, Duncan, using the Path of Naked Necessity and disguised as a priest, rounded a corner and came face-to-face with a fellow Naked Necessitator: a third-year boy, as petrified as Duncan, the two of them sneaking so noisily through the gravel that neither had heard the other coming.

Duncan wrote later:

> If he had uttered a single sound, I would have lived up to my surname—I would have shrieked and begun a babbling confession. But his face in the moonlight reflected such a remarkable amount of fear concentrated in such a small space that I found my tongue first and, shaky but firm, let him know that this—whatever this was—would not be tolerated at Blythe Academy. Continuing on, as much from my own exquisite terror as anything else, I proceeded to drive the demons out of the boy with such overwhelming success that I believe he—certain he could never match the conviction and fervor of the mouth-frothing apparition he met that night—eventually abandoned the priesthood as a vocation and started a brothel on the outskirts of the Religious Quarter. Meanwhile, as he ran away from me, gasping over gravel right out of the Academy, I was shaking so hard my teeth ground together. How close I had come to discovery! What was I to do?

What Duncan did, cynically, was volunteer for "tryst duty" as much as possible, which meant that he joined the ceaseless wanderings of the old night watchmen, supposedly on the lookout for those lean and compact boys, their dark wolf eyes shining, who might defy curfew in hopes of bedding a female student. (I performed a valuable service, whether hypocritically or not. And much of the time, frankly, we caught female students sneaking into the boys' rooms.) This helped, but there were still unwelcome encounters with unexpected teachers or priests at unfortunate times—"Why, I was just checking the window to make sure it was securely locked"—and pricked buttocks from sudden jumps into rosebushes to avoid Bonmot, whom Duncan could not lie to. (The crushed bushes only made the gardener more relentless. Bittern complained to Bonmot several times, but Bonmot was not ready to believe him.) As his fellow history professor Henry Abascond once said to Duncan at a meeting of teachers, "A taste for the night life, have you? A taste for the dark, the shroud?" in typically pompous Abascond fashion. (And he wasn't joking about it, much as others thought he was referring to my area of study. I thought for one paranoid moment that he and Bittern had formed a conspiracy to ruin me, but there was only one genuine conspiracy: my conspiracy to ruin myself.)

Of course, nothing lasts forever, least of all desperate, ridiculous sexual melodrama, and Duncan would prove no exception to the cliché. But that day was as yet far off. In the meantime, Duncan reveled in his love for Sabon—you could see it in his distant enthusiasm at our lunches in the courtyard: a brightness to his eyes, a sheen to his skin that was impervious to rainy days or scholarly disappointments (or the more sympathetic interpretation, that it was the effect of the fungi).

Still, I noticed that Bonmot scrutinized us both with a certain suspicion, no matter how pleasant our conversations. With me, I believe he was just worried—looking for signs of a despair that might lead me to again cut my wrists—and with Duncan, searching for something hidden that Bonmot could not quite, for all of his wisdom, figure out. (I am sure that if not for my secret studies, he would have found out about Mary much sooner. But rumors that I snuck around at night had, to his mind, more the feel of hidden tunnels and underground depths than of secret assignations with students. My prowess, in his eyes, was the prowess of research and obsession.)

I did not meet Sabon until ten months after I returned to Ambergris. Duncan did not seem eager for me to meet her—perhaps he was afraid Mary would know he had confided in me about their relationship, even if inadvertently; perhaps he was afraid something in our conversation might give him away to Bonmot. For whatever reason, for a long time I continued to hear about Sabon secondhand, through the mirror of Duncan's love for her.

For this first part of their relationship, I cannot bring myself to blame Sabon, not for their mutual seduction. She eventually ruined my brother in many different ways, but at first she made him see a different life—as if all these years there had been another Duncan Shriek, or the possibility of another Duncan

Shriek, completely different from the person I knew as my brother. Because they could not be seen together, they devised complex ways of meeting in public. Mary would invite Duncan to one of her parents' parties along with all her other teachers, and then seek Duncan out for a "fatherly" dance or conversation.

Similarly, Duncan began to make the most of social functions at the Ambergrisian Historical Society by inviting his students to attend for "educational" reasons. Most students would not show up, conveniently leaving Duncan required to escort Mary for the evening. (You can sneer all you want, Janice, but that *was* the primary purpose. In fact, I also met other people there who were useful to my career. I remet James Lacond there, for example, long before he broke with the Society. You are suggesting I was not just incompetent, but actively sabotaging myself, which is not the case. It was coincidence that Mary sometimes appeared at those events, which were so public that there could be no chance of an assignation.) It was through his attendance at these events that he had his first real conversations with James Lacond, an active member of most of Ambergris's cultish "research" collectives—the beginning of a friendship that would affect Duncan in many ways.

Duncan discovered that he didn't even mind dancing and that, "with a drink or two in me," as he puts it in his journal, he could "endure chitchat and small talk." He began to put on some weight, but it looked good on him, and his new beard, prematurely shot through with gray, gave him a scholarly and respectable appearance. He discovered that people liked to hear him talk, liked to hear his opinions, something that had only been true at the very beginning of his career. Suddenly, he saw a future in which he might actually settle down with Sabon.

Duncan's journal expresses no guilt for his AHS deception, or the many other deceptions "forced" upon him over the next two years. (My journal could not express such guilt—after all, my journal is an inanimate object, although you are doing a fine job of forcing it, by tortuous miscontext, into confessions it would not otherwise make.) Nor does Duncan's journal offer much in the way of gray cap research over the next two years. Sabon might have inspired him, but she also took up much of his time. (True, but by then I had other professors unwittingly carrying out my research.) Sabon had so altered his perceptions that a journal entry from the time reads:

All my research, even the gray caps themselves, seems remote, unconnected. There might as well not be a Silence, a Machine, an underground. I feel as if I have emerged from a bad dream into the real world. It does not seem possible that one person should be able to lead two such lives at the same time. (And a third life, in a sense. I could not put aside my conversations with Bonmot. I could not find a way to completely discount the spiritual—not when, in some sense, I was becoming so much a part of the world that, in the particles of it that became the particles of me, I sometimes thought I sensed a kind of *presence*. It maddened me—that I could not be certain of its relevance. That I could not be sure.)

But just because Duncan no longer believed that his life depended on the gray caps did not mean the gray caps no longer believed in Duncan, as he would soon find out.

9

The sounds from the ceiling have stopped. The sounds from the hole leading underground have not stopped. Curiously, I am calm. I'm somehow glad, even though I can see Mary's necklace of admirers and the marble staircase, can see her books hovering like crows or bats in the green shadows of the ceiling. Age does that to you, I think. It makes it impossible to have a memory that is not colored by the future.

Still, during that time so many years ago, Duncan and Mary's romance progressed into its second year, randy and light-of-foot, although punctuated by awkward—but not fatal—events, such as a very tense parent-teacher conference during which Duncan almost fainted when Mary's father jokingly asked, "So what are your intentions with our daughter?"

Meanwhile, my gallery never fully recovered from my absence. Those artists who had not stolen their art from my walls deserted me in more subtle ways: a parade of apologetic or sniveling excuses is how I see them in my mind, usually delivered by proxy, the artist in question too cowardly or embarrassed to tell me in person. My little dance with death had been only one of several extreme actions that year: half a dozen writers and artists had died, either from their excesses, or from being murdered by rivals during the Festival. (Which, mercifully, you'd missed during your travels; I wish I had missed it as well. I had to work devilishly hard to protect the Academy from the gray caps that year.) The authorities, namely the family Hoegbotton, thought it wise to lay the blame for such maladies at the (comatose, oversexed, overdrugged) feet of the art community. Excess was "out," a new austerity—inappropriate for our great, debauched city, but completely appropriate to my new condition—was "in."

My suicide attempt had only placed an emphatic exclamation point on a year ruinous to all who enjoyed good, clean fun. (You forget the now-pervasive influence exerted by Frankwrithe & Lewden, which led to many of these mishaps. You should, historically, see this as an action by Hoegbotton & Sons against F&L, not against your friends.)

So my gallery stuttered on in an altered state, reduced to selling reproductions of reproductions of famous paintings, and unsubtle watercolors of city life created by people who would otherwise have made honorable livings as plumbers, accountants, or telephone salesmen.

Nearly broke, I had to find other sources of income. From time to time, Sirin still gave me article and book assignments—"My dear Janice," he would say, "come work for me full-time," a perilous agreement if ever there were one. I also received the leavings of Martin Lake, who sometimes gave me—as Sybel later put it—"the financial equivalent of a mercy fuck" in the form of preliminary sketches for paintings that Lake's new gallery, which Sybel had fled to when my fortunes faded, was selling for many times what I'd ever made off him. All in all, my attempt had killed me.

But it hadn't killed me physically—not as Duncan was being killed physically. That second year of his romance with Mary Sabon coincided with a definite worsening of his fungal disease. Sometimes it left him so weak and drained that he could not teach his classes—although this did not mean that if his disease went into remission by nightfall he would not take the Path of Hypocrisy right up to Mary's window. These symptoms varied with the seasons, as shown by a brief examination of the "symptom lists" he kept:

SPRING
Vomiting
Diarrhea

Cramps
Dry mouth
Shortness of breath
Violent mood swings

SUMMER
Dizziness
Blurred vision
Shivering
Profuse sweating
Excessive salivating
Violent mood swings

FALL
Vomiting
Diarrhea
Cramps
Violent mood swings

WINTER
Delirium
Blurred vision
Nausea
Violent mood swings

Duncan was convinced he had contracted these symptoms as a result of his encounter with the Machine. I was convinced the "violent mood swings" had nothing to do with his fungal affliction and everything to do with a malady known as "Mary Sabonitis."

Luckily for their relationship, which otherwise might have been punctuated by episodes more suited to a madhouse or a sick house than an institution of learning, the symptoms came and went like the summer storms that had always plagued Ambergris. (Ironic, that. Because now there is no slower turning to the world than with this disease, this gift in flux, in flow. I might as well be turning into a tree, putting down roots. The yearning in my flesh calls out to the yearning in the ground. Nothing can be made that is not a part of me, that will not eventually become me. "I want for nothing and hunger naught," as some crackpot old saint named Tonsure once said before they buried him underground.)

Admittedly, his disease sometimes brought with it great joy, no doubt also caused by the fungi. An episode during the second year of his affair with Mary best describes the extremity of effects that his body could force from him:

I felt a slight disorientation that morning when I woke in my teacher's quarters. A kind of half-hearted dizziness, a prickling in the skin: a harbinger of encroaching symptoms. However, the sensation faded, so I went to my classes anyway. I remember seeing Mary in the back row of my "Famous Martyrs" class at the exact second that my mouth went as dry as the blackboard. I remember thinking it was just her presence that had affected me. For the first twenty minutes I was fine, livening up my lecture by telling some old jokes about Living Saints that Cadimon Signal had related to me at the religious academy in Morrow. Then, suddenly, I could feel the spores infiltrating my head, my limbs—they clambered over my sinuses, got between me and my own skin. I couldn't breathe. I couldn't move. The spores began to seethe across my eyes, bringing a stinging green veil over my sight. I did the only thing I could do, the thing I have learned to do, still the hardest thing. I relaxed my arms, my legs, my neck, my head, so that I entrusted my balance to the fungi . . . and damned if I didn't stay up. Damned if I didn't continue to live, although I felt like I was drowning. I sweated from every pore. I felt nauseous, disoriented, dizzy. I felt as if the gray caps were searching for me across a vast distance—I could feel their gaze upon me, like a black cloud, a storm of eyes . . . and still the tendrils spread across my vision, blinding me . . . and then, as soon as they had finished their march from east and west, meeting somewhere around the bridge of my twitching nose, all of the discomfort faded and I could . . . breathe again. Not only could I breathe, but I was *flying*, soaring, my body as light as a single spore, and yet so powerful that I felt as if I could hold up the entire Academy with one hand. A fierce joy leaked into me, sped from my feet to my waist to my arms, my head. I could not have been happier had I been the sun, shining down on everyone from on high. And in that happiness, I did not even really exist, except as a connection, a bridge, an archway, linked with a hundred thousand other archways that extended up and down my body in a perfect crisscrossing pattern of completeness. And I cannot help feeling, even as the spores just as suddenly relinquished their hold and left me gasping and white, that what radiated into me was a thankyou from the thousands that comprise the invisible community that has become my body. (Later, Mary told me that I had kept talking through the entire episode, albeit with slurred speech.)

Do I believe him? I've seen too much not to. But, then, Sabon saw exactly what I saw, and she couldn't be bothered to take the leap. She decided, somewhere along the way, to ignore, to miss, to go blind, to *see through*.

After Duncan had recounted some of these "episodes" to me, it was hard to laugh when he began to sign his infrequent postcards, "Your Brother, the Fungus Garden." (But I was—I was a transplanted fungal garden torn from the subterranean gardens of the gray caps. As the seasons came and went, I was the end of the journey for a great exodus, a community of exiles that colonized me and tried to observe the same seasonal rituals—to bloom and ripen and die in accordance with their ancestry. They were homesick, but they made do with what they had: me. And I, poor sap, was in turn able to experience with each season some new explosion of fertility, selfish enough in my pleasure to endure the counterbalanced pain—and to only hope that when in remission my affliction was not contagious. In this way, I remained connected to the underground even though absent from it. One day I will dissolve into the world, will become a gentle spray of spores, will settle on the sidewalk and on trees, on grass and soil, and yet still *be*—watchful and aware.)

Perhaps more disquieting was that, unknown to me, each week brought Sabon's flesh necklace, and thus Duncan's final humiliation, closer.

I had an intimation of the future when, two years into her relationship with Duncan, Sabon finally visited me at my gallery, probably at Duncan's request. (No—she decided to do that on her own. You were my only family besides Mom. She was curious. It's your guilt showing through here—that you weren't supportive, that you were so negative despite never having met her. It strikes me now, Janice, that as much as we talked over the years perhaps we never talked about the right things.) You might well ask why she waited so long, why I waited so long, but I think she must have realized how deeply I disapproved of my brother sleeping with a student. (I'll grant you this now: you seem to have a sixth sense for impending tragedy. At the time, it just seemed like pettiness on your part.)

By then, I had begun to shed even my less respectable artists. But my gallery still maintained an aura of the respectable. I kept it Morrow-clean and replaced each departed painting with some admirable imitation. After that strange cold winter, the weather in Ambergris had been near-perfect for more than eighteen months. Good weather meant more walk-ins, and more walk-ins meant more sales. A few more tourists and I might again be as green as mint-scented, tree-lined Albumuth Boulevard.

So at first I saw Mary Sabon as only another potential buyer. Besides, from Duncan's feverish descriptions, I would have expected someone taller, wiser, more voluptuous. She was short but not slight, her frame neither fat nor thin, and from her shiny red hair to her custom-made emerald-green shoes, from the scent of perfume to the muted red dress that hung so naturally off her shoulders, she radiated a sense of wealth and health. (She *dressed up* for you, Janice, in her Truffidian Cathedral best.)

She nodded to me as she came in and wandered from wall to wall, glancing at the paintings with nervous little turns of her head. Her hands, held behind her back, clutched a purse. She had not yet attained the artful guile of poise and positioning that would someday make her the center of attention. The necklace had not yet begun to form.

"Can I help you?" I asked, half rising from my desk. I remember wondering if I might interest her in one of the pathetic landscapes that had come to fill my walls—indeed, whether the listed prices were high enough to match her wealth. I had, at that time, some masticated and mauled views of Voss Bender Memorial Post Office—popular since Lake's success—as well as some nicely watered-down panoramas of the docks and the River Moth. All made respectable by the nearby presence and divine quality of two Lake sketches of fishermen cutting apart the carcass of a freshwater squid.

She turned to face me, smiled, and said, "I'm Mary Sabon." Despite her nerves, she carried herself with an assurance I have never had. It rattled me.

"Mary Sabon," I said.

She nodded, looked down at her shoes, then up at me again. "And you, of course, are Janice. Your brother has told me a lot about you." And laughed at her cliché.

"Yes. Yes, I am," I said, as if surprised to learn my own identity. "So you're Sabon," I said.

"Indeed," she replied, her gaze fixed on me.

I said: "Do you know that what you're doing could get Duncan fired by the Academy?"

It just came out. I didn't mean to say it. Ever since the Attempt, I haven't had any tact. (Ever since? You've never had any tact!)

Sabon's smile disappeared, a look of hurt flashing across her face. In that hurt expression I saw a flicker of something from her past coming back to haunt her. I never found out what it was.

"We love each other, Janice," she said—and *there's* a surprise, a shock. Something unexpected brought to the surface by the clacking of keys against paper: she's just a girl. When we met that first time, she was just a girl, without guile. I am ashamed of something and I'm not sure what. She was young. I was older. I could have crushed her then, but did not know it. (Dead. It's all dead. It's all gone. Senseless.)

"We love each other, Janice," Mary said. "Besides, your brother is a historian. He teaches for now, but he's working on new books . . . And, besides, I won't be a student forever."

I think now of all the things I could have said, gentle or cruel, that might have led away from a marble staircase, a raised hand, a fiery red mark on her cheek.

I sat down behind my desk. "You know he's sick, don't you?"

"Sick?" she said. "The skin disease? The fungus? But it disappears. It doesn't stay long. It isn't getting worse. It doesn't bother me."

But I could tell it did bother her.

"Did he tell you how he got the disease?" I asked.

"Yes. He's had it since he was a boy, when he went exploring. You know—BDD. It comes and goes. He's very brave about it."

Never mind the magnitude of Duncan's lie; it was the BDD that caught me. All the breath left my body, replaced by an ache. Before Dad Died was something between Duncan, my mother, and me. (And yet here you are, sharing it in a manuscript that might be read by any old drunk off the street.)

"Are you all right?" she asked.

There must have been a pause. There must have been a stoppage, a shift of my attention away from her.

"I'm fine," I said, leaning back in my chair. "As long as you know about it."

Yes, the fungus left his skin for weeks, sometimes months, but when it returned, it was always more insidious, more draining of his energy. How could I possibly explain to her about Duncan's obsession with the underground, especially now that he swore it no longer obsessed him?

She smiled, as if forgiving me for something. The simplicity of that smile charmed me for only a moment. Simplicity, where no simplicity should exist. She would always be complex, complicated, devious, in my mind.

"I want to buy a painting," she said.

I had a feeling this was her last-ditch effort to make nice. She would buy my friendship.

"A painting," I echoed as if I were a carpenter, a butcher, a priest, anything but a gallery owner.

"Yes," she said. "What do you recommend?"

This was a good question. I wanted to recommend that she never see Duncan again. That she leave Duncan alone before she hurt him irrevocably. That she never return to my gallery because . . . because . . . Did I say these things? No. I did not. I held my tongue and pointed out the most expensive items in my gallery: the two squid sketches by Lake called, perversely, "Gill" and "Fin."

She nodded, smiled, looked at them, then looked at me. "They're very nice. I'll take them," she said, and, turning, blanched as she noticed the price.

I let her buy them, although I could see they were too expensive even for her. (She didn't have much money. You made her spend two months' allowance on those paintings. I bought them from her afterward so she'd have money to live on.)

We exchanged minor pleasantries. At the door, purchases in hand, she turned back to me, smiled, and said, "Maybe someday I can join you and Duncan for lunch with Bonmot."

For lunch. Under the willow trees. Just the four of us. How comfortable. How perfect. We would eat our sandwiches in the glare of the summer sun and talk of flesh necklaces and how they form and do not form in this forlorn city by the River Moth. Just now, even in remembering this suggestion, I feel that I am drowning.

A blackness grew inside of me, or the fungus overcame me, or any of a number of conditions or situations that you may, reading this, imagine for yourselves, and I said:

"I wonder. What route will Duncan take tonight? The Path of Remembering You or the Path of Forgetting You."

The painting of the Voss Bender Memorial Post Office actually looked quite striking in the light that pierced the windows and gave my humble gallery a golden hue. The details of that painting became etched in my memory as I stared at it until I could no longer feel the reproach of her gaze and I knew she had gone.

My gallery was empty again. I was alone again. And that was as it should be.

Although I *saw* Mary on Duncan's arm a dozen times after that, the next time

I *spoke* to her directly was at the party where she stood waiting for me at the foot of the staircase, the dagger of her comment about Duncan held ready.

Ironic, really. I have reached out across time and space to construct a mosaic of her in a harsh light, only to find that now, when she shares a room with me, that light fails and finds her nearly . . . harmless.

Perhaps I have never really understood Sabon. Perhaps she remains the type of cipher who seems more remote the more words I devote to her. Fading into the ink, untouchable.

The fungus in this place has eaten into the typewriter ribbon. I'm typing in sticky green ink now, each word a mossy spackle against the keys. If I could turn off the light, no doubt my sentences would read themselves back to me in a phosphorescent fury—the indignation of creatures uncovered from beneath a rock. (Equipment failures should never be part of your narrative. That's the first lesson Cadimon Signal ever taught me.) My ink has defected to the cause of the gray caps; not so my blood.

I have made Mary Sabon, deservedly so, as much of a villain in this afterword as the gray caps, and yet I could as easily have offered her an escape—even a fragile excuse could have absolved her for the way my heart feels right now. If only she had offered up something of herself. But she never has: you could pore over her books for a hundred years and never find anything personal. Whether Duncan had a better idea of her true nature is debatable. It is debatable that *Sabon* knew her own heart. (No—she knew. She knew who she was more perfectly than anyone I have ever met. I think that is why I loved her, and why she did what she did.)

At the party, after I had slapped her—even then she did not offer anything personal. All she did was wave back those who would have otherwise taken me away. She waved back the onrush of beads from her flesh necklace. They retreated, gleaming and muttering.

"What is it you really want, Janice?" she said, smiling. "Would you like the past back? Would you like to be successful again? Would you prefer you weren't a washed-up has-been with so few prospects she had to agree to help out with a party for an artist she used to agent?"

I had an answer, but it wasn't what Sabon expected. No, it was far more than Sabon expected.

But I should probably start over, even here, and step back into the role of brittle chronicler of that which I would have liked to influence . . .

Dry facts, as dry facts will, have mushroomed and moistened in recent years, along with the popularity of her books, so that now I can enter any bookstore or library and discover information about her childhood—inspiration, education, perversions, diversions, etc.

Her books, their titles like curses—*The Inflammation of Aan Tribal Wars, The Limited Influence of Gray Caps Upon Ambergris, A Revisionist History of the City*—parrot each other when opened to the biographical note, with selective information added to the end of successive notes like the accretion of silt in the Moth River Delta. Why, I happen to have a couple of her books right here. Imagine that.

The notes from her third book, *Reflections on Ambergris History,* and her latest, *Confessions of a Revisionist: The Collected Essays of Mary Sabon,* differ only by degree. I have combined them below for ease of dissection.

ABOUT THE AUTHOR: Mary Sabon has lived in Ambergris for her entire life. During the War of the Houses, she received her history degree from the Blythe Academy, where her teachers included author Duncan Shriek. (1) Sabon has written 16 (2) books over her distinguished twenty-year (3) career, including *The Role of Chance in the History of the Southern Cities; Trillian as Reformer: The Influence of Pig Cartels on Ambergrisian History;* (4) *Magical Ambergris: The Legacy of Manzikert IX; Nature Studies with My Father; The Gray Caps' Role in Modern Literature: The Dilemma of Dradin, in Love;* (5) and *Cinsorium: Rethinking the Myth of the Gray Caps.* (6) At 47, (7) Sabon remains (8) the most vital and beloved of Ambergris's many historians, shedding light on history and her fellow historians alike. (9) Her early interest in nature studies no doubt arises from her parents David Sabon and Rebecca Verden-Sabon, the former a noted naturalist best known for having coined the term "Nativism," and the latter a gifted nature illustrator. (10)

Perhaps my annotations can be of help regarding this reeling litany of Mary's accomplishments:

1) . . . *Blythe Academy, where her teachers included author Duncan Shriek.* Over the years, Sirin has decided whether to include Duncan based on two factors: (1) To what extent the book guts Duncan's theories, and (2) The level of Duncan's limited notoriety at the time of publication. If the book openly attacks a theory or theories in Duncan's work—at least half have—and makes that aggression its thesis, the phrase disappears from the sentence, a phantom limb waiting to be reattached. As for notoriety, now that Duncan has disappeared, possibly for good, I imagine he will magically reappear in the author's biography, trapped there for all time. (Or magically reappear *right here.*)

2) *Sabon has written 16 books* . . . Alas, the number continues to rise, each new eviscerating tome kept in print by a necromancy beyond my understanding, and each leading to a more complete flesh necklace. What is Sabon's appeal to readers? Why is she always more popular than Duncan? (And why should the answer interest us? Get on with the underground adventures.) In page after page of exquisite prose, much of which I cannot bring myself to read, Sabon has, over the years, reassured her readers, made them feel intelligent, offered rational commonsense explanations for even the most miraculous and profound of events. (Although even she cannot explain away the Silence!) It doesn't seem to matter if her answers are wrong or incomplete. It does not matter that her answers often diminish the complexities of the world—leach it of its sorrow and its joy in favor of a comforting numbness, a comforting sameness: the husk of a starfish, not its living body. (And yet, you must admit, Sabon enlivens the corpses with wit and glamour.)

Duncan, conversely, liked to provoke his readers, poke them with a sharpened stick, to emphasize the supreme unknowable irony of the world and then, in marching toward the truth, unearth new mysteries, so that every so-called solution begged a hundred questions. The reader left Duncan's books shaken and unmoored from what he or she had always taken for granted.

In short, if reduced to a single point of punctuation, Sabon's work would have been a period (sometimes an emphatic exclamation mark!), Duncan's a question mark. Closed doors. Open doors. All shrouded, all revealed. (It could just be that I wrote bad books.) The average reader likes to return home after a long journey, not be left stranded in the middle of nowhere, with dark coming on and the printed pages a desert devoid of comfort. (You make my books sound like mirthless lumps of coal hidden at the bottom of a dry well, Janice! I refuse to believe you didn't see the humor, the enthusiasm, in my books. Replace "desert" with "a mysterious foreign land," with all the danger and excitement that entails.)

3) . . . *over her distinguished twenty-year career.* Unfortunately, this number also continues to rise, although riddled with inaccuracy. Seven years after Sabon graduated from Blythe, the author's note read "ten." Ten years after her graduation, the note read "fifteen." Regardless, I'm sure Bonmot was always glad to see a mention of Blythe Academy bereft of any hint of scandal.

4) The Influence of Pig Cartels on Ambergrisian History . . . The most unintentionally humorous book I have ever read. At its core, Sabon's atrocity is based on Duncan's observation in an article for the Ambergrisians for the Original Inhabitants Society's *Real History Newsletter* that Trillian the Great Banker fell from power due to his battle with the leader of a powerful pig cartel over the favors of a woman (you can't be sure my mention sparked her book—the anecdote is, more or less, common knowledge), which prompted Sabon to devote a 175-page book to the futile task of trying to convince the reader that pig cartels have wielded immense power throughout Ambergrisian history—and all the sentences that I read at least, are as breathlessly long as this one. (I admit, the book did bewilder me, as did its popularity. But we're all entitled to one bad book. I'm sure the pig cartels were flattered, at the very least.)

5) The Gray Caps' Role in Modern Literature: The Dilemma of Dradin, in Love . . . The only dilemma, to my way of thinking, being how to dignify as "literature" such a collection of angst, stupidity, and old wives' tales. At least Sabon left my brother out of this one.

6) Cinsorium: Rethinking the Myth of the Gray Caps . . . I don't feel up to addressing this book for now. It requires more explanation than I have the strength to give it. Besides, Nativism was born from it, and that's too horrible to contemplate at the moment.

7) *At the age of 47* . . . Thankfully, this number also continues to rise. One day it, and she, will pass on to the Infinite. (As will we all, without a little bit of luck or planning. And then none of this will matter to anyone, not that it matters to many people at the moment, anyway.)

8) *Sabon remains* . . . "Remains" best describes the current content of her books: the remains of Duncan's theories, devoured and spat out by Sabon. (That's the way it often happens, although usually, I think, the author stolen from is already dead or senile. Still, the sting of it is there, I cannot deny it.)

9) . . . *shedding light on history and her fellow historians alike* . . . This latest addition to the Sabon Canon (or cannon) at least begins to acknowledge that most of her books feast off the carcasses of other historians.

10) This mention of Mary's parents reminds me that I have lied a little for the sake of dramatic tension, I think. There was one time I saw Mary before she visited my gallery. I just didn't realize it was her.

I saw her with her parents at Blythe Academy once, surrounded by the controlled chaos that is the start of the spring semester. A spray of sudden greenery from the trees, the clatter of shoes on walkways and stairs as students—nervous and excited—tried to find their classes. As I passed by on my way to visit Duncan, one family caught my eye by their very stillness. They stood in the center of the courtyard and also at the center of a kind of calm. The girl stood, legs slightly apart, staring down at the ground, schoolbooks held carelessly in one hand, a pensive look on her face. Her parents stood like towers to either side of her, the space between them containing a daughter not quite belonging to the same world.

Their unlined, unremarkable faces expressed no great joy or sorrow, or none that I could discern, and yet I could feel a tension there; the presence of some overwhelming emotion. I almost felt as if I were a witness to some kind of ritual or ceremony. Was the girl's head bowed in prayer? As I walked away, I turned to watch them, and it seemed as if they were receding from me at a glacially slow pace.

That must have been Mary's first year at the Academy, and I find it interesting that even then I noticed her, before Duncan ever pointed her out to me, before I even knew who she was.

When I read Sabon's biographical note in her various books, what I envision when I come across the sentence beginning "Her early interest in nature studies . . ." arises not from her gallery visit, but from that first glimpse: of twinned parents standing guard on either side of a daughter whose face is tilted toward the ground. Something about their wary stance still worries me now, even after my research has made of them more than silent statues.

In fact, my research has somehow lessened their pull on my imagination, for the facts do not particularly impress. (They impressed me!)

Given that David Sabon's most important contribution to natural history consists of helping to edit a revised edition of Xaver Daffed's classic *A History of Animals*, perhaps it would be best to simply note his presence and move on. However, his peculiar (dangerous!) attitude toward the gray caps, delivered in the form of speeches to many a meeting of the Ambergrisian Historical Society (smoky, jaundiced events punctuated by coughs, grunts, and unintelligible murmurings from octogenarian senilitians), should be documented somewhere. Where better than an afterword?

David Sabon preached a *strain* of Nativism (otherwise known as "a good way to get yourself killed"), although not quite the same one later popularized by Mary. David Sabon not only believed that gray caps possessed "no more natural intelligence than a cow, pig, or chicken" but that they should be treated "much as we treat other animals." As the transcript for one memorable speech reads, "Gray caps should be used to support our labors, for our entertainment, and for meat."

Although David Sabon later claimed that "and for meat" had appeared in the speech by mistake (transposed from a speech on the King Squid), the cutthroat Ambergris newspapers had no qualms about printing headlines like DAVID SABON RECOMMENDS SNACKING ON GRAY CAP BEFORE DINNER and NEW "ARCHDUKE OF MALID," DAVID SABON, LIKES A NICE BIT O' GRAY CAP BEFORE BED. Surely Mary Sabon, lone seed of a loon's loins, became indoctrinated with her father's attitudes at a very early age, setting the stage for her own irresponsible theories. (Perhaps so, but Mary always seemed embarrassed by her father's activities.)

While David Sabon's forebears included no one more distinguished than a barber in Stockton and a minor judge in Morrow, Mary's mother, Rebecca Verden-Sabon, came from newly minted stock. Her father, Louis Verden, began his career as a jeweler but went on to illustrate a number of scientific texts, although his best work appeared in *Burning Leaves*, a creative journal he eventually art directed and to which I sometimes contributed when I had no work from Sirin. Verden also illustrated a series of paranoid (not paranoid enough) Festival pamphlets for Hoegbotton & Sons, including *The Exchange, Bender in a Box, Naysayer Mews, In the Hours After Death*, and *The Night Step* (all in collaboration with the darkly humorous, underrated writer Nicholas Sporlender, whom I once bumped into by mistake—underground, oddly enough).

Rebecca became her father's apprentice and eventually took over editorial duties at *Burning Leaves*, although not until my gallery had turned to dust and ash. Before that, she specialized in illustrations for advertisements or to accompany scientific texts. In some ways, it could be argued that Rebecca's work for her daughter's first book, *The Inflammation of Aan Tribal Wars*, gave her more exposure than all her previous work combined.

⁂

Duncan's parent-teacher conferences with David and Rebecca continued for several semesters. I have this rather humorous vision of Duncan in his office, talking solemnly with Mary's parents and then, once he has smiled reassuringly and guided them out the door, frantically jumping out of his office window, on his way to a tryst with their daughter. (I honestly thought I was protecting her, and that she could make her own choices. After all, she was already a young adult. She knew her own mind.)

Apparently, the famed naturalist suffered from a peculiar form of blindness: an inability to see anything under his nose unless it crawled or flew or swam or galloped, for that keen observer of the natural world never realized what Duncan and Mary had been up to until he was told by a third party.

"Thank you," he'd said to Duncan. "Thank you for taking such good care of our daughter."

And in his way he had, hadn't he?

10

Mary and Duncan, Duncan and Mary. As with all utopias, especially those based on love, someone, thankfully, always comes along to say, "No—this is not right. No—this should end." Why? Because the true path Duncan always took to Mary's window was the Path of Denial, a path with which I was familiar. For example, take my current situation. I have begun to run out of money, although the owner of this establishment doesn't know it yet. He believes I just haven't had a chance to go to the bank, what with all the typing. (Real life, intruding on the recording of real life. How odd.)

Besides, I'm akin to a curiosity—he makes a healthy living from letting loathsome types peek around the corner at me. "That's Janice Shriek. She used to be famous." Some slack-jawed gimp is peering from behind a glossy wooden beam right now. I am ignoring him—he will not receive even a sliver of my attention.

I do like the smell of beer and whiskey and smoke, however. I do like the busy times when they are all chattering away in there, happy as a bunch of click-clacking gray caps holding a half-dozen severed heads, as in "days of yore."

Duncan only started coming here again in earnest after he fell out with Bonmot. When it all came crashing down, he called the Spore of the Gray Cap his home once more; again became the Green God of the Spore. Many a beer was consumed here. I wonder sometimes if Duncan ever came back during those happy-unhappy hours and sat looking at the corner, where all that can now be seen is a hole.

Now why would Duncan fall out with Bonmot? Could it have been over love? Possibly. If we turn to Duncan's journal, to the entry where he recounts to Mary Bonmot's fateful discovery along the Path of Remembering You, we shall soon find out. The ink was not yet dry on his grief when he wrote:

Glimpsed. Detected. Surprised. Held. Ensnared. Ensnarled. Entrapped. Captured. Stricken. No hope of understanding. He'd caught on, grasped, and comprehended, with no hope of acceptance. If I could make a fence of these words to keep him from us, I would, but it's no use. It's over. I am no longer a teacher. You are no longer my student. In a sense, we are released from all of it—the hiding, the sneaking around, the lying, the delicious forbidden feel of your lips against mine.

(There I go, romanticizing it—putting words between myself and the hurt. I disgust myself sometimes.)

I took the Path of Remembering You well after dark. I don't remember anything about my trip, except the absentminded scratches from a rosebush in the gardens and the frozen position of the stars. It was cold, and I was glad to pull myself up into your open window and into your smooth white arms. Your skin, as always, awakened my senses, and I trembled from the power of your eyes, the soft place at the base of your neck, the soap smell of you, the miraculous hollows on the inside of your thighs.

And, afterward, intoxicated by the feel and scent of you, the taste of you on my hands, my lips, I swung happily back into the cold, certain I would see you the next night; even the sudden tight prickle on my left arm, my right foot, that presaged spore-pain only added a spark to my mood. The stars swam and spun, and the solid, cold buildings seemed to sway with this happiness in me that was you.

But, my love, no happiness ever went untested. No happiness ever lasted unchanged, untransformed. It doesn't mean happiness has to end, just that it takes on new patterns, new shapes.

It happened by the willow trees where I first saw you, that flickering shiver of a glimpse, and yet that red hair like a fire burning through the trees. It was by those trees, along the path where I walked a happy man, that the stone table where I spent my lunch hours came into view. It lay at the very heart of the willows like a black cave, not a stone at all, and the dark green leaves of the surrounding bushes glistened with reflected light. And, my love, someone sat at that table, and even in that uncertainty, I knew who it was and all of the life left my gait. I could tell my happiness was about to change.

Bonmot sat at the table, dressed in his most formal clothes, as a Truffidian priest would on sacrament day at the Cathedral. Glittering robes, with gold thread woven through them. Even in the dark, they glittered.

I looked into that dark and I could not see his eyes. "Bonmot," I said, "is that you, Bonmot?" Even though I knew already that it was him.

He said nothing, but motioned for me to sit beside him at the table. I didn't hesitate, Mary—I sat next to him willingly. Any excuses about the cold, the lateness of the hour, would have been crushed by the weight of the stone and that gaze. So I sat and made a joke and remarked on the cold and said, "Should we have a midnight snack, then, instead of lunch?" and trailed off because throughout my nervous monologue Bonmot had said nothing. He stared at me with no expression on his face, the staff leaning against the stone bench, the medallion hanging around his neck on a silver chain. I clutched the table so hard that the stone abraded my fingers.

Now, finally, he spoke, each syllable unbearably clear against the cold night air. This is what he said, my love. I can't forget it. I can't sleep tonight because of it. He said, "It's no use, Duncan. I know. Once I too had a secret that made every breath I drew a lie, and so it's no use for you to talk of other things. Because *I know.* You have compromised your student, Mary Sabon."

There was silence for a full ten seconds and then I began to talk. I could not stop talking. Every word was a denial of what he had said. Every word placed such a distance between you and me that it made me physically ill—and yet I did it because I thought it was the only way to save us. And so I babbled on—what was Bonmot talking about? How dare he? Didn't he know me better than that? I had just been out taking a late walk. Didn't he know I helped to keep boys *away* from female students? Didn't he realize I was a colleague, a professional, a person who would never do what he accused me of? After so many talks in the gardens at lunch—so many wonderful conversations—how could he possibly consider— why, it was an outrage—why, I had been a model teacher—why, I was a published historian—I was—I was . . . and, finally, at some point, I realized that he had heard none of what I had said, and that his look of sorrow had transformed his face from granite to skin and flesh and bone. And I stopped talking. I looked away from him. My body shook. I could already anticipate everything he was about to take away from me, and I thought it meant the end. Really, The End.

He said: "There are no more lunches under the willow trees for us. You are no longer a teacher at this academy. I expect you to gather your things now and be gone before dawn. As for Mary, she will finish out the next two semesters and earn her degree, but if you ever set foot in this place again, she will be expelled in a very public way. I have had my fair share of scandal, Duncan. I will not let friendship or anything resembling it destroy my good works at this school. Good night, Duncan."

I did not even notice when he left because I thought I had lost you. I thought those words meant not just the end of my career as a teacher, but the end of us. But now, as I tell you all of this, I realize it is not the end—it just signals a change. A change for the good. We've been desperate and in love, which can be a great thing. It lends an urgency to all we do and say. It means that we do not take lightly each other's bodies or our hearts. It means we love each other fiercely and with no artifice between us.

But this is not the only kind of love we can have—it's not the only kind of passion. What we have is a flame like your hair, but there's another kind of excitement in the freedom to admire each other in public, without fear. There is a charge that comes from sharing our lives through more than just midnight trysts and frantic letters like this one. And this is why, finally, having lost everything tonight, I am still oddly hopeful, Mary. Mary. Your name is still such a revelation to me, your body always reminding me of the first time so that your touch makes me weak with the miracle of this thought: I am with Mary Sabon. I am loving Mary Sabon.

I am writing this by lantern light in my office. As dawn begins to gray the city, I can almost see your window from where I sit. The air is sweet and cool. I have two cases full of books and other personal belongings. In a few minutes, I will leave this academy, perhaps forever. I will leave only two things behind me: in my desk, for you to take when you will, that copy of Cadimon Signal's *Musings on the Many Faces of Ambergris* that you so much wanted—it was supposed to be a birthday present—and this letter, protected by our favorite hiding place. Please, if you have read this far, don't cry. Everything will be okay. I promise.

Please do not abandon me.

Love,

Duncan

Please do not abandon me, he writes in this journal entry that awkwardly transitions into a letter that could have been written by a nineteen-year-old, which he rips out of his journal, signs, and leaves for her—only for it to return to him four years later to be reunited with its fellow pages. He did not tear out related pages and send them to her. He did not send her the page right after his tearful but triumphant farewell, the one that contained this passage: "I have lost one of my best friends. I have lost a friend because of my own stupidity. Who will understand now? Who will I be able to talk to?"

Who will understand now? Here's the heart of it, what began to eat at Duncan. He told Bonmot so many things—sometimes in abstract, sometimes nonspecific, but still with enough detail that Bonmot could respond with all of his training and intellect. Me, I was neither historian nor priest, neither artist nor subject of art. Mary? Too young, he must have known on some level. Fine for the physical, but not to discuss such mysteries with. (Not true, and unfair, and judgmental, and unworthy behavior, even from you. I did not discuss the underground, the gray caps, my disease with her to *protect* her. And, yes, because she was young, but not because I didn't think she could understand—but because I was afraid I would scare her. That she would think me a crackpot, a false prophet, a madman.)

In fact, he did not tear out the *first* draft of his second page, which is identical to the second draft, except for the speech he attributes to Bonmot:

There are no more lunches under the willow trees for us. You are no longer a teacher at this academy. I expect you to gather your things now and be gone before dawn. As for Mary, she's just a child. She is as much your victim as this academy. Have you ever thought how this might hurt her? And I don't mean your status as her teacher, but you, Duncan, you in particular. How many obsessions can you sustain in your life? How many masters can you serve? Survive?

Did he suppress this part to save Mary from hurt, to protect Bonmot from her resentment? Or to make himself look better? (It doesn't really matter *now*, does it? One would think you were more intent on defending Mary than destroying her. You should decide what your purpose is.)

✸✹✺

I thought writing all of this down would help me place events in their proper order and context. Instead, the sequencing grows hazy. I stand at the base of the stairs at Martin Lake's party, the scarlet imprint of my hand still warm on Mary's face, about to respond to her careless words. What did I say? I'm not sure it matters anymore. The harder I focus, the faster the sharpness I desire and deserve dissipates, as if it all happened at the same time, or backward, and we only now approach a beginning.

Is there any real reason, other than bad luck and ill-timing, that Mary and Duncan could not still be together? Is there any reason it could not have been Mary and Duncan that I walked toward down the stairs, the flesh necklace/noose undone before it ever formed, its pieces resolved into smiling, appreciative faces? The imprint of my hand on Mary's face transformed into the loving touch of a sister-in-law? I might not be here now, the darkness of the ceiling muted only by the purple tiers of fungus that encroach at such speed. (No purple fungus ever grows with good intent in this city, Janice. You must have known that. It is a breed bred for spying, the source of myriad fragmented reports collected in the depths of the city's underground passages.)

But words will never persuade the past. Bonmot did fire Duncan. It did signal the beginning of the end (in one sense, but only in one sense) for my brother and Mary.

I remember that Bonmot told me about it during one of our sessions in the Truffidian Cathedral. I didn't have unbridled sex anymore, so I had, as you may have guessed, turned to "religion." That didn't last, either, because it had little to do with faith, but at least it gave me an excuse to spend time with Bonmot. We were standing in the very place where he later died, among the pews closest to the door.

"Janice," he said. "I've had to do something. I hope you won't hate me for it."

"I don't think I could hate you, Bonmot."

"You might. I've had to let Duncan go. Because of Mary. I think you already know what I mean?"

For a second, it was very quiet. I was shocked. Duncan hadn't had a chance to tell me. I hadn't seen him in days.

"Did you really have to?" I asked. I think I was worried, at first, as much about how it might affect my relationship with Bonmot as about Duncan.

"Yes. I had to."

He bowed his head, and we prayed.

How did Mary respond to this news? For a long time—for longer than I might have expected—she stood by Duncan. Duncan told me a week later, an echo of passion in his voice, that Mary had smuggled a letter to him through her unsuspecting parents. (Bonmot had left it up to Mary to tell her parents, and she never did.) In it, she begged him to wait for her. Either Duncan's line of romantic blather had ensorcelled her or she found the general notion of separated lovers, forced to check their desires, tragically romantic.

"A year and I can be with her," Duncan told me. "We'll find an apartment. Settle down."

"Have some kids?" I said. "Find a respectable day job? Stop skulking around belowground?"

A bitter smile twisted his face, but he did not reply.

(It may have seemed bitter to you, but I was mostly aghast at your lack of faith. I truly thought back then that Mary and I shared the same beliefs about the underground. In my dreams, I led her through those tunnels as if I were still a boy of fifteen, her sense of adventure as acute as my own.)

Mary might beg him, but Bonmot's begging days were well behind him; the old priest would never forgive my brother. His superiors in the Truffidian hierarchy used the incident to further humiliate him within the church. Nor would the Academy as a collective of teachers forgive him. Although Bonmot made no attempt to spread the news beyond informing them that Duncan had left the staff, Duncan's fellow instructors found out. How could they not? Their lack of forgiveness would take many forms, the worst of which would further hound my brother to the outer edge of his chosen field. (I was more concerned about getting from them the data they'd collected while working unwittingly on my many projects.) Many (not so many; certainly not, I thought then, enough to scuttle any future career aspirations) of his former colleagues wrote for history journals, or edited them, or had written books. With them as gatekeepers, with their long memories, it became less and less likely that Duncan's theories would ever find print in respectable publications again. (Respectable? Disreputable, really. Hundreds of pages of print a year devoted to concealing or sidestepping the truth. *They* were on the fringe the entire time and didn't know it.) Thus, Duncan's excommunication from Blythe further isolated him from anyone but Mary. (Mary *and you*, which certainly wasn't my idea of a happy family.) Duncan's journal reached new levels of bathos (it was genuine sadness at the time, but even proper melancholy is worthy of scorn in retrospect) in listing those who had abandoned him, in pages and pages of affronted pride. I'll spare you all but a snippet of it.

Atriarch, Elizabeth—Assistant dean of student affairs, made a mock ritual of me dancing with her at school functions. Next to Bonmot, her support was the most helpful in continuing my underground studies. She had once accompanied the famous Daffed on one of his odd specimen exhibitions into the Southern jungles, and she had learned to love the muck and mire of slogging through vegetation. I fed her a steady diet of harmless but exotic stories about the underground, and in return she looked away as my classes grew more and more esoteric. Now, I might as well be a shadow to her. (Everyone was a shadow to that woman. I should not have taken it personally.)

Balfours, Simon—One of the guards I used to evade while making my way to trysts with Mary; he liked to joke with me about the Hoegbottons. The one time I saw him in the street since, he barked out my name like a curse, and followed it with real curses. (Since dead, of a heart attack, falling while on duty. I can't blame him for his response—I made a fool of him.)

Binder, David—A stuffed shirt fool, head of Morrow Studies, who used to chatter on endlessly while I was trying to get to my next class. Now he's gone silent as dumb stone, as useless to me now as he was to my research. (I stand by my assessment, especially now that he, too, is dead, run over by a motored vehicle.)

Bittern, Ralstaff—The gardener! Even the gardener won't talk to me, won't look at me. Although, in truth, he never liked me much. But I thought he at least enjoyed matching wits with me in his efforts to uncover the scope of my midnight perambulations. It seems I was incorrect. (Now he's the gardener for the grounds around the Truffidian Cathedral, and his attitude is absolutely the same. He spits at me when he sees me.)

Cinnote, Fiona—Indigenous Tribes Studies. Beautiful in her own way. She used to laugh at my jokes. I used to laugh at hers. There was a world-weariness behind her eyes that made me think she had an interesting history. But she had an affair with Binder, for Truff's sake. How dare she judge me! (And how dare I judge her, truly. I actually thought about suggesting lunch, but she quit the Academy and mounted an expedition to the Southern jungles, never to be seen again.)

. . . and on, and on . . .

When it came to Blythe Academy, all Duncan could think of for several years was how he had been wronged by them. He couldn't see how he'd hurt the Academy, or his fellow professors. There was nothing in him, then, that was able to accept the guilt of his misdeeds. (Perhaps not on the surface, Janice. But I've made up for it since. I think I've made up for it thrice over. But I guess *no one makes it out*, a line Lacond was fond of quoting from Tonsure.)

Even worse, these were people Duncan had never mentioned to me or hadn't known while at Blythe. He had never cared about them before, but their features came into sharp relief after he believed himself wronged by them. (I have no comment, no defense.)

So Duncan became absent from Blythe Academy, no longer roaming its halls, its gardens, its classrooms. The effect of Duncan's sudden removal on Mary, paradoxically, was an unlikely blossoming. Released from the constant "tutelage" and the equally lustful pressure of Duncan's ideas, she, Bonmot told me, had become one of the school's best students. With Bonmot to guide but not smother, Mary began to develop her own theories, the seeds that would eventually lead to disagreement and betrayal. (You find her theories totally without merit, Janice, yet claim that I constricted her intellectual freedom like some monstrous . . . monster.

You can't have it both ways. I don't deny I made some mistakes, as I'm sure you'll soon demonstrate, but I'm not totally at fault. I'm not sure anyone is at fault.)

I can only guess how no longer having access to the Academy affected Duncan's studies of the gray caps. I imagine it hurt him to the core, if he could even register that pain above the intensity of his lust for Mary. (Wrong again! Wrong! You are setting new records for presumption in this account. By the time of my expulsion, I had nearly completed my experiments. There was little else I could set my students to doing that would not arouse suspicion. My classes had, by that point, become mockeries of classes, mockeries of studies. The students themselves sensed it. That the results were inconclusive does not mean the experiments were incomplete. I just moved my laboratory and studies to another location—namely, my own body. And quite a schooling that proved! As I began to live with my condition, and then find ways to control it, it became less of a disease and more of a transformation.)

A week after Duncan told me about his expulsion from Blythe Academy, the late afternoon brought not only rain and the murmur of prayers from the Religious Quarter, but also a knock on the door. Duncan stood on the porch in the rain, his hair plastered to his head and puddles around his booted feet. Gray as a mushroom dweller, and smelling of mildew. Eyes like phosphorescent green circles with dead black centers. For a startled second, I saw him as Mary would later—not of this world, but not having left it. Half-invisible spores, caught by the porch light, formed a hazy halo around his head. His hair had begun to thin and I noticed, with a pang of recognition, the emergence of gray at his temples. And yet, once again, he was fleeing the ruins of a self-made disaster. A part of me could not sympathize.

"This is becoming routine," I said.

"Can you find me a job?" he asked, grinning. "I'm broke." As matter-of-fact as that. With the old glow of fragile confidence you find in people held together by nothing more substantial than affection (and fungi).

"Hello to you, too," I said, walking back into the apartment to find him a towel, vaguely happy that I would not be asked to scrape mushrooms off him this time.

As I threw the towel in his face, I said, "Of course I can find you a job. There are lots of available positions for a paranoid, discredited, fringe historian with a fungal disorder who has recently been laid off for laying his students."

Duncan winced. "Student. Singular."

"Singular. Plural. Does it really matter?" I turned away from him. "So. Should I go or do you want to?" I asked. "Neither of us really has a choice. It's not like my gallery is going to pay your bills when it doesn't even pay mine."

"Go?" He stared quizzically at me for a moment, and then he understood. "You should go. What if he disapproves of me now?"

"You assume he knows."

"He knows everything. And what he doesn't know, he finds out quickly. You should go."

So I went. And that was the start of something altogether different.

✦

Sirin's office occupied part of the second floor of Hoegbotton & Sons' headquarters on Albumuth Boulevard. The dull mass of red bricks always smelled of packing sawdust and exotic spices. It had gained a kind of inbred notoriety due to a novel that had used the offices as a prop to its fading plot during its climactic scenes. The building had survived not only that malaprop, but centuries of other challenges—from the Gray Tribes, to Festivals gone bad, to fires set by outraged monks from the Religious Quarter protesting unsavory business practices. (Not to mention the ongoing assault on its editorial domains by a certain pair of increasingly toothless and shrill Shrieks.) "There are only two times not to trust a Hoegbotton: when you're selling and when you're buying" was a common saying down at the docks.

Sirin's office—a haven for culture within the blunt instrument of greed that formed the building proper—had a seasonal quality to it. In the winter and early spring, Sirin's rosewood desk would be buried in contracts, manuscripts, proposals, financial information, and related books, all in preparation for publication. (Not then, but soon—perhaps even within three or four years—one of those manuscripts would be Mary's. She truly was gifted at one point. And prolific—positively fecund—once she got started.) As the year progressed, his desk would slough off much of the clutter, until, by autumn, all but the finished books had vanished, and the magazines or broadsheets pregnant with reviews, both bright and dark, had taken their place. Then winter would once again obscure the lovely rosewood of his desk with the weight of things promised and things promising. His office had the most wonderful smell: of parchment pages, of ink, of newly printed books.

Remembering this as I type, I suddenly see not just one trip to Sirin's office, but many, over several seasons, a pleasant overlay of memories as sensual as any heated groping of bodies in the back rooms of a guest house. I see the perpetual but graceful aging of Sirin, which for him manifested itself solely in his hair, which whitened and receded, while the rest of him stayed exactly the same. I see the constant rush and withdrawal of the papers on his desk. I see the sudden and inexplicable disappearance and reappearance of his legion of secretaries. The blur of colors and motion outside of his windows. The steady permanence of his smile, his desk, his butterflies. (It's difficult to shake off the feeling, isn't it, Janice? Difficult because you don't want to. Neither do I.)

One of the more distinctive aspects of Sirin's offices, beyond the sheer expansive clutter on his desk (early spring, then, was it?), and the lingering odor of cigars and vanilla, were the tubular glass enclosures a Morrow glassblower had made for him. They lay clustered on the table behind his desk, near an oval window that overlooked Albumuth Boulevard. Each had tiny holes cut into the glass and contained a caterpillar, chrysalis, or fully formed butterfly. (Certainly, little bound his butterflies to the past, or the present. As they emerged glistening from their tight houses, they knew nothing but the moment. Sometimes I envied them.)

I had often observed Sirin puttering over his charges as his secretary showed me in, but this time he stood there lamenting a dead butterfly. Sirin looked tanned and well-rested beneath his crisp gray suit and burgundy shoes, any graceful effect ruined by a glaring multicolored bowtie that a clown would have been ashamed to wear; it was his only vice, besides tricking people. His hair had by now receded to reveal more and more of his narrow, intelligent face.

I had known him for many years, and yet I knew little or nothing about him, really.

Sirin spun around at my approach. (Butterflies and moths lived inside his head, Janice, just as mushrooms lived inside of mine. This made it difficult to hear.) He fixed me with the famous stare that could pierce walls and bring confessions from even the most hardened Truffidian monk.

"Look at this," he said, gaze bright but disturbed behind the gold frames of his glasses. "My favorite sapphire cappan has been colonized by the emissaries of the gray caps. It's a sign, perhaps." His outstretched hands, smeared with fungal spores and bearing the crumpled corpse of his beloved butterfly, belonged to a piano player, not an editor and writer. (I often thought his piano playing was a step above his editing, to be honest.)

We met halfway between the door and his glass habitats. I stared at the creature in his hands. True enough—the dead butterfly was completely encrusted with an emerald-green fungus. The outstretched wings had sprouted a thousand tendril colonists, topped with red and resembling a confusion of antennae. It looked like some intricate wind-up toy covered with jewels. It looked more beautiful than it could have alive—not just a butterfly choked with fungus, but a completely new creature. Even the texture of its exoskeleton appeared to have changed, become more supple. I stared at it with sudden irrational fear. It was too similar to the process that had begun to claim my brother. (I am neither butterfly nor fungus, and I chose my fate, but I appreciate your concern.)

Sirin's voice brought me back to the present.

"It's a shame, Janice," he said. "A terrible waste. A tragedy of Manzikertian proportions. I should never have left." He had recently returned from a "vacation" in the Southern Isles forced upon him to avoid the backlash from his role in the Citizen Fish Campaign, about which the less said the better. (Even an aging historian such as I, Janice, must consider that statement a challenge: Senior members of the Hoegbotton clan had suggested Sirin temporarily disappear after it became known through a leak to the city's broadsheets that Sirin had been behind Citizen Fish, an effort to fill the recently vacated Antechamber position with a stinking, five-day-old freshwater bass.)

"You had no choice," I said.

A dismissive shrug. "We might have won the election. Anyone would have been better than Griswald. He'll last a few weeks, perhaps, before they tear him down. Figuratively, one can only hope. A shame."

"Yes," I said. "It is." But I wasn't sure if he meant the butterfly or something more elusive, more dangerous. The distance between us grew with each new utterance.

Sirin turned toward his desk, butterfly still cupped in his hands, and seemed startled by the cacophony of papers, books, pens, manuscripts, newspapers, and contracts that greeted him. Most prevalent were the manuscripts, which had been so thoroughly lacerated with red pen marks that they looked as if they were bleeding out. (Sirin the Invasive, I used to call him. Always trying to put his stink on a poor writer's immaculate style. Always intimidating people with his little red pen. I used to joke that if he had had to use his own blood to make his marks he'd have been stingier with his criticism.)

"Sit, sit," he said, gesturing to a chair piled high with books. "Just push those off."

Bent almost double by the burden, I did as he suggested. As I sat down, I could not help but notice a ragged piece of paper, in his handwriting: "Did the arrival of the Manzikert family in some way trigger a change in the gray caps? Did the arrival of M ruin our chance to understand them?" (That is another thing I will never forget about Sirin: his ragged notes, the emissaries of authorial destruction.)

So Sirin, too, had his finger on the pulse of a mystery (or simply a note mimicking or correcting some book he planned to publish). I sometimes thought that should Sirin and Duncan ever sit down for a serious talk, all mysteries would be solved, revealed, undone. (No—not true. An altogether uglier scenario comes to mind.)

Sirin laid his tiny burden down on the desk in front of me, then sat back in his chair, arms crossed, and stared at me, an odd smile flitting across his face. Perhaps he was already contemplating his escape, or perhaps it was one last smile of pain for his sapphire cappan. An exotic jewel, the butterfly looked ever more beautiful in the light streaming from Sirin's window.

"I heard a rumor," Sirin said, "that Duncan has left Blythe Academy under peculiar circumstances. Is this true?"

"He has left, it's true," I said. "There is nothing peculiar about it, however. A difference of opinion, really. Nothing that would get in the way of his being hired by someone else."

"Janice. Is Duncan determined to destroy every career he makes some progress toward?" (Typical of the bastard.)

I gritted my teeth. "It was an amicable parting of the ways."

"I hear otherwise," Sirin said, but dismissed my nascent protest with a wave of the hand. "Not that it matters much."

I'm confused now. I can't remember if we had this discussion in his office or somewhere else, if I'm thinking of another conversation. As I try to imagine his office during our meeting, I see books that belong to other eras, other encounters. I'm fairly sure that *The Exchange & Other Stories* by Nicholas Sporlender had not yet been published, for example, and that that book of essays about Martin Lake wasn't published until several years later, either. Why, now that I really look, I can see a cane in the corner of Sirin's office, although he didn't use one. And over there—glimmering darkly, like some expanse of black lamplit water—a starfish

Duncan never showed him. No, actually, it's a pair of the same glasses I brought with me to Lake's party. I can see that now.

Does that mean Sirin knew what Duncan knew? About the glasses? (You worry me, sister. The one thing you had going for you was a kind of grim, lurching linear progression. You seem to be losing that now.)

It's darker in here than before, but I can see better, if that makes any sense. The spores are thick. I shall ask the bartender to bring me a fan, or to open the window. I can't afford to leave again now. It's getting too late to rewrite. All I want to do is move forward. All I want is to look ahead. Typos will proliferate. Sentences will wind up nowhere. I don't care.

But we were in Sirin's office, attempting to throw off the weight of accumulated memory.

Sirin told a joke of some kind, but I didn't understand the punch line. We sat there uncomfortably for a moment before I said, "I came here to see if—"

"You came here to find work for Duncan, and possibly for yourself. Your gallery is failing. Duncan was indiscreet with a student. Tell me why I should help you?"

No respite from that uncanny knack he had for knowing things. I said the only thing I could say: "We've always done good work for you. Rarely missed a deadline. Our private lives have never affected Hoegbotton."

Sirin laughed at that—or perhaps I am again remembering some other meeting—and as his body shook with that not unsympathetic laughter, a strange black dust rose from his suit.

He sat forward, elbows on the desk, fingers templed. His features took on a sudden intensity. He said: "I am going to recommend you both for positions. Temporary or permanent, who can tell? Something horrible is about to happen that will provide an opportunity for you both to find work. *The Ambergris Daily Broadsheet* will soon become the only reliable source for information. They will need reporters. Between the two of you, you should be able to supply that need and do a good job." (Just do a good job? Nothing was ever so simple with Sirin, which is why I kept well away from him.)

This information stunned me. "How do you know?" I started to say, but then shrugged. I had given up trying to understand how or why Sirin knew so much, or why it continued to surprise me. Someday, I was sure, Sirin would write a book that explained it all.

"It doesn't matter why, does it? I'm offering you employment." (Witty, yes. Clever, yes, with a core of hidden sadness, but also deadly in his way.)

He leaned forward, offered me a card from the end of his long fingers. I liked looking into his eyes, used to experience a tiny tremor from the effect of that gaze.

"Visit the editor at the *Broadsheet*," he said, "in about six weeks. When it all begins."

"Six weeks is a long time to wait," I said. Ahead, in those six weeks, lay a period of the doldrums—Duncan stalking Mary from afar, unable to get close, while I piloted the doddering skeleton of my ever-less-seaworthy ship of a gallery. At times, sitting at my desk with no customers on the horizon, I could actually feel the room begin to list from side to side, the gallery anchored to nothing more permanent than perpetual debt.

Sirin sat back in his chair. "Not as long as you might think." His gaze softened. "I cannot guarantee you anything, Janice. No one ever receives what might be called an ironclad guarantee. Now, I have another appointment, so you'll have to excuse me. If you're lucky, perhaps you can turn your work for the *Broadsheet* into a book for me. We'll see about that later, depending on whether or not Ambergris is still standing at the end of this."

And that was the end of my meeting with Sirin. As I left, he had returned to his butterflies, clucking his disapproval of the fungus that had swallowed up his sapphire cappan.

Two things stayed with me from that encounter. First, the name on the card: "James Lacond." Lacond—thick, stinking of cigars, rumpled, pinkish, rambling—would soon play a large role in Duncan's life. But as I stared down at the name and tried to understand that our lives would be changing in six weeks, he seemed nothing more than a bit player. This was when it first occurred to me that perhaps Sirin had not received his information about Duncan in quite as intuitive a way as I had thought. As I left, I could have sworn that I saw a manuscript with a title page reading "The Role of Chance in the History of the Southern Cities" pinned between two volumes of *The Lore of the Ancient Saphant*. Even now, the thought of that title, Sabon's first book, causes an involuntary shudder.

(Like those hallucinations you were having a few paragraphs ago, this is clearly impossible. Mary did not publish her first book for four years. For two of those years, I saw her drafts. Such marvelously light, sensual drafts. I would only reluctantly apply my red pen to them, for to edit her, often in the afterglow of making love, was almost to draw upon her skin, to criticize her very form—which I could not do, for she was perfect in every way.)

Within the hour, Sirin, that elegant man, would disappear from Ambergris for three years. Where he went, what he was doing, no one would ever know.

✶✷✸

A fight broke out in the bar a couple of minutes ago. As I typed, I listened to the raised voices for a few minutes before the screech of chairs and a heavy sound, like a table being overturned, marked its escalation to something more serious. For a moment, I wanted to go out there. I felt insular, removed. I wanted to talk to someone. Anyone. Instead of just "talking" to whoever is reading this account.

I have wondered, more than once, who will be reading this after I am gone. I am faced with the distinct possibility that the owner of the Spore will read it—or at least glance at it. (Wrong—I got here first.) If this is so, thank you for your hospitality. I wonder what you'll make of these spore-stained pages. (I wonder what he'll make of my notes. Except I'm not sure I'll leave the pages here when I'm done. I might move them somewhere safer.)

There.

The bar is silent now. Someone is breathing deeply. Someone is typing and breathing deeply. We're getting close to the end. I can see Mary at the bottom of that staircase, waiting patiently for me to destroy her world.

There's a hole behind me, you know. I may have mentioned it. They've filled it in, but on breaks from typing I've been reopening it. I've cleared away a lot of rubble in the last few days. Something also seems to be working at it from the other side. Maybe it's yet another indication of the Shift, or maybe it's just an old-fashioned intrusion. I guess I'll find out eventually.

✶✷✸

Five weeks after my talk with Sirin, a man later identified as Anthony Bliss walked up to the entrance of a Hoegbotton storage house near the docks. He nodded to the attendant, who stood inside stacking boxes, and then, according to a witness, held out his hand with something in it. The attendant, John Guelard, straightened up, nodded back, and took a step toward Bliss. Bliss tossed the object to the attendant. Guelard caught it with one hand, cupped it with his other hand, and then frowned. He tried to pull his hands away from the object, but he was stuck to it. Bliss nodded, smiled, and walked away into the crowd, while Guelard writhed on the ground, his skin turning rapidly whiter and whiter while beginning to peel off in circling tendrils of the purest white . . . until nothing remained of him but glistening strands of fungus. The strands of fungus began to darken to a deep red, and then exploded into a gout of flame. Within minutes, before water could be pumped to the scene, the storage house had burned to the ground, taking a considerable portion of Hoegbotton & Sons' imports for the month with it. The object Bliss had tossed to Guelard had been a kind of spore mine bought from the gray caps: Frankwrithe & Lewden's first overt action against their mortal enemy, Hoegbotton & Sons, in what would come to be known as the War of the Houses.

PART II

It is perhaps too cruel to think of Tonsure not only struggling to express himself, to communicate, underground, but also struggling aboveground to be heard as [historians try] equally hard to snuff him out.

    —Duncan Shriek, from *The Hoegbotton Guide to the Early History of Ambergris*

1

"Let no man nor woman say
they crossed me and lived to tell
unless in grave discomfort ever after!"

"What ho! I see Sophia's Island
before me, weighted by the night,
as like an echo as a ghost."

"Might we shed our ghastly fate
and shed with it this war
that we never should have waged?"

What do you most vividly remember about the War of the Houses?

Even as recently as six months ago, some brazen young reporter asked me that question, having taken the time to track me down in my apartment: a ruin crowded with the detritus of a lifetime of false starts. I can't even remember what broadsheet he represented, to be honest.

I was surly and morose after a long day of serving as a tour guide for the type of people I call the Ignorants and the Rudes, and I had begun to take on some of their less savory characteristics. Besides, he was *very* young; even as a child, Sybel had never been that young. I doubted this one had been alive at the start of the war.

"What do you most vividly remember about the War of the Houses?" he asked me.

You could see dust motes floating in the air behind his head, revealed by the sunlight of the open window. I rarely opened that window anymore. I didn't like what it revealed about my apartment: the worn red carpet, the sequined dresses half hidden on hangers in a corner, draped over a dumpy old sofa chair; the dozens of paintings I'd rescued from my gallery, none of them worth a thing. I even had two ceremonial swords from Truff knew where—and dozens of picture albums I hadn't had the heart to pull out in years.

The place needed a serious airing out, although to the reporter's credit he didn't so much as wrinkle his nose, even when a plume of dust rose from the impact of his sinewy buttocks meeting the seat of the second sofa chair.

"What do I remember?" I echoed. Truff, his face was smooth and bare of worry, even in that light. Does every innocent share that look? "Why, the opera, of course," I said.

His eyes brightened and widened, and he began scribbling on a useless little pad he had brought with him.

"When we were reporters during the war—especially by the middle of it—we didn't have paper," I said in a helpful tone. "We had to jot notes on handkerchiefs using our own blood. Usually when the ink ran out."

He looked up, startled, his brown hair sliding down over his even browner eyes, then stared at his pad with an almost guilty expression until I cackled—a sound that startled me more than him—and he realized I was joking.

"Are you upset with me for some reason?" he asked, all semblance of reporter gone. Suddenly he was just a kid, the way Duncan had once been a kid.

I stared at this nascent reporter and sighed, sat back in my chair and said, "No. I'm not upset. I'm old and tired. Can I get you something to drink? Or eat? A friend made me some pastries. I think they're still around here somewhere." I started to look beneath the pillows assembled at my feet.

"No," he said, a little too quickly. "That's all right. I just want to know more about the war, about the opera."

He had lips that would always be full and yet empty of expression or inflection. A serious mouth, without even a hint of an upward or downward curve to reveal whether he was an optimist or pessimist. Because of that alone, he might someday become a good reporter, I thought. Or a good card player.

But now he was sitting there, waiting for my answer and sweating, the sweet young scent of him filling my apartment.

"It was a war," I told him. "A lot of people died. A lot of buildings were destroyed. It was hell—and for what? I don't think anyone knew *why* after a while."

He nodded as if he understood. But how could he, really? We'd been reporters during wartime and we didn't even understand it. As my father always said, a reporter is a mirror, not a window, which makes it doubly painful. You don't just let it flow through the glass of your perspective; you stare back at it.

Already a lump was forming in my throat. My apartment looked unbearable. My leg was heavy and inert and aching.

I rarely tell any reporter what I remember—to them I give platitudes, clichés, spirals of brave words that mean nothing. Because it's painful. Because we lost so much during the war.

"No one makes it out." Those were among Samuel Tonsure's last written words, according to what Duncan had uncovered at the fortress-monastery of Zamilon, and it's a good piece of life advice: *No one makes it out.* Enjoy what you can while you can.

I was tempted to repeat Tonsure's wisdom to the reporter, but I had already begun to feel self-conscious, and irrelevant. Besides, he had a question.

"And what about the opera?"

I smiled and leaned forward, staring into his pretty face and untroubled eyes.

"What I remember about the war," I said, "is that right in the middle of it near the very epicenter of the conflict, when hundreds of men, women, and children might be blown up or turned to spores in the next week, the creative powers that be in Ambergris decided to stage the most ridiculous folly in the city's entire ridiculous history: an opera."

And what an amazing enterprise *that* was, the opera described in advertisements as:

THE ROMANCE OF

AMBER & GRIS

Authored by: Anon
Sponsored by: Concerned Citizens
Directed by: Sarah Gallendrace
Staged at: The Trillian Opera House
—if still standing
Starring: Various & Sundry Talents—as available

A Wicked "Mutual Satyricon" of Both Parties to the Current Conflict, whilst Containing a "Poignant Love Affair" Stolen Whole from The Distant Past, by way of Subterfuge and Subplot. An Opera—with what Music can be Spared From The War Effort—Overseen by Sarah Gallendrace, the Genius Behind the Production of Voss Bender's Opera *Trillian*.

Price of admission negotiable at the door.

In hindsight, no matter what happened, the opera would be the one great success of the war, the only sign that there might still be a city called Ambergris afterward.

The city at that time—after more than two years of conflict—had begun to tear itself apart, like a beast that hates itself with a passion born of long familiarity. Every night, the deafening thunder of bombardment, the lights in the sky—the purple, red, or green of fungal bombs—the continuous, monotonous noise, so febrile, soaking into the very ground so that even the strange new flocks of crows, come to peck at our dead, became married to it, their cries the perfect mimic of fungal mortar fire. (No one knew whether they were about to duck death or bird shit.) And in the morning: the self-inflicted wounds, buildings sliced in half or crumbled into dust, the great, slashing scars in the earth . . .

In the weeks before the announcement of the opera—ragged hand-lettered posters nailed to charred posts and crumbling walls—a fear had begun to overcome many of us: a fear that Ambergris, as a place or an idea, could not last, that it might fall for the first time, and fall forever. With the fear came a terror of our own mortality that we had put aside through the first years of the war. With the evidence all around us that the city itself might die, we could no longer ignore thoughts of our own individual fates. Now we all seemed to shine with a clarity that imbued our forms with a figurative kind of light, a light we had not had before. It shone out through our eyes, our mouths, our movements. It made us all noble, I suppose, this fatalism, in a disheveled, unwashed way. (Such a lovely way to put it, but all I saw was grime and dirt and blood and death. The only real beauty lay underground, and it was a deadly beauty. How strange to be caught between such extremes.)

When Hoegbotton & Sons and Frankwrithe & Lewden came together at Borges Bookstore the week before the opera to announce a ceasefire, we all relaxed a little. We all let down our guard. If they could call a ceasefire for an opera, then perhaps they might one day call a ceasefire for more important things.

It had been a hard (not to mention dangerous) two years for Duncan and me, chasing after this or that story. We needed the rest. We needed the comfort. (The opera occurred, I felt later, almost out of the collective consciousness of the city—an impulse toward a remembered harmony Ambergris had never really known. When I heard the rumors of the opera's impending production, I thought of them as horrible lies, intended to make us hope. It never occurred to any of us that one night House Hoegbotton and House Frankwrithe & Lewden would find themselves entangled in a temporary peace, and we would find ourselves in front of the Trillian Opera House.)

The night of the opera, we formed a party of five: me, Sybel, our employer James Lacond in the middle, Duncan, and Mary. Sybel, Lacond, and my brother served as an impregnable barrier to any potential unrest involving myself and the Lady Sabon. Sybel had recently reentered my life as a runner for Lacond and sometimes stayed at my apartment, just like old times.

"An opera?" Sybel had said when I told him. "Is there a building left standing to stage it in?"

Miracle of miracles, the Trillian Opera House stood conspicuously intact between two mounds of red fungi—seething rubble that had once been a bank and a restaurant. Granted, a huge wedge-shaped gouge (the classic indication of a fungal bomb) broke the opera house's skin, running from the roof down to the second floor and exposing the rough-hewn timbers that formed the building's skeleton. Such a minor wound, compared to so many buildings that had collapsed, unable to withstand the insidious veins of invading fungus.

It was dusk and the blood clot of a sun sawed through the opera house's wound, lit the street with a deep orange light that I had never seen before. We waded through this light, our party and many others approaching the opera house. A smell permeated the street that made us anxious to get inside—the all-too-familiar stench of mold, afterbirth of some fungal weapon, fired a week ago or a day ago or an hour ago. One could never tell.

The doors, unharmed, swung open on their rusty gilded hinges, ready to receive us all, whether Hoegbotton, Lewden, or neutral. No one would be turned away who wanted a seat, even though certain seats would require more bartering than others. (Tickets in such a context would have been too specific a madness. It was such an odd experience to enter the opera house that night, in that context, after so many years of stealing away at lunch for a performance, or taking students there for an assignment, or going with you, Janice.)

As I recall, Mary and I looked magnificent in our sequined dresses, perfumed and powdered. I had taken from a safe place the finest of my outfits from the height of the New Art's popularity. A curving neckline. An audacious black hat. Shoes made from lizard and mole skin. A handbag of a texture and design rare in any but the most southern of the Southern Isles. My hair was still a bit of a mess—that could not be helped; scarcely a mirror survived in the city, most fragmented by bombardment or wrinkled by filaments of fungi. For me, wearing such clothes reminded me of what had been, which made me sad—but also made me stand taller, for back in my glory days I had practically owned the opera house. I cannot remember what Mary wore, but whatever she wore, it could only presage future glory.

Mary and Sybel and I had one thing in common: none of us had succumbed to any of the fungal diseases that had so ravaged the general population as a side effect of the ceaseless bombardments. The same could not be said for many of those who surrounded us as we jostled our way through the door.

Toad-like James Lacond, ever-present cigar between his lips—his usual Nicean Reserve—had a patch of tendrils, a brilliant green, growing off the left side of his balding head. Nothing in his sour demeanor, however, revealed even the slightest discomfort. (As always, for a fat man he moved with surprising grace.) "Lie down with the gray caps," he was fond of saying, "and you make your peace with them, in one way or another."

My brother, however, tight-lipped and nervous (because I expected, with no truce yet spoken or implied, that you and Mary would fight the entire evening; why, the war was at times the least of my worries, even though I could sense the gray caps in the floorboards, their symbols and signs everywhere), showed more of the strain. A silvery-purple "birthmark" writhed upon his forearm like a living tattoo. Who knew if his clothes hid some greater embarrassment? (They didn't. I could now maintain control, at least for a while. Had I manifested in my full fungal state, it would have cleared out the opera house.)

Some of those around us had even incorporated their misfortunes into their costumes. As we walked into the antechamber, stairs on left and right leading up and down, the gold-painted walls and somber red curtains unable to hide the gouges in the floor, the gutted, silent bar awash with signs of flame, we encountered these fashion marvels. The full extent of Ambergrisian ingenuity or insanity became clear. One woman had actually created a body-length trellis over which to cultivate the deep blue fungi ravishing her, the fronds forming a full dress, complete with train. Others had fashioned earrings or other accessories from their symptoms. (It says something that we had come far enough not to be shocked by what we saw that night. How quickly people adapted to such extremes; and how, secretly, I was glad of it, for it made me normal for a time, no more or less afflicted than anyone else, especially in Mary's eyes. Later, of course, it would help me not at all, once the "ordinary" citizens of Ambergris conveniently forgot the strangeness, the surreal quality, of the city during wartime.)

Mary gasped when she saw the woman with the trellis. Sybel and Lacond turned withering expressions of contempt toward her that she pretended not to see. Sybel had never been underground, but he had a way of adapting to each new situation as it presented itself. Lacond, meanwhile, had not gone as far belowground as Duncan, nor for as long, but he was marked for life by it, nonetheless: an encrusted blackness sometimes shone through his pores.

"You'd all better get used to it," Lacond muttered. "There'll be much more than that to get used to before the end."

Sybel scowled; I knew Lacond's pronouncements sometimes struck him as both vague and pretentious.

But you may wonder how, even with so great and ponderous a weight as James Lacond between us, Mary and I could walk so calmly into the opera house as members of the same group. The circumstances of war, as well as her keeping her distance and being eclipsed by the mushroom moon known as Lacond, didn't hurt, but you must also remember that the two semesters of Bonmot's ban had long since passed into history. The ban, along with much else from before the war, had become so remote that sometimes I could not find these details in my memory, or could not find them with a sharpness that made them real.

So I had, for the duration of the conflict, suspended my judgment of many things, including Mary. I had even become reconciled to the idea that Duncan and Mary might make a life together. Indeed, you might say that the war, for a time, created another kind of excitement for Duncan and Mary, an urgency to replace what they had lost now that they could no longer sneak around Blythe Academy. (Yet you were still so tense, your smile so forced, your politeness so impolite.) I did not speak to her, but we both laughed at Duncan's jokes, and made comments to each other indirectly, through Duncan or Lacond. Sybel, for his amusement, tried to create situations in which Mary would have to talk to me, or vice versa, but was never successful.

Through the sweat-stained, boot-scuffed antechamber we walked, all of us crowded together as we climbed the stairs to the balcony, having to ignore our own sour smell.

Then, a rush of stale air in our faces, followed by another, even staler, blast, as we walked onto the balcony and beheld the opera house!

We stared down at row upon row of worn gilt seats, rapidly being filled by the people sitting in them, saw the orchestra pit filled with the febrile scratchings of musicians tuning their instruments, and beyond that, the plain wooden stage, half hidden by burgundy curtains that had great, gaping holes in them, revealing the scurrying singers behind the veil, the grunt and nudge of set pieces moving into place.

The more we looked, the more small details came into focus, the grandeur fading upon closer inspection. Plaster cherubim placed at the corners of the balcony, framing our view, had grown old, fissures of wrinkles aging them to appear wiser, and more malevolent than innocent. Every seat had a sweat stain from years of use. Every filigree and swirl of decorative paint on the walls or ceiling had a crack, a dent, a fault line. It had always been that way, and the familiarity of it comforted me.

Then Duncan gasped.

"Look," he said, pointing toward the ceiling. Only Lacond did not make a sound when he saw it. Even Sybel swore, under his breath.

It seems odd now that we had not seen it before all else, as if we wanted at first to deny its existence.

Looking up, as we walked forward to the edge of the balcony seats, we slowly came to recognize the source of the clear, clean, but undeniably green light that served as our illumination. (The rational mind can absorb only so much of the strange without damage.)

"What is it?" Mary whispered.

"The remains of a fungal bomb," Lacond replied.

"Half exploded," Duncan said. "Fused to the ceiling."

The wound we had seen from the outside of the opera house had provided scant evidence of the damage suffered by the building. The center of its mosaic dome—a stylized scene of Morrow cavalry riding to Ambergris's defense during the Silence—had disappeared, the shards of its dissolution having simply vanished, assimilated, replaced by an intense green that shed its light in waves upon the stage. The green had eyes, or so it seemed, for it manifested itself as a series of circles or nascent fruiting bodies.

My breath caught in my throat. My neck grew sore from staring up at it. You could see through the green to the stars in the sky beyond, as if the green were no more substantial than gauze, than fog, and yet it sparkled and spun, each particle of it, as it shed the light that allowed us to see as we found our seats.

Lacond noticed that I could not look away from it, even as I sat down.

"Nothing you haven't seen from the outside in," he said as kindly as he could. His bulbous eyelids twitched, the cigar working up and down between his teeth, caught in his grouper-like lips. The sweet spicy smell of the cigar calmed me. "A fungal bomb that misfired, like we said. It hit the glass and stone of the dome and formed a substance . . . well, unlike anything I've ever seen. An interesting effect. And stable. It'll stay there for a long time, or at least for the next four hours." He laughed.

"Almost a piece of New Art all by itself," Sybel said, grinning.

"Beautiful," Duncan said, staring up at it. "Absolutely beautiful."

"Horrible and shocking, I would have thought," Mary said—a distant murmur, a whisper lost in a current of air.

"Quite a climb up there that would be," Sybel said. "I think I could do it, though."

"You'd climb a rainbow if you could," I said, earning a half-hearted scowl.

I tore my gaze from the ceiling. I had to. Otherwise my thoughts would have remained up there, trapped, during the entire opera. (It stunned me to see such a thing aboveground. It reinforced a thought that had come to me more and more frequently during the war: if that which belonged belowground came aboveground, why should I remain aboveground? I was like a sailor who falls overboard and reaches for the light, only to find that the light is false, and he has descended into even greater depths.) And yet, haven't we all seen things much stranger since the beginning of the Shift? Thinking of that ceiling now, I'm oddly unmoved. I've been undone by too many miraculous sights, both holy and unholy.

No one had tickets, but that didn't mean we had good seats. Even during the war (especially during the war!), there remained hierarchies, and hierarchies within hierarchies. Lacond could have sat in the orchestra area with one guest, but that would have meant leaving the rest of us behind. Guided to the top row, we had to lower our heads for fear of bumping them against the balcony ceiling (a comforting white, that ceiling, at least). The seats were hard wood—hard indeed for an opera that promised six acts and only one intermission. Above us, the dome; below, the fatal curving lunge down to the ground floor seats (which, from that perspective, seemed to go on forever), then up and through them to the orchestra pit and the stage. The balcony smelled like old rotten books. No one had cleaned it for ages. That which from afar had looked both smooth and spotless was, up close, tawdry and sad. Only Sybel, with his lithe frame, seemed comfortable.

Perhaps I remember the opera so clearly because it was the last time anyone saw so many enemies occupying the same space without trying to stick a literal or figurative knife into one another. Agents from both sides of the conflict attended the opera that night, carefully guided through separate entrances, one of which consisted of a large hole in the wall. Anyone considered neutral had been positioned in the middle section of the ground floor, farthest from the exits. (Which made me laugh—should the two sides lose composure and attack each other, the neutrals in the middle would suffer greatly for their nuanced stance.)

Imperious members of the House Hoegbotton, already resembling scions of Empire in their somewhat presumptuous frocks and pleated trousers—if made a bit cadaverous, cloth sliding off elbows, from having to ration their food—made the forced march to their seats. Fixed stares. A few nervous smiles. Many of them wore medals they had awarded to themselves for wartime bravery.

The Frankwrithe & Lewden side was entirely different. They sidled in, wore mostly black, tried to stay in the shadows—except for their leader, L. Gaudy, who entered in what I can only call a "costume" of bright red, transformed by the green glow of the fungal light to a pulsating, brackish purple. He stood for several minutes, staring over at the Hoegbotton side, hands on his hips. A wide grin had seemingly paralyzed his face. (There was some discussion as to whether this bold figure truly was L. Gaudy, or one of the many actors hired by Gaudy to portray him at official events, the real Gaudy having developed an understandable fear of assassination attempts over the past two years. Regardless of whether it was Gaudy or pseudo-Gaudy, a healthy shiver of fear fled down my spine at his appearance.)

In the neutral section, we saw Martin Lake and his lover Merrimount take their seats, surrounded by the remnants of the New Artists, all looking rather tattered and downcast. (Their day was done. No opera could resurrect them.)

Martin and Merrimount had chosen to wear half evening gown, half formal suit, and I could almost smell the aggressive cologne that had become Martin's "signature smell," even though his sponsorship of it gained him no monies during the war. (You make it sound like an actual ceasefire, this opera. Janice, we were all armed to the teeth, like pirates sailing down the River Moth looking for a ripe place to build a city. You couldn't move through the hallway toward the restrooms without bumping into someone's concealed bulge of a gun or knife, or worse. And when you did get to the men's room, it was full of spies exchanging information.)

We took the sadly amateurish hand-printed playbills off our seats and sat, Lacond still occluding all sight of Mary on the other side. In the expectant green light, the muted chatter of people still entering the opera house, the pauses in conversation as three or four times it appeared the opera was about to begin, I had a glimpse, an echo, of my former life. For an instant, sitting there, my buttocks rapidly beginning to ache from the hard seat, I had the illusion that I had conjured up the resources, out of full-on ruin, to create an opera. For just that period between taking our seats and curtain rise, I felt powerful again. An awful feeling. I could see Edward's slack face in the insane asylum, feel the ribbon of red rising from my wrist. I did not want that life back, not really.

Besides, the illusion was ruined anyway by a brief encounter on the way to the bathroom before the opera began. Narrowed and wrinkled by the years, Merrimount's jester face suddenly came into view.

He nodded and said, "Did you have anything to do with this opera, Janice?"

"No," I said. "Not me." Caught. Accused.

"Ah, right," he said. "I thought maybe you had." A pause, and then, "Do you think this is what the New Art has all been leading up to? An insane opera performed during wartime?" His smile was all teeth, and then he was gone.

I hated the elation that made my face flush, brought out a little shiver of happiness. Merrimount had talked to me. (Very sad, sister.)

I told Duncan about the encounter, across Sybel's thin chest and Lacond's broad belly, and before he could respond, out of the darkness I heard Mary say, "If so, it's been a waste. Everything leading up to this one performance. They should have saved it up for after the war."

I laughed, and Sybel, like a good former manager, said to Mary, "Merrimount means that except for him, Martin, and Janice, every member of the former New Art movement of any consequence is involved in this opera. It's the only thing they've been able to agree on long enough to bring to the public attention."

Mary nodded, held her tongue. She knew Sybel didn't like her, and she knew Sybel didn't like her because I didn't like her.

"Admittedly, a captive audience," Duncan said, "with nothing else to do except hunker down in their homes."

"True," I said. "I suppose there is a hint of desperation in it."

Desperation during those days could not be hidden at the opera. In such close quarters, the truth of our diets would begin to manifest as a sour smell of stale bread and vegetable broth and, oddly enough, doorknobs. Some enterprising individual had discovered that many of the doorknobs in the city had been made from sawdust and ox blood. If heated and distilled, a doorknob could be eaten, given an extremity of hunger.

"Martin and Merri are living on the kindness of friends and neighbors, you know," Sybel said.

"If he's painting at all," Duncan said, "it's with borrowed canvases and stolen paints. He'll get the odd job here and there, but work must be scarce."

"Yes it is, my dear Duncan," I heard Mary whisper, "but you don't need to worry."

He didn't need to worry because Mary's parents had conspired to acquire an apartment for her out of the way of both the local Hoegbotton and F&L militias, in an area that had not yet been the target of attacks or skirmishes. Mary, meanwhile, had yet to realize that, having taken Duncan in, she might have more worries than the average person where the gray caps were concerned. (She had less to worry about. Trust me. I protected her well.)

My gaze burned through the darkness that protected Mary.

"What are your plans after the war?" I asked Duncan.

Was that the hint of a smile on my brother's face?

Mary answered for him, making Sybel sit up and pay attention, as if he had a bet riding on the answer: "The same as now. To continue my studies. To write books, like Duncan's."

Well, it was true that she continued her studies during the war. In fact, the war often had no impact on her whatsoever, not emotionally. But she didn't want to write books like *Duncan's*. She wanted to write books *like* Duncan. That became clear soon enough.

A hush fell over the audience. The lights could not dim, but the curtain could rise. It chose that moment to do so. I could either stare into the now silent darkness or turn toward the stage.

The curtain rose. The green light was very much like the green light in this place, as I type this afterword. Here, I am on the stage. There, I was part of the audience.

Not that there's much difference.

The opera began.

Despite Gallendrace's valiant efforts, it soon became clear that the opera would be a rather muddied affair. What more could one expect under the circumstances, hampered by lack of funds, lack of time, donated costumes and sets, and the short-age of many other supplies? But a certain unnecessary complexity also wreaked havoc with the production—too many parts and not enough actors. Further, men played most of the female parts and women played most of the male parts, which created a dissonant musical effect, tenors and sopranos popping up in the most unexpected places. It became increasingly difficult to keep track of all but the most major characters.

Still, the main story line had the kind of familiarity that is difficult to lose in translation, especially when you're in the middle of the conflict in question. As in real life, the opera carefully related the particulars of a deadly war between merchant families.

To put it plainly, what hawkish Sirin had anticipated so accurately was an economic invasion of Ambergris by Frankwrithe & Lewden, the type of invasion that only coincidentally results in bloodshed. For years, the constant pressure exerted by Hoegbotton & Sons on F&L in their home markets around Morrow had hindered Frankwrithe's attempts to expand into Ambergris—although a tenuous toehold had been gained through influence on Antechamber book bannings and through bookstores large enough to ignore Hoegbotton intimidation. However, mere months before my enlightening trip to Morrow, F&L had managed to take over its governance from a failed monarchy, in the process issuing a decree banning all Hoegbotton agents and imports from the city. Hoegbotton found itself unable to mount an effective counteroffensive. (In part, F&L took advantage of H&S's temporary shift of attention to trains and railways, a fixation that emanated from Henry Hoegbotton, the hoary but clever patriarch of the Hoegbotton clan. Henry Hoegbotton—of whom not enough has been written; if not for my present circumstances, I would attempt the biography myself—had hoped for an era of economic domination over all of the South, to the very tip of the last atoll of the Southern Isles, and all of the North, including the frozen Skamoo in their spackly ice huts. Many experts speculated that Hoegbotton might then wage "a holy war of commerce" against the closed markets of the Kalif's empire. However, such a vision required Hoegbotton to overextend itself so much that it became unable to effectively respond to a threat like being banned from Morrow.)

This new vision on the part of F&L explained the large numbers of their operatives that had dominated my view from the window of my (comfortable, furnished) prison(-like) cell. Emboldened by victory at home, F&L sought to bring their trade downriver, staking their chances not only on their diversification into a superior brand of typewriter, the Lewden Model II—a version of which I am typing on now and which I swear and sweat by; if only this fungus would not keep nibbling on the accursed keys—and long-distance telephone services. In fact, many infiltrations of Ambergris began as the result of F&L agents installing telephone poles: not only did F&L inject liquid explosives into hollow portions of these poles, but the installers themselves formed a secret army of espionage in the city. F&L also funneled more and more funds into Ambergrisian banks, hoping to create influence in those quarters.

Hoegbotton, naturally, resisted, and matters came to a head over Sophia's Island, a curling finger of an atoll located north of Ambergris in the middle of the River Moth. The "Sophia" of Sophia's Island was none other than the wife of Ambergris's founder, Manzikert I—they had used it as a summer residence many hundreds of years ago. Now, it occupied a strategic position in the northern trade routes: whoever controlled the island could levy all sorts of tariffs, and use the island as a storeroom to boot. An obscure lease on the island had been given to the rulers of Morrow, the Menite Kings, as a thank-you for their aid to Ambergris during the Silence. Despite the fall of the Menite Kings, the lease had never been withdrawn, and Frankwrithe & Lewden used it as pretext to lay claim to the island, with predictable results. The conflict that had begun on the island had spread to Ambergris, and had probably been an excuse to initiate open warfare.

The opera attempted to convey the entire origin of the conflict in song using a motley collection of servants, bankers, merchants, and soldiers—a chorus of voices that stumbled ragged about the stage—while a forbidden love affair between members of the Hoegbotton and Frankwrithe clans—a plot device old long before Voss Bender took his first, tottering steps—played out in the foreground. A subplot involved two servants, one from each clan, and the odd appearance of a man from the Nimblytod Tribes, who observed from on high (in this case, two boxes set atop each other), and provided sporadic narration—much to the disgust of Sybel, who muttered to me about "stereotypes." The ghost of Sophia Manzikert also made many an appearance, fated to roam her beloved island as all manner of skullduggery occurred around her, and she unable to stop it.

A hail of catcalls and whistles abused the singers when Sophia's Island first appeared as a series of earth-colored potato sacks stitched together and held up by men dressed in black who were still, tragically, visible in the green light. As the island sailed toward the singers rather than the other way around, atonal booing drowned out the voices coming from the stage.

Pieces of the music had clearly been stolen from Bender's *Trillian*, as might be expected with Gallendrace in charge. The orchestra was short a flutist, his place taken by a rather aggressive whistler. (In fact, the entire orchestra sounded like the "scrittling, scratching brittlings of a skeleton crew," as one wag put it.) A few holes in the floor of the stage—apparently there had been no time to repair them—resulted in Sophia's ghost at one point pitching headfirst into the orchestra pit, much to the delight of the audience, which stood and clapped. (We might have been glad to have an opera during wartime, but that didn't mean we had given up our essential nature as Ambergrisians.)

The (almost) corresponding holes in the curtain made scene breaks tantalizing, and scandalous, in that the audience could see the flash of thigh and buttock in the frenetic thrashing of costume changes. The set changes proved much less dramatic, as Gallendrace had chosen to use the set to suggest rather than illustrate, letting unpainted wooden boxes and other unconcealed objects serve as placeholders for the imagination.

Still, it was a passable attempt at an opera. The orchestra lurched on even after Sophia fell on top of them. The singers had good voices—they had convinced the great retired baritone Samuel Rail to make a short appearance. However, the hole in the ceiling, even clogged with fungus, changed the acoustics in such a way that sometimes those voices came to us profoundly curdled or twisted; at times, I felt as if I were hearing the voices of gray caps, not human beings at all.

Halfway through the second act, my legs beginning to fall asleep, I turned in my seat and looked back. Some ten rows behind us, I caught a glimpse of Bonmot with some of the teachers from Blythe Academy. I waved; he waved back. I was inspired for a moment to go talk to him, perhaps even join them—after all, Duncan had his Mary and Lacond had his Duncan, and Sybel was too busy being angry about the depiction of his people to be of much use to me. But it was then that Sophia fell into the orchestra pit, and as I turned back to watch the ensuing chaos, the moment was lost. By intermission, Bonmot had left for some reason (along with several others in the audience!), although not before Mary had made a great show of going over and talking to him, abandoning Duncan for several minutes. (She didn't do it to *hurt* me, Janice, but to *help* me. She worked hard to try to repair the rift, thought that a ceasefire for the warring Houses might also mean a ceasefire for House Bonmot and House Duncan, but it was not to be.)

After intermission, the set design devolved even further, and the plot became ever more ludicrous, featuring a plethora of ghosts, and even an appearance by a wingèd fairy—a device so pathetic I thought violence might break out. The singers desperately tried to cover for these faults with stellar, sometimes over-the-top performances, voices drowning out voices, dissonant not in their individual talents, but as a group.

By the middle of the fourth section, I seemed to have missed some essential act of communication. I had lost the thread of the narrative, I suppose. Actors dressed in deep red uniforms identical to those favored by the Kalif's soldiers began to appear on the stage, to much clapping and cheering from all of us. Finally, some real costumes! Some spectacle to satiate our lust for pomp. They poured onto the stage in a tight pool, almost as if a bottle of wine had overturned and leaked across a table. In their midst, we saw the white turban of a Kalif's commander as he fired his guns across the stage with a great crack and recoil. The audience roared once more, for he presented a fine sight on that stage, singing or not singing, with his dark beard and mustache, his piercing gaze.

He aimed at a singer and s/he fell—Sophia again, poor Sophia, so fated to fall. The leak of blood, miniature mimic of the soldiers' progress, that spread across the front of Sophia's white dress, had the effect of renewing our love for the opera. Such melodrama! Such an authentic battle scene!

From the rising screams and shouts onstage, we naturally expected one clear soprano or alto would rise above, drawing together the threads of chaos. The Kalif's men would drop their guns and swords. They would become part of a great chorus of voices, or a powerful counterpoint. The lovers would reunite. The houses would reconcile. The curtain would fall, then rise again, that our applause might become more specific, rewarding our favorites.

But none of these things happened. Not a one of them.

Instead, the music began to lose its harmony, become discordant, and momentarily returned as strong as ever as a section of foolish woodwinds held their ground. It then dissolved into individual horns and violins before falling away into silence, leaving only the sounds of struggle.

Silence from the audience, for a moment. (Some of us were just glad the musicians had stopped playing.) Finally, we began to understand. We did not know it to be true all at once, and each of us reached our conclusions separately. But understanding did come to us, some with gasps, some with shouts or screams, others in a silence born of dread or amazement. Under the green light, anything was possible, even an invasion.

When the white-turbaned commander drew his sword and cut Sophia's head from his neck and held it, dripping and white, by one gloved hand, we knew any performance had ended minutes before. As we had sat there, watching the opera, the Kalif's troops had invaded Ambergris. (For me, it was a few seconds later, when Sarah Gallendrace appeared onstage, her belly cut wide open, her impossibly pale hands trying to stanch the flow. That's when I unfroze.)

The flag of the Kalif was unfurled on the stage. The moat created by the orchestra pit became so cluttered with the most unmusical of things—dead, hacked-apart people and the remnants of the set, cleared with methodical precision—that it was no great leap for some of the soldiers to bridge it and start firing into the audience.

Now, in the most orchestrated event of the entire evening, House Hoegbotton and House Frankwrithe & Lewden gave their reply. It was animal, guttural, and in almost perfect unison. With a great shout of both outrage and fear, out came guns previously hidden. Out came the knives, the swords. While the neutrals—I saw Martin and Merrimount running for an exit—tried to extricate themselves from their now utterly indefensible position, Hoegbotton and Lewden, Hoegbotton and Frankwrithe, came together in a unity of purpose. You could see it in their eyes, that, for a time, all differences would be laid aside to defeat a common enemy. They poured up toward the stage, firing, stabbing, while the Kalif's soldiers, under the calm command of their leader, laid down a murderous fire. Bodies fell in the aisles, cut to pieces. The smell of blood and gunpowder rose from the stage. Billowing smoke, caught and distorted in the green light. The utter panic and dissolution of those who had never thought their night might end like this, some in their distress running back and forth as if caged, unable to find their way out.

Those of us in the balcony seemed to have a better chance than most, unless the front entrance lay blocked. We began to make our way to the stairs and down. We were much calmer than those on the ground floor. Just as the stage had, during the performance, been remote from our rarefied location, so too the violence. We had the sense of it spreading slowly, the stain of the Kalif's soldiers like some natural force, one that had its own rhythm of invasion, one that would allow us to casually take our leave.

Lacond had pulled his pistols from their ankle holsters. Sybel wielded a particularly deadly looking knife so long I wondered how he'd managed to conceal it. My brother had, in his protectiveness for Mary, let his fungal disease overtake him further, so that one eye lay clear and blue while the other had become overgrown with a green curling substance that magnified its intent and size. His right arm he had allowed to become a kind of fungus club, black and shiny. The look on his face told me he was ready to die for Mary, right there, right then. (And perhaps endure a minor maiming for you and Sybel.)

We took cover behind the battering ram of Lacond, who cleared a path for us by shoving people out of the way. My last glimpse of the stage showed that the Kalif's soldiers had advanced farther into the audience, the Ambergrisian resistance becoming more of a rearguard attempt to let the majority escape, rather than anything resembling an offensive.

Then down the cramped stairs, stinking of sweat, and out the front door into the night, running, all too aware now of the new sound of what would turn out to be the Kalif's mortars, set up to ring the city. Shells hurtled through the air, poorly aimed and indiscriminate. (We knew them as the Kalif's because the unique sound had no parallel to H&S weapons. And unlike F&L bombs, they did not become a writhing explosion of fungi and spores. They just smashed into things and sent shards of those things crackling across the space between, then lay inert. Why we feared those mortars more than the weapons of the Houses, I do not know. Perhaps the sheer unfamiliarity of them. We had grown accustomed to our other assailants.)

And that was our night at the opera, which I remember more clearly than all the rest.

It had been a strange, strange war long before the opera—two years of watching Ambergris, like some sun-drenched, meat-gorged reptile, make one of its random attempts to molt, to shed its skin, to become something new. All across the city, from the narrow alleys of the ruined Bureaucratic Quarter to the wide bustle of Albumuth Boulevard, we could sense it coming. Odd alliances formed under stark orange skies. The vertical invasion of telephone poles, for example, once a random dotting, had become a concerted march from the docks into the city's scaly white underbelly. Guns poured in with the telephones, both originating from the Kalif's empire (although often by way of F&L's agents, already gathering in the city, fly-thick and as black-swarming). The guns came in every size and description, most of them oddly bulky and gleaming with the kaleidoscopic reflection of unknown metals. They smelled both new and old at the same time, smelled of far-off places, as if the metal had soaked up the essence of the foundries and factories that had produced them. The guns frightened me. They seemed like an emanation from some future Ambergris, some place that did not yet exist, but soon would.

Outdoor café life became charged with danger and interruptions. Shootings and stabbings became all too frequent. (The novelty of guns was too much temptation for the average Ambergrisian.) Motored vehicles began to reemerge—dark, dank metallic beetles long dormant—as new Hoegbotton resources brought barrels of sticky black fuel into the city.

The very air smelled different—it had a charged quality, as if we were all breathing tiny particles of gunpowder; our lungs burned even without the impetus of pollen in the spring, and, in the fall, even on days when the air wasn't cold and dry. (This was not your imagination—the spore content of the city began to change, to be transformed. The gray caps had begun the process of slow but inexorable translation/transformation that would culminate in the Shift.)

At the time, none of us thought much about these changes. Ambergris, for all its history, its secrets, its allure, had always been dirty, sickly, on the verge of crumbling back into itself—battered, babbling, incoherent in its design and intent. We all thought that, ultimately, the molt wouldn't take, and the reptile that was the city would sink back into the mud a little, its skin ever more mottled from the experience.

Into this strangeness, this bubble of trapped amber, in which everything and nothing was happening all at once, the war intruded. Suddenly, what had seemed random had form and structure: it was Us against Them: a Hoegbotton many of us could not tolerate against Frankwrithe & Lewden, an Other that was far worse: an invader, usurper, the likes of which we had not known since the Kalif's temporary Occupation generations before.

It was in this atmosphere that we became reporters for *The Ambergris Daily Broadsheet* under the guidance of the *Broadsheet*'s editor and publisher, James Lacond.

Duncan, in the absence of Mary—still, in those early days of the war, imprisoned by the two-semester ban—decided to take it upon himself to visit Lacond and make the arrangements with him. I can't say I minded Duncan going instead of me. I had made some inquiries about Lacond and discovered a man of many vices—he smoked at a ridiculous rate, he drank, often while on the job, he swore constantly, and he sometimes participated in the dangerous fungal drug trade. (All vices you once possessed, Janice!)

At first, Duncan found Lacond to be cantankerous and irritating. He seemed unable to understand the value of adding us to his stable of broken-down journalistic nags. However, he had met Duncan before, read his work, and even reviewed one of his books in the past, and that made him warm to us. (Warm to me. I don't know if he ever really warmed to you. It certainly wasn't your fault—he was, without much doubt, a blustery old fart. The day I went to see him, James had already begun a downward spiral. I think this is why he wound up liking me when we got to know each other better. He saw in me a fellow lost soul, an underachiever, a candidate for an early reputational grave. As I was to find out, I had crossed his path as his expectations were decaying—journalism was as much a low point for him as for us. When I came upon him—bloated, red-nosed, squat, a cigar in his mouth—setting type for the printing presses that clacked and rattled and sobbed behind him, I sensed a stubbornness, a refusal as yet to acknowledge his fate. He was talking fast, his stubby fingers working the type in and out of position with an unexpected grace. The man liked plain shirts, over which would hang striped suspenders, holding up pants that he tucked into short boots. He often muttered to himself—always muttering to himself as long as I knew him, whether about the price of ink or the vagaries of typefaces.

("What do you want?" he asked, never looking up from his work. He didn't need to look up. I could guess our connection from the faint black stippling around his chin, his ears. He had been underground. And when he finally did look up, he recognized the same in me. After that, any reluctance on his part was mere economics.)

For Lacond, by fate or fortune, or both, was the founder of the Ambergrisians for the Original Inhabitants Society, a historical organization known for its outlandish theories and high fatality rates. As Duncan wrote in his *Early History of Ambergris* several years later:

> Never has membership in a historical society been so fraught with peril. Every two or three years, another few members succumb to the temptation to pry open a manhole cover and go spelunking among the sewer drains. Inevitably, someone gets stuck in a drainpipe and the others go for help, or the gray caps, presumably, catch them and they disappear forever. One imagines the helpful AFTOIS members waving their official membership cards at the approaching, unimpressed gray caps. When not conspiring to commit assisted suicide, the AFTOIS publishes *The Real History Newsletter*.

This newsletter would later become Duncan's eccentric flagship as he led a fearless crew of "fringe historians" into the uncharted and unclaimed waters of Oblivion. These hardy men and women subsisted at the far reaches of popular acclaim and derived what little sustenance they could from peripheral mentions in the lesser-known broadsheets and journals—lingering in the brackish backwaters of footnotes in papers by their more famous colleagues. (Mary's footnotes would eventually take on this preservative quality, often the only extant mention of any number of historians, myself included. Although some felt gratitude, for most living in the margins proved a grim and unfulfilling existence.)

Our dad loved historians, of course, but he had always hated journalists. He considered them the juvenile, larval stage of the historian, and as with certain reptilian or insect species that eat their own young, he believed they should be done away with for society's greater good. I remember he used to call journalists "Historians without the wisdom of perspective."

As Duncan used to say, though, after the war, "Father was wrong. Journalists are just frightened people with notepads who are trying very hard not to get killed." It was, paradoxically, a boring time, what with all the running around. All we did was skulk and hide, then run somewhere. Record what we saw—the aftermath of an explosion, an outbreak of illness, a battle—run somewhere else. Hide. Report. Run. Hide. Report. Run.

"Bring me the story!" Lacond used to bellow from his chosen spot behind the typesetting machine. "There's a story out there—find it now!"

Even as, some weeks, he was reduced to paying us for those stories with bread, vegetables, and milk.

Bring me the story! This command became our lives. Rather than a slow, bleary-eyed stagger down to the gallery, my day would begin—in the deepest part of the night—with the telephone ringing. I would fumble for the phone, offer a mumbled "Hello?" A voice, usually Lacond's, sometimes his assistant, would whisper "123 So-and-so Street—there's been a bombing." If the phones weren't working, it would be a knock on the door from a runner, usually Sybel, who'd taken the job because there was nothing else for him in the city. Where once Sybel had dressed outrageously, now he wore clothes that allowed him to blend right into the wall. "To each time and place its own apparel," he told me. "Not that I don't miss the bad old days." (Miss them? He was still *living* them. Acting as a runner for a broadsheet gave him a certain amount of neutrality in sections of the city critical for him to reach if he wanted to continue providing "substances to those who desire them," as he was fond of saying. It certainly made it more convenient for Sybel to slip me my "peace of mind," as he called the tincture I required. As for Sybel's wartime clothes, they hardly taxed his skill at camouflage. You should have seen what he wore while in his natural element, the trees. Except . . . you *couldn't* see him there.)

I would then rush into a shirt and trousers—the only practical clothes for a woman in such circumstances—shove big black boots over cold feet—and careen out the door, pen and notebook clutched in one hand. In my pants pocket, the dried mushrooms Duncan had given me. If a spore bomb exploded near me, I was to swallow them as an antidote. Of course, this only helped against F&L's unconventional weapons. I would still be vulnerable to the shrapnel bombs of H&S.

I cannot think—through all of our transformations of position, location, and function—of a change more bone-crunching than that which made us reporters. I had never counted physical endurance among my attributes, but now I had to call on hidden reserves almost every day. I kept spraining my ankles, too, whether running toward a story (or away from one that had proven too hostile), walking across an uneven island of pavement disfigured by fungi, or fighting to avoid being trampled by a mob of fleeing citizens. Eventually, I wrapped both ankles in bandages before I went out, hoping that the extra support would help.

Considering the ease with which death had found our father, it can only be luck that saved us. Sometimes, as we stared at the smoldering remains of a grocery store, the clerks reduced to red ash, the stench unbearable, I wondered if I wasn't trying to kill myself all over again.

(If so, then the entire city was trying to kill itself. One of the strangest things about the war for me was the calm in the midst of violence that sometimes came over people—a state of grace, or denial, perhaps. I can remember watching from one end of a street as a fungal bomb blew up a few blocks away. It was one of those hideous creations that, dissolving into a fine purple mist, travels forward from the impetus of the blast and enters the lungs of anyone in its path, making of them brittle statues that disintegrate at the slightest touch or breath of wind. I ducked into a side alley, even though I was already immune—the purple mist would encounter and be neutralized in my lungs by the green mist already residing there—and watched as people ran by, screaming. There was no help for them, no help I could give. Across the street, though, I saw a man in a long overcoat standing calmly by a lamppost. He had on thick glasses and he had covered his nose and mouth with a mask of cloth. As the mist washed over him, bringing with it the usual, if incongruous, smell of limes and lemons, he did not panic. He just stood there. As others were brought up short in midflight, rendered motionless, their eyes rolling into their sockets, a light purple fuzz hardening on their lips and eyebrows, crawling up their legs, this man stood there for a moment, and then went on about his business. Over time, as more and more precautions were taken, you would see people going about their daily lives with a calm, with a sense of peace, that astounded me. Only in Ambergris! For, incredibly enough, very few people fled the city during the war. Stockton and Morrow combined received no more than a few thousand refugees.)

Poor Duncan, meanwhile, had different afflictions. His seasonal fungal diseases intensified under the stress, until he jokingly said to Lacond that at times he could lean against a fungus-covered wall and no one would see him. His trench coat grew oddly empty or full depending on the virulence of the attack, a hat hiding most of the tendrils that insisted on colonizing his scalp. Thick coatings of cologne helped disguise the reek of decaying mushroom matter—at least until the second year of the war, when so many people had contracted their own fungal diseases that disguise was no longer necessary. (Often, Janice, I was flexing my newfound control of my affliction. My changes in shape, in density, were but responses to the spores in my immediate surroundings. They were how I defended myself—and, not coincidentally, *you*. Although sometimes I was hiding an awfully big gun under my coat; some threats are best met with bullets.)

But this was not the full extent of my brother's handicap. The rest, in those early days, was expressed by his longing for Mary to return to him. I can remember the two of us running down a deserted alley, my swollen ankles killing me, Duncan's disease in full bloom—tendrils of bright green fruiting bodies shooting forth from his hatless head like flares signaling the enemy—while behind us, through the billowing smoke of an H&S grenade attack, some dozen F&L irregulars chased us, intent on making us pay for someone else's transgression . . . and as we ran, Duncan wrote a love letter to Mary—a jotted phrase or two at a time, scribbled on a thrice-folded piece of paper. One such "letter" ends, "Must wrap this up, my love! Would like to write more, but am late to an appointment." Truff knows how he smuggled them into Blythe Academy and, later, Mary's parents' house.

Blythe Academy stayed open for one and a half of the two semesters Mary needed to complete her degree, although the professors and priests continued to use it as a safe haven after the students had been sent home. For the coursework

Mary and all the students in similar straits still needed to complete, Bonmot made weekly rounds to their parents' houses. Typical of him, he ignored the danger implicit in crossing barricades and encountering militia checkpoints. I imagine him, solid, strong, in his green robes, walking down the street, impervious to the bloodshed occurring all around him. To be a priest during that war required a certain amount of dissociation from the real world.

I knew what it was like to lead such a life—it conferred an illogical form of *immunity* by forcing you to become separate from your surroundings. You *had* to separate yourself, pull yourself out of the context swarming all around you. There was no choice. To allow yourself to become part of it would have meant a kind of death. (Odd you should think that, Janice, because most of the time, while not attending to my job, I was fleshing out theories of history at odds with that opinion. To me, the events of the war—the chaos—mimicked the worst qualities of my precarious relationship with Mary. My own body seemed able to express emotion through transformation. As I felt, so the world around me felt, or vice versa. I did not, of course, believe that my mental turmoil created the conflict—this was a metaphorical connection only, but no weaker because of it. Would it not be true, I began to think, that a historian could best explain those periods of history that most closely imitated the events or significant emotions of his own life?)

I'm sure some of the regulars here at the Spore of the Gray Cap remember the insanity of the war—there are certainly enough gray beards and grizzled voices among them. Even this green glass that provides my only light beyond candles— this glass that distorts the quick, rhythmic stride of walkers making floorboards creak, the random punctuation of a cane—has experience of the war: it was caused by clear glass fusing with a fungal bomb. The result is beautiful, if unintentional. (And since the glass seems to shift and re-form every so often, who knows if an end result has yet been reached? Perhaps it is transforming into something else altogether.)

But the intensity or scope of the conflict never gave me pause—it was the nature of the weapons. It was as if the gray caps had come aboveground in disguise and started to slaughter us. Guns now shot fungal bullets that, upon hitting flesh, burrowed deep into arteries and created thoroughfares of spores that hardened within seconds, making the victim as brittle as any coral from the Southern

Isles. Certain special fungi could serve as bombs or mines or grenades, decomposing a body in seconds, or releasing spores that choked the victim to death. Telephones soon became dangerous, used as the emissaries of assassination—the victim would pick up the phone only to hear a high-pitched scream that burst the eardrums and the heart (said screams very similar to those attributed to the giant "gray whale" mushrooms that became common in Ambergris immediately prior to the Silence). Henry Hoegbotton's brother Frederick died in this manner, as did several other merchants. (Did F&L realize what they were doing when they found a way to procure such weapons from the gray caps? Probably not. They probably didn't have a clue. They just wanted results.)

One of our first joint reports dealt with the issue of the new weapons.

BOMBS ARE BREAD
by D. J. Shriek

This past weekend, a disturbing new fact has come to light regarding the weapons being used by House Lewden: they can be eaten. In certain parts of the Merchant Quarter, which has sustained heavy bombing damage in recent weeks, citizens have been hunting through the rubble not for other survivors or the bodies of loved ones, but for the bombs themselves.

Dr. Alan Self, a physician employed by a House Hoegbotton militia, confirms this information. "I don't know how it started, but because of the food shortage in parts of the city, starving people have begun to eat the remains of House Lewden's infernal fungal bombs," he said.

The core of these bombs does not explode, but serves as the delivery system for the bomb—ballast, of a sort. The ballast is high in protein and appears to have no harmful side effects, as of yet.

Some kinds of fungal bullets appear to share these properties.

"They have a short half-life," according to Sarah Mindle, one of many Hoegbotton employees recruited to fight in the increasingly confused civil war. "After about five hours, most of them become inert, harmless."

High in nutritional content, these bullets are also being harvested by the poor and those cut off from food by the barricades and militias of the various warring factions. Of course, finding the bullets can be hazardous. Knowing when they have become harmless requires yet another set of skills.

"I wait until [the bullets] lose their purple tinge," Charles Jarkens said. Jarkens is a homeless man whose wife died in a bombardment at the beginning of the war. "I wait for that, and I wait until they get a little orange around the base of the bullet. That's when I know they're good to eat."

In an unverified and extreme case, a family whose son was killed by a barrage of such bullets resorted to removing them from the body and eating them.
What no one can as yet explain is exactly how House Lewden procured such weapons, nor why Hoegbotton & Sons have not yet deployed captured weapons against F&L. Some speculate that the blockade of Ambergris by F&L ships has led to such a reduction in food stores for Hoegbotton's various militias that the Lewden weapons are, in fact, being deliberately detonated for use as food.

As might be expected, such incendiary stories led to Lacond's offices being bombed so many times that he eventually moved his printing presses, under cover of night, to a secret location in the forests outside of Ambergris.

"Let them stop me now!" he would say, face flushed with defiance. "Those pompous, homicidal swine can blow me up as much as they like—the presses will keep churning out the pages!" (The war, I must say, revitalized Lacond for a time.)

While the fuel lasted, motored vehicles brought the broadsheet in every morning, and fast runners—usually boys and girls from ten to fifteen years of age, the only group with the stamina for the job who had not already been conscripted by the Hoegbotton militias—would distribute it to a few safe or neutral locations, where it instantly sold out. Distribution was dangerous, and sometimes our runners did not come back. Sybel kept at it for a time, but it wore on his nerves.

"I can't take it," he said one morning. Dark circles had formed around his eyes and he had developed a habit of blinking rapidly, his left hand subject to uncontrollable quivering no matter what his mood. "I can't take it. I can't take it." (What he couldn't take was working so many jobs at once. Although he did have several disturbing episodes involving either militia members who robbed him at gunpoint, or bombs.)

Lacond had come to love our work by this time, so he let us use Sybel for our personal missions, which didn't mean he was in any less danger—just a different kind.

"You must be doing a good job," Lacond said once, while all three of us sat on the floor of his office, sweaty and exhausted. "Both sides want your heads on a platter."

Thus, it became wiser for us to publish our reports under pseudonyms like Michael Smith and Sarah Pickle. I even began to sleep in different locations, seldom returning to my apartment for fear of a fungal bullet to the back of the head.

And yet, on certain days, in certain parts of the city, you could walk down a dozen streets and not even realize a war was going on—if you could rationalize the mortar fire as thunder. Markets were open, people walked to work, the telephones operated (even if few wanted to use them), restaurants served what food they had. The Religious Quarter, for political reasons, remained largely safe, with both H&S and F&L doing a respectable trade in foodstuffs and clothing—sometimes while fighting raged only a few blocks away. (War was also an opportunity for the native tribes, the Dogghe in particular, to make a killing supplying food and collaborating with the enemy—either enemy.) A few times, I was even able to meet with artists and gallery owners, regaining a little respect from them because of my new profession.

This sometimes sense of safety was in part caused by a retrenchment by both sides following the first seven or eight months of the war. House Lewden's original probes centered on feints to the southeast and southwest, with the aim of control of H&S headquarters and the docks. But after several intense battles, F&L had been restricted to the northern third of Ambergris. They controlled part of the docks and a portion of Albumuth Boulevard, but they could not smash through to H&S headquarters. Recovering from the initial shock, H&S had found the morale and discipline to hold their ground. Thus, the "front" became relatively stable, except for some porousness due to spies, sneak attacks and, eventually, the Kalif's mortar fire. The regularity of it became a kind of comfort. (I was never comforted. The whole conflict had troubled me from the beginning. Just trying to guess the reasons for gray cap involvement bothered me. Never before had they backed one faction over another, or even seemed to recognize the difference between factions—or, if they did understand the difference, to care. Why now should they change tactics? Also, their weapons were everywhere, but *they* were nowhere to be seen.)

Still, it could not go on forever. The city was in real danger of becoming less than a city, of becoming rubble and black smoke and piles of bodies—of becoming twenty different cities that only loosely formed a country called "Ambergris."

Duncan sensed this, but could not really articulate it. (I anticipated it as a feeling deep in my ever-changing body, but could do nothing about it.)

"We're near the end," he said one evening eighteen months into the war, as we sat in the smoldering remains of the Café of the Ruby-Throated Calf. It was more or less neutral ground now that most of it had been destroyed by mortars. At least we could count on no one trying to kill us as we sat there, protected by overturned tables and a few strategically placed shrubs. The service was terrible, but, then, all the waiters were dead.

Duncan was pale but whole, face dark with dirt, a flurry of cuts rubbed red. We were drinking a couple of bottles of Smashing Todd's Wartime Stout, which we had found—miraculously whole under a fallen, splintered door—in an abandoned store.

"Near the end?" I prompted.

"Yes," he said, and took a long pull on his beer. "We're near the end. Something has to give. Someone has to blink. To change. It can't go on this way. It can't."

"It's done a fine job of going on this way for a while now, Duncan," I reminded him. I took a sip of ale. It was warm, almost hot, but the bite of it still tasted good.

"Maybe I mean *I* can't go on this way," he said.

"You mean, being paid in eggs, cauliflower, and milk?" I said.

He laughed, but I knew he was thinking about Mary, always Mary.

How to express the overlap between war and blissful domesticity? For this was the time of Duncan's purest happiness—when, for those few months before they began to tear each other apart, he had Mary's body, her mind, and the little apartment they shared. Mary had come free of her Academy obligations a couple of months before and graduated with honors. Bonmot had no hold over her anymore, except for the hold created by her gratitude. She and Duncan moved into an apartment off Albumuth Boulevard. A nice little arrangement. In his journal he wrote of a contentment that served as a welcome respite from his aboveground and underground adventures, almost as if Manzikert had confessed to enjoying sewing.

> I wake early to make a pot of tea and to cook up some eggs. We have matching placemats but the plates are all mixed up. A few I bought have some kind of whale motif, while others Mary stole from her father's house, and these have a tracery of ivy on them. I like mine better. But the forks are all the same.

It was almost as if he had lost his mind. Didn't he know the Family Shriek is condemned to wander above- and belowground like the most transient of Skamoo nomads? Or like the foraging armies of the doomed infidel Stretcher Jones? (No, I most certainly did not know this, Janice. Until Dad died, we were most assuredly stay-put people. Nothing fated us for a lack of domestic bliss. Besides, without that fragile calm, I don't think we could have survived the war. It's odd what stays with you. *I still* remember the tracery of ivy on those plates she stole, and the pleasure she got from the theft, and the tiny and not-so-tiny cracks that those plates acquired over time from the constant echo of bombardment.)

What for me had always been like quicksilver, the intense heat of a caress that faded from my memory over time, was for him long, and drawn-out, never far from his thoughts. Another typical entry, from several weeks later, read:

> In the morning: sunshine and her. I'm not sure which I'm more enamored of. This freedom after so much heartache seems almost unreal. She's here, in front of me, sleeping. I can watch her as long as I like—catalog the elements of her beauty, from her rose-colored mouth to the fine down above her upper lip to the soft line of her nose to the long lashes that frame her closed eyes to the neck with its delicate glide to the lightly freckled arm that slid out from beneath the sheets during the night. I should wake her. I should. But I can't. She's so peaceful right now, and the world outside is not. I gain strength from watching her like this, and I hope I give it back to her as well when she is awake. I must cut this short—the mortars are going off again, and she is beginning to stir.

(That's a nice entry, if atypical for more than a short while. I almost feel as if I was trying to convince myself with that entry, considering the horrors of the world around us. I went home to her every night after hours of hard, dangerous work. Under even the best of circumstances, I would hardly have made what you would call a stable lover. But with bombs exploding everywhere, screaming shells digging into the street only blocks away, and the random violence of the militias, I was very unstable. There were times when the danger brought us close together, when we didn't need words or other constraints, like it had been back at Blythe. And then it was good. But the rest of the time, I struggled to love her despite the tense, closet-like atmosphere. I admit it—there was no way to preserve the allure of the forbidden, of having to sneak into her room at night. Now I was the man who snored at night and sometimes, choking on the spores in my throat, woke gagging. I think I began to scare her almost from the beginning. This was everything she hadn't seen yet. She wasn't ready for me. She was brave in many ways, but not in that way. And I can't blame her.)

We sat there in the café and watched as, across the street, six Hoegbotton irregulars took up positions behind a stand of trees and began firing into the buildings, from which came spiraling the distinctive crimson bullets that had become known as "Lewden Specials." Two of Hoegbotton's men went down writhing and clutching their chests. An F&L supporter fell from the third story of one of the buildings and landed with a wet thud on the pavement below in a confusing welter of blood and bone.

And we just sat there, watching and drinking our ale. Really, it was tame next to what we had already seen. Really, it was expected. So we sat there for another half hour and talked while men killed each other across the street.

✣

Then, of course, the Kalif invaded during the night of the opera performance, and we suddenly had a new topic to write about.

KALIF'S MEN SURROUND CITY:
OCCUPATION, PHASE II? ONE MAN'S OPINION
D. J. Shriek

The Kalif has in the past given us telephones, guns, and a variety of delicious cheeses. Now, it appears that the current Kalif wishes to give us two things we already have in abundance: bombs and war.

Clearly, the Kalif has forgotten the essential lessons of history. During the first Occupation, before the Silence, the citizens of Ambergris set aside their petty squabbles long enough to thoroughly demoralize and defeat the Western Menace.

Now the Kalif has returned, bombarding the city with mortar fire from the outskirts. Despite a brief foray into Ambergris, apparently for the sole purpose of ruining our enjoyment of a humble but entertaining opera, the Kalif seems generally reluctant to send his troops into our streets. Apparently, he believes he will not need to enter Ambergris, that we will simply capitulate like some Stockton ne'er-do-well.

He may be wrong in this assumption, however. Instead, his actions appear to have united enemies whose only previous commonality was an ampersand.

Along Albumuth Boulevard yesterday, this reporter saw elements of House Lewden's Twelfth Militia and House Hoegbotton's Fifth Irregular Infantry (or the "Filthies," as they're commonly known) moving in concert toward the docks, intent on rooting out any of the Kalif's men unlucky enough to still be in the area.

Besides this circumstantial evidence, respected sources tell this reporter that

Hoegbotton & Sons and Frankwrithe & Lewden may orchestrate a general cease-fire, the main goal of which will be to ensure the Kalif's defeat prior to the resumption of hostilities.

The broadsheets accompanying the Kalif's mortar fire haven't helped the Kalif win much support, either. These odd, half-shredded love letters to our great city indicate that the Kalif has come to "liberate the citizens of Ambergris from chaos and tyranny."

"Frankly," says the typical man on the street (at least typical among those who are still alive and not crawling with fungal bullets), "I thought we were already doing a good enough job of that ourselves. This is our squabble. Between us and those bastards from F&L. The Kalif should stay out of it."

The broadsheets also indicate that "To preserve the rare antiquities and collective wisdom of the Religious Quarter, the Kalif has decided to stepped in and bring an end to the conflict."

"Stepped in," indeed.

Many of us wondered why Stockton, Nicea, and other Southern cities had not intervened in the conflict—after all, their trade was profoundly affected by this split between merchant houses. Now we knew—they had been calling on a higher power, and although it had taken almost two years for that august entity, the Kalif, to take notice, take notice he had. He would have needed little real pretext; after all, in each Kalif's heart must burn the desire for revenge upon our city for earlier defeats.

The scream of the Kalif's mortar fire—often indiscriminate or ill-timed—was a welcome contrast to the whine of fungal bullets, the garrulous chatter of Hoegbotton guns. (As the city was at war, so, by then, was my body. The rumblings of my belly, where fungus fought fungus—much remarked upon by Mary in her less charitable moments—matched the Kalif's invasion. The sharp pains that sometimes annihilated my chest hurt no more or less than the spiraling flight of bullets through the Ambergrisian air.)

Perhaps more insanely, no one paid the Kalif's troops much attention once we knew H&S and F&L had united against them. Even the day they came marching down Albumuth Boulevard on a daylight raid in a long, proud column of red, we ignored them. We had suffered through too much war. Either we could not digest this new threat, or we felt no need to.

This, then, is how things stood that year on the threshold of the Festival.

2

There came a night so terrible that no one ever dared to name it. There came a night so terrible that I could not. There came a night so terrible that no one could explain it. There came the most terrible of nights. No, that's not right, either. *There came the most terrible of nights that could not be forgotten, or forgiven, or even named.* That's closer, but sometimes I choose not to revise. Let it be raw and awkward splayed across the page, as it was in life.

Words would later be offered up like "atrocity," "massacre," and "madness," but I reject those words. They did not, could not, cannot, contain what they need to contain.

Could we have known? Could we have wrenched our attention from our more immediate concerns long enough to understand the warning signs? Now, of course, it all seems clear enough. Duncan had said the war could not continue in the same way for long, and he was right.

As soon as Duncan and I saw Voss Bender's blind, blindingly white head floating down the River Moth two days before the Festival, we should have had a clue.

"There's a sight you don't see very often," Duncan said, as we sat on an abandoned pier and watched the head and the barge that carried it slowly pull away into the middle of the river. A kind of lukewarm sun shone that day, diluted by swirls of fog.

"It's a sight I've never seen before, Duncan," I replied.

F&L had cut apart a huge marble statue of Voss Bender that had stood in the Religious Quarter for almost twenty years and loaded it, piece by piece, onto the barge, displaying a remarkably dexterous use of pulleys and levers. There lay the pieces of Bender, strewn to all sides of his enormous, imperious, crushingly heavy head. About to disappear down the River Moth. As vulnerable-looking in that weak sunlight as anything I had ever seen.

"I wonder what the people who live along the banks of the river will think about it," I said.

"What do you mean?" Duncan asked.

"Will they see it as the demolition, the destruction, of a god, or will they be strangely unmoved?"

Duncan laughed. "*I'm* strangely unmoved."

In part, we had come to the pier to relax. We were both still a little rattled from a close call the day before, when we had arrived at what was supposedly the scene of a bomb attack only to find the bombs exploding as we got there. My hair was dirty and streaked with black from the explosion. My face had suffered half a dozen abrasions. Duncan had had a thumbnail-sized chunk of his ear blown off. Already, it had begun to regenerate, which I found fascinating and creepy at the same time. (Do you want a glimpse of something even more fascinating? The real problem was: it wasn't my ear. That had been blown off a long time before.)

"I think it's sad," I said. "They're carting off all of our valuables, like common thieves."

Until then, F&L had contented themselves with bombing us silly day and night. The steady northward stream of goods, art, and statuary had only started in the past week. It should have been a clear sign that the war was about to change again. After all, F&L, with their fungal mines, bombs, and bullets, seemed to have a direct line to a certain disenfranchised underground group.

"Actually, Janice," Duncan said, as he dipped his ugly toes in the Moth, "I hesitate to try to convince you otherwise, but I think the sight of Voss Bender's head floating vaingloriously down the Moth is very funny. So much effort by old F&L, and for what? What can they possibly think they will do with these 'remains' when they reach Morrow? Rework the marble into columns for some public building? Reassemble the statue? And if so, where in Truff's name would they put it? We hardly knew where to put it ourselves."

"Maybe you're right," I said, "but that doesn't mean it can't be sad, too."

Did I already say that there came to be the most terrible of Festival nights? It burned down the Borges Bookstore. It stopped the war between F&L and H&S. It stopped the love between Duncan and Mary, too. Snapped it. Was no more. Never again. (It brought an end to many things, this is true. But the Festival had nothing to do with ending my relationship with Mary. I caused that all by myself.) There had never been a Festival like it, except, perhaps, during the time of the Burning Sun. There may never be another like it again. (Why would there need to be? Every week since the Shift began, some part of the city is as raw as during Festival time.)

As far as I can remember, our father had never had anything to say about the Festival. (Not true. In his essay "The Question of Ambergris," he wrote [I paraphrase from memory]: "At the heart of the city lies not a courtyard or a building or a statue, but an event: the Festival of the Freshwater Squid. It is an overlay of this event that populates the city with an alternative history, one that, if we could only understand its ebb and flow, the necessity of violence to it, would also allow us to understand Ambergris." Statements like this led me to my explorations of Ambergris. I remember trying to read my father's essays at an early age, and only understanding them in fragments and glimpses. I loved the mystery of that, and the sense of adventure, of the questions implied by what I *could* understand.) However, he did say one or two things about the gray caps. I recall that at the dinner table he would ramble on about his current studies. He had no gift for providing context. He would sit at the table, looking down at his mashed potatoes as he scratched the back of his head with one hand and pushed his fork through his food with the other. There was always about him at these times a faraway look, as if he were figuring something out in his head even as he talked to us. Sometimes, it would be a kind of muttering chant under his breath. At other times he was genuinely talking to us but was really elsewhere. He smelled of limes back then, our mother having insisted he wear some cologne to combat the smell of old books brought back from the rare book room of the Stockton Library. But since he hated cologne, he would cut up a lime instead and anoint himself with its juice. (I enjoyed that smell of books, though, missed it when it was gone—it was a comfortable, old-fashioned smell, usually mixed with the dry spice of cigar smoke. I came to feel that it was the smell of learning, which provoked the sweat not of physical exertion, but of mental exertion. To me, book must and cigar smoke were the product of working brains.)

At one such dinner, he looked up at us and he said, "The gray caps are quite simple, really. I don't know why I didn't think of this before. So long as what you're doing doesn't interfere with their plans, they don't care what you do—even if you cause one of them physical harm. But if somehow you step across the tripwire of one of their 'activities,' why, then, there is nothing that can save you."

(I remember that, too. "Tripwire." A word I'd never heard before he used it. Why did he use that word? It fascinated me. While teaching at Blythe, I used the term in connection with the Silence. Had the Silence been caused by some kind of triggering of a "tripwire," a set of circumstances under which the gray caps thought they could activate their Machine successfully? If so, what particular stimuli might have come into play? Could we predict when another such attempt might be made? And yet, even after the most minute study of ancient almanacs, historical accounts, the works of a number of statisticians such as Marmy Gort, and anything else we could lay our hands on, I still could not divine those finite, measurable values that might have created the ideal conditions. I concluded that the gray caps' extraordinary ability to collect information, coupled with their additional spore-based senses, made it unlikely that we would ever be able to know. This did not stop me from continuing to try. Or continuing to ask the most important question: why build a Machine? And what—exactly—did it do?)

We were to find out during the Festival of the Freshwater Squid that year just what happened when Ambergris collectively sprung a tripwire. For the bad Festival was like the antithesis of the Silence, sent to convince us that any semblance of law in the city was illusory, that it could not truly exist, whether we thought it resided in the palm of an obese, elderly Hoegbotton, a thin, ancient Frankwrithe, or the wizened visage of a Kalif none of us had ever seen.

⚜

The night of the Festival, the sun set red over the River Moth. Most of the crepe paper lanterns that people had set out had already been crushed by rubble or by the motored vehicles of opposing forces. The Kalif's men had stepped up their bombardment of the city from without. They made no pretense anymore of aiming at anything in particular, their bombs as likely to crack open a hospital ward as a Hoegbotton sentry post. Really, it was as random as a heart attack. Why worry about what you cannot defend against? So we walked the streets as calmly as we had before the war, when we hadn't been hunkered down against threats like a fungal bullet to the brain from some trigger-happy F&L recruit.

No, gunfire couldn't get to me. What terrified me as I looked out from my apartment at dusk was the proliferation of red flags.

On the way back from our journalistic assignments that day, before we turned in our now infamous "The Kalif Yearns for Every Ambergrisian's Head" article, the flags of the gray caps had appeared in multitudes—rhapsodies of red that seemed, like the ever-present fungus, always on the verge of forming some pattern, some message, only to fall apart into chaos again.

As we approached Lacond's offices in the late afternoon, the wind picked up. It rattled the gravel on side streets. It brought with it a strange premature twilight, and a smell that none could identify. Was it a smell come up off the river? It seemed bitter and pleasant, sharp and vague, all at once.

The light, as Martin Lake might have said, had become different in Ambergris.

We left Lacond's offices tired and ready for rest, Duncan to his and Mary's apartment, me to my own place much farther down Albumuth Boulevard in the opposite direction. (Not even Lacond could demand we cover the Festival, not that year. The Kalif's troops were an unknown factor—they made us nervous, as had the uneventful Festival the year before.) Sybel had decided to take me up on my invitation and stay with me that night, just in case. Either we'd celebrate the Festival together or defend ourselves against it. (I left ample protections; I'm sorry they were not enough.) We had all been through many Festivals. We were old pros at it. We knew how to handle it.

I had thought about making the trek to our mother's mansion, but Duncan had assured me he could keep her safe. (She was quite safe, for several reasons, not least of which was her location: far enough upriver that the Kalif's men had not requisitioned the house, and far enough from Ambergris that she would come to no harm from the gray caps.)

Dusk had become night by the time Sybel arrived, breathless from running. After I let him in, I bolted the door behind him.

"It's not good out there," he said, gasping for breath. "The trees are too still. There's a silence that's . . . like I imagine what the Silence must have been like."

That was a thought. I felt light-headed for an instant, a conjoined chill and thrill. What if, tonight, we were to experience what the twenty-five thousand had experienced during the Silence, the city to become another vast experiment?

"Nonsense," I said. "It's just another Festival. Help me with this."

We pushed a set of cabinets up against the door.

"That should do it," I said.

Outside, a few dozen drunken youths passed by, shouting as they stumbled their way past.

"Death to the Kalif!" I heard, and a flurry of cursing.

"They'll be lucky if they survive the hour," Sybel said. "And it won't be the Kalif that kills them, either."

"When did you become so cheerful?" I asked.

He gave me a look and went back to loading his gun. We had pistols and knives, which Sybel had managed to purchase from, of all people, a Kalif officer. There was a booming black market in weapons these days. Some wags speculated that the Kalif had invaded Ambergris to create demand for inventory.

Meanwhile, the gray caps had spores and fungal bombs, and Truff knew what else.

"Do you think we're much safer in here?" I asked.

Sybel smiled. "No. Not much safer."

There seemed about him that night more than a hint of self-awareness, mixed with that rarest of commodities for Sybel: contentment. (It was only rare to you because you never saw him in his natural element.)

We didn't board up the window until much later, fearful of losing the thread of what was going on outside. The full moon drooped, misshapen and diffuse, in the darkening sky.

Through that smudged fog of glass, we watched rivulets and outcroppings of the Festival walk or run by. Clowns, magicians, stiltmen, and ordinary citizens with no special talent, who had put on bright clothes and gone out because—quite frankly—in the middle of war, how much worse could the Festival possibly make things? True, without the great influx of visitors from other cities there wasn't nearly the number of people that we had become accustomed to seeing, but Sybel and I still agreed it was a more potent Festival than had been predicted by the so-called experts. (Including us, Janice, in our column in the *Broadsheet*.)

Then the merrymakers began to trail off. Soon the groups had thinned until it was only one or two people at a time, either drunk and careless, or alert and hurrying quickly to their destinations. Every once in a while, something would explode in the background as the Kalif's men kept at it. The bright orange flame of the shuddering explosions was oddly reassuring. As long as it stayed far away from us, that is. At least we knew where it was coming from. (Yes, with all the force of His benevolent, if distant, love.)

Sybel and I sat there looking out the window like it was our last view of the world.

"Remember when we used to host parties in abandoned churches on Festival night?" Sybel said. He looked very old then, in that light, the wrinkles around his eyes and mouth undeniable.

"Yes, I remember," I said, smiling. "That was a lot of fun. It really was."

At least, more fun than the war. I didn't want to return to those days, either, though.

Sybel smiled back. Had we ever been close? I search my memory now, thinking of the glance we exchanged back then. No, not close, but *comfortable*, which is almost more intimate. In the preparations for countless parties, in seeing Sybel day after day at my gallery, a deep affection had built up between us.

"Maybe after the war, I can . . ." The words felt like such a lie, I couldn't continue. "Maybe the gallery can . . ."

Sybel nodded and looked away in, I believe, embarrassment. "That would be good," he said.

We continued to watch the city through our window: that fungi-tinged, ever-changing painting.

Finally, it began to happen, at least three hours after nightfall. A stillness crept into the city. The only people on the street were armed and running. Once, a dozen members of a Hoegbotton militia hurried by in tight formation, their weapons gleaming with the reflected light of the fires. Then, for a while, nothing. The moon and the one or two remaining streetlamps, spluttery, revealed an avenue on which no one moved, where the lack of breeze was so acute that crumpled newspapers on the sidewalk lay dead-still.

"It's coming," Sybel muttered. "I don't know what it is, but it'll happen soon."

"Nonsense," I said. "It's just a lull."

But a chill had crept over me, as it seemed to have crept over the city. It lodged in my throat, my belly, my legs. Somehow, I too could feel it coming, like a physical presence. As if my nerves were the nerves of the city. Something had entered Ambergris. (Creeping through your nervous system, the gray caps' spores, creating fear and doubt, right on schedule. I'd put the antidote in your food, but an antidote only works for so long against the full force of such efforts.)

The streetlights went out.

Even the moon seemed to gutter and wane a little. Then the lights came back on—all of them—but they were fungus green, shining in a way that hardly illuminated anything. Instead, this false light created fog, confusion, fear.

Sybel cursed.

"Should we barricade the window?" I asked.

"Not yet," Sybel said. "Not yet. This might be the end of it, you know. This might . . ." Now it was his turn to trail off. We both knew this would not be the end of it.

We began to see people again on the street below. This time, they ran for their lives. We could not help them without endangering ourselves, and so we watched, frozen, at the window, beyond even guilt. A woman with no shoes on, her long hair trailing out behind her, ran through our line of vision. Her mouth was wide, but no sound came from it. A few seconds later, some *thing* appeared in the gutter near the sidewalk. It tried to stand upright like a person, tottered grotesquely, then dropped all pretense and loped out of sight after the woman. The roar of the Kalif's mortar fire followed on its heels.

"What was that?" I hissed at Sybel. "What in Truff's name?"

Sybel didn't reply. Sybel was whispering something in his native language, the singsong chirp of the Nimblytod Tribe. I couldn't understand it, but it sounded soothing. Except I was beyond being soothed.

Then a man came crawling down the street, shapes in the shadows pulling at his legs. Still he crawled, past all fear, past all doubt. Until, as the Kalif's mortars let out a particularly raucous shout, something pulled him off the street, out of view.

Silence again. I was shaking by that time. My teeth were grinding together. I'd never understood that your teeth could actually grind involuntarily, could chatter when they weren't grinding. Sybel made me bite down on a piece of cloth.

"The sound," he whispered. "They'll hear you." (If they heard you, it is because they "heard" my protections on the door of your apartment—my attempt to help you may have endangered you instead.)

The street lay empty, save for the suggestion of shapes at the edge of our line of sight.

Suddenly, the Kalif's mortar fire, which had been progressing in a regular circle around the city, became erratic. Several explosions occurred at once, quite near us, the characteristic whistle of destruction so banal I didn't even think of it as a threat at first. The ceiling lifted, the floor trembled, dust floated down.

Then nothing for several minutes. Then another eruption of explosions, farther away. On the outskirts of Ambergris, gouts of flame lit up the night sky, whiter than the moon. Slowly, as the fires spread, it became clear that the conflagration was forming a circle around Ambergris.

We watched it spread, silent, unable to find words for our unease.

After a while, Sybel said, in a flat voice, "Did you notice?"

"What?"

"The Kalif's mortars have been silenced."

"Yes, yes they have," I said.

Nothing rational told us that the Kalif's positions had been overrun, but we knew it to be true regardless. Someone or something had attacked the Kalif's troops. And yet not even H&S or F&L would have been foolhardy enough to launch an attack on so unpredictable an evening as Festival night.

That is when we decided to board up the window. Some things should not be seen, if at all possible.

🟦

Shall I tell you Duncan's crime during the Festival, in Mary's eyes? While Sybel and I boarded up my apartment window, Duncan was leading Mary to safety—just not a safety she had expected or particularly wanted. It was not the safety provided by a living necklace of acclaim and warmly muttered praise. It was not the kind of safety that reinforces trust or love. For where could Duncan possibly be safe with the surface in so much turmoil? I think you already know, my dear reader, if you've followed me this far. Some of us read to discover. Some of us read to discover what we already know. Duncan read Mary the wrong way. He thought he knew her. He was wrong. How do I know? His journal tells me so. It's all in there.

I took Mary underground as the Festival raged above. Truff help me, I did. Why I thought this might be a good thing for us beyond ensuring our immediate survival, I don't know. The Kalif's men were too close to our home, and I could sense the gray caps getting even closer. The spores in my skin rose to the surface and pointed in their direction. My skin was literally pulling in their direction, yearning to join them—that was how close to turning traitor my body had become. Besides, some F&L louts were five doors down, beating an old woman senseless. It seemed clear they'd reach our door before long.

"Do you trust me?" I asked Mary. She was pale and shaking. She wouldn't look at me, but she nodded. I don't know if I've ever loved her more than at that moment, as she left everything familiar behind. I kissed her. "Get your jacket," I told her. "Bring the canteen from the kitchen."

And then we set off. The place I meant to take her was underground, yes, but a place rarely inhabited by gray caps. The entrance lay halfway between our home and the F&L thugs. We had to hurry. We were scurrying to a rat hole before the other rats could catch us. I had my greatcoat on, which I had seeded with a few varieties of camouflaging fungi. I was carrying an umbrella for some reason—I don't even remember why anymore. Except I remember joking with Mary about it, to make her laugh, at least a little bit. But she was too scared, frozen. I really think she thought we were both about to die. Thankfully, I was more or less human right then, or she would have been out of her mind with terror. When you can't count on your lover to stay in one consistent shape . . .

We beat the F&L thugs to the entrance by a few minutes—we could hear their cries and catcalls, the swish of their torches, smell the bittersweet decay that coated anyone who handled fungal weapons for too long—but they passed us by as we descended ever deeper into the hole, down a ladder.

"Where are we going?" Mary asked me. I don't know if she really wanted an answer or not. She smelled like fear, her perfume gone sour.

"Keep following me," I told her. To her, it was dark as we came to the end of the ladder and into a tunnel, but my eyes were different than they had been. I could see things she couldn't. I could see markers in the tunnel. I could see colors spiraling out of the dark. I held her hand—cold, and clutching my hand desperately—as we walked through the passageway. It was wet now—we were wading through thick, shallow water, the tunnel beginning to slope downward, so we had to be careful not to slip. Through the darkness, I could see the sightless eyes of certain mushrooms, the fiery green of creeping mosses. We could hear dim, dumb shudders above from some kind of bombing: I remember being, insanely enough, happy to hear that sound. Surely it would make Mary realize we could not have stayed aboveground?

Of course, as a corrective counterbalance, the smell coming from below us was rank, stifling. And then, as if to undo all of my reassurances, there came the sound of scuttling, of scattering. That's when I think her spirit really broke and she began to panic. She pulled away from me, to turn back, to run. I held on to her wrist, would not let go. I had to put my hand over her mouth to stop her from screaming.

"We're lost, my love, if you make a sound," I said. "We're dead. You understand?" She nodded, and I took my hand from her mouth. Her eyes in the dim light were white and wide.

The sounds came from below us, moving fast. Something wanted out. Something wanted to reach the surface. It wasn't my place to stop it even if I could, which I couldn't. There was no time to do anything but what I did: I pulled Mary inside of my greatcoat and pushed her into the side of the passageway, my coat covering both of us, and the coat itself covered with the protective spores. They had begun to take root and form fruiting bodies. I had to hope it would be enough.

The scuttling sound and the smell became more intense. I could tell Mary was still stifling her screams. She was shaking, her body tight against mine. Nothing at Blythe Academy, or in her relatively short life so far, had prepared her for anything like this moment.

Then they were all around us—gray caps, racing up the tunnel, speaking in clicks and whistles. One even brushed against my coat, but they were in such a hurry that they did not stop, and before long there was silence again, save for the echo of their progress to the surface. Something was going to happen tonight; my instincts had been right. It would be much safer belowground than above, because tonight even the gray caps would be on the surface. I shuddered, pulled Mary closer.

"Can you go on?" I asked her.

"I think so," she said, her voice calmer than before.

I've often wondered since if that was the point—if it was in that tunnel, as the gray caps passed by, that she made her decision. If she had decided then that she refused to believe any of it, no matter what she saw. If she was going to disown me, discredit me because of that moment. Or this moment. Or the moment after that. I'll never be sure, but I do wonder. For me, though, the moment was a sweet one: to smell her hair, to feel her next to me, to know we were both still alive, and together.

Meanwhile, in the darkness caused by the boarded-up window, Sybel and I awaited our own fate. We had no recourse to the underground, no thought that it might be safer there than where we were.

Sometimes we heard strange sounds that could not have been real—gurglings and shouts and screams, but oddly twisted, as if distant or distorted. At other times, it sounded as if soldiers fought with swords on the street below. The sound of leafy vines growing and intertwining at great speed. The sound of buildings collapsing—a dull, muted roar, then the sweet exhausted sigh of wood or stone hitting the ground. A smell, sharp yet musty, began to enter the apartment.

Sybel began to rock back and forth, holding his arms over his knees.

"We should leave," he said. "We should get out of the apartment. Find a high place."

"Don't say that," I said. "This is the safest place to be."

Sybel smiled and gave me an odd look. "The Borges Bookstore was the safest place to be, and they burned it down."

Sybel was beginning to scare me.

Something scratched at the outside of the door. A slow, tentative sound. It could have been anything. It could have been the wind. But the breath died in my throat. I realized every nerve in my skin had come alive in warning. I shut my eyes for a long time, as if willing the sound to go away. But it did not. It became louder, gained in confidence, precision. Scrabbling. At the door. At the window. I heard it sniffing the air. Reading our scent. I shivered, caught in the grip of nightmare. If we hadn't boarded up the window, it would have been looking in at us at that very moment.

Sybel moaned, took me by the arm. "Janice, I think we have to leave."

I held the gun tight, so tight my knuckles ached. "But where can we run to, Sybel? And how do we get out of here? I don't think it's possible now."

"Do you think you could slide out of the bathroom window?" Sybel asked.

A knock at the door before I could reply—but not at the height I'd expected; lower, much lower.

I stifled a scream. "It's too close. It can hear us right now. It can hear us talking. It knows what we're going to do." I held the gun like a club. I was no use to anyone. The fear had gotten too far into me. This wasn't like trying to kill myself. I could face the fear of that now, but not this fear—this was too different, too unfamiliar.

Sybel grabbed me by the shoulders, whispered in my ear, "Either we go through the bathroom window or we're dead. It's going to come in here and kill us."

"Yes, but Sybel," I whispered back, "what if there's already one at the bathroom window, too? What if they're already back there?"

Sybel shrugged. There was an odd, fatalistic light in his eyes. "Then it doesn't matter. We're dead. I'll go first. If they get to me, go back into the apartment and lock yourself in the bedroom, and hope dawn comes soon."

I hugged him. I've never been more terrified than at that moment—not even now, writing this account. I don't know what came over me. I'd seen the horrors of war, become clinical and precise in the cataloging of them, but somehow this was more personal.

The thing at the door knocked again. Then it spoke.

In a horrible, moist parody of a human voice, it said, "I have something. For you. You will. Like it."

Was this the first time in Ambergris's history that a gray cap or a creature sent by the gray caps had spoken to a resident of the city? Most assuredly not—history is littered with the remains of those who have had such conversations; at least a dozen, two dozen. And yet, that night more than one hundred people reported having such contacts. What did it mean? At the time, no meaning would have penetrated my fear. (Mostly meant what a clever mimic, a parrot, means: nothing. A lure. Bait. A tripwire. A distraction. Delivered by their drones. Now I wonder if this was another harbinger of the Shift.)

❄❄❄

We made our way to the back of the apartment, to the bathroom. I helped Sybel clamber up to the window. Behind us, the creature with the wet voice was banging on the door like a drunk and making a low gurgling laugh. "Let me in!" it said. "Let me in! I have something for you."

"Quickly," I said to Sybel, as he fumbled with the latch. "Come on!"

Sybel undid the latch. He looked down at me.

"Open it," I said, bile rising in my throat.

I flinched as Sybel opened the window, gun held ready.

Fresh air entered the apartment. Fresh air, the distant sounds of battle, the roar of flames in the middle distance, over the silhouette of rooftops, but nothing else.

Sybel pulled himself through. Then it was my turn.

The creature began to pound on the front door. It began to laugh—great, rippling waves of laughter. Perhaps it was calling to others of its kind. (It was gathering its strength—it had nothing but a collective consciousness; it was but the sum of its spores.)

I stood on the toilet seat and pulled myself up to the window ledge by pushing off against the wall with my left foot. A narrow ledge, a narrow window.

The banging behind me had become splintering.

Sybel offered his hand and pulled me through.

The splintering had become a rending. The door would be broken down within the minute.

Sybel shut the window behind us. The night was glistening with stars masked by patches of fog; there was a chill to the air. The fires on the edges of the city raged on.

Shivering, pistol stuck through my belt, knives in my pockets, as much a hazard to myself as to others, I stumbled out onto the second-floor roof. There wasn't much room. I had to engage in a close shuffling dance with Sybel so we could both leave the storm drain for the roof proper.

Behind us, a muted roar. A shriek. Something I'd never heard before, something I never want to hear again. (No matter where you are now, I'm afraid you'll be hearing it again. What we all heard in that moment of the war was the first groaning, rust-and-flesh-choked stirrings of the Machine. It fed off of that energy. It needed it. Forever after, my finely tuned senses could hear that hum, that vibration, in the ground. It terrified me.)

How do you control your fear at a time like that? I couldn't. I could barely stop from wetting myself. Bombs are different. Reporting is different. This time, I couldn't get outside of myself. I couldn't get outside.

"What now, Sybel?" I asked. I was breathing hard. I think I might have been whimpering.

"Now, we go higher," Sybel said.

Looking at him, I saw a sudden confidence in him that I had not seen before. As a Nimblytod, high places were his birthright, no matter how long he had lived in the city.

So we went higher, following the curve of the roof to a point where we could pull ourselves up to the next level and the next, until we were on a real roof—a slanted, tiled affair a block away from my apartment. We couldn't see over the other side of it, and we didn't want to. On that side lay an unimpeded view of the street—and whatever had come through the door to my apartment.

We tried to be quiet, but the creature somewhere below had already heard us. Was tracking us.

Sybel knew this better than I.

"It's at the bathroom window. It's coming out onto the rain gutter," he said. He looked to our right. Three feet separated us from the flat roof of the next building. It was higher, but we could see the edge of a wall in the middle of that roof.

"We need to jump to the next roof," I said.

Sybel nodded.

He went first, so he could help me if I didn't quite make it. A smooth, graceful run; the leap up into the night; and then landing on all fours on the other side. I tossed my gun and knives over to him. I could hear scuttling sounds behind me. There was a smell now, like rotted flesh, but mixed with a fungal sweetness.

I ran toward the gap as fast as I could and jumped, the ground spinning below me, the flames to the west a kaleidoscope; came down heavily on the other side.

Sybel helped me up and we ran for the wall. Once behind it, out of sight if not out of smell, Sybel handed back my pistol and knives.

We could already hear it sniffing our scent from the other roof. We could sense its enjoyment. The sound of that thing slowly coming toward us will never leave me.

"It knows exactly where we are," Sybel whispered.

We could hear it getting closer and closer to the gap between the roofs.

I was babbling by then. Praying to Truff, to Bonmot, to anyone I could think of. Even now, in this afterword, with the hole in the ground behind me, my type-writer slowly turning into fungal mush, I am babbling, thinking of that moment.

We waited. We almost waited too long. Its smell came closer, came closer. It jumped onto the roof—we could hear it leap to clear the gap with an effortless stride, heard its claws scrabble to find purchase on our side. It couldn't have been more than twenty feet away.

"What do we do Sybel what do we do?" I kept saying, over and over again.

"Be calm and quiet, Janice," he said. "Just be calm. When I say, stand up and fire at it."

I looked up at the few stars through the moonlight, the clouds and the smoke that had begun to move in over the city. It was a cool night. I could feel the rough chill of the stone wall against my back. The seconds seemed to stretch out for a very long time. I had time to think about my gallery, to wonder if it would still be standing in the morning. I had time to think about Duncan and Mary, and to ask myself if I had been too harsh, if it had ever been my place to disapprove. I experienced a twinge of regret—that I had never married, never had children, never lived a "normal" life.

You understand, I hope: I thought I was going to die.

We almost waited too long. We thought it was farther away. But then it began to run at us. It had played its game of Stalk as long as it wanted to—now it meant to finish us. It was talking as it ran at us: "I have something for you something for you something for you you will like it you will like it you will like it," like the chant of some senile priest counting beads cross-legged in the Religious Quarter.

That's when we rose, in our fear. We rose up, and we emptied our pistols into it. It was dark as the night and yet transparent—you could see the stars through it when it got close. It was thick. It was thin. It had claws. It had fangs like polished steel. It had eyes so human and yet so various that the gaze paralyzed me. It was indescribable. Even now, trying to visualize it, I want to vomit. I want to *unthink* it.

Our shots went right through it. It veered to the left, misjudged the distance, and struck the wall in front of us, reared up again. We shot it again—tore great holes in its fungal skull, its impossible body. It roared, spit a stream of dark liquid, and tried to come up over the wall at us. Sybel stuck the muzzle of his pistol under its soft-rigid chin and pulled the trigger. The recoil sent the creature screaming and stumbling to the edge of the roof, and then over—falling. Still talking. Still telling us it had something for us that we'd like.

We stood there, numb, for a moment. Some things cannot be described. Some things can only be experienced.

Gone was the fear. I couldn't feel it anymore. I just couldn't. I had no room for it; it had no room for me. It had other places to go, other people to visit.

"Come on," I said to Sybel. "We have to get off this roof. There might be others. They will have heard. We'll seek refuge in the Religious Quarter. It might still be safe there."

Off the roof and into the night.

And how did that feel, you may ask. It was terrible, I tell you. Terrible. It was an experience to inoculate you against horror forever.

✶✿✶

Meanwhile, Duncan and Mary traveled ever farther into the depths . . .

So down we went, ever down, until the tunnel leveled off and an odd green phosphorescence that even Mary could see began to rise from the walls, the ground. Now we walked across a thick green carpet of blindly grasping tendrils. Soft and silent, so that our every sound was sucked into that which we trod upon. Ahead, we could see nothing but the continual wormhole of the tunnel, with no possible deviation, no other possibility.

"How much farther? Where are we going?" Mary asked, her voice flat and dull.

"Not much farther," I told her, heartsick at how every step seemed to make her more distant, even though we walked shoulder-to-shoulder. "We're going somewhere we can be safe." As safe as we could be anywhere, at least.

The fungi on my body had come alive the farther down we traveled. They pulled at my coat, they curled across my chest. They knew they were home. They wanted to return, but I wouldn't let them. If they returned, I would never leave.

At the same time, I could hear Mary next to me, her every sound magnified by my heightened senses. Her breath, the nervous movement of her hands, the tread of her shoes.

"I don't know why this is necessary," she said at one point, the fear gnawing at her face in the green light.

"We have to," I said. "If we'd stayed aboveground, we might be dead by now." The dim dumb hum and throb of explosives somewhere over our heads punctuated my point. The emptiness of the tunnel just confirmed it.

And yet we were not alone. Mary just couldn't see them, floating in the air around us, as oblivious to us as Mary was to them, conforming to their own rituals and needs. I still didn't know what they were, nor could I even describe the shape of them. Perhaps they were red-tinged megaspores, diaphanous, translucent. Perhaps they were some other organism altogether. I'd learned long ago not to wince when I walked through one.

"You trust me, don't you?" I asked her while all around us the tendrils swayed, and the green was not one green but a thousand shades of it, and the intensity of the voices in my ears made me want to shout to be heard, although I knew no one could hear them but me. The blind voices of the fungi, calling out. So beautiful. So unbearable.

"I don't know if this is about trust," she replied. "This isn't real, Duncan. I don't accept that this is real. You've fed me a pill. I'm having visions." It was odd to see her, usually so strong, so weak when out of her element.

I ignored her. The fungi were like pale hands beneath our tread. I had to carry her for a while. "We're almost there," I said.

"Almost where?" she asked, trembling in my arms. "Almost dead?"

What can I tell you about our escape to the Truffidian Cathedral? What, I wonder, will put it all in the proper perspective? I hardly know where to begin, but, then, that's not unusual. There's no balance between measured prose and raw experience that does not end in mediocrity or a slow burn into oblivion.

It happened like this: Sybel and I left the shelter of the roof and began to make our way through back streets and alleys to the Truffidian Cathedral. It was the only landmark I could think of that might be safe.

"What if the Cathedral's been overrun?" Sybel asked.

"Then we go somewhere else," I said. "But we have to try."

Sybel knew as well as I did that we couldn't sit still—we couldn't stay on that roof and wonder what might be coming over the ledge next.

The world we found ourselves in was silent. In some places the lamps were on, and in others they were not. Where they were on, they illuminated everything in purples or greens. The purple and the green both came from spores. The spores were heavy in the air; so as not to breathe them, we tore strips from our clothing and put them over our mouths and noses.

Was it effective? I'm still alive today, but at the time I could not get over the uncomfortable feeling that I was breathing in thousands of tiny lives, that I was one step away from becoming Duncan.

I said that the world was silent. Do you understand what I mean by that? I mean that there was no sound anywhere in the city. The spores clotted the air, muffled noises, sucked the sound out of the world. We lived in silence. It was like a Presence, and it was watchful. As we sidled along a wall, keeping to the shadows for long moments, I felt that each spore was a tiny eye, and that each eye was reporting back to an unseen master. A heaviness grew in my lungs that I've never felt since. The air was trying to suck words as yet unspoken out of me, and snuff them, stillborn.

Silence and haze. The purple and green of the spores made the air heavy, made it hard to see more than two feet in front of us. It was a kind of fog, through which we could just make out the distant flames that signified the destruction of the Kalif's army.

But I don't mean to suggest that this silent haze was empty. It wasn't. As we picked our way through streets turned foreign, unrecognizable, hints of movement suggested themselves, almost out of view, always on the periphery. We did not turn to look at whatever walked there, for fear this would make it too real. That which watched there ignored us, went on past—saving energy for other, more important missions, no doubt. But this made it no less frightening.

Nor did it blunt the effect of the human catastrophe that came out of the haze and lingered for far too long in our vision. Some lampposts played host to bodies swinging from ropes, heads lolling, tongues distended, skin pulled back in caricatures of smiles. Other bodies crowded the street, stumbled over in the dark. Pieces of people that appeared to be carefully cut apart, not the victims of mortar fire, but in precise stacks: legs, arms, torsos. The moon overhead like the knuckle of a fist pressed against a dirty window.

And always the motion, so unnerving that at one point I fired into the dark, screamed into the shadows, "Come out! Come out, you bastards!"

Sybel didn't even try to stop me. He just stared ahead and kept walking. His gaze was haunted, his face vacant. Not all fears are the same. I met mine on the roof; Sybel met his on the streets.

We reached the outskirts of the Religious Quarter by taking two steps forward, a step sideways, a step back, two forward, always almost seeing the vague delineation of ghosts, flitting and circling.

The Religious Quarter rose out of the mire of night as an outline of domes and steeples, highlighted by the flames that lay miles behind them. In that light, it looked unearthly, bizarre, not of Ambergris. Still, we entered it, in the hopes that that way lay safety. We allowed ourselves to come under the influence of those spires, those outcroppings of alcoves, all silent, all dead, not a priest in sight. (Probably cowering in their basements for all the good it would do them.)

We were on a street called Bannerville. I remember that. The streetlamps there were bare of the terrible burden of death. Some of them worked. Glowed green. At the end of Bannerville, we'd turn to the right and we'd be a block away from the Truffidian Cathedral.

A strange surge of joy or recognition overtook us, all out of proportion to our reality. We began to run, to laugh, abandoning our shuffle through the shadows; with safety so close, it was agony to walk. The worst seemed past. It really did. I was already thinking about what I'd say to Bonmot. I was already thinking about that, Truff help me.

Sybel had stopped holding my hand. He was a little behind me at this point. We were almost at the end of Bannerville, not more than twenty feet from safety. Overhead, a streetlamp flickered free of the green glow that pervaded the rest of the city.

We were both about to turn the corner. I could hear Sybel's heavy breathing as he ran. Then I heard an unfamiliar sound—a sound trapped between a gasp and a moan—and when I turned to look back at Sybel, all I could see was a mist of blood, floating out in streamers. I stopped running and stared. I couldn't breathe for a second. Nothing of him was left—not even his shoes. Nothing at all. His dissolution was complete. Utter. There was such a final and terrible beauty to it that I thought it must be an absurd magic trick, a horrible joke. But it wasn't, and the laughter caught in my throat, became a sob. Sybel had died, almost in front of my eyes, less than a block from the Cathedral. A moment later, I realized it must have been one of F&L's fungal mines, but for an instant it seemed more deadly, more immediate—something personal.

When I tried to move—away from the blood mist? toward it?—I put pressure down on my right foot, felt a shock of pain, and fell to the ground. That's when I realized that the mine had also erased my right foot, shoe and all. There was now just a stump. Nothing else. I lay on the ground, panting, and watched the blood dribble out of the part of the wound that hadn't been cauterized. The silence had been transformed into a pounding of blood in my ears, a slow, aching pulse. It reminded me of the blood I'd let spurt from my wrists, and for a moment I was content to watch it leak out of me—all of this liquid that constituted me at a level more basic than brain or mind, soul or spirit. I almost let it happen. I almost decided to lie back and let it happen.

But then I thought of poor Sybel and something changed inside of me. We had come so far. We had almost made it. I started to shout or scream then, but not words, nothing as coherent as words.

I took the strip of cloth from around my mouth and made a crude tourniquet to stop the bleeding. Around me, the blood mist that had been Sybel writhed in strands of gorgeous crimson, already dissipating.

I got up, grit in my teeth. I began to hop around the corner, toward safety. I don't know how long it took, or even what was happening around me—all I could focus on was the sound of my remaining shoe against gravel as I hopped, pain in my left leg from balancing the weight of my entire body. At some point I fell and could not get back up. I remember crawling until I reached the great doors of the Truffidian Cathedral, rising long enough to shove those doors open, pushing my way inside, and then falling to the floor.

Everyone inside the Cathedral was dead. I lay where I had fallen, next to a corpse. We stared at each other, eye to eye, and it took me a while to realize that somewhere in the background, near the altar, something was moving.

Once we reached our destination, I set Mary down. We stood in a large, circular cavern. Green lichens coated the floor. The walls reflected red-and-green, spores floating through the gold-gray light. I had made a throne of mushrooms for her, lavender and silver. I had sent into the air perpetually twirling strands of emerald fungi, like shiny crepe paper. I had carved a table to appear from the ground, and upon it set a cup of pure cold water from an aquifer. And beside it, three mushrooms—orange, blue, and purple—that would not only feed her but leave her feeling strong and calm.

I had spent a long time preparing for that moment. And yet, I must admit, not everything in that cavern lay under my control. How could it? Something was laughing in a corner, at a pitch no ordinary human ear could hear. Something nonhuman. It almost sounded like human speech. Things crept and crawled through the murk. A smell like rotted mango permeated the cavern. But, still, this was as safe a place as you could find belowground. It was my laboratory, my refuge. I knew everything here, including the thing that laughed. I knew them all on the most basic of levels. I relaxed as Mary wrapped her arms around me. I thought she would appreciate all that I had given her. But she wouldn't talk to me, and she refused to look around. I couldn't talk to her, either. Instead, I turned away so she wouldn't see the veins of emerald creeping up my face.

They stayed for hours in that secluded cavern, sitting or standing. They spoke, if at all, in whispers, and sometimes not even whispers because some new threat would approach every few minutes, requiring utter silence.

"I was happy," Duncan wrote in his journal. "I thought we were reaching a new closeness, one beyond words. That the extremity of our situation would make us as one. Instead, we were growing further apart with each passing minute. Now, I am confused by my happiness that night. Was I blind?" (Was there a moment when I switched from the epiphany of discovery to the weight of discovery? I don't know, except that one day I realized that knowledge—especially secret knowledge—had become a burden.)

Mary's assault began from that moment, from the moment when her mind refused to accept what she had seen, for she maintained her distance all the way back up to the surface the next morning.

From that moment, it was only a matter of time until the flesh necklace, until I would confront her at the base of the stairs. It smoldered in her eyes, as indelible as the mottling of fungus on Duncan's body. All of her scholarship, all of her will, would be focused on making what she had seen as unreal, as distant, as possible. Who could blame her? I could, and did, even if Duncan lacked the nerve. It was a failure—a failure of love and of imagination.

While they waited underground, I lay on the cathedral floor, gray caps walking among the bodies, me dead and yet not dead, seeing yet sightless, staring up at a ceiling that depicted the glory of the Truffidian cosmos. It almost might have been a premonition of Sabon's flesh necklace. It too was incongruous to its surroundings. It too was dead and yet not dead, blind yet had eyes. But mostly I had not a thought in my head as I tried to survive by playing dead next to such a weight of bodies. I had no room for grief at that moment. I had no time for tears. In that moment, I began to relax. I began to give up my self. I had no choice. I had nowhere to hide, nothing to hide with.

That is the night I stopped being a reporter and became something else entirely.

3

The closer I get to the end, the closer I get to the beginning. Memories waft up out of the ether, out of nothing. They attach themselves to me like the green light, like the fungi that continue to colonize my typewriter. I had to stop for a while—my fingers ached and, even after all that I have seen, the fungi unnerved me. I spent the time flexing and unflexing my fingers, pacing back and forth. I also spent it going through a box of my father's old papers—nothing I haven't read through a hundred times before. Drafts of history essays, letters to colleagues, perhaps even the letter he received from the Kalif's Court, if I dig deep enough. On top, Duncan had placed the dried-up starfish, its skeleton brittle with age. (I kept it there as a reminder to myself. After your letter to me—which, while reading this account, I sometimes think was written by an entirely different side of your personality—I wanted to remember that no matter how isolated I might feel, separated from others by secret knowledge, I was still *connected*. It didn't help much, though—it reminded me how different I had become.)

I've put the starfish on my table here, as something akin to a good luck charm. Perhaps it will help me finish.

Next to the starfish, I found seashells, dull and chipped—the last remnants of our most noteworthy vacation. I was ten, Duncan six. Our dad had gone on sabbatical from his position as a history professor at the Porfal College of History and Advanced Theory (or as Dad called it, "Poor Paul's Collage of Hysterics and Advanced Decay") in Stockton. I cannot recall ever taking a weeklong vacation before or since. Dad had bought berths on a river barge for us. Mom was relaxed, happy. Dad was as calm and at peace as I've ever seen him.

I remember one habit he picked up during that vacation. He liked to take a stalk of sedge weed and hold it in his mouth like a pipe, gnawing on the end, a wide-brimmed hat shading his face. We'd sit in the deck chairs and read, or watch the countryside go by.

In those days, the west side of the River Moth was almost entirely uninhabited. We saw strange animals come to the water's edge to drink; they would look at us with curiosity, but no fear. Once, we saw odd, short people dressed in outlandish clothes, staring across the water at us with a peculiar intensity. The water formed a mirror in which our images reached out to theirs across the waves—stretched, unreal.

We took the barge down to the Southern Isles, where we spent four days on the beaches. We couldn't afford to go farther than the northernmost island of Hathern, with its black sand and the melancholy ruins of the long-dead Saphant Empire, but we still had a good time.

Mom refused to go *in* the water, so she had to put up with Dad splashing water at her. Dad loved to swim—although "bob" or "float" might more accurately describe what he looked like when he took to the waves. Mom loved to watch the sunrises and sunsets from our little rented bungalow. During the day, she would walk along the beach for hours, and always brought back shells and shiny rocks for us. Sometimes Duncan and I went with her, sometimes we stayed with Dad.

At dusk, we sat on a blanket together and Dad would make a fire, cooking fish over the flames. I can't remember if he bought the fish or caught them. I don't remember him being much of a fisherman.

Then Dad would lecture us in a teasing way about the mighty Saphant Empire.

Pointing to the black-gray nubs and jagged walls drowning in the sand and sea, suffused with the orange of sunset, he would say, "Those are the result of war. A naval conflict and then the survivors fought on this very beach. There used to be a city here. Now, just what you see. And then . . . and then!" And then he would find a way to bring pirates and adventures into his history lesson.

I didn't give his words about war much thought at the time. The ruins were just great rocks to climb on, tidal pools to explore. That men had fought and died there hundreds of years ago seemed too remote from our vacation to be real.

Another time, Dad presented me with a tiny hermit crab in a white coiled shell.

"Don't hurt it," he said, "and leave it on the beach when we go."

"I will," I said, marveling at the feel of its tiny legs against the skin of my palm.

The sand crunching between my toes; the heat and breeze off the sea, the lights of boats far offshore.

Mom looked after Duncan for most of the trip, because he was young and needed constant attention. (I remember only the vaguest flash of sunlight, the most tenuous thread of a memory of water—it was all too idyllic for me to retain, I suppose.)

It is one of the only times I can recall the full attention of my father upon me. Five years later, he would die. Eight years later, my mother would bring us to Ambergris and the house by the River Moth. Twenty years later, Duncan would feel the first twinge of the fungal colonization occurring within him. Twenty-five years after our long-ago vacation, I would try to kill myself. Thirty years later and the War of the Houses would almost kill us all.

How can such a pleasurable memory as a childhood vacation coexist comfortably with memories of the war? How can the world contain such extremes? I thought about such things as I lay among the bodies in the Truffidian Cathedral. Each question begat another question, so that soon the questions seemed to contain their own answers.

I lay there for a very long time, gazing at nothing and no one while the gray caps rummaged all around me, each syllable of their clicking speech a knife slid between my shoulder blades. I do not know what they were looking for, nor whether they found it. I could hear them rolling bodies over, rifling through the pockets of the dead. Once, a clawing hand brushed against the side of my face. I could feel someone or something looking at me; I refused to look back. I could *feel the breath* of one of them upon me, smell the spurling tangle of scents that clung to them like their skin: must and mold and funk and dust and a trace of some spice.

And then, finally, the stained glass above me refracted the light of the sun, and it was dawn, and the gray caps were gone, and I was still alive, surrounded by hundreds of the dead, the blood upon them dark and caked.

Stiffly, like an old woman, I propped myself up, struggled to raise myself onto my foot, stared around me at the carnage.

The dead did not look peaceful. The dead did not look planned or purposeful, or *at rest*, or any other combination of words that might signify comfort or the rule of law. Legs and arms lay at unnatural angles, torn or contorted or dislocated from torsos. Mouths were caught in extremes of pain and fear and surprise. Dried blood and gathering flies. Skin a pale yellow tinged with blue. Great wounds, like vast claws, had cut into chests leaving dull red furrows. A row of heads disembodied. After a while, I had to stop looking. I had to stop myself from looking.

I wish I could have told you they looked beautiful.

That is when I resolved I would never become one of them. I had to find a way out. (Even if it meant typing up an afterword in bad light, on a limited budget, for a potential readership of thousands or none?)

Painfully, hopping, I made my way through the bodies, pushed open the double doors with a supreme effort, and walked out into postwar Ambergris.

Afterword, aftermath. I'm shaking now, and I don't know if that means I'm hungry or that I'm afraid of what might come out of that hole in the ground behind me. Or if I'm upset thinking about the aftermath of that catastrophic struggle between Houses, gray caps, and the Kalif. Between me and my now traitorous leg. Between Sybel and the fungal mine he never saw. Between Duncan and Mary.

As I hobbled through the city that morning, still in shock, using a stick as a crutch, it became clear that we had been having a bad Festival for many, many months. Buildings reduced to purple ash. Corpses still unburied, but frozen by needlings of fungus, which, mercifully, took away any smell. I marveled at the number of people who walked through the city with a blank look in their eyes; I was one of them. A look of sadness, yes, but beyond sadness—a sense of dislocation, of desolation. We were encountering Ambergris as survivors and asking a question: Is this really our city? Is this really where we live? (I thought it went deeper than that—the listlessness, the fatigue. It seemed to indicate a confusion, a mental flinch, an inability to understand if we'd won or lost. How could we tell?)

Collapsed buildings lay impaled on their own columns, which still reached toward open sky. Streets strewn with garbage and bits of torn-up flesh. Relics of past ages splintered into unrecognizable thickets of wood and metal. The Hoegbotton headquarters, which had survived any number of F&L attacks, had been brought low on that last night—looted and gutted, the stark black of extinguished fire racing up the interior walls toward the lacerated ceiling. The ever-present smell of smoke and of rot, which we had grown accustomed to over the last few years, but which, on this particular morning, had a sharpness, an intensity, that we had not experienced before. The Voss Bender Memorial Post Office had been ransacked, and little metal boxes, some of them melted and deformed from fire, littered the cracked steps. Elsewhere, whole neighborhoods of people worked to tear down barricades erected to keep out the Kalif's men, or F&L's men, or the gray caps. If I could have flown crow-like over the city, I would have seen it as a crumbling eye pierced through the center and smoldering at the edges where the abandoned mortars of the Kalif lay surrounded by the bodies of the slain.

It will sound odd, but I realize now that if I had looked closely enough, I could have seen physical evidence of the beginning of Mary's attacks on Duncan's books. Stare long enough, hard enough, with the appropriate intensity, and Duncan's theories were all there, woven into the brick, the stone, the wood, even inhabiting the wind that came down and whispered through narrow streets backed up with rubble. And, in the sheer remembered violence of bloodstains, burnt wood, crippled brick: Mary's retort, her refutation of him. As Mary walked through some other part of the city that day, through some other aftermath, what did she see? What could she see but the embodiment of her father's Nativism theory? Everything cataloged as the most natural of disasters. (Truly a stretch, Janice, if ever there was one!)

I understand now, remembering *my* walk through the city, that the glittering flesh necklace surrounded a neck that supported a head filled with maggoty ideas. Filled with images that do not connect, and which will always make it impossible for Sabon to recognize the truth in Duncan's theories. She has found her own personal history; she has written it to drown out the truth.

In a sense, almost every word, every sentence, every paragraph she has written about Ambergris since the war has been an attempt to undo my memories—what I saw during that war, what I saw that night with Sybel beside me, what I saw afterward, walking through the city. And, of course, everything she saw belowground. (This is nonsense. Mary reacted no differently than many other Ambergrisians. A deep sense of denial pervaded the city, but how can you blame any of its inhabitants? They still had to live on in the city. It must have been much worse after the Silence. Imagine your loved ones being spirited away one night and you unable to do anything except go about your daily business and hope that you, too, would not be subject to the same fate.)

Eventually, on that first morning after the war, I found myself at Blythe Academy. I had hopped and hobbled my way there after an hour or two, my journey aimless and funereal. An ache and an emptiness had begun to gnaw away at me. A glimpse of the familiar acted like an anchor.

For some reason, I had assumed that the desecration of the Truffidian Cathedral would have extended to Blythe Academy as well, but this was not the case. I saw a few broken windows, two overturned benches, an area of burnt grass, and a singed section of roof, but the willow trees remained the same as always. Priests and teachers bustled across the lawn, cleaning up the debris. The air of activity, of honest labor, gave me hope.

I sat down on a bench, hoping that somehow the memory of those long-ago conversations that had so calmed me then might calm me now.

Instead, a shadow fell across me. I looked up, and there stood Bonmot, staring down at me with a grim smile upon his lips. His face was grimy with soot or dirt. He had a long, shallow cut running down his left cheek. Bonmot, in that moment, looked invincible, even though he had become more vulnerable than I could then know. (Whose faith wouldn't falter for at least a moment in the midst of such inexplicable carnage?)

His grim smile softened to concern as he saw the condition of my foot—or, rather, the lack of a foot.

"You're alive," I said, in wonder. By now, the lack of sleep, the terror of what I had gone through, had taken me somewhere else entirely.

"You need to see a doctor," Bonmot said. He crouched down beside me, gently cupped his hand under my calf to better examine the wound.

"Not really," I said. "There's nothing to be done now. It's mostly cauterized. I washed the rest of it. The flesh is clean. I spent all night with a mob of corpses in the Truffidian Cathedral. You may wish to investigate."

He bowed his head, looking at my stump. "I know. I've heard. You were there?"

"Yes," I said. "Pretending to be dead. Please, don't worry about the leg."

He stared at me. "Janice, you need to have it looked at anyway."

I laughed, an edge of bitterness in my voice. "I suppose," I said, "but who will look at it? I've been limping around this broken old city of ours all morning. And I've seen little that isn't mangled, mashed, cracked, twisted, or dead."

"It won't take long to rebuild," he said. "You'll be surprised. All of this will be behind us someday." A pause. "Have you heard from Mary?"

This, then, was the closest he could come to asking about Duncan.

"No, I haven't," I said.

(And you wouldn't, not for a few days. I had returned Mary to our apartment, which had been ransacked but not ruined, and we took up again the unhealthy non-bliss of our domestic lives together—a little more silent around each other, a little more reserved, a little more distant. She became fond of saying I was "suffocating" her in those first few days after the war. I had no response. I needed comfort from her. I *needed* her.)

I started to cry. I was still talking, my face still set in a half-grimace, half-smile, but I was crying. "Sybel's dead," I said.

And then, even though he had a thousand responsibilities that day, Bonmot pulled me to him and held me as, sobbing, I told him about all of the dead.

The losses kept piling up. When I visited my gallery, I found the inside had been gutted by fire. All of my inventory had disappeared yet again, taken by looters or flames. The artists blamed me, even though I was convinced some of them had stolen their own work off my walls. I wasted time. I wasted money. I thought I could resurrect the gallery, but without Sybel, I was lost. I did not have the requisite number of "friends with money," as he had liked to call them. I reopened for a short time, but I could no longer attract even mediocre talents. I was left with a half-dozen elderly landscape oil painters as clients. Clearly, I was doomed.

Looking back, the war signaled the end of so many things that the dying throes of my gallery must be considered no more than a buried footnote in the history of that period. For example, the war certainly ended my right foot—there's no doubt about that. I'm tempted, whenever someone asks me what I remember about the war, to point to my grainy toes and say, "Ask my foot."

As a hidden perk of so many people having lost limbs, the art of wooden limb construction had reached new heights. I personally picked out the wood for my replacement from the very best strangler figs on the west side of the River Moth, near where Sybel had grown up. My foot might even have been made from a tree Sybel had once climbed. Maudlin, I know, but I don't care about the sentimentality of that thought.

I had Judith Aquelus, a sculptress, collaborate with the wooden limb experts at Similian's Arm & Leg Shop, to create the unique artifact that is my right foot. I had Judith carve a miniature, stylized version of the opera house stage on it on which the Kalif's soldiers could be seen, making their acting debut.

No amputee should be seen in public without a Judith Aquelus creation. A foot and a cane: the perfect accessories for such necessary tasks as walking to the grocery store for a loaf of bread! With my cane and my new wooden foot, I have attained a whole new level of eccentricity. Why, I've become my own work of art—my only option, considering that creating art and selling art had proven so unprofitable for me.

The funny thing is, the green fungus that has colonized my typewriter and makes it harder and harder to complete this afterword has also begun to infiltrate my wooden foot. I am becoming a rather small forest. In my own way, perhaps I'm experiencing what Duncan went through. (Dead wood does not equal living flesh. There's nothing to compare to that heart-choking prickle of another life entering your skin and flesh.)

Since that first foot, I have found it hard to resist having more made when I can afford it, or carving them myself. In my more whimsical moments, I'm tempted to leave a trail of feet through the city. One day a foot may be all that is left of me.

"Do you like it?" I asked Duncan the first time I showed it off to him.

"It's very much you," Duncan said. (I'd had too many strange experiences with my flesh to be too empathetic. The sloughing off of flesh, the losing and regaining of it, had become too normal an experience.)

"It itches," I told him. And this is still true now. The foot, with its lithe straps and silver clasps, itches like hell at the oddest times.

"I itch all the time," Duncan said, not to be outdone.

On that particular day, down by the docks, watching the ships come in, Duncan was very pale. You could see, if you looked closely, that the hair on his head was not really hair ruffled by a breeze, but a black fungus lazily swaying back and forth. There was a further suggestion of movement under his coat. I doubt anyone else saw it—or wanted to see it.

"Do you miss him?" I asked Duncan.

"I miss him terribly," he replied. (I missed the everyday normalcy Sybel had brought to my life. Dealing with you, Janice, was an up-and-down experience, often full of melodrama. As much as I loved Bonmot, my conversations with him had always had some religious subtext. But speaking to Sybel was so natural and effortless and free of judgment that I didn't even miss the experience until it was over.)

"If it itches really badly," he said, "I could probably find a way to grow you a fungal replacement."

I ignored him and asked, "How's Mary?"

He didn't answer.

I had to stop to clean off the typewriter keys. The green fungus had become too insidious. The keys weren't striking paper, but bunching up in emerald moss, the paper itself reflecting a series of ever more vegetative marks. I couldn't get it all off, but enough of it is gone that I can continue typing for a while. I'm not sure when I will run out of time; there are so many factors to consider. When will the patience of the Spore's owner run out? When will I tire of what increasingly seems a pointless exercise? When will something crawl out of the hole in the ground behind me and put an end to my speculations?

I think it's morning outside, but I haven't bothered to check. I had thought it was lunchtime earlier, but it turned out that my stomach had it all wrong. If it is morning, the sky is probably gray and undistinguished, flecked with rain. It's that time of year when sudden showers appear and make of the city stark out-lines, robbing it of color and texture. A welter of umbrellas appears on the streets and people walk quickly to their destinations, with no appreciation for anything around them.

4

Afterwords. Afterwards. Afterwar.

The war had been jarring, numbing, senseless. In its aftermath, the balance of power remained much as it had before all the bloodshed. The Hoegbottons controlled Ambergris and F&L controlled Morrow and Sophia's Island but lacked the military and political will to enforce their ridiculous tariffs. The Kalif's mauled troops retreated across the River Moth even as their merchants advanced to secure deals with the Hoegbottons to rebuild the city and import new products. (Oddly enough, the Kalif's troops could be said to have ultimately achieved their goal, if not in the preferred way. For, after all, hadn't they liberated the citizens of Ambergris from chaos and tyranny through their sacrifice?)

After the war, Ambergris forgot the real enemy—Hoegbotton & Sons still railed against Frankwrithe & Lewden or the Kalif, but provided no warning against the gray caps. People gratefully went along with this mass denial. Wasn't it easier to blame F&L than an amorphous, faceless enemy that hid underground and attacked seemingly at random? (To be fair, the still unknown way in which F&L had acquired fungal weapons confused the issue—F&L did look like the sole instigator. After all, didn't the gray caps periodically erupt from their hidey-holes during the Festival anyway?)

The terrible, cold beauty of the truth appealed to no one. Every few weeks, for several years, one or two, or three or four, people were killed by a leftover fungal bomb or a new one planted by someone—the gray caps or F&L, I assume, but who could tell the difference? H&S did nothing to prevent this, and tried hard to stop Lacond from reporting it. We were a city and a people unable to face our coming annihilation, incensed over an enemy that posed not a quarter of the threat. In a way, we lived in a fairy tale, convinced that someone else's actions or inactions might save us. As day after day passed without Ambergris being invaded, we flinched less and less, let down our guard. No one was going to destroy the city—only rumors could do that, the thinking went, only idle talk. If we pretended otherwise, the enemy could not creep out at night and make us all disappear. Permanence had become a thing from the past.

(I didn't think much had changed, but if it had, it had changed for the reason most eloquently put by the historian Edgar Rybern: namely, that barbaric institutions and individuals can benefit society, while "civilization" can, in its most benign forms, prove barbaric. This led me to two conclusions germane to the war. First, that the very act of F&L coming into contact with the gray caps and then into contact with H&S had irrevocably changed all three parties; and second, that stated goals aside, all three of these institutions have been thrown off-kilter by the war. Now, whether they realize it or not, each new decision pulls them slightly further away from their original purpose. What effect this might have, I could not tell you.)

For Duncan personally, the end of the war meant two things: that Lacond was available to help him limp back into a shadow career in print—it became apparent at war's end that Lacond could only keep one of us on, and, even if I had wanted to stay, it wasn't going to be me—and that Mary's patience with him was almost at an end.

The slow withdrawal, the retreat from love, went on at the same time Lacond began recruiting Duncan for his eccentric obsessions. (No more eccentric than my own obsessions, Janice. Lacond and I understood each other in a way that made me no longer feel quite so alone.)

How did Mary withdraw? Let me count the ways. She no longer tolerated my brother's erratic schedule. She no longer found his eccentricities endearing. She no longer found his fungal diseases tragic, his endurance of them brave. (I'm not sure she *ever* felt that way about my fungal diseases. It was more that she put up with their side effects to be with me.) The small apartment they shared became claustrophobic. Duncan's journal skirts the reason behind the feelings:

> I cannot find my inspiration in this place—I have to go down to the Spore or Lacond's apartment to write, or I just stare at the page. I don't know why my apartment has become so stifling, but it has. There's nothing in it to spur me on to create. Except Mary, of course.

But Mary spent more and more time with friends. Sometimes she even stayed at her parents' house. Duncan had no chance, no choice. How could he? He didn't have the experience to combat it, to see the signs. To Duncan, sadly enough, the only way to get her back was to keep showing her the truth, even though it was clear to anyone with any sense that he'd need to start *lying* to her if he wanted to keep her. (A cynical view that would only serve as a short-term solution. And I was neither so naive nor Mary so experienced as you make out.) Every time he showed her the truth, she pushed him farther away. Duncan wrote in his journal:

> I feel as if I am living by myself again. She isn't really here anymore. She's a husk or a shell. Her eyes are dull. Her hair is dull. Her words are weighted and slow. She doesn't listen to me. I am killing her.

But the truth also meant accepting that the day-to-day domesticity didn't suit him either, especially for long periods of time. I will spare you the contrast between the journal entries that detail with a silly kind of joy the beauty of her snores early in their relationship and the dull snarl of his comments on those self-same snores near the end. Or, take this terse entry only a month before disaster: "another night of odd smells." Sometimes he would be almost apologetic: "She could easily have complained about the frequency with which I spored. Or how I tracked in strange green mud from time to time. But she didn't."

Even then, I think he wanted to stay with her. I don't believe he ever understood that he might actually lose her. (I couldn't, back then, imagine a tolerable moment without her—and, in all honesty, tolerable moments since I lost her have been fewer and less intense.) After all, he'd never been through a breakup before—unlike me, who had been through dozens. I had become an expert on broken relationships. It had become ritualized with me, each battle with its own histories, its own decorum, and its own rules of disengagement.

Duncan and Mary managed to stay together in their little apartment for a few more months, but like the starfish that rapidly became brittle, their love had died long before they acknowledged the fact. The bond between them had broken, snapped, and although Duncan was still in love with her—even though I don't know if he *liked* her anymore—she was not in love with him. Their situation frayed, unraveled. They had screaming arguments, tearful reunions. Duncan would seek refuge at my apartment, only to go back, over my objections.

He wrote in his journal at some point near the end:

I feel as if she is made of clay or wood or stone. There is no longer any of the lovely fluidity that made me lust for her, although I lust for her still. I keep thinking that it will just take time—that, in time, she will reconcile herself to that night and to what she saw. That she will understand the strange beauty of it. That her understanding of it will lead her to an understanding of me. Until then, she complains about the amount of time I spend away from her, with Lacond and "that stupid society," as she calls it, and then, when I do spend time with her, she complains that I smother her. She cringes in distaste when my fungal disease flares up. I must keep myself wrapped in a bathrobe, away from her critical eye, when I feel it coming on. I cannot relax around her. My love for her is making me old. I keep thinking back to that night. The rush of joy I felt because she would finally see what I had seen, that we could finally share it. And I wonder how I could have been so naive.

Duncan never thought of disavowing his findings, of putting the underground behind him, denying what he had found. He was, however, capable of self-blame:

How could I expect her to believe what I myself scarcely comprehended at times? Sometimes I wish I had been able to find another way. Sometimes I wish I could undo it all, start over. But I don't think she will let me.

Soon, they barely talked to each other . . . then, one day, he came home from Lacond's offices and she was gone. He thought that she had just stepped out for a moment, until he found the note. He left it with his other notes. It is right here beside my festering typewriter. It reads:

My Love:

I *do* love you, but I am not in love with you anymore. You want me to see things that aren't there. You want me not only to see the impossible—you want me to think it beautiful, a revelation. That night was a terrifying experience for me, Duncan. And with your insistence that I believe, you have begun to frighten me.

There's no way to rescue us. I can't keep living with you. I hope that in time we can become friends, but for now we must be apart. Besides, we both have books to write, and neither of us can be creative in this situation.

Do you know how hard it is for me to leave not only my lover but my teacher? But I have no choice.

Thank you for everything you have taught me, everything you have shown me about history and about the world. I'll never forget that.

I'll end here, for now, because, as you know, too many words can be a trap.

Love,

Mary

P.S. I'm leaving you the apartment until you can find your own place.

The difference between what we need and what we want can be an abyss. For example, I want more light in this accursed room, but I need lunch because my stomach is grumbling. Duncan would always want Mary, but did he need her? In a way, he didn't. In a way, like the writer who pursues his art above all else, Duncan did not need anything other than access to the underground. (You make me out to be a theorem in search of expression, rather than a human being.)

Next to Mary's note is a letter she wrote to a friend. I don't know how Duncan came by it. I don't like to guess in this instance. (It was a low point for me, intercepting her mail. It was a brief insanity, a madness created by love. I only did it once or twice. I'm still ashamed of it.) The letter explains the situation much more baldly, and must have driven Duncan a little crazy when he read it.

> Duncan has become ever more himself. I left him because I couldn't take any more of his ravings about the gray caps. Everything is focused on the gray caps. Even if he did love me, I'd never be more than ancillary to those damn gray caps. It didn't help that my parents hated him for, as they saw it, spoiling the innocence of their little girl. And because he was impossible to live with, and because he was like a child—he always wanted to be in love, so when he wasn't in love with me, he was in love with his studies. He wore me out. He was so intense. How can anyone be so intense all of the time? I couldn't breathe, or think. And his opinions on my research! Always picking at it, always so sure he was right and I was wrong. I don't think that I would ever be more than a student in his eyes, so I had to get away from him. Yes, I loved him, but, sometimes, as I am discovering, you need more than love.

(A mental shudder. A sudden moment of self-awareness—was I like that? Yes, I probably was. But I don't know if Mary ever understood the great strain I was under, how what I sought was of the utmost importance. That it meant nothing more or less than safeguarding the fate of everyone who lives in this city, perhaps in the world. And still. And yet. I knew she had taken something from me, that I had been valuable to her. I had given nearly as much as I had taken. I'd been her mentor and she'd been my student, no matter what grief I had caused her. I took some small comfort from that.)

And that was the end of it. Or so I thought. For although Mary was free of Duncan, Duncan would never really be free of her, or her flesh necklace.

As Duncan's romantic fortunes waned, his fortunes as a historian waxed again: a flowering in miniature, given the heights he had ascended to in his youth. Although those who did speak a kind of truth about the gray caps and Ambergris's past were condemned to the fringes, they did have their own organization: the Ambergrisians for the Original Inhabitants Society. Most of Duncan's postwar hopes of self-expression reached fruition through AFTOIS.

AFTOIS had once again become Lacond's passion—and in its limited way, it flourished for a time after the war—so that the *Broadsheet*, which paid the rent, often suffered from his neglect. (Indeed. It never quite failed when he was in charge, but some years after I took over production of the *Broadsheet*, I would have to put it out of its financial misery, much to the delight of our many enemies.)

"The important thing," Lacond said to me once, "is that we get the truth out in some form, that we document what is happening. So that at the very least, there will be a record that someone knew about it."

This struck me as an absurd statement. "Why?" I replied. "So that when the abyss opens up you can stand on the edge and shout down, 'I told you so!'?"

Lacond looked at me as if I hadn't understood anything he'd said.

When I told Bonmot about this exchange, he said, "Yes, but without Lacond, how much more mischief would Duncan get into?"

A good point, I had to admit. Because Lacond spent much of his time in those years after the war making Duncan his second-in-command. Without Lacond, the loss of Mary might have hit Duncan harder than it did. (How much harder could it have hit me? I hardly left my apartment for months. Lacond had to drag me out of my bed to get me to work for him. For years afterward, I would feel this hollow space in my stomach, in my lungs. Sometimes, I would think of her and I couldn't breathe.)

Lacond had a perverse effect on Duncan. Lacond made Duncan want something he thought he had given up on long ago: the restoration of a measure of legitimacy. (I might have reconciled myself to living without respect, but that didn't mean I didn't fight hard against it. Years would pass between a chance at even the most minor legitimate publication opportunity, but I never gave up.) Lacond kept telling Duncan that if he published enough essays in the AFTOIS newsletter, he would eventually get noticed again.

"Enough essays in a marginal journal read by a couple thousand fellow crackpots?" I said to Duncan when he told me. "A path to greater glory? I don't think so, Duncan. I really don't. You should attempt another book—you might find a publisher."

Duncan shook his head. "Not now, not yet. I can't even think about a book—my thoughts are too fragmented. But essays—yes, I could do essays. And Lacond might be right, you never know."

Ridiculous! Yet Duncan believed it. As he wrote in his journal:

Sometimes I read through the letters I kept from my glory days, when readers could acquire my books easily and in quantity. There were people back then who understood me, who realized I told the truth. I can't imagine that all of them have died in the twenty years since, or that there aren't new readers who might appreciate my books. I just need to find a way to reach them again. And if I can't reach them, perhaps I can reach Mary again. It's easy for Mary to dismiss Lacond, or AFTOIS, but it might alter her perception of me if . . . but it is too much to hope for, to think about.

(I did believe this then, perhaps naively, but over time my emphasis would shift. I no longer thought books would be my salvation. I no longer thought in terms of publication, really, but more in terms of accumulating knowledge and making as much of it public as the public could stand.)

Didn't Duncan see that Lacond had been trying for years—decades—with less success than my brother? Not any more than he saw that, for all the time he spent in the shadow of the huge oak tree outside her parents' house, hoping to catch a glimpse of her, Mary was traveling along a very different path. How could someone so smart be so foolish? But Duncan persisted. (I had no choice. I thought Mary and I could eventually be friends. I justified my hauntings of her by telling myself that I was watching over her, protecting her. The truth? My heart, caught between hope and pain, could not bear never seeing her, even if seeing her meant only the slightest glimpse of her through a window—a silhouette that, for many months, could still transfix me.)

Bonmot used to say that "The limits of our imagination are the limits of our free will." Duncan could not imagine a life that did not include Mary and the gray caps. I sometimes wonder how different it would have been if he could have wrenched himself free of Ambergris and set sail for the Southern Isles, lost himself in the waves and the wind, adopted a different obsession.

(Janice—*all* obsessions are the same. They vary little in the essential details. You refuse to believe that my search for knowledge wasn't so much personal, wasn't so much for myself, but out of a fear for the future of our city. I pursued Mary out of a fear for the future of Duncan Shriek. There wasn't much holding me to the city besides Mary, to be honest. As I continued to change, I needed to make up reasons why I shouldn't just venture underground and stay there. I could have planted myself in a dark, moist corner of the gray caps' world and taken root. I could have allowed the fungi to colonize me, taken in the breath of their sleep and woken in a thousand years to a far different fate. So was it love, after a certain point in time? Probably not. It was probably just a grasping for some kind of normal life. But can you blame me?)

If only Duncan could have apologized to Bonmot in a way that Bonmot would have accepted. But he wouldn't. I think Bonmot was more fragile in his faith than he let on—I think he believed that if he let Duncan back into his life, it would affect his character, would erode his integrity. Duncan could have used Bonmot for balance during those times. He could have used someone other than a sister with one foot who had nightmares about being buried alive in a pile of corpses. Because Lacond really did have him convinced—they'd go to those lunatic meetings of their lunatic society, and Duncan would think that because three hundred people showed up and listened to him he was making progress. (Lacond was enough for me. Lacond never made me feel as if I were damaged or deranged, the way Bonmot could even during the best of our conversations. There's a whiff of righteousness in the most humble servant of Truff that is a terrible, terrible thing. But Lacond taught me confidence and endurance. Every year of his adult life, he had written down his bizarre, unpopular theories and, through his society, made them available to the public. And every year, most people rejected his work, or feigned indifference, or found his theories an unkind reflection or comment on the man himself. Yet he never stopped, never gave up. It's more than I could have done.)

I went to one AFTOIS meeting. That was enough for me—one glance at the agenda handed out by a portly woman with a purple scarf wound endlessly around her neck, as though a purple constrictor had a choke hold on her—one glance convinced me I would not be coming back:

THE AMBERGRISIANS FOR THE
ORIGINAL INHABITANTS SOCIETY
WEEKLY MEETING NO. 231
—As Presided Over by Society President James Lacond—
—Minutes Taken by Linda Pitginkel—
—Incidental Music Provided by "George the Flutist"—
—Refreshments Baked by Lara Maleon—

ORDER OF EVENTS

(1) Recital of the Society Motto: "In pursuit of truth, for the truth, by the truth. Against inertia, against ease, against the false."

(2) Introduction of Speakers [James Lacond]

(3) Rebecca Flange reads an excerpt from her book *The Crimes of Tonsure: The Role of Poison*

(4) "What Is the Truth—How Shall We Approach It and Its Importance to Our Understanding of the Gray Caps"—speech by Sarah Potent

(5) "Channeling the Dead—Its Impact on Our Understanding of the Gray Caps"—speech by Roger Seabold

(6) "I Am the True Descendant of Samuel Tonsure"—speech by James "Tonsure" Williams

(7) "Evidence for the Existence of a City-Sized Fungus"—speech by Frederick Madnok [as read by Harry Flack in Mr. Madnok's absence]

I think the agenda alone should give some insight into the kinds of buffoons with which Duncan had aligned himself. He had gone from writing legitimate books to writing legitimate articles to teaching at a legitimate school to scandal and heartbreak, and now lived a sad existence at the very fringe of his chosen field.

(Again, unfair. I appreciate your protectiveness, but the truth is often so strange that one cannot, at the outset, discard even the most ridiculous of theories, the silliest of suppositions. Remember how I let my students do my research for me? This was a similar situation—I was always searching for the sliver of truth in the outlandishness presented at those meetings. Even the most absurd theory might have in its core details, its foundation, some hint of information about the gray caps, something to be salvaged or redirected. I attended those meetings for that reason, not because I *believed* everything I heard, or even wanted to be associated with all of them. But who else, Janice, would publish my "crackpot theories"? No one after the war except, ultimately, Sirin. And even *he* didn't do it properly, as you—my benign, self-chosen executioner—well know.)

Certainly, I was used to dealing with strange people—I've never met an artist who wasn't at some level a deeply strange or estranged person. But this was different. These were people on the edge of the edge of sanity. Oddities. Carpenters who, in their spare time, developed paranoid theories about House Hoegbotton that grew to full fruition in the dark, glistening spaces of their imaginations. Stay-at-home wives who, bored, had bought into the more lurid broadsheet headlines.

Self-hating bank clerks making a pittance who had curdled inside and defended the gray caps because they would have cheered if the gray caps had risen up and taken over the city. People who believed they were the reincarnation of historical figures like Tonsure. And, on the fringes of those fringes, homeless people who used the meetings to take shelter. The mentally challenged who had been discharged from the now-destroyed Voss Bender Memorial Mental Hospital. I even thought I spied a gray shape that resembled my former fellow inmate Edward at one point, although when I looked again, he was gone.

And those were just the audience members.

How the spittle flew during the meeting I observed! The sour taste of vitriol! The sad, lonely, pathetic, nervous, neurotic, psychotic, exposed underbelly of the city.

"In my opinion, Tonsure was a gray cap disguised as a priest."

"The grace with which the fungus leapt from tree to tree astounded me."

"I didn't realize I had the gift to channel ghosts until I was twelve."

"In the vast, empty spaces beneath the city, this huge fungus has taken over and means to envelop us in its clammy grasp."

"Being a woman, I am more attuned to the feelings of inanimate objects."

And Duncan wanted to become their leader: the Lord of the Disinclined. Disinclined to work. Disinclined to hold a job. The Disenchanted who had never been enchanting, except, perhaps, as children. No wonder Mary hated that group. I hated that group. We could have taken an oath of solidarity on that much, at least. (And yet, they, and I, are much closer to the truth than those who scoffed at our organization, regardless of the sometimes illegitimate evidence provided at those meetings. I sense a certain amount of snobbery in your remarks, Janice, as if the only people worth a damn are artists or writers or playwrights—but look back on your own description of the New Art and the New Artists. Were they really any different, except that the results of their obsessions and imagination were more forcefully inflicted upon the world? Sometimes a theory or idea is as strangely beautiful as that expressed by any painting, even when it's articulated by those who are not articulate.

(Let me tell you what I saw that day, at that meeting. I saw a woman trying to come to terms with the death of her sister by inexplicable means. She did so by taking what facts she knew about Samuel Tonsure and bending them to a theory that attempted to reconcile the irreconcilable. In that forced assimilation of fact and fancy, Janice, there might have been a fragment of truth, even if only a psychological truth. Perhaps by seeing Tonsure in a different light than I, she advanced my understanding of him one tiny increment.

(Sarah Potent's diatribe about the truth, taking as her basis Stretcher Jones's rebellion against the Kalif and expanding it to include many of the unanswered questions about Ambergris's past—wasn't she, in disguised form, asking the same questions we all have asked from time to time? Does she deserve vilification for trying to think her way through all of this?

(Could you have missed the beauty of Frederick Madnok's theory that Ambergris is "shadowed" from below by a giant fungus, wide as the city and deep as the city is tall, through which catacomb the tunnels of the gray caps? Could you not see the utter precision and craftsmanship of his many diagrams? The humor of the labeling—a sense of humor that tells the reader that Madnok *knows* how outlandish his theory may sound.

(There is an art, Janice, to being an outsider, a skill to being a good crackpot. Some people decide to become writers of fiction and this is considered a legitimate endeavor. Others decide to make their expressions of the imagination more personal. I, for one, gained more from that meeting than from any novel I have ever read!)

But the fact is, Duncan didn't see them as they really were, only as he wanted them to be: a society of visionaries, of dreamers, of revolutionaries. Apparently so enthralled by them that he lost his wits for a time, Duncan became antisocial and avoided me. (Who could blame me, considering your attitude then? So similar to your attitude toward Mary. Oh, the irony, considering her attitude toward AFTOIS.) As these crackpots began to take up more and more of his time, he began to forget to bathe. He didn't change his clothes for weeks on end. He babbled to himself. (I missed Mary terribly. I missed her so much, Janice. I don't know if you can conceive of how much I missed her.)

Worst of all, Duncan assumed more and more responsibility for the AFTOIS newsletter, as Lacond became sicker, meaning that Duncan wrote less as his increased editorial duties ate up his time.

Like Lacond, Duncan did not censor theories in conflict with his own. Duncan believed, given the inability of most "experts" to absorb the truth about the gray caps, that all outlandish theories should be given an airing, regardless of their validity. He thought that this would make minds receptive to the unusual and improbable, "softening resistance," as he used to mutter, "to reality. A kind of general insurrection against the complacent surface of things." (For all the good it did me.)

To this end, the journal, which he edited more and more "in the name of" the still-living Lacond—even writing essays under Lacond's name—became even more eccentric, and thus ever more dismissed, unread by a populace living in denial. (But some of these theories were beautiful and elegant, no matter how wrong-headed. For example, "morelmancy"—divination of the future from mushrooms . . . or, as you called it, much to my amusement, "a flowering of spores, long dormant, a colorful array—of insanity." Not everything beautiful has to be true to have value, you know.)

At least Duncan had seen the truth, or a kind of truth, firsthand. All the rest of these people sitting in their glorified clubhouse listening to why intelligent mushrooms were going to rise to the surface one day and kill everyone—and, in some cases, why they were going to enjoy the experience—these people hadn't seen the truth. They just didn't know any better—they were guessing. They were lonely and screaming out for company, or for something to keep out the darkness. Even a crackpot theory is better than no theory at all. Than nobody. Than an abyss.

Like the hole that lies behind me, leading Truff knows where. (Truff may not know where it leads, having more important things on His mind, but you and I both know it leads into the underground. Let me evoke Truff in a more appropriate context: for Truff's sake, stop being so melodramatic!)

What were Mary and I doing while Duncan decided to go slumming? I'm so glad you asked. Mary was establishing the beginnings of her brilliant career, which would eventually result in the creation of her stunning flesh necklace. Meanwhile, I climbed farther down the ladder of success. I said goodbye to my gallery one murky spring day.

I stood there alone on the street, and Sybel said, "It had a good run. You accomplished a lot. You shouldn't be too sad. How much longer could it hold together anyway?"

"Once, you said this was just the beginning, Sybel."

"Did you really believe me? I just told you what you needed to hear."

"No, you're right. You're right."

I turned to look at him and he was gone, of course. I had to collect my thoughts for a moment after that. Then I walked away without looking back, for fear of bursting into tears.

※🦋※

Escape, escaping, escaped. I'd done it. I was no longer in even the most remote danger of being considered a success. I would have to begin again, in a city I did not entirely trust to help me. I loitered in the same circles, lounged in the same antechambers of vice on occasion, but it was only pretense—a kind of fading after-glow that did not warm the face.

I threw myself on Sirin's mercy once more. Sirin had taken up his long-ago position at Hoegbotton, with nary a whiff of rumor as to what skullduggery he had involved himself in while he was gone. (I don't know what he knew about the Hoegbottons to provide him with such protection, but it must have gone beyond mere evidence of embezzlement, adultery, or vice.)

But while Mary received from Sirin first-class treatment in the form of her first book contract, I got a job as a tour guide to Ambergris, my "office" on the first floor of the newly rebuilt H&S headquarters building. Although we rarely saw each other, Sirin and his rosewood desk lay directly above me. Sometimes I would look up at the ceiling tiles and imagine I saw butterflies fluttering out from between the cracks. There were days, I admit, when I seethed, ground my teeth, floated silent curses toward that ceiling. (The worst admission of all, I suppose, is that I introduced Sirin to Mary a few weeks before the war. It was largely on my recommendation that Sirin, upon his return, inquired with Mary as to the possibility of a book. I didn't tell you for the obvious reasons.)

To be fair, without my gallery and the tattered, faded cloak of respectability it had conveyed, I could no longer command a prestige position—and Sirin had found younger, cheaper writers for the article assignments that had once gone to Duncan and me. So, five days a week, a trickle of tourists would find their way to my office and sign up for such ridiculous tours as "Gray Cap Haunts and Habitat"—which consisted of showing them where various famous people had been "disappeared" or killed by the gray caps, then descending into the basement of the newly rebuilt Borges Bookstore, a place in which no gray cap had ever been seen. Another favorite tour was the dusk-to-midnight "Haunted Ambergris" expedition, to which I had to bring a measure of acting skills I did not possess, and a ream of notes to read from, since the stories all blended together otherwise. (I imagine I might have been good at this kind of work, if you'd ever given me an invite.)

But the worst tour, over time, was "Literary Highlights of Ambergris," since, as Sabon's popularity grew, I would be forced to take them past whatever expensive hovel she was currently renting, where they would gawk and circle, certain they would soon catch a glimpse of the author peering out from behind a curtain.

"This is the home of the controversial and talented Mary Sabon," began the official spiel I was made to mutter and cough to tourists who may or may not have cared very much.

"It is in this house that Sabon wrote much of her book *More Banal Banalities*, which disproved many of the more paranoid theories about the gray caps." And so on and so forth.

Sometimes, Sybel stared out at me from a nearby tree, sporting a not-unsympathetic smirk on his face and dressed in his most familiar outfit: the wood-land greens and browns of his youth.

"Gently, Janice," he would soothe. "It's not so bad. It could be worse. I know all about worse."

"Worse? How much worse could it get?" I would ask him, but by then he was already a mote of dust spiraling at the corner of my eye, and me having confused myself and tourists alike by having spoken aloud.

The more I reflect on it, Sybel had it right: I was, considering the condition of my foot, lucky. My status as Old Relic counterbalanced the crippling whorls of my wooden toes and the grain of my soles. I could diverge from the script to tell stories about the places we visited with a knack for detail and intrigue and per-sonal panache that few other guides could match. I truly had been there when *that* happened, or *this*, or *this*. To pay for my past crimes against public decency, against modesty, I would even sometimes have to guide people to the site of my poor gutted gallery, there to recite a history of it and the fabled New Art. (Do you really believe that Sirin didn't experience a shiver of perverse satisfaction from forcing you to go back there? I'm sure he did; how could he not?)

I didn't mind the job too much in those early years, if I'm to be truthful, espe-cially when I didn't have to do the "Haunted Ambergris" tour, and before I had to stand outside Mary's home like a fool. At least part of the time a horse and buggy would be employed so I didn't have to drag my leg around. And business gradually became more robust: the cessation of hostilities soon brought a new wave of the curious—not curious enough to venture over for the Festival, but curious enough to explore during the daylight of other seasons.

Besides, I often contrived to arrive at the Blythe Academy right before lunch, so I could allow those bright-eyed travelers from Morrow or Stockton or Nicea to wander as they would, within reason, while I sat down for a sandwich with Bonmot. At a stone bench. Under the fabled but now considerably more wizened willow trees.

"Tough crowd today?" Bonmot would almost always say, making me smile.

"I'm not a comedian or a juggler, Bonmot. I don't have to entertain. I just have to lead them around to interesting places."

"You are such a kind tour guide," Bonmot would say, trying not to laugh. "To teach them the responsibility of finding their own entertainment."

"Why not? That's what *I* have to do."

I wish I could say my lunches with Bonmot felt the same as before, but they did not. Yes, a similar sense of contentment, of ease, lingered over those conversations, but it became a more fleeting thing; it did not last as long or affect me as power-fully. Our discussions had limits; we had acquired scars. Bonmot never discussed Duncan, and I, not wishing to give up even the faded pleasure of those lunches, never pressed the point.

If the situation had changed, so had Bonmot. The war had changed him.

"You're hesitant sometimes now," I said to him once, during an uncomfortable silence. "You halt on the verge of saying things."

Bonmot nodded. "You're right. I halt because I am not certain anymore. The things I thought I knew do not always seem *right* when I say them, so I say them first in my head, and then speak. Otherwise, it's as if I were mouthing sawdust. And I miss people who have died, and sometimes when I speak, I see them, because this priest or that priest who has passed on had taught me the truism I was about to say."

He stared at me with a knowing sadness. "I liked it better when I knew every-thing."

A barking laugh. And an echo from Sybel, standing in the willow tree, whis-pering to me: "*I liked it better when I knew nothing.*"

For my part, I found it odd to sit there watching the current crop of fresh-faced students make their way across the courtyard—lithe, flushed with success, seem-ingly innocent—and know that it was just a few years ago that Mary and Duncan and Bonmot had played out their appointed roles of lust, love, secrecy, and discovery. The war lay like an insurmountable black wall between then and now.

⚜

I should have mentioned before that the beads of Mary's flesh necklace actually did have faces and names. As I stood at the base of the stairs, the scarlet imprint of my hand still warm on Mary's face, about to respond to her hateful words, I remember turning away from her for a moment to stare at them. Let me identify them for you as they come into focus in my memory, that you may know them if you see them: John Batte, Vice-Royal under Bonmot, rose to the post of Royal following Bonmot's death, and is a staunch supporter of Sabon's work, even going so far as allowing her access to previously closed Truffidian archives. Sarah Cryller, currently the ambassador to Ambergris from the House of Frankwrithe & Lewden, is a newly risen star still bright-burning who at one time hoped Sabon might defect to her publishing company. The oft-mentioned Merrimount provided Sabon's "in" to the creative community at large and appeared at many of her book release parties. Jessica Hoegbotton, scion of the House of Hoegbotton, main liaison between the public and Sabon's words, is the one who laughed loudest at Mary's joke about Duncan. Daniel Griswald, Antechamber of the Truffidian Church, has teeth that glint like fangs when he grins, which is more often than a stone gargoyle, and who, in his infinite wisdom, has failed to ban any of Sabon's books, instead embracing them and recommending them to his congregation. And, finally, Mathew Daffed, one of Duncan's colleagues at Blythe Academy, is now among his most outspoken critics.

And others, still others, whose faces blur even as I conjure up their names. Why did I invite them? Because I had to—Lake demanded it. Even as I condemned them with my gaze, I found that I was surprised—surprised that they should have so disliked my brother, surprised at the fear rising from their faces like steam. (Some of them have been scoundrels at times, but most of the rest of them have caused me no harm, even as they continue to send Mary to her triumph.)

⚜

At first, I received updates on Mary's progress through Bonmot.

"Mary has sold her second book," Bonmot told me one fall, the willow trees impervious to the change of seasons even as, across the street, oaks became an indignant red-and-orange, and then bald, and a strange whisper of flame spread through the city.

"Her second book," I said.

It was almost unbearable to receive such information from Bonmot, when every day I could hear the creak and shift of timber above me as Sirin walked between his desk and his precious butterflies. (Worse, worse—I found she had taken up with another man, her own age, the son of her father's best friend, someone she had known for years. Someone comfortable. Someone safe. Someone with a "III" in his name. I could tolerate the books, because I knew they contained a little piece of me in them, but I could not tolerate that relationship.)

"Yes. It's called *The Inflammation of Aan Tribal Wars*. I've had a look at it, and it's excellent. Very well researched. She's a credit to the school."

As Duncan was not, went the tired old, silent old refrain. (Bonmot never forgave me, not even at the end. I couldn't understand that. I'd have forgiven him had our situations been reversed, but, then, I am not a priest. I did see him sometimes, in the last few years before he passed on. When I took walks in Trillian Park, I would discover him sitting on a bench as I turned a corner. He would look up, and our eyes would meet before he could turn away. Those few times, I would see a peace within him that faded as he recognized me. I wouldn't stop to talk—it was too painful, too maddening, to understand that he could not move past my lapse of judgment. Later, back in my apartment overlooking Trillian Square, I would sit on my balcony drinking wine, analyzing the moment in the park, searching my memory of our brief encounter for some hint of recognition on his part that did not include bitterness or rancor. Sometimes I convinced myself, sometimes I did not.)

Bonmot—to his credit, or perhaps not to his credit—never realized that I might prefer not to hear such details, such confirmation of Mary's success. Later, when he better understood the humiliation of having to stand outside of her various residences and tell tourists about her, Bonmot stopped telling me. He must have realized by then that her ascent was self-evident.

"That's nice," I mumbled. "I am sure it is a very interesting book she has written." Through a mouthful of my chicken sandwich, looking out of the corner of my eye for my bumbling tourist charges, to make sure they had not gotten into too much trouble.

We studied Truffidian religious texts at lunch sometimes as well. I found them soothing. *My God, keep my tongue from evil, my lips from lies. Help me ignore those who slander me.* Although I could no longer bring myself to attend services in the newly renovated Truffidian Cathedral or any other enclosed space, I took some measure of comfort from the hymns and sayings. *Guardian of happiness, in whose presence despair flees, with Your great compassion grant me the ability to welcome what may come with calm and grace, to experience happiness and joy.* When I read them aloud before sleep, the nightmarish images would recede, the red mist of Sybel's death dissipate. *May You find delight in the words of my mouth and in the emotions of my heart.* The sensation, when I went to bed, of lying down among a row of corpses would lessen, become tolerable. *The wise must die, even as the foolish and senseless, leaving their possessions to others.*

"Do you like being a tour guide?" Bonmot asked me at one lunch.

"I do," I said, before I could think about it. If I'd thought about it, I would have said no.

"Why?" he asked, no reproach in his voice, just a genuine curiosity. He had hinted more than once that he could find me a comparable job with the church, but turning my religion into a daily chore, complete with choir, didn't interest me.

"Why?" Why did I like working as a tour guide? In those early years: "Because I get to be outside a lot. I get to see the city afresh, from the perspective of those unfamiliar with her."

Because it took me away from Duncan's world. Because it allowed me to relive, in daydream reveries, my past successes week after week. Because I met interesting people, some of them men, though I had learned to be more discerning than in the past. Because those who I guided saw me not as a failure but as part of the heritage, the history, of Ambergris. And there was something to be said for not trying quite so hard. I arrived in the same place, I had begun to notice, regardless of the amount of effort.

But I could never truly escape Duncan, just as Duncan could not escape himself. And ultimately I wouldn't have wanted to. Except for my father's writings, Duncan is my only link to my father. Duncan is still here, I hope, in the flesh, while Dad speaks to me in shards of meaning gleaned from the fragments Duncan kept of his journals, his scribblings and essays. All of it is work-related; Dad appears never to have written anything that was not related to work, or, at least, such writings weren't found when Mom cataloged his things.

I've gone through all of it twice before lugging it here along with anything else I wanted to salvage from Duncan's apartment. Most of Dad's papers are so dry, so dusty, that I've begun to understand that he lived in his own little special-ized world. His work galvanized and, perhaps, electrified, other historians with its sense of rarefied knowledge, but there's nothing for the rest of us to hold on to. Sometimes I think Duncan took it upon himself to "translate" our dad's work into a form that might be palatable to the public. (I thought maybe he knew, maybe something in the papers would solve my mysteries. It never did.) Sometimes I think that Duncan would have been better off becoming a plumber, a carpenter, a blacksmith, a merchant, a missionary.

Nothing of our personal history made it into Dad's work, even though that his-tory had some relevance. Some said, not without a hint of mockery, that you could trace our family's history on my mother's side all the way back to the founding of Ambergris by John Manzikert—that one of the anonymous, unremarked-upon members of the ship's crew, George Bliss, had been our distant great-to-the-umpteenth-power grandfather. Over the years, among our shadow relatives—aunts, uncles, grandparents, cousins, "shadow" because they lived in far-off cities like Nicea and we saw them rarely—an entire mythology had grown up around Bliss. Stories of Bliss fighting off gray caps, of his friendship with Samuel Tonsure before Tonsure disappeared, vague references to the underground—all apocryphal, of course. (Apocryphal? Maybe, but I enjoyed those stories growing up. Those stories reaffirmed my birthright to crawl around in dimly lit places.)

Dad used to joke that he had married Mom as part of his research into the history of the city.

"Your mother, children," he said once, "figures prominently in my current research. She's fodder for my essays. Certain experiments, certain experiments cannot be conducted without her—or, if conducted, do not"—and he stared point-edly at Mom and then back at us—"yield the same results."

Sometimes when he said this, he would hold her close from behind, nuzzle her neck. Mom would give a sly, quick smile then, before pretending to be of-fended as she pulled away from him, and I remember that smile, because it gave me the first clue that there might be an adult world existing above or on top of the one in which we dwelt as children.

Mom had a problem laughing at herself; she never knew if people were laughing with her or at her, so she never fully gave herself up to it with other people—Dad was the only one who could make her laugh in a way that seemed effortless rather than forced.

As for whether first-generation Ambergrisian blood flows through our veins, I don't know, but I think our dad believed it did. (And if it didn't before, Janice, the city probably flows through my veins now, in altered form, whether I want it to or not. An entire world flows through my veins these days.)

✲❀✲

While upstairs Sirin worked on making Mary the flavor of the decade and downstairs I labored at scraping out a living, Duncan fleshed out his theories and his articles, which would one day culminate, or dissolve, in his *Early History of Ambergris* tour guide book. (Or at least culminate in the unexpurgated version that has still never seen print.)

In those days, sentences crawled out of Duncan's skin, paragraphs exhaled with each breath. On a winter's morning, you could almost see them forming in the white smoke of his speech. (For all the good it did me—most of the sentences and paragraphs didn't coalesce into longer works, or if they did, I sacrificed them to the AFTOIS newsletter.)

Sometimes I thought the Spore of the Gray Cap made him prolific—that in a space neither above nor belowground, he felt in the most perfect balance—and thus balanced, ballasted, he could write without self-consciousness. Certainly, the owner loved his presence—"fringe" or not, they'd never had a historian use their tavern as a work space. Of course, Duncan brought more business with him than I ever did, in the form of his fellow crackpots. Lacond even indulged for a time, before his illness made that impossible.

The following note in Duncan's journal exemplifies his approach:

Should the historian's personal life happen to coincide in some way with the history he has chosen to write about—if the personal history "doubles" the public history—then an alchemy occurs whereby the historian, in a sense, becomes the history. That is, once rendered in all the signs and symbols at the historian's command, the history he has written becomes, for him, the story of his own life. This fact may not be obvious to the reader except in flashes and flickers of reflected thought, where the passion of the historian for the story peers out, naked, from the page. There, for a flicker of a moment, we find the historian exposed, if only the world decides to correctly interpret the clues. (I didn't write this. I was quoting another historian. I can't even remember which one.)

In expressing this theory—a theory that calls for the historian to internalize a selected portion of history as part of his or her life; or, more specifically, to map historical events to personal events—Duncan was deeply influenced by the work of the idiosyncratic Nicean philosopher-historian Edgar Rybern. Rybern believed that the personal politics of each individual distorts their view of history. As Rybern wrote in his book *Approaches to History* (a book Sabon violently disapproved of, even during her days at the Academy):

Such a person never merely traces the outline of the past. Texts do not sit side by side on the shelf, but intermingle, entering into conflict and confluence with one another until the probable emerges from the impossible. Reduced to rubble, such sources provide the raw building material for a theory of greater import and durability. However, the story that emerges from this process does not interest such a historian. The tale told is mere preamble to explanation, preamble to a more personal theory. In such a process, the chronology and lineage of the acts depicted in the narrative depend on the prejudices and experiences of the individual's psyche, and the subconscious impulses embedded therein.

Based on Rybern's musings, Duncan began to ask himself—in countless articles published in the hapless AFTOIS newsletter, and in countless conversations with Lacond—"Why not *consciously* distort history by focusing on those portions and patterns that have the most relevance or resonance to one's own life?"

Such a slant would, presumably, intensify the empathy that the historian has to those particular historical events. For example, I, as a historian, would be most at home describing the history of various mental wards and the effects on the psyche of mass slaughter witnessed up close.

If every individual mind can be said to exist within a lively morass of prejudice and subjectivity, then the pursuit of the objective becomes a futile, laughable goal—in effect, a lie; especially in a field such as history, where every day, every hour, every minute, the historian becomes more distant from the core occurrences under observation. (A simplification, true, but essentially accurate. Not that it matters to anyone anymore. History is about to catch up with us, and what I've really learned is that anything connected to the printed page becomes a kind of tombstone, marking the death of the past.)

Lacond, for all of his faults, understood this about Duncan. (After all, he, like me, had been underground at least once or twice, and came away from it having paid a physical price.) In one issue of the newsletter, Lacond wrote:

> When Duncan Shriek writes about the Silence—as he has been known to do within these very pages—he quite literally, in my opinion, writes also of his personal silences over the years, the way in which he has been silenced—by others, by his own mistakes—and all the similar silences, suffered by us all. In a sense, he has made Ambergris's history personal. He may be too good a historian to invade his text, but certain parallels emerge again and again—allusions to Tonsure's descent into silence and despair and subsequent reemergence in the form of a book being especially prevalent.

Those experts who bothered to refute Duncan's theories—mostly Sabon—pointed to the dangers of the personal history approach. Sabon wrote an essay for the H&S collection *Impersonal Perspectives: Objectivity in Ambergrisian History* (which probably sold about five copies):

> The irrefutable fissure in any theory of "personal history" lies in the impulse to find a plateau far above sheer fact, to reveal a lesson or universal "truth" that can be mapped to an individual life and intertwined with a complicated intellectual disdain: contempt for accuracy, rejection of contradictory evidence, confusion of conjecture with truth, resistance to correction.

Sabon had a point, of sorts. Not that Duncan's theories were flawed—no one ever dared to test their veracity through underground research. But when Duncan began, a few years later, to write his *Early History*, he looked to what he was writing for some indication of how to live his life, so that instead of finding what in history could become personal, he let the personal become history. (You might be right, but the reading public never had a chance to discover the truth or falsehood of it, either in the book or in reality.)

Unfortunately, in my opinion, the parallels that Duncan sought did not always exist. As I told him once, "Nothing in your studies will ever explain the death of our father." I don't think he believed me. He would have believed me even less if I had told him Bonmot and Truffidianism might be able to help him with that mystery. (Of all your incarnations, your transformation to the cause of organized religion baffled me the most. I certainly didn't begrudge you your conversion, though—all I envied was the time you spent with Bonmot.)

⁂

I've finally found something personal of Dad's in among all the dry discourse—tucked away inside a box inside another box. A canvas sculpture of a mushroom, about twelve inches tall. Part of his personal history, you might call it, and the symbol of a rare hiccup in the respect my parents showed each other.

That respect manifested itself in the way our father avoided invading Mom's space. Our parents were as separate and yet together as any two people could be, and I've often thought that when Dad died, the reason it took Mom so long to create again is that Dad created the space for her to be able to make her art.

Dad did not enter some rooms of our house in Stockton—in particular, Mom's studio. There, she would relax and sketch, paint, or even work on sculptures, her studio window providing a magnificent view of the forest. She knew that Dad would never enter, not even for a quick visit or to remind her of some dinner party they had to attend, not even when she was out of the house. And she did the same for him—his office formed a country forbidden to all of us.

Some days, they would be in their separate spaces and the house would seem quiet, but Duncan and I could sense a kind of tingle or hum in the silence, a potent energy. Because we knew that, in their separate spaces, in their own different yet specific ways, both of our parents were *creating*. That feeling of applied industry, of work, permeated our awareness in those years before Dad's death.

Which is not to say that our parents didn't take joy in their creations, or want to share them. But there was a space to work and a space to share their work. The living room served as that latter area. If either wanted to share in the flush of post-inspiration, out the pages or painting would come to the living room. On that neutral ground, they would present their findings and receive their praise. Dad would read from the loose-leaf pages crumpled in his hand while Mom would murmur, "Lovely. Inspired. Very original." Or Mom would unveil a sketch or study or painting and discuss the spark that made it coalesce into being, while Dad would say, "Wonderful use of color. I love the way you've drawn that figure.

Beautiful." (Such compliments would be tenfold in intensity, Janice, should you or I share our early experiments. I can still remember how much praise they lavished on you for your first paintings. They loved your work unconditionally.)

In that separate space and that shared space, I think I can see the secret of their happiness. Each could feel the other's presence in their separate spaces as powerfully as in their shared space.

But the living room also served as a place to seek assistance. If stuck, if faced with conundrum or puzzle, dead words or dead paint, one would stomp out into that middle ground and, by certain signals, make it clear the other was needed to brainstorm possible solutions.

On our dad's part, the signal involved much crinkling of papers and long, deep sighs (I perfected my own sigh listening to his), perhaps even an artificial propensity to make noise by banging into furniture. On Mom's part it was more direct, because to get to the living room she had to pass Dad's office. A quick slap of the palm against his door on the way to common ground usually got his attention.

What always surprised me is how quickly the other parent would halt in his or her own labors and come out to the living room. Sometimes it was just to listen to the other vent, sometimes to offer practical suggestions.

Only once, to my knowledge, did one or the other cross a boundary. Our dad one day decided to try his hand at sculpture, but not just any sculpture. He wanted to use wire and canvas, to combine sculpture and painting, in a sense. I could see from the expression on Mom's face what she thought of this idea, but she loaned him the supplies and for a week he worked on his own New Art. You could hear him bumping into things in his office, cursing sometimes, coming out to beg more supplies from Mom. Duncan and I both expected great things. (Or, at least, *something*—or, as Janice put it at the time, some *thing*.)

Finally, Dad had finished, and we all gathered in the living room for the unveiling. The sculpture stood on a table near the couch, covered by a bedsheet. Mom stood to the side, arms crossed, while Dad explained the concept.

"I wanted to reveal the true shape of everyday things. This is the first of a series of studies that combine painting and sculpture into a new hybrid," he said.

With those words, he pulled the sheet away, to reveal . . . a canvas mushroom, wires under the canvas giving it a shape.

"A mushroom. Made of canvas," Mom said.

"Well," Dad said, "I haven't painted it yet."

Mom went back into her studio.

I went back to reading.

Only Duncan had the decency to walk up to our dad and tell him how much he liked it.

Dad never crossed the line into the arts again.

I don't think I was fated to be granted the kind of connection our parents often had, and I don't know if I learned enough from our parents' example. The dynamic changed too much after Dad's death, and our careers took us too far apart to allow it, but I imagine this connection, this understanding, is something that Mary and Duncan shared before they grew apart. (All too briefly, I'm afraid. Some months it was there, some months it wasn't. You need to know a person for a long time to develop that kind of trust. We didn't have enough time.)

"Nativism," Duncan said to me once, "is like a prolonged case of mass suicide."

I mention this because History and my reincarnation as a tour guide continued to intersect in a number of ways, against my wishes. For example, evincing a cruel kindness, Sirin managed to finagle me a nonpaying position on the toothless horror that is the Ambergris Tourism Board, in a nod to my past status as an "iconic figure in society in general, etc., etc.," as one of the other board members greeted me before slumping back into a kind of half-drool, half-reverie that looked quite pleasant.

I joined the board at the perfect time: it seemed to be trying to make itself obsolete. The first day I reported for service, the board decided to mount a rather muddled campaign to discourage tourism in the city because, as one gout-ridden veteran of many a real or imaginary war put it, "These fools. Must protect them. Too many deaths. At Festival time. Darlings deserve better." I almost pointed out that fewer tourists meant more of a chance, statistically, that local residents would be the targets of violence or "odd events," as the broadsheets now sometimes termed encounters involving gray caps. But I kept my mouth shut. After all, it was only my first day on the job, and I wasn't yet sure I wanted to burn any bridges. (If you'd taken your duties more seriously, perhaps some of AFTOIS's positions would have received a sympathetic hearing from those old bastards. As it was, I can't recall you doing anything at the public meetings of the board but taking up space.)

As a result, for two years, in the months leading up to the Festival, the board paid for posters to be put up that depicted dead dogs in a variety of unkind and teeth-grimacing positions, complete with titles such as DEAD DOGS. DEAD TOURISTS. IT'S ALL THE SAME TO US. STAY OUT OF AMBERGRIS AROUND FESTIVAL TIME.

The posters appeared to result in insulted—but not fatally insulted—tourists, if the large number of people letting me lead them around the city and babble about dead people and old buildings was any indication. I certainly didn't mind this change, but posters or no, a more profound and negative transformation had begun to change Ambergris. The invisible yet necessary buffer between the professional and the personal slowly eroded, and for this I blame Nativism.

I'm sure that blaming Nativism for *anything* will be seen as blasphemy by many readers, but then, you've made it this far—you can't give up now. So, if you haven't become irrevocably jaded, perhaps even revolted (or revolting), by the preceding pages, I dare say you'll hardly even twitch when I say: *I blame Nativism.* Not the specific form of insanity displayed by Sabon's father—not that brand of Nativism. No, I refer to the form that Duncan called "the final outcome of the war": an attempt to become blind, deaf, and dumb as a most peculiar and pathetic method of semi-survival. (It allowed people to function in their day-to-day lives, rather than boarded up, gibbering in fear, in their homes. I'll give it that much.)

As Sabon's kind of Nativism spread throughout the Southern cities by way of her books and essays, it infected the tourists who subjected themselves to my tours. Over time, I no longer needed Bonmot to give me updates on Mary's progress. Instead, her flock of black crows feasting on the carcasses of Duncan's investigations could be clearly seen in the eyes of the visitors I guided from one banal site to another.

I can't say I minded these intrusions into rote routine at first. As I told Sybel when he accompanied me on these jaunts—and he was always there in some form—each recital of the same information became more stale than the last, until I was like some crippled, half-senile goat or sheep, chewing and rechewing the same yellowing stalks of grass. It was a relief when the replies to my jaded bleatings began to change from polite nods or the obvious questions or the occasional attempt at wit, to observations such as "Mary Sabon wrote about this place in her book on Nativism. You should mention that next time."

"What a good suggestion!" I would reply. "I'll be sure to do that," and try to carry on as if nothing offensive had been said, if they would let me.

Sometimes they also came seeking wish fulfillment: "Do you think we might see Sabon on this tour?"

To which I would reply in a clipped but neutral tone, "Not on this tour." Not even if we stood for a week in the shade of the large oak tree outside her ancestral home.

Even more jarring, though, were the questions out of nowhere—broadsides I was in no position to absorb, meant to torment me—that opened a door where no door should exist.

"Are you any relation to the Duncan Shriek mentioned in Sabon's books?"

Most of the time, my interrogator exuded a naive good humor as natural as sweat when asking the question—wanted only to know that I was not just an expert but intimately *involved* with the information I imparted, whether we stood inside the old post office or outside of some tavern with "Spore" in the title.

I had no problem providing graceful answers in such cases, although each time it did surprise me—and more than surprise me, it changed the world so that I saw my brother's influence in everything.

"Nativists are like Manziists or Menites or any other religion," Duncan said once. "Just as righteous, just as right." No wonder their questions changed my worldview.

As Nativism conquered the city and the entire South, I found the door to my misery widening and darkening, so that a belligerent quality entered the voices of those asking the questions.

One particularly grueling and hot summer afternoon a few years before the Shift began in earnest, I heard the words, "Are you Duncan's sister?" delivered in a tone somewhere between fervent eagerness and bloodlust.

My surroundings, which had faded to the usual blur—my mouth spewing a stream of familiar words while my mind went elsewhere—came back into sharp focus.

The tour group and I stood in the middle of Voss Bender Memorial Square, in front of a fountain depicting Banker Trillian's victory over the rival banker-warriors of Nicea. Around the square stood the ancient buildings that had once served as Trillian's headquarters. In between, a pleasing and aromatic mixture of green-and-red blossoms signaled not only the arrival of the summer's wildflowers but House Hoegbotton's crass attempt to memorialize the struggle that followed

Voss Bender's death. I had set the tour group loose on the square for a few minutes, and they currently wandered here and there, staring at everything with a freshness I could not understand.

I faced my interrogator, who doubled in an instant. A woman had spoken, but her husband stood beside her, just as resolute and nervous. Both of them had reached the far end of their fifties, the woman gray-haired and stuffed into a form-less flower-print dress, matched to white stockings and blocky wooden shoes.

"I can't say I much cared for the mad glint in her eyes, or the thick red smile she gave me," I told Duncan later, relaxing in his apartment.

In fact, I looked at her as if she were a huge mushroom that had erupted through the courtyard tiles.

"That was no mad glint," Duncan replied. "That was the spark of righteous purpose."

Her husband, stocky muscle half-turned to fat, wore spectacles and, bizarrely, the kind of trousers and tunic that had gone out of style long before Old Fart had capitulated to New Fart—close to the kind of museum pieces I spoke about during the tour.

Helpfully, their jaunty name tags, affixed to the continents of their chests, disclosed not only names but locations. Mortar and Pestle, as I came to think of them, hailed from my birthplace of Stockton. Somehow, this did not reassure me.

"Are you Duncan's sister?" Pestle asked again. This time it felt as if she'd poked me in the ribs with her finger.

"And what if I am?" I asked.

Mortar remained impassive while Pestle gave me a blank look, as if she hadn't expected a question in return.

"We'd have a message for him if you were his sister," Mortar said in a gravelly baritone, shifting uneasily. I could tell that this conversation hadn't been his idea, but that he'd decided to make the best of it.

"Really? You'd do that?" I said. It wasn't really a question, and I'd like to report that I delivered those words with the appropriate amount of withering scorn, but that's not true. I was truly caught wrong-footed by the idea that two tourists could walk up to me and *presume* in such a way.

Mortar balanced on one leg for a second while Pestle hesitated; she definitely hated being asked questions.

"Absolutely. Absolutely that's what I'd do," Pestle said, finally.

"And what would the message be?" I asked her. I shouldn't have bothered. I could have ignored her. I could have moved on to the next part of the tour.

Pestle frowned and her face achieved a certain narrow intensity. "Why, I'd ask you to tell him that he's wrong and that the Nativists are right."

"And that he should stop trying to scare people with his theories," Mortar added.

Mortar and Pestle stood there, waiting for my response while the sun baked us all. My gaze fled to two swallows chasing insects through the searing blue sky, and I wondered how it had come to this. Had I misjudged how far I had fallen, and was falling still? Where will it end? Can it end? Should it end? My fingers are green with spores. That cannot be a good sign.

※₩※

I could have told old Mortar and Pestle—for whom I now feel a mounting affection where no such affection should exist—that Duncan was closer than they might have thought, and perhaps they would like to meet him? But I don't think they really would have wanted to meet him. That the person they had pictured in their minds actually existed would probably have confounded them. Unlike Nativism, which existed precisely so people could avoid being confounded.

Nativism, to my mind, had become the next "phenomenon," like the New Art before it, except in a different discipline. You didn't have to paint anything or enjoy art to join it. You didn't have to react or interpret or express yourself. Nothing so active. You just had to believe in a theory and mindlessly recite it to others with any minor variations you might have added to it in the meantime. (Not much different from the chants some of the imprisoned Truffidian monks used to drive the fear from their hearts.)

Nativism would become so popular that not long after Mortar, Pestle, and I had our enlightening conversation in Bender Square, the Ambergris Tourism Board, against my sole and emphatic "No—hell, no," vote, added a Nativism tour to my busy schedule.

What did this new tour consist of? Our standard "Gray Cap Oddities" tour combined with a few extras, like a view of Sabon's family home, Blythe Academy, and some carefully selected and cultivated fungus-infested walls—"Ooh, very pretty, very awe-inspiring," most tourists would coo—and a lot of extra propaganda that made my teeth hurt. I never thought that I would ever be required to repeat the name "Sabon" so many times to so many strangers.

"Am I Duncan's sister?" I finally replied. "Yes, I am. Do you know him?"

"We know of him," Mortar said, almost cleverly.

"But you don't know him?"

"No, not personally," Pestle replied.

They didn't even know you, Duncan," I told him later. "Hadn't met you even once. And yet it was as if they thought they did know you—personally."

"Oh, I see. I thought perhaps, given your use of his first name, that you were old friends of his."

"The price of reflected fame, I guess," Duncan said, staring out the window into the courtyard. "It's enough to have read about you."

At least I got the courtesy of an embarrassed look from old Mortar. Pretty Pestle, though, went right on pounding away.

Eventually, I managed to rescue myself from the Nativism tour, but it took almost a year. People liked the irony of a Shriek, any Shriek, narrating that tour—at least the ones who had read Mary's book, and too many of them had read Mary's book. (Even me. I'm surprised you make no mention here of the time *I* took your Nativism tour. I've never seen anyone have to hold in so much irritation for such a long time. I only did it because for a time I contemplated joining the fray. If they wanted to use my life for their mass hallucinations, then I should at least have made a little extra money off it. Can you imagine the furor if *Duncan* Shriek had become a tour guide?)

Cinsorium: Rethinking the Myth of the Gray Caps was a book we needed during those reactionary rebuilding years as much as we'd needed Sabon's pig cartel book a few years before. It was the book that made the rift between Duncan and Mary permanent. As Duncan wrote in his journal after reading it, "For the first time, my body understands what my mind accepted long before: Mary is never coming back to me."

In her book, Sabon alternately refuted Duncan's theories about the gray caps and cribbed from them—as if she had ground Duncan's ideas down to specks of glitter and then used them to decorate her own creations. (Perhaps it wouldn't have hurt so much if I hadn't given her a copy of my own *Cinsorium* when we were at Blythe, inscribed "My dearest Mary—here's the heart of me. Treat it gently. Love, Duncan." She couldn't have treated *my* Cinsorium more ruthlessly in *her* Cinsorium if she'd honed the book's boards to a fatal sharpness and then stabbed me with them repeatedly. I can forgive her for most things, but not that.)

"So that is the message you would like me to relay to Duncan?" I asked Pestle, to make sure.

A triumphant look from Pestle. "Yes, thanks. That would be wonderful. But we have more to tell him."

"I rather thought you might."

✾✾✾

As everyone knows, Nativism consists of two major ideas, but most people do not realize that only one of them is unique. The other has been around for centuries. Sabon's innovation consisted in how she put the two together and then slapped her father's crowd-pleasing title of "Nativism" on top of it all like the final slice of bread on a particularly messy sandwich.

What was the first part of this magnificent theory? To start with, Sabon floated the thought—I can't even credit it with the term "idea"—that the gray caps were the degenerate descendants of a local tribe similar to the Dogghe or the Nimblytod (without asking either tribe how they felt about being lumped in with the gray caps, and without consulting their extensive oral histories), but a tribe that had been colonized and then subjugated by several variations of fungus found in both above- and belowground Ambergris. She claimed that the mighty city that had existed before Manzikert I razed it had housed a Saphant-type civilization predating the gray caps. She even went so far as to suggest that the gray caps had been a servant class to this hypothetical other race. (I found it highly ironic, given the fate of my books at the hands of reviewers, that by postulating this "other race" and leaving that question as the book's central mystery, she so captured readers' imaginations that no one thought to cry out, "Where's the proof?")

Pestle said, "Tell Duncan that he doesn't need to worry about the gray caps."

"They say you don't need to worry about the gray caps, Duncan."

"Ah, but I know that they worry about us, and that worries me."

Duncan did a rather unconvincing imitation of a shuffling gray cap. If I hadn't seen him do it before, I wouldn't have known what he was trying to do.

"Half-wit."

"*Unappreciative pedant. But what else did they say?*"

"Also tell him," Mortar added, without a hint of threat, "that he might want to go into another line of work."

"*Ho ho! Haven't you said the same to me sometimes, Janice? So how can you complain?*"

"*Do you want to hear the rest or are you going to be difficult?*"

"I'm sorry," I said to M&P, remembering a valuable bit of advice from Sybel about how it's never too late to correct your course so long as you've not yet run aground. (Because Sybel was, of course, an *expert* on sailing metaphors.) "I'm sorry, but I was joking. I'm not really Duncan's sister. I just like to claim I am sometimes, you know, because it makes things more interesting. My apologies."

I turned to the rest of the tourists, who had regrouped in front of me and had become a little too interested in my conversation with M&P.

"Now, as we continue, notice the telltale Trillian period details in the building across the square—in particular the fluted archways, the broad columns, the fine filigree. Also note—"

"I don't believe you," Mortar said, with the kind of earnest emphasis that can be interpreted as sternly polite or quietly angry, depending on your inclination.

Not for the first time, I remember thinking that perhaps it was time to change careers again.

The second part of Nativism reflected an odd prejudice that Duncan had tried to refute in his own book: most historians (and laypeople) thought of and wrote about the gray caps as if they represented a natural phenomenon, as immutable, faceless, and unpredictable as the weather, and, therefore, best understood in the aggregate, like the change of seasons or a bad thunderstorm. (Would that the Nativists had treated the gray caps like weather and tried to divine, from certain signs—a lowering of the temperature, a particular type of cloud, a strange hot wind—what the gray caps had planned for us.)

As Duncan wrote in his book so many years ago:

Looking back at all of Ambergris's many historical accounts, the answers to three basic yet profound questions are always missing: (1) in the absence of a strong central government, how does Ambergris manage to avoid fragmentation into separate, tiny city-states? (2) What cause could there possibly be for the fluctuating levels of violence and personal property damage experienced during the Festival? (3) Given the presence of members of over one hundred contradictory religions and cults in the city, what prevents occurrences of holy war?

For Duncan, the answers always returned to the gray caps, who, by use of hidden influence (the first physical manifestation being Frankwrithe & Lewden's use of fungal weapons) and a multitude of carefully engineered "spore solutions," kept the population balanced between anarchy and control. To Duncan, this meant that it served the gray caps' interests for Ambergris to lurch ever forward, never truly disintegrating or cohering, but instead always on the edge, teetering.

However, Mary and her Nativists refused to believe in conscious gray cap machinations. In an article for *Ambergris Today,* Mary wrote:

> Time and again, apologists blame the gray caps for our own follies and misdeeds. Such a position abrogates personal responsibility and is as irresponsible as those religions that attribute deeds to the sun, moon, or sea. We are, ultimately, responsible for our own actions, our own history, and our own happiness. I do not refute any claim that the gray caps are vile and degenerate creatures, or that they have not influenced our city in a negative way. But they have not done so with *intent.* Their story is not that of an overarching conspiracy, of careful control over centuries, but instead the pitiful tale of a subjugated race that acts with the same instinct and lack of planning as any of the lower animals. For us to confer intent upon them—or to seek intent from them—turns us into victims, unable to fashion our own destinies. I reject such crackpot ideology.

Mary mercilessly picked away at any attempt to prove that the gray caps had exhibited conscious thought or causality, no matter how minor. For example, in a letter to the editor for a broadsheet, Duncan wrote about what appeared to him to be a side effect of the gray caps' efforts: (I did not. I considered these effects to be as intentional as all of the overt harm done to us by the gray caps.)

> The very spores that keep the population in thrall also undertake many beneficial tasks. For example, Ambergris has stayed relatively disease-free throughout its history, with no documented plague as has occurred in Stockton and Morrow. Whether intentional or not, these benefits should not be overlooked.

Mary skewered this idea, writing in a subsequent issue, "Does the absence of disease lead one to the immediate conclusion that some force other than common sense and hand-washing is protecting us?" (I am ashamed to admit that her letter to the editor, in response to my own, sent a little thrill down my spine. I know she wasn't responding to me personally, but it was still direct communication of a kind.)

"It all sounded so logical in her book," Duncan complained to me as we looked down at Trillian Square from his apartment window. Below us, M&P and the rest of the tourists were milling about, not sure what to do. "It doesn't matter that her proof is as insubstantial as mine."

"Yes," I said, "but can't you provide proof, Duncan? Can't you do something?"

"How? With another article for AFTOIS? All the mentions in the world in Mary's books do me no good. I'm offered a few interview opportunities, but only if I play the role of clown or eccentric. Anything I said to them would be tainted and instantly discounted. Better not to speak at all."

Earlier, I had sighed and turned back to Mortar and Pestle.

"You're right. I wasn't joking," I said. "Duncan is my brother. So I'll let him know what you said next time I see him. Now can we—"

"And give him this letter," Pestle said, pulling a sealed envelope out of her pocket and handing it to me.

I took it from her as if she had given me a dead fish. What further surprises could the day hold? How patient should I be? It was difficult not to see them, on some level, as Sabon's personal emissaries, sent to torment me.

". . . and give him your letter," I continued, lying. I threw it away, unread, at the first opportunity. "But I have a favor to ask in return. I need you to relay a message for me."

That surprised them, but Mortar nodded and said, "That only seems fair."

The main appeal of Nativism to Ambergrisians was that it freed them from any responsibility to think about or do *anything* about the gray caps, while reassuring them that this was the most responsible thing they could do. And, in my opinion—I can already hear the howls of outrage, but I am unmoved—it absolved Ambergrisians from any guilt over the massacre perpetrated by Manzikert I.

"Not to mention that it saved them from having to worry about another Silence," Duncan said. *M&P had disappeared from view. The square below was relatively quiet.*

"Not to mention," I said.

Perhaps the speed with which House Hoegbotton and House Frankwrithe & Lewden embraced Nativism proves Duncan's theory. What better way for the gray caps to protect themselves than by convincing the Houses? (I think this enters the far reaches of that land known as the Paranoid Conspiracy Theory, Janice.) Meanwhile, those of us not as devoted to blind ideology have had to suffer through the Nativists' huge rallies, their righteous speeches, their letter-writing campaigns when anything the least bit threatening to their worldview has the audacity to step out into the light. I would imagine that even Sabon never realized that Nativism would become so popular, or that it would drive her book sales for so long. (Although, you must admit, the mechanics of the Shift have put a stop to her momentum.)

I had personal reasons for rejecting Sabon's theory. Sometimes, during my tours of duty, I would see Sybel standing in the nearest available tree behind some mob listening to a Nativist speaker. He'd look back at me and shake his head, sadness in his eyes. After all, he'd been killed by a very specific deployment of the gray caps' weapons. I'd lost a foot. It was hard to blame either outcome, ultimately, on the random, the unexplainable. At least, I refused to do so.

"But how can we pass on a message from you?" Pestle asked.

"Easy," I said. "It's for Mary Sabon. She is, after all, the leader of you Nativist types."

Mortar had already begun shaking his head, about to protest that they didn't know Mary, that they'd only read her books, but I waved these objections aside, pulled them both close.

Before the war, before Sybel's death, before I became a gallery owner, this is what I would have said to them, either in a whisper or a roar: "First, let me point out that if you don't deliver this message for me, I will have Duncan bring the gray caps down upon you like a plague so you can see for yourself just how motivated they are. So I suggest that as soon as I stop talking, you start searching for Sabon. I want you to tell Mary to stop misleading sycophantic morons like yourselves. To stop making it seem like everything in our lives is under our control, to stop undermining everything my brother has ever worked toward. To stop killing him by degrees, in public. To stop wasting your time and his time with these ridiculous theories of hers that only apply to her personal demons. To stop to stop to stop to stop to stop."

But I didn't say that. I was Janice Shriek, former society figure, and I'll be damned if I let any two-bit tourists just off the slow boat from Stockton get under my skin.

✦✦✦

What drove Mary to the cruelty of showing her "affection" for Duncan as mentor by tearing down all he had built up—and doing so after he had already become comfortable as a ghost—I do not know. Perhaps it was not just fear. Perhaps it was out of envy. Perhaps it was to show she could do it all better.

The practical effect of Sabon's resurrection of discussions initiated by Duncan was that Frankwrithe & Lewden bought the rights to his books from Hoegbotton & Sons and proceeded to publish them in a badly edited, hideously expensive, horribly abridged omnibus entitled *Cinsorium & Other Historical Fables* (Dad would have punned it as *Sin-sore-ium & Other Hysterical Foibles*), an edition intended solely for the library market so that scholars could peruse it as part of their primary text exploration of Sabon's books. The rights Duncan had sold to Hoegbotton were all-encompassing and he could do nothing but accept a trickle of royalties from publication of the omnibus. He could not stop the butchery of his original texts. (Nor could I afford to object anyway, my income having dropped off precipitously since AFTOIS could not sustain me by itself.)

The omnibus received scant attention from reviewers—it was considered a historical curiosity, reflecting the "hysteria and ignorance of a less enlightened time," as one of the few notices put it—meaning that kind readers like Mortar and Pestle only encountered Shriek through Sabon's filter. One hates to think of Duncan struggling to express himself while F&L and his beloved Mary struggle to snuff him out, but that's exactly what was happening.

Despite Sirin's assertions from time to time—rebutted by Lacond at many a furious AFTOIS meeting, where according to Duncan, the issue came up continually—that Sabon meant no harm by her actions—perhaps even the opposite—and that neither did Hoegbotton in selling the rights to Frankwrithe & Lewden, I'm certain she resurrected him merely to more effectively destroy him. Whether she meant to or not. Nativism, as it turns out, was an excellent descriptor for Mary's own actions.

What made me angriest, though, is that Duncan didn't even seem to mind, as if accepting her right to take advantage of him. (I couldn't hate her for it. And even as the sight of butchered chapters and paragraphs cut me to the quick, part of me thrilled to see *any* of my words back in print, in any form.)

⁂

No, what I said to Mortar and Pestle with sincerity and with hope, as I handed them my cheat sheets for the rest of the tour was simply, "If you do ever see Mary, tell her that Duncan sends his love." It's a pity I couldn't maintain my composure later, on a certain marble staircase, but I've never claimed to be consistent.

Then I put my arms around Mortar and Pestle and turned all three of us to face the tour group.

"I'm afraid there's been a change of plans. These two fine upstanding citizens from Stockton will be leading the rest of the tour. Enjoy!"

I left them without regret, Mortar and Pestle speechless, and climbed the steps to Duncan's apartment overlooking Voss Bender Memorial Square, where we talked for quite some time, while below, through the open window, we witnessed the slow disintegration of the tour group.

The Ambergris Tourism Board—caught between their dead dog slogans and their sense of profit, between my protestations of being "confused" as to the message we were trying to convey and their certainty that I'd known exactly what I was doing—contemplated firing me, but couldn't quite summon the nerve.

Most days since, I've been glad they didn't.

5

Sometimes—only sometimes—I wonder who I am writing this account for. Who will read this? Will they care? I am past the delusion that I'm writing an afterword for Duncan's *The Early History of Ambergris*, and I suspect that you, dear reader, if you've come this far, are past that delusion as well.

Sometimes, I think I'm writing out of anger and sadness, out of a sense of injustice—a sense that my life, that my brother's life, should have been easier, that we should have been more successful. At other times, I think I'm writing this account to preserve some part of me after I'm gone. Or that I am in some sense trying to write past those bodies in the Cathedral, or my red ribbons for wrists, or Duncan's heartbreak.

There are certainly those who would prefer I not write this account—they'd prefer to have the same image of Janice they've always had, the same thoughts about Duncan. A more full-bodied likeness would ruin all of the stylization they've spent years accreting to both of us. (Who are these people, so intent on our ruin? Your oft-mentioned flesh necklace? Janice, no one *cares* enough to create an image of us—and they haven't for years.)

Then there are those who simply hate what Duncan represents, those who cannot accept the truth and thus must reject the messenger along with the message. It's common enough in life, isn't it? Mary is a prime example. She's still waiting there, at the party, but I honestly don't want to write about that yet. There are more important things to discuss first, and it's possible I won't have time to finish this account, but I'll soldier on because there's nothing left to do.

A gate. A mirror. A door.

Somewhere there's a door, surely?

One afternoon, after I had guided a family from Stockton on a tour centered around Trillian the Great Banker, Sirin appeared at the head of the stairs leading to the second floor. He beckoned to me with one long, graceful finger, and disappeared up the steps.

His office was the same as it had always been, down to the butterfly paradise residing in glass flasks at his back.

"I have a job for Duncan," he said, without preamble, smiling from behind his desk.

At the time, Duncan hadn't yet begun to "benefit" from the pittance Frankwrithe & Lewden would pay him for the infamous omnibus and still made his marginal living editing the AFTOIS newsletter for a Lacond whose health had begun to fail. So the money would come in handy. But I couldn't imagine that Sirin, whose current fortunes depended on the continued publication of the great Mary Sabon, would have anything of value for Duncan.

"What sort of job?" I asked, sitting down heavily. My stump was throbbing against the strap and wood of my artificial foot. If Sirin had been a kinder man, he would have met me on the first floor.

"A writing kind of job," he said, and smiled again. "The sort of writing job I think might appeal to Duncan, if presented to him in the right way."

I already didn't like the sound of it.

"What is it?"

"We have a pamphlet we need written. The original writer proved unreliable and it's scheduled for publication in less than three months."

"Unreliable how?"

"He was blown up by a stray fungal bomb."

"Oh."

"But," Sirin hastened to add, "it had nothing to do with his assignment. Wrong place, wrong time. Strictly."

"What's the title of the pamphlet?"

"*The Hoegbotton Guide to the Early History of Ambergris.* Do you think Duncan would do it?"

I didn't know how I felt about this proposition. Sirin had more or less abandoned us after the war. On the other hand, he had gotten us a job during it. He had helped Mary more than us of late, but no one could say his choice didn't reflect good business sense.

"A travel guide?" I said.

"Yes. A travel guide. Duncan will have to understand that up front. There will be no place for his outlandish theories in the piece, unless they add an element of entertainment. We don't want to upset the tourists—think of the effect it would have on your own business." Again, the smile, the upturning of the lips as his eyes acknowledged the debt I owed him for my position.

He named a compelling price for completion of the project.

"I'll try," I said. "Thanks for thinking of us."

I don't really know how I felt. My expectations of influence and power had decreased so rapidly and so monumentally that I believe at the time I felt Sirin was bestowing a great honor on Duncan. I believe I thought that Sirin was attempting to usher us back into the ranks of the Privileged, the Chosen. I was mistaken, but can anyone blame me for hoping?

At the door, I turned and asked, "Why didn't you give the assignment to Mary Sabon?" (And if not Sabon, surely a member of her flesh necklace would have welcomed the opportunity?)

"She's busy with other things," and then, catching himself, "but more importantly, she's not the right person for this. Your brother is somewhat unique in that regard."

✦✦✦

It did not take much convincing—by then Duncan had begun to chafe under the restrictions and limited audience of his AFTOIS soapbox. He welcomed the opportunity to do something different. (I welcomed the promise of money.)

"It'll be like old times," he said in this very room. "It will be like before the war."

His right eye writhed with gold-green fungi. His left index finger had formed a curled purple tendril, like a fern. His neck was encrusted with a golden patina that pulsed like the skin of a squid. His smell was indescribable. Yes, it would be like old times.

For two months, Duncan lugged thousands of pages of books, magazines, and old papers down here. For weeks, he labored on this very typewriter, creating his early history of the city. I believe he thought he might be creating a Machine of his own, made from the city's leavings. (The assignment came at the right time—it came as I was attempting to synthesize and explain all that I had learned over the years. It took two months, yes, but also thirty *years* to write that account. My findings might have been destined for a travel guide, but that didn't mean I had to make them shallow or incomplete.)

I left him to it, after a while. I stopped in every few days to see how it was going, but that was all—I had my own life to lead, and an ever-growing list of tourists to exhume the city's highlights for . . .

When Duncan showed me pieces of his essay so that I could report to Sirin on his progress, he did so by reading selections of it to me aloud.

"The importance of squid to the Ambergrisian economy cannot be overstated," he would say.

"Not squid again," I would say, and he would make a hushing sound.

"Certainly the rebel Stretcher Jones learned to appreciate the freshwater squid, as it sustained his army for long periods of time when they were relegated to the salt marshes on the fringes of the Kalif's empire," he would intone.

I would catch Sybel's eye and he would fold his arms and shake his head, while I nodded in agreement. (How like you to conjure up a dead man to agree with you.)

"The type of cannonballs used by the Kalif during the Occupation proved useful in the creation of walls during the rebuilding efforts." (A very interesting fact that many a tourist would have found useful, if it had survived Sirin's sword.)

And on and on. It didn't sound much like a tourist guide, based on my experience guiding tourists around, but at least Duncan was making progress toward completion. I didn't think it productive to give him advice until he had finished it.

✳✳✳

But, at the end of two months, Duncan bypassed me completely and sent his finished manuscript to Sirin via courier. It was six hundred pages long. Of those six hundred pages, two hundred and fifty pages consisted of long, convoluted footnotes, some of which had their own footnotes and additional annotations. I think he knew what I would have said had I read it first.

Sirin called me up to his office, where we could both contemplate the green-stained pages that lay in an awkward lump on his desk. Some of the pages looked like dried, veined lettuce leaves. Others had the consistency of moist glue. Still others had a dark phosphorescence to them. I could have sworn I could hear a low hum coming from the pile.

"What," he asked, "am I to make of this?"

"It does look a bit long," I said.

Sirin spluttered. "The length? Are you looking at the same pages I am? The length is not really the issue. I mean, certainly, the length is an issue, but not *the* issue. Have you read it?"

"Only the parts Duncan read aloud to me."

Sirin sat back in his chair, a look of disgust on his face.

"Everything I hate about AFTOIS is in this manuscript, and then some, Janice. Every old wives' tale, every fear, every paranoia. He even tries to tie your father's death into his web of gray cap conspiracy theories."

"Is it really that bad?"

"Janice, not only that, but he attributes any number of insane theories to James Lacond that sound beyond the pale even for that old rogue."

I didn't bother to tell him that this was intentional. Duncan had disclosed to me that Lacond's reputation had been so compromised by his obsessions that he found it useful to let others use his name as cover for those theories that might discredit them, while he wrote under his own pseudonyms. ("James Lacond" became a house name at the newsletter. It got out of control, but it felt good, too. A kind of self-destructive impulse embedded in it, a way of acknowledging our own irrelevance, but reveling in it. It embodied Lacond's self-deprecating manner. I merely played off this in the *Early History*. Ultimately, Sirin ignored it and left it in, much to our delight.)

"You can't edit it into shape?" I said instead, already knowing the answer.

"No, I can't," Sirin said. "I can't save this." A pause, a calculating stare. "Why? Do you think you can?"

"Maybe," I said, knowing the real trick would be to get Duncan to agree to change even one comma of it. (How little you understood me, Janice.)

I met Duncan at the Spore again, in this room. As I approached the door, the flickering light within played a trick. I thought I saw his shadow, impossibly vast, curled around the edges, *snap* into a more human shape. A gurgle and whine that coalesced into a human voice.

"Janice," came a throaty greeting, then, "Janice," in my brother's true voice.

I hadn't entered the room yet. He couldn't have seen me. (Not with my own eyes.)

When I did enter, I found him pale and shrunken, folding and unfolding his arms.

"You've come from Sirin," he said. It was not a question.

"Yes."

"So you've seen . . . you've seen my early history?"

"Yes."

"And he has read it."

"Yes."

He looked up at me, his gaze suddenly desperate.

"Does he like it?"

"Does he like it?" I echoed. "No, Duncan—he loves it. He absolutely loves it. He asked for a travel guide version of an early history of Ambergris and you gave him a tome large enough to contain every Truffidian hymn ever sung—and half of it in footnote form. He absolutely despises it."

Duncan began to mutter to himself. It was a habit he'd developed in the years after the war. It did not endear him to many people.

"But I've finally gotten it right," he said. "I've finally documented all of it."

Sirin had let me read some of the manuscript in his office. It was riddled through with strange symbols, strange characters. It contained much that was personal to Duncan's life. It rambled. It made sense only in spurts. I felt, reading it, that several different people had collaborated to write it, only two or three of whom were sane or had consulted with the other writers. (I agree. It was a bad time. I could not control my shape. I could not get my bearings. Keeping myself cooped up in that room, working on the essay, I let other parts of me infiltrate the text with their opinions. From hour to hour, my body changed, making it hard to concentrate on my task. In the end, it all *seemed* right to me, but there were so many of *me* then.)

Duncan frowned and looked away (to hide a mushroom blossoming on my cheek). "So he doesn't want it."

"Duncan," I said, "I'm not sure even AFTOIS will want it. It doesn't make all that much sense."

Duncan stood, pasted a smile onto his face, kept to the darkness.

"What about you, Janice?" he said. "You could edit it. You could give Sirin what he wants. At least some of what he wants. And I'll save the rest for something else."

This response shocked me. The old Duncan—or at least a Duncan who wasn't this vulnerable—would have taken his manuscript back from Sirin. But I remember making excuses for Duncan as I stood there. The times had passed us by. Duncan needed money to pay for his tiny apartment and his space at the Spore, so we had to take what we could get. But I never really understood why he didn't fight for himself more, why he gave in so easily. I'm not sure I ever will. (Because, Janice, I was *becoming* what I believed in. I was *becoming* it. And it might have been strange and unknown, never to be recognized, but it meant more to me than words on a page by then.)

"I can try," I said.

"Thanks! Thanks," he said, so pathetically grateful he even gave me a hug. "That'll work out fine then. Go tell Sirin," he said. "Go tell Sirin. Make Sirin happy." (I needed you to leave. I was getting ready to change again, and sometimes now when I changed, I would *assimilate* things around me.) So I went to tell Sirin.

What had taken Duncan two months to write took me three days to edit. I simply discarded anything that didn't make sense and tried to keep anything that hinted of a chronological history. Duncan read over the result mournfully, added a few more footnotes, changed some of my line edits, and gave me his approval in such an offhand way that I was even madder at him for the ease with which he had given up.

Perhaps I should have been more empathetic, though. In his journal from the time, I find this entry:

> How will I die? Not that way, not me. For me it will be the slow decay, the failure of my senses, the graying of the world, the remaindering and misunderstanding of my books, followed by the very forgetting of my words, the pages wiped clean of all marks, and so too the wiping clean of me, my brain sinking into slow senility, utterly alone, no vestige of past family and friends left to me until, finally, when I am dust, I shall unleash a sigh of forgetfulness and leave not a trace of my existence in the world . . . But until then, if the black bough taps against the windowpane, I shall ignore its brittle invitation—and in all ways and in all things I shall not dignify the name of that which will one day take me.

Rather vainglorious melancholy, and contradictory, too, but clearly indicative of the depression Duncan sometimes fell into during this period. (Janice, that whole quote is from one of the Kalif's genealogists, who wrote potboilers on the side! Context, Janice, context. Or is my handwriting so bad you couldn't read the attribution?)

When I brought the revised essay to Sirin, he still didn't care for parts of it, but with his deadline approaching, he had little choice.

"Besides," he admitted, "a little eccentricity will probably seem quaint to the tourists."

Among those eccentricities, in that first edition, were entries in the appended glossary for both Duncan and for Sabon, alluding to what no longer existed:

SABON, MARY. An aggressive and sometimes brilliant historian who built her reputation on the bones of older, lovestruck historians. Five-ten. One-fifteen. Red hair. Green, green eyes. An elegant dresser. Smile like fire. Foe of James Lacond. In conversation can cut with a single word. Author of several books whose titles I quite forget at the moment.

SHRIEK, DUNCAN. An old historian, born in Stockton, who in his youth published several famous history books, since remaindered and savaged by critics who should have known better. His father, also an historian, died of joy; or, rather, from a heart attack brought on by finding out he had won a major honor from the Court of the Kalif. I was ten. I never died from my honors, but I was banned by the Truffidian Antechamber. Also a renowned expert on the gray caps, although most reasonable citizens ignore even his least outlandish theories. Once lucky enough to meet the love of his life, but not lucky enough to keep her, or to keep her from pillaging his ideas and discrediting him. Still, he loves her, separated from her by the insurmountable gulf of empires, buzzards, a bad writer, a horrible vacation spot, and the successor to Aquelus/Irene.

. . . this last bit of cuteness a reference to the entries for the Saltwater Buzzard, Samantha, the Saphant Empire, Scatha, and Maximillian Sharp that lay between his entry and Sabon's. Even here, toward the end, he could not give up on Mary, no matter how much he should. And no matter how I begged him to delete it—to delete both of them. (I also left numerous clues to the fact that I was fronting Lacond's various misshapen theories, but I doubt the reading public caught them, butchered as they'd been by the editing process.)

�֍֎֍

The Early History had been saved, but the effect was minimal. Serious journals do not review travel guides and tourists rarely remember who wrote them. More importantly, no new work was forthcoming from Sirin for Duncan or for me. And

Duncan, for the first time, I think, clearly understood that there was no way back for him. He would continue to haunt the fringes of his former career, and I would be an apparition that appeared as a warning to travelers and passersby.

It was almost like a joke. Me, living on as a ghost. Do you know how ghosts manifest themselves in Ambergris? They haunt you as travel guides. They lead you to old buildings. They educate you on the history of the places they haunt.

Once I realized I was a ghost, I became much happier.

⁂

Sometimes, as I may have mentioned, I go outside at night, just for a break. Night is so different from day for me. I cannot keep the ghosts out as easily at night, and the cot I have had brought in here is somewhat uncomfortable. My leg grows cold from the fungus that enraptures it, but I don't mind the feel of it.

On a good day, I have been averaging several thousand words. It's true I return to certain paragraphs and pages and revise, but mostly it's ever forward. I can't hope to create something perfect, but perhaps I can create something that's *alive*—assuming I can finish it. Right now, I see no reason to imagine I will ever stop typing this afterword. The hours float by so quietly and without event that there seems nothing else worth doing. What would I want to do? And what will I do when I'm done?

But we *are* getting closer to the staircase, the party, the necklace, with each word. I can almost *sense* the ending, even if I can't see it yet. I'm so prolific I surprise myself—I keep filling up pages. I keep creating new sections, new chapters.

All the same, I'm tired. My prose, I've noticed, becomes by turns more plain, more linear, only to jump out into time as if in a desperate attempt to maintain momentum. Even if it doesn't feel like it, I cannot be far from the end, even if I end too abruptly. It may be that my fatigue will outweigh my momentum, that it will rush the ending and send you, dear reader, out of this riveting true-life account far sooner than necessary or proper. If this should occur, I refuse to apologize. This is an afterword or an afterward—I can't remember anymore—and no one reads them. No one cares what they contain. By the time the afterword appears in a book, the story has already ended. Why, if I wanted to, I could write one hundred pages on obscure Truffidian rituals to offset my fear. It is not without precedence. It has happened before.

What's left to tell? Many years passed, in much the same way as they had passed before. Sabon's star continued to ascend. I was forgotten, although I continued on as a tour guide and cantankerous member of the Ambergris Tourism Board. On rare occasions, they called upon me to make short speeches at the re-dedication of certain historical buildings, or to make appearances as one of several fossils at various dinners mummifying the War of the Houses.

Duncan was forgotten, except for Sabon's continued cruel resurrections. Bon-mot died—in the long view of things, one moment he was there and the next he was not—much to my ever-growing sadness. I would sit at the old stone bench with my sandwich at lunchtime and try to conjure up the image of those wonderful conversations, that gravel voice, but it was never the same. Memory may be all we have, but it's a poor substitute for flesh and blood.

And still, even as he seemed to make little progress regarding his theories, Duncan was changing, becoming other, the process always ongoing. He never recovered fully from Sabon (or AFTOIS, for that matter), rarely expressed interest in other women, never took enough of a break from his work to notice them, really. Sometimes, Duncan later confessed to me, he would still haunt Sabon from the shadows outside her current house, or her current lover's house. (I went a little crazy at times. Late in the game, I set traps for Mary in the AFTOIS newsletter, using Lacond's name for crazy theories that I thought she would be forced to refute, wasting her energy and, at the same time, unknowingly engaging me in a kind of dialogue. It never happened, to my knowledge.) Between his obsession and my tour guide job, we were a veritable team of stalkers, me during the day, him at night. (The only thing that comforted me: she never married. Surely that meant something?)

Somewhere along the way—I don't know exactly when—we grew old, Duncan and I. Old and yet defiant; if not wise, then wizened, at least. Exactly as we had always been, only more so. *No one makes it out.*

Even as we stayed the same, the city changed again and again, as it always would, its grime-smeared head, its soiled towers, its debauched calls to prayer the same, and yet always it changed. I grew to love and appreciate it more than I ever had before. It was all I knew, and I knew it almost too well by now. (Yet neither of us ever found out if it loved us back.)

Then, some four or five years ago, the Shift began to affect Ambergris, disrupting the flux and flow of the city. All became unpredictable, save for one constant: as once it had become colder, now the city seethed with heat, even in the winter and spring. With this heat has come the rain, sliding down in oily sheets, or mumbling to itself in little gusts and flurries, or dissipating into a fine gray mist.

In a *Broadsheet* article Duncan cut out and stuck into his journal, the strangeness of the rain is remarked upon in detail:

> This rain behaves oddly sometimes. It forms funnels in the sky. It falls one way on the left side of Albumuth Boulevard and at a different angle on the right side of Albumuth Boulevard. It delivers a puzzling bounty: fish and tiny squid and crabs that are not native here. They lie struggling in piles of seaweed as alien to the city as we are to them while crowds form around them, or do not; many among us try to ignore such happenings.
>
> Over the River Moth, the rain behaves as if with a conscious will, for there it will sometimes form columns on two sides with no rain between, and the air there, as one eyewitness put it, "turns to darkness with a weight and smell unlike the rest of the sky." (A door, Janice.)
>
> With the rain has come, again, as in the old days, a proliferation of fungus, so that the business of mushroom culling and cleaning is once again very profitable. And yet the gray caps have become absent even during the deep night.
>
> That no one knows what these signs mean may be more troublesome than the signs themselves.

Even House Hoegbotton, in the past three years, has looked askance at the weather, seemed oddly humbled by an enemy it can neither predict nor defeat.

With the heat and rain have come the agents of House Frankwrithe & Lewden once again, infiltrating Ambergris, although this time with no discernible gray cap support. And yet, with murder on the rise and rumors of war constant now, our nerves have once again become as frayed as they were on the eve of conflict so many years ago.

None of this has helped the tourist trade. The number of people attending my increasingly rote tours has dropped off. Incidents such as having to walk around a three-foot crimson mushroom suddenly erupting from the pavement near their feet, or ducking a torrent of tiny silver fish delivered by a thunderstorm, has positive novelty value to only a select few.

I know that even these simple statements of fact about the Shift will outrage some readers, most of them Nativists. To them, there has been no Shift. To them, the continued "strangeification of the city," as Duncan once put it, has no pattern to it, no rhythm or cause. Some still deny anything odd is happening at all, pitiable fools. I suppose, in our usual way, even those among us who admit to the Shift have begun to become accustomed to it. (We shouldn't become accustomed to anything anymore. We are beginning to live in our own future, and it *should* feel strange.)

Perhaps this will make it more personal, more real: at the beginning of the symptoms of the Shift, James Lacond fell ill. When I say he fell ill, I mean that his fungal disease finally overwhelmed him, as it had sometimes threatened to overwhelm Duncan. (Alas, he hadn't traveled far enough underground, or for long enough. Which is worse than going too far. I told him more than once that he needed to experience more, to know more, inside his body, to survive it. He refused the advice.) He was forced to retire to a back room in his own offices while Duncan ran everything in his name, instead of just part of it. After a while, he couldn't hold on any longer and almost literally faded away.

(No one knew how ill he was until after he passed away. Janice, you should have visited him toward the end. I was there every day, hunched over a chair beside his fungus-riddled bed, trying to pry an intelligible word from between the rotted teeth of the poor feeble wreck, to no avail. "Hmmmm bwatchee thoroughgard stinmarta," he would say to me with the perfect clarity of those beyond hope. I would nod wisely and continue to work on my own diatribes against Nativism and all the other dangerously deluded theories.

(He smelled of the rum I gave him to soothe his agony. He smelled musty, like rooms not opened to the air since the Silence. It's true I loved him dearly and I helped him as best I could, but you could never say he was a substitute for Bonmot—that would be unfair to both of them. More correctly, when I looked at him, I saw a mirror of my own future self: gray-bearded, addlepated, a half-century's study of history dribbling out of my brain through a mum-mumbling mouth. I cannot say it comforted me much, and yet how much more tenderly I cared for him because of it!

(There might have been no coherence to his speech, but Lacond could still write at times. Once, he drew me close and showed me some words scribbled on a scrap of paper: "I am concerned that disintegration and ensuing death will blunt my ability to continue to coherently put forth my usual arguments with the customary vigor." It made me laugh, and that made Lacond smile, as much as he was able. I nodded, to let him know I understood. When he did pass away and I assumed the editorship of the AFTOIS newsletter, it seemed natural to continue, to dig up an almost endless series of "newly discovered" papers by the old rogue, as if he still mumbled nothing-nothing-nothing in my ear.

(Early one morning, I entered Lacond's room to find a fine misting of glistening black spores clinging to the white sheets, and no sign of a body. The sheets smelled vaguely of lime. I knew what had happened. It had taken so long to happen that I didn't feel grief in that moment. I just felt a sense of purpose.

(I rolled up the sheets and walked with them down to the River Moth. As I walked, I scooped up black spores in my hand and let them fall. On Albumuth Boulevard. On the cobblestones of the Religious Quarter. Smeared them along the walls in the abandoned Bureaucratic Quarter. Abraded the bricks of H&S headquarters with them. Dropped them on bushes and on park benches.

(When I got to the river, I tossed the sheets into the water and watched them drift and unwind, the last spores, drunk with moisture, disappearing from sight.

(Of course, I saved a vial of the spores to spread underground. No part of Ambergris was going to get rid of James as easily in death as in life.)

❈

Somewhere, somewhen, in the last year, my (our!) mother also died, out in her mansion by the river. Her neighbors found her sitting in a chair, staring out at the water. She looked happy, they said, but no one likes dying, so I don't see how that could be true. She looked as if she understood everything, they said. Or, at least, understood more than I ever did, despite my restless searching.

The strange thing is, the night before she died, the telephone rang at about three in the morning. When I answered it, there was no voice on the other end. Maybe it was a wrong number. Maybe she had decided there was nothing left to say. Maybe she just wanted to hear my voice before the end. I don't know.

This was in the spring. The trees all around her home were in bloom—white-and-pink blossoms that drooped heavily from the branches. The lawns strewn with petals. It didn't seem like the time for a funeral. The scent of the flowers drove out the scent of death.

Duncan and I accompanied the casket back to Stockton, over the River Moth by barge, and then by mule-drawn carriage. We buried her next to our father in the old communal cemetery next to the library where our father had spent so much of his time. There weren't many people there for the ceremony: a few relatives, the Truffidian priest, an old friend of Dad's—an ancient fossil of a man, stooped, bent, and a little confused (throughout the ceremony, the clasps of his suspenders hung over his shoulders, where he had flung them up while using the gents' room)—and a couple of young people whose parents had known Mom. Standing there, surrounded by tombstones and bright green grass, it didn't quite seem real. It didn't seem true.

We didn't stay in Stockton long—we had no connection to it any longer. It seemed like a foreign place, somewhere we'd never visited before. (Ambergris will do that to you—it becomes so central to your life that any other place is a faint echo, a pale reflection, a cliché in search of originality.)

When we arrived back at her mansion, we realized how much of a storehouse it had become—she had so filled it up with things, made by her, bought by her, and placed by her, that it almost didn't seem as if she had left. (And yet, as it turned out, most of it had been stored on behalf of other people, the house emptying with each new relative who stumbled inside.)

"She was always so distant," Duncan said, as we stood in the hallway looking at all of the portraits and photographs of family members she had collected over the years. We had an entire constellation of relatives we could seek out—some we'd met at the funeral—but, really, why bother now? It was too late. We'd been taken to a foreign place, and since then all the old bonds had snapped like rotted rope. The people we'd met in Stockton were just polite faces now, and I only resented that a little bit. Part of me was relieved to excuse myself from all the work it would have taken to hold on to those relationships. Better that they remain photographs, vague smiles and handshakes and fondly remembered hugs from childhood. We had been cast adrift by Father's death, and we had taken to it, in our way.

"She was always so distant," Duncan said again. It took me a while to hear him, in that empty and cavernous place, surrounded by the images of so many dead people. There were as many tombstones framed on the mantel in that place as puncturing the earth in the Stockton graveyard.

When I did hear him, I turned toward him with a look of irritation on my face. "*She* wasn't distant. *We* were distant. We were odd and surly and *distant*. We crawled through tunnels and we didn't talk much and we were always alone in our own thoughts. Not much of a family, if you think about it. We never knew how to be there for anyone else. So *how do we know?*" I said, and by now I'd raised my voice. What did it matter in that place? It would just echo on forever, the sound captured in the swirls of the staircase, floating down into the flooded basement. "How do we know it wasn't *us?*"

Duncan's face scrunched up and turned red, and I could tell he was fighting off tears. It was difficult to know, though, because most of the time he couldn't produce tears anymore—or if he did, they were purple tears, semi-solid, that hurt as they slid out of his tear ducts. It's a measure of how accustomed I'd grown to Duncan that this didn't seem odd to me.

"I hardly ever visited her," he said. (I meant I hardly ever saw her. I did visit her, but I never saw her. I tunneled up through a dry corner of the basement and left her gifts from the underground—things I thought she might appreciate. I'm sure she knew they came from me.)

"She didn't mind. She was a solitary person. That was her choice."

Before Dad Died, she had been as sunny and well-adjusted as the rest of us. (We were never well-adjusted, Janice.) But that death had killed us all as surely as it had killed our father. How could we deny that?

Surrounded by the awful weight of Mom's things—the rugs, the paintings, the sculptures, the books, the bric-a-brac of collecting gone wrong—it seemed all too apparent. While the river, oblivious, gurgled and chuckled to itself outside the window. (Everyone always tells you that you become more alone as you get older. People write about it in books. They shout it out on street corners. They mumble it in their sleep. But it's always a shock when it happens to you.)

We couldn't keep the house. (How could we keep the house? We made all the inquiries, but it was impossible—Mom had been too much in debt, her money so ancient it didn't really exist except as run-down property.) And we couldn't keep much *from* the house (because it wasn't ours!). But I couldn't bear to lose the hallway of portraits and photographs. Somehow, to lose the only tenuous connection between ourselves and those people we should have known felt as wrong as seeking them out, trying to enter into a relationship with strangers. (Those polite protestations of "we should make plans to get together," which no one really ever believes, as we stood there by the gravesite in Stockton. Why did I make that effort for strangers and not for my own mother? I truly don't know. Unless I had truly believed that she would outlive me. Or that she had died a long time ago.)

"I'm not coming back," Duncan said as I closed the door behind us and we walked out into the glorious hot spring day, the sun lithe and yellow above us, the River Moth smooth and light and glistening beyond the mansion.

In the sun, he had a diaphanous look to him. He seemed like an avant-garde sculpture, a person from a myth or fairy tale. The light slid through his face. In the sudden glow, I could see the white hairs at his temples, the gray-and-white of his beard, the lines that had sculpted his mouth, his forehead, the way his eyes had sunk a little into the orbits. He was old. We were old. Prematurely.

"Not coming back?" I said. "Back here?"

"I'm not coming back," he repeated, but he wouldn't meet my gaze.

And he didn't. He didn't come back. I saw him only one more time.

✾✾✾

The owner of the Spore came in here again, muttering about unpaid bills. I gave him a smile and tried to fend him off with a couple of coins I'd hidden in a sock. Apparently, he has realized that he has begun to let me have this room for free. I wonder if he would understand if I told him I am standing vigil for Duncan. There is an old Truffidian ritual where you wait for a dead loved one out of respect. For three days, you wait as if for a resurrection, but what you are really waiting for is your own grief to subside, just a little. But the fact is, Duncan might crawl out of that hole in the ground behind me at any moment. (True enough. But you shouldn't have waited for me.)

The owner liked Duncan, but if Duncan came crawling out of the underground, the owner and his friends might have set upon him with clubs. I will have to leave soon, one way or another, so it strikes me that now might be a good time to tell you about the last time I saw Duncan. The very last time, three weeks before Martin Lake's party. Surprise, surprise—this is the last time Mary saw Duncan as well, although she didn't mention it to her flesh necklace while vilifying my brother at the party. I guess she didn't think it important. Perhaps her fear had become too great by then.

The reason Mary saw Duncan at all was because Duncan, throughout everything that had happened, had never given up on her. He was still trying, right up to the end—although the end of what, I don't know, and may never know. (I hardly know myself, Janice—I don't even know where you are now. I finally "creep out of that hole" as you put it so eloquently, and you're nowhere to be found—just this profane, infuriating, opinionated account.)

✦✦✦

Dusk of a spring day, and I sat at my desk in the Hoegbotton & Sons building on Albumuth Boulevard. The weather had been strange as usual. The sun shone hazy through a layer of fog: a faint shedding of light through glass doors festooned with flyers and broadsheets proclaiming the restorative virtues of various Ambergrisian tours.

I had put a lamp or two near my desk, and since the weather had scared off my fellow tour guides and, apparently, any potential customers, I was spending my time paying off my bills and writing letters of circuitous regret to the artists who blamed me for losing their artwork during the war. Yes, I still owed money to a lot of people. I don't believe most of them are going to get anything, though—I've given all my money to the owner of the Spore.

I was in the middle of calculating how much I could give to Roger Mandible and also pay my rent, when *it* dropped from the ceiling, onto my desk. I suppressed a scream, internalizing it as a long, violent shudder, but backed away from the desk, holding my pen like a knife.

Anticlimax. It took me a second to identify what had dropped onto my desk, because the desk was so cluttered. The only unfamiliar object proved to be a pair of peculiar glasses, right side up atop a program from an old Voss Bender play. A red triangle of fabric had been knotted around one arm of the glasses. I circled the glasses slowly, looked up at the ceiling once or twice, my impromptu weapon still raised above my head. Still nothing there. Anyone observing from the street would have thought me crazy.

My heartbeat began to slow. I lowered my pen, set it down on the desk, and sat down, chuckling at my own fear. Glasses. Stuck to the ceiling? Falling onto my desk? I still could not grasp the chain of events. Had a colleague or tourist stuck them to the ceiling months ago and they had finally succumbed to gravity? At least I seemed to be in no danger. It would make a semi-interesting story to tell my fellow tour guides in the morning.

I picked up the glasses. The metal was warm to the touch, almost sinewy, but eyelash thin. A strangely golden, pinkish hue suffused the frames, the texture both rough and smooth. The lenses shared the thinness of the frames, but of a different order: thin as a dragonfly wing. The lenses too were hot, and my questing finger recoiled when the minute translucent scales that comprised them almost seemed to move under my touch, though it must have been the texture of finger and lens combined that produced the sensation.

I laughed when a hum rose from the glasses. I had the sense of a practical joke, of a whimsy that was almost within my comprehension, not of any danger. A vibration mixed with a sound, I thought, but I could not at first tell if this was simply the shaking of my own hand, a ringing in my ears.

I tapped the glasses against my desk. A sound tinny and fine, like the sound of a tuning fork, emanated from them. Out of the same sense of curiosity that pulls the wings from flies, I first tried to bend the glasses, and when that failed, break them against the side of the desk. Fully engaged in a series of experiments now, perhaps glad to turn my fear into aggression, I took a penknife from the drawer and tried to scratch the lenses. I could not.

Then I set the glasses down, more confused than before. What should I do with them?, I wondered. Outside, the fog had deepened, come hard off the River Moth. No one had entered the office during my explorations. No one would. The fading sun had shrunk to a feeble white point outshone for brilliance by the luminescence of the fog.

I took a closer look at the red swatch of fabric. It did not look as if it belonged with the glasses. It did not have the same elegance or precision. With a slightly trembling hand, I unknotted it from the glasses. Now it looked familiar. The shade of red, the triangular shape. Where had I seen it before? I remembered a moment before I saw words written on the fabric in a familiar hand:

> Put on the glasses. Follow the red path.
> Do not be afraid.
> Remember BDD.

Duncan. The red swatch was a piece of a gray cap flag, most commonly seen atop a wooden stake driven into the ground near any gray caps that had not returned underground during the daylight. Suddenly the flag and the glasses seemed very connected indeed. My mouth was dry, my heartbeat rapid again.

Put on the glasses? The thought had never occurred to me. I held the glasses up to the lamplight and looked through them, but did not put them on. Up close, they smelled like lavender and brine. Although the "scales" of the lenses distorted my view of the fogged-in window, I suffered no change of perspective, no clarity or fuzziness. These were not prescription lenses.

The scrap of red cloth on my desk stood out from all the mundane, colorless bits of minutiae that had begun to take over my life—the bills, the relentless letters from angry artists, the descriptions of various tours of the city, all the awkward geography of my daily life. And in the middle of it all, a scrap of color, a scrap of blood, a scrap of message.

What harm, after all, could there be in putting on a pair of glasses?

I stared out at the fog-shrouded sky. I walked to the door. I opened the door and walked outside. The fog clung to my skin. The faint tinkle and chime of distant conversation. The melodious roar of a motored vehicle. The smell of flames. The taste of metal. Could these glasses allow me to see through the fog? Could they undo the mist? I still held them in my left hand, away from my body, as if they might explode and shower me with shards.

Before Dad Died.

I hadn't seen or heard from Duncan in months.

I put on the glasses. They fit snugly against my nose, the arms sliding neatly over my ears; again they pulsed, as though alive.

For a long moment nothing happened, and in that moment I grinned. My poor brother had me staring through distorted dragonfly lenses into a world of mist. What was new?

But then the frames tensed, tightened around my ears. For a moment I experienced an intense heat, but so briefly that I did not have time to make a sound.

Then the glasses began to fill up with blackness. The blackness oozed from the top of the frames and, with a methodical precision, filled first one distorted scale and then the next. Slowly, as I stood there fascinated and horrified all at once, the liquid occluded my vision, replacing it with its own reality.

When the blackness was complete, the fog no longer existed, swept away, banished, along with all things unclear, diffuse . . .

My world now consisted of two . . . levels? Layers? The world I knew had become subservient to a second world. It is not so much that the world I knew disappeared, but that it, still sharply in focus, became the translucent background to a new world. I could distinctly see the street, the stores opposite my office, the streetlamp on the corner, the two women standing under the streetlamp, the pigeon asleep atop the lamppost, the facade of store fronts that extended down the street—every solid brick or stone of it.

What stood revealed, however, made my reality seem very poor indeed. How to explain it? I was never a very good painter—how now to paint with words a picture that few if any have ever seen? (Start with color. Start with symbols. Start with texture. Start with hue. Start anywhere, but start!)

Example: across the street, the printer's store front . . . it was "painted over" with a living swath of minute, glowing red fungus. In among this fungus moved slow accumulations of emerald light, harvesting it. How can I describe it when I couldn't even paint it for you? The vision defeats the pen. It would take a better writer than I to begin to describe the least of it.

Every building—*every surface*—had symbols and words written upon its sides: glowing and bold, in phosphorescent greens, yellows, reds, purples, blues. Arrows and road signs in a foreign language. The etched equivalent of clicks and whistles. Like the difference between the city before and during the Festival of the Freshwater Squid—when the lights festoon every balcony, every flourish of filigree. Now I was looking at the city as the gray caps saw it, I began to realize. Conveniently portioned out and mapped and described for their benefit. This was their city, still— this overlay the skin of their control. It was like a dream and a nightmare all at once. On the edges of my vision, I could see things moving in ways that seemed unnatural. In the air, a million spores leapt together, suffusing the sky in a vermilion orgy of renewal, the sky itself more dusk than dawn, the stars pale ghosts, larger and more opalescent than in our world. "Scents" hung in the air, in clouds and yet not-clouds, ripples and veins of texture that were not ripples or veins of texture.

BDD. BDD. I repeated the acronym over and over to myself. I tried to be calm. What had Duncan written? *Follow the red.* I should follow the red, and trust in Duncan.

Follow the red. There, before me, appeared a red path composed of tiny writhing tendrils. If I took off the glasses—could I take off the glasses?—I knew I wouldn't see the path, wouldn't see the fungus. Did I want to try to rip off the glasses and leave Duncan to his own devices? For a moment I hesitated, and then I followed the red path through the transformed city.

My self dissolved into . . . something else. How do I describe? How do I begin? Where do I begin? (Oh for Truff's sake, Janice! Start at the beginning. Proceed to the middle. Finish with the end. Muddle through.) The city darkened to black, with people like quicksilver flashes against that background, each composed of a thousand brushstrokes of individual whorls of activity. The red path erasing itself behind me, urging me on by erasing itself more quickly if I slowed.

Perhaps I should start with color. Perhaps I should try to paint it for you. The way an artist layers paints, these glasses layered information. Or, as an artist layers paints to reveal, to accentuate, some facet, some theme, some previously unknown truth, so these glasses revealed a different city, a city which the gray caps had returned to, recolonized, without our knowledge. (Never left, Janice, dear sister. They never left. The glasses didn't reveal what was hidden. They merely showed what had always been there throughout the centuries.)

Everything had become a negative of itself so that the fog snuck in like coal smoke and the dark, hard brick of buildings became as light, as insubstantially white, as glass. Burned into this real world, the world by which we are assured of our own foundations, our own existence—by which I mean our bedrock; assuming, of course, that the world interpreted by our senses has any objective reality—burned into it, I tell you, were all the signs and symbols of the gray caps.

Superimposed. A nice word, but not the one I'm searching for, because this might imply some ethereal, unreal attribute for something that was all too unbearably real.

What I am trying to say is that the real world, the world I had known for over fifty years, no longer held true when confronted by this other world that existed on top of it and yet also within it.

But what, really, did I see as I walked that red carpet toward the Spore of the Gray Cap? I saw a phosphorescent cloud of green spores dancing in the midst of the fog, the glistening, swooping fullness of them almost that of a single, sentient entity. I saw a wall of brick covered—clotted?—with insect-harsh letters and symbols, in a welter of colors so diverse it destroyed the imagination. I saw long, centipedal creatures rippling and undulating, blending into the translucence of the brick. I saw stretching out before me, threading its way through a street littered with clumps of glowing yellow, blue, green spores, a continuing trail of red splotches, etched into the street as if by a painter.

As if in a dream, I followed the path. I had no choice.

The trick was not to flinch at the suddenly mobile, unlikely things that might sputter and lunge into the corner of your vision. The trick was to imagine it was all a dream, to lie to yourself as much as possible. Sometimes I felt as if the skin of the city had been torn away to reveal another place—a parallel world that shared only a few points of similarity with ours.

(Ah, well, perhaps no one could have done it justice, or injustice. How to describe something not so much seen as observed through some sixth sense, some place between eye and brain that should not exist. Some who see it for the first time go mad. A monk living in the fortress at Zamilon saw it and jumped from the fortress walls. It didn't drive Tonsure mad only because so many other revelations overwhelmed his senses. You did well, sister. Very well. Better than Mary.)

Duncan waited for me in this very room. He sat on a chair near the hole in the ground, table in front of him. He couldn't be seen from the doorway. I sat down in the chair opposite him. With the glasses on, the entirety of the room shone in shades of violet and gold; things floated in the air, things like clear jellyfish.

With the glasses on, Duncan's body was transformed. Fungus moved across the outlines of his bones, reshaping him, slowly, patiently. Or was it fungus? I caught a glimpse of brown-gold cilia, of protrusions eerily reminiscent of a giant starfish. He smelled of stagnant wine left out overnight. He smelled of sewers scoured clean with an essence of honeysuckle and sandalwood, with the sewer smell still lingering in the background. Rotting flesh. Cinnamon. Blended into a smell, a vibration, never intended for a human nose.

"Can I take the glasses off now?" I asked Duncan. I didn't like seeing him this way.

"Don't you wonder?" he said, his voice throaty, harsh. "Don't you wonder what you're looking at? I would if I were you."

Something about the way he held his head—his head an oval of incandescent light, his neck a slab of mottled darkness—made me think he was drunk.

"Are you all right?" I asked him. Something told me to run away from him, to get away, to wrench the glasses from my head. (Those were good instincts.)

"I said—don't you wonder?" he replied, and smashed his fist down against the table. Orange spores rippled from his fist and across the whorled grain of the table. For an instant, it looked as though the table had burst into flames. Then it dissipated and the orange evaporated into nothing.

"Yes—I wonder. I wonder about the way you look. I wonder why you chose this way to bring me here. But I asked—are you all right?"

A rough laugh. "Have I ever been *all right?* In your experience."

"Yes. I've even seen you laugh on occasion."

Duncan held out one hand and I could see that it was engulfed by the pointed translucent pseudopod of some creature.

"Remember your letter?"

"Which one?" I asked. There had been so many letters. Letters litter the floor of this place even now.

"Golden strands of connections. No one is alone. Everything is joined. When someone dies, there is a keening across the lines. Something of that nature."

He was definitely drunk, or not himself. (Oh, I was myself—the self I'd been suppressing for years.)

"I remember," I said. "What does it have to do with this, now?"

Duncan laughed. "Everything! Because you were more right than you knew. What you are looking at, my dear sister, is the starfish I showed you so many years ago. It never died—it just shed its skeleton and its corporeal presence: Skeletonless and invisible, it has expanded to encompass my body. It feeds off of my disease."

I didn't know what to say, so I said nothing.

"In the gray caps' world nothing ever really dies—it just *transforms.* To other flesh. Other spirit. Other vessels. Look at it from their perspective and it's quite beautiful. It flenses me of disease, but at a cost. It brings me closer and closer to the world you see through those glasses."

You'll doubt me now, dear reader, even if you didn't already, even though this is all true. I doubt myself. I doubt the evidence of my eyes. Doubt was a great friend to my father. To Jonathan Shriek, it was the Great Ally. "Doubt," he would say, raising a finger, "is what will see you through. It is a great truth." Dad doubted every word he'd ever written. He told me so once, in the living room, at the end of a long, exhausting day. Every word. I thought he was joking, but now I can see that he wasn't.

So you can choose to disbelieve if you wish—whatever part you want to disbelieve. But don't disbelieve my intent: to set the record straight, to explain Duncan to you, to explain myself.

"Take off the glasses," Duncan said.

"I'm not sure I want to now," I replied. I had begun to understand that there could be worse things in the real world than what I saw through the glasses. Even as the invisible starfish made its slow orbit of Duncan's body, feeding off his disease, cilia rotating madly.

I took off the glasses. It was no surprise to me when they scurried to the middle of the table and crouched there, waiting. Waiting for what? Me to put them on again?

Without the glasses, Duncan came into focus as . . . assimilated, made over in the image of some gray cap's imagination. A camouflage that seeped into the flesh so that it became entity, identity. He was slow and fast in that attire, that disguise, that incarnation. Swift and slow. He formed runnels of himself, the "particulate matter" of his left arm shining and purple, studded with the hoods of thousands of tiny mushrooms. The arm extended like a trickle, a slender stream, ending in a formless puddle of flesh. The strands of his other arm coalesced, recombined, came undone, came back together again.

Of his body, the less said, the better. (It was definitely not my best day.) There was nothing left to him that was Duncan, except for his eyes and a wry smile like liquid gold with a vein of granite running through it.

"What happens when it begins to infiltrate my brain?" Duncan said, though I'd said nothing. "I don't know. Maybe I'm no longer Duncan. Maybe I begin to know all there is to know about the gray caps."

But by now I was not afraid. I really wasn't, I was surprised to find. He didn't scare me. He was my brother, no matter what. I'd become accustomed. I realized now that even from the first time he'd stumbled into my apartment, covered in mushrooms, I had known it would come to this one day. (You weren't scared? Maybe because it wasn't happening to you. Me, I was fascinated and terrified at the same time.)

I reached out toward the shimmering, simmering writhing of his arm and touched him lightly.

"Tell me what happened," I said.

"We were both drunk," he said.

"Who?"

"Mary and me." He choked out the words.

"Where?"

"At a gallery opening. This afternoon. I happened to be there and she happened to be there. We had both had some wine before we met, and I guess that's why she didn't ignore me. She seemed in a good mood. She'd just finished a new book. She wanted to talk about it. I didn't mind. There was something about both of us, and the day, that allowed it. Everything from before had become ancient history."

I didn't believe him. That they had met by accident? That they had happened to attend the same gallery opening? Unlikely, knowing my Duncan. But I let it pass. (It's true. You're right. I planned it, down to the last detail. One last chance. I wanted to show her everything—all of it, from root to root, cavern to cavern.)

"Did you . . . did you look like you look now?" I asked him.

Duncan scowled. "No. I had control. I was keeping it all in. She didn't see any of this. I'm sure I looked a little fatter than when she'd last seen me, from everything I was keeping bottled up inside. But that's all."

"What happened?"

Duncan looked over at me, his frown enough to tell me before he said anything.

"We went outside. I began to talk about my theories. I had the eyeglasses in my pocket. Like I said, we were both a little drunk. We'd shared some pleasant memories from the Academy. I'd made her laugh. Now I think she was taking pity on me. At the time, I thought I saw in her face, her movements, a willingness to be friends again. And I couldn't help myself. I just couldn't. I pulled out the glasses. I told her to put them on. She giggled and said, 'What's this?' and then she put them on. She looked so beautiful then. I could not bear it. I think at first she thought it was a kaleidoscope, or some sort of party trick. At first, she laughed in delight. She let me take her by the hand and walk down the street. But somehow . . ."

"What?" I asked.

"Somehow, she guessed what she was looking at—she saw something that frightened her, something that made her so frightened that she got mad. She flung the glasses into the street. She began to curse me. I think she would have hit me if I hadn't backed away. I followed her for a while, to make sure she got back to the gallery safely. And that was it. I left her and came here. Then I sent my glasses to find you."

"That was it," I echoed.

After a pause, I said, "What did you think would happen?"

Duncan shrugged. "I don't know. I guess I thought she would finally see, that if she could see as I saw, then I could make everything all right."

Instead, in her fear and his distress, he had finally realized that he would always be alone, that he would never have the luxury of a normal life.

He winced at the look on my face.

"Janice! I didn't think it would make everything like it was before, but I thought it would make her see that I'm not a crackpot, not a liar, not crazy. At least that . . .

I spent a long time making those glasses for her, so she could experience it." (Ten years. It took ten years of research to make them. But no one wanted to see through them when I was done, except you, Janice, and you already believed me.)

"Did you really think that it could end well?" I asked.

The look of grief he gave me made it hard to judge him.

"Do you know how long I've protected her, looked out for her?"

I began to wonder whether Duncan's madness lay more in his inability to put Mary behind him than any of his more outlandish obsessions. (I had to try. I had to make the effort. Even if I knew how useless it was from the moment I entered the gallery.)

"Anyway," he said, "it's over now. I don't think I'm long for Ambergris, at least not aboveground."

"Going on another trip?" I asked.

"Not a trip. I wouldn't be the first. There are others down there. In the dark, rejecting the false light, as Bonmot liked to say. It's a choice. We all have a choice. So I think I'll travel there again."

"For good?" A panic threatened to overcome me, a panic that at first had no source.

"Probably. There isn't much left aboveground for me."

Which is when I realized, dear reader, that there wasn't much left aboveground for me, either. What would it mean to be a tour guide for the rest of my days, fated to point out landmarks that would always be personal for me, signs of success and failure? What kind of life would that be? Would I wind up like my mother? Perhaps I would try to kill myself again at some point, when the loneliness of it got too bad. Or perhaps I would let it happen to me, go through the same routines day after day, allow myself to fall into repetitions that masked the truth. And some days wonder, *Did Duncan make it? Did he find some kind of final truth? Did he find some kind of final happiness? Could it have worked for me?*

It might seem more like surrender to you, but right now it feels like defiance.

"You should join me," Duncan said. "They've moved the Machine. I have to find it before they bring it aboveground. Because when they do that, they'll be coming with it." He gave a little laugh, almost a yelp, as if something had stung him. "So it really doesn't matter where we are—above or below. It really doesn't."

"Coming aboveground?"

"The Machine is a door, Janice. But the flaw in it wasn't about the door itself. It was the location. They have to bring it aboveground. They have to reclaim the city. To use the door, to get back to wherever they came from. I've studied it. I've gotten close to it. It could take me to a new place."

As he had written in his journal:

> Ghosts of images cloud the surface of the machine and are wiped clean as if by a careless, a meticulous, an impatient painter. A great windswept desert, sluggish with the weight of its own dunes. An ocean, waveless, the tension of its surface broken only by the shadow of clouds above, the water such a perfect blue-green that it hurts your eyes. A mountain range at sunset, distant, ruined towers propped up by the foothills at its flanks. Always flickering into perfection and back into oblivion. Places that if they exist in this world you have never seen them or heard mention of their existence. Ever.

"It's great detective work on my part, Janice," he said. "I just had to wait long enough and be patient. I just had to let the fungus eat me alive. The door is opening. The gray caps are almost ready. There will be a green light in the sky and between the towers another world will arise. Something Tonsure wrote in his journal put me onto the trail, of course—something about the fortress of Zamilon. So why not go to meet it? Why wait? No matter where it leads me."

It was at this point, even with all that I had seen, all that I knew, that I thought for a moment that my brother *was* crazy, that Mary was right, that everything he had ever told me was a lie; that he was more insane than Lacond had ever been; that Mary had been fleeing, as she'd written to her friend, a madman; that I had been living a life fueled by reports delivered from the insane asylum of Duncan Shriek's brain. It has certainly occurred to me that the readers of this account may have reached that conclusion many, many pages ago.

"Are you sure?" I asked. "Are you *sure*?"

Duncan had been steeped in decades of alternative history, discussing his theories with the dead by way of their books, and with the living, yes, but an assortment of crackpots and eccentrics such as to make the Cult of the Lord's Botches look positively mundane. He had developed a skin as tough as oliphaunt hide. (Yet it occurs to me now that I've never really wanted to be a historian, let alone a journalist. I've always wanted to create history, even if no one ever realizes what part of it I helped create.)

But I saw the look when I said that. The sudden, unexpected, hurt look. Was I going to second-guess him? Betray him?

"Yes, I'm sure," he said.

"Then that's good enough for me," I said, and smiled.

When he rose to hug me with his fungal arms, I let him, and I hugged him back and tried not to shudder. (That moment saved me. If you had stopped believing in me too, I would have been lost.)

Then I took the glasses and left, not knowing that I'd be back soon enough.

✶✹✶

I received one last postcard from Duncan before he disappeared. It had lodged on the doorstep, caught in a crack in the wood, as if it were an errant leaf. It read: *It's time.* That's all, just: "It's time." And it was true. Everyone we cared about was dead or lost to us. Why stay above?

Worried, I visited his apartment, where I received partial confirmation that he had left: the door stood open a crack, and inside, other than a large trunk, it was empty of anything important to him. As I walked through those bare rooms, I remembered something else I said to him, when we had finished talking about the Machine.

I told him, "No matter what you do. No matter how much you publish. No matter how much you transform yourself, you're going to die. Aren't you?"

He laughed, even though his eyes weren't his, and gave me a grin that showed his teeth.

He said, and it sent a shiver through me and a calm such as I had never felt before, "There may be a way."

Sybel and Bonmot stood there like ghosts, gazing over that empty apartment. We were all wondering what was in the trunk, I think.

✶✹✶

There may be a way. I've thought about Duncan's words for a long time now. I have pondered what he might have been suggesting, and I think I know what he meant. I just don't know if it could really be true. Do I believe deeply enough in everything he's shown me?

I thought back to Duncan's account of the Machine and the underground. To him, it was another aspect of his quest, his obsession, no matter where it led. For me, it looked like a way out, a door, as Duncan had described it, or an open window into blue sky. What had it looked like to Tonsure, I sometimes wonder.

6

I fell asleep for a while. I couldn't help it. I've been pushing myself to the end ever faster, taking fewer breaks.

I dreamt while I slept. Edward was in my dream. Neither of us had really ever left the insane asylum. We sat there in matching straitjackets in uncomfortable chairs, facing each other. We were surrounded by huge orange-red-and-black mushrooms. The sight of their amber gills above us, slowly breathing in and out in a susurrating mimicry of conscious life, was strangely calming to me.

"Where have you gone?" I asked him.

"Underground," he said.

"What did you find there?" I asked.

"Acceptance, everlasting life, and mushrooms," he said, and smiled. It was a lovely smile. It radiated outward to suffuse his entire face in a golden light.

"Is that all?" I said. "Was it worth it? Did you have to give up anything?"

"My fear. My consciousness. My former life."

"What was that like?"

"Do you remember those trust exercises they made us do? Where one of us would fall into the arms of the others, and you just had to fall and keep falling and believe that they would catch you?"

"It was like that?"

"It was like that. Except imagine falling for a hundred years before you're caught, looking at a black sky full of cold dead stars in front of you, and the abyss at your back." (I think you were absorbing a line or two from my journal entries in your sleep.)

"You're dead," I said. It wasn't an accusation.

"Probably," he replied.

By then, we had shed our straitjackets and we stood in the lonely dull courtyard that the asylum had swallowed whole. At the far end, twelve elegant emerald mushrooms on long stalks were being guarded by two round rolling puffballs that glistened with sticky sea-green spores in an odd approximation of the asylum's lawn bowling facilities.

"I'm sorry," I said, although I didn't know what I was saying sorry for.

"It's okay, Janice," he said.

Then he walked away from me down the alley, getting smaller and smaller until he disappeared into the cluster of mushrooms.

Isn't that odd? I remember thinking in my dream. Isn't that odd? And I don't even know what it means.

When I woke, I thought I saw Sybel standing over me, but I was wrong. I was quite alone in my cot, in this dismal back room.

✻

I have left out so much, and yet there is no time now to go back and put it in its proper place. I've had no time to explore my (brief) conversion to Truffidianism under Bonmot's guidance after my unfortunate accident. I've not dwelt on my two miscarriages. Or that I was a drug addict for most of my adult life. That I loved Sirin, for many years, in secret, and that we slept together a few times four or five years ago. That—and I am so sorry for this—that I am the one who told Bonmot about Duncan's relationship with Mary. (I suspected. At the time, I would have been beyond furious; I never would have talked to you again. But now I see that that isn't what destroyed my relationship with her.) That I stole Duncan's journal from his apartment months before he left for the underground, long before I acquired the trunk. (Again, I had a suspicion it was you.) That there are definitely things walking up and down the tunnel at my back. That not everything I have told you is the truth as Duncan saw it. That my typewriter glows so brightly that I no longer need a lamp to see. That Duncan's glasses are in my shirt pocket, dormant, waiting for me to put them on.

None of that is important next to what I *do* have time to share with you, because I think I finally made Mary Sabon see—really *see*. It wasn't Duncan. It was me who did it.

How? A stroke of good fortune, and Truff knows I deserved one. About two months before Duncan's final disappearance, I led a group of insufferable snobs around the city—the type who sneer at anything genuine and delight in the false; the less truthful the better. Yet they turned out to be falsely snobbish themselves, once I saw them in another light—one was Martin Lake's new agent, David Frond, and two were his friends, visiting Ambergris for the first time. It was truly a miraculous intervention. When David found out who I was, the look he gave me made it clear he had thought I was dead. The thrill rising in my chest was because he knew my name at all.

After we talked for a while, David offered me a job rounding up Lake's old artist friends and getting them to display their work at a gallery show doubling as a party for Lake's fiftieth birthday. With any luck, he'd let me coordinate the party as well, he said. It was certainly a better offer than anything Sirin had brought my way in quite some time.

"It will be a regular parade of ghosts from Martin's past," he said, smiling.

It would be a parade of ghosts from my past, too, and I wasn't sure I liked the thought of that. Still, I needed the money if I wanted to keep my apartment. The tour guide business had been bad of late.

And, oh, the dead, the ghosts, cataloged but never accounted for among the living. The people I have known who thought they knew me. Each astonished face I tracked down vied more seriously for the winner of the most-startled-Janice-is-alive contest. Each astonished face would be a way to shore up Lake's ego by showing what a mediocrity Insert First & Last Name had turned out to be.

Most of them were people who had been oddly absent whenever I'd been in any kind of real trouble, coincidentally enough. During the ceremonial slitting of the wrists. During the gallery's financial woes. While I was in the hospital reconciling myself to the empty space where once five toes had cavorted like penned-up rutting pigs.

No, if it were to be a party of my peers (of veneers and sneers, more like), then it would just be my luck that I uncovered "acquaintances" or "not quite friends" or outright enemies. Most of my lovers had vanished during the war—they'd survived *me*, but, still, somehow, the sight of bloodshed scared them—seeking out less eventful lives in Stockton, Morrow, or Nicea. Bonmot and Sybel had both died, of course, and Sirin—through his writing—had ascended to a place where he was, in a way, untouchable. Sybel, of course, was by my side throughout all of the planning for the party; how could I possibly plan a party without him?

When I think of the people I knew back then, I realize that each of us had such private, personal, and immediate experiences that discussion with anyone about them, let alone achieving some kind of joint catharsis, would be meaningless—like a Blythe Academy reunion that invited only strangers from different years. The jargon used might have some kind of similarity, but beyond that, an aching void. That had been the whole point of the New Art—pour all of that empathy into the work, leaving only the surface as a connection to other people. I wonder now if any of it was worth it to any of us.

Still, despite reservations—and, trust me, I had reservations about many of them—I managed to exhume enough of Lake's long-dormant, sleep-tinged, hibernating friends and their dusty, packed-in-storage-for-decades artwork to earn my salary and be kept on for the party.

My main duty at the party? To herd the ruminant artists, to keep them happy. In the background, I would also help with the invitations, and in return, I would not only receive more money, but a promise of a position at a gallery—a promise I'm sure I must have known would never be kept, no matter what happened at the party. I was beyond that kind of respectability, and some part of me may even have been proud of that.

Four artists showed up for the party that night—any more and I wouldn't have been able to handle them, or their egos. After all, I was getting close to an age when women of much greater strength than I had retired to an early dotage on some pleasure barge or houseboat sailing idyllic down the River Moth. I was also worried about my brother, and therefore not in the best of moods. I cannot say that I cared that much about party preparations or "reparations," as I used to joke in the days before the party—with the cook, a sardonic man of my age who lifted my spirits and tried to lift my blouse on more than one occasion.

Lake had decided that the party should be held at the refurbished and renovated Hoegbotton Hotel. It had previously served as a glorified safe house, most active during Festival days, and thus had to be taken apart almost brick by brick to become a "hotel." For example, such features as iron bars on guest room windows did not convey the right message. Nor, for that matter, did the "safety crawl spaces" that led to tunnels, that led to the River Moth. No, it had all been stripped away as if the gray caps and the Festival were now some remote happening—remote in time and space and even remotely unbelievable, from some period of ancient history that could not be verified by even the most reckless historian. A kind of silly rumor—a scary story told to children before bedtime by unenlightened parents. (I blame such innovations as the telephone. Such prosaic devices make it difficult for people to believe in the *other* until it stares them in the face and takes a swipe at them.)

To replace such outdated structures came wide staircases of marble bought from the Kalif at ridiculous prices and large glass windows that any lout with a plank of wood would find irresistible come Festival time. They had scented candles and handmade bedsheets made by the few Dogghe tribesmen who hadn't been slaughtered by our ancestors, and chairs and tables crafted by carpenters from the Southern Isles. Every floor had its own telephone on a pedestal, conveniently located near the staircase. The smell of new stone, new furnishings, and clean sheets was so un-Ambergrisian that as soon as I stepped into the place, I knew no locals would be checking in for a night's rest and relaxation.

The party would take up the ground floor, centered around the banquet hall, while the artists' gathering/gallery would be located on the second floor, in a smaller room.

✻

That night was calm but for a steady drizzle and drip of rain, the moon missing, but the streetlamps making up for it. A breeze blew into the reception area. It felt cool as I waited for the Four Ghosts of Lake's Past to arrive for the party.

I stood in the doorway, smoking a Smashing Todd's Deluxe cigar and nursing a glass of cheap red wine from the kitchen staff's stock. I intended to enjoy my evening by indulging myself early on, so if things went hideously wrong, I would still have a memory to look back on with fondness.

I watched the night as it passed by me on Albumuth Boulevard, one of the last times I had a chance to just relax and observe, as it turned out. And yet, a feeling of peculiar intensity came over me. I saw it all with such precise detail, in a way that I cannot put into words. It was not that the world slowed down or that I saw anything hidden in it, although I knew there was more in front of me than I could see—I had the glasses in my pocket to remind of that. It was more that my gaze *lingered* for once. It lingered and held, as if I was parched for that little glistening of light off water in the gutter as a motored vehicle rumbled past. As if I was hungry for the exact way a street vendor cocked his head while rattling off a list of his offerings. The quiet syncopation of conversation half-heard and then gone as people walked by. The lamppost opposite the hotel, illuminating the facade of a closed bank door. The quick-low cry of a nighthawk circling somewhere above. The feel of the street through my shoes. The grit of the doorway against my shoulder as I leaned on it. The bliss of the cigar's trembling surge of flavor, the biting smoothness of the wine.

I think I already knew then that I was not long for such sights.

✻

The four artists arrive on time—two by an old-fashioned carriage, another by hired motored vehicle, a fourth on foot. Sonter, Kinsky, Raffe, and Constance were their names: a motley rabble of ragtag talent, and none of them had ever so much as scaled a small mountain of acclaim except through the long-ago benevolent influence of Lake's hand upon them.

Sonter looked ancient and creaky, like a narrow, withered boat with bad caulking—on the verge of a watery death, perhaps. A decade spent on an island in the middle of the River Moth had done him no favors. Kinsky had become broad and looked defeated but brave, the gray circles under his eyes negated by an animation lacking from the others. Constance maintained a look of perpetual outrage that made me roll my eyes before I could help myself. Only Raffe, though aging—and, I realized with a shock, probably my own age—appeared in any way serene or accepting of Fate.

I greeted them. They were polite. That was all I expected from them.

Raffe said to me, "You look tired. Can we help with anything?"

Which comment, for some reason, made me want to cry.

I took them upstairs to the temporary gallery—a room converted from its original function as a bar. The lighting was all wrong and I hadn't been able to hang the paintings the way I would have liked due to an incompetent helper, but at least a small throng had gathered there already. I don't remember my welcoming speech, I just know that, for a moment, an emotion welled up in my throat that came close to affection for those I was introducing. After all, they were survivors just like me. They were also artists, and for twenty years of my life all I had done was introduce artists. Was there a sad twinge for my lost gallery? Of course, but these days there is a sad twinge about everything—to the point that I begin to wonder if it's my heart that's gone bad, rather than anything to do with my memories.

Besides, it can't be avoided. Bonmot once told me, "If you don't feel a certain sadness toward the past, then you probably don't understand it."

After my introduction and short speeches by the artists, the adoring if small-in-numbers public pushed forward to engage the Obscure, Sonter somehow evading the crush and coming up to me.

"I heard Mary Sabon will be here tonight," he said. "Is that true?"

The peace I had been experiencing left me.

"I don't know," I told him. "I didn't see her on the guest list."

That had been my one petty triumph—I'd managed through sleight of hand to get Mary Sabon uninvited from Lake's party, said sleight of hand involving an unmailed invitation and a sidewalk gutter leading to the nether depths. Somewhere *down there* a gray cap might be clutching that invitation as I write this account. It might be its most treasured possession.

So I hope you will understand in advance that my later actions were spontaneous, perhaps even unplanned. I did not go to the party, as some claimed in muttering whispers afterward, to confront Mary. I had done my best to make sure she would not be there at all. (I believe you.)

Sonter opened his mouth to question me further, but I shut it with a well-aimed appetizer delivered on raised foot, the appetizer rescued from a passing waiter's tray with an ease I almost never experience. Sonter turned away immediately.

There may have been an expression on my face that made him turn away. It may have had nothing to do with the appetizer. I would not rule it out if I were you.

※※※

For the next two hours, I attended to the artists, explaining their paintings to those who required an explanation. It was hard work. Some of the paintings came from the kind of obscure symbolism that either baffles me or brings out my inventiveness, but the old potent phrases from the past came back to me from the void of memory soon enough.

"Vibrant use of color."

"Brave application of the oils."

"The composition accentuates the face, for nicely subtle symbolic effect."

This part I enjoyed, I admit. It made me feel free. For a brief time, while pointing out the detail of a sudden azure thrush in the dull emerald undergrowth at the bottom of one of Raffe's paintings, I could pretend Lake was still my client, that my gallery still served as the nexus of the New Art. I even caught the eye of a former lover from across the room, and he smiled. You could say I was happy.

Then they pressed me into duty helping downstairs, in the banquet hall. David Frond's idea of a menu included lark's tongues and frog's legs, fish eggs and lemon pie, squid soup and oliphaunt kidneys. It was quite an ambitious spread, worthy of the obese gastronome Manzikert III himself. It wasn't hard to imagine another time, another place, in which this would have been a party for Duncan, had luck been on our side. A string of alternate scenarios in which we rose to the top and stayed there, instead of being diminished by time and our own enemies. (Would it have been so much better that way, Janice?)

Ill-suited for such work, I hobbled back and forth past the extravagantly costumed guests as they cavorted across the dance floor—half hunter, half flushed rabbit—escorting notables with polite conversation about the weather—there was quite a drumming of rain outside by then—or about the history of the fluted archways in the lobby that the Hoegbottons had stolen from some ruin down south.

Some of the people I escorted, I remembered coming into my gallery as children or young adults, but none of them remembered me. Scions of Hoegbotton's mercantile empire, officials from foreign cities, even a nervous-looking emissary from Frankwrithe & Lewden (more than likely a hostage). I don't know why I had to escort them, and I didn't much care. (Lake's agent probably feared they would get drunk and cause a scene.)

Then followed a period of rest for this old woman, where I just stood in the gallery room on the second floor and smiled at patrons of the arts as they glided by, drinks in hand. The artists had all joined the reverie on the ground floor, but I welcomed the respite by then.

The party had reached that unfamiliar point where, in contrast to past events, I stood outside of it, looking in. I was far away, and very tired, remembering with regret the cigar I had had to abandon when the artists showed up. Remembering that my brother was missing and feeling powerless to do anything about it.

There is, I have to say, a perfect anonymity at a party like that, in the role chosen for me. You can pretend by remaining silent that you are invisible and yet all-powerful. The way the conversation intermingles so that you do not hear any words, just a kind of spiraling hum, or babble, or crescendo—and you can then, if you listen hard, hear the individual words and phrases, but not in a way that makes any sense. Duncan was hundreds of feet below me by then, working his way to the heart of a mystery. I know he had to be because he was nowhere near me anymore (although closer than you think), and it seemed to me in that moment that he really wouldn't be coming back.

And, also, I was thinking about how you can bring the hum, the babble, the crescendo low—bring it all low with a single accusation, a shout, a scream, perhaps even, yes, a shriek.

I might have stayed in that trance forever, enjoying a measure of melancholy contentment, if I had not heard someone, probably Sonter, say, "Mary Sabon is here" as he walked by the doorway.

The party jolted into focus again.

Sabon? Here? But she hadn't been invited . . .

I surveyed the thinning gallery crowd. No sign of her. So she must be downstairs. I don't know why my first thought was to hunt her down, but I got up, pushed through a wedge of drunk people, and escaped to the top of the marble staircase.

At the bottom of the steps, surrounded by the glittering necklace of flesh that always surrounded her now, stood Mary Sabon. My attempts to keep her away had been useless. She was like an apparition to me, an apparition that had manifested itself in flesh and blood and makeup. Sabon transcended any attempt to ward her off. She had risen above that.

I had not seen her in years, except in newspaper photographs or granular dust jacket likenesses. She looked younger than she had any right to be, and there was a glow to her skin, and a sheen to her hair, as if she were feeding off the heat and light given off by her swirling necklace of admirers. Admittedly, I almost couldn't see her, surrounded by that necklace. But such perfect poise. Such caked-on rouge. Such hypocrisy. There she was, telling her flesh necklace a series of stories to beguile them with her charm, to make them un-realize what the war and Duncan had been warning them about for years.

I couldn't banish her, so I decided to punish her instead. (You could have left the party. Would that have been so hard?)

I was, admittedly, a slow, deliberate stalker; anyone could have evaded me, had they been able to see me over the tall individuals who kept blocking my path. It took me ages to reach the last step, what with my cane and my wooden foot. What would I do when I reached her? What would I say? Perhaps, I thought, in a moment of panic, I should take off my foot and throw it at her and retreat to the gallery. But that was absurd, and she hadn't seen me yet. She was too busy talking about herself.

I had reached the last step when I heard her remark about Duncan.

"Duncan Shriek? That old fake? He's not a human being at all, but composed entirely of digressions and transgressions."

I laughed for a moment, out of surprise more than anything, but also out of affection for my brother, because it was true—except her tone made it obvious she didn't mean it affectionately.

Mary heard my laughter because it was out of place with the rest of it—an echo too remote from the original sound. She looked around and saw me just as I finished hobbling down the stairs, making a mockery of their convenience. I suppose if they'd had a dumbwaiter I could have winched myself down instead.

Thus I descended to the foot of the stairs. The marble shone like glass, like a mirror—my face and those of the others reflected back at me. The assembled guests slowly fell apart into their separate bead selves. Blank-eyed beads winking at me as they formed a corridor to Sabon. Smelling of too little or too much perfume, of sweat. Shedding light by embracing shadows. A series of stick figures in a comedic play.

I walked right up to Mary. Red hair she still had in abundance, although I would not like to conjecture how she kept out the gray. She wore a dark green evening dress with brocade straps. Her gaze was contemptuous, perhaps, or merely guarded.

Ignoring my presence—something she would have done at her peril in the old days—she repeated, "Duncan is composed entirely of digressions and transgressions. Assuming he's still alive."

As she said this, she took a step forward and turned and looked right at me. We stood only a foot or two apart.

I stared at her for a moment. I let her receive the full venom of my stare. Then I hobbled forward and I slapped her hard across the face. She grunted in surprise, seemed stunned more than hurt.

She wasn't that much taller than me, really. Not as tall as she'd seemed while I was coming down the stairs. And not as young as she had seemed, either. My hand came away covered in makeup.

The imprint shone as red as her hair, as flushed as the gasp from the necklace of flesh. It lit up her face in a way that made her look honest again. It spread across her cheek, down her neck, swirled between the tops of her breasts, and disappeared beneath her gown. If the world is a just place, that mark will never leave her skin, but remain as a pulsing reminder that, at some point in the past, she hurt someone so badly that she wound up hurting herself as well.

"Once upon a time," I said, "no one knew your name. Someday no one will again."

The wide "O" of the mouth, the speechless surprise, the backward step, the hand raised toward her cheek, the fear in her eyes as if she saw herself already as dust. That slap would tease a thousand tongues in a dozen cafés that week, until even the swift-darting swallows that so love our city repeated it in their incessant, insect-seducing song.

To her credit, she waved back the guards. She waved back the onrush of beads from her flesh necklace. They retreated, gleaming and muttering.

"What is it you really want, Janice?" she said, smiling through her pain. "Would you like the past back? Would you like to be successful again? Would you prefer you weren't a washed-up has-been with so few prospects you had to agree to assist to help out with a party for an artist you used to agent?"

But I had nothing to say to her.

Instead, I turned to look at the assembled fawners and sycophants, the neophytes and the desperate, to make sure they were watching. Then I took the glasses from my pocket—and flung them at Mary's face. I didn't know I was going to do it until the instant it happened, and then it was too late to un-wish it.

In midair, the glasses opened up and, like some aerial acrobat of a spider, attached themselves perfectly to her face, the arms sliding into position around her ears, the bridge settling on her nose.

Mary was staring at me as the scales of the lenses filled with that amazing blackness—and she began to scream as soon as the top half of her pupils disappeared, a scream that grew deeper and more desperate as it continued, and continued. It was as if she had forgotten she could close her eyes. All she had to do was close her eyes, and, after a time, I began to hope she *would* close her eyes.

She stumbled, caught herself, blinked twice, stopped screaming—but, no: she was still screaming, it was just soundless. A look had come over her that destroyed the unity between mouth, eyes, forehead, cheekbones. Before me, she became undone looking through those glasses.

She fell to her knees, now grappling with the glasses, but they did not want to come off. Her precious flesh necklace didn't know what to do—it dithered, came forward, retreated, unable to reconcile this moment of Sabon's life with the last.

Raffe and Sonter were the first to recover from their shock, pushing through the crowd to come to Mary's aid. Sabon was slack-jawed, moaning, and saying a word over and over again. It sounded suspiciously like "No." Sonter tried to pry the glasses off while Raffe comforted Mary. But they still wouldn't come off.

Finally, mercy flooding back into me, I stepped forward and plucked the glasses from her face; they scurried across the floor and rolled up into a ball. Sabon's face went slack, and I saw a momentary flicker of pain—the ghost of regret, perhaps?—and then it was gone. Her eyes rolled up into her head and she fainted.

The flesh necklace, now adding their cries to the growing cacophony, parted to let Raffe and Sonter carry Mary away, Sonter cursing my name. Even in unconsciousness, a look of utter terror and helplessness marred her face.

No one else wanted to pick up the glasses, so I did. After all, they were mine. I folded them and put them back in my pocket. They were still warm.

I was trembling and exhausted; watching Mary struggle had taken all of my energy. I still cannot decide if it was relief or horror that drained me. I still can't decide if what I did was right or wrong.

What had Mary seen? I don't know. I had stopped wearing the glasses more than two weeks before. Released from Duncan's expert guidance, they had become stranger and stronger somehow, as if they now pierced through layers of reality deeper than even the gray caps were meant to see. But whatever she saw, it was the truth—in one massive dose.

I've thought about whether I should put them on again—I've thought about it the entire time I've been typing up this account. Might I see *all the way through*? Might I see through the golden threads, if they exist, to something else entirely? Or would I just fall, and keep falling?

I do know this—sometimes, afterward, I've had a daydream in which I seek Mary out once the glasses come off, and I find her weeping in a corridor in the bowels of the hotel, and I sit down beside her and I hold her close and I say, "Please—forgive me." But sometimes in the daydream I'm also saying, "I forgive you, Mary. I forgive you."

7

I bought a few newspapers after I came here, but all they can tell me is that "Sabon is recovering from a bout of exhaustion." None of them mentions my role in her exhaustion.

And that is all I know, and all I want to know.

I halted on the edge of an abyss when I left Mary, I think. I halted on the edge of a kind of Silence. I needed to write it down, try to make some sense of it outside of my own head. Draw the poison.

But I've shed my last skin. I've no more skins to shed. I can't start over again—

I've started over too many times before. You won't believe me. *I* won't believe me, either.

Maybe all of this was prevarication and excuses and not an afterword at all. Not an essay. Not a history. Not a pamphlet. Just an old woman's ramblings. Maybe I don't want to think about that hole in the ground behind me and the decision I have to make. But if so, at least it's over now. I have told you everything I meant to tell you, and more.

As I sit here in the green light and review these pages, I see what Duncan saw when he wrote in this room—the sliver, the narrowness of vision, the small amount we know before we're gone—and I realize that this account was a stab in the dark at a kind of truth, no matter how faltering: a brief flash of light against the silhouette of dead trees. This was the story of my life and my brother's life, my brother and his Mary. (How could you think to tell such a story without me by your side, Janice?)

And, somehow, I have kept separate, hidden away in my mind, one single image of joy before disaster: my father, running across the unbearably green grass. And not what occurred after. Not what happened after.

I want that kind of joy, that epiphany, or a chance at it, at least, even if it kills me. (Must I echo to you your own words? That we are all connected by lines of glimmering light. How many times those words kept me alive, made me see approaching light in unending darkness? As Bonmot used to say in his sermons: "We are vessels of light—broken vessels, broken light, but vessels nonetheless." Fragments across the void. It's time to find you, Janice, and see what you've gotten yourself into.)

But you're free now, regardless of what this was—after word, afterward. I release you to return to what you were before. If you can.

As for me, it is time to abandon even this dim green light for the darkness. I've put as many words between myself and this decision as I can, but it hasn't worked. There's a space between each word that I can't help but fall into, and those spaces are as wide as the words and twice as treacherous.

A shift of attention. Another place to go. That's all it is. I'm not afraid anymore. I'm not frightened. Everyone is dead or disappeared or disappointed. I ask you, who is left to be afraid of? This is After Dad Died. This is After Mom Died. This is an entirely new place.

I think it is time for one last walk outside. One last look at this crazed, beautiful, dirty, sad, glorious city. Sybel and Bonmot and my mom and all the rest are waiting for me out there in some form or another—a whisper on the breeze, the rustle of the branches, a shadow across a wall, and, perhaps, there will be time for one last lunch under the willows, my glasses safely in my pocket. Then I'll come back and decide whether or not to seek out Duncan, whether to put on these glasses and face whatever Mary saw.

No one makes it out, Samuel Tonsure once said.

Or do they?

A (BRIEF) AFTERWORD BY SIRIN

My role in all of this is complicated and compromised because I know or knew almost all of the people mentioned in Janice's manuscript, not least of whom was Janice herself. I was always fond of Janice, perhaps more than I should have been, but confronted with her typewritten manuscript, I felt much as I had felt several years before when confronted by Duncan's six hundred pages of early history: overwhelmed, irritated, fatigued, intrigued, and perplexed. I've always thought Janice had the best intentions, but also that her biases and her own obsessions sometimes led her to suspect conclusions. Many of these suspect conclusions had made their way into the afterword she left behind, and this explains, or helps to explain, my actions with regard to it. I hope.

✸❀✸

I found the original typewritten pages in the back room of the Spore of the Gray Cap. I had gone there searching for Janice, as she had not shown up for her job in over a month. Since we had a professional history, I felt an obligation to find out what might be wrong. In fact, given our personal history, I felt more than an obligation—I was worried about her.

Given the events that had taken place at Martin Lake's party—events accurately described in Janice's account—I thought it likely she was "hiding" from a sense of shame or embarrassment. I never realized she might be writing a highly inflammatory, perhaps even actionable, history of her life and her brother's life.

When I found the manuscript, it lay in a disorganized mess of pages beside her typewriter. The typewriter had become clogged with a green lichen or fungus; the entire shell overtaken by the spread of this loamy green substance. If I had arrived only a day later, the manuscript also might have succumbed to this same affliction.

I examined the pages briefly—long enough, however, to ascertain who had written the text and to note the comments added by Duncan, whose handwriting and attitude are familiar to me from our association over the years.

Beyond the desk, on the floor near the wall, a series of loose boards partially covered up a hole that led down into the ground. Once I saw the hole, I left quickly, pausing only to gather up the manuscript pages.

After I returned to my office with the manuscript and read through it, I was baffled as to what to do next. While many of the sections dealing with Ambergris's recent history had a general ring of truth to them, these were inextricably interwoven with sections that contained the most outrageous accusations and assertions. What was true and what false, I might never know.

Neither could I corroborate any statements made about Janice's family—despite the mention of family papers and Duncan's journal in the manuscript, no such documents had been in evidence at the Spore of the Gray Cap. Worst of all, the manuscript did such a disservice to the reputation and character of my author Mary Sabon that from a purely professional point of view I was disinclined to attempt publication. However, paramount above all other concerns, I sincerely believed that Duncan or Janice would walk into my offices at any moment to reclaim the manuscript. So, for several years, I held on to it. I could not bring myself to destroy it. Nor could I bring myself to let the public have its way with the account.

However, it gradually became clear that Janice and Duncan had disappeared, possibly forever. Oddly enough, the owner of the Spore still swears that Janice never left his establishment on the day she would have finished her account—that she simply disappeared from the room, presumably through the hole in the floor. Similarly, the owner claims he never saw Duncan during the time Duncan must have been adding his comments to the manuscript.

That Duncan had been missing for several weeks before Martin Lake's party is supported only by the unsubstantiated statements in Janice's manuscript. As he was unemployed at the time of his supposed disappearance, no one, not even members of AFTOIS, noticed his absence. Still, it is true that he has not been seen in Ambergris since commenting on Janice's manuscript. It has been almost four years.

As for Janice, not much more is known about her whereabouts. The current rumor is that a person fitting her description fell (or was pushed—we will never know) into the path of a motored vehicle on the same day Janice seems to have finished her account. Supposedly, a wooden foot was found near the scene, but the body was too badly mangled to be identifiable.

Figure 1: Janice Shriek's typewriter. As the reader can see from this photo, the typewriter keys had been infiltrated by mushrooms. Many of the keys were brittle and fell off within weeks of taking the machine out of its room at the Spore of the Gray Cap. The typewriter disintegrated entirely within five months.

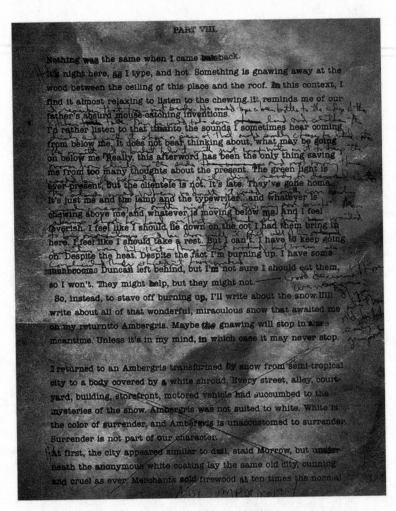

PART VIII

Nothing was the same when I came ~~backback~~.

It's night here, as I type, and hot. Something is gnawing away at the wood between the ceiling of this place and the roof. In this context, I find it almost relaxing to listen to the chewing. It reminds me of our father's absurd mouse-catching inventions.

I'd rather listen to that than to the sounds I sometimes hear coming from below me. It does not bear thinking about, what may be going on below me. Really, this afterword has been the only thing saving me from too many thoughts about the present. The green light is ever-present, but the clientele is not. It's late. They've gone home. It's just me and the lamp and the typewriter...and whatever is chewing above me, and whatever is moving below me. And I feel feverish. I feel like I should lie down on the cot I had them bring in here. I feel like I should take a rest. But I can't. I have to keep going on. Despite the heat. Despite the fact I'm burning up. I have some mushrooms Duncan left behind, but I'm not sure I should eat them, so I won't. They might help, but they might not.

So, instead, to stave off burning up, I'll write about the snow. I'll write about all of that wonderful, miraculous snow that awaited me on my return to Ambergris. Maybe the gnawing will stop in the meantime. Unless it's in my mind, in which case it may never stop.

I returned to an Ambergris transformed by snow from semi-tropical city to a body covered by a white shroud. Every street, alley, courtyard, building, storefront, motored vehicle had succumbed to the mysteries of the snow. Ambergris was not suited to white. White is the color of surrender, and Ambergris is unaccustomed to surrender. Surrender is not part of our character.

At first, the city appeared similar to dull, staid Morrow, but underneath the anonymous white coating lay the same old city, cunning and cruel as ever. Merchants sold firewood at ten times the normal

Figure 2: A reproduction of a sample page from Janice Shriek's manuscript. Despite Duncan's admonishment about the unimportance of Janice's description of a transformed Ambergris, I did not delete the text as he requested; nor did I delete anything in the manuscript that Duncan edited out. After careful consideration, I did, however, delete a half-dozen paragraph-length oddities that bore no discernible relation to the rest of the text, since I felt that these digressions would distract from the text more than they added to it. The careful reader will note that the page reproduced above contains one of these deleted segments.

Once it was clear the Shrieks would not be coming back, I pulled out the manuscript again and reread it. In the three years that had passed, many strange things had happened in the city, so that even the most bizarre parts of the account no longer seemed quite so ridiculous. But there was still the issue of its portrayal of Mary. I decided to show Mary the manuscript and let her decide its fate. It may seem that I abrogated my responsibility in doing so, but I felt I had no choice.

To my surprise, Mary told me Hoegbotton & Sons *should* publish it. She was quite adamant about it, and further instructed me not to delete or soften any references to her, regardless of how unflattering. She became very emotional on this point, and I had the impression she wished I had shown her the manuscript the day I had found it.

Obeying Mary's wishes, I did not make many edits of substance in preparing Janice's account for publication. I did, in some instances, smooth out the text—for example, fixing the grammatical errors in those sections written in exceptional haste. Likewise, I corrected all spelling errors. Where Janice had alternate versions of a page or scene—which occurred with some frequency—I chose the more polished of the two. I also untangled Janice's handwritten corrections from Duncan's comments, deciding that placing the latter in parentheses and removing parentheses from Janice's text was the most elegant solution to a potentially wearisome problem. Where she spent too long on a subject, or lost focus completely, I did excise text, but the entirety of these deletions constitutes only five or six paragraphs in total. I may have erred too far on the side of preservation in this case—some of the discussion of Duncan's theories strikes me as tedious—but better tedium than claims I was overzealous in my editing duties.

I also deleted Duncan's final comment on Janice's manuscript, which he wrote on the page following her last chapter. I did this not because I wanted to, but because I *had* to. The comment was illegible. I had several handwriting experts examine the sentence. None could come to any agreement as to how it might have read. The most coherent interpretation? "Confluence of light between towers and being there at the right time leapt forward." I include the phrase here despite my best instincts to do otherwise. My sole addition to the text consisted of fleshing out one or two scenes where Janice's descriptive powers deserted her, but only in cases where I had been privy to the same information.

A further complication concerned the fungal contamination of the pages, coupled with the haphazard way in which the pages had been stacked on the table at the Spore. On some pages, the words were barely legible, and many pages or sections were out of order, several lacking the page numbers that might have allowed me to easily sequence them. I erred on the side of chronological order—even though Janice did not always adhere to such an order—but it is possible I made a few errors in my sequencing.

Therefore, I have clearly made editorial decisions with regard to Janice's manuscript which some may consider to be too invasive, no matter how slight. But what is not true, despite the rumors, is that *An Afterword to the Hoegbotton Guide to the Early History of Ambergris* represents an elaborate deception on my part. Not only is the manuscript genuine (see the reproduction of a sample page herein), but I had nothing to do with writing it. Nor is Hoegbotton & Sons only publishing it now due to the sharp upturn in sales of Duncan's books.[1]

I have no doubt that the publication of this book will generate fierce discussion about the merits of Nativism, about the aims of the gray caps, and about the nature of the Shift that has increasingly disrupted life in Ambergris. Some will feel that Duncan is about to be vindicated in the most dramatic of ways.

In preparing the manuscript for publication, I have, for that very reason, experienced fresh doubts about making it available. We live in a very volatile time and I would not want this book to be a catalyst for extremism. Nor, I would hope, will readers jump to unsupportable conclusions having read it. I know that many people are clutching at whatever they can to make sense of the odd events that, on certain days, seem destined to overwhelm all of us. My sincere hope is that this book will not push anyone over the edge.

As to the current whereabouts of Duncan and Janice, I must fear the worst,

---

1. Some on my editorial staff have suggested that we should include an unexpurgated version of Duncan's *Early History of Ambergris* as an appendix to this edition. However, I cannot acquire that text, as I returned my only copy to Janice and do not know what she did with it. Moreover, an edition that combined Janice's manuscript with the complete *Early History* would put even Hoegbotton's hardbound edition of its seventy-five Southern Island travel pamphlets to shame for sheer size and verbiage.

although rumors,[2] as rumors will, continue to flourish in the current atmosphere of paranoia and fear.

And yet, despite the strife and violence chronicled and presaged by this volume, the enduring image I have of Janice and Duncan is a peaceful one. It is, oddly enough, of Janice in that room in the Spore, calmly typing away—from the bar folks' perspective, in a sliver of green light between the doorway and the corridor as once they saw Duncan, but farther and farther away, across green glass and green grass, and fading, fading as the light fails once more.

2. No evidence exists to support supposed "Duncan Sightings" at Zamilon and Alfar, for example.

"When they give you things, ask yourself why. When you're grateful to them for giving you the things you should have anyway, ask yourself why."

—Lady in Blue, rebel broadcast

MONDAY

Interrogator: What did you see then?

Finch: Nothing. I couldn't see anything.

I: Wrong answer.

[howls and screams and sobbing]

I: Had you ever met the Lady in Blue before?

F: No, but I'd heard her before.

I: Heard her where?

F: On the fucking radio station, that's where.

[garbled comment, not picked up]

F: It's her voice. Coming up from the underground. People say.

I: So what did you see, Finch?

F: Just the stars. Stars. It was night.

I: I can ask you this same question for hours, Finch.

F: You wanted me to say I saw her. I said I saw her! I said it, damn you.

I: There is no Lady in Blue. She's just a propaganda myth from the rebels.

F: I saw her. On the hill. Under the stars.

I: What did this apparition say to you, Finch? What did this vision say?

1

inch, at the apartment door, breathing heavy from five flights of stairs, taken fast. The message that'd brought him from the station was already dying in his hand. Red smear on a limp circle of green fungal paper that had minutes before squirmed clammy. Now he had only the door to pass through, marked with the gray caps' symbol.

239 Manzikert Avenue, apartment 525.

An act of will, crossing that divide. Always. Reached for his gun, then changed his mind. Some days were worse than others.

A sudden flash of his partner, Wyte, telling him he was compromised, him replying, "I don't have an opinion on that." Written on a wall at a crime scene: *Everyone's a collaborator. Everyone's a rebel.* The truth in the weight of each.

The doorknob cold but grainy. The left side rough with light green fungus.

Sweating under his jacket, through his shirt. Boots heavy on his feet.

Always a point of no return, and yet he kept returning.

I am not a detective. I am not a detective.

Inside, a tall, pale man dressed in black stood halfway down the hall, staring into a doorway. Beyond him, a dark room. A worn bed. White sheets dull in the shadow. Didn't look like anyone had slept there in months. Dusty floor. Even before he'd started seeing Sintra, his place hadn't looked this bad.

The Partial turned and saw Finch. "Nothing in that room, Finch. It's all in here." He pointed into the doorway. Light shone out, caught the dark glitter of the Partial's skin where tiny fruiting bodies had taken hold. Uncanny left eye in a gaunt face. Always twitching. Moving at odd angles. Pupil a glimmer of blue light at the bottom of a dark well. Fungal.

"Who are you?" Finch asked.

The Partial frowned. "I'm—"

Finch brushed by the man without listening, got pleasure out of the push of his shoulder into the Partial's chest. The Partial, smelling like sweet rotting meat, walked in behind him.

Everything was golden, calm, unknowable.

Then Finch's eyes adjusted to the light from the large window and he saw: living room, kitchen. A sofa. Two wooden chairs. A small table, an empty vase with a rose design. Two bodies lying on the pull rug next to the sofa. One man, one gray cap without legs.

Finch's boss, Heretic, stood framed by the window. Wearing his familiar gray robes and gray hat. Finch had never learned the creature's real name. The series of clicks and whistles sounded like "heclereticalic" so Finch called him "Heretic." Highly unusual to see Heretic during the day.

"Finch," Heretic said. "Where's Wyte?" The wetness of its moist glottal attempt at speech made most humans uncomfortable. Finch tried hard to pretend the ends of all the words were there. A skill hard learned.

"Wyte couldn't come. He's busy."

Heretic stared at Finch. A question in his eyes. Finch looked to the side. Away from the liquid green pupils and yellow where there should be white. Wyte had been sick off and on for a long time. Finch knew from what, but didn't want to. Didn't want to get into it with Heretic.

"What's the situation?" Finch asked.

Heretic smiled: rows and rows of needle lines set into a face a little like a squished-in shark's snout. Finch couldn't tell if the lines were gills or teeth, but they seemed to flutter and breathe a little. Wyte said he'd seen tiny creatures in there, once. *Each time, a new nightmare.* Another encounter to haunt Finch's sleep.

"Two dead bodies," Heretic said.

"Two bodies?"

"One and a half, technically," the Partial said, from behind Finch. Heretic laughed. A sound like dogs being strangled.

"Did the victims live in the apartment?" Finch asked, knowing the answer already.

"No," the Partial said. "They didn't."

Finch turned briefly toward the Partial, then back to Heretic.

Heretic stared at the Partial and he shut up, began to creep around the living room taking pictures with his eye.

"No one lived here," Heretic said. "According to our records no one has lived here for over a year."

"Interesting," Finch said. Didn't interest him. Nothing interested him. It bothered him. Especially that the Partial felt comfortable enough to answer a question meant for Heretic.

The curtains had faded from the sun. Tears in the sofa like knife wounds. The vase looked like someone had started a small fire inside it. Stage props for two deaths.

Was it significant that the window was open? For some reason he didn't want to ask if one of them had opened it. Fresh air, with just a hint of the salt smell from the bay.

"Who reported this?" Finch asked.

"An energy surge came from this location," Heretic said. "We felt it. Then spore cameras confirmed it."

Energy surge? What kind of energy?

Finch tried to imagine the rows and rows of living receivers underground, miles of them if rumor held true. Trying to process trillions of images from all over the city. *How could they possibly keep up?* The hope of every citizen.

"Do you know the . . . source?" Finch asked. Didn't know if he understood what Heretic was telling him.

"There is no trace of it now. The apartment is cold. There are just these bodies."

"How does that help me?" he wanted to say.

Finch usually dealt with theft, domestic abuse, illegal gatherings. Flirted with investigating rebel activity, but turned that over to the Partials if necessary. Tried to make sure it wasn't necessary. For everyone's sake.

Murder only if it was the usual. Crimes of passion. Revenge. This didn't look like either. If it was murder.

"Anyone live in the apartments next door?"

"Not anymore," the Partial replied. "They all left, oddly enough, soon after these two . . . arrived."

"Which means they made a sound." *Or sounds.*

"I'll interrogate anyone left in the building after we finish here," the Partial said.

What a pleasure that'll be for them.

Still, Finch didn't volunteer to do it. Not yet. Maybe after. Not much worse than door-to-door interviews in unfriendly places. Many didn't believe his job should exist.

"What do you think, Finch?" Heretic asked. Just a hint of mischief in that voice. Laced with it. Just enough to catch the nuance.

I think I just walked in the door a few minutes ago.

The bodies lay next to each other, beside the sofa.

Finch frowned. "I've never seen anything quite like it."

The man lay on his side, left hand stretched out toward the gray cap's hand. The gray cap lay facedown, arms flopped out at right angles.

"Might be a foreigner. From the clothes."

The man could've been forty-five or fifty, with dark brown hair, dark eyebrows, and a beard that appeared to be made from tendrils of fungus. That wasn't unusual. But his clothes were. He wore a blue shirt long out of fashion. Strange, tight-fitting long pants. Dirty black boots.

"He's not from the city," Heretic said. Again, an inflection that bothered Finch. A statement or a question?

What's on his mind?

Finch squatted beside the bodies. Took out his useless pen and his useless pad of paper. Above him, the Partial leaned over to take a picture.

The dead gray cap looked like every other gray cap. Except for the one glaring lack.

"I don't know what caused the injury to the other one, sir."

I don't know what caused the leg situation.

"When we find out," Heretic said, "we will be just as understated."

The exposed cross section, cut almost precisely at the waist, fascinated Finch. He almost forgot himself, poked at the tissue with his pen.

The cut had been so clean, so precise, that there was no tearing. No hemorrhaging. Finch could see layers. Gray. Yellow. Green. A core of dark red. (A question he was too cautious to ask: *Was it always that dark, or only in death?*) Within the core, Finch saw a hint of organs.

"Is this . . . normal?" Finch asked Heretic.

"Normal?"

"The lack of blood, I mean, sir," Finch said.

Gray caps bled. Finch knew that. Not like a stream or a gout, even when you cut them deep, but a steady drip from a leaky faucet. Puncture wounds healed almost immediately. It took a long time and a lot of patience to kill a gray cap.

"No, it's not normal." The humid weight of Heretic was at his side now. A smell like garbage and burnt glass. Made him nauseous.

"None of this is normal," the Partial ventured. Ignored.

Finch looked up at Heretic. From that angle: the pale wattled skin of Heretic's long throat.

"Do you know who . . ." Finch hesitated. Gray caps didn't like being called "gray caps," but Finch couldn't pronounce the word they did use. *Farseneeni* or *fanaarcensitii*? The Partial circled them, blinking pictures through his fungal eye.

"Do you know who that is?" Finch said finally, pointing at the dead gray cap.

Heretic made a sound like something popping. "No. Not familiar to us. We cannot *see* him," and Finch understood he meant something other than just looking out a window.

"Have you . . . ?" Couldn't say the whole sentence. Too ridiculous. Terrifying. At the same time. *Have you eaten some of his flesh and picked clean the memories?*

But Heretic had been around humans long enough to know what he meant. "We tried it. Nothing that made sense."

For a second, Finch relaxed. Forgot Heretic could send him, Sintra, anybody he knew, to the work camps.

"If you couldn't decipher it, how will I?"

Then went stiff. Richard Dorn, a good detective, had questioned Heretic too closely. Nine months to die.

A bullet to the head. In that case.

But the gray cap said only, "With your fresh eyes, maybe you will have better luck."

Heretic pulled a pouch out of his robes, opened it. Finch rose, stood to the side as Heretic sprinkled a fine green powder over both bodies. Could've done it using his own supply, but Heretic enjoyed doing it. For some reason.

"You know what to do," Heretic said.

In time, a memory bulb would emerge from both corpses' heads. Did the *fanaarcensitii* rely too much on what made them comfortable? No autopsies, just mushrooms. But also hardly any experts left to perform them.

Nausea crept back into Finch's throat. "But I've never. Not a gray cap. I mean, not one of your people."

"We don't bite." The grin on that impossible face grew wide and wider. The laughter again, worse.

Finch laughed back, weakly.

"Write down whatever you encounter, whether you understand it or not."

Mercifully, Heretic looked away. "A gray cap and a man. Dead in such a manner. We need to know *everything*."

"Yessir," Finch said. He couldn't keep the grimace off his face.

Heretic seemed to take it for a smile. As he walked past on his way to the door, he patted Finch's elbow. Finch shivered. A touch like wet, dead leaves sewn together and stuffed with meat.

"Report in the morning," Heretic said. "Report and report and report, Finch." The laughter again.

Then Heretic was gone. The hallway shadows ate him up, the apartment door opening and closing.

Finch could hear his own breathing. Shallow. The sudden panicked drumming of his heart. The butterfly blinks of the Partial, still snapping photographs.

Took a breath. A second. Closed his eyes.

A sunny day by the river. A picnic lunch. A tree with shade. Long, cool grass. With Sintra.

2

No obvious bullet or stab wounds. No tattoos or other marks. Grunting with the effort, Finch turned the man over for a second. He seemed heavier than he should be. Skin warm, the flesh solid. From the position of the arms, Finch thought they might be broken. A discoloration at the edge of the man's mouth. Dried blood? When Finch was done, the man settled back into position as if he'd been there a hundred years.

No point checking the gray cap. Their skin didn't retain marks or burns or stab wounds. Anything like that sealed over. Besides, the cause of the gray cap's death was obvious. Wasn't it? Still, he didn't want to assume murder. Yet.

Out of the four "murders" in his sector over the past year, two had been suicides and one had been natural causes. The fourth solved in a day. Disappearances were another subject altogether.

He stood. Looked down at the tableau formed by the dead. Something about it. Almost posed. Almost staged. But also: the man's neck, half hidden by the shirt collar. Was it . . . twisted? Who could tell with the gray cap. Impossibly long, smooth, gray neck. (*Did that mean Heretic was old, this one young?*) But also torqued.

Finch glanced up at the tired, sagging ceiling. About ten feet.

"They look like," Finch said. "They look like they both *fell*."

Could that be the sound the neighbors heard?

"The spore camera's first shot is of them on the floor," the Partial said.

Finch had forgotten him.

Turned, stared at the Partial. The Partial stared back. Taking Finch's photo with each blink.

"I could . . ."

"What?" the Partial said. "You could what?"

I could tear out your eye with my bare hands. Not a thought he'd seen coming.

"You know what I think?" the Partial said.

Finch tamped down on his irritation. Tried to remember that, in a way, none of the Partials were more than six years old. Disaffected youths no matter what their age. All pale. Or made pale. Humans who'd gotten fungal infections and liked it, Truff help them. Got an adrenaline rush from heightened powers of sight. Enhanced by fungal drugs autogenerated inside the eye. Pumped into the brain. In a sense, their eye was always looking back at them.

I'll never know what you think. Not in a million years.

"You *volunteered* for that," Finch said. Pointed at the Partial's eye. "That makes you crazy. So I don't need to know what you think."

The Partial snickered. "I've heard it all before. And you'll never know what you're missing . . . But here's what I think, whether you want it or not. That man's not really human. Not really. I should know, right? And something went wrong. And maybe they didn't die here but were, I don't know, moved."

Finch gave the Partial a long glance. Turned to kneel again by the man's body. The second half of what the Partial had said made less sense than the first.

"Just do your job." *I'll do mine.*

The Partial fell silent. Hurt? Seduced by something new to click?

Finch really didn't care. Something had caught his attention. Two fingers of the man's left hand. Curled tight into the palm. Grit or sand under the fingernails. Finch got to his knees, leaned forward, took the man's hand in his. The warmth of it surprised him, the green spores already ghosting into the flesh. He pried the fingers back. Revealed a ragged piece of paper. A pulse-pounding moment of excitement.

Then he pulled it out. Released the fingers. Let the arm fall. Shielding the paper from the Partial with his body.

Normal paper, not fungal. Old and stained. Torn from a book? He unfolded it. Two words, written hurriedly, in black ink: *Never Lost*. And below that some gibberish that looked something like *bellum omnium contra omnes*. Self-contained, or once part of a longer message?

Definitely torn from a book. On the back a printed sentence fragment, "the future can hold when the past holds ambiguity such as this," and a symbol. Somehow familiar to Finch. Although he didn't know from where.

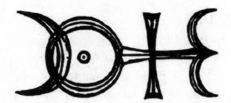

Stuck the paper in his boot before the Partial could blink that he'd found something. Got up. Pulled gloves from his jacket pocket and put them on. Opened the pouch at his belt.

Heretic had forgotten the preservatives, but would blame Finch if it wasn't done. Corpses didn't last long otherwise. Within forty-eight hours, you'd be breathing them, as the spores did their work.

Carefully, he sprinkled a blue powder across both corpses. Not spores this time, but tiny fruiting bodies. The powder smelled like smoke from the camps to the south. Or the camps smelled like the powder. Pointless to wear the gloves after the hundreds of fungal toxins and experiments that had been released into the air. The millions of floating spore-eyes. Yet still he did it.

Blue mingled with green. The green disappeared as he watched, colonized by the blue. The two bodies would not decay now. They would linger, suspended, until Finch returned to collect their memories.

". . . and know you don't want to eat the memories," the Partial said to Finch's back. Sounding triumphant.

Finch's thoughts had been so far away he'd missed the first part.

"Is that all?" Wanted to laugh.

Did they talk this way together in the barracks near the camps where the gray caps housed them like weapons? Spewing out each day and night like black ants. Foraging on the flesh of the city. Observers and security both.

"You're afraid of change," the Partial said. "Of being changed. That's why you hate me."

Swiveled abruptly in his crouch, hand on his gun. Met the Partial's corrupted gaze.

"Is that all?" Finch repeated. "I mean, are you done with your picture-taking?"

No skill when every blink was an image. No honor in a perpetual voyeurism. A kind of treason against your own kind. "It warps the privacy of your own life," Wyte had said once, as if he knew. "Permanent occupation. I wouldn't want to live that way." Yet now Wyte did. And so did Finch. In a sense.

"I'm never done," the Partial said. "And if you've got a past, you should be worried. They'll work through all the records someday. Maybe they'll find you."

Funny thing is, Partial, Heretic already knows my past. Most of it. And he doesn't give a fuck. That's not who I'm worried about.

Wanted to say it but didn't. Unsnapped the clasp on his holster. The fungal gun trembled there like a live thing. Wet. Dripping. Useless against a gray cap. Very useful against a Partial. *Still human, no matter how much you pretend.*

"Get the fuck out of here."

"I see everything," the Partial said. *"Everything."*

"Yes," Finch said, "but that's unavoidable, isn't it?"

The Partial stared at Finch. Seemed about to say something. Bit down on it, hard. Walked out into the hall. Slammed the door behind him.

Leaving Finch alone with the bodies.

⁂

Now Finch can see the frailty death has lent them. Now Finch can see the vulnerability. The way the light uses them in the same way it uses him. He walks to the window. Looks out across the damaged face of Ambergris.

Six years and I can't recognize a goddamn thing from before.

Harsh blue sprawl of the bay, bled from the River Moth. Carved from nothing. The first thing the gray caps did when they Rose, flooding Ambergris and killing thousands. Now the city, riddled through with canals, is like a body that was once drowned. Parts bleached, parts bloated. Metal and stone for flesh. Places that stick out and places that barely touch the surface.

In the foreground of the bay stands the scaffolding for the two tall towers still being built by the gray caps. A rough pontoon bridge reaches out to them, an artificial island surrounding the base. The scaffolding rises twenty feet above the highest tower. Hard to know if they are almost complete or will take a hundred years more. Great masses of green fungus cling to the tops. It makes the towers look shaggy, almost as if they had fur, were flesh and blood. A *smell like oil and sawdust and frying meat.* At dusk each day the gray caps lead a workforce from the camps south of the city. All night, the sounds of hammering and construction. Emerald lights moving like slow stars. Screams of injury or punishment. To what purpose? No one knows. While along the lip of the bay, monstrous fungal cathedrals rise under cover of darkness, replacing the old, familiar architecture. Skyline like a jagged wound.

Twenty years of civil war. Six years of the gray caps.

To Finch's left, southwest: smudges of smoke, greasy and gray, above the distant mottled spectacle of the Spit, an island made of lashed-together boats. A den for spies. A sanctuary for the desperate and the lawless.

Beyond the Spit, the silhouette of the two living domes covering the detention camps. Broken by the smoke, hidden by debris. Built over a valley of homes. Built atop the remains of the military factories that had allowed the two great mercantile companies, House Hoegbotton and the invading House Frankwrithe & Lewden, to dream of empire, to destroy each other. And the city with them. Finch had fought for Hoegbotton. *Once upon a time.*

Between the domes, the fiery green glitter and minarets of the Religious Quarter, occupied by the remnants of native tribes. Adapting. Struggling. Destined someday to be wiped out. He can see the exposed crater at the top of the Truffidian Cathedral. *Cracked. All the prayers let out. Nothing left.*

To Finch's right, on the north shore: the Hoegbotton & Frankwrithe Zone. Huge tendrils of reddish-orange fungus vein into the rocks lining the water. A green haze obscures any view of what might be left on the north shore. Six years ago, the HFZ had just been northern Ambergris: wild, yes, but not infected. Then, under sustained attack by the gray caps, the rebel army had retreated there. So much heavy armor, munitions, and ordnance had gone in, along with twenty thousand soldiers, that it is hard for Finch to believe all of it could just vanish or molder. Yet, apparently, it had. They'd gone in and the gray caps had created the Zone around them. Only the rebel commander they called the Lady in Blue and some of her soldiers had escaped the trap.

Once, the HFZ had grown in size every day. Now, it has stopped, covers about ten square miles. Almost every citizen can see it. For all the good that did. *Will the rebels return?* is the question everyone asks, even now. When the wind is strange—gusting this way and that without purpose—great glittering particles from the north drift orange and purple and blue across the bay into Ambergris. Even the gray caps don't enter the HFZ except by proxy. Content to let the remnants of the rebels wander through a toxic fungal stew, goes the theory. Almost like another camp, without fences or guards.

Except, no one comes out of the HFZ.

Beyond the towers, beyond the bay, the far shore of the River Moth. Distant. Unattainable. Beyond that, although Finch can't see it, just feels it: the easternmost edge of the Kalif's empire, the Stockton Commonwealth to the south, the Morrow Protectorate to the north. Between them and Finch: security zones. Blockades. Set up by the surrounding countries. All three as determined as the gray caps that no one gets out of Ambergris. Even as they send in their spies to steal the city's secrets.

Finch turns away from the window. It leaves him sad and cold and frightened. The towers especially. What will happen when the gray caps have finished them?

A view like that could drive a person mad.

3

"When the time comes, right, Finch?"

Back at the station, which used to be Hoegbotton & Sons' headquarters. High ceilings. Hints of gold leaf and mosaic. Dull light from tiny round windows set in rows across both side walls. A tortured light that never gave any hint of the weather outside. Sometimes in the early morning and late afternoon they had to use old lanterns. The chandeliers had been ripped out long ago.

Back at his desk with the other detectives. The must of fungal rot from the green strip of carpet running from the front door down the middle. The whole back of the room hidden by a curtain. Smell of bad coffee from the table that also housed their only typewriter. Shoved up against the far wall. Next to the holding cell.

Ten desks. Seven detectives. Skinner, Gustat, Blakely, Dapple, Albin, and Wyte furiously scritching away on their notepads with sharp pencils. Some on the phone. All of them like schoolboys in an incomprehensible class. None of them likely to ask questions of the teacher.

Only a weak hello when Finch had walked in. Too much effort. Not yet over the paranoid morning jitters. Ever more difficult to know what to say. How to act. They all assumed the gray caps spied on them. Difficult to remember all day long. Especially when strange things happened with just enough irregularity to make them think *that was the last time.* The air pungent with old and new sweat. Laced with some underlying funk that was almost sweet.

Albin, just off the phone, out of the corner of his mouth: "I'm not risking my life for a lost dog. Too many Partials there. Besides, it's an old Hoegbotton neighborhood." Albin, the Frankwrithe & Lewden man. Finch might've shot at him back during the war. Former scientist. One of the few not killed by the gray caps or snatched by foreign powers in the chaos of the Rising.

Finch's mood had soured on the way back to the station. A tortuous route. The gray caps had banned bicycles and motored vehicles four years ago. Too many suicide bombings by rebel sympathizers. Not much fuel anyway, and no one outside the city willing to resupply, even on the black market. Too dangerous. And few alternatives since the horses had been eaten long ago.

Instead, makeshift bridges over the canals. Through a sector where a lot of gray cap buildings had gone up, scrambling the landscape. Changes didn't correspond to any map. Sliced through existing apartment complexes, divided or blocked streets. Displayed an arrogance about the way things had been and were now that angered Finch.

Then a mob to avoid at the corner of Albumuth and Lake, when he'd almost made it back. One of the huge blood-red drug mushrooms hadn't yet released the morning ration. Not Finch's problem. But the addicts were mad. They wanted their fix. *Wanted out.* They stood beneath the slow-breathing deadwhite gills waiting for the purple nodules that also fed them. *Wanted oblivion. A nice trip into waves of light and a past that didn't include dead bodies and nightmares.*

Maybe someday he'd join them. Instead, another rickety bridge over another canal. Had looked down at his frowning reflection in the silver-gray water and hadn't recognized it. Broad shoulders. Still muscular but losing some of it. Too much alcohol. Not enough nutrients in the gray caps' food. The man lingering in the water seemed at least forty-five, not forty. The hooded eyes. The paleness of the face. Wavery. Indistinct. Never in focus.

"When the time comes, right, Finch?"

"Sure, Wyte," Finch said. "When the time comes."

"You'll know what to do." The voice, once so deep and gravelly, had changed since Finch had first met Wyte. Become soft and liquid, lighter yet thicker.

"I'll know what to do."

The ritual conversation.

Ritual had a purpose. Ritual cordoned off fear. Ritual made the abnormal ordinary. The memory hole beside each of the desks. The deep green vein running the length of Wyte's arm. Pushing up ridgelike against the fabric of Wyte's long sleeve. Like the green carpet leading back to the curtains and what lay beyond.

Finch took his gun from its holster. Recoiled from the touch of the grip.

"For Truff's sake," Finch said. Laid it on his desk with a squelch.

The gun had been issued by the gray caps. Dark green exoskeleton, soft interior. Its guts stained his hand. Reloading didn't seem like an option. It had been seeping a lot lately.

"I wonder if it's dying on me," Finch said. To Wyte, who sat at the desk to his left.

Should I have been feeding it?

Wyte grunted. Reflexively writing up reports on nothing in particular. Lost husbands. Unidentifiable corpses. Vandalism. Finch had cases, too, but nothing that couldn't wait.

"Hate these things," he said, again to Wyte. Again, to indifference.

Heard Blakely muttering to Gustat: ". . . they're saying that we're addicted to a special mushroom that grows out of our brains." Gustat chuckled but it wasn't funny. Rumors could get a detective killed by some desperate citizen. *Any excuse that didn't slip through the fingers.*

Finch rummaged in a drawer. Found a worn handkerchief. It predated the war. He'd gotten it from an expensive clothing store farther up the boulevard. Didn't know why he kept it. Luck? Grimacing, he picked up the gun with the handkerchief. Shoved the thing into a space under his desk. Next to the box with the ceremonial sword his father had given him. Brought back from the Kalif's empire twenty years before. Wrapped in cloth. Finch could always get to it in a pinch. Made him feel perversely safer knowing it was there. In its gleaming scabbard.

"I'd rather get shot than use that gun," Finch said, too loud. Not sure if he meant it.

Gustat and Blakely, joined at the hip, looked up, glared. Both had a flushed look. Like they'd been drinking.

"Shut up, Finch," Blakely said.

"Yeah, shut up," Gustat echoed. Fiercely.

This caused Dapple to bring a case file so close to his eyes it hid his face. Dapple was the worst of them. He'd been an artist once. Landscape painter. Watercolors. Popular with the tourists. No market for that now. No landscapes to speak of that you could spend hours painting without taking a bullet for your troubles. Sure to become a druggie, or a creature of the gray caps in his cringing way. At least Gustat and Blakely, even though they annoyed Finch, still had their wits about them.

Almost as if to cover for Finch, Wyte asked, "So, Finchy, just how bad was it?" "Finchy" sounded closer to his real last name, so Wyte often called him that. To avoid slipping up.

Finch turned toward Wyte. Hadn't wanted to. No telling what he looked like.

Wyte: a tall man, late forties, with a handsome face, powerful shoulders and chest. Tattered olive suit. Eyes gray. A spark of green colonizing the brown of each pupil. Right temple: a purple birthmark that hadn't been there yesterday. Smelled of cigarette smoke to cover the stench of mushrooms. Even though cigs were hard to come by. Once, he could have entered a crowded bar and all the women would have found a way to stare at him.

"A double," Finch said. "In an abandoned apartment. One gray cap. One male human." Then told Wyte the rest.

"Dancing lessons gone terribly wrong," Wyte said. His grin only manifested on the left side of his mouth.

Skinner, next to Wyte, hazarded a snicker. But Skinner snickered at everything. Finch didn't find it funny. He was still seeing the bodies. Skinner expressed too much zeal pursuing cases that involved the rebels. Why hadn't Skinner become a Partial?

"This is nothing good, Wyte." *Good* equaled *will go away quickly.* This could linger.

Wyte, as if realizing his mistake: "Do you want me to take the memory bulbs?" "No thanks."

Who knew what a memory bulb would do to Wyte in his state? Finch didn't want to find out. The late Richard Dorn had sat at his desk for nine months after the gray caps had forced him to eat a memory bulb despite his wasting disease. Dead. Turning into a tower of emerald mold. The desk sat in a corner now, abandoned, a smudge on the seat of the chair.

Worse for suspects kept in the holding cell. Bring in a thief, do the paperwork, then the gray caps decided. Attempted murder? Might be disappeared by morning. Or sent to the camps. Or let off with a fine. The guy Blakely had brought in the other day was still there. Slumped in a corner. Clearly thought his life was over.

Never bring anyone in unless you have to. Unless you're certain.

"Are we in trouble on this one?" Wyte asked. Black patch on his neck, slowly moving. Nails a faint green. A whiff of something toxic.

Not the same kind of trouble.

Finch shrugged. "Who knows?" A routine call could turn into disaster. A disaster could go away overnight.

Wyte leaned back in his chair, hands behind his head. Red stains on the shirt's underarms.

Finch had known Wyte for more than twenty years. They'd fought in the wars together. Known the same people before the Rising. Played darts at the pub. Had drinks. Sudden gut-punching vision: of his girlfriend back then, a slender brunette who'd worked as a nurse. Laughing at some joke Wyte had made one night, the days of Comedian Wyte now long past except for the occasional flare-up that just made it worse.

Some cosmic mistake or cruelty, to work cases together when Finch had once worked for Wyte as a courier for Hoegbotton. Each a reminder to the other of better times. Since then, Wyte's wife, Emily, had left him. He'd taken up in a crappy apartment just north of the station. Never saw his two daughters. They'd been smuggled out to relatives in Stockton before the Rising. Finch couldn't work out how old they might be now.

Someday Wyte will be a silhouette on the horizon. Someone familiar made distant.

And Wyte sensed it.

"You can help with the fieldwork going forward, Wyte," Finch said. *If you don't become the fieldwork.*

"No problem. Be happy to."

"I'll put my notes in order," Finch said, "and after I use the memory bulbs, we'll start in on it. Tomorrow."

Wyte wasn't listening anymore. Gaze far away. Disengaged. Apocalyptic thoughts? Or maybe he was just registering the inside of the building. They all conducted an unspoken war against the station. It tried to make them forget its strangeness. They tried not to forget.

Finch turned back to his desk and started sorting through the mess. Hadn't organized it in a week. Hadn't had the energy.

Mirror. Pills to protect against infection. Spore mask for purified breathing. Writing pad. Pencils. Telephone. Broken telephone. Folders on open crimes. Folders on closed crimes. Paper clips across the bottom of drawers. A list he'd made of complaints from people who had called him, thinking he could help. Usually he couldn't.

Maybe once, early on, he had convinced himself he could do some good, sometimes even imagined he was a mole, getting close so he could strike a blow. Imagined he was in it to defend Ambergris from the enemies that surrounded it. Imagined he was protecting ordinary citizens.

But the truth was he'd been tired, had stopped caring. Broken down from too much fighting, too many things connected to his past. And when that spark, that impulse, had returned, it was too late: he was trapped.

"I'm not a detective."

Heretic: "You're whatever we want you to be, now."

If he just left one day, what would happen to Wyte? To his other friends? To Sintra? And: Did they know about Sintra?

Nothing seemed missing from his desk. Still, a good idea to take stock. Lots of things disappeared during the night, or were replaced by mimics. More than one detective had screamed, picking up a pencil that was not a pencil. Finch took out the piece of paper he'd found in the dead man's hands. Placed it in front of him. What could the words mean? Finch took out a writing pad, scrawled

Never Lost.
Bellum omnium contra omnes

across the top. Stared at the strange symbol. It looked oddly like a baby bird to him.

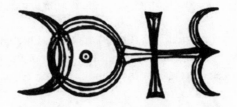

Randomly ripped from a book to write on? Or something more? Abandoned the question. Wrote:

> *two bodies*
> *fell*

Thought about the Partial, daring to contradict Heretic. Heretic's secret amusement. What did that mean? At least he knew what Heretic on the scene meant: the gray cap must suspect the case had some connection to the rebels and their elusive commander, the Lady in Blue. She who was now larger than the city and yet not of the city. Most saw her hand in any act that seemed to cause the gray caps grief. Although such acts of resistance seemed rarer and rarer. Some thought she didn't exist. Or was dead.

The trapped rebel soldiers. The Lady in Blue.

Was the fate of either better or worse than his?

⁂

Finch sees again, back across six long years, the columns of tanks and infantry in retreat, traveling through the city toward the north. Recognizes with hindsight that the path they took had been chosen by the gray caps. Forced by the rising water.

Distant explosions had split the air as the gray caps attacked stragglers at the end of the column. Even then, small-arms fire no longer registered with Finch unless it was close by.

Despite the risk, many people had come out to watch the rebels. From the roadside. From balconies. Peering out of windows reinforced with metal bars. To bear witness to the rumbling tread of the tanks. To remember the faces of the troops: pale and dark, old and young and middle-aged. Beneath green helmets with the intertwined H&S/F&L insignia that rankled so many. Armed with automatic weapons, bayonets, knives. Most in uniform. Many damaged. A welter of bandages on heads, legs, arms, that hid evidence of strange fungal wounds.

One man's face held Finch's attention. Salt-and-pepper beard, creases in his forehead, wrinkles that made him look as if he were squinting. A red patch on his cheek. Body slumped, then tensed, against the lurching of the tank. A gaunt hand clutching his Lewden rifle, knuckles prominent. Gaze turned forward, as if unwilling to acknowledge the present.

Which had made Finch realize again that these men and women leaving, they were the same ones who had fought one another during more than three decades of the War of the Houses, broken only by armistices, cease-fires, and the dream of empire. The ones who had brought ruination upon Ambergris in so many ways before the Rising.

Yet they were still from Ambergris, of Ambergris, and even Finch felt it in his chest, Wyte standing there beside him with his Emily. Almost as if Ambergris itself was retreating, leaving behind only ghosts and children. But also leaving a perverse giddiness. A sense of celebration at seeing such a mighty force. The retreat portrayed as a new beginning. The lull before the launching of a great offensive.

Even the tanks were part of Ambergris. They'd come out of the eighty-year-old metal deposits found in eastern Ambergris that had catapulted the city out of the past but not yet into the future.

Rebel tanks had two turrets: one pointed ahead, one unseen beneath that pointed at the ground. Specially built to open up and deliver bombs to underground gray cap enclaves. Once, their rough syncopated song had been heard all over the city. Juddered through the ground into the walls of buildings and tunnels alike. Like a kind of defiant echoing growl.

In retreat, though, it was the singing of the troops as they left that Finch heard, their voices ragged over the rumble of the tanks. Patriotic songs composed long centuries before. A refrain that had started as a prayer by the Truffidian monks.

> *Holy city, majestic, banish your fears.*
> *Arise, emerge from your sleeping years.*
> *Too long have you dwelt in the valley of tears.*
> *We shall restore you with mercy and grace.*

City of wounds. City of wounding. For a moment, Finch had felt the urge to climb up onto one of the tanks, to join them in what was then the wilderness of North Ambergris. But Finch wasn't one of them. He'd had no officer to report to. Had bought his own weapon. Off the books, off the record. An Irregular, fighting alongside other Irregulars in his neighborhood. Defending their sisters, brothers, parents, and neighbors against the invaders.

After the last tank had rumbled past, Finch had gone back with Wyte and Emily. To await the next thing. No matter what it might be. *The need to work. To eat. To have shelter.* People were already telling themselves things might still be better under the gray caps than during the War of the Houses, at least. Joked about it. Like you might about a passing storm.

Waiting it out at Wyte's house. By candlelight. Drinking. Laughing nervously. Trying to forget. Finch's father dead almost two years.

Just after midnight: a sound like a giant flame opening up and then winking out. A devastating *whump*, as of something hitting the ground or rising from it. When they looked outside, they'd seen a dome-like haze above the north part of the bay. Green-orange discharge like sunspots. They'd just watched it. Watched it and not known what to say. What to do. Barricaded the house. Spent the rest of the night with weapons within reach.

In the morning, a paralyzing horror. Across the bay, when they slipped out through back alleys to get a clear view: the seething area that became known as the HFZ, and no sign of anyone alive. No sign of the tanks. No messages from the rebel leadership.

Thought but not said: *Abandoned. Gone. On our own.*

Then the realization, as the gray caps began to appear in numbers in the streets, and as their surrogates the Partials began to help occupy the city, that the war was over for now. That each citizen of Ambergris would need to make some kind of peace with the enemy.

Always with the hope sent out across the water toward the HFZ: that the tanks, the men, might come back. Might reemerge. That the rebels were not dead. Destroyed.

Lost.

4

Midafternoon. A soft, wet, sucking sound came from the memory hole beside his desk. Finch shuddered, put aside his notes. A message had arrived.

Some detectives positioned their desks so they could see their memory holes. Finch positioned his desk so he couldn't see it without leaning over. Tried never to look at it when he walked into the station in the morning. Still, the memory hole was better than the dead cat reanimated on Skinner's doorstep, message delivered in screeched rhyming couplets. Or the mushroom that walked onto Dapple's desk, turning itself inside out. To reveal the message.

Exhaled sharply. Peered around the left edge of the desk. Glanced down at the glistening hole. It was about twice the size of a man's fist. Lamprey-like teeth. Gasping, pink-tinged maw. Foul. The green tendrils lining the gullet had pushed up the dirty black spherical pod until it lay atop the mouth.

Finch sat up. Couldn't see it. Just heard its breathing. Which was worse.

The gray caps always called them "message tubes," but the term "memory hole" had stuck. Memory holes allowed the detectives to communicate during the day with their gray cap superiors. Finch had no idea if the memory holes were living creatures or only seemed alive. Fluid leaked out of them sometimes.

Once, impulsive, Finch had crumpled up the wrapper around the remains of his lunch and shoved it down the hole. Lived in fear the rest of the day. But nothing had happened. When he'd thought about it since, it had made him laugh. Heretic, down there, hit in the head with a piece of garbage. Maybe cursing Finch's name.

Now Heretic's message vibrated atop writhing tendrils.

Finch leaned over. Grabbed the pod. Slimy feel. *Sticky.*

Tossed the pod onto his desk. Pulled out a hammer from the same drawer where he kept his limited supply of dormant pods. Split Heretic's pod wide open. Spraying slime.

Beside Finch, Wyte winced, got up for some coffee.

Disgusted, or was it too close to home?

"There's no pretty way to do it, my friends," Finch called out. "Just look away." No one acknowledged him this time. Too usual. Even Finch's refrain.

In among the fragments: a few copies of a photograph of the dead man, compliments of the Partial.

And a message.

Pulsing yellow. An egg of living paper. He pulled the egg out of the shattered pod. Began to massage it until it spread out flat. Kept spreading, to Finch's surprise. Then began to unspool. Like a long, wide tongue. And kept on growing.

That was unusual enough for the other detectives to gather round.

"What in the hell is that?" Blakely asked, Gustat beside him. Dapple shyly peeked over Blakely's shoulder. Albin and Skinner were out on a call or they'd have been right there too. Anything to waste time.

"Looks like Heretic's given you a long to-do list," Gustat said. Too young to have known anything but war and the Rising.

Finch said nothing. By now, the pliant paper had grown to drape itself over both sides of Finch's desk, sliding into his lap. Clutched at it. Saw the rows of information in the reed-thin, spidery print common to gray cap documents. He let out a long, deep breath.

"It's the records of everyone who ever lived in the apartment of the double murder I was at this morning. Going back . . ." He checked as the paper finished unspooling. "Going back over a century. More."

Pulse quickening. *How am I supposed to investigate* that?

MORDEN, JONATHAN, OCCUPANCY 3 MONTHS, 2 DAYS, 11 MINUTES, 5 SECONDS—WORKED IN FOOD DISTRIBUTION IN THE CAMPS . . .

WILDEN, SARAH, OCCUPANCY 8 MONTHS, 3 DAYS, 2 MINUTES, 45 SECONDS— NEVER LEFT THE APARTMENT EXCEPT FOR GETTING FOOD. HAD THREE CATS. LIKED TO READ . . .

A sudden panic. Smothered by the past. Lost in it.

Tried to get a grip. Wadded the paper up, pocketed the photographs. While the other detectives gave out nervous laughs. Returned to their desks. Frightened again.

No one wanted this kind of case.

A sudden anger rose in Finch. *Did Heretic really think that this list would be helpful?* It was scaring the shit out of him.

Wyte had been standing behind the others, holding his coffee mug. Loomed now like an actor from backstage, suddenly revealed.

"A lot of information," Wyte said.

Finch glared at him. Hands splattered with yellow and green. "Find me a towel."

Wyte put down his coffee, rummaged in a desk drawer.

SILVAN, JAMES, OCCUPANCY 15 MONTHS, 3 DAYS, 1 HOUR, 50 MINUTES, 2 SECONDS—COLLABORATOR WITH A SPLINTER REBEL FACTION . . .

HUGHES, SHANNA, OCCUPANCY 1 MONTH, 2 WEEKS, 3 DAYS, 10 MINUTES, 35 SECONDS—KILLED BY A FUNGAL BOMB . . .

"Maybe they got it from the old Bureaucratic Quarter?" Wyte whispered out of the side of his mouth as he leaned over to give Finch the towel. Smell of sweat mixed with something sweeter. "Maybe they just copied it down?" Returning to his desk, receding into the background.

"It's half encrypted with their symbols, Wyte," Finch said. Tried to correct for the disdain in his voice. "It contains surveillance information. They collected it themselves."

From underground. Using a million spore-eye cameras. Somewhere, he knew, in one of a series of images captured by the gray caps: evidence of his past that Heretic didn't know about. *Finch as a Hoegbotton Irregular fighting against Frankwrithe & Lewden in the War of the Houses. Finch standing side by side with F&L soldiers against the gray caps before they Rose.* What he'd done.

Except the gray caps didn't have the time to pore over that many images unless given a good reason. And Finch hadn't. Only Wyte knew the truth.

GILRISH, MEGHAN, OCCUPANCY 10 MONTHS, 3 WEEKS, 6 DAYS, 14 HOURS, 15 MINUTES, 6 SECONDS—OWNER OF A GROCERY STORE . . .

BARRAN, GEORGE, OCCUPANCY 2 YEARS, 1 WEEK, 5 DAYS, 7 MINUTES, 18 SECONDS—DIED OF OLD AGE . . .

Finch stared at the first rows of names on the paper. The sheer density of information defeated him.

Kept thinking about the bodies. Saw them lying there on the floor of the apartment. *They dropped in out of thin air.*

Why there?

A riddle wrapped in a puzzle. Perversely comforting, that the memory bulbs might hold the answers.

Never lost.

Bellum omnium contra omnes.

Never lost.

Said it three times under his breath. Wondering if Wyte was staring at him. Still didn't dislodge an answer.

"Well," Finch said, out of the corner of his mouth, "do you know what those words mean? *Bellum omnium contra omnes?*"

But Wyte was done talking to him about the case.

Sometimes the overlay of reality seemed a sham. One day, he would turn a corner on a rubble-strewn street. Pass through an archway into a courtyard. Be back in that other, simpler world. When he worked in the same building but as a Hoegbotton courier. Not as a detective. When he worked for Wyte, not with him.

Am I dead? he thought sometimes, walking down that green carpet he remembered from a different city, a different time. *Am I a ghost?*

Six in the afternoon. Time to leave. He packed Heretic's list in a satchel and holstered his miserable gun. Watched Blakely and Gustat put on spore gas masks "just in case." *Just in case of what? Just in case there's one fungus in the whole damn city you haven't been exposed to yet?*

A nod. A handshake or two. Muttered goodbyes to Wyte. Then they dispersed. The night shift would arrive soon. Partial patrols outside started in only two hours. Curfew. Gray caps lurking. You rarely saw more than one, but that was one too many. A detective's badge might help or it might not.

The others headed north, up Albumuth. Wyte was a hulking shadow hanging back at the rear. Finch went south, but not home. Not yet. First, he had to pick up the memory bulbs from the crime scene. But he also had decided not to trust the Partial. Wanted to interview some of the residents of 239 Manzikert Avenue himself.

A different route than that morning. Late-afternoon sun like dark gold against brick walls. The street sloped on an incline before following a gentle curve downward. Tight high walls of shoved-together tenements and lofts. Hoegbotton territory, before the Rising. Finch brushed by a man or woman covered up in robes. Another person ducked into a doorway, face made a question mark by an old gas mask that might or might not keep spores out. Stain of blue-green lichen in the gutter. A rancid quality to the air.

Faintest hint of the bay from the cross street. Mostly obscured by mansards and rubble. Glimpse of the two towers. Did the sky match? Or was it darker between the towers? Had a bet going with the other detectives about the purpose of the towers. To dull the fear.

A hint of shadow moved behind him as he rounded a tight corner. It made him cautious. It made him paranoid. He stopped a minute later. Pretended to tie his shoe. Managed a backward glance. Nothing.

Imagined it?

Wouldn't put it past Heretic to have him followed. Or maybe it was just some ragged kid hoping to mug a passerby. As he rose, Finch made sure to pull his jacket back. To show his gun. Such as it was.

239 Manzikert Avenue was a dark vertical slab of stone and wood with blackened filigree balcony railings crawling up the front. Trees left black leaves and rotting yellow berries on the steps. If the berries had been edible, the steps would've been clean.

Ornate double doors stripped of the metal that had once served as inlay. Steps guarded by a three-legged cat that hissed. Then hopped away. Beyond the doors, a hallway studded with lights so dim it would've been hard to read by them. Finch stepped inside. The feeling of being followed shut off. Like it'd been attached to a timer inside of him.

The floor squeaked. Freshly waxed. It hadn't been waxed in the morning. Finch smiled. Old Hoegbotton trick. Cheap security. *Bell the cat.* He went squeaking to the stairwell. Already knew the elevator didn't work.

The outside light couldn't seem to push through the tiny windows set into the walls. The stairwell got darker the farther up he went. But, gradually, more evidence of people. A dog howling. The flushing of a shared toilet. A screaming child. A mother's raised voice. The smell of something spicy being cooked for dinner. Filtered through the exhausted, stale funk of a place in which too many had lived in close quarters for too many years.

Finch knew not to start on the first couple of floors. No one liked to live that low if they had a choice. *Ambergris Rules.* Better to live next to a corpse than one floor above the gray caps' underground realm. His father had taught him that.

Stopped at the fourth floor. Just to be safe. Fourth or sixth. Anyone on the fifth was long gone. Either after the corpses arrived and before the Partial came to talk to them. Or after the Partial came to talk.

Finch had a simple formula. A polite knock. Short questions, in a friendly tone. Didn't like to go in like Blakely, guns blazing. Or like Gustat, using threats to coerce. They got information, sure. But not always the right information.

He worked the long line of closed doors to either side of the discolored, torn carpet. At the fifth door, a mother answered, holding her son. Maybe five or six, born around the time of the Rising. The mother looked worn. Pale and thin. Probably starving herself to feed the child. Probably thought that holding the kid would make Finch play nice. The kid's open, eager face confounded Finch. Almost like seeing another species. Parents kept their children hidden. Went out to forage for them. Finch's father had done the same for him. During the wars.

"What do you want?" she asked.

Finch decided he wanted nothing. Asked a couple of easy questions. Showed her the photo of the dead man. The woman didn't recognize him.

Tried a couple more doors. A middle-aged man in a tank top and shorts answered holding a frying pan. For defense? For dinner? Either way, he didn't know anything, hadn't seen anything.

Neither did the old married couple who might've lived there for forty, fifty years. Might even have recalled when 239 Manzikert Avenue hadn't been a dump. The man stood behind the woman, peering out with the kind of distant stare Finch associated with the camps. The wife had a blotch of purple on her forehead that might've been a birthmark or might've been fungus.

The next interview went better. A man of about sixty answered. Slight build. Large blue eyes, accentuated by the wrinkles in his forehead. A cultured voice. He wore a too-tight dinner jacket. The points of the collars on the white shirt beneath stabbed the flesh of his neck. His wrists showed from the dark ends of his cuffs. He looked like a child in a straitjacket.

As Finch questioned him, he slowly realized the man had dressed up for the interrogation. Had heard him at other doors down the hall. Soon, the man was asking him to come in for tea. Polite in a way that hadn't been common in Ambergris for years. Finch guessed violinist or theater owner. Either that or he'd once been the doorman.

He didn't know anything about the murders. (Finch couldn't recall when he'd started calling them *murders*, but the word felt right.) Thought the man in the photograph looked familiar, but couldn't place him. In the way people do when they're trying to help.

Then the man asked if the people living there had been of use.

"People living there?" Finch echoed.

"Yes. There were people living there. A man. A woman."

"Really?"

"Yes. I don't know their names."

Didn't know anything else, either.

Who was lying to him then? Heretic? The Partial?

Remembered Heretic's strange mood as he headed up to the fifth floor.

In the apartment, the bodies lay much as before. Except that each had sprouted a thick, emerald-green stalk topped by a nodule. The detectives called them memory bulbs. No one could pronounce what the gray caps called them. Sounded like a word between "loam" and "leer." An aqua-colored nodule for the man. Bright orange for the gray cap. Which meant Finch had learned something new.

The bodies still looked peaceful. Even with the dull light streaming through the open window. The man looked better preserved than when Finch had seen him that morning. Sometimes death did that. For a time.

A figure stepped out of the back room. The Partial, grinning. "Shit." Finch's gun appeared in his hand. Heart pounding.

"I'd aim that somewhere else if I were you," the Partial said. Fungal eye blinking and blinking. *Recording.*

Finch transferred his gun to his left hand. Shook his right. Green liquid hit the floor. *Goddamn gun.* Wiped his hand on the side of the couch.

"Did you follow me here?" Finch demanded.

One eyebrow arched. "Getting paranoid? Afraid you'll be found out?"

Snarled, "Why do you keep saying that?"

The Partial smiled. Triumphant. "Everyone has something to hide."

"Why didn't you tell me two people lived here?" he asked the Partial. "A man and a woman. Did you question them? And where are they?"

A preternatural calm to the Partial as he countered with, "Tell me what was in the dead man's hand."

Finch stepped back. Took in the narrow face, all slab of tongue and uncanny black-green left eye. Right eye atrophied from the repurposing. Dull orange lichen lived there now. The tongue moved like Finch's pet lizard's tongue. Tasting the air. The amount of energy that went into the eye meant they had to suck on gray cap–provided mushroom juice seven or eight times a day. *Looked like green pus.* What was their name for themselves? A gray cap word. Sounded like *grineeknsenz* or something just as ugly. Rumor had it they'd made a pact with the gray caps. That soon they'd be made more like the gray caps, in return for their service.

"Nothing important," Finch managed finally.

"Isn't that for me to decide?"

"It's for Heretic to decide. It'll be in my report."

"I hope it is." The Partial's gaze was cold and dark. "We notice more than the gray caps, Finch. And we're more prepared to use what we find than they are."

That surprised Finch. Was the Partial criticizing Heretic? *Safer to ignore it.*

"What did the people who lived here tell you?"

"Nobody lived here."

Finch chewed on that for a moment. Was the Partial *hiding* something from Heretic? He patted his satchel. "I've got the entire list from Heretic of anyone who lived here." *Idiot.* "You're saying it won't include the two who lived here?"

"They don't live here," the Partial said, a hint of warning in his voice. "They don't live anywhere anymore. They didn't know anything important."

Dead, then. Disappeared into the abyss of history.

Appalled, Finch said, "Heretic knows this?"

The Partial nodded, folding his arms. "Don't take anything from the bodies this time except for the memory bulbs. I'm supposed to guard them. I've been here all day. Someone will always be here."

The way the Partial said this made Finch think the man, the abomination, was applying for martyrdom. Did the Partial think Finch was weak just because he hadn't allowed the gray caps to take his eye? Part of Finch wanted to hit the Partial in the mouth for that. Instead, he squatted next to the man's body. Looked so peaceful.

Was he alive for a time? In the room? Was he fighting the gray cap? Fleeing him?

The Partial, from in front and above him: "I'll watch. Just to make sure."

Make sure of what?

"Stay where I can see you."

"Such distrust," the Partial murmured.

Finch knelt beside the man's body. Pushed aside the matted hair on the man's head to get a good grip on the stalk. Held the bulb in his hand. *Sticky, porous, rubbery.* Gently twisted it off the stalk. A *pock* sound as he detached it. He put the bulb in his pocket. Pulled the stalk out at the root. Left behind a round indentation about a half inch deep. Blood began to fill the small wound.

That'll leave a scar.

Let loose a yip of nervous laughter. Shut it down.

But the Partial still noticed it. "I knew you didn't want to eat their memories."

Finch ignored the Partial. Repeated the process for the gray cap. *No blood, no pock sound.*

"You might be the first person to ever eat a gray cap's memory bulb. Aren't you the lucky one."

Finch rose to face the Partial. "Pathetic idea of security, by the way. One Partial. First thing any intruder will want to do is shoot out or cut out your eye. Followed by cutting off your head to make absolutely sure." Said each word slowly. Savored each.

The Partial wasn't smiling now. The eye twitched. He advanced on Finch until he stood inches away. Finch looked into that ruin of a face and tried not to turn away in disgust.

"Finch. Finchy. Whoever you are. You're not as smart as you think. I'm not the only one here. We've got this whole building staked out. If anyone comes here, we'll see them. The spores will see them."

Bellum omnium contra omnes. "Never lost" in a dead man's hand.

"Who would come here? And why?"

"Followers of the Blue." The Partial seemed on the verge of saying more. Caught himself.

But Finch had heard enough. A grin broke across his face. *Didn't turn back soon enough.* He gave the Partial a last poisonous stare.

"What? Nothing more to say?" the Partial called after him as he headed down the stairs. "I'm disappointed, Finchy . . . Someday, though, Finchy, someday . . ."

Out onto the street, amid the black leaves. The rotten fruit. A memory bulb in each pocket. Looking now for the signature of the rebels in every figure that he passed.

Followers of the Blue . . . The Lady in Blue.

A thousand tales told about her by now. Told by old men to young men. Told by mothers to sons and daughters. Most are about her voice. No one agrees on where the Lady in Blue came from, but everyone agrees that during the worst of the War of the Houses her voice was heard coming from courtyards, buildings, even underground. Or seemed to. Some thought she was an opera singer transformed by grief over a slain lover. That she was in some way the voice of the city, coming up from the earth. Believed this even though it could not be true. None of it could be true.

Then her voice started coming to the people on the radio stations of House Hoegbotton and House Frankwrithe, before the Rising. In those interim years when the Houses combined forces to confront the true insurgents. The enemy hidden in the ground.

Finch remembers some of those broadcasts. Listened to them with his father. Near the end.

The Lady in Blue would begin in a low, slow voice. Almost the murmurs of a lover. Her voice would build in volume and strength. Until she was exhorting the people of Ambergris to stand firm against not only the "underground invader," but also against the avarice and selfishness of its own leaders.

That her voice came from everywhere was reinforced by background noises in her broadcasts. Many different settings. Sometimes the sounds of the River Moth behind her. Sometimes a windy tower. Sometimes a water-clogged basement that she would claim was actually an underground gray cap stronghold. Often, she sounded weary. So incredibly tired. And other times strong, defiant.

Then the gray caps Rose, and Hoegbotton and Frankwrithe alike became the rebels. Dead. Dispersed. Fled. Lost. But the Lady in Blue survived, and by surviving she seemed to have again become greater than herself. Neither the green of the Hoegbottons nor the red of the Frankwrithe & Lewdens, but all the colors mixed together. People clung to the hope that she would return in force to save them. Even though she'd never been more than a voice on the radio to most of them.

Finch has seen the gray caps' files on the Lady in Blue, of course. Knows that she was born Alessandra Lewden in the Southern Isles. Received her education from various private schools in Morrow and Stockton. Then became Alessandra Hoegbotton in a politically advantageous marriage arranged during a brief truce between the Houses. Wife to the opera singer Joseph Hoegbotton, who was shot dead by an insane rival after a performance. After which Alessandra disappeared for several years. Until House Hoegbotton needed her for their latest propaganda tool: radio broadcasts. Across enemy lines. The disembodied voice of the self-described "Lady in Blue" coming out of houses and the back rooms of cafés.

Unclear from the files if Alessandra had given herself over entirely to Cause Hoegbotton. But it didn't matter when Cause Hoegbotton and Cause Frankwrithe-Lewden came together. The Lady in Blue just became more powerful. Sometimes, she was the only thing connecting the two factions.

But fascinating to Finch: her voice coming over the radio had driven the gray caps insane with anger. At first, they did not understand this new invention, brought to Ambergris by the busy scientists of the Kalif's empire. So for a time her voice seemed to come from everywhere and nowhere. Magically. Or a magic that was beyond them, unaffected by spores or fruiting bodies. You could not re-create radio using fungi. You could not spy on it from within.

The gray caps, the files revealed, had spent at least as much time trying to track her down as preparing for the Rising. But they could not locate her. They flooded tunnels. Sent spore armies rushing down remote streets. Blocked off passageways. Still, they couldn't find her. Which made Finch, even conflicted, admire her, reading the files. Understanding the cost of being constantly on the move. Constantly in flux.

Sometimes that cost came through over the radio. A mad howling. As if the city were a creature gone insane. Capturing the sounds of warfare. Of demolition. Of fighting with the gray caps or the Partials.

But for the last several months Finch knows there have been no radio broadcasts from the Lady in Blue. From Alessandra Lewden. Little or no organized rebel activity anywhere in the city. Meanwhile, the towers continue to rise in the bay. People grow more and more used to their situation. Becoming cynical about the Lady in Blue. Distrust reborn between former Hoegbottons and former Frankwrithes. Even Wyte's noticed it.

The fact is she hasn't saved Wyte, him, or anyone from six years of living under gray cap rule.

5

Home is an apartment in a twelve-story run-down hotel. He'd moved there six years ago, three months after the Rising, two years after his father's death. In its day, during the worst of the fighting between House Hoegbotton and House Frankwrithe, it had become famous as a kind of sanctuary. Far enough away from the battles to be neutral. Near enough to the merchant quarter to be profitable. Everybody trying to make money on the war.

But those days are gone. Outside the hotel, a statue of a dead composer stands guard beyond the crumbling steps that lead to the gaping front door. Powder-burned, nose shot off, one raised arm just a stone stump. A raving madman lives near the statue. Finch has no idea how he survives the gray caps' patrols at night.

Inside, the lobby is dank and dim and molding. An old crooked photograph on the wall captures a few signs of the hotel's lost luxury in a scene from some long-ago party. A strain of pale green lichen has infiltrated the faded burgundy of the carpet. Gives the floor a spongy feel and sheds a disconcerting, ghostly glow that leads Finch through the entrance after dark.

Elsewhere, bulbs burn fierce or dull, like mismatched cousins. Always, a ghastly yellow haze. A curling faded wallpaper that sometimes isn't. Smells that change by the hour, dictated by the currents in the basement. Walls knocked out. Old furniture piled high. A courtyard through the middle of the hotel. The basement is awash in water, an intrusion from the River Moth.

Finch knows many of the people in the building by name. A kind of survival strategy. Strangers mean danger. Like a leftover slogan from the old days when Hoegbotton gangs purified their neighborhoods of the "F&L scourge," and F&L gangs returned the favor. He doesn't know how safe his presence makes those around him, but he does his best. Tries to notice what's going on. Likes to believe he is doing what his father would've done.

The crumbling sign on the roof still reads "otel Mur t." Crows nest in it.

Sometimes Finch hides behind the sign.

Peers out across the skyline, toward the bay, from its shelter.

His apartment was on the seventh floor, but Finch ignored the dirty marble stairs and the stubborn elevator. Followed the wormy carpet into a darkened courtyard instead. A snarl of bushes and long grass along the path. At the center, a ragged vegetable garden of tomatoes, carrots, squash. Didn't know who tended to it. He turned left, pushed open the first door, took familiar steps down into the dark two at a time.

Bottom of the stairs. Finch turned right, faced a door at the end of a stub of hallway.

Rebecca Rathven lived there. He could hear the sounds of water, the slap of fish surfacing, coming through the air ducts. Mixed, sometimes, with Rathven's cackling laugh as she read something funny in her books. On a quiet night, the odd sounds traveled as far up as Finch's floor. Finch liked the sounds. And he liked Rathven. Found her useful. Found her interesting. Sometimes in a sinister way.

Who takes a flooded basement as an apartment in a hotel full of empty rooms?

Finch knocked. Heard footsteps. A pause. An appraisal through the peephole.

She was used to visitors, but still cautious. People came to Rathven for information from the past. They came to her if they'd lost the thread. They came to her to talk. Why? Finch, like most people, had books, but Rathven had a *library.*

That library changed with every visit. Rathven kept shifting the stacks against the inroads of the river. People who owed her favors helped her create barricades of wooden beams and homemade sandbags. He'd told her to move, to go higher. But the effort, *all of those books . . .* she said she would, but she hadn't yet. Might never.

The door opened wide enough for Finch to smell soggy pulp. *Trying to save the unsalvageable.* A wavery yellow light crept into the hall. Rathven's long face appeared, tilted up at him. Startling white skin, almost translucent. Looked at times like something broken. Then like something strong. Dark hair shot through with lighter strands. Thick black eyebrows, hazel eyes, high cheekbones, thin lips curled in a smile. Blue dress and brown sandals. Finch could never tell her age. Somewhere between twenty-five and thirty-five. Had never found a way to ask.

"Finch." The word invested with some secret amusement. "Come in?"

Smiled, shook his head. "But I do have something for you. A list. A long list."

"A list of what? Laundry list? Shopping list? Enemies? Friends?"

Finch laughed. "You should've been a detective."

"I *am* a detective," she said. The ritual refrain.

"List of names," he said. "People who lived in an apartment where two murders took place. And you'll love this: it's more than a century of names."

Not quite a frown, but a kind of quiver to the lips. A caution entering the eyes. She'd guessed the source. Not hard, really.

Rathven had been in the work camps for three years. Had the brands on the bottoms of her feet, the red-gold marking of fungus she could hide but never forget. There was a pulsing sensation sometimes, she'd told him. A restlessness. He'd never asked what else had happened to her there. Didn't really want to know.

She helped him because he'd gotten her brother, Blaine, who went by the name "the Photographer," out of the camps and into the hotel. Dozens of old cameras in the Photographer's fifth-floor apartment. The man used the cameras to take thousands of photographs of water. Funded that obsession by running a black market for goods. Finch bought or traded with him like everyone else. Using gray cap vouchers, food pods, or salvaged items.

If the Photographer ever cut him off, or Rathven ever stopped helping him, Finch knew it would feel like a punch to the kidneys. *Friendship or need?*

He leaned over, pulled the list from his satchel. Felt tired suddenly, like he'd stolen something from her but realized it too late. "Could you read it? Tell me if any names are familiar. Maybe from your books." Would pay her in information and fungal antidotes, like usual.

Rathven took the paper gingerly. Prodded the spongy edges with one finger. "Only if you tell me why."

"Recent murders."

The color went out of her face.

"Got a piece of paper?" he asked.

She nodded, reached behind her. Handed him an old envelope. Return address from somewhere in the Southern Isles. *Might as well be some imaginary place now.*

Drew the symbol. Handed the paper back to her. "Do you know what this is?"

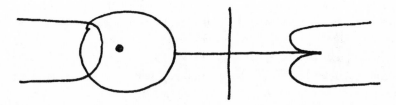

A disdainful glance. "It's a gray cap symbol, of course. Very poorly drawn."

"Can you check it out? I've seen it before. But I don't know what it means."

"Sure. I don't know how long it will take."

"That's fine . . ." Lingered, unsure how to ask for more. Then just said it: "Another favor. Memory bulbs tonight. Can you check on me? Call, or knock on the door if the phones are out? In an hour or two?" No idea when Sintra would get there. No point taking chances.

Now came the frown, as he knew it would. But she nodded. "I will. I will, Finch. Don't worry." Reached out to squeeze his arm. Then withdrew her hand quickly. As if she'd shown weakness.

He stared at her now. Smiled. Sometimes he felt a closeness with her he shared with no one else, not even Sintra. She'd never fought the Rising. She'd just read her books, preserved them. Protected them. Shared them. Eked out a living making crafts. At least, this was the story she'd told him. A small part of him still wondered why she'd been taken to the camps. Or why she'd been let go. *"I was too sick to work,"* she'd told him. But she'd never looked sick to him.

"The gray caps like to confuse randomness with purpose," Wyte had said once. But Finch didn't believe that. Just believed they kept the purpose buried deep.

"Thank you," he said. The words came out a little ragged. "Long day. I'll call when I take them. If the phones work."

"I'll come up and knock if I don't hear," she said. In return, he knew he'd have to help push back the encroaching river one more time. Each task had its own price with Rathven.

She shut the door, taking the light with her.

Finch's apartment was near the end of the hall. Had to negotiate a hothouse wetness to get there. Tendrils and caps of red-and-green fungus sprouted from the walls. Gray caps only cared about keeping the streets clean. No help from his next-door neighbors, either. Almost like they thought it gave them camouflage.

No one around, except his cat, Feral, a big brute of a tabby, crying to be let in. Bumping up against his legs while Finch made shushing sounds. Feral was loud, always trying to trip Finch and bring him down to eye level.

Sometimes the little old man in the apartment opposite heard Finch and came out, but not tonight. A former accountant, the man liked to sit in a shaft of sunlight from the hall window. Smile and talk to himself and nod, and read from the same ragged book.

Two minutes to unlock and then relock. Only Sintra knew the sequence. Still not comfortable with that idea. Had thought about changing the key.

Flash of another dark room. A worn bed. White sheets dull in the shadow. Didn't look like anyone had slept in it in months. Dusty floor. Two corpses.

Flipped a switch. Relief when the lights actually came on. Faded floral print wallpaper. Rootlike edges to the frayed beige carpet. Worn-out furniture.

Relief at being able to hang up the role of detective in the closet, along with his jacket. To let the tough exterior come off like a mask worn for a festival.

"Hold on for Truff's sake," Finch said to Feral as the cat ran to the kitchen through the living room.

Feral had wide round eyes. They gave his owlish face a perpetual look of surprise. Finch had rescued him as a kitten from a fungus that had wound tendrils around the animal while he slept. Still had purple patches on his flanks, sometimes growing, sometimes not.

No sign of Sidle, his windowsill lizard. Never really knew if it was the same lizard anyway. Felt compelled to pretend for some reason.

After feeding Feral, Finch put the two memory bulbs on the kitchen counter. Poured himself a glass of Trillian's Premium Whiskey, aged eighteen years. An F&L brand trading off a famous name. Something no self-respecting H&S man would've drunk before the Rising. He had six bottles left in the closet. Next to the boxes of cigars. These had been his father's habits, his legacy. Nothing better had replaced them. The smell of cigar smoke made him feel like his father was right there, beside him.

Cigars. Whiskey. Both working as a kind of peculiar clock or timer. When they ran out, would his life as Finch run out, too?

Heretic's touch like wet, dead leaves sewn together and stuffed with meat.

Dinnertime, but he wasn't hungry.

A long, shuddering sigh as he sat in the old leather chair next to the couch in the living room. Under the light of an old glass lamp shaped like an umbrella that he'd taken from the lobby. Watched the dusk dissolve into night.

On the far wall hung three of the hotel's original tourist scenes of Albumuth Boulevard. A far better view than the one from the small balcony abutting the kitchen. All the balcony could show him was more of the night sky, a sliver of the two towers, and the alley below. *A view saved for emergencies.* A second view could be had from the bathroom by opening the small latched window and standing on the toilet. Finch could look down into the courtyard whenever he wanted. Between the two sight lines, he had as much forewarning as he could expect. If what came after him was human.

Not a bad place. At least he had a separate office next to the kitchen and extra bookcases, overflowing, on the wall closest to the door. He'd made them from planks torn up from the rotting eleventh floor.

Even before the Rising, Finch had enjoyed reading. So many nights at the old house in the valley he and his father had sat reading in silence, separate yet together. To block out the night. The wars. Now the gray caps' camps lay so close that a crushed foundation under a heap of garbage was all that remained of the house. Nothing left but the books and other things he'd rescued.

Some books had been bought during cease-fires. Before the Rising destroyed the idea of bookstores. A few had come from his grandparents, who had returned to the Southern Isles when he was ten. Memories of them were like spent matches dull against a sudden darkness. He leafed through the books for signs of them sometimes. *A folded letter. A note that never dropped to the floor.*

But most of the books had been his father's, rescued from the old home. About a dozen Finch knew from long repetition, part of his father's home-schooling when it was too dangerous to go to class.

His father had started out as a brilliant engineer. In his youth, he had served in the Ambergris military in that brief, bright window when they'd taken on the Kalif's empire. He was with the troops as they advanced into a desert strewn with oases and hunched trees with gnarled black branches. As they took the Kalif's lands, and contemplated their own vision of conquest. As they were pushed back.

With Finch's mother dead in childbirth, his father had raised him after the war. A strange life, seesawing between wealth and poverty. Father's many important yet strange friends. His connections with Hoegbotton & Sons. And yet sometimes things had been bad enough Finch's father had supported them doing odd jobs and trading books for food. Or burning books for fuel.

Back at the old house, there had been many photographs of his father. The broad-chested muscular form of the man, tight in that characteristic Ambergrisian uniform of olive green. Wedge of a hat tilted to the side as was the fashion. On a hill or in a city or atop a tank. Surrounded by fellow soldiers or alone. Always smiling. Eyes dark dots looking into the camera. Seeming aware of future fame, but not of how it would come. Nor of how far he would fall.

Finch had chosen "John" for his new identity because it was his father's name. "Finch" was just a common bird, a creature no one would ever notice. He'd burned all photographs except one the night he'd changed his name. Displayed on the mantel, it showed his grandparents just arrived from the Southern Isles. At the docks with their suitcases beside them. Looking faded, remote, and confused. Grandpa had been a carpenter. Grandma a homemaker. There were no relatives on his mother's side. His father was four years old in the photo. This image was all Finch was willing to risk.

Once, Sintra had asked about the people in the photo. He'd said he didn't know them. That he'd found the photo on the street and liked it. True, to a point. Hadn't known the four-year-old. Never really knew his grandparents. Just another nonmemory from a lost life, and most days he didn't regret that.

On the back of the photograph, his father had scrawled a few lines: "Sometimes a man will see in his own image a desert, and it is the need to make that desert bloom which drives him again and again to action, as hopelessness compels us to our end. Sometimes, too, a man will flee in the enemy's direction, eager to weather any punishment—physical or mental—that proves he is still alive. Or, he does so from a pride that lies to him, tells him he can change what seems unchangeable." From a book? His own thoughts? Finch would never know.

Feral jumped up on his lap. Began to purr as Finch petted him.

The rough-smooth taste of the whiskey scratched and soothed his throat. He sank farther into his chair. Maybe Sintra would come by tonight.

Never lost.

"Yes, I know, fat boy," Finch murmured. Could sit there all night. Forget what he had to do and pull out a book that he'd read three or four times already. Pretend he lived in a better world.

Turned on the small radio on the table next to him. Feral stopped purring for a second. Only one station across the dial: the gray caps' station. Gone any cacophony of voices and music. Usually just a single signal, filled with cryptic clicks and whistles. Punctuated by propaganda delivered in flat tones by human readers. ". . . A *spy is caught and killed just outside the Zone . . . Sector 509 has been scheduled for renovation. Anyone living there should relocate immediately.*"

But, tonight, nothing. That made thirty-seven days of static. What did it mean? Was it just another slackening of attention? Or something more serious? Finch had noticed a pattern. The new dislodged the old. A puppet government in place for six months dissolved when the gray caps turned to building the camps. Electricity no longer reliable since they'd started in on the two towers. These failings brought a twisted optimism. *Maybe they can't do everything at once.* Or maybe there was a purpose to all of it that he just couldn't see.

He pushed a complaining Feral off his lap. Walked back into the kitchen.

The memory bulbs lay on the counter. Vaguely round. Pitted and whorled. Smelling of both salt and offal. Already rotting?

Finch looked down at the cat, which had followed him expecting a treat. Wondered what would happen if he fed a bulb to Feral.

"You want to eat one of these and I'll eat the other?" he asked Feral.

The cat walked back into the living room. Finch laughed. "Smart choice." Picked up the phone receiver, dialed Rathven's number. A crackling interference. *At least it's working.*

Through the static: "I'm taking one now. Give it an hour. If I don't call back, check on me."

"I will. Be safe."

"Thanks."

Finch put the receiver down. *Be safe.* Don't slip on the carpet. Don't fall out the window.

Which poison first? Finch picked up the orange one. *Get the worst over with first.*

Each time he ate a memory bulb, he became someone else. *Different* when he returned.

These would be his fourth and fifth. The first had belonged to a girl of ten and had given him nightmares for a year. Montages of a ragged doll. Soup made with dog bones. A bleak apartment without even wallpaper. Turned out there'd been no foul play. Her parents dead, she'd starved to death. The second had been a young man, the third a young woman. A double suicide unspooled in his head. Left him with longings he didn't know he had. Regrets that weren't his. Memories of people he didn't know. Or want to know.

Finch had never eaten two in one night.

How many would change him by just a little too much?

Fuck it.

Opened his mouth wide. Placed the bulb on his tongue. The taste of the gray cap bulb was dry. Like dirt and sand. The worst part was you had to eat them whole. Crunch down on the ridiculous size of it until your jaw ached. No good cutting them up, grinding them down to paste, adding them to food or water. Ruined the effect. His skin prickled as his mouth took in the strange texture, the taste. An odd, sickening blend of cinnamon-pepper-lime. Sour breath.

Dread, and yet also a thin layer of anticipation. To be taken out of his own life. If only for a little while.

He stumbled into the chair. Feral butted his head up against his slack arm.

Memories didn't come out the way one might expect. Nothing logical or ordered about them. Almost as if you were standing on a street corner as a motored vehicle raced by. As it passed you, a thousand pieces of confetti flew up. You had to try to catch as many of them as you could before they hit the ground.

Finch closed his eyes.

Leaned back.

Let it hit him all at once.

Come to:

At the bottom of a well. Layers of rough stone spiraled up to a distant pale light. A wriggling mass of worms or insects or something thick and strange pushing down through the light, extinguishing it. Sudden image of a monstrous City, balanced atop a single building greater than anything ever built in Ambergris, and it all housed in a cavern so huge that the ceiling is lost in blue-tinged darkness.

Come to (faster now):

A stumbling, jerky run through a tunnel. A surrounding mob of gray caps click and whistle with insane speed. A glimpse of blue sky, winking out. A burning motored vehicle, ancient model. A parade with a huge black cat caged and orange-yellow-green lights spread out along the route. Superimposed: an enormous grub drowning in a sack of its own liquid skin. A dark-green frond of fungus five stories high. Blood, lots of blood, pooling out across the ground. A man's face, in extreme agony, suddenly gone black in silhouette, turning into a huge door made half of volcanic rock and half charred book cover. And on top of the door a smaller door, and a small door set into that one. Hand on the doorknob. Opening . . .

Come to (slower now):

A stone fortress in a desert. Spinning out into open space—falling, falling, falling. And then a face Finch recognizes, the dead man's, smiling. Beatifically. More mud and dirt and the smell-sound of a river nearby. Side view of water flowing, ear to the grass. Something licks the moisture from his eyes before huffing and going on its way. Falling again, through black fabric studded with stars. The dead man falling, too, staring right at Finch, expression oddly calm. Words from the man's mouth in the clicks and whistles of the gray caps' language. And then, a sudden and monstrous clarity that can never be put into words.

Come to:

Moving slowly among a thousand swaying fungal trees in a thousand vision-shattering shades of green. Nearby, a rotting tank with the insignia of the Houses on its side, asleep under the fruiting bodies. The sound of footsteps. A hint of movement other than spores, strained through the heavy sky. Hunting for something. But what? A man. Moving in front of them. Night. Strange numbers and words spilling out emerald against a field of darkness. Shadowing the man. The orange sky dominated by the shambling hulks of floating fungal fortresses. *Things* crawl and fly and swim between the fortresses. Running now, just yards behind the man. But the man was turning to face them. The man was looking right at him when he disappeared. Winked out. Leaving only the smile. And that only for an instant. An intense feeling of confusion and surprise. Then: falling through cold air and couldn't feel his legs.

Returned whining. Keening. A low, animal sound from deep in his throat. Lay curled up on the chair. Sweating. Things crawled around inside his skull. Didn't know how much time had passed.

An enormous grub drowning in a sack of its own liquid skin.

Coughed. Sat up.

A rotting tank with the insignia of the Houses on its side, asleep under the fruiting bodies.

Feral rubbed up against his extended arm. Finch got up, made it to the phone, dialed Rathven, said "One done, one to go" when she answered, and hung up. Grabbed the second memory bulb. Collapsed back to the chair.

A monstrous City, balanced atop a single building.

Started laughing. Didn't know what was so funny or why he couldn't stop.

Falling through cold air and couldn't feel his legs.

Wondered how much this would mess him up.

6

The night half over. *Something important slipping away?*

Drank more whiskey, and let it swirl around his mouth. Held the burn in the back of his throat. Followed by numbness.

The sounds out in the dark beyond the window hadn't made him shudder or start for a long time. Skitterings. Moanings. A cut-off shout of alarm.

A spotlight of lavender and crimson painted itself across the far wall of his apartment, then leapt away. Once, Finch had seen a shoal of spores take the form of a huge, bloated green monster. Spiraling red eyes. It had bellowed and dived into a neighborhood to the north.

Smashed itself into motes against the ground.

A child might see that and cry out in delight.

Sidle, quick-shadow, scuttled up the side of the wall near the window. Pursuing moths that had flown into the apartment. Sidle was a happy little predator with bright black eyes. Didn't care about anything but his next meal. Finch could put him in a cage with a branch and water, and Sidle would be content his entire life. So long as he got fed.

"I guess we'll soon find out what kind of bastard he was," Finch said to an oblivious Feral. Feral was looking up at the wall. Mesmerized by Sidle's stalking of the spiraling moth. Finch wondered how many Sidles Feral had caught over the years.

Finch forced the second bulb into his mouth. Chewed it into a dull paste as he moved from the chair to the couch. Lay down. Swallowed.

The room spun a little. Righted itself.

The ceiling had a few odd discolorations but nothing to suggest infiltration. *Invisible spies.* Who lived upstairs, anyway? Sometimes lately he had heard a person pacing across the floorboards in the middle of the night.

After a minute or two, Finch sat up. Nothing seemed to be happening. Nothing at all.

The dead man sat in the chair next to him, smiling.

"Uhhh!" Finch leapt to his feet.

The man was flanked by a Feral grown large as a pony. A Sidle grown as large as a Feral. They both looked at him the way Sidle had been looking at the moths.

"Sit down," the man said. An order, not a suggestion. In a strange accent. The man looked much younger than he had on the floor of the apartment. Had lost the fungal beard.

Finch sat down slowly. Didn't take his eyes off the man. Left hand groping across the cushions. Where was his gun?

"I've been waiting for someone like you," the man said. "You won't understand it, but I'm going to give you what I know. Just in case."

The window behind the man no longer showed the city. What it did show was so impossible and disturbing Finch had to look away. And yet the image entered into him.

The man said Finch's name. Except he didn't say "John Finch." He used Finch's real name. The one buried for eight long years.

Finch tried to slow his breathing. Failed. Chest felt like something was going to explode.

He must be *inside* the man's memories.

Then why is the man sitting across from you?

"Who are you?" An obvious question. But it kept pounding against the inside of his skull. So he had to let it out.

The man laughed.

"I didn't say anything funny."

"More to the point," the man said, "who are *you*? And who are you with?"

"Shut up. This is just one of your memories. Manifesting in me. It isn't real."

Blindingly, unbelievably bright, a light like the sun shot through the window. The night sky torn apart by it. Through the tear: a turquoise sea roiling with ever-changing patterns.

"You don't have to understand it. Not now," the man said.

Didn't know if he was inside a mushroom or outside the universe. Glimpses of the city from on high: each street, each canal, an artery filled with blood. Hadn't known there could be so many shades of red. Spiking into his eyes.

"Be careful," the man said, echoing Rathven, and took Finch's hand. The man's hand was warm. Callused. *Real.* "Don't lose yourself, no matter what happens."

The man and Feral and Sidle disappeared. The window became a huge mouth, and they were all nothing more or less than memory bulbs within it. Finch fell through the same skein of stars he had seen in the gray cap's memory.

Woke up:

Teetering on the battlements of an ancient fortress, looking out over a desert, the sand flaring out for miles under the seethe of dusk. Moments from someone else's childhood. A parent's death. Sitting in a blind. Crawling through tunnels.

Woke up:

A cavern glittering with veins of some blue metal, huge mushrooms slowly breathing in and out. Seen in a flash of light that faded and kept fading but never went out: more caverns, an old woman's face, framed by white hair; another woman, in her twenties, her thirties, her forties. A shadowy figure hobbling down a street.

Woke up:

The insane jungle of the HFZ, almost floating above it, through it, coming out into a clearing ringed by twelve green men planted in the ground, arms at their sides, their mouths opening and closing soundlessly. And the jungle was made of fungus, not trees, poured over trucks and tanks and other heavy machinery junked and rusted out and infested with mushrooms, some of it still slowly, slowly moving. And back to the fortress, at the edge of a man-made cliff, many hundreds of feet above the desert floor, and out in the desert a thousand green lights held by a thousand shadows motionless, watching. A sound of metal locking into place. A kind of mirror. An eye. Pulling back to see a figure that seemed oddly familiar, and then a name: *Ethan Bliss*. Then a circle of stone, a door, covered with gray cap symbols. And, finally, jumping out into the desert air, toward a door hovering in the middle of the sky, pursued by the gray cap, before the world went dark.

Wake up . . . Came out of it seconds, centuries, later. To find Feral and Sidle watching him. Feral on the floor near the couch. Sidle on the windowsill, a large black moth trapped between his clockwork jaws.

The phone was ringing and ringing. Reached out for it. Put it to his ear.

"Are you okay?" Rath's voice.

"I'm going to be fine. I think."

Hung up.

Closed his eyes.

TUESDAY

I: The *fanaarcensitii*. You said he had fallen from a great height. Did anything you saw in the memory bulbs support that idea?

F: Instinct. I didn't trust what I saw.

I: Why not?

F: Because I haven't felt the same since I ate them. Because they were scenes out of a nightmare. I don't know.

I: There's one strange thing in all of this.

F: Just one?

I: A mention of a fortress. In a desert. Do you know the name of this place?

F: No.

I: I think you do.

F: I don't even know if it was real or not.

I: Is this real?

[screams]

1

Woke to a weight on the bed next to him. Went rigid. Sucked in his breath. Reached for his gun. Then relaxed. Recognized the smell of her sweat, some subtle perfume behind it. Sintra Caraval. The woman who had been part of his life for the last two years. She smelled good.

He could feel her staring at the back of his head. Her breath on his back. He smiled. Didn't open his eyes. She kissed his neck.

She was naked. Smooth, soft feel of her breasts against his shoulders. He was instantly hard. Opened his eyes. Turned over on his back. Sintra turned with him so she was nestled under his left arm. A surge of happiness startled him. Through the window: dim light creating shadows out of the darkness. Her brown skin somehow luminous against it. She'd told him she was half Nimblytod, half Dogghe. Tribes that had lived in Ambergris since before settlement. Before the gray caps.

Even in the darkness, Finch knew her face. Thick, expressive eyebrows. Green eyes. Full lips. A thin scar across the left cheek he'd never gotten her to talk about. A nose a little too long for her face, which gave her a questioning look.

An exotic lilt to the ends of her sentences as she whispered in his ear: "I let myself in. I wasn't trying to startle you."

He started to get up, to lock the door. She pushed him back down. "I locked the door behind me. No one else can get in."

Finch stopped resisting her. The key was the greatest act of trust between them. Was that good or bad?

"Sintra," he said sleepily, bringing his right arm around to cup one warm breast. "I could get used to you. I really could." Not really listening to what he was saying. Still waking up. Reduced to the kind of meaningless words he'd mouthed at fifteen. Having sex in his room with the neighbor's daughter while his father was out.

"You could *get used to me?*" she said.

When mock-angry with him, she raised her eyebrows in a way he loved.

"A bad joke," he said. Hugged her closer. "I'm already used to you." Kissed the top of her head. Relaxed against her, the shudder that had been building up overtaking him. Then gone.

Then, more awake: "Let's escape. Tonight."

He'd worked it out in his head hundreds of times. Along the shore of the HFZ at dusk.

A rowboat. Not a motorboat. To the end of the bay. Then either west to the Kalif's empire or south to Stockton. West because it was easier to get through the security zones in the desert. He knew places there. Places his father had shown him on maps.

Escape. Now.

Imagined she was grimacing, there, in the dark. The way she always did when he mentioned it.

"Bad night?" she asked.

"Just don't betray me," the man said, and took Finch's hand.

"Confusing night."

"Tell me later."

Then she was kissing him and he was kissing her. Tongue curled against tongue. The salt of her in his mouth. A hunger. A need. His hand between her muscular thighs. His cock in her hand. A pulse. A current that made him want to touch, to kiss, every part of her. Warmth and softness at his fingertips. Burning in her hand. An intake of breath. A little sighing cry. He turned and turned until he was above her, his forearms brushing her shoulders. Moaned as he slid into her and kept kissing her. Dissolving his poisoned thoughts. Not thinking at all. Becoming someone else.

She felt so good that he had to stop for a moment. Locked his elbows to hold himself up over her, looked into her eyes, her hands on his chest.

"I love your neck," he said, and kissed it. "And your eyes." Kissed her eyelids. He could see her better now, light colonizing shadows.

She wasn't smiling back. Wasn't responding.

"John," she said, looking worried. "John, you're crying blood."

She wiped a too-dark tear away with her finger.

"Am I?" he said, trying to smile, and came with a long shuddering groan before the thought could hit him.

Occupational hazard.

———

Later. Lying in bed together. Feral pushing his head against a bedpost, already wanting breakfast. The blood tears had stopped almost as soon as they'd started. Remembered Wyte had told him it could be an after-effect of eating memory bulbs. It hadn't hurt. It had just surprised him. He'd daubed his eyes clean with a bathroom towel. Had stared for a moment at the worn face of the stranger trapped in the cracked mirror.

A desert fortress. An army of silent gray caps. And Ethan Bliss, Frankwrithe & Lewden's top man for so many years.

Pushed the thoughts aside. Sintra would have to leave soon. *The place on the back of her neck where she liked to be kissed. Soft brown hairs. Crisp salt taste.*

"How was your work yesterday?" he asked her, holding her tightly to him. Skin so warm against his body.

"The same as always."

What did that mean?

"The same as always," Finch echoed. "That's good."

"I guess," she said. She sounded distracted.

Still didn't know what Sintra did, or even where she lived. Remnants of the Dogghe and Nimblytod had carved out a defiant kingdom for themselves in the ruined Religious Quarter. But Sintra might not even think of herself as one of them, integrated into the city. He'd never asked. Sometimes he daydreamed of her being a rebel agent. Comforting. Utterly unreal. But that didn't matter.

"I'm lonely. Even with you."

"Someday, it will be different . . ."

That she preferred him not knowing hurt him. Even though he understood the sense of it. Even though they made a game out of it.

"Where do you work?"

"In the city."

"And what do you do?"

"Answer questions. Apparently."

He'd known everything about his past girlfriends. But even in their lovemaking Sintra seemed to change from week to week.

Exhausting. Exciting. Dangerous.

Still missed the normalcy of the one time she'd stayed long enough to make breakfast. A surreal, sublime morning. They'd met at a black market party the night before. Taken off his detective's badge, gone as a civilian wanting some fun. Bumped into each other on the makeshift dance floor. In someone's basement.

Everyone there expecting the gray caps to blast up through the tiles and send them to the work camps.

"Your day wasn't as good, I can tell," she said now. Bringing him back.

"I have a difficult case."

"How difficult?"

He sat on the chair and talked to me. The cat was as big as a pony and the lizard was as big as a cat. And me, I was as tiny as a reflection in Feral's eye. A perverse nursery rhyme.

"Difficult enough. A gray cap cut in half. A dead man. In an apartment. But they seem to have fallen from the sky . . ."

Sintra sat up, looked at him. "Where were they found?"

Finch stared back at her. Surprised by her sudden interest. Sometimes he shared details as an act of faith. But not on something that might pull her down with him.

"Down by the bay," he said. Waited.

Sintra considered him as he'd considered her. Then changed the subject. "Is that why you were crying? Because of what the memory bulbs showed you?"

"Yes." Propped himself up on an elbow. Shuddered, winced. An aftershock? Pressure in his head. Like his brain had outgrown his skull.

Sintra hugged him. Kissed him. He laid his head against her chest. She scared him sometimes. Both from her presence and her absence.

"Maybe it was a bad reaction to a drug," she said. "Maybe you inhaled a bad spore."

Back before the Rising, Sintra said she had been a doctor's aide.

"Unlikely." He and his fellow detectives got fed antidotes every few months. One perk of working for the gray caps. He stole extras for Sintra and Rathven. Sintra always took them with her. Never used them in the apartment.

"But it's over now."

"Yes. It's over."

He broke off the embrace. Feral was cleaning himself in a shaft of light by the window. Sidle was motionless on the windowsill. Drunk on the new sun.

Sintra wrapped the sheets around her and stood up, walked toward the window. Leaving Finch naked and exposed on the bed. Watching her as he put his underwear back on. Remembering the first time they had made love. How he'd checked the sheets, the pillows after she'd left. Wanting to breathe in more of the smell of her. How there had seemed to be no trace of their sex. Only his memory of the act. As if he had entered a ghost.

She turned to stare at him, framed by the window.

"I'll come back in a night or two," Sintra said. "That's not long."

"No, it's not long," Finch said. Thinking of the station. The other detectives. Work fatigue washed over him.

Memory holes and Wyte and Heretic and wanting to scream, to just start shooting.

"Maybe I'll even spend the night. If I can," she said. A curious look on her face, like she was testing him. She held her hands behind her back, one leg slightly bent, her body bronzed and perfect to him. "What do you think of that?"

Must have been obvious what he thought, because she couldn't take the weight of his gaze. Looked away. Leaned down to pick up her knapsack, retrieve her clothes.

Not that he doubted she felt the same. He knew why she kept her distance. The same reason he did.

Except, it's not working for me.

A long kiss. A final hug.

And she was gone.

All he could feel was the ache in his thighs. The damp spot on the front of his underwear, colder now than before.

⁂

Just once, Sintra left something behind. Finch keeps it hidden in a desk drawer. No reason for him to keep it. But no reason to get rid of it.

Written in longhand, Sintra's concise notes are about mushrooms, which no longer come with any field guide. Ignorance can lead to death, even though since the Rising the gray caps have kept the streets clear. Personal curiosity? Something to do with the black market? Has she helped someone she shouldn't help? Given aid to some group the gray caps are hunting down?

Does it make her a spy to have this information, or just pragmatic? Does it make him complicit to keep it, or just sentimental?

This incomplete list doesn't include fungal weapons. These mushrooms all perform certain tasks or "work" within the city. If any have a secondary or tertiary purpose it is unknown at this time.

(1) Tiny white mushrooms almost like star-shaped flowers—found most often around surfaces where dead bodies have recently lain or where some conflict

has occurred. Like the chalk outlines used by detectives pre-Rising to mark bodies? Warnings, or . . . ?

(2) *Green "spear" mushrooms with sharp, narrow hoods and long, slender stems—four or five will be found around a building targeted for transformation. Three days after the appearance of these green spear mushrooms, the building in question will begin to look moist or spongy, due to infiltration from below. By the fourth or fifth day, it will begin to crumble. By the sixth day, the building has blown away in the wind. On the seventh day, a new structure has usually blossomed, overnight. This new structure may take any of a number of forms, all fungal-based.*

(3) *Red "tree" mushrooms with huge caps and strong, thick "trunks" or stems— these can grow up to eighty feet high and are much more resistant to storms and high winds than other kinds of mushrooms. They appear to have a filtration system that gives them stability by letting air pass through millions of "pores." In a sense, they float. An examination of distribution patterns from any height reveals that they have been "planted" in regular patterns forming rough "spokes" radiating out from the bay, interrupted only by the HFZ and the Religious Quarter. They regularly expel from their gills a smaller, purple mushroom with a strong euphoric effect and high levels of digestible protein.*

(4) *Purple "drug" mushrooms with ball caps and almost no stems—dispensed from the red "tree" mushrooms, these purple mushrooms are clearly meant to serve as "crowd control" by giving the people of the city sustenance and making them dependent. These mushrooms create a strong addiction by affecting the pleasure centers of the brain. They also create hallucinations intended to pacify, most drawn from happy memories.*

Definitely her handwriting. She's slipped more than one message under his door while he's out. Tells himself: *I'll throw it away when I know more about her.* But nine months have passed since he found the note. She hasn't told him anything more than what he knew before.

Yet caution loses out when she walks through the door. Remembering how, on days when he's expecting her and she's late, the fear creeps aching into his muscles. Finds himself gulping air like water. Thick and heavy. Lost. *Never lost.*

2

After Sintra had left, Finch fed the cat, grabbed a quick bite, and cleaned off with a couple of pails of once-used bathwater. Fresh shirt, same pants, same jacket. Kicked Feral out to explore on his own while he went down the stairs to the courtyard, then the basement.

Rath's pale, angular face peered out from behind the door. Evaluating him. Looking for something.

She let Finch in without a word. Through a hallway brightened by walls painted light green. Probably to conceal rot. Then into a larger area with a few chairs, her strange library to either side. Beyond, where Finch had never gone: the start of entropy. The bruises of gray and blue stains spread across the ceiling. Disappeared into the darkness of a tunnel.

"Nothing new, I see," Finch said.

Rath laughed. "Not that you'd notice."

Finch brushed by her to sit in an armchair on a blue throw rug. Rising above him, water-damaged paperbacks and hardcovers had been stacked unevenly on warped shelves. The shelves perched on stilts to fend off any sudden rise in the water level. The weighted smell of moisture seemed both fresh and claustrophobic.

"Coffee?" she asked. The usual.

Hesitated, said, "No. Tea, please." Didn't know why.

Rath disappeared into the tunnel. Did she have a kitchen back there? Maybe a bedroom. Maybe more books. A whole troupe of clowns. The thought made him smile.

Stray pages saved from long-drowned books caught his attention as he waited for her. Red eye peering from monstrous face. Lines of scrawl in an unknown language. Diagrams of buildings or plants or motored vehicles. A black-and-white photograph of a gaunt five-year-old girl in a ragged dress standing in the muddy track of a tank.

Truff knew who had lived here before, collected the books originally. Or how long it had taken Rath to organize it all. Or how much she had added to it, scavenging across the city. The collection was an ever-changing scene of preservation and dissolution. So many things saved only to be destroyed by time. Always with the water gurgling its way along the floor. Sometimes fish would get trapped, their fins brushing against pipes or grillwork and making a sound like quills over skulls.

She came out with a teapot and two cups on a tray. Set it down on the table between them. Poured him a cup.

"You sure you want this?" she asked. Skeptical.

"Yes." Took the tea gladly. His head still hurt. The tea tasted different. Better. Drove out the lingering taste of the memory bulb.

"I haven't looked at the lists," she said, sitting opposite him in a low wooden chair with a green blanket atop it.

"Didn't expect you to yet," Finch replied. "What about the symbol?"

"Now, *that* I did get around to," she said. "If only because it was easy."

"I've seen it, I've just never known what it meant."

"You're not alone. We know more about what the symbol is associated with than what it means."

A broken version was scrawled by the gray caps as a warning, Rathven told him. At the beginning of the city's history, when the gray caps sent back the eyes of Ambergris's founder, the whaling captain John Manzikert, on the old altar now drowned by the bay. Manzikert, who had slaughtered so many gray caps and driven them underground.

"It looked like this," she said, drawing it for him:

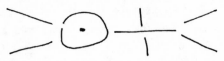

It had figured prominently in the recovered journals of the monk Samuel Tonsure, Manzikert's fellow traveler underground. Had appeared in unbroken forms at various times since, at crucial moments in history.

"Give me an example," Finch said.

"The Silence," Rathven said. "That symbol, according to the accounts I have, appeared everywhere, all across the city."

Finch gave her a sharp look. "I never heard that." But an intense feeling overtook him, telling him that he *had* known. Just forgotten.

Rathven shrugged. "I'm just telling you what's in the histories. Half the books down here mention the Silence, so it's not hard to track down."

The Silence. Seven hundred years ago, twenty-five thousand people had vanished from the city. The only survivors had been aboard the ruler's vast fleet of fishing ships, fifty miles downriver at the time. Many a horror story had been written about the Silence. It had shaped Ambergrisian life ever since. Especially attitudes toward the gray caps. Everyone had believed the gray caps had done it. When they'd Risen, some people said it was because of Manzikert's genocide against them, and because of something they hadn't finished during the Silence. Revenge, after waiting patiently for centuries. Of course, who could confirm that? The gray caps said less now that they were aboveground than when they'd been below.

"A broken symbol means a broken pact, some believe," Rathven said.

"I found it on the back of a scrap of paper used to scribble a note. Torn from a book. It probably isn't connected to the case." Wanted to move on for reasons he couldn't identify.

"Probably." In a tone that said, *Why waste my time asking me to research it then?*

Took the photo out of his pocket. "I want you to have this while you research the list."

Rathven took it. Winced.

"What?"

"He's dead, Finch."

"Of course he's dead. It's the murder case. I need to know who he is. It's very strange. I can't get my head around it. I need your help."

And there's no one in the station I trust to thoroughly check out that list.

"Are you sure you *want* to tell me more?" Rathven said.

People came to Rathven who the gray caps would count as enemies. Seeking information from her library. Information from *her.* Finch turned a blind eye. But someday somebody was going to test Rath's neutrality, her ability to put it all in a locked box.

A sound distracted him. A sudden retreat of water somewhere in the darkness behind him. He'd seen fish "walk" up out of that darkness. Watched them gasping as they tried to be something other than fish. Once, Finch had heard a splashing like oars, from deep in the tunnel. Had asked Rath, half serious, "Is there something you want to tell me?" She'd ignored him.

Finch put down his tea. Leaned back in the chair. *Do I trust Rathven more or less than Sintra?*

"A dead man and a dead gray cap. In the same apartment. The gray cap is just a torso with arms and a head. No blood. True, it's a gray cap. But maybe they weren't even murdered. Maybe murdered, but not in the apartment. I didn't get much out of the memory bulbs." *Not much I can share.*

It felt good to talk. Drew the tension out of him. Got rid of a strange echo in his head.

Rathven nodded, looking serious. "Didn't get much? So you got *something*." She waited, expectant.

"I haven't given you enough?" he asked with mock shock. "No. That's not all. They seem to have fallen from a great height. Maybe from the walls of a desert fortress. I have to file a report today."

Do I sound crazy?

"What other clues?" Rathven asked.

Suddenly irritable: "Jumbled memories. Including a conversation with the dead man. Must have imagined that."

"What?"

"Just what I said! Are you deaf?" *The man laughed again. Blindingly, unbelievably bright, a light like the sun shot through the window. The night sky torn apart by it.*

Realized he'd shouted at her. "Sorry."

Rath gave him a look he could not interpret. "You're not the same today," she said.

"Do you think I can do what I do and not be changed?" Spitting out the words. "Take memory bulbs? Work in the station?"

"I don't care," Rathven said. "If you change too much, I won't let you back in here." An intensity behind her gaze. Seeing someone or something other than Finch. *Couldn't even imagine . . .*

"Sorry," Finch said. The words took an effort. Gritted his teeth. Said it again. *Fuck!*

Rathven looked down. Took a sip of tea. Said, "So the dead man was talking to you?"

Fair enough. Move on. Realized that he needed to take more care with her. *She's not one of the detectives at the station.*

"It must have been," he said. "Imaginary, I mean."

"What else?"

"Nothing else. Just the piece of paper that symbol was on the back of. Some words. *Never Lost.* And then *bellum omnium contra omnes.* Ever heard those words before?"

"No," she said. Still, Finch sensed interest.

"You don't know what it means?"

"How would I know what it means if I've never heard it before?"

Couldn't bring himself to say "sorry" again, so he said nothing. "Maybe you're asking the wrong question. *Bellum omnium contra omnes.*" Rathven said it like an echo from another world. As if it had no meaning at all.

"How do you mean?"

"I *mean*, does it matter what it means? Why did he have words on a scrap of paper when he died? Pretend for a second that it's any word. Any word you know: city, cow, apartment, saucepan, book, paragraph."

"A code? A password?" Felt foolish for not seeing it before. "Might not mean anything at all."

She pointed at him. "And that's what makes it valuable."

"But why? Why have part of it in gibberish?"

She shrugged, gave him an impish look. "I'm not the detective."

I'm not a detective either.

"We should be detectives together." Relaxing into their time-worn call and response.

✦

"They're here and then they're there, and sometimes they don't know the difference, and if you let them, they'll keep making that the whole point of everything they're doing to the city. They'll break you down by not telling you what you already know, should already know, because that's the way they operate. Knowledge is the lack they seek in us, and when they find it, they turn the key, open a window, and it's all back to where we started."

Finch endured the rant from the madman outside the hotel, then made his way back to the station.

The suspect from yesterday wasn't in the cage. Instead, an old woman with light blue eyes staring from a face crisscrossed with wrinkles. As if from behind a fence of her own making. She could've been a thousand miles away for all the help Finch could give her. Ignored her as a casualty. Ignored Albin quietly feeding her questions like he was at a zoo. Continued on to his desk.

More of the same from the detectives around him. Indifference, absence, fear, boredom. Blakely and Gustat as always inseparable, whether in agreement or argument. Skinner out on a call, about to tell a man his missing wife was probably dead. Dapple drawing something on a piece of paper. Lost in another world.

Wyte had turned away from him for once and was hunched over as if Finch were trying to cheat from him on a test. He looked bulky, blotchy.

Finch leaned over. "Don't let your pencil burn up."

Wyte grimaced, said, "I'm busy, Finchy. Really. I am." And kept writing. It looked incomprehensible to Finch.

"Last will and testament?" Wished he hadn't said it.

"Shut up, Finchy," Wyte said. Still scribbling.

"I'm not pathologically reporting on evidence I haven't gathered yet," Finch said, "and they haven't come to cart me away."

"You're just lucky," Wyte mumbled.

A light green stain began to spread across the back of Wyte's blue shirt.

Finch cleared space on his desk. Brought the typewriter over. One of the best models Hoegbotton had ever made. A hulking twenty-pound monster that reminded Finch of just what Ambergris could accomplish back in the day. Hundreds of thousands had been shipped out to cities up and down the River Moth. "Combat-ready" went the slogan, and it wasn't a joke.

Looked at his notes. Didn't want to tell Heretic about everything he'd found. Not until he knew more about what the words meant. Discounted the symbol entirely. Even though it had burned its way into his head. *"Focus on what you can control. The rest is just distraction."* Something his father used to say.

What could he report that was *solid*? A few moments gazing into space. Then he started to type. Stopped when he got to a part that bothered him.

Both memories contained images of a desert fortress. Both memories contained images of falling.

From a great height? Maybe.

Finch took a sip of his coffee. He'd washed the cup beforehand to make sure no fungus, visible or invisible, had taken root. Sometimes the gray caps did strange things with the mugs during the night.

Both memories contained images from the HFZ.

I think. How would I know, never having been there?

From analyzing

"My memory of . . ."

both memories it seems certain that the gray cap

Fanaarcessitti? Fanarcesittee? Always typos in these reports.

that the fannarcessitti was in pursuit of the man. But I don't know
why.

*Then Sintra was kissing him and he was kissing her. Tongue curled against tongue.
The salt of her in his mouth. His hand between her muscular thighs. A hunger. A
need. Something that didn't exist outside the sanctuary of his apartment.*

Recognized the strength of that need, the danger of it, on the way to the station.
He exhaled sharply. *That way lies madness.*

More to the point, he shouldn't even have been on this case. Not many people
made the distinction between what detectives did and what Partials or gray caps
did. Never do police work anywhere near your own area. Never let the people
where you lived know your job. And yet, 239 Manzikert Avenue was only a mile
from the hotel. Why had Heretic put him in charge? Didn't trust Wyte anymore?
Or was there some other reason? Leaned forward in his chair. Had to make some
progress. *Just dive into it.*

The man's memories had more coherence than the fannarcessitti's
memories. I could not tell if this was because the fanarcesitti's
mind had been more confused and disjointed at the time of death or
because, as a human, I could more easily read the man's memories.

Nothing during the experience brought me any closer to knowing the
identity of the man.

I wish the memory bulbs had been more useful.

But he had seen *one* person he recognized. He leaned back and thought about
Ethan Bliss. What he knew. What he didn't know.

First, the impersonal. Bliss had fought for Frankwrithe & Lewden during the War of the Houses. Behind the scenes. No one seemed to know for sure what he did for F&L. Secret ops? Bliss had joined the political wing. Risen quickly to become F&L's number one man in Ambergris. Had been instrumental in forging the alliance between the F&L and the Lady in Blue. Then, right before the gray caps took over, he dropped out of sight. Probably returned to his native Morrow, only to reappear a couple of years ago. Because of how Morrow had suffered from the gray caps having cut off the flow of water? Ships suddenly resting on a dry riverbed. Trade disrupted. Drinking water scarce.

This new Bliss had reverted to spying. Had connections to the Spit. But hadn't made common cause with the rebels, according to Finch's informants.

Although, when you paid informants in food and clothing, how valuable could your information be? More valuable? Less?

All of this made Bliss of special interest to any detective who hated foreigners messing around in Ambergris business. Finch could've used Bliss as a snitch, perhaps, but hadn't. He was wary of who Bliss might be working for now. If he worked for anyone other than himself.

Second, the personal. Bliss had been at his father's house a couple of times when Finch was maybe twelve, thirteen. He could recall looking through the kitchen window to see Bliss and his father in the garden. The smaller man compact, unmoving. His father unruly, animated, throwing his arms about, pointing at Bliss and demanding something. And yet, seeing the two figures there like that, Bliss had seemed in his silence and self-possession to be the one in charge.

Thought, too, that Bliss might've been in one of the photographs he'd burned before becoming Finch. But Bliss was one of many visitors. During the few peaceful years, there had been lots of parties at their house, with people from both sides.

Finch had seen Bliss give speeches, too. One, in front of the Voss Bender Memorial Opera House, to a crowd of almost ten thousand. He'd looked striking in an evening coat and tails. A chestful of honorary medals that made you notice the glitter more than the man. Urging *cooperation* and *common cause* in that silky voice when, just a year or two before, behind the scenes, he'd caused House Hoegbotton so much grief. Bombings. House-to-house battles to clear insurgents. Fighting in narrow streets where tanks were no help, but where F&L fungal bullets worked just fine.

Third, whatever the gray caps knew about Bliss, if they knew about Bliss. Finch couldn't remember pulling the file on him. He'd have to put in a request. Which he hated doing. Couldn't know what Heretic would "request" in return.

Took out the form anyway. Wrote in what he needed. Under "subject," he filled in Ethan Bliss's name and a few others. For cover. If Finch put in his report that he'd seen Bliss in the dead man's memories, Bliss was as good as dead. Or would want to be. And Finch couldn't be sure what it all meant until he questioned Bliss. Which wouldn't happen if Heretic got hold of him first.

Why the hell was Ethan Bliss in the memories of the dead man? Typed:

```
Perhaps a fannarcesitti would be more useful in reading the man's
memories?
```

What would a gray cap see? Baiting Heretic gave Finch a grim satisfaction. Gray caps hated eating human memories. Almost as if there were a taste, a smell, that repulsed them. Finch couldn't recall Heretic ever eating one. Could human memories harm a gray cap?

```
It is not entirely clear that these deaths are murders, rather than
accidental. The two may have died somewhere else and been brought
to the apartment. Residents of the apartment building have no
additional information. Rumors that two people lived in apartment
525 cannot be confirmed.
```

Just covering himself in case whatever game the Partial was playing went south. Yet, stubbornly, couldn't bring himself to mention the scrap of paper. Despite the fact the Partial knew about it. Had the Partial told Heretic? Maybe. Maybe not.

Finch pushed his chair away from the typewriter, hands behind his head. The report made no sense. Composed of smoke and shadows. Doubted Heretic would find it convincing. What did it mean that the dead man had *spoken* to him? Another thing he hadn't put in the report. Some instinct had warned him against it.

Ripped the paper out of the typewriter carriage. A mechanical tearing sound loud enough to make all the other detectives turn toward him in one motion that seemed choreographed.

What the hell are you looking at?

Realized he'd said it out loud.

Jammed his report into a pod, along with the request for files. Shoved that down the memory hole gullet. *Choke on it.*

A minute later: a sound coming from the damn thing. *Incoming.* The pod. The tendrils. Hammer. Egg. Extraction. A message from Heretic.

STAY LATE TONIGHT TO MEET

"Fuck," Finch said.

"Is it bad?" Wyte asked.

"Why do you always ask that question?"

"Why is the answer always yes."

"Then you shouldn't ask it."

Staying late always unnerved him.

Have to get out of here.

"Come on," he said to Wyte. It would do Wyte some good, too. "We're going to go talk to Ethan Bliss."

If they could find him.

On a table near the desk in his apartment, Finch has a map of Ambergris from before the Rising. It covers the whole table, renders the city in perfect detail. He has no idea what it's made of. Never tears. Never wrinkles. His father had given it to him when he was thirteen. "You'll never need another." Made a mark on it with a green pen every time he sent his son on an errand to a new location. Insisted Finch take the map with him everywhere. Even though it was heavy. Even if Finch had been to a place before. "The streets are shifty. I want to make sure you don't get lost."

The errands? Collect letters. Drop off packages. Say a single word or phrase. *"Shipping lanes." "The weather is too cold for this time of year." "Mr. Green says you are a lucky man."* Never to the same people. Old, young, male, female, each one with secrets behind their eyes. He played it like a game. Delighted in the mystery of not really knowing the rules. Then he'd return, a human homing pigeon, to their house.

"Official business," his father said. He held an important position for H&S because he was a war hero. Anyone could tell that from all the photographs of him fighting against the Kalif, and from the people who came over to visit. Some of them wearing funny hats and uniforms.

But by the time Finch was seventeen, his father had stopped sending him on these errands. He'd felt discarded. Hadn't understood then that his father had turned to others when Finch began to ask questions. When he began to have a sense of the secrecy behind his missions. *A tallish, dark-haired, serious boy with few close friends his age, taught at home by his father.* Those journeys across the city had meant a lot to him.

But he'd kept the map, used it for his new job, which his father had gotten for him. Courier for Hoegbotton business interests. Running invoices and shipping inventories between the main offices and the warehouses at the docks. Sometimes, if the conflict heated up, if F&L cut off certain roads, he had to find alternate routes.

Trade "has to keep on an even keel, no matter what," his boss Wyte liked to say. Wyte, seven years his senior, with an office in the brick building on Albumuth they'd both work at after the Rising. Even then Wyte had seemed too large for the world around him. Desk too small. Him too clumsy. But to Finch he'd been the height of authority.

The map shows that brick building, with a green mark by it. It also has detailed views of the Bureaucratic Quarter, the Religious Quarter, and what had unofficially been known as the Merchant Quarter before the wars. Albumuth Boulevard, the great snake wending its way through almost every part of the city. The valley that had been the home of so many citizens. The docks. The swampland to the north.

A view of Ambergris that had remained essentially unchanged for centuries. Had survived early incursions by the Kalif, the cavalry charges of Morrow back when it had a king instead of the F&L. Had even survived the Silence.

But could not survive the Rising.

The gray caps have a kind of see-through paper. A slight greenish tint, barely noticeable. It feels light as a leaf, but is very strong. Finch has stolen two sheets of it, taped them together to form an overlay to his old map. On this overlay he charts the changes he has observed, using a dark pencil that he can erase at will.

In the evenings, when too restless to sleep but too tired to read, Finch will turn on the light in the study. Or use a lantern if the electricity is out. Review the overlay. Search for what he knows has been made different again. Then render a section bare with handkerchief and water. Build it up again, redraw it all. A change in the lip of the bay. Or in the HFZ. A row of houses that has burned down. A drug mushroom that erupted from the pavement. A new gray cap house or cathedral.

Lately, he has been charting the retreat of the water. Right after the Rising, the canals from the bay into Ambergris had been like the fat fingers of a grasping hand. Now they are withered, the "thumb" almost dry, the others shriveling. Like his father's blue-veined hands in the clinic near the end. A disease he'd picked up early in life, fighting the Kalif. It got into his lungs first, and spread. No cure except death.

Remapping takes the kind of concentration that empties out the mind. In the old house, before they became vagabonds together, his father had created something similar in his locked study. Much bigger, with even more detail, laid out across a huge table fit for a banquet. Color-coded to show Hoegbotton and Frankwrithe territories within the city. Green and red. Along with blue for those narrow reefs of neutrality. Over time, his father would chart weapons depots on that map. Troop concentrations. Hidden storehouses. Usually Hoegbotton but some Frankwrithe positions, too. His father's overlay was actually a black sheet that perfectly hid the map. And a tablecloth over top of that.

How many guests invited into that place had been served drinks on that table, never realizing what was hidden beneath?

At seventeen, mad at his father for no longer using him as a courier, Finch had stolen the key. Started sneaking into the study when his father was out. Found the map. He used to stand there, it naked before him, and memorize the progress of the war in his head. It looked like lively abstract art. Symbols in search of context.

Finch doesn't draw directly on the old map because he doesn't want to forget the past. Hopes that one day that lost world will return. The overlay is only temporary, he keeps telling himself. Even as the changes become more and more permanent.

His map is a crude facsimile of the original. He has only the dark pencil to record the changes. Nor can his map chart the changes in the people around him. Or tell him what to do next.

One day, his father surprised him in the study. He stood at the door with a guarded look on his face. Finch stared back, frozen. There seemed to be nothing he could say. His father walked up. Put the black sheet over the map. Replaced the tablecloth. Muttered, "This didn't happen." Took the key from him. Escorted him out.

They never talked about it again. But in that moment of shock, when Finch heard the door open, it burned his father's map into his head. Every detail. Every nuance. And even now, looking at his own map, the overlay, he sees it. Sees that room.

Knows every inch of Ambergris. Even the parts he hasn't yet visited. Even the parts still changing.

3

Tracking down Bliss took three tries. Wyte had an address for a townhouse Bliss sometimes used for meetings, in an old Hoegbotton stronghold southeast of Albumuth. Finch could still see the slashes of faded paint on the pavement, left by groups of Irregulars. Who knew how old the marks were? A code that told a secret history of the city. *Gray cap passed by here Tuesday . . . Food and ammo in the second house on the left . . . Stay clear of this intersection after dark.*

They found the house on a street that had once been part of a wealthy district. Trees lined the sidewalk, but not a leaf on them. Gravel where grass had been. Silence all around. The houses to either side derelict husks. A burned corpse with no arms right on the steps. Which should've told them Bliss wasn't there. Flies had settled on the torn-up face like a congregation. A slender whiteness had begun to push up through the black. Stalks of fruiting bodies. Rising. In another twenty hours, nothing would be left.

"Nothing inside," Finch said, coming back out.

"Let's visit Stanton," Wyte said.

Stanton, one of Wyte's druggie snitches, lived a few blocks down. Behind Stanton, Finch saw a tarp draped over a soot-gray alley mouth. A bundle of his possessions to one side. A crumbling brick he used to protect himself at night. Before the Rising, Stanton had been a banker. Or, at least, that's what he'd told Wyte. Probably an addict then, too.

Wyte always kept a few extra purple mushrooms in his overcoat pockets. Stanton, in a kind of makeshift robe, clung to Wyte like *he* was the drug. Wyte a plank of wood in the River Moth and Stanton trying to stop from drowning. Except all he ever did was drown.

"Where'd Bliss go?" Wyte asked Stanton.

The thirty-year-old Stanton lifted his gaunt, balding head. Red-eyed, wrinkled face. "Down by the abandoned train station. Four streets over. Corner of Sporn and Trillian. He was just there yesterday."

Wyte put three purple mushrooms in Stanton's hand. Stanton received them like they were worth more than one day's relief. The huge red mushrooms that dispensed the drugs stuck to a strict schedule. Monday and Friday. Stanton had already gone through what he'd gathered the day before. Finch didn't think he'd last another month.

When they left Stanton, he was trembling under his pathetic shelter. Eyes wide open and dilated. Gone someplace better. Someplace temporary.

The train station was empty. But way in the back, under the shadowed arches populated by pigeons and bats, they found a gambling pit. Almost a grotto, for all the fungus surrounding it. Fuzzy clumps of muted gold and green hid the entrance. Cockfighting. Card games. Betting black market goods.

Not much of a conversation. Wyte stuck his gun up against the lookout's cheek. Convinced her it would be better just to lead them in. The hardened men and women they surprised, lantern-lit and reaching for knives or guns, thought better of it, too. But they had a hard time restraining the roosters. One fire-red, the other a muted orange. Razor talons moving like pistons.

A heavily muscled man in his twenties who had done some piecework for Bliss gave him up, quick. Called Bliss a slang word for foreign. Even though the muscled man looked foreign himself. Seemed to dare any of the others to argue with him. They didn't.

Wyte and Finch receded into the gloom. Shoved the lookout inside. Barricaded the door from the outside with a couple of heavy rusted barrels. Hoped there wasn't a second entrance. But knew there always was. Got the hell out before anyone could start thinking about an ambush.

"Fuck, but I hate this job!" Wyte exclaimed, as their boots kicked up water pooling between rows of bolted-down chairs alongside the abandoned track.

Said he hated it, but looked a lot happier than at the station.

The address turned out to be a modest-looking two-story apartment building west of the Religious Quarter. Shoved up against more of the same, with the billowing dome of the northernmost camp beyond.

Finch recognized it as a former Frankwrithe & Lewden neighborhood. It had retained some sense of order. Of discipline. A few men with red armbands stood on the sidewalk like guards. While people traded goods.

Finch was nervous. Always worried when they went to F&L places that someone would tag him as an ex-Hoegbotton Irregular. Maybe want to put a bullet through his brain. He would've liked to have told the detectives in this sector what they were doing, but the gray caps frowned on cooperation. They liked to keep the stations as separate as possible. Make themselves the conduit.

It began to drizzle. Had been damp and warm all day. A mist gathered around Finch. Moistened his hair, his face. Green sweat had darkened the armpits of Wyte's shirt and now leaked through his overcoat.

Would Wyte hold up? Truff, please let him hold up.

Inside. Down the hall. Gun drawn. Leaking.

Wyte always went first now. He'd accepted that role voluntarily. It only made sense.

At the green-gold-purple splotched door of Bliss's apartment on the first floor, Wyte signaled his intent. The door didn't look that strong. Wyte would batter it down. Finch would storm through behind him.

A strange mewling whine came from inside. Just strange enough to make Finch shiver.

Finch mimed, *Wait.*

Took out his handkerchief, turned the knob.

The door opened.

Wyte was through before Finch could stop him, yelling, "Detectives! Hands up! Weapons down!"

Finch followed. Heart like a hammer. Gun squirting out a little between his hands in his hard double grip.

The first four rooms: empty, trashed. Someone had destroyed or ransacked everything. Tables, couches overturned. Books shredded. Torn pages everywhere. A smell of shit or rot or both. And blood. Lots of blood. Sprayed. Pooling. But no bodies. From the looks of the furniture, the arrangement had always been meant to be temporary. Or at least, it was now.

In the back bedroom they found the source of the mewling.

"Oh fuck," said Finch.

"Is that him?" Wyte asked.

"Yes."

Ethan Bliss had been nailed alive against the far wall, above a bed. His face was crusted with blood. White shirt red. Blood welling from his punctured extremities. His hands and feet still twitching as he tried to pull free of the green nails that looked like hard mushrooms. Whimpering and looking down at them through eyes crusted by something purple and brittle.

The eyes through the crust registered Finch, Wyte. A bright red mushroom had been rammed into his mouth. But he'd managed to get most of it out.

In a muffled roar: "Don't just stand there like a couple of fucking idiots. Get me down!"

Bliss began to weep.

Finch held Bliss while Wyte worked at the hands and feet. *Too close.* Sweat. Funk. Some underlying sweetness that was worse. For a sixty-year-old man, Bliss was wiry and muscular. Odd. To be here with someone who had been so well-known. Nailed to a wall. Blood all over the place. Would've been a scandal before the Rising. Now it was just another day on the job.

It took ten minutes to get him down. They tried to wipe the crust from his eyes. Managed to smear his face with green residue from his wounds. Looked like pollen dusted over the blood.

Wyte muttered, "Should we take him back to the station?"

Finch shook his head. "No. Let's do it here."

They took him to the couch in the living room. Pulled the couch upright. Wyte pushed the glass off it using his sleeve. Finch found towels in the kitchen, brought them back and offered them to Bliss.

Bliss angrily waved Finch off.

"No, not yet," he said.

"For Truff's sake, aren't you glad to be alive?" Wyte said.

Finch gave Wyte a hard look. "He's probably in shock."

"Shock's overrated," Bliss said. "Hand me that red mushroom. The one they stuffed in my mouth."

It had fallen onto the bed. Finch went back and got it. Wondering if Bliss would recognize him. Probably not. Finch had changed his appearance completely, and Bliss had last seen him about twenty years ago.

Bliss smeared the remains of the fungus, soft cheese consistency, all over his hands and feet. Glistening. Already he had stopped bleeding.

"Now the towels," he said, taking them from Finch. He glared at Wyte, then Finch. "Who are you anyway? How did you find me? What do you want?" Even in anger, he had a youthful face. One of those faces that got more rigid as it aged.

But you could still see the boyish features under the wrinkles. Under the neatly trimmed mustache.

Finch stood in front of Bliss. Wyte to the side, tapping his foot. Restless. Disturbed by something.

"I'm Finch. This is Wyte." Finch showed Bliss his badge. "You don't look happy. Should we put you back up there?"

"I wasn't dying," Bliss snapped. "Someone would have come along." Emphasis on *someone* made Finch think Bliss knew exactly who.

Bliss at the old desert fortress, turning slowly at his approach. A sound of metal locking into place. A kind of mirror. An eye. Then a circle of stone, a door, covered with gray cap symbols.

"Who did this, Bliss?" Wyte asked, kicking a broken chair out of the way. "Whose blood is all over the floor? Who'd you piss off?"

Bliss appeared not to hear this question. He stared instead at Finch. Measuring him. Like a light had clicked on behind his eyes. That weathered face had hardened remarkably, even as it managed a good imitation of a smile. Said to Finch, "You look familiar to me, Detective. Do I know you? You obviously know me."

Wyte barged in, to Finch's relief: "Shut up. We're asking the questions."

Bliss registered Wyte as if for the first time. Said in a smooth voice that drove in the barb. "Why don't you find who did *that* to you, instead of wasting your time with me?"

"I said, shut up!" Wyte slapped Bliss across the cheek. Hard.

Finch had never seen Wyte hit a suspect who hadn't tried to hit him first.

Bliss took it quietly. Cursed. Put a hand to the mark. Like it had happened before. Or like pain was just an inconvenience to him. "What do you *think* happened, *Detective*? They surprised us, lit us up, and didn't leave much behind. Ten of my best men."

Finch, supporting Wyte: "Answer the question, Bliss. *Who* did this to you?"

An exasperated sigh that seemed to signal a decision.

"A new man, from the Spit. He asked a lot of questions about gray caps. About the towers."

"What's his name?"

"He kept telling it to me over and over so I wouldn't forget. Even while they butchered my men. *Stark.*"

"Just Stark? What's his full name?"

Wyte broke in. "I know about Stark. He's only been here eight weeks. He's from

Stockton. New blood. He's been liquidating the opposition the past few weeks." Wyte was the station's Stockton expert. Ran a few snitches in that organization.

"And we've been *letting* him?"

Wyte shrugged. "Makes our job easier, doesn't it?"

Finch gave him a look that said *we'll talk more about this later*. Found it odd that Wyte knew something he didn't.

He turned to Bliss. "Why the hell did he leave you alive?"

Bliss shrugged. "Maybe he wanted to send a message."

I don't believe you.

"What kind of message? To who?" Wyte asked.

Silence.

"Take a guess about what he wanted, Bliss," Finch said.

"Part of what he wanted to do was to hurt me. He enjoyed that a little too much. I think he would have done it even if he hadn't wanted information."

"Anyone with him?"

"Just his god-awful muscle. His second-in-command goes by the name of Bosun, like on a ship. He's built like a kind of wiry circus strongman with a bullet-bald head. Once you see him, you recognize him forever. He's the one who lifted me to the wall with one hand and drove the nails in with the other while Stark watched. All this *before* they asked me any questions."

"What questions, Bliss?" Wyte asked.

No response.

Finch showed Bliss the photograph of the dead man. "Do you know him?"

Bliss stiffened, glanced up at Finch. "Again, it would be nice to know *why* you're here?"

"Look at the photo, Bliss." Bliss looked.

"This man is dead."

"Yes, but do you know him?" Finch asked again.

Bliss shook his head. "I've never seen him before."

Lying? Or truly confused?

"What about these words?" Finch took out a piece of paper on which he'd written *bellum omnium contra omnes*.

Saw the surprise on Bliss's face. Saw that surprise change to something vaguely cat-like and unreadable. Knew whatever Bliss told him would be truth diseased with lie.

"Stark asked about something similar," Bliss said, gaze distant. "But I wouldn't know anything about that."

Wyte made an exasperated sound. "Let's finish this at the station. Interrogate him there." To Bliss: "If you cooperate, maybe it won't come down to a bullet and a memory bulb."

Most men would've gone a little pale. Bliss just sat there staring daggers at them. A defiant little man who had once run half the city.

Finch pushed. "Maybe you're right, Wyte. I'd like to know what deal you made with Stark for your life. You don't mind a trip to the station, do you, Bliss? You've got nothing to hide, right?"

Bliss erupted up off the couch like a man twice his size, flung the lamp at Wyte, knocking his gun away. Completed the motion by slamming Finch on the side of the head with surprising strength. Dazed, Finch fell over a low table, banging his knees. Bliss bolted for the kitchen while Wyte was still scrambling for his gun.

"Fuck! Finch, stop him!"

Finch got up off the floor, drew his gun, stumbled toward the kitchen. Wyte was two steps behind.

Beyond the kitchen: a flight of stairs leading down. Finch could hear running footsteps but couldn't see Bliss. Had no choice but to charge down the stairs, only to be greeted by another hallway. Then a quick, tight corner. Wyte had caught up, and they barreled around like a couple of slapstick comedians, sliding into each other.

Caught a glimpse of Bliss's white shirt through darkness.

"Bliss! I'll shoot! Don't think I won't!" Could Bliss even hear him?

He lost Bliss in the shadows again, but got off a round or two. Hit nothing but wall. Cursing himself for not having checked the rest of the apartment. Collided with Wyte taking a second corner. Wyte was already breathing hard.

They collected themselves. Opened the door that greeted them. Another long corridor, with a door at the end.

"Fuck! How big is this place?"

They sidled up to the door. Finch got down low on his haunches, put his hand on the knob. Now he was breathing hard, but not because he was winded.

"Cover me high," he said, glancing up at Wyte. Blood singing in his ears, fingers a little numb.

Wyte nodded, face impossibly long and thick from that angle, chin jutting, expression priest-solemn. Finch turned the knob and pushed the door open. Slowly rose, knees already aching.

"Goddamn it."

An empty room ten feet square, the walls made of cinder blocks painted white. A single bulb for light. No windows. No other door.

They kept circling it with guns drawn, like Bliss would appear out of nowhere. *Never lost.*

Except now he was.

4

Where had Bliss gone? The question haunted Finch as they left the apartment. Didn't know if anyone had heard the shots. Or if Bliss still had people who might be watching. "Secret door?" Wyte had suggested, almost as if it didn't bother him. But they'd found nothing. They'd have had to tear the place apart. Brick by brick. Didn't have the tools or time for that.

They passed addicts with the familiar purple stains across their skin. Men in the ill-fitting uniforms of janitors for the camps. Somebody pissing in an alley. Faded posters on a long crumbling wall, showing pictures of members of the short-lived puppet government. Another blood-red mushroom looming over them big as a tree. Every week there seemed to be more of them. Next to it, a blossoming flower of a building atop the squashed remains of the local grocery store. Soft humming sounds came from an interior obscured by fleshy window flaps.

Where had Bliss gone—and how was he involved?

Finch replayed that moment over and over. Bliss running for the kitchen. Bliss in his memory bulb dream. Trying to reconcile those versions with the Bliss he remembered from before the Rising. The way Bliss's gaze couldn't settle on one thing. As if his mind worked faster now. A growing sense that this new Bliss hadn't been stripped of prestige and security but had *traded* it for something else.

Wyte seemed agitated, and Finch thought he knew why. So he said, "It's my fault. We should've taken him in from the beginning, like you suggested. I didn't need to question him first. And I forgot to check out the rest of the apartment."

Wyte's neck had an orange stain on it. Fingernails that had turned black. A smell like a distant sewer drain. But he'd been worse.

"I hit him, and I spooked him," Wyte said. "I'm as much to blame as you. Maybe more. But that's not the point, Finchy."

Here it comes.

Wyte stopped walking, faced him. Finch had his back to a crumbling wall veined through with fungus so blue it looked black. An overlay of scattered bullet holes. Across the street, a laughing pack of Partials shoved a couple of prisoners ahead of them. A middle-aged bearded man with a bandage across his forehead and angry rips in a shirt discolored pink. A woman who could have been the man's wife, her long black hair being used as a leash by one of the Partials. Just a jaunt around the block before getting down to business.

"Look, Finch," Wyte said. "I'm your partner. And you keep *keeping* things from me. I hadn't even seen the photo of the dead man until you showed it to Bliss. And where's the list Heretic gave you?"

Wyte will never adjust. It made Finch sick deep in his stomach.

Finch pulled Wyte back to the wall with him. The Partials had moved on ahead, oblivious to anything but their prisoners, but he didn't want to take any chances. In a whisper: "Listen to me. I'm just trying to protect you."

Wyte stared at him for so long that Finch had to look at the ancient dislodged stones of the sidewalk. A sudden hunger for a past when Wyte hadn't been this way. A feeling so strong he felt water in his eyes.

Each word meant to wound, Wyte said: "I don't need protecting, like I've told you. Back in the day, *I* protected *you*." Then self-importantly, when Finch said nothing: "I'm going to work for the rebels soon. I know someone who knows someone."

This shit again. Once every few weeks.

Something snapped in Finch. Felt it in his head like the sudden eruption of a migraine.

He shoved Wyte up against the wall. Didn't care who was watching. Felt the air go out of the older man's lungs. Those eyes scared by what they saw in Finch. Skin clammy. Some of Wyte's shirt wasn't really a shirt.

Finch said as calmly as he could: "You are not going to be a fucking spy for the rebels. You are not going to be a fucking spy for the rebels. Ever. *Do you understand?*"

"Get the fuck off of me!" Wyte hissed. Twisting in Finch's grip. Head angled toward the sky. Shoulders arched back like he was trying to take off his coat but had gotten his arm stuck.

"You're not. And do you know why not? Because you've been colonized. And it's gone too far. *And they'll never take you.*" *Never take you back. Never want you now. Too late.* "And if they did, you'd probably be spying on them. For the gray caps. Without even knowing it. Which is why you can't." *And you'd be leaving me with a station full of detectives who hate me because I didn't abandon you.*

He released Wyte, pushing off him. Creating space between them in case it turned into a fight.

But Wyte stayed up against the wall. What was the look on his face? Didn't matter. It was the way he stood. Finch had seen the same tired stoop in workers from the camps. Seen it at times in Rath.

Continued on now that it made no difference: "The closest you'll get to working for anyone is wringing intel out of that ragged bunch of Stockton contacts you call a network." Trailed off.

Wyte's self-disdain when he turned to Finch made him look angry or righteous. A darkness there that might have been spores coming up through his skin.

"Better than doing nothing, like you."

"I don't do nothing. I do what I *can*. There's a difference." Hands clenched into fists. Face contorted. Close to being out of control. *What if he's right?*

Stood there while Wyte opened his mouth to say something.

But Wyte didn't say anything, just let out his breath with a shudder. Finch watched warily as Wyte reached into his overcoat pocket with a hand that trembled slightly and took out a flask made of battered silver and tin, the once-proud H&S insignia marred by fire burns.

Finch had given it to Wyte on his birthday ten years ago. Emily hadn't liked it. Thought her husband drank too much anyway. Didn't need to "make it into a ritual" as she put it. But that didn't stop her from joining them when they'd stood on the step outside of the house to share a smoke and whatever Wyte had put in the flask. Remembered its quick glint as it picked up the sun or a streetlight.

"It's got good brandy in it, Finchy," Wyte said. "The last bit I've been hoarding."

"You're not going to hit me?"

"What for, Finchy? What'd be the point?"

Finch grimaced. Managed to transform it into a thin smile. "Some brandy might be a good idea." He patted Wyte's ruffled overcoat back into place. "I'm sorry, Wyte. I'm sorry."

And he meant it. Turned away. Disgusted with himself. Who had the bigger burden? The one who had to watch the other person endure or the one who endured?

Wearily, Wyte said: "How could you know? What it's like living with something else inside me. While on the outside I keep changing."

Worse than a dead man talking to me?

Finch didn't want to think about it. Took the flask. Downed half of it in a gulp. Felt the liquid rage through his capillaries. Like a forest fire that left ice behind it. He handed the flask back. "Good stuff." They started walking again.

Wyte laughed. "Still can't really hold it, can you? Any more than you could when you were working for me."

Slapped Finch on the back hard enough to make him stagger.

Fair enough.

✻

Wyte. The story.

He'd gone to investigate a death about a year ago. By himself. No one else in the station. The call sounded simple. A man found dead beneath a tree, beginning to smell. Could someone take a look? Most days, not worth bothering with. But it was a slow morning, and Wyte took the job seriously. The woman seemed upset, like it was personal.

The body was down near the bay. Beside a cracked stone sign that used to welcome visitors to Ambergris. *Holy city, majestic, banish your fears.* No one was around. Not the woman who had called it in. No one.

The man lay on his back. Connected to the "tree," which was a huge mushroom. Connected by tendrils. The smell, vile. The man's eyes open and flickering.

Wyte should have left. Wyte should have known better. But maybe Wyte was bored. Or wanted a change. Or just didn't care. He hadn't seen his kids since they'd been sent out of the city. He'd been fighting with his wife a lot.

He leaned over the body. Maybe he thought he saw something floating in those eyes. Something moving. Maybe movement meant life to him.

"Who knows? Just know that it's a dumb move."

A *dumb move.* That's how the detectives would say it during the retell. At their little refuge, not far from the station. Blakely had discovered the place. In front of what used to be the old Bureaucratic Quarter. Looks like a guard post. Nondescript. Gray stone. Surrounded by a thicket of half walls, rubble hills, and stunted trees. With a moat that's really just a pond that collects rainwater. From the inside, it's clear the structure is the top of a bell tower pulled down and submerged when the gray caps Rose.

Always half out of their minds with whiskey or homemade wine, or whatever. When they told the story. *A dumb move.* Like they were experts.

"Point is," Albin would say, because Albin usually told the story, "he leaned over, and the man's head exploded into spores. And those spores got into Wyte's head."

White spores for Wyte. Through the nose. Through any exposed cuts. Through the ears. Through the eyes.

Although he fought it. Twisted furiously. Jumped up and down. Cursed like the end of the world. So at least he didn't just stand there and let it happen.

"But by that time, it was too late. A few minutes later and he's just somebody's puppet."

Wyte became someone else. The "dead" man. Someone who didn't understand what had happened to him. Wyte ran down the street. Taken over. Screaming.

"Screaming a name over and over. 'Otto! I'm Otto!' because that was the dead man's name. Wyte thought he was Otto."

Or most of him did. Wyte, deep inside, still knew who he was, and that was worse.

Sometimes, out of a casual cruelty, a kind of boredom, one of the other detectives, usually Blakely, will call Wyte "Otto." Until Finch makes him stop.

"Well, they found him a day later. Once they figured out who the dead body was. Cowering in a closet. Saying 'Otto' over and over again."

In the dead man's apartment.

"A caution to us all."

Then they would clink glasses and bottles, congratulating themselves on being alive.

Truth was, they told the story less to humiliate Wyte than to keep reminding themselves not to take any chances. *Ambergris Rules.* No dumb moves.

Wyte got Otto out of his head. Eventually. Most of Otto. But not the fungus. That became worse. The gray caps couldn't or wouldn't help. Maybe they saw it as some kind of perverse improvement.

No one had ever found out who had lured Wyte there. Or why.

Finch knew they never would.

They split up. Wyte headed back to the station. Finch decided to return to the apartment on Manzikert. He'd have more than his fill of the station later.

"Do I mention Bliss?"

"If it comes up, no. His file's already being pulled. That's enough for now."

"He made us look like fools."

"We made ourselves look like fools."

Black trees. Odd fruit. Pissed-off cat. Hallways that still squeaked from wax. The stairwell still collected darkness. But a silence had crept in, too. An emptiness that hadn't been there before. No sounds of a mother and child. No smells of cooking.

On a hunch, Finch stopped at the fourth floor again. Knocked on the door of the man who had dressed up for Finch's mild interrogation. Held his badge up to the peephole.

The door creaked open. A Partial stood there. Stockier than the one who had cataloged the crime scene. His face even paler. Red teeth. As if he'd been eating raw meat sloppily. Dressed in black dyed leather, but wore beige boots. Like he'd been caught trying on someone else's clothes. In the belt around his gut, two holstered guns and a hammer, of all things.

Finch held the badge in front of him.

"I'm the detective on the case in apartment 525," he said. "Where's the old man who lives here?"

The Partial considered him for a moment. The glittering black eye was flickering madly. But the rest of him was like a chilled tortoise. Arms at his sides. Almost paralyzed.

"Gone," he said slowly. Making the syllable linger.

"Gone where?" Finch asked.

"Gone somewhere else," the Partial said with an effort.

Like you, my friend. Wondered if the flickering eye meant his attention was elsewhere. *Reviewing not recording.*

A new thought, horrifying him. "Are they *all* gone?"

The eye stopped flickering. Blinked twice. In a more normal voice the Partial said, "The building has been cleared."

Cleared how? Escorted out and rehoused? Sent to the camps? Liquidated?

But he didn't ask, just nodded. Smiled. Stepped back.

The Partial parroted the nod and receded from him into darkness. Shut the door.

Finch stood there a moment. This place was now a Partial stronghold. *No witnesses.*

He took the stairs to the fifth floor in leaps. As if running fast might prevent the crime that had brought him here. Bring back the old man in the too-tight suit.

The door. The gray cap symbol, glistening and obscene. The hallway. The bedroom, empty. The living room; no sign of the Partial.

The bodies.

Correction. Body.

The gray cap's body had disappeared.

Finch stood there a moment, brought up short. Trying to process that sudden . . . *lack*. Then realized: Heretic must have removed the body. If not, they'd send Finch to the camps. *Scapegoat*. Returning: the chill that had come over him talking to the red-toothed Partial. It hit him as it hadn't before. This case was a threat to his life. To the little security he had. His apartment. His relationship with Sintra.

But the man was still there, under a blanket someone had thrown over him. *The dead man sat in the chair next to him, smiling.* In the same position. The blue of the preservatives still stippling his features. *The man laughed again. Blindingly, unbelievably bright, a light like the sun shot through the window. The night sky torn apart by it.*

Finch went over and pulled the blanket back from the man's face. Sat on the couch, looking at the body. He would have to meet with Heretic soon. The thought unnerved him. Wished now he'd asked Wyte for the whole flask. Wished he could just go home. Find Sintra waiting for him.

"You know what those nonsense words mean," Finch said to the man. "You know why it's important."

Peaceful. The man looked peaceful, to be so dead. How perfectly preserved in the light from the open window. Ignoring how that light changed as it was interrogated by the space between the twinned towers in the distance.

Finch got down on his knees. Searched the body again. Not the careful search of yesterday. *Fuck the spore cameras. Fuck the Partial.*

Roughly, he rolled the body over and went through the pockets. As if he'd killed the man himself.

There must be something else.

But, no, there wasn't. Just lint in one pocket. A few bits of sand and gravel, maybe a grain of rice?, in the other.

He began to rip up the fabric. It tore easier than he would've thought. Hurting his hands. Red lines on his palms. Aching wrists. Still nothing. No hidden pockets. He forced himself to stop tearing.

The upturned corners of the man's lips seemed to say, "You'll never solve me."
I'm not a detective.

But he would be judged as a detective. Convicted as a detective.

A desert fortress. The HFZ. A phrase. *Never lost.* Falling from a great height. A gray cap even the gray caps couldn't identify. An operative from Stockton who was on the same trail. Another operative, probably from Morrow, attacked by Stockton spies and appearing in a dead man's memories. Now disappeared.

Stark. Bosun. Bliss.

It would drive him mad, he realized. If he let it.

I need a better gun.

Looked at his watch.

5:20.

Time to leave.

Let the horror show begin.

5

Back at the station.

5:50.

No sign of Wyte. The other detectives had left, too, except for Gustat, who was frantically packing up his things. Finch looked at the smaller man with a kind of scorn. Gustat ignored him in his haste. Strange horselike footfalls across the carpet. The croaking bang of the door behind him.

Then it was just Finch.

Soon the curtains at the back of the room would part. Night would truly begin.

Wyte had placed a hasty typo-filled report on Finch's desk about the situation in Bliss's apartment. "John Finch" typed at the bottom. *Brave of you, Wyte.* A blotch of purple obscured a few words in the middle. A smudged green thumbprint on the left corner. Wyte had tried to wipe it away, which just made it worse.

Under it, another sheet, handwritten, with some crude facts about Stark.

"Stark is now the operational head of Stockton's spy network."

Stating the obvious. No one started liquidating the competition unless they were already secure in their position.

"He carries a sword."

Who didn't, these days? Thought about pulling his own sword out. As he did several times a week, when he thought the others weren't looking.

"*He has a taster for his food . . . He's a psychopath . . . He's been seen . . .*" well, practically everywhere and nowhere, if Wyte's information was correct.

Nothing solid. Nothing that linked Stark to the case except Bliss saying Stark had asked him about those words they'd found on the scrap of paper. *Bellum omnium contra omnes.* Wondered what Bliss would've said if he'd shown him the symbol too.

Finch kept a stack of cigars in his desk in a box converted to the purpose. He took one out. Trillian brand. Several years old. Common and popular in its day. A little dry now.

Nothing new in this city. Not whiskey. Not cigars. Not people.

The kind of thing his father used to say.

He cut the tip. Used his oil lamp to light it.

The ash was even. The burn slow. He puffed on it, waiting. *The congregation will be here soon enough.*

His thoughts went back to Wyte's flask. In a flush of inspiration, Finch went over to Blakely's desk, opened the top drawer. Sure enough. Something plum-colored in a bottle. Homemade cork. He pulled it off. Took a whiff. Rotgut, but good enough. Took a couple of swigs right from the bottle. His throat burned. His tongue felt numb.

Saw double for a second. Another puff on the cigar fixed that. Went back to his desk.

Waiting this way, helpless, his vision became apocalyptic, false. In his mind, mortar fire rained down on the city. Artillery belched out a retort. Blasted into walls, sending up gouts of stone and flame. The war raged on, unnoticed by most. He was an agent of neither side. Just in it for himself.

Tried to think past the evening's torment. The walk back to his apartment afterward. In the dark. Thought of who might be waiting.

If he didn't screw up before that.

A little after six, the gray caps began to arrive. *The night shift.*

The first one pulled aside the curtain. Had emerged from the awful red-fringed hole at the back. Perfect parallel to the memory hole. Only much larger. Finch could see the gray cap's face under the hat. Pulsing. Wriggling. The eyes so yellow. What did they see that he could not?

The gray cap stepped forward, onto the carpet.

In the light of day, on certain streets, Finch could almost pretend that the Rising had never happened. But not here. Not now. Any fantasy was fatal. Any fear.

Finch walked out onto the carpet. Puffing. Feeling the brittle squeeze in his chest even as he released the smoke from his mouth. Let the cigar burn down toward his fingers to feel the distracting pain.

A strong scent of rotting licorice as the gray cap pushed past him. Ignoring him as it sat down at a desk. Gustat's desk.

One.

Nine more. One for each desk. Along with whatever familiars they had decided to bring with them.

Finch wished he had a club. A knife. Anything. The fungal guns didn't work against gray caps. Thought again about the sword. About bringing it across Heretic's rubbery neck.

He drove the image away as irrational. Heretic had asked him to be here. If Heretic ever wanted him dead, he'd send a present to his apartment. Or dissolve him into a puff of spores in front of the other detectives.

Five times he'd stayed after hours. Survived each encounter. But talking to a single gray cap during the day was different from being among many of them after dusk. It brought back memories of the war. It reminded him of night duty in the trenches, the crude defenses House Hoegbotton had created for its soldiers. Sighting through the scope at some pile of rubble opposite. Hoping not to see anything. Feeling the sweat and fear of the others to each side. The flinch and intake of breath at the slightest movement.

Two.

Three.

Four.

Moving past him. Soft rustle of robes. Hushed sigh of their breathing, as if they slept even while awake. Oddly heavy footfalls. A smell that ranged from sweet like syrup to rank and disgusting. Did they control it? Were there signals they gave off humans could never read? *Those eyes. That mouth. The ragged claws on the doughy hands.*

Sitting at the desks like distorted reflections of their daytime counterparts. He had never learned their names. Thought of them only by the names of the humans who'd been assigned the same desks. Or once had. So there sat Dorn, and there sat Wyte, and there were Skinner and Albin.

The fifth was Heretic. He'd brought something with him. On a leash. Finch didn't know what it was. Couldn't tell where it started or ended. It had no face, just a sense of wet, uncoiling darkness. Like an endless fall off a bridge at night, under a starless sky, into deep water. That one glimpse and Finch never looked at it directly again.

The light in the room had faded to the dark green preferred by the gray caps.

"Do you like my *skery*, Finch? Do you find my *skery* pleasing to the eye?" Heretic asked in a voice rough yet reedy, standing in front of Finch. Emphasis on *pleasing to the eye*. As usual when Heretic tried out a turn of phrase. "No? That's a shame. The *skery* is a new thing, and useful to us. Very soon, it will save us a lot of effort, allow the Partials to do other work."

Finch had no answer for that.

Together, Finch, the gray cap, and the *skery* went to his desk. At night, Heretic walked with a kind of effortless forward movement. More at ease and more deadly. As if daylight affected a gray cap's equilibrium.

Heretic sat down, dropping the leash. The *skery* went right to Finch's memory hole and began worrying the edges with its wet gobble of a mouth. Cleaning it of parasites.

Finch put out his cigar in the ashtray at the edge of the desk. Stood in front of Heretic. *Take the initiative*. In a calm, flat voice, he said: "I went back to the apartment. The body . . . one of the bodies was missing."

"I took it away." A clipped quality behind the moistness. Some continuing thread of amusement. The eyes looked as though embedded in a rubber festival mask. "We're testing the body for a variety of— —." The word sounded like *tilivirck*.

Finch nodded like he understood.

"We also harvested another memory bulb from the man."

Utter paralysis. Unbidden: an image of Sintra's face as he entered her. The way she sighed and relaxed into him. As the blood of his tears dropped onto her cheeks, her lips.

"What did you see?" Finch asked.

Heretic shook his head. A simple motion rendered alien, frightening. "Perhaps you should tell me first, Finch. What you saw."

"It's in the report," Finch said. Too quickly.

"The report. It's all in the report. How could we forget? Perhaps because the report was disappointing. Very disappointing, and not what we've come to expect from you." Still a secret amusement there, mingled with the threat.

His stomach lurched. The room felt hot. At the other desks, the last of the gray caps had sat down. At their feet, their familiars curled, mewled, foraged.

"It's only been a day," Finch said.

"Finch," Heretic said. "Are you telling me everything?"

Bliss had disappeared from a ten-foot-square room. With no windows.

"I left out nothing important," Finch said. "Up to that point."

Heretic said something in his own language that sounded like a child arguing with a click beetle. Then, a half-expected blade held to the throat: "What about the scrap of paper the Partial says you took from the body?"

The symbol. The strange words. What would Heretic tell him about the Silence if he asked? Nothing. He'd kill Finch. Or worse.

Out of sudden fear, a strange calm. Later, he realized it felt like losing control even as he gained it. An echoing faint laughter that became the sound of hammers working on the two towers in the bay. That became water slapping against the wall in Rathven's basement.

Words left his mouth. "There was a man in the memories I recognized. I didn't put it in the report because I wanted to investigate first. It related to the paper in the dead man's hand." Lying.

Falling through cold air and he couldn't feel his legs.

"Explain."

"A man called Ethan Bliss." And then the flood: "A Morrow agent active for Frankwrithe & Lewden, during the War of the Houses. I tracked him down today with Wyte, but he . . . slipped away. I'm following up. I put in a request for his file along with my report."

If we can't find him, we'll go after Stark.

Heretic seemed to consider that, then asked, "And the scrap of paper?"

"I'm still investigating what it means. I'll put it all into my report for tomorrow."

"And the list I gave you, of people who lived in that apartment?"

Finch relaxed a little. "I'm still working on it. By tomorrow afternoon I should know more." *If Rathven's finished by then.*

Heretic considered this statement for a long time, then said, "You have withheld information from me. You haven't even finished with the list. From now on, you will report every day. You are to tell me *everything*. Do not leave it to your judgment."

Finch opened his mouth to speak. Heretic said words that sounded like *kith vrisdresn zorn*. Snapped his fingers.

The *skery* wound itself around Finch's legs and tightened. Sudden tingling paralysis. He could not move away. Could not fall. Choking on his own breath. The paralysis brought with it an image of an endless field of dim stars, one by one extinguished. A gulf and a void. Finch was as afraid as he had ever been in his life. Because he didn't know what he was looking at, or why.

Try to breathe. Slowly. Breathe slowly.

The *skery* curled its way up to his chest. Around his neck. It pulled tight so he was gasping in his motionlessness. He felt something like sharp leaves or thorns up against his neck. An impression of lips. A sharp, smoky scent. Half the field of stars had gone out. There was more darkness than light.

From behind Finch's desk, from a thousand miles away, from behind a thick wall: Heretic. Saying, "A *skery* is not as bad for you as what I could bring with me."

The *skery* curled back down Finch's body. Released him. He stumbled forward, hands on the desk to stop from falling. The field of stars so bright he almost passed out. Then the desk came into focus. Prickles of sensation came back into his legs. Neck already sore and throbbing.

"Do you understand me, Finch?" Heretic said. "We can make it quite clear who you really are. To everyone. Or we can just put you in the camps. Or we can do much, much worse."

Finch had killed a gray cap once. As an Irregular. Before the Rising. Out in the confusion of civil war. With a knife and a gun. He thought about that now, looking at Heretic.

Heretic: "How did Bliss manage to escape you? I expect that in your report by tomorrow night. You will leave your report on your desk. I will read it. If I am not satisfied, I will visit you. Find ways to convince me that you are more valuable alive than a memory bulb. Do you understand?"

"I understand," Finch managed after a moment. Throat sore. Burying his anger deep. Just wanting to be away from there. Just wanting to be somewhere he might fool himself into calling *safe*.

The gray cap rose. "You'll find Bliss's information in the 'memory hole' by your desk in a few minutes."

Heretic walked toward the back, holding his *skery*. Rivulets of golden spores swirled up from his footfalls. Sparkled in the murk like tiny blinking eyes.

Against all good judgment, against his shock at the *skery*'s touch, Finch spoke. "What happened when you took the dead man's memory bulb?"

Heretic half turned, the look on his face murderous. "I did not eat the memory bulb. That was another *fanaarcensitii*. He saw nothing. He died within minutes, in horrible pain. Apparently, you are very, very lucky, Finch."

A long peal of that awful laughter before Heretic disappeared behind the curtain.

Afterward, Finch couldn't sleep. Stomach churning. Couldn't get rid of a crawling sensation. Half his mouth felt numb. The other half tingled like a faint electric shock. His legs moved slowly, a deep ache in both muscle and bone.

Had returned to his apartment to find a note from Sintra shoved under the door: *Can't make it tonight. Tomorrow night.* Found that a bad mood could get worse.

He went up to the roof of the hotel, a fifth of whiskey retrieved from his kitchen, and let a nagging Feral come with him. Carried the cat's comforting weight, like a purring loaf of bread, in the crook of his left arm. In his other hand, the file on Bliss.

The stairs above his floor had been so colonized by moss and lichen that they didn't creak. Dark. Dangerous. But Finch didn't care. He'd lost his way anyhow, was in need of something sturdier than self-pity.

A hatch in the ceiling where the stairs ended led to the roof. He switched Bliss's file to under his arm, next to a protesting Feral. Set down the whiskey long enough to push open the hatch without losing his balance. Picked it back up, and stepped through with Feral. Into a bracing wind. A wash of stars set against the black-and-green-tinged sky.

Except for the bit obscured by the dilapidated sign, Finch could see the whole city from here. One reason he'd chosen the hotel. The view from the roof helped him with his map overlay. Made him feel more in control, being able to see so much from one place. The soldier in him always wanted the best possible recon.

Muted lights from the buildings to either side. Like he saw them through a black curtain. Even the two towers seemed dulled, the emerald glow humble. A few sparkling clouds of spores, in blue and yellow, danced far out in the sky, to the south. Otherwise, just the inward-focused white of the camp domes, balanced to the north by the humming glitter of orange-green HFZ. The air didn't carry the smell of mushrooms. As if a fresh breeze had come from outside the city.

A tall figure stood near the edge of the roof, looking out. Finch stiffened, making Feral hiss. He groped for the gun he had left in the apartment, Feral jumping from his arm. Then Finch realized it was just the Photographer, Rath's brother. The man who liked to take pictures of water and ran a black market store out of his apartment.

Finch had seen the photographs. Stacked up next to the cameras. Plastered to the walls. Blown up, miniaturized, blurry, in focus. On anything that might serve, or re-serve, as contact paper. As if the Photographer looked for one particular thing in the water. As if not interested in water at all, searching for something he hadn't found yet.

A fifth of whiskey was enough for two.

The Photographer turned as Finch approached. A slow, unconcerned motion. Finch had never seen him anything other than calm. Or maybe his mood was always resigned to whatever new thing came next. Didn't know what had happened to him in the camps. Didn't know much about him at all, except that he trusted the man. Which made little sense. He was so clearly damaged. So indifferent to Finch's help in getting him out of the camp.

The Photographer nodded.

Finch passed the bottle to the Photographer. The man took a sip and handed it back. He stared at Finch with an unreadable gaze. A white face and a watchful mouth, with an upturn to the lips that could make him look devilish. The eyes and cheekbones didn't match the mouth. The eyes were almost vacant, except for a deep-set glint. Finch thought of that glint as curiosity or obsession. The high cheekbones gave the Photographer an aura of deep or deeply denied suffering.

"Anything new out there?"

"A few things." His voice a thin reed.

"Anything I should know about?"

The Photographer shrugged, looked out at the night. "More activity at the towers, just a little while ago. An emergency? Quickly solved, if so. Nothing there now. A few spore discharges to the west. Can't tell if they're human or mechanical. But not much, no . . . What happened to you?"

An involuntary snort. He must look as ragged as he felt. The Photographer had never asked after his health before.

"I came across something that didn't like me," Finch said. No desire to share the details. Thinking about how he had to hold out for another day before seeing Sintra again.

The Photographer nodded as if this made sense. Returned to his contemplation of the view. Didn't care much for small talk.

Slowly, stiffly, Finch lowered himself into a chair. A few feet away, Feral was munching on something he'd caught.

A couple lightbulbs hung near the rotting sign. The outer arc of their light just barely caught the edge of the chairs. Enough to read by.

Eyes adjusted to the dim light, Finch began to go through Bliss's file. Two laughably old photographs. One so dark it was just a silhouette with a hint of jaw leering out of a smudge. The report itself was brief, pithy, in the spidery script of gray cap transcriptions. Translated from their original files. *Which took what form?* Probably were worse things than memory holes down below.

Finch already knew most of what was in the report. Bliss's rise within F&L ranks. The compromise with Hoegbotton. The alliance with the Lady in Blue. But he was somehow surprised that the gray caps knew it. Made him wonder about the extent of their intel before the Rising.

Buried in the middle of the report, Finch found a list of aliases under which Bliss had operated: *Charles Dinley, George Graansvoort, John Letcher, Grant Shearwater, Dar Sardice.* And, most improbably, Jasper Marlowe Anthony Blasio. A typo? An error in the transcription?

Dar Sardice proved the most interesting. The other names had been ways of disguising movements across checkpoints within the city. Dar Sardice had been used much earlier, during Ambergrisian-Hoegbotton campaigns against the Kalif. "Dar Sardice" had been Frankwrithe's man keeping an eye on the progress of the war. From behind the Kalif's supply lines. The cover? Independent merchant and businessman. With an established trade route that cut through over eight hundred miles of desert dotted with fortified towns. The whole Western Front. Against which the Ambergrisian Army had thrown itself with unparalleled ferocity. From which it had eventually retreated. *"It was just too large,"* his father had said once. *"It was overwhelming. The wide, hot, empty spaces. The strangeness of the towns. The fact we didn't speak the language."* Left a trail of broken, bombed equipment behind. Trucks. Tanks. Mortars.

A desert fortress. A fall from a great height. Ethan Bliss as Dar Sardice, turning up in every major theater of a desert war. Then appearing again not long after as F&L's man in Ambergris. Popping up in the dead man's memories. Had disappeared when cornered, after having been nailed to a wall just a few minutes before.

Was he looking at a secret that should be obvious? If so, it eluded him the more he tried to pin it down.

Beside him, the Photographer stirred. "I am going to go back inside. Do you need anything from me?"

"Just information," Finch said, and downed some whiskey. He enjoyed the way it spread out from his throat, his stomach. Settling him as it mixed with the afterburn of the cigar.

"What kind of information?"

On a hunch, feeling like his back was exposed: "Seen anyone strange around the hotel recently?"

The Photographer replied with a kind of odd regret, as if speaking out of turn: "Yes, I have."

Suddenly more alert: "Describe them?"

"Two of them, today. They came separately. The first I saw around noon. A tall Partial. He was on the stairs when I saw him. Coming down." A look of disgust on the Photographer's face.

The same Partial?

"Coming down from where?"

"I don't know. I was on the fifth floor. He was coming down."

Could've been anyone. Could've been here for any reason. And nothing he could do about it.

"The second?"

"He stayed outside the building. It was late afternoon. A bald man. Dangerous-looking. He talked to the madman by the statue. Didn't like what the madman told him. Then looked up at the windows for a while. He stayed off to the side smoking a cigarette. Got impatient and walked into the lobby for a moment, came back out, and left almost right away."

A description that matched what Bliss had told them about Bosun, Stark's muscle. Which meant they'd had watchers on Bliss's place. Watchers who had identified Finch incredibly fast. Now they were checking out where he lived. He didn't like that. Didn't like it at all.

Definitely time to have a talk with Stark.

"Tell me if you see them again? Or anyone else who doesn't live here?"

The Photographer nodded. Then he was taking long strides to the hatch, as if he suddenly needed to be somewhere. The hatch creaked open, and he was gone.

Off to Finch's left, Feral was stalking something new around a couple of wooden boxes. Finch went back to his whiskey. Wondered if Bliss/Dar Sardice leading them to Stark meant Stark would lead them back to Bliss. And who was Stark, then? Just another Stockton man, or something else?

All the while trying not to think of the *skery*. Curling up his leg. Wound around his neck.

Failing.

WEDNESDAY

I: When did you first decide to contact Stark? Before or after Bliss?

F: I was just investigating two deaths. Following orders.

I: And to you that meant scheming with *all* of the city's enemies?

F: No, that's not it at all. That you—

[screams, garbled recording]

F: *Why did you do that?* Why? I'm *talking.* I'm *talking.*

I: But you're not saying anything.

1

On their way the next morning to track down Stark . . .

Wind and spray of rain against Finch's face as they sped across the bay toward the Spit. Glad of the cool water soaking his hair. But he had a hard time keeping the filter-mask over eyes, nose, and mouth from clouding up. It itched, made him sweat. Made Wyte, as he turned toward Finch, look like something meant to frighten children. But better safe than dead. Even the gray caps didn't know what lived in the air above the bay, the water corrupted by runoff from the HFZ. *Tiny assassins. Cell disruptors and breath-stealers . . .*

Finch stood at the prow of the gray cap boat, the only kind allowed out on the bay. Wyte beside him, skin on his arms green. Not from being seasick. The boat was big enough for eight or ten. Empty with just the two of them. Slight upward lurching push as it expelled water below the surface to propel them forward. Looked like any other boat from afar. *Except it acts like it's alive.* Route preplanned by the gruff Partial who had met them on the shore. Who had shoved a mushroom into an orifice on the hull that looked uncannily like a memory hole. Somehow the boat knew where to go. How to return.

Finch's shoes were sinking into the loamy sponge of the "planks." Tried to remember to bend his knees to keep his balance. But balance was a precarious thing. Tongue dry, stomach aching. The *skery* had done something to his muscles. Made him feel like he'd wrestled a giant all night. Didn't like that. Didn't like being robbed of his natural river-legs. Finch had liked the water, once. With childhood friends, names now lost—*Charlie? Sam?*—he'd gone down to the docks to fish. Pushed a canoe out into the current. Later, working for Wyte, he'd gotten up close to the big ships docking to unload and take on board H&S goods.

Ghosts of early-morning conversations with Wyte ran through Finch's head.

"Most of my informants have gone dark. Stark's influence. Taking care of leaks and stirring up hornets."

"You've got to know more about Stark than what you left on my desk, Wyte."

"No. Not a thing. We don't even know if that's his real name."

"Nobody's real name is just Stark, Wyte."

Wyte had arranged for a Stockton operative named Stephen Davies to act as a go-between with Stark. They'd approach the floating pontoons at the northeast edge of the Spit. Much safer than from the land side. A maze of ruins there. Ideal for ambush. No cover. No way to retreat.

Spies came into Ambergris simple and alone, first stop the Spit. Over the water. In the darkness, as if newly born. With nothing on them that the gray caps might want. Nothing that their masters wouldn't want taken. They built up their resources over time. Using whatever money or influence they'd brought from Stockton, Morrow, or even more distant lands. Sometimes the Spit was the last stop, too.

"Truff love foreigners, trying to take advantage of our fucked-up city."

"Stark'll be no different. Where was Stockton during the Rising?"

"Waiting to pick the bones clean."

Trying to pump themselves up. Convince themselves they were still loyal to Ambergris. Hated how the masks made their voices tinny.

"Davies seems in awe of Stark."

"Sure it's not fear? Though most of them are probably past fear or awe by now . . ."

Wyte just shrugged. Finch knew he didn't want to think about that. Didn't want to know what shit might be waiting on the Spit.

Hints of bobbing islands in the waves now. Some of them too close to ignore. Yet Finch ignored them. Corpse islands made from workers who had died in the camps. Reborn as floating compost for fruiting bodies. And far, far below them, the decaying docks, the drowned part of Albumuth Boulevard. All of the dead, still in the buildings where they had worked or lived, the onslaught of water so sudden. Slamming into them. For a time lit up by the strobing of the giant squid that had patrolled the bay. Long since gone, driven out by the pollution. Finch couldn't take it. Not this morning.

"Water can behave like a person," his father used to say. Treacherous. Tides and swirls and eddies. Sucking boats down with them.

The past didn't seem like another world. The past seemed like it had never happened. Couldn't have happened. The leap to *this* too hideous, too nightmarish. Better to have no past at all. Suddenly, he needed Sintra. Needed her badly. Could almost smell her perfume. Wanted to be back in his apartment, next to her.

"Where do you live?"

"A place with four walls, and a ceiling."

"What are the neighbors like?"

"Noisy. Sad. Temporary . . ."

Resented Wyte irrationally for a moment. As if Sintra could've replaced him on the boat. Backed him up. Except she couldn't.

"What can you hear from your window, Sintra?"

"The sound of detectives asking questions."

"Finch." Wyte made it sound like a warning, jolting him from his thoughts. "Over there." Pointing, like he wanted a distraction, too.

Just behind them: another boat. Much larger, coming in from the southeast. Flat-bottomed. Lagging in the water.

Finch had brought his gun against his own better instincts. Drew it now. Then looked closer and holstered it.

"Just prisoners," he said. *Could as well be us.*

Wyte took a second look, nodded.

Soon the boat slid past their prow, heading for the towers. It held about thirty people from the camps. Guarded by two gray caps and a Partial. The men and women dressed in the dull sack robes of their status. Some wearing old-fashioned masks that might or might not work. Heads bowed not from prayer but from hopelessness. Thin, with light-green skin. Shoulders slumped.

"During the *day?*" Wyte said, almost pleading to be told he was wrong.

"During the day," Finch said, annoyed. Best just to be thankful not to be in the camps.

The Truffidian priest in the back of the boat caught Finch's attention. In full regalia, down to the golden chains. The same priests had walked side by side with Ambergrisian infantry invading Kalif lands. The gray caps had broken them. Treated them almost like pets now. Their eyes locked, the older man bowing his head to avoid Finch's stare. Noted the hooded look. The slight shake. He was on the gray caps' drugs. Did this in return for his fix. *Turncoat.*

Wyte: "In the old days, he'd have died for that. And not quickly."

And so would we.

"What?" Wyte said.

"Nothing."

Against his will, pulled to it by the immensity, Finch's gaze slid beyond the work camp boat. To the towers in mottled green, with darker blues writhing through. Protected by scaffolding, they seemed to flutter and be alive. Portions like lungs. Breathing. The tops, two hundred feet high or more, lost in clouds and rain and odd magenta shards of lightning. A wide pontoon bridge led out to the towers. A semi-permanent island at the base housed the workers. Several boats had docked there. Dozens of gray caps stood guard.

Past the towers, back the way they'd come, Finch could just make out the hunched group of buildings that included the apartment with the dead man and gray cap. Was the Partial there, staring out at him? Talking to Heretic? *Hiding something from Heretic?*

"When will they know the towers are finished?" Finch wondered aloud.

"Roofs, Finchy. When you see roofs on top. That means it's done."

Joking? Serious? Didn't know anymore when Wyte was lucid and when not. Didn't know what to encourage.

The *wrongness* of the railing at the prow suddenly got through to Finch. Should be grainy, splinters needling his hands. Instead: soft, fleshy. He took his hand away like the railing was boiling hot.

Through the rain, the Spit was revealing itself. Gone with surprising quickness from a brown line in the distance to something with substance and texture. Rows of boats moored side by side by side, twenty or thirty deep. Still floating, bobbing, even as they were falling apart and half-sinking. A leaky sovereignty. A chained-together legion of convicts treading water. All of it shoved up against the shore, against the remains of the Religious Quarter. If the gray caps ever decided they wanted to truly cut off citizen from citizen, they'd burn the Spit, place a wall between it and the Religious Quarter. They'd root out the Dogghe and Nimblytod from the Quarter like so many weeds. Shove them all into the HFZ and be done with it.

Limits to what they can do? Or to what they want to do?

The boat began to slow. Soon they bumped up against the docks, gently. Prow kissing wood. Finch jumped off the boat as it lay wallowing there, followed by Wyte. Took off their masks. Breathed in the metallic air. Tossed their masks back in the boat. The boat sighed, shutting down until their return. Didn't know what would happen to anyone who tried to board it while they were gone. Knew it would be bad.

No sign of Davies. An avalanche of other boats before them, a scattering of tall buildings, natural and not, dull-glistening far beyond, through the rain. Buckets tied to the dock gurgled and filled, emptied. A blue dinghy. Oily water. Rotting planks.

"Got a plan if Davies doesn't show up, Wyte?"

Wyte didn't answer.

A bald man appeared at the edge of the empty docks, weapon holstered. Just appeared. Finch couldn't tell where he'd come from. Wyte drew his gun for both of them.

Face like a boxer's, the nose wide from repeated blows. Scar over the left eye, under the right eye. *Same knife stroke?* Barrel chest. Thick arms. Wearing a blood-red vest over a dark-green shirt. Black pants, blacker boots.

The man came forward with hands held in front of him. Like he wanted to be handcuffed. Something was in his hands, though. *An offering?*

He dropped what he'd been holding onto the ground. A wooden carving of a lizard caught in some kind of trap.

The man said, in some misbegotten blend of accents, "I'm Bosun. Davies couldn't make it."

Close enough now that his face was like a carved oval bone. Scrubbed clean of anything except directness. Some sort of spice on his breath. A smirk Finch didn't like any more than the name.

Wyte gave Finch a glance. Knew Wyte was thinking the same thing. Bliss had named Bosun as Stark's right-hand man. Someone who didn't flinch from torture. Who seemed to enjoy it. Who'd helped wipe out Bliss's whole team.

"What happened to Davies?" Wyte asked, stepping back to create a little space. Finch faded to the right, so he'd be out of Wyte's line of fire. Kept his hand on his belt. Near his holster.

"Davies couldn't make it," Bosun repeated. "Stark's waiting. Come. Now."

Bosun started walking back toward the maze of gathered boats. Didn't seem to care about Wyte's gun. Finch wondered who might be watching from the row of dark glass windows that formed the first wall of boats.

"What guarantees do we have?" Finch called after Bosun. Wanted to ask, "What's with the lizard, you fucking lunatic?"

Bosun, without looking back: "None, beyond this: We won't hurt you unless you try to hurt us. And we won't try to fuck you, either. Unless you try to fuck us." A deep rasp similar to laughter. Him receding farther toward the maze while the two detectives stood there.

Finch stared at Wyte. Wyte stared at Finch.

"Are we really going to go in there?" Wyte asked.

Finch looked back across the bay, saw how far they'd come. *Who on the Spit would risk angering the gray caps?* Thought about the *skery*. About how easy it would've been for them both to go down in a hail of bullets if someone waited behind the windows of the first line of boats.

Shrugged. "Just think of him as Davies if it makes you feel better." Hiding his own unease.

They stepped around the lizard carving like it might do harm. On impulse, Finch went back and stooped with a muttered curse. Picked it up. As Bosun had no doubt intended him to do from the beginning.

Followed Bosun into the darkness.

✦✦✦

Once, Finch's father had shown him an old tobacco pipe. "This pipe contains the world," he said. Finch might've been fourteen, still running errands like a loyal son. His father was ten years removed from the campaigns against the Kalif, and rising fast within House Hoegbotton. They sat at his ornate desk in the study of the old house. Dad on his soft red silk chair. Finch on a stool to his left. Souvenirs his father had brought back from the desert served as grace notes. A rifle used by the Kalif's men. The steering wheel from a tank. A scimitar that he had promised would one day be his son's.

A sunny spring morning, mottled shadow coming into the room from the long bank of windows against the far wall. Faint honey smell from the tiny white flowers that came with the manicured bushes that lined the avenue in front of the house.

"A pipe?" Finch said. Incredulous. Expecting a trick. Maybe a magic trick.

His father pointed to a hole in the side of the pipe. "Look inside."

Warily, Finch put the pipe to his eye. Gasped in delight. Because the glass magnified the image revealed through the hole. And the world did indeed exist there. A whole map of the known world. There was a dot for Ambergris. The line of the River Moth. The city of Morrow marked to the north, Stockton some fifty miles south, on the other side of the river. The Southern Isles down below the Moth Delta. The Kalif's empire covering the whole west beyond the Moth. Exotic city after city marked in that vast desert, the plains and hills beyond. To the east, jungle and mountains that remained uncharted.

"There's a hole on the other side, too," his father said.

Finch turned the pipe around. Stared into another tiny piece of magnifying glass. Black-and-white photos of twelve men and women confronted him.

"Who are they?"

"Spies," his father said. "The owner of this pipe ran a network of spies. The map on the other side is really a code. It tells the owner something about the spies whose pictures you're looking at. Each one lives in a different city marked on the map. But you have to know the code to know which goes with which city. And what other information is being given to you."

Finch took his eye away from the pipe to look at his dad. "How fun!" he said, because he didn't know what to say.

"No," his father said, frowning. "No, it's not fun. Not really. It's deadly serious." A look like he was trying to tell Finch something Finch just couldn't understand at the time.

Finch remembers that pipe when he's working on his overlay. That tiny view of a huge world, which makes him realize the limitations of his map. That beyond it, beyond Ambergris, there's something more. Though it's easy to forget.

It's the pipe he's thinking about as he enters the Spit with Wyte. About those spies, who had led exciting, dangerous lives all across the world. But who were still, at the end of the day, captured inside a pipe.

Bound by rules.

Moved around a board against their will.

Or thought they were.

What's the difference?

2

Through the doors of boats. Through many doors. Always with sudden water between them. Gray, blue, black, depending on the shifting clouds above. The distance wide enough to make them jump. Then narrow as a line of blue. As the boats rocked, lashed together by rope that groaned. A marsh smell. A fish smell. Mixed with the odd old-new smell of paint curled back in a snarl or crisply flat.

Into spaces seeping water from old wounds, the texture of warped planks beneath their feet weathered in a hundred ingenious ways. Across decks that announced them through the creak caused by their weight, wood singing a dull protest. Up or down steps always too deep or too shallow.

Following the wide back of their silent guide, Wyte the worse off for being taller, having to contort his frame into whatever shape awaited him. The doors got smaller then larger, then smaller again. Oval. Rectangular. Square. Inlaid with glass. Gone, leaving only a gaping doorway and a couple rusted hinges. Once, a flapping triangle of canvas with an eye painted on it in green and red that seemed to follow Finch's stumbling progress.

And what in Truff's name is this supposed to represent? The thought came to Finch more than once, looking down at the whittled wood from Bosun. The trap. The lizard caught in it. The carving brought his thoughts to Sidle, made him feel, absurdly, like Bosun had been inside his apartment. Who created such things? Who had the *time*?

Bosun stopped suddenly, turned back to look at them from just inside a doorway.

Wyte ran into Finch before he could stop himself. Lulled by the stilted rhythm of their progress. Finch just able to stop falling.

"What? Are we there already?" Wyte asked, peering over Finch's shoulder. Could feel his breath, hot and thick.

Bosun smiled. A thin smile. Nothing humorous about it.

They stood precariously outside the doorway, on a tiny deck, backs to a cabin wall. A trough of water lapping between boats. A heron croaking through the slate-gray sky.

"Toss your guns," Bosun said.

"Why should we?" Wyte asked.

"No guns allowed with Stark."

"Too bad," Wyte said.

Bosun said, "Drop them in the water. Or I'll leave you here."

Framed by the doorway, gray water shadows leaking all over him, Bosun didn't look human. Didn't look real. Seemed to be receding from them while all around the sounds of the Spit became stronger. Like a drumbeat that faded in one place, picked up with a different tempo in another.

Wyte said, "Again, why the *fuck* should we do that?"

"Because," Finch said, "we don't know where we are." *And if he'd wanted to kill us, he'd have done it already.*

Bosun's smile widened while Wyte cursed, said, "Do you know who we work for?"

We work for monsters. We work for ourselves.

As if in a dream, Finch watched himself toss his gun into the water. It entered like a diver, headfirst. The water parted for it. Disappeared without a splash. A kind of relief came over him. A kind of acceptance. *The gun had been nothing but trouble. The gun had always caused problems.*

Wyte gave Finch a look of betrayal. Hesitated. Bosun receded farther. Wyte could shoot Bosun. Then they'd be lost, in hostile territory. Or Wyte could miss and Bosun would be gone anyway. Or Wyte could get rid of his gun and Bosun would leave them. But Finch didn't think that would happen.

He tugged the gun from Wyte's reluctant hands. Threw it in the water as Wyte muttered, "A mistake, Finch. A mistake."

Finch demanded it of Bosun: "*Stark.*"

"Stark," Bosun said, nodding.

Then Bosun was just a wide back again, a kind of door himself. Leading them somewhere dangerous.

But a few minutes later, Bosun stopped again. This time inside an old tugboat. Finch right there beside him, back sore from stooping. Wyte behind them, still in the last, much larger boat. Exuding a muddled aura of defeat.

Then he was gone. Finch could sense it. Wyte there, behind him. Then not. A kind of wind or impact punching the air. A muffled shout. Cut off. Finch turned and saw just the outline of doorways receding in a ragged infinite number back the way they'd come. Nothing but shadow otherwise. Whirled around to Bosun, deck rising and falling beneath his feet.

Bosun stood there. Arms folded, watching.

Finch fought the urge to close the distance. To hurt Bosun. Fought it. Knew that self-control would save his life. Maybe save Wyte's life. Knew now, too, that Stark didn't give a shit about gray cap retaliation. Didn't care that Heretic would be after him if he snuffed out two detectives.

"Where's my partner? Where are you taking him?" Tried to keep his voice level.

If you hurt him . . .

Bosun shrugged, said, "Doesn't want to see him. Just you. Wyte's not safe. We don't know where he's been. You'll see him later. Take off your shoes."

"Take off my *shoes*?" It was unexpected enough to make Finch forget Wyte for a moment.

"Shoes and socks. Need to see your feet. That going to be a problem?"

"Why the fuck would I care about my shoes after giving up my gun?"

Over the side went Finch's shoes and socks. Stood there, hopping, as he showed Bosun the bottom of first one foot, then the other. Wondering where this would end. Furious, worried, scared.

Another part of him looked down from a great height, puzzled. *When did being a detective mean this?* He was investigating a double murder. He was working for an occupying force that could make Stark disappear in a burst of dandelion-like spores. And he didn't have his shoes. He didn't have his socks. He didn't have his gun.

"Are we done?" Finch asked. "Is this almost over?"

Impassive bullet of a head swiveling toward Finch. Dark eyes glinting. "Turn out your pockets."

"Why?"

Bosun pulled out his gun. "No good reason."

Finch raised his left arm, palm up. "I'll do it. I'll do it."

There was a lot more than he'd thought. A copy of the photo of the murder victim. A folded up note from Sintra, the first and almost only thing she'd ever written to him. *Dear Finch—I made you coffee. Thanks for a great night. Love, S.* His current identity papers. A few semi-worthless paper bills from before the Rising. A strange coin, notched along the edges, that he'd kept for luck. A scrap of paper with nonsense words written on it, an odd symbol on the back.

In the end, Bosun returned all of it to him.

"Worthless."

But he'd lingered on the scrap of paper. Far longer than necessary to read it.

3

Thirty minutes? Longer? Finch lost count of the doors. Lost count or didn't care. His back throbbed from hunching over. From crawling, then climbing, Bosun's form always ahead of him. They were in the heart of the Spit now. Bigger boats—almost ships—lay near the center, places where you could forget you were on the water. Masts rose up like barren trees. Warrens of rooms, through which Bosun walked sure-footed, never losing his bearings.

Passed through a bar of sorts, with homemade booze in reused bottles. Women flirted with dull, rumpled men with beards and strange black hats. A few loners with a calculated threadbare appearance. Beyond the bar, the sound of spirited bartering in back rooms for black market goods. Selling guns, food, maybe even information.

Where was Wyte now? How far behind or ahead? Still alive, or thrown over the side to follow their guns? Began to wonder if Wyte would wind up like Bliss or like Bliss's men. Nailed to a wall? Bleeding fungal blood?

Even stranger ideas began to enter his head. That Rath in her basement, doling out information, was someone he'd made up out of convenience. That Sintra had no mysterious life beyond his own. That he'd written the words on the scrap of paper pried from the dead man's hands. That the soreness around his neck came not from the *skery* but from sleeping in the wrong position. That he would wake up to find Sintra was his wife. The gray caps had never Risen. He still worked for Hoegbotton & Sons as a courier, but Wyte was an obedient wire-haired terrier he'd bought for Sintra. There was no Spit. No bay. No towers.

Instead, they reached Stark's headquarters: through one last doorway, hinges splinters of wood, the door missing. *Ripped apart? How long ago?*

Bosun straightened up, Finch beside him. Stepped into a room aboard some kind of ferry. Passenger seats stripped out leaving the metal skeletons of chairs. The high, curving ceiling showed in faded paint a scene from an opera, people in balcony seats applauding. Below that hung a chandelier from which almost all the glass was gone.

A long wide space stretched out before them. Like a dance floor. Timbers stained with dark red swirls and smudges. The soft smell of soap couldn't dull the sharp assault of the blood.

At the far end: a couple of chairs, a desk, and a large figure hanging a painting on the wall. As they approached, Finch recognized the painting as a reproduction. It showed the Kalif of another age demanding fealty from a defiant Stockton king. Back when Stockton had kings. Hunting dogs stood in the foreground, but fiendish, with forked tongues and jowls curling back to reveal metal daggers. The composition more surreal than photographic. All of it the echo of a time lost to the present.

The large man nodded to them even as he kept moving the painting. Trying to catch it on the nails in a wall covered with bullet holes and dark bloodstains. Splatter had swept across the divide between wall and floor.

Finch noticed now the dark sheets in the farthest corner. Roughly man-sized.

"You found Bosun, I see," the man said. A deep voice. "Or he found you. Either way, you're here. Finally." The painting caught on the nails. Held. "There."

The man turned toward them. "You can call me Stark."

Stark made a tall space look small. A height that warranted a girth that could have been muscle or fat. Or both. The truth of it hidden by a trench coat. Frank-writhe & Lewden army issue. With old medals from the Kalif's empire pinned there: black glint with a hint of gold against the steep gray of the trench coat. A hawk face, with dark pupils swimming in too much white. A strong nose and a chin that jutted: two halves of the same beak. A knife in his left boot sheathed in a silver scabbard that shone as if polished every hour. Finch mistrusted that knife immediately. Reminded him of the squeaky floors at 239 Manzikert Avenue. *Look at the knife while the blow comes from somewhere else.* What else did the trench coat hide? A sword?

Stark didn't come forward. Didn't offer his hand. Just stood there. The painting behind him. Now Finch saw that Stark hadn't been trying to hide the bullet holes, the blood. Instead, the painting had been placed between them.

"Sit," Bosun growled, shoving Finch forward into a chair. Stark sat down behind the desk. Bosun stood to the side, reaching for a piece of dark wood on the desk. One of many. Started carving. Quick, accurate cuts. So fast his hands were a blur.

"Where's Wyte?" Finch asked.

Stark pursed his lips, ignored him, and said, "What did you think would happen? I'm curious. You thought you two would just walk in here, into *my place*, and you'd take me away to your shitty little station for questioning? Come back with an army if you want that, and come in shooting."

Finch, pressing: "What have you done with Wyte?"

Stark stared to the side, exhaled loudly. He seemed to breathe through his mouth. "John Finch. Why do you think people are so stupid?"

"Are they? Stupid?" Finch said, too aware of his bare feet. The floor was cold.

"Take my predecessors," Stark said. "They knew I was coming. They knew their superiors weren't pleased with them. Yet they took no precautions. They were *still here* when I arrived. I think they deserved what they got, don't you?"

Anger rising. "If you've hurt my partner . . ."

Stark dismissed his concern with a wave of his hand. "Don't start making threats you can't back up. Wyte is fine. You'll see him soon enough. But he's a tad too . . . fungal . . . for my liking. Or yours, from what I've heard."

"What about my gun?"

Stark smiled, revealing teeth stained red. Finch recognized the signs of addiction to a stimulant found in the bark from a tree that grew in both Ambergris and Stockton.

"You can join your gun," Stark said, "or you can shut up about it. I'm not here to talk to you about *guns*." The stained teeth made Stark resemble one of the shambly dogs latching on to its prey in the painting behind him. But the way he stared at Finch wasn't doglike. It reminded him of the older men in the Hoegbotton Irregulars. They too had looked crazy. Like a black flame burned within them.

"Taking my weapon might lead to strong actions by my superiors." Hated Stark for forcing him to use the gray caps as a shield.

Bosun dropped a carving of a cat onto the desk, stepped back. It looked like Feral to Finch. Made him obscurely worried again. Behind him, the sounds of knife on wood again.

Ignoring Bosun, Stark said, "We all know what *superiors* you mean, Finch. You mean those fey, gray-hatted, walking talking shit-stalks. But the fact is I don't care. I haven't cared since I came here, and I will continue not to care until I leave. With as much of Ambergris smoldering behind me as I can manage. So here's a question for you: Why do you work for them? I mean, really? *Why?* Besides fear, of course. Besides a leaky roof over your head and a plate of mashed-up mushrooms on your kitchen table. Do you *like* working for them?"

Finch had never answered that question. Asked: "Why did you leave Ethan Bliss alive?"

Stark nodded in appreciation. "My question is better than yours, but, still— good for you, changing the subject. I took out his team because I don't like surprises, and Bliss seems full of them. Why'd I leave him *alive*? Well, maybe I thought Bliss made enticing bait. Maybe I wanted to see who would come creeping around if I left him alive . . . and here you are."

The smile was a little too painted on, the comment too blunt.

"What did Bliss promise you? And where can I find him?"

Stark sighed. "You're not getting it, Finch. Bliss reminds me of a toy I once had. A mechanical toy. By the time I got it, who could tell what the hell it was or what it was supposed to do. Its uniform or fur or whatever it had wasn't there anymore. It had no eyes, just eyeholes. Mostly it mumbled and marched in place when you wound it up. Who knows what Bliss started out as. I doubt he even remembers. So, where is he? It doesn't matter to me. And if you take my advice you won't let it matter to you, either."

Sudden anger burned in Finch's chest, kindling for pride. "I'm not here to ask your advice."

"Oh, but you are, *Detective*. You want to question me about that nasty double murder you're investigating. You want to know things only I can tell you. What is that but asking advice?" The black flame lit up his eyes. Lent his speech a subdued yet incandescent fury.

Finch leaned forward, into the teeth of Stark's strength. "What do you know about the murders?"

Stark chuckled. "Finchy—that's what Wyte calls you, I think. Finchy, I've been here two months. Why would you think I'd know anything about the murders, except that they occurred? Why, I'm just an immigrant, still getting my land legs. Imagine how many questions I have for *you*."

Finch reached a decision. Slowly pulled the photo of the dead man from his jacket pocket. Slid it across the desk.

"Do you know this man?" The more questions Finch asked the fewer he'd have to answer. Or so he hoped.

Stark made a show of examining the photo, waved it at Bosun, who said, "Already saw it," and went back to his whittling. Stark returned the photo to Finch.

"No. I don't know him. But he looks peculiar. Like he's having a very bad day, and it might get worse. Like he's also sick of this freak show you call a city. Like he might just have decided to hang it all up and go on vacation."

"Is that so?" Finch said, staring at the painting on the wall. "Maybe you should leave with him." The blood. The bullet holes. Did Stark actually *know* anything? Tried to set aside his irritation. Knew he was just sick of Stark insulting his city.

"Don't try to be clever—it doesn't suit you. Here comes another one," Stark said, glaring over Finch's shoulder.

Bosun had finished his next carving in record time. Set it on the desk with something akin to sincerity. A man with a mushroom head. *Wyte?*

"What about the words *bellum omnium contra omnes*?" Finch asked. "Why did you ask Bliss about them?" Bosun had already seen that, too.

"Bosun," Stark said, "did you ask Bliss about that mouthful? Bella . . . bella . . . Finchy, a little help?"

"*Bellum omnium contra omnes.*"

"No," Bosun said. "Don't know what that means. Just nailed him to a wall. Didn't ask him anything."

"You're lying."

"I don't lie," Bosun said, smacking Finch across the back of the head.

Stark spread his hands in a cryptic gesture. "See, Detective? You really don't understand who you're dealing with at all. But now *I've* got a question: Why didn't you arrest Bliss? Bosun says you and Wyte came out of his apartment empty-handed. When Bosun went back inside, Bliss wasn't there. Where'd he go? Did you reach some kind of agreement with him? Except if you had, you wouldn't be asking me where he'd hidden himself."

Confirmation that Bosun had been following them.

"What would I arrest him for? He was the victim. He'd been tortured and his men liquidated."

"Torture's a strong word, Finch," Stark said. "And you're not telling me everything, I'd be willing to bet. You Ambergrisians are naturally clever. Like a fox is clever. Like a rat is clever."

Ignored Stark. Changed tactics. Asked, "Why did you come here?"

"Vacation."

"How long do you plan to stay?"

"As long as my vacation lasts."

"Why did you target Bliss?"

"For fun."

"Do you have any information about the double murder we're investigating?"

"In the apartment on Manzikert Avenue? No."

"Do you like the camps enough to live in them for the rest of your life?"

Stark rose suddenly, seeming to increase threefold in height. "Threats, Detective? Come on! You can do better than that. You have no other clues. You're getting pressure to solve the case. Or maybe not. Maybe you just want to know what's going on because it's eating you alive, not understanding what you're looking at. Such a big mystery, so many ways to disappoint your bosses, only one way to please them. But, then, I'm not here to guess at your motivations."

"Again, then, *why are you here?*"

"Isn't it obvious?" Stark said, gesturing at the blood, the bullet holes. "I'm here to fucking clean house. Clean house and, along the way, maybe make my mark. Nothing wrong with a man turning a profit and helping his country at the same time." Stark pulled a file out of a desk drawer, tossed it across to Finch. Then leaned forward, hands on the chair. "Here's a little something to help us both."

Finch picked up the file. "What's this?"

"A transcript of a . . . conversation . . . two Stockton operatives had a couple of weeks ago. With a gray cap."

That got through. Incredulous: "You interrogated a *gray cap*? Are you insane?"

Stark: "Sane as a lamppost, Finch. Sane as a lamppost. And come to think of it, the whole experience was a little like interrogating a lamppost. A lamppost with teeth."

Some private joke passed between Stark and Bosun that made them both chuckle.

Bosun said, "Grays don't like us much."

Stark, smirking: "No, they don't. Not that you'd ever find me in a room with one of those things. You don't have to teach me, not old Stark. Bosun might be able to take one on, but there's nothing subtle about his approach. It's like a wolf ripping into a pheasant.

"Now, I'm giving you a copy of this transcript because whether you believe it or not, I *like* you . . . even if your name probably isn't Finch any more than mine is Stark. And I especially like you because according to rumor you've killed a gray cap or two before. I imagine you haven't forgotten how? So take a look. See what you think. Does it help with your murders? I can't tell you what to think. But understand this: I'm doing you a favor. I'm bringing you closer to the truth. You might even have a chance of getting out of this alive if you do your job right. That should be valuable to both of us."

Finch, through clenched teeth: "Why shouldn't I give you up to the gray caps?"

Another carving. A woman. Reclining. Crudely made to emphasize her breasts. Didn't want to know who it was meant to be.

"You could. But will I be here when they come? Maybe I won't. Maybe I'll be at your apartment. With a gun. Or maybe I'll be over at *Sintra's* place. *You* don't know where she lives, do you? But maybe *I* do. Maybe I'll be there. She'd be worth the trouble I think. She might even like it."

Finch started to rise. *To do what?* Bosun just as quickly pushed him back down, shoving a gun hard into his ribs. Grinding pain. He stifled a grunt.

"Not smart," Bosun said.

Stark hadn't moved. "Just something to think about, Finch, that's all."

"Where's Wyte?" Finch asked. Because if he didn't ask that question he'd be screaming at Stark.

Stark's smile faded. He ran both hands beneath his eyes, as if to clear cobwebs.

"That's such a dull question. Here's a better one. Ever wonder why they let anyone *stay*? On this godforsaken 'Spit'? Why they don't just raid it and wipe us all out? No clue? Seriously? Well, I'll tell you anyway. It's because they want to send spies back with us, Finch. Little grimy bastards. Most of them too small to see with the naked eye. But luckily not small enough to escape a microscope. And they're spying on everything. Even you. While you're just trying to do your job. How about that, Finch? How does that make you feel?"

"Fuck off," Finch managed, trying to stanch the torrent of words.

But Stark wasn't finished: "For that reason, as much of a shit hole as this city is, I don't look forward to going back to Stockton when this is all over. They put you through hell for decontamination. Weeks. Some spend months. So, to answer your question: you'll get Wyte back soon enough. He won't know where he was or what he saw. But he'll be intact. Except for some skin scrapings. Just in case."

Bosun placed a carving of a boat on the desk. "We get your boat, too," he said.

"No, no, Bosun," Stark said, irritably. He shoved the boat off the side of the desk. "That would be mean of us. Almost cruel. How will they get back to the station otherwise? Can you imagine how cut up their feet would be? How sick they'd be of squishing down on something soft and not knowing if it was a banana peel or something alive and deadly. Why, they might not make it back *at all* by land, going through that gauntlet with no guns, no shoes. No nothing."

"Thanks," Finch said. Making it sound as much like an echo of "fuck off" as possible. The sudden thought that he might have to kill Stark to be free of him.

"Time to leave now," Stark said with a big neighborly smile. "Just know we'll be watching you. Watching and checking in from time to time. I've given you information. You owe me information back."

Almost against his will, biting on the inside of his cheek: "How do I contact you?"

"Oh, you don't, Detective. I'm only here on the Spit to finish cleaning up. I'm not staying on the Spit. That would be suicide. I'll be in touch. Or Bosun will." Pointed with his head to the pile of bodies under blankets. "Poor Davies there, I'm sorry to say, did not clean up well. You might not want to tell Wyte about that, although I'm sure he can guess."

As Bosun led him out, Stark said, in an uncharacteristic tone, like a wistful afterthought, "The towers will be done soon, Finch. Ever wondered about what *that* might mean for this miserable city?"

Silence as they took the boat back across the bay. Finch lay on the deck of the boat. Not giving a shit about how it breathed into him. Staring at the sky. Gray cloud ribbons, the rain now just mist. A hint of cold, something unexpected for the season. Wyte stood above Finch. Fuming. Livid. Jut-jawed about how easily they'd abducted him. Bruises on his face and hands long and narrow from that foreshortened angle.

Finch felt the smooth glide of the boat through thickish water. The way the deck gave a little under his weight. Like he was lying on top of another body.

No gun. No shoes. Just what was left in his pockets, because Bosun didn't want it.

Stark: "I'm here to fucking clean house."

Heretic: "A skery is not as bad for you as what I could bring with me."

Bliss: "You look familiar to me, Detective. Do I know you?"

And the dead man laughing at all of them.

Beside Finch's head, Wyte's feet. In black boots dirty with algae-like fungus. A tiny community. A miniature of the city. Finch imagined he could see creatures there. Creatures who lived out their unaware lives in a state of naive happiness. A sharp smell, like petrol mixed with pepper. The friction of their discourse on that slick black hillside.

He turned his attention back to the sky. Ignored the three crimson tendrils coming out from under Wyte's overcoat. The weariness wasn't from confronting Stark. The weariness was from continually being threatened.

"Wyte. Just so we're clear—you're not thinking about making a deal with Stark. To replace Davies and your other Stockton contacts?"

"No." Didn't sound convincing.

"You're so full of shit, Wyte." Exasperated because back in the day Wyte was the one lecturing him about being naive. Telling him not to trust the ship captains at the docks when what was in their hold didn't match the invoice. Always warning him about getting fooled.

"I'm not going to make any deals!"

Pressing: "What did Stark's people talk to you about then, Wyte? Scratch that—*who* are Stark's people?"

"Nobody! No one," Wyte protested. "They didn't talk to me. I had a hood over my head. I never even saw them. And how do I know you didn't decide to trade information with Stark?"

"Because I didn't, Wyte. You know why? Because he's not like your Stockton contacts from before. You can't really deal with someone like Stark. He'll cheerfully sell you a knife and then slit your throat with it before you've even given him the money."

"I *know* that. Tend to your own house."

"Fair enough."

A silence that spread and spread until it reached the sky. Not really mad at Wyte. Mad at Stark for making him powerless. For humiliating him.

Thick stalks of green appeared at the left edge of his vision. He turned his head. It was the underside of the two towers. The cross-section of scaffolding and support. It seemed alive. Made of vines wrapped around sinews that convulsively wove and rewove themselves together. Thought he saw a dead fox in there. Thought he saw a face.

Then they were past, and it was just the gray again.

Everyone has a theory about the two towers. Finch has heard them all, mostly at the detectives' nameless refuge. When they first decided on the location, they'd had to take the bell out of the bell tower to make more space. A grunting, straining ordeal. To get it down. To shove it out of the one window without destroying the place. It had sunk slowly. Much to their mutual amusement. "It should've sunk like the stone it is," Blakely had said. "Something about the clapper," Wyte had said. "The air trapped inside?" Finch: "Bullshit. It's just being difficult." Could still see it in the water below. Dark and rippling. A shape like the bullet head of some monstrous fish.

Talk of one tower had led to talk of the others.

Skinner: "I hear the towers are being built over the ruins of the old gray cap library. For some ritual."

Wyte: "I heard it's a power source for more electricity. When it's done, the whole city will be lit up again. They're nothing if not practical."

Gustat, snorting his disdain, "Lit up for sure, because it's a weapon. Why else out in the bay? From there, it looks over the whole city. It'll shoot out some kind of energy. Another way to control all of us. First thing they'll do is destroy the Spit."

Blakely: "You're full of shit. It's a huge statue to their god. Or a memorial. Whatever, those are just its legs."

The "island" around their refuge is just floating debris that has matted round. Encouraged by them. Camouflage. Stability. Someday, the whole thing is going to rot. They'll have to go elsewhere. Or maybe by then the city will be theirs again and they'll have their pick of pubs. Won't have to be part of the same chain gang, the same galley crew.

One day they might even get around to building a bridge. But for now, the detectives have built a place to moor a boat, and used the boat to bring across an amazing amount of booze. Salvage from every murder scene. Every call of domestic abuse. A history of Ambergris in alcohol, from Smashing Todd's to Randy Robert's. A smell like sweat and beer. Better than the smell of the station. No electricity, but they've hidden an icebox in the waters below the rotting floorboards at the far end of the main room. Keeps cold enough. They bring food as they have it. Stock the place with gray cap rations too. Tastes like crap, but the food—if that's what it is—never goes bad.

Gustat: "What god? They don't worship a god. They're too practical, like Wyte says."

Albin: "Too practical? By what measure? This is just them working up to another Silence. Better hope the rebels get to it first."

Dapple, uncertainly: "Not true. They can kill us all now if they want to. They don't need more help."

Albin: "Not enough of them for that."

Blakely again: "Some people think it's some kind of gate. They swear late at night you can see things moving through it. That you can see strange stars."

The detectives never talk about work. But, rumor? Rumor is like news from some far distant, more exciting place. Especially about the two towers.

Once, Finch offered his opinion. "They've got limits, first of all. You can see that already. They couldn't control the effects of the HFZ. They need help from the camps to build the towers. When the towers go faster, they put up fewer other buildings. The electricity goes out. Or their radio station goes silent. They have *limits*."

Blank looks. Not getting it. Much easier to think of the gray caps as some implacable force. Like the weather. Something that can't be fought. Because the fact is: if the gray caps want, they can disappear your friends, your family. It doesn't take unlimited resources to do that.

Wyte and Finch aren't allowed at the hideout anymore. Once it became clear Wyte would never really get rid of his affliction. Ever since Finch decided to back him anyway.

5

Finch and Wyte returned to the station in time to witness the end of a rare fight. Blakely and Dapple had gone at it. Under the glow of spectral lamps, the gaze of the tiny windows. Not caring if the gray caps were watching.

Blakely faced them. Standing on the mottled green carpet right where it reached the desks. Nose bloodied. Dapple with his back to them. Hair rising in tufts like he'd been startled. Fists up, too. Albin watching from his desk. A peculiar look of interest and boredom on his face.

Back when it had mattered, Dapple had been a Hoegbotton man. Blakely had been with Frankwrithe & Lewden. Both stared at each other now across a battlefield of other people's betrayal.

The other detectives gathered around.

"I won't do it," Dapple was saying.

"You've done it plenty of times before. Looked behind the curtain," Blakely said with a kind of cruel confidence. "What's different now?"

"I was forced to those other times. None of you did anything to help."

Finch doubted the fight had started there. Or that either remembered what it had really been about. Blakely was famous for baiting others. Daring them to look behind that damned curtain. *Enter the haunted house. Walk through the graveyard at night.*

After Stark and Bosun, Finch felt like he was watching Blakely and Dapple from on high. Heard Wyte mutter from behind him, "Dumb fucks."

Blakely saw them first. Lowered his hands. Tension losing out to puzzlement.

"What happened to your shoes, Finch?" Said with contempt.

Dapple turned, looked too. His eyes were red.

"Nothing as exciting as what was happening here," Finch said, pushing through them, Wyte tightlipped behind him. Over his shoulder, "Whatever play you're practicing for, I'm not paying to go see it."

That got a laugh, though not from Blakely or Dapple. Spared Finch from having to talk about his shoes.

As he and Wyte sat down, Finch tossing Stark's file onto his desk, they got plenty of stares. Looks that said *you'll get questions later.* For now, though, the Blakely-Dapple spat was still more interesting. Skinner was already trying to get them going again, asking Dapple, "Are you just going to take that from him?"

On top of the clutter on Finch's desk: a note to call Rathven. Felt a spark of excitement. Picked up the receiver. Dialed the number. Waited while it rang. Stomach growling. Didn't think he could take more gray cap rations, though. Might wait to eat until he got home. Hunger focused his thoughts. Made him sharper. For a while.

Still ringing.

Wyte, searching through drawers: "I've got an extra pair of shoes somewhere. Too big, but . . ."

Still ringing. He'd try later.

"If you find them, I'll take them," Finch said. No hesitation. Didn't want to take another step without something on his feet. Too easy to pick up something nasty. Sudden memory of his father kneeling to tie his shoelaces. Eight? Nine? Saying, "*Mud between your toes in the river, no one cares. Set one foot outside this house onto the street, I'll never hear the end of it.*" Sounds of his grandparents in the background, arguing about something long forgotten. Father's bristly face inches from his, mouth transformed by a smile. "*Let's go for a walk, shall we?*" Never knew when that meant his father had to meet someone, or if it really was just a walk.

Finch called another number. A number Sintra had given him. None of the phones on their way back had worked. Felt a helpless need to tell her she might be in danger. That "a man named Stark" might be following her.

Experienced an odd relief when no one picked up. Because, really, how could he tell her? Without telling her too much?

All you have to do is play along with Stark and he won't touch her.

How *had* Stark known about Sintra? Bosun casing the hotel? Then following her home? Along with the unworthy thought: *Maybe that's what you should do.*

A perverse pang of jealousy.

A sound of triumph from Wyte, who had produced a scuffed old pair of shoes. "Socks still in them!"

Wyte tossed them at his feet. Wyte had left his fingerprints all over the socks. Blotches of red and black. With a grimace, Finch put on the socks, then the shoes. Too big, but they'd serve.

"Thanks."

"Sure." In a whisper: "Now we just have to get new guns. There might be some in the supply cabinet, but Skinner has the key on his desk."

"Lost your guns, too?" Never live it down.

Finch shook his head. "No. I'm going to get a real gun. Something more reliable. I'm done with guns that leak."

Wyte raised an eyebrow at that. "You sure that's a good idea?"

"If I put a bullet in Stark, I want it to count."

"If you put a bullet in Stark, make sure you've got a good reason. And that you've taken care of his men," Wyte said.

Finch had no answer for that. He looked around. Blakely was by the coffee maker. Laughing at something Gustat had said. Dapple was hiding behind his desk, pretending to work. Trembling. Let the gray caps figure that one out from their surveillance. Skinner and Albin had disappeared for the moment. Good. No one except Wyte was watching.

Picked up the file. Opened it. Saw the Stockton logo. TOP SECRET stamped in red across the top. Scrawled note from Stark, in a spidery script: "My gift to you, Finch. Let me know when you crack the case. If it doesn't crack you first." *Bastard.*

"What is it?" Wyte asked.

"I don't know." And he didn't. Not really.

He started to read, hesitated, then began handing pages to Wyte as he finished them. Wanted to say, "Don't share this with anyone." Instead said, "Remember, Wyte, you told me not to protect you . . ."

And, if you have made a deal with Stark, you'll just be feeding back to him what he already knows . . .

REPORT 2A-ATC-001

Originating Agents: Classified, pending investigation

Interrogation location: 22 East Lake Street

Transcription: Classified

Details:

* 14.3 minutes of a damaged 60-minute tape.

* Breaks in the tape—of unknown length—are indicated in the transcript by "****."

* Brackets around a word or phrase indicate poor sound quality and therefore doubts as to the actual word or phrase.

* There are three voices on the tape, labeled Agent #1, Agent #2, and Subject.

* * *

Agent #1: Is that thing turned on?

Agent #2: Of course it's fucking well turned on. It might say something we need to remember.

Agent #1: Then remember it. Don't put it on tape . . .

Agent #2: No. I want it all on the tape. So we don't [forget] . . .

Agent #1: That Stark's orders?

Agent #2: What the hell is that?

(Sounds of a struggle, followed by labored breathing. Tape turned off, then turned on again.)

Agent #2: Get . . . that thing away from me.

Agent #1: Goddamn it they're tough bastards. Even I forget sometimes. Okay, put it on the tape. Doesn't really matter, does it?

Agent #2: You want to ask it the questions?

Subject: I will [answer] no questions.

Agent #1 or #2: Shut up.

(Loud slap. Sound of a chair falling down?)

Agent #2: Be careful. Be careful. It hasn't even started talking yet.

Subject: Long and painful for you . . . your insides will explode, your lips and cheeks split open. Your brains feed the birds.

Agent #1: Cheery fucker, isn't he? And they're all like that.

Subject: I do not know the answer to your questions. Your question sounds
like a [question]. It does not sound like an answer. Do you have an answer?

Agent #1: What were you doing when we caught you? Simple question.

Agent #2: Oh, do it right. Do it right . . . For the record: Subject was
intercepted and brought to this location after stepping out of a strange
door. Like a secret panel or something, which closed up after him.

Agent #1: You stupid fucking mushroom. Answer the question. Answer now
and save yourself.

Agent #2: For the record, the Subject drew a symbol on the table. In some sort of
golden dust. Kind of a half circle then a circle then a line with another line
across it. Then two more half circles at the end. I'll draw it later.

Agent #1: More bullshit. Shove some more water into it. Only thing that works.

(A sound like water being poured from a jug. Splashes. Sounds of gasping. A cracking sound.
A shriek. Silence for a long time, but no cut in the tape.)

Agent #1: Can you hear [me]? I know you can hear me.

Subject: I hear [you]. [You will] all die. I will myself see you afloat in the
canal. Cultured. You are not—

* * *

Agent #1: Just more water then.

Agent #2: It'll die.

Agent #1: Don't care.

Agent #2: Don't you think Stark should—

Agent #1: The hell with Stark. He's been here, what? Three seconds?

Agent #2: Record shows [name redacted] authorized additional water torture on the Subject.

Agent #1: Shut the fuck up and help with this.

(A gurgling, thrashing sound. Spluttering. Silence.)

Agent #1: Now, once again, where'd that door come from?

* * *

Subject: . . . been where you were not. But you'll never read them. Not before we finish the towers.

Agent #1: What is behind the door?

Subject: Nothing for you. Too late.

Agent #2: Now I'm getting impatient with this. Maybe this will help you. Remember.

(Long, prolonged scream. Not human.)

Subject: Don't do that again. Don't do that again. Don't do that again. Don't—

* * *

Agent #2: He doesn't [know] what he means. I should just kill him now.

Agent #1: Not yet. Not yet. Tell me, mushie, about this gold. Where'd it come from?

(From here on, Subject's words are more garbled, as if its mouth had been damaged. Accuracy of transcript compromised.)

Subject: Not a [filo] left. Not one. What [indecipherable] would take me like this?

Agent #2: What about the gold?

Subject: Yes, lots of gold there. Lots of gold other places, too. Gold is everywhere. Gold and green. The light, the water . . .

Agent #1: Do you mean the door? Or do you mean real gold?

Agent #2: Should we start on his legs? Fucking thing [smells] like shit. I think he's rotting.

Agent #1: Other places? What do you mean, other places?

Subject: Someday we will move other places but you will still only be here.

Agent #2: Give it up. He's hallucinating.

Agent #1: Just wait. Mushie—tell me just a little more, and maybe we'll let you go. Back underground where it's safe. Would you like that?

Subject: No place is safe. For you.

* * *

Subject: No more. No more. You, maybe if you [know] what it says there. Maybe you will not [indecipherable gray cap word].

Agent #2: We'll let you go if you just tell us—what is this weapon the rebels have?

Subject: [stream of gray cap swear words]

Agent #1: What about this address, then? The chapel at 1829 Northwest Scarp Lane. This rebel safe house. Ring a bell? Has it got something to do with the weapon? Our sources say it has something to do with the weapon.

Subject: Make me sleep. Burn me. Take me back to where I was.

Agent #2: He doesn't know anything about it. That much is clear.

Agent #1: Start on his legs.

(Prolonged screams.)

* * *

Agent #1 (panting): It's done. It's over.

Agent #2: Where do you think you're going?

Agent #1: He's not going to say anything else. If he is still alive—and I doubt that—kill him and throw him in a canal. No, wait, cut him up. Dump him somewhere they won't find him for a while.

Agent #2: And what the fuck will you be doing while I'm doing [that]? That's going to take me a long fucking time.

Agent #1: I've already got plans. And they don't include waiting around here. We've gotten all we're going to get.

Agent #2: You're staying. Stark's orders. I'm telling you—

(Sounds of something heavy falling over.)

Agent #2: . . . Not dead! It's got a hand free.

Agent #1: Shit. Get that other light on. Get it on quick.

(Banging on the door. Calling out to some third agent.)

Agent #2: Open the fucking door! This isn't funny. I don't see it now. It was here just a second ago. Is it in the fireplace? Dammit, at least throw a gun back in here. And unlock the fucking door. I can't see a fucking thing.

Subject: But I can.

(Screaming for three minutes, then tape cuts off.)

6

Finch stared at his desk for a while after he'd read the last page. A kind of primal horror rose even as he tried to tamp it down. Mixed up with a question: *What does Stark want me to take from this? How does it help him for me to have this?*

Wyte finished. Handed the pages back like they had been dipped in poison. "How'd they think they'd get away with that?" he said. Voice haggard. "Killing a—"

"Don't say it." Finch stood. "Let's go for a walk." Took the file with him. Wyte trailed behind. Down that emerald carpet, past the crumbling marble tables at the front that once served as cover for receptionists. Through the massive, worm-riddled double doors, gold leaf long since peeled off and sold. Along with the inlaid iron bars.

Walked out into the light. Onto Albumuth Boulevard. Above them rose a sharp finger of red bricks, jutting. Only sign the building had ever had five stories instead of two. Ahead, the rough stone barricades that discouraged suicide bombers. Lichen sensors in purple-and-green dotted their surface. Beyond that, the dirty street. Just a few people in gas masks walking past. Huge black insect eyes. Trench coats. Gloves. Hunched over. Not looking in their direction.

Finch pulled Wyte to the side. Against the faded brick wall. Who knew if it was safer. But it felt safer. Reminded him of when Wyte used to bring him out here and patiently explain how he'd screwed up back when he worked as a courier.

"Why don't you tell me what you think."

Wyte looked at him for a second as if to say "You really want my opinion?" Then, slowly, "Two Stockton agents kidnapped a gray cap who came out of a secret door. Maybe a door leading to the underground? One of the agents worked for Stockton before Stark arrived. The other probably came with him. There was a third agent outside as a precaution while they interrogated the gray cap."

"Water torture," Finch interjected. "Take note of that. Not something I'd've thought to use." Thinking of his encounters during the war.

"So they interrogate the gray cap. Pretty brutally. And they ask him about the door, and the gray cap seems to make a connection between this door and the towers."

Agent #2: For the record: Subject was intercepted and brought to this location after stepping out of a strange door. Like a secret panel or something. Closed up after him.

"And there's another connection, Wyte. If you can appear out of a strange door that disappears, you can *disappear* out of a door that *appears*, perhaps."

Wyte: "Bliss?"

Bliss or Dar Sardice. Warming to this task now. Relishing the idea of figuring it out. "Remember that Bliss knew exactly which mushrooms to use for his wounds."

"True," Wyte said, but he frowned, like he didn't totally agree. "So then they talk about gold, but not real gold. The gray cap seemed to be taunting them a bit. And after that, they're following up on information that led them to believe the gray caps know about some weapon the rebels have."

Agent #1: Do you mean the door? Or do you mean real gold?

Agent #2: We'll let you go if you just tell us—what is this weapon the rebels have?

"And there's that mention of the two towers." Finch searched through the pages, found it. "Here—'been where you were not. But you'll never read them. Not before we finish the towers.' And then one agent asks about the door again. What does that mean?"

Wyte shook his head. "I don't know."

They stood there. Looking at each other. As if the answer might appear between them through sheer force of will.

What did Stark know? Maybe he didn't know anything. Maybe he was flushing out information like he'd flushed out two detectives by messing with Bliss.

"A rebel weapon. Strange doors. Gold that isn't gold. The two towers." Finch laughed. "Fuck if I know what it means." And he didn't, not really, even though answers kept niggling at the edges of his thoughts.

"But maybe we know how Bliss escaped," Wyte said.

Using magic. Using trapdoors. Maybe he turned into a door himself. Finch put that aside for later.

"Heretic is going to want another report. By tonight." He'd promised not to leave anything out. Didn't dare leave anything out. "At least we've got a couple of addresses." Finch wondered if Wyte was as relieved as he was at the prospect of having real leads.

"Want me to check them out?"

Finch: "Just the one."

Wyte: "Which one?"

"Where they tortured the gray cap."

Where they both died because they didn't finish the job properly. Searched for it in the transcript, pointed to it with his finger: "22 East Lake Street. But for Truff's sake, *use a proxy.* Get one of your snitches to do it for you. Watch from down the street just in case. If the gray caps have the place under surveillance, you don't want to just walk right up to it."

"What about the other address?"

Lowering his voice as a Partial passed by on the other side of the street: "If it's a real lead and not something Stark stuck into the transcript to fuck with us, it's too dangerous. A rebel safe house? Not even clear the gray cap knew what they were talking about? Wyte, that's a job for Partials. I'll put that in my report to Heretic. But I have to leave out the part about a tortured gray cap, and where we got the information. Which means, we need to check out the torture address ourselves."

"What am I looking for?"

"I don't know."

Wyte didn't seem to care. "Shouldn't take more than an hour or two there and back. Maybe a little more if I check in with some of my snitches along the way." His expression had become tighter, more defined. As if Finch was filling him with purpose, the thing encroaching on Wyte beaten back. For now.

Finch clapped him on the shoulder as they went inside. Wyte grabbed his coat. Lumbered over to Skinner's desk, swiped the key as Skinner watched. Went over to the supply cabinet. No longer caring what they thought. Got a gun, loaded it, and headed for the door with what almost looked like a skip in his step.

Blakely stared at the door Wyte had disappeared through: "What, you finally agreed to marry him?" With a leer.

Finch ignored him. Time to call Rath again.

Rath's voice crackled and hissed through the bad connection. Sounded like she was buried deep in a watery cave.

"Finch," she said. "I've got news. I think I've found out about—"

"What I wanted to know?" he said. Before she could say "the dead man."

"Yes."

A prickle of excitement. Along with a sobering wave of caution. He still didn't know for sure who had given up Sintra to Stark.

Kept his voice calm. "I'll come by after work." Fought the urge to say he'd be right there.

"You don't want to know now?" Disappointment in her voice.

"Busy. I'll catch up with you later." Hoping she'd understand. *They're listening.*

Click. Either Rath had hung up or the line had gone out.

A sudden elation wouldn't leave him. Made him give out a little laugh. Even though he knew it was premature. Usually you knew who the dead person was to begin with. The trail was three days cold by now.

How to frame it all for Heretic?

Finch thumbed through Stark's report again. Thought about his encounter with Stark on the boat. Bliss's disappearance. Bliss's appearance in the memory bulb dream.

What could he tell Heretic?

Blakely, Skinner, and Gustat were working at their desks. Once upon a time, he might've consulted with them. But the Wyte situation made that impossible now. Sometimes he thought they even liked Wyte better than him. Wyte couldn't help it. Finch could help it. Didn't have to side with Wyte.

The phone rang. He stared at the receiver for a second. *Sintra? Rathven?*

Finch picked it up.

"Hello."

"Finchy!" Stark's voice. Strong and smooth. A shock hearing it on his station phone. "I see you've read the transcript of our little drama, since Wyte's already hotfooting it over to where Number One and Number Two heroically sacrificed for the greater good."

Finch leaned forward. Shielded the receiver with his hand. In a low voice: "How did you get this phone number? Don't you know—"

"Don't I know what, Finch? That I'm one of your informants, calling in as scheduled? To ask: Did you like what you read?" A mischievous lilt to the words. Blood behind it.

Play Stark's game or just hang up? Blakely was giving him an odd look. Dapple too.

Finch turned his back on them, phone on his lap. "Yes, I did. I did like it. So long as it's true. I would have liked to heard the conversation myself."

"Oh, I don't think so," Stark said. "I don't think you would've liked that at all. It's quite melodramatic. Practically bathetic. The kind of thing that would've lent itself to opera, back in the day."

Except then I'd know if you'd left anything out. Or put anything in.

"How about the Subject?" Finch asked. "Did the Subject get away?" *Does Heretic know about any of this?*

"Alas, the Subject didn't get far. A tragic case of smoking in bed. Happens all the time. After the Subject finished with our poor agents, the Subject went to sleep. A sound, sound sleep."

"I don't know what that means."

"Oh, you know what it means, Finch."

"What do you want, then?"

"What do I want? Nice of you to ask." Stark's tone had gotten colder. "I want lots of things. So many things it's hard to know where to begin. Money's always good. Especially *gold.* I could also use a *weapon.* You know, to defend myself against the rebels. Think you can deliver that? After all, I've delivered for you."

"What you've delivered are rumors," Finch said. "What you've delivered is information we don't know will lead to anything important."

A pause. Then, "I'm not sure I like your attitude, Detective. Maybe I should be working with someone else. Maybe I should be working with your girlfriend. Or your friend Rathven. Or your partner, Wyte. Or even that madman who lives right outside of your hotel. Would you prefer that?"

Managed a calm tone. "No. I think the arrangement we have will be fine." Realized he'd curled his free hand into a fist. Knuckles white. Nails biting into his palm.

Laughter on the other end. "I thought you might say that. I thought you might see it my way. It's all on you now. Just remember: we'll be watching."

Hung up before Finch could reply.

7

Back on the roof of the hotel. Where Finch could see it all from on high. See it clean and remote. Banish pointless images of ripping out Stark's throat. Shooting him dead in the street. If Heretic doubted Finch, killing Stark wouldn't help anything. He'd filed his report before he left. Stuffed it down the memory hole with misgivings. Would it be enough?

Wanted clarity before he saw Rathven, knew he wasn't going to get it.

The sun was going down. Watched the orange-yellow shimmer. Tried to ignore the towers, but that was impossible. The light made them a fuzzy green, as if dusted with pollen. The glare hurt his eyes.

The Photographer would be coming up soon. Finch had knocked on his door on the way up. Thin shadow through slit of door. Pale face rising from someplace submerged to meet his request. Told him that what he wanted would take thirty, forty minutes.

Too restless to sit. Hands in the pockets of his jacket. Left hand clenched around a piece of paper, a time line:

Stark arrives—disappearing door—gray cap tortured—two murders—strange phrase on scrap of paper—Bliss—men murdered—Bliss disappears—two towers near completion—Stark gives us information—Heretic presses re the case . . .

How much of it was really connected?

Agent #2: For the record, the Subject drew a symbol on the table. In some sort of golden dust. Kind of a half circle then a circle then a line with another line across it. Then two more half circles at the end. I'll draw it later.

Now he had to reconsider the gray symbol on the torn piece of paper. Had preferred the case when it all seemed to be about Bliss.

Within the hour, he'd know the identity of the dead man. Part of him wanted to know. Part of him thought he wasn't going to like the answer.

He'd included almost everything in the report for Heretic except the tortured gray cap. *Put some heat on Stark.* And nothing about Rathven. After all, Finch hadn't even spoken to her yet. But he'd had to mention the words on the piece of paper. Called it a possible password.

Wyte had returned before Finch had filed the report, with nothing to add but a bad mood. Looking like shit again. His informant had found nothing at the address, because the building had burned to the ground. No witnesses. "Nothing except this." Wyte had tossed a carving onto Finch's desk. Crudely like a gray cap. Along with some information from his informant: Bosun was Stark's younger brother. Known in Stockton as a brawler and boozer. *Interesting, but what to do with it?* Stark was still a question mark.

The hatch behind him opened. Out unfolded the gawky frame of the Photographer. Once upright, he walked across to Finch. Holding something that seemed to absorb the light in his long fingers. Compact. Functional. Deadly.

"Here, take it," the Photographer said. As if Finch needed prompting.

Finch loved the weight as his right hand closed over it. Had a cold, comforting heft. A Lewden Special: a vicious snub-nosed semiautomatic. He'd used one during the wars. Taken it off a dead man. Liked it. Liked it almost too much. Could reload quickly. Accurate fire. Used bullets that ended things. Bullets that exploded inside the body. Would cause even a gray cap an acute case of indigestion. Finch hadn't expected something this good.

Gave the Photographer a sly look. "What, exactly, did you do before the Rising?"

On the Photographer a smile looked grim. "I took photos." No other information was forthcoming.

Finch looked at him for a moment, then dropped it. "Ammo?"

"Yes," the Photographer said. Handed over ten clips. Twenty bullets in each.

Finch's eyebrows rose. He'd only asked for five clips. Looked at the Photographer as if to say *What do you know that I don't?*

"How much?"

"Nothing now. Maybe a favor, later."

"Just make sure to ask while I can still grant favors." Wry laugh.

"Or while I still need them." The Photographer's expression revealed neither humor nor the lack of it.

Listening with only one ear. Thoughts wandering back to the transcript. The two towers. A strange door. *The rebels have a weapon.*

Which rebels? came a question from a voice in his head. *The ones in Ambergris or the ones in the HFZ?*

They turned to watch the city at dusk. The unexpected phosphorescence in places. As if the sun's death throes. The now-dull green glow rippling from the bay. The towers were still being worked on nonstop. Finch could almost imagine them complete now.

"What do you think the towers are for?" Finch asked the Photographer.

A gleam of interest entered the Photographer's dead black eyes. "Sometimes I dream. I dream it's a giant camera. And it's taking pictures of places we can't see."

Rathven let him in without a word. She locked the door behind them quickly.

"There have been strangers in the building the last couple days," she told him.

"I know," he said. *Some of them may even have been here to visit you.* Glad of the weight of the gun in his jacket pocket. Trust wasn't something Finch gave up lightly. But he was willing to give it up.

"Why do you think they're here?"

"No idea." Not entirely true.

The water had receded for the moment. Leaving odd marks on the floor and walls beyond the main room that gave evidence of tides and eddies. Remains of minerals. Remains of books that hadn't survived. A broom leaning against the wall, used to sweep away water. The stacks and stacks of books. That odd darkness of a tunnel leading . . . *where?* And where did she sleep?

Rathven took two books from an old sofa chair. Put them on the table. An old oil lamp flickered across the books, which were tattered and stained. Mold and worms had been at them. A thick mustiness made Finch sneeze. The gray caps' ridiculous list lay sprawled beneath the table.

She asked him to sit. He didn't like that the chair was so comfortable. Felt like he could fall asleep in it. Wanted to ask, in a conversational way, "So, did a man named Bosun visit you? Maybe a man named Stark?" But didn't. That conversation could wait. As for warning her, she had plenty of reasons to be careful already.

She pulled up an old wooden chair. Turned it around, leaning her arms against the back. Looking tense. Unsettled. The straight, unflinching stare she gave him undermined by quick glances toward the tunnel. Was she expecting someone to appear?

"Do you need tea or coffee?" she asked. He only liked tea now for some reason, but wanted neither at the moment.

"I'm tired, Rath. I'm not in the mood. What did you find out?"

Rathven winced. "Just the information, right?"

"What's wrong?" he asked, feeling he'd insulted her. "Something's wrong."

She stared at him with those large hazel eyes. "You're not going to like what I found out."

Finch laughed. Until the tears came. Doubled over in the grip of the chair. "I'm not going to like what you found out? I'm not going to *like* it?"

Glanced over, wiping at his face with his sleeve. Saw her confusion.

"Rath, I haven't learned anything I *liked* since Monday. There's nothing about this case that I've found *likable*. Nothing. This morning I went out to interrogate a suspect and came back without my socks, my shoes, or my gun."

That brought a curling half smile, but her eyes were still wary. As if the idea was both funny and horrible to her. "Your socks? Walking around in your bare feet? *In Ambergris?*"

He nodded. Sobered. "So, what did you find out?"

A deep breath from Rathven. She looked like a creature used to being in motion stopped in midstride. Asked a fundamental question about its own existence.

"Yesterday, I read all of the names on your list. That took a long time. Then I made a much shorter list of any names I recognized."

"Like?"

"People with any historical significance. I didn't recognize anyone I knew personally. But there were a few names from the past. A minor novelist. A sculptor. A woman who was a noted engineer. I thought I'd look them up in various histories. See if they had connections to anyone in the present."

"A long shot." But he admired her for having a process.

"Yes. At the same time, I also started checking names from the past thirty years with what city records still exist. But I didn't get far."

"Why?"

Rathven leaned forward, balancing on two chair legs. "Because I came across information about one of the names on the list. Someone who lived in that apartment a long time ago."

"Who?"

Rathven said the name. It meant nothing to him, but rang in his head like a gunshot.

"Duncan Shriek," he repeated. "Who was he?"

"Good question. It took some research, but I thought I'd heard the name before. Not sure where. I had to borrow a couple of books to find out."

"And?"

She seemed reluctant to answer, which made Finch reluctant, too. As if he needed her to go slow to protect himself. From a feeling that had begun to creep up from his stomach.

Tightening his chest.

She sucked in her breath, continued: "And I did—I found out a lot about him. Shriek was a fringe historian. He had some radical ideas about the Silence. About the gray caps. They wouldn't seem radical to us now. They'd seem mostly right. But by the time anyone would've been able to see that, he was gone. Disappeared. Over a hundred years ago."

Suddenly, Finch felt disappointed in her.

"What's the connection to the here and now? How does this help me?"

Rathven leaned back again. "Take a look at the two books on the table."

The feeling in his stomach got worse. Finch looked at her. Looked at the table. Back at her. Straightened in the sofa chair. Picked up the books gently. Felt the dust on his hands.

Turned to the title page of the first. *Shriek: An Afterword*, written by Janice Shriek with Duncan Shriek.

"Janice? His wife?" A strange emotion was rising now, unconnected to the feeling of dread. A formless sadness. A watchfulness.

"No," Rathven said in a flat tone. "No. His sister."

"Is it fiction? Nonfiction?"

"A kind of memoir by Janice with comments by Duncan. She was an art gallery owner. A major sponsor of many artists back then. She went missing, and so did her brother. Both around the same time. But it's the other one you really need to look at."

Finch put down *Shriek: An Afterword*, picked up the other book. "*Cinsorium & Other Historical Fables*," he read. "By Duncan Shriek." Felt a twinge of irritation or resentment. Couldn't she get to the point?

"Look at the inside back cover. Of the dust jacket," Rathven said.

Turned to the back. Found the author's photo staring out at him. A confusion overtook him that snuffed out rational thought.

The man could've been forty-five or fifty, with dark brown hair, dark eyebrows, and a beard that appeared to be made from tendrils of fungus.

"Fuck."

The man laughed again. Blindingly, unbelievably bright, a light like the sun shot through the window. The night sky torn apart by it.

The photo was ancient. Stained. Falling apart. But it didn't lie. The face in the back of the book matched the face of the dead man in the apartment.

Light-headed. Cold. He sat back in the chair, the books in his lap. *Cinsorium* closed so he didn't have to look at the photo. *Never lost.*

"When did he live there? *Show me the entry.*"

Rathven reached down to get the list. "It's already folded right to it." Handed it to him.

SHRIEK, DUNCAN, OCCUPANCY 17 MONTHS, 5 DAYS, 15 HOURS, 4 MINUTES, 56 SECONDS—WRITER AND HISTORIAN; LEFT SUDDENLY, DISAPPEARED AND PRESUMED DEAD.

"That's impossible," Finch said, letting the list slither out of his hands to the floor. "That's impossible."

Felt exposed. Vulnerable like never before. The semiautomatic at his side was no protection at all. *Stark, lips drawn back in a leer. Bosun and his psychotic carvings. Bliss as a young F&L agent staggering across the Kalif's desert. A dead man talking to him, flanked by a cat and a lizard.*

Rathven nodded. "It's impossible. But it's him."

The books felt too heavy in his lap. "Or his twin. Or his great-great-grandson."

"Do you really believe that, Finch?" Rathven asked.

"No."

No, he really didn't. Not in his gut.

Suddenly, the double murder had a sense of scale that expanded in his mind like Heretic's list. A time line almost beyond comprehension.

How to escape this?

I am not a detective.

He understood Rathven's look now.

Haunted.

Being haunted had started for his father during the war against the Kalif's empire, in the engineering arm of the Hoegbotton army. Something had gotten into his lungs during that time. The doctors at the clinic, toward the end, still couldn't find a solution. Something about dust. Different kinds of dust. Dust from the road to empire, thousands of years old. Dust from the retreat. Dust from trying to hold Ambergris together. Dust from betraying it.

Earlier on during the campaign there had been a feeling of optimism, a heady confidence. House Frankwrithe had been beaten back to Morrow. The gray caps seemed once again in decline, and because of the war effort Ambergris now had a powerful military.

As his father had said once, "They didn't want it to go to waste. And they feared that the young officers might be too ambitious left at home. And there was this kind of claustrophobic restlessness hard to understand now, perhaps. People wanted to be part of Ambergris, but to be *out* of it at the same time. They felt cramped, hemmed in—and the eastern flank of the Kalif's empire was so close, and the Kalif spread so thin, defending all of that territory. It was too tempting. Too easy."

One of his father's first tasks was to get the Hoegbotton army across the Moth in a way that allowed quick return. He accomplished this with boats, with floating bridges that could be taken apart and reused in other ways. From there, "the Fixer," as he came to be called, participated in more than a dozen battles. Helping take defensive positions. Solving how to get across supposedly impassable mountains. Whenever they needed an engineer, he was there. And he had the photographs to prove it, the ones Finch had since consigned to the flames: his lean, clean-shaven figure posing in front of a canyon, a cityscape, a smoldering tank. If the posture seemed more stooped, more resigned, the smile a little more faded as time passed, it could have been the natural process of aging. If not for Finch knowing that, eventually, what his father had found there would kill him.

He'd told Finch one day that he'd imagined he would be able to quit the military, take on the civilian projects that he preferred. Saw, he said, a grand new age of architectural expansion, as in the days of Pejoran. A city reimagined and rebuilt in a way that meant more than just restoration or renovation. Mineral deposits that fueled a war effort could fuel a peace effort.

But it didn't happen that way, as if the dust of empire that slowly changed his father had changed Ambergris, too. House Hoegbotton's race to acquire territory in the name of Ambergris meant not engaging insurgents at its exposed flanks: holding cities but not holding land. Until, finally, a slow collapse back to the River Moth, leaving behind as evidence of their passage more than a few half-breed children, abandoned equipment, and all of Finch's father's engineering projects. His father had had photos of these, too. In a separate album. He used to thumb through it at night with Finch on his lap, as if to deny what had happened next.

Images from some other life. A few of a woman with the distinctive features of the west. Faded. Worn. Lost.

His father had returned to an Ambergris exhausted in some ways, with House Frankwrithe eager to resurrect itself in people's hearts because House Hoegbotton neglected the home front to focus on the Kalif. Food shortages, electricity shortages.

In the decade that followed, Finch's father rose to become a strangely neutral figure. As the divide between Hoegbotton and Frankwrithe became narrower, as the city devolved into regions and factions and neighborhoods, he found himself working in government as a former war hero. For bridges. For reconstruction of roads. For anything that could bring back, even for just a month or a year, stability to a district or side.

"It was like fighting a guerilla war of engineering," he told Finch once. "I'd rebuild it. Someone else would smash it."

Finch believes that being found out was a kind of relief for his father. To give up the exhaustion of playing sides against each other. Of having to find work. Of having to be so secretive. Being a fugitive didn't weigh on him as heavily.

Thinks about this as he struggles with the mystery that is Duncan Shriek.

Is Duncan Shriek the dust, coming down across a century, that will kill him?

8

Could be a twin. Could be a great-great-grandson. But wasn't.

Finch walked up the stairs to his apartment, holding the two books. Rath had tried to get him to stay longer. As if she didn't want to be alone with what she'd found out. But *he* had to be alone with it.

Still at a loss. You could plod along for years thinking you were holding on, that you were doing okay. That you might even be doing a little good. Then something happened and you realized you didn't understand *anything*. A sudden shuddering impulse for Sintra that he understood was reflexive. Wasn't real. Was about forgetting. Even though he needed to remember.

The stairs seemed to go on forever. Like a throat swallowing him up.

Finch had shielded Rath from his confusion. Asked her to do more investigative work. Suggested there was a rational explanation. Even though he didn't believe it. Even intimated he knew something he couldn't share.

How long until Heretic knows? Maybe he already knows.

He came to the seventh floor. Saw that his apartment door was open a crack. Which drove Duncan Shriek from his mind and brought Stark back. Stark and Bosun. Unless it was Sintra?

Would she have left the door open?

Strange, how calm he felt. Had he played out the scenario of intruder in his mind too often to be surprised?

Finch placed the two books on the floor. Took out his Lewden Special and released the safety. Nudged the door wider. Saw the gray and black silhouettes of his living room furniture, the kitchen beyond, and the window directly ahead of him. A hazy green-white light came from outside.

No one there.

No sign of anyone having been there.

Maybe they'd already left.

Maybe he'd forgotten to close the door. *Not likely.*

Slowly, Finch entered, sighting along the gun's barrel. Still felt like ice water ran through his veins. Saw even the darkness in preternatural detail.

Stood to the left of the window. In the shadow of bookcases. Listening. Heard someone breathing in the next room. Someone moving around. *What if it is Sintra?*

Decided to wait there. Let whoever it was come out into the living room. Now, finally, his heart pounded. Images of mistakes flashed through his head. Of Sintra with a bullet hole through her forehead. Or Wyte.

The bedroom door opened. Out came a shadow. Finch couldn't see the face. Couldn't see a weapon, either.

"I've got a gun. Stay where you are, or I'll shoot," Finch said.

The shadow stopped, quick glance toward him. Then ran for the window.

The window?

Already moving forward, Finch squeezed the trigger. The roar of the Lewden Special. A thick splintering sound from the bookcase opposite. He'd missed.

The figure leapt. Closing the distance, Finch leapt with him. A circle of green light had appeared. Rimmed with fiery gold. Shot through the middle with purest black. The figure went through the circle—and Finch went too, slamming into the shadow's back. Grabbing hold of the shoulders. Gun still in his hand.

The blackness extended. *Past the floor.*

Gasped, screamed. Overcome by the sense of falling. Held on to the figure, which was trying to throw him off. Finch's face felt like it was burning. The blackness was absolute.

Falling into the throat of a *skery*. Falling into nothing. Falling through the window. To their deaths. His stomach kept dropping and dropping. He kept screaming and screaming.

And still they fell.

Nothing lost.

All lost.

THURSDAY

I: Why do you hate Partials?

F: I don't hate them.

I: We all have a job to do.

F: I don't like cameras.

I: Where did you go during the party?

F: Nowhere. Home. I went home.

I: You were seen on the street after curfew. By a Partial.

F: It was someone else. No. No. Please. Don't! [sounds of weeping] I
didn't go anywhere. I don't remember.

I: Who was it? Stark? The Lady in Blue? Bliss? Someone else?

F: All of them. None of them. Doesn't matter what answer I give. *Your*
answer is always the fucking same.

I: I can make you remember.

1

Light. Blinding him. They both fell heavy and sprawling across some unforgiving surface. Gun skittered out of his hand. A shooting pain in his left leg, ribs. Cried out. Lost his grip on the man's shoulders. Every scrap of skin *crawled*. As if he'd passed through a cloud of hornets. Spasmed for a moment, his muscles not obeying his commands. Brain on fire. Worse than the *skery*. Came to rest gasping. Rough stones with something soft between them. An intense clapping sound rose up. Faded.

The other man rolled to the side. Started to get up. Finch reached out. Caught a booted foot. Pulled the man back down toward him. He opened his eyes just a slit against the terrible light. Saw the man's face.

"Bliss! Bliss!" Finch hissed. Still in the grip of darkness. He dragged Bliss closer as the man kicked, struggling to get free. Jumped on top of him. Punched him in the kidneys. Once. Twice. Three times. Knuckles aching. Bliss grunted. Finch delivered an elbow across the face, through Bliss's guard. Bliss went limp. Saw the man's eyelids flutter, his eyes almost roll back into his head.

Finch got up, staggering. *What did you do to me?* Keening. Kicked Bliss in the ribs. A bark of distress and Bliss curled onto his side.

Meant to launch another kick, but was brought up short. The ground around them had caught his attention. Dull red tiles. Yellow-green weeds thrusting up between them.

Looked up. In a sudden panic, he realized that the terrible light was the sun. He stood in the middle of an empty courtyard. A rusted, crumbling fountain. Blank azure-amber eyes of some long-dead hero astride a rusting horse. Mottled brown fish spouting air beside him.

Above the wall facing him: the looming white dome of one of the camps. Took a quick glance behind. The green shimmer of the two towers just visible through an archway leading out. A flock of pigeons circling. The clapping sound.

He was between the Spit and the Religious Quarter.

On the other side of the bay from his apartment.

The sun was out.

In the middle of the night.

Finch began to shake. Fought down nausea.

Said, gasping the words, "What the fuck did you *do*, Bliss?" Almost couldn't stop saying it. Taste of grit in his mouth. Skin still twitching.

Bliss raised his head, still on his side. Through blood-greased teeth: "Don't be frightened. We went through a *door*. Like any other door."

Finch kicked Bliss again for that. This time he didn't cry out, just lay there. Found his gun. Squatting beside Bliss, Finch shoved the muzzle against the man's left cheek. Forced Bliss's face against the stone.

"Answer my questions. Answer them without any bullshit," voice calmer than he felt.

This wasn't the first time he'd put a gun to someone's face. But he was threatening a man who, in his former life, had made speeches and led parades. A man now reduced to snooping in apartments after dark.

"I'll answer them! Stop hitting me." Startling bloodshot white of Bliss's eye trying to look up at Finch from that extreme angle. Face already darkening with bruises like a stormy sky.

"Get up," Finch said. He pulled the smaller man to his feet by one arm. Looked around. Two exits. The archway behind him. Another on the far side. Didn't trust the broken windows blinding him with the sun. Anyone could be watching.

Finch dragged Bliss into the darkness of the nearest archway. The contrast of shadows after the extreme light almost left him blind again. Black sunspots everywhere.

Pushed Bliss up against a whitewashed wall turned gray. Bricks exposed through the mortar like dark red teeth in a rotting mouth. Got close to Bliss so he could force the gun under the man's jaw. Pinned him to the wall with a fist wrapped around his shirt collar.

His hands were steady now. Shock hadn't set in yet. Maybe it never would.

Bliss was wheezing from the pressure of the Lewden Special against his windpipe. Trying to swallow.

"Now. Tell me what just happened." He eased up on Bliss's throat.

Bliss coughed. Managed, in a hollow voice, "Like I said, nothing to panic about. We just went through a door."

Something switched on in Finch. *Stark threatening him. Heretic and the skery. Falling through darkness with Bliss like moving through the doors on the Spit, like traveling through the gullet of a skery large as a behemoth.*

Smashed Bliss across the face with the Lewden. Felt a satisfying *give* as metal met flesh and laid open Bliss's right cheek. Bliss made a sound more like surprise than pain. Began to slump but Finch held him up. Blood flowed down the side of Bliss's face. Spattered onto his shoulder. Another puzzled sound. Like he couldn't believe Finch was doing this to him.

"You already said it was a door, Bliss. Tell me something new."

Bliss's head drooped toward his chest. Finch slapped him lightly.

"Stay with me, Bliss," Finch said. Released his grip on Bliss's collar. "Here." Handed him his handkerchief. "Keep it."

"Thanks," Bliss said, with more than a hint of something deadly behind the word. He held the handkerchief to his face, the gray-white soon soaked with red.

"If you tell me enough I'll let you go," Finch said. Tried to sound reasonable. As reasonable as he could while he kept the gun trained on Bliss. Truth was, he didn't know what he was going to do with Bliss. Or to him.

After a moment, Bliss said in a dull tone, "We went through a door to another part of the city. Across a kind of bridge."

"That's how you escaped the first time. There was no hidden exit."

"No, there wasn't," Bliss said.

"It was night just a few minutes ago." Couldn't keep the confusion from his voice.

"From the position of the sun, I'd say it's noon now. Maybe it's the next day."

"The next day?"

"Yes. If we're lucky. You surprised me. I didn't have time to be . . . specific."

Impossible. Like a story told about the gray caps to frighten children. Fought the urge to bring the gun smashing down on Bliss's face again.

Focus on what makes sense. Ignore the rest.

He was in a courtyard, the tiles warm and rough beneath the shitty shoes Wyte had lent him. There was a breeze. The sun was out. These things were real.

"What were you doing in my apartment?"

Bliss put more energy behind his words suddenly. "Finch, listen to me: you don't want to know. It isn't what you find out that's going to keep you alive. It's *where you're standing.* You're in the middle of things you can't control. It's too big for you. You shouldn't be worried about me, or what I was doing. You should be worried about yourself."

"Answer the question."

Bliss must have caught the returning menace in Finch's voice. He tried to smile sheepishly, as if embarrassed. Said in his polished but shopworn voice, "I was looking for information on you."

"What did you find?"

"Nothing. I didn't have time to find anything."

"Who do you work for?"

"I work for Morrow," Bliss said.

"I don't believe you." He didn't. Not really.

"My answer won't change no matter how you rough me up."

Finch doubted that. Bliss's face was covered in blood. But more damage could be done.

"Let's go back to what I asked you after we took you down off that wall. Why were you in the dead man's memories?" Bliss looked genuinely surprised. By the question? Or being asked it? "I ate the dead man's memory bulb. I saw you. I saw you near a desert fortress."

A kind of mirror. An eye. Pulling back to see a figure that seemed oddly familiar, and then a name: Ethan Bliss. *Then a circle of stone, a door, covered with gray cap symbols. And, finally, jumping out into the desert air, toward a door hovering in the middle of the sky, pursued by the gray cap, before the world went dark.*

"Memory bulbs are unreliable. You know that. You can see almost anything in them."

Finch would never be able to tell when Bliss was lying.

"What do the two towers have to do with all of this?"

"Who says they do?"

"Stark."

Bliss made a dismissive spitting sound. "Stark's a thug. He's nothing. Knows nothing."

"Yet he killed all of your men and nailed you to a wall."

Bliss grimaced, like he'd swallowed a mouthful of dirt. "That was beginner's luck. His days are numbered. In this city you adapt or you die."

Finch still didn't believe him.

"Like you've adapted? Gone from Frankwrithe spymaster to politician to something else?" Then, on an impulse: "What were you doing during the war with the Kalif? Working for F&L and Morrow? For Hoegbotton?"

Bliss smiled, though his eyes were cold. "I was doing my duty for my city."

"Which city?"

"Like I said, you adapt or you die."

"What did you promise to Stark to save your life?"

"Nothing. Stark's a smooth-talking thug. Anything he got I gave him because I wanted him to have it. Because nothing I have would've stopped him from killing me if he got it into his head to kill me."

"Then what did you want him to have?"

Bliss just shook his head.

"How do you travel between doors?"

"Maybe there are some things I'm never going to tell you."

The sunlight, the fact it shouldn't be sunlight, kept getting into Finch's head. Disrupting his thoughts.

"Let's talk about the towers again, then."

Bliss's expression had gone neutral. No one, looking at the spy's face, could've known what he was thinking. "The towers are close to completion. And the gray caps are putting all of their resources into those towers. Ignoring everything else. Even their Partials. But, still, they have an intense interest in this case. Curious, isn't it?"

"Any theories?"

"You already know more than you should. Enough to get you killed."

A weariness came over Finch. His skin still felt *wrong*. What would happen if he faded away with Bliss still there? Where would he wake up? The nausea was getting worse.

"Here's a theory. It just came to me. I might as well try it out on you. I think my murder victim saw you, Bliss. I think he saw you because you were somehow involved with his murder. Maybe you took him through a door like the one you took me through. Maybe the door closed on the gray cap. But you led the victim to his death. The only thing is: I don't know *why* you would do it."

But Bliss was done. He lowered the handkerchief from his cheek. "Are you going to try to take me to the station now? Or just start hitting me again?" Defiant. Almost smug.

For one terrible moment Finch had the sense he hadn't been hurting Bliss at all. That it was all an act. A light shone in Bliss's eyes that seemed shielded from the moment.

Finch let out a deep breath. Lowered the gun. Shoved Bliss away from him. "Go. Get the fuck out of here."

Bliss looked surprised. "Just like that?"

Finch gave a tired smile. "Just like that. I've run out of questions. And you'd just jump through a door before I got you back across the bay." He was going to be sick in a second. Didn't know how much control he'd have then.

"Letting me go doesn't make me forget what you've done to my face, Finch."

"I could've done worse. Don't come near my apartment again, Bliss, or I'll kill you." *Don't come near Sintra. Don't come near Rathven. No one.*

The spy's voice went cold, condemning. "When you see me again, it will be because I *want* you to see me. And not before."

Finch turned around. He really didn't want to see Bliss leave.

Bliss said, "You could escape, you know. You could just disappear."

"I tried that once," Finch said. "It didn't work. I'm still here."

A pause. Then a sound like darkness imploding on itself, a brief flash of green-gold light.

Bliss was gone. The scent of limes hung in the air.

Cursed and shuddered as he realized something: Bliss's hands hadn't been bandaged. They'd looked good as new. *Who healed that fast, even with fungal help?*

Bent over. Threw up his guts onto the courtyard tiles.

When he'd recovered, he sat down heavily on the edge of the fountain. Bone-tired.

Wondering what day it was.

Ten doors knocked on. Three doors that actually opened for him. Only the last one had a working telephone inside. An apartment a few blocks from the courtyard. He flashed his badge. An emaciated woman in a flower pattern dress let him in, checking first to make sure none of her neighbors on the ground floor saw her do it. Eyes large and bloodshot. Anywhere from forty to sixty. A purple growth on her left shoulder like a huge birthmark.

Inside, a bald man in socks but no shoes sat in a wicker chair facing the wall in a spare living room. Staring at a crappy painting of a beach in the Southern Isles. Wore a stained white undershirt and brown shorts.

The woman went to stand beside the man, protective hand on his shoulder, while Finch leaned on the kitchen counter.

Dialed the station. Wyte's number. Listened to it ring once, twice, ten times. His mouth was still dry, vision a little blurry. Jacket dirty. His hair full of grit. Wyte's extra pair of shoes scuffed from kicking Bliss. A sound in his ears he couldn't identify. Tired because he hadn't slept? Or because of stress?

A click, and someone said through the crackling, "Wyte's desk."

"Who's this?" Finch asked.

"Blakely. Who's this?"

"Blakely? It's Finch. Where's Wyte?"

"Finch. Where the hell have you been?"

Now he'd find out. "Have I been gone that long?"

"Just the whole damn morning." Blakely sounded rattled, and a little drunk.

Perverse relief. He'd only lost a half day, maybe less.

"I had to follow up on a lead. Can you pass me over to Wyte?"

"Wyte's not here. Heretic came in. Smoldering mad about your case. He ordered Wyte to go investigate an address. It related to something in your report, I think. Wyte was told to take Dapple with him. Poor bastard."

"Crap." Consequences of being honest with Heretic. "How long ago did they leave?"

"An hour. Maybe a little more." That meant he could still catch up with them. He was already on the right side of the bay.

"By boat?"

"Yes. Western canal."

What experience did Wyte and Dapple have investigating rebel safe houses? Partials and their snitches usually followed up on those kinds of leads. A spark of anger and guilt. Anger at Stark for giving them the information. Guilt at himself for putting it in the report.

"Remind me of the address?"

"1829 Northwest Scarp Lane. Wyte made sure I wrote it down."

"Right," Finch said.

The edge of the Religious Quarter. Dogghe-controlled territory. A low-grade war still going on between the native insurgency and the gray caps. The war they'd all forgotten. Either the gray caps no longer saw that insurgency as a threat, or the towers took up all of their time now. Or Finch just wasn't in the loop.

"Putting Dapple and Wyte together. That's like a suicide mission."

"No shit, Finch. But Heretic wanted it done, said Wyte knew the area."

"Only because he was a shipping manager for Hoegbotton, Blakely." Twelve years ago. More.

"*I* wasn't the one who sent them out there," Blakely said, irritated.

The crackling became a roar, flooding the phone, then subsided after a minute.

"Blakely? You still there?"

"Barely. Listen, there were two messages for you. One from someone called Rathven. Another from a woman who just left her name as 'S.'"

"What'd they say?"

"Just to call them. You should get back here. Soon. People are saying strange things, like the towers will be finished this week. We're all on edge."

Didn't know you cared.

"I've got to find Wyte first."

"You're an idiot," Blakely said, hanging up.

The woman stirred. An accusing stare. Hand still on the man's shoulder. "Are you going to go now?" she asked. It didn't take much effort to realize the gray caps or the Partials had done something to her husband. No stretch at all to blame the stranger with the badge.

"One more call and I'll leave," he said.

She held his gaze for a second. Then turned to the painting as if it were a window.

Finch dialed the number Sintra had given him. Rathven could wait.

A voice answered after a moment. Finch wasn't sure it was her.

"Sintra?"

"Finch?"

"Yes."

"Finch." Relief in that single word, but also something that he couldn't identify. "I was worried. I went by your apartment. Your door was open. You weren't there. Are you okay?"

More than they'd said to each other in person sometimes.

"I'm fine." An ache rose in his throat. His hand on the receiver shook. No, he wasn't fine. Exhausted. Starving. Still trying to process losing twelve hours in a blink of an eye. Holding it together because he had no one to hold it together for him.

"Are you back home? I came by, and when I saw the door open I locked it."

"Thanks for that."

"Where are you, Finch?"

Where was he? Clinging to a lifeline. He'd meant to warn her to be careful. But, somehow, talking now, it felt like he was talking to a stranger. A voice in his head told him he should be careful. How had Stark found out about Sintra? What if *Sintra* had told Stark? About him? Was that possible?

"I'm working on a case."

"But why was your door open? Things were knocked over, as if there'd been a struggle."

"I'll tell you later."

"Can I come by tonight?"

Lump in the throat. "Sure," he said. "I just called to hear your voice. Tough day."

"Finch," she said. "Is everything really all right?"

"No," he said. Made a decision, leapt out into the abyss. "Not really. I'm about to go into a dangerous situation near the Religious Quarter. There's an address we're supposed to check out."

"Then don't go. Just don't go."

"I have to. I don't have a choice." *Not with Wyte out there with only Dapple for backup.*

"You're scaring me, Finch," Sintra said.

"I'm going to hang up now," Finch said. "See you soon. Be safe." A click as the phone cut out. Didn't know if she'd heard him or not.

The woman watched him without saying anything. Even as he told her thanks. Even as he left a gray cap food voucher on the counter. Even as he backed out into the corridor.

Relax your guard in this city and you were dead.

2

An hour later, Finch stood on the ridge and stared down. Far below, the dull blue snake of a canal. Two detectives in a boat. Slowly making their way northeast. Finch was about three hundred feet above them. Wyte was a large shadow with a white face, the boat a floating coffin. Dapple had been reduced to a kind of question mark. Not a good place to be. Anyone could've been on the ridge, looking down. Lucky for them it was just him.

A steep hillside below Finch. Made of garbage. Stone. Metal. Bricks. The petrified snout of a tank or two. Ripped apart treads. Collapsed train cars pitted with scars and holes. Ragged, dry scraps of clothing that might've been people once.

A dry smell hung over it all. Cut through at times by the stench of something dead but lingering. He'd been here before, when it had just been a grassy slope. A *nice place. A place couples might go to have a picnic.* Couldn't imagine it ever returning to that state.

The weather had gotten surly. Grayish. A strange hot wind dashed itself against the street rubble. Blew up into his face. Off to the northeast: the Religious Quarter. A still-distant series of broken towers, steeples, and domes. Wrapped in a haze of contrasting, layered shades of green. Looking light as mist. Like something out of a dream from afar. Up close, Finch knew, it reflected only hints of the Ambergris from before, the place once ruled by an opera composer, shaped by the colors red and green.

The canal led into the Religious Quarter, but Wyte and Dapple would have to disembark much earlier. Their objective lay just outside the Quarter.

Finch's gaze traveled back down the canal, toward civilization. Zeroed in on a series of swift-moving dots some two hundred feet behind the boat. Dark. Lanky. Angular. Using the bramble on the far side of the canal as cover. Partials. Trailing Wyte.

Stared down at the story unfolding below him with a kind of absurd disbelief. Swore under his breath. Took the measure of the Partials down the barrel of his Lewden Special. But it was a long shot. Literally. He lowered the gun.

Maybe Wyte knew about the Partials? What if they were providing support? No. Blakely would've mentioned that. Blakely would've told him about Partials. Probably sent to make sure Wyte did as he'd been told. Was *the* Partial with them, or was he back at the apartment guarding a dead man?

For a moment, Finch just stood on the ridge, under the gray sky. Watched with envy the wheeling arc of a vulture like a dark blade through the air.

Easy to turn away. Heretic didn't expect him to be there. Wyte didn't know where he'd gone. Finch could say he'd been investigating some other lead. Could go back to the station. Forget he'd seen any of this. Wait for them to get back. If they came back.

Bliss: *"It isn't what you find out that's going to keep you alive. It's where you're standing . . . You shouldn't be worried about me, or what I was doing. You should be worried about yourself."*

Bone-weary. Hungry. Bliss's words still in his thoughts. The long fall through the door still devouring him. Finch looked back the way he'd come. Looked down at Wyte and Dapple. Remembered Dapple calm once, at his desk, stealing a moment to write a few lines of poetry. Remembered Wyte training him as a courier for Hoegbotton. His patience and his good humor. Long nights in their home, laughing and joking not just with Wyte but with Emily. Back before the end of history.

Now he was standing on top of a mountain of garbage, trying to figure out how he'd gotten there.

"Fuck," he said to the vulture. To the false light of the Religious Quarter. "Fuck you all."

Then he was descending the ridge at an angle. Trying to put enough shadow, enough debris, in front of him and the canal that the Partials couldn't see him.

This was going to get worse before it got better.

Finch caught up to them as they were mooring the boat to a rickety dock under a stand of willow trees. Shadowed by a lichen-choked, half-drowned stone archway that led nowhere now. The canal had a metallic blue sheen to it. Nothing rippled across its surface. The gray boat had that mottled, doughy look Finch hated. Like it was made of flesh.

He said nothing. Just came out of the shadow of the trees and leaned against the arch. Waiting for Wyte to see him.

Looping one last length of rope round a pole, Wyte did a double take.

"Finch?" he said. "Finch." A slow, hesitant smile broke across his troubling face. A sincere relief that softened the sternness of his features. "It's good to see you."

Dapple jumped off the boat. "How'd you know where to find us?" he demanded. The anger of a desperate man.

"Relax. Blakely told me," Finch said. "I was already on this side of the bay."

But Dapple's face darkened at the mention of Blakely. He looked more nervous than usual. The body language of a mouse or rat. Twitching. Had two guns. Both gray cap issue. One drawn. One stuck through his belt. He wore a mottled green shirt too big for him and black trousers shoved into brown boots. Like a doll dressed for war.

As ever, Wyte hid himself in a bulky, tightly buttoned overcoat. An angry red splotch had drifted down his forehead. Had colonized half of one eye. Cheek. Chin. The splotch had elongated and widened his face. Made his head more like a porous marble bust. He wore black gloves over his hands. Red and white threads had emerged from his sleeves. Wandered of their own accord.

As Wyte trod heavily closer, he extended his hand. Gave Finch a thankful look as they shook. Wyte's grip was strong but *gave*. Like the glove was full of moist bread. Finch suppressed a shudder from the sense of *things* moving inside each finger.

"Where were you this morning?" Wyte asked. Dapple stood behind him, eclipsed.

"I'll tell you later."

"Why not tell me now." Finch heard the fear in Wyte's voice.

"No," Finch said, laying the word down hard.

Wyte considered that for a moment. Like it was a wall between them. Looked back toward the boat as if thinking about getting back on it. "Did Blakely tell you our mission?"

"I told Wyte we should just. Should just run," Dapple said, breaking in. "That this is going to. Going to get us killed." Sometimes Dapple stopped in mid-sentence. Like an actor trying to perfect a line.

"Listen, Wyte," Finch said, ignoring Dapple. "I came down off the ridge. There are Partials following you. A few hundred feet behind. They're probably watching us now."

Or they've got a spy on you, Wyte, and they don't need to watch us.

Wyte grimaced. Dapple stared at the water like he expected something to erupt out of it.

"What do we do." Dapple asked. Didn't seem to expect an answer.

"Shut up, Dapple," Wyte whispered.

"Carry out our mission. Come home alive. Like always." Finch putting emphasis on *our*. An ache in his throat. Knew Wyte would understand that Finch wouldn't have come down the ridge for anyone else.

No matter that you're not always the Wyte I remember.

A sudden spark in Wyte's eyes. Something that glittered. Began to fade almost as soon as it had passed through.

"Like old times," Wyte said. A wry grin. "Like when I taught you how to deal with ship captains down at the docks." His voice was crumbling like a ruined wall. The edges of words worn away.

Finch was too tired to take the brunt of that. "We should get moving."

He wanted action so he wouldn't have to think.

About any of it.

3

The haze of the Religious Quarter came closer and closer. A fake fairy tale city-within-a-city above them. Of those following, no sight. Just the sound of gravel once, dislodged. A distant muttered curse.

After a climb, the ground leveled out. They came to a long, tall wall parallel to a rough road. Ahead, the wall ran on into the distance, buckled and cracked in places. Like it was having trouble restraining what it had been made to hold back. Coming over the wall: the lime scent, the rich greens of the Religious Quarter. Fungus and trees wedded in a vast alliance. Looked like nothing more or less than a fiery explosion, frozen in time. Bullet holes in the wall, in dozens of places. The blackish spray of old blood where someone had gotten unlucky. Under it all, a latticework of fungus. Faintly visible. Faintly green-glowing.

"This is Scarp Lane," Wyte said. "I was here before the Rising. Tree-lined. Nice homes. Bars and restaurants and dance halls. Little alcoves for people to put up offerings to their gods. You could indulge in your favorite vice and then walk right over and pray it away. Between the wars, it used to be a nice row of wrought-iron streetlamps and sidewalk vendors."

Finch frowned. *Used to be.* Wyte didn't usually indulge in *used to be.*

Nothing for it but to follow the wall.

People began to appear in doorways. Leaning against rusting lampposts. On balconies. Dark in complexion. Wore strange hats. Stared you in the eye. Challenged silently why you were here. Sometimes as many as six or seven. Loitering on a street corner. Any time Finch saw more than four people gathered in one place, he figured the gray caps had used their resources elsewhere.

"Put your badges away," Finch said, suddenly.

Dapple had been holding his badge so anyone could see it. Protested, even after Wyte made his own disappear.

"Seen any Partials here?" Finch asked.

"No."

"Seen anyone who would give a shit about your badge?"

Dapple didn't respond.

"And you won't, either," Finch continued. "Not this close to the wall. Except for the ones following us."

They'd be heavily armed. Probably with fungal weapons. Moving in a tight formation. If they were doing more than shadowing Wyte and Dapple, gray caps might be following, too.

From below.

The chapel at 1829 Northwest Scarp Lane pushed out from the wall. It had once been a modest two-story church topped by a silver metal dome. Now that dome was spackled and overgrown with rich burnished copper-bronze-amber mold that met a sea of mixed sea greens and blues creeping up. Little rounded windows in the dome. Perfect firing lines.

Beneath, the green-and-white paint of the rounded walls had peeled away to reveal dry dark wood beneath. In the center, a large ornate double door. To either side, hollowed-out alcoves that Finch didn't think led anywhere. In front of all three, a facade of archways.

A horseshoe-shaped barricade of six or seven tanks with a sandbag wall curved from just beyond the side of the chapel to around the front of it. The tanks nestled together as if sleeping. Been there seven years at least. Burnt out. Crumbling. Faithful old Hoegbotton insignia still visible on the sides. Delicate snow-white mushrooms had overtaken them. Fernlike green tendrils grew from their rusted tops: all that was left of the men that had been flushed out.

Less than one hundred feet between the chapel entrance and the sandbag wall. Anyone could have manned it. At any time. Rival armies and militias had marched and retreated across that damaged ground for more than forty years.

No one in sight now, in either direction. Yet another kind of sign.

"Great fucking place for an ambush," Finch said, as they stood outside the chapel. At their backs, beyond the tanks and sandbags, a warren of streets. Burnt-out schools, apartments, abandoned businesses.

"I don't like it, either," Wyte said.

"What if it's a test? A test to prove our loyalty?" Dapple said. "And it's not a rebel safe house at all."

"Shut up," Wyte said. Shifting his weight from foot to foot as if something pained him. To Finch: "If anyone is in there, we ask a few questions. Try to get some information to satisfy Heretic. Get out."

Finch nodded. If anyone was in there, Finch didn't know if they'd get many words in before the shooting started. Rebel safe house. Three detectives working for the gray caps, with Partials backing them up. Be better off turning in their guns, asking for mercy. Maybe.

Dapple looked close to tears. "We should get. The hell out now."

"Changed your mind? Then why don't you stay out here," Finch said. "Guard the door. Duck inside and tell us if you see anything suspicious." Dapple would be less dangerous as a guard than backing them up.

"With Partials out here?" Dapple protested.

Finch checked the magazine in the semiautomatic. Released the safety. "You'll do it, Dapple, and you'll be happy about it. And Dapple? Don't run away. We'll find you."

"Enough!" Wyte said. "Let's get this over with."

The language of men scared shitless.

Wyte put his hand in the huge left-side pocket of his coat. The one with the growing verdigris stain. The one with his gun in it.

He walked through the middle doorway, Finch behind him.

Dark and cool inside. A second door just a few feet after the first. Wyte pushed it open. Finch covered him.

As his eyes adjusted to the gloom, Finch let the room come to him. The smell of moist, rotting wood. A high ceiling that made every step echo up in the rafters. Two sets of pews, in twelve rows. Leading up to a raised wooden platform with an ornate, carved railing. Beyond that, red curtains. The supports for a chandelier hung down from the ceiling. But there was no chandelier. On the right side of the dais, an iron staircase curled up toward the dome.

"What the hell is that?" Wyte said, pointing.

As his eyes adjusted, Finch could see that a long, low glass-lined counter ran along the right side of the dais. Couldn't tell what was inside it.

"I don't know."

Finch drifted ahead of Wyte. Walked up the carpet with Wyte behind. Climbed onto the platform from the steps built into the right side.

The counter. Under the smudged glass, a series of arms and heads. The arms looked like prosthetics. Didn't understand the heads with their hollow eye sockets any better.

"Why in a church?" Wyte asked.

Finch shushed him.

Beyond the counter: a doorway covered with a tapestry of Manzikert subduing the gray caps.

Finch motioned toward the tapestry with his Lewden Special.

Wyte shook his head. Too dangerous. Too unknown.

Finch nodded.

Wyte retreated into the shadows to the left of the counter. Pulled the gun from his pocket. It looped spirals of dark fluid onto his overcoat. Finch bent at the knees, put the counter between his body and the doorway. Aimed at the tapestry.

"Is anyone there?" Finch said. Loud enough to be heard in any back room.

Something fell. Like a jar or tin.

"Is anyone there?" Finch repeated. His heart felt like a fragile animal inside his chest. Trying to get free. Being battered in the attempt. Kept switching the gun from hand to hand. So he could wipe his sweaty palms on his shirt.

A kind of hesitation from beyond the doorway. A kind of poised silence. Then a careful movement swept aside the tapestry. A short, thin woman walked out.

She stood behind the counter as Finch rose, gun at his side. Wyte reappeared from the shadows.

The woman's gray hair had been pulled back into a tight ponytail. She wore a formless blue dress with a black belt. Her face was heavily lined. Her mouth drooped on the left side as if from a stroke. Or an old wound. Finch thought he could see the whispering line of a scar across the cheek.

"Point your gun somewhere else, Detective," she said, staring at Wyte. Her voice had gravel in it. Finch had no doubt she'd commanded men before.

The seepage had become a constant spatter against the wooden floor. But Finch couldn't tell if it came from the gun or from Wyte.

Wyte lowered his gun.

"Who says we're detectives?" Finch said.

Her eyes were the color of a knife blade. "That's a gray cap weapon."

"We're investigating a murder," Finch said. "That's all we're here for."

"All?" she echoed.

Finch wondered what they looked like to her. Wyte transforming. Him tired and dirty. In Wyte's crappy shoes.

Wyte asked, "What's your name?"

No answer.

"We could bring you in for questioning," Wyte said.

"But you won't, because I'm an old woman," she said in a whisper. "Because you're decent men."

Wyte snorted, losing patience. "A night in the station holding cell might make you more talkative."

The full, hawklike intensity of her stare focused on Wyte. "You want a name? It's Jane Smith."

Wyte opened his mouth. Closed it again.

Finch gave Wyte a wary look. Said to her, "What are all these parts doing here?"

"This is a business. People who've been released from the camps come here if they've lost a leg. Or an arm."

"Or a head?" Finch asked.

"You seem to be keeping yours, Detective," she snapped.

Wyte said, "Are you the Lady in Blue?"

Finch knew he'd meant it as a kind of joke. But Wyte's voice couldn't convey a joke anymore.

A look of disbelief spread across the woman's thin features. The wrinkles at the sides of her eyes bunched up. She began to guffaw. The roughest, crudest laughter Finch had ever heard from a woman.

When she had recovered, she said, "You should leave. Now."

"*Bellum omnium contra omnes,*" Finch said. Put as much weight as he could behind the words. As if he meant to physically move her with them. Couldn't have said where the impulse came from, to say it. Wyte gasped.

Her eyes opened wide. The color in her cheeks deepened.

"There is a way," she said. Hesitated. As if she'd made a mistake.

Finch repeated the words: *bellum omnium contra omnes.*

Her features hardened. "I don't think I know what you're talking about after all."

"I think you do," Finch said. He hadn't given the right response, but he'd been close.

Wyte pulled out his gun, brushed past Finch, and shoved it in the woman's face.

"Wyte . . ." Finch said in a warning tone.

"No, Finch," Wyte said. "I'm sick of this. Sick of it. She's lying. You want this to go down like Bliss all over again? Well, I don't." Wyte pushed the muzzle into the woman's forehead until the discharge dribbled down her face. She closed her eyes, winced, said again, "I don't know what it means. I don't."

"Wyte, *this won't get you what you want,*" Finch said.

Turned his pale, monstrous head for a second. "Hell it won't."

"For Truff's sake, Wyte! Put down the fucking gun!"

"If I do, she's going to kill us," Wyte said. The gun slipping in his grasp. Finger still tight on the trigger. "Can't you feel it? We're going to *die here* because of her." Voice small and low. His shape beneath the overcoat in the grip of some terrible insurrection.

The woman's eyes fluttered, closed again. Waiting for the bullet while Wyte waited for his answer.

No way to get to Wyte before he shot her.

Saved by Dapple calling out in alarm from beyond the door. "Partials!"

Wyte looked toward the door. Lowered the gun. But something was swimming in his eyes. Something that wasn't part of him. Not really.

The woman leaned down, fast.

The front of the counter exploded in a cloud of dust and debris.

The force threw Finch up against the rail, drove Wyte down to one knee. Wyte's gun skittered across the floor. A piece of wood had grazed Finch's left arm. His ears rang from the blast. Through the wreckage of the counter, Finch could see the cannon of a gun that had done the damage. Mounted on a metal stand.

The woman had leapt to the spiral staircase. She was shouting to someone above her. Coughing, Finch got off a shot that bit into the steps at her heels. Then the darkness took her.

Wyte recovered his weapon, started to move toward the stairs. Finch followed, then stopped. Pulled at Wyte's coat sleeve.

"Fuck. Wait."

"Wait, Finch? *Wait?*" Straining against his grip. "Goddamn it, *she's getting away!*"

The sound of gunfire. Coming from the top of the chapel. And a torrent of boots on steps from beyond the tapestry door.

"No! Didn't you hear Dapple? And there's a whole fucking army coming."

"Shit," Wyte said. No longer pulling away.

They ran back down the carpet. Past the pews.

Bullets sprayed in a torrent against the outside of the chapel walls. A muted cry from Dapple.

Brought them up short at the double doors.

Finch looked at Wyte. Wyte looked back at him. Knew they were thinking the same thing. *Better outside with Partials than trapped inside with the rebels.*

Finch heard the sound of the tapestry parting just as they burst through the double doors. Out into the light. Stumbled over Dapple lying on his back in the dirt between the doors and the archways. Face slack. Clipped by a fungal bullet. Left shoulder turning black. Neck covered in looping veins of dark red that made him look like an obscene map. Convulsions already. Eyes distant. Muttering through a mouth flecked with spit. His guns beside him.

Finch looked up to see Partials behind the sandbags, among the tanks. Dozens of them. Pale faces. Dark clothing. Aiming up at the top of the chapel and the sharpshooters pouring fire down on them.

Frozen for an instant. Caught between two bad choices. Didn't know how Dapple had gotten hit.

Then a roar from next to him. *Wyte* was roaring. Standing straight up. Not caring if he got hit. Finch could just see the Partials moving back and forth behind their shelter. The liquid muzzle flashes.

"No, Wyte!" But it was too late. Wyte was shooting at them, and shooting and shooting. Bullets stitched through the dirt. Smacked into the stone of the archways.

No chance for finding common cause now. They had to get away from the front door.

"Wyte! Come on!" Shoved Wyte toward the alcove to their right. Finch dragging Dapple, who had gone silent with shock. Wyte still blazing away with his gun, gone mad with the pressure. Goading them. Laughing at them. Their confused pale faces in Finch's confused vision like smears of fat.

Between the alcove and the archway in front of it: enough cover to get Dapple out of sight and Finch mostly out of the line of fire.

But Wyte, oblivious, was beginning to scare Finch. A fungal bullet ripped right into Wyte's arm as he shot back at them. The bullet just stuck there. Absorbed by Wyte's body.

Finch got off a couple shots at the Partials. Semiautomatic bucking in his hand. Smelled the acid smoke of the aftermath. None of the Partials went down. Had about ten bullets in the gun. More clips in his pockets.

But they'd still get shot to pieces. Now the double doors had opened. Rebels were firing back at the Partials. From the doors. From the dome.

Wyte jammed another bunch of sticky nodules into his gun from his right front pocket. Kept right on firing. The noise was hellacious. Wyte's bullets made an echoing thwack sound. Finch's a deeper crack. The Partials' return fire was like wood popping in a fire. The smell of the fungal bullets musty and metallic.

A scream from one of the Partials. Another scream. Finch, back up against the wall, shielding Dapple, had only a partial view.

A fungal bullet hit the dirt well to their right. Veins of red spread out across the ground. Seeking. Searching. Stopped next to a lizard sunning itself, oblivious to the threat.

"What's happening, Wyte," Finch shouted above the roar.

"I'm fucking killing them. Killing them all," he roared.

A conventional bullet clipped the side of Wyte's head. Left a bloody track. A runnel of flesh coming off. He roared again—this time with pain. Directed his fire to the left, toward the rebels or more Partials. The response was a fresh hail of bullets that sent even Wyte back into their shelter for a moment. Finch kept squeezing off rounds blind. Trying to aim high but not too high.

Wyte's face shone bright. His eyes were large and dilated and he was smiling.

"The bullets don't hurt," he kept saying. "They don't hurt at all."

"They'll hurt you eventually, dammit!" Finch got off another round.

Dapple convulsed. Blood rushed out of his mouth. His eyes stared toward the sky. Lifeless.

"Fuck."

Finch grabbed Wyte's shirtsleeve. Pulled him in close. Green pallor. Tongue purple. Eyes like black marbles shot through with gold worms. A bullet lodged in his left cheek. Coin-shaped. Like a curious birthmark.

"Wyte! We've got to get out of here. *Do you understand?*"

Wyte seemed to wake up. Spittle came out of his mouth as he said, "We'll go right through the Partials." Firing with his straight right arm as he talked. Bullets slamming into his side. Finch could hear them making impact. Being absorbed. "There's an alley behind them. Up or down the street you're dead. But if we're fast, right through the Partials works."

"How the fuck does that *work?*" Finch shouted at Wyte.

"I go out first, shielding you," Wyte said impatiently. Almost with a snarl.

"With your body?" Finch said, incredulous. "That's crazy."

Grinned at him. One eye on the street. "It's all fucked up. What's one more thing? Trust me, Finch."

"You'll die if you do this, Wyte," Finch said.

"No. I won't." Never heard Wyte so confident.

A bullet spiraled into Wyte's left thigh. He didn't even flinch.

Grim smile. "I love you, Wyte." And he did, he realized.

A smile back from Wyte like it was the old days before the Rising.

Later, in memory, it would be a fractured mix of shouts and screams and bullets flying and Finch running into the back of Wyte to keep as close as possible. Tripping over the things crawling off Wyte's legs. Wyte exploding out from their shelter, overcoat thrown aside to reveal a body become *other*. A garden of fungus. Arms ballooning out into sudden wings of brilliant purple-red-orange. Legs lost in shelves and plateaus and spikes of green and blue. Back broader and insanely strong and gray. Head suddenly elongated and widened. As he ran a high-pitched scream came from his mouth that frightened Finch and bloodied the ears of the Partials.

The bullets. Wyte kept taking them like gifts. They tore through his limbs, lodged in his torso. Leaving holes. Leaving daylight. That closed up. And running in the shadow of that magnificence, as Wyte's scream became a roar again and they were assailing the ramparts of the Partials, he felt as if he were following some sort of god, his own gun like a toy as, from the shelter that was Wyte, he shot back at the chapel to keep the rebels pinned down.

Wyte's voice came out incomprehensible and strange now. Guttural and animallike. No part of him in those moments that was human. Once he looked back at Finch to make sure he was still there. The whites of his eyes colonized. His pupils looking like something trapped. Trapped forever inside its own flesh.

For a while it was as if Wyte had lent Finch that kind of vision, because he could see the bullets coming. As if Finch were floating overhead, watching. And it was ecstasy or some kind of odd heaven. The surprise that eclipsed the Partials' pale faces as Wyte overran their positions. Wyte trying to outrun something he couldn't outrun. Tendrils from his chest racing out to impale them. The weeping muzzle of his gun taking them in the legs, the heads. Faces trampled under his charge. Fungal eyes still clicking and clicking as the bodies lay dead. While even the rebels' fire had become scattershot from the shock of the new. From seeing the glory that Wyte had become. The monster.

Then it all came crashing down and Finch was in his skin again. In that one last look back he saw it all as a crazed tableau of men fallen, falling, firing, or running at an impossible speed. Almost distant enough as they made it to the warren of streets beyond to think of them as the silhouettes of broken, spasming dolls.

Realized he was roaring, too, like Wyte. As the tears ran down his face. As he kept firing behind him long after the enemy had faded into time and distance.

4

Breathless. Aching. Side hurting. Wyte trailing bits of things into the rubble behind them. Waiting for a bullet in the back of the head that never came. The acrid smell of spent ammo. A shambling halt under the shadow of the arch. The boat still tethered in the canal. The sky dark gray.

Wyte was still coming down from whatever had possessed him. Voice slick with some hidden discharge. Muttering: "Like wheat. Like paper. Just shredding them. Just running through them."

Finch babbling back. Exhilarated. Heart still beating so hard in his chest.

Wyte's face had regained a semblance of the normal, skin sealed over the bullets. Already now looking drawn, diminished. Finch kept seeing Wyte killing the Partials.

Wyte had rebuttoned his trench coat. The lining torn. Hung down below the hem. Mud-spattered. Blood-spattered. About a dozen bullet holes in it. Small orange mushroom caps peeked out from the holes. Others had burst through the fabric. Around the buttons, purple fungus rasped out, probing.

"Wyte, Dapple's dead," Finch said.

"I know, Finch. I saw. Get in the boat."

Finch climbed in and sat down. Held himself rigid as Wyte made the difficult negotiation of casting off and jumping in without capsizing them. Wyte sat down opposite. The boat glided across the water, back the way it had come. Like magic.

"You saved my life, Wyte," Finch said. And it was true. Monstrously true. Kept staring at Wyte with a kind of awe. Wyte's strength had manifested in a way Finch still couldn't quite believe.

"But not Dapple," Wyte said. "Dapple's dead. And I feel beaten and bruised all over."

Had Wyte passed a point of no return? More things that had colonized him peered out from the collar of the coat. Spilled out from his pants legs. Erupted in red-and-green patterns from his boots. A stench of overwhelming sweetness. Of corruption.

"Don't go back to the station," Finch said. "Not today."

"We were sent there to die, weren't we?" Matter-of-fact.

For my sins.

"Maybe we weren't," Finch said, thinking about the Partial standing over Shriek's body. Lecturing him about how Partials saw more than gray caps. "Maybe it's all falling apart. In front of our eyes. Everything."

Wyte made a wet clucking sound. He was trying to laugh. "Didn't it fall apart a long time ago?"

Knew Wyte was thinking about his wife, his kids, the little house they'd shared together so long ago.

Finch didn't want that in his head, shot a glance up toward the ridge. Anyone could pick them off. Anyone. "Stay at home. I'll figure it out. Call you."

Wyte nodded again, almost slumped over in his seat. A kind of glow had begun to suffuse his features. Green-golden.

Or you'll call me. Suppressed a shudder.

Finch's vision blurred. Too many things to keep inside. Every time he thought he'd tamped down one thing, another came rushing up.

A long silence. A complex smile played across Wyte's blurring lips. Finally said, "You know, Finch, I think we're a lot closer to solving this case."

A double take from Finch. A stifled smile. "Yeah, Wyte. Sure you do. Rest now. Sleep. I'll keep watch."

Wyte nodded. Closed his eyes.

A flake of something floated onto Finch's shoulder. Then another and another. He looked up to see that it was snowing. It was snowing in Ambergris.

As the white flakes drifted down, Finch on a hunch looked back. The white dome of the farthest camp had disappeared, replaced by an impression of billowing whiteness. An outline of what had once been. Realized that bits of fungus were raining down on them.

Raindrops followed, thick but sparse. Finch blinking them away. He laughed then. A wide laugh. Showing his teeth.

The "snow" still coming down. Falling onto Wyte's slack face. Melting away. Into him.

By the time Finch made it back to the hotel, he was almost asleep on his feet. Keeping him awake: left shoulder on fire. A bullet hole through the right arm of his jacket. Would've nicked him if he'd been a fatter man. A sharp pain in his ankle when he climbed the steps to the lobby. Stomach empty and complaining. Even after he bought some sad-looking plums. On credit. With a threat. From a woman who'd set them out on her stoop like a row of Bosun's carvings. Ate them on the way back to the hotel. Slowly.

Passed the Photographer inside. Grunted a hello. The Photographer just stared at him.

Lots of love to you, too.

He turned left in the courtyard, descended. Stopped at Rathven's door. Knocked.

A slow, reluctant opening. Long wedge of light. When Rathven looked up at Finch he thought he saw the secret knowledge they shared shining through her eyes.

A frown hardened her face. "What do you want?" She had one arm behind her back, hiding something. Wore severe pants and a shirt that almost made her look like an Irregular.

"You called me. Remember?"

She seemed to consider that. Almost as if she couldn't tell if he was lying. That she couldn't remember making the call.

"Can I come in?" Finch said, pressing.

"No. I mean, *not now.* You look like a wreck. What happened to you?"

Felt exposed there, in the hallway.

"Just let me in," he said, pushing at the door. Seeing if it would give. Seeing if she would give. "Of course I look rough. It's been a rough day."

"Stay where you are," Rathven said. She was stronger than she looked. The door hadn't even trembled. Or she'd wedged something behind it. "Are you drunk?" she asked.

Brought up short by the question, he shook his head. "No, of course not. At least tell me why you called." Felt like he had stone blocks attached to his legs. His vision was swimming. The words he said came both fast and slow. Didn't wait for her hesitation, said, "Don't tell me it was nothing. Something's obviously wrong. You're not yourself."

A fire in her hazel eyes. A kind of scorn in the set of her mouth. Her rigid stance. "Do you blame me?" she spat out. "And you—you're not 'yourself' either. I don't know who you are. You work for the gray caps but you help me get someone out of the camps. You help people in this building but then you go off and do Truff knows what during the day. For them. For *them*. You're in a good humor. You're in a bad mood. Sullen. Distant. Suddenly friendly. You like coffee, then suddenly you like *tea*. Why *wouldn't* I be wary?"

The words hit him like a blow to the head. Felt the corridor swirling.

"I have to sit down," he said. "If I have to, I'll sit down right here." The nausea had come back. Kept seeing Bliss and the tunnel they'd fallen through. Holding on to Bliss's shoulders had made it real, hard to shake off.

Rathven, continuing: "You bring me these lists. These lists of dead people. And you say research them, and it turns out you're investigating the murder of someone who *couldn't possibly have been alive*. It's a burden knowing that. Thinking that maybe you're not even working on a murder case. That maybe you're just crazy."

Each word like a length of rope Finch tried to hold on to as he fell. Slipping away under his grasp. Burning his palms.

He saw the floor coming up on him, then the ceiling above as he managed to land on his back. Shoulder feeling crunchy, like ground-up glass. Hand scraping against the floor. Crumpled into darkness. But, thankfully, not Bliss's darkness. Weightless. No nausea here. No thoughts.

Except the original one: *What was Duncan Shriek doing in that apartment?*

Ghosts of light pearling across the uneven surface of ceiling beams. Came to his senses in his own apartment, on the couch. A lamp on the stand by his head. Rathven leaning forward to stare at him. Her gun on the table between them. A battered old revolver. Heavy. The kind of thing that at close range would take your heart out, throw you across the room. Not what Finch would've expected from her. Curled up next to it, Heretic's list, returned, along with *Shriek: An Afterword* and *Cinsorium & Other Historical Fables*.

With an effort, he pulled himself into a sitting position.

"How long was I out?"

"Just a few minutes." Rathven wasn't smiling.

A sudden, suspicious thought. "How'd you get me in here?" Reached for his own gun. Found it still there. Tried to make a graceful motion away from it. Too late. Looked up to see Rathven frowning again.

"What are you afraid of?" she asked. "That I'm really strong or that I had an accomplice? Or that I'm going to shoot you?"

"No, I meant—"

"My brother helped bring you in here."

Finch nodded, ran a hand across his face. His hand felt like lizard skin. In his head a sound like waves.

Slowly realized the apartment didn't look the same. Thought it was him at first, vision blurry. But no: books tossed on the floor. Paintings smashed or askew on the walls. His other furniture knocked over. The kitchen trashed, too. Winced from pain in his shoulder.

"Shit, Rathven. What happened?"

"I don't know. It was this way when we came up. There've been too many strangers in the hotel lately. Why do you think I'm carrying a gun now?"

"You didn't before?" Ignored the look she gave him. "I've got to get cleaned up," he said.

"I'll wait."

He checked the table in his bedroom, with the maps on it. On the floor. The overlay was torn and had a boot print on it. Of the Partial? The one he hated? Much as he'd hoped during Wyte's mad charge, he hadn't seen the man.

The map his father had given him was intact. Still on the table. The bed was tossed. Pillows on the floor, sheets pulled back. Mattress had knife marks in it.

Finch considered that for a second. Then went into the bathroom. Shower didn't work. A thin trickle of water from the sink. He took off his clothes slowly, knees creaky. Like an old man. Washed himself clean with a washcloth. Waiting patiently for the water. Cold. Bracing. A lot of sandy dirt. Especially on his feet. He put on clean clothes. Same jacket. Bullet hole and all. Found some socks and an old pair of boots. Felt a little bit more human. Still, the face in the mirror looked defeated, pinched. Eyes he didn't know stared back at him.

He walked into the living room to find Rathven with a broom, sweeping up broken glass in the kitchen. She'd already wrestled many of his books back onto their shelves.

"Rath, you don't need to do that," Finch said.

"No, I don't," she said. Kept sweeping.

Whoever had trashed the apartment had left Finch's whiskey alone. He found a glass. A generous pour. Let the taste burn in his mouth. *Sterilize me.* Grimaced as his shoulder tightened. Could've been worse. Could've been the right shoulder. Interfered with drawing his gun. Or his sword.

He picked up a chair with his good arm, righted it. Sat, watching Rathven in the kitchen. Admired how she could focus so single-mindedly on the ordinary.

"Seen Feral?" he asked her.

"No. I'm sure whatever happened scared him."

"Was the door open when you brought me up here?"

"No, it was closed. And locked. I had to get your key out of your pocket."

Relief. Sintra. Though how many hours had just anyone been able to walk in?

"Do you know a man named Ethan Bliss?" Had to ask the question.

A break in the rhythm of her sweeping. "Bliss? No."

Finch wasn't convinced. "Ethan Bliss. Smaller than me. Dark eyes. You might have known him as a Frankwrithe & Lewden supporter before the Rising. . . . He was the one in my apartment last night." *Although he didn't have time to trash the place then.*

No reaction. Which was a kind of reaction.

"We fought," Finch continued. "It's part of why I look this way."

Rathven leaned on the broom. Eyes narrowed. "How does *he* look?"

"I don't follow y—"

"Because I wouldn't know. I've never met him."

"Never even seen him? He used to be a powerful man for Frankwrithe before the Rising."

"No."

Hard to read her. Had, for that reason, sometimes been tempted to request her file from the gray caps. Resisted the urge. Didn't want to have Heretic asking him why.

In a low voice, "Are you investigating me?" Her tone said, *After all the help I've given you.*

"No, of course not." Scrambled for cover: "Could you do me a favor? He has a couple of aliases I need checked out."

Finch searched for a piece of paper. Wrote down *Graansvoort, Dar Sardice.*

The truth: he couldn't really imagine Rathven hurting him. Not on purpose. Suspected her of hiding something. But that might have nothing to do with him. Everyone in the city kept secrets.

She looked at the names on the piece of paper.

"It's all getting more and more complicated, Rathven. Hard to keep it all clear in my head."

"More complicated than Duncan Shriek?"

"Much more complicated." *Doors that were more than doors. Wyte become something greater and lesser than human.* Suddenly, the city was several cities. Time was several times. As if he'd been looking at his map and the overlay, and suddenly realized *more* overlays were needed to really see Ambergris.

The confusion must have shown because she gave him a half smile. A kind of peace offering. "I'll be finished soon. Then you should get some sleep."

In the apartment Bliss can visit anytime he wants to?

He tried to smile back. "But why did you call? Really?" Teetering now. *Two towers. Heretic's skery. Wyte's improbable charge. Dapple sprawled in the dirt. Dead.*

She held his gaze for a moment longer than was comfortable. As if trying to convey something to him that could not be said aloud.

"Sintra came by the hotel this morning."

"I know. She told me."

"Did she tell you she came down to see me?"

Finch, suddenly alert: "No . . ."

"Did she tell you she asked about your case?"

"It was a short phone call." Already marshaling stones, sandbags, the wreckage of tanks as a barricade.

"Well, she did, Finch," Rathven said. "She asked me about the case. We talked about it."

"And you told her about Shriek?" Incredulous.

Flat, dead tone. Not a glimmer of humor in her eyes.

"No. She already knew."

Feral came to the door scratching about ten minutes after Rathven had left. Frantic as Finch undid the locks on his apartment door. Complaining about the tragedy of not having been fed. That there should be such injustice in the world. Despite himself, Finch smiled.

Finch locked the door behind Feral. Once again shoved a chair up against the doorknob. Put down twice the normal amount of food for the cat. Then lay down on his couch, forcing himself to eat a packet of gray cap rations. The packet was porous. The contents a swelling purple. In his mouth, it tasted like onions and salt and chicken. Knew it was not.

Welcomed the utter fatigue. It emptied his head. Made it hard to think about unthinkable things. He'd go back to the station in the morning. Sort it out. Somehow. The apartment still looked like shit, but not as much like someone had trashed it. Actually found himself hoping it had been Bliss, come back to finish the job. Otherwise, Stark was already upping the pressure. Or, there was an unknown element out there.

Too tired to sleep. Poured himself another whiskey. Sat down with *Shriek: An Afterword* and *Cinsorium & Other Historical Fables.* He was facing the apartment door, with his Lewden Special wedged in beside his left leg. So he could reach across his body to draw it. Sitting upright eased the pain in his shoulder.

Cinsorium looked like a kind of abridgment of Duncan Shriek's theories. He started to read it, then put it down. Needed something first that gave him more of a sense of Duncan's character.

He picked up *Shriek*, began to skim it. Saw at once the conceit: Duncan's voice in parentheses, commenting on Janice's history of a broken family and the first war between the Houses. Skipped to the end, read the editor's afterword. Duncan's disappearance. His sister's disappearance and possible death. The manuscript found in a pub Finch figured must've gone under or been destroyed years ago. With notes scrawled on the pages by Duncan. Which meant he'd still been alive when Janice went missing.

Finch turned back to the beginning. Charted Duncan's rise and fall as a historian, a believer in fringe theories about the gray caps. Almost all of them now proven true. Obsessed with a student at the academy where he'd taught history. A long, unhappy love affair. Duncan turned into a stalker. Discredited. Become unbelievable. Skipped Janice's own rise in the art world. Beside the point to Finch. He found Janice an exasperating narrator. She hid things, lied, delayed the truth. To undermine and slant. Like a particularly crafty interrogation subject.

Gradually, he got a sense of the tragedy of Duncan's life. How close *Shriek* had been to success. To being a kind of prophet. An injustice, his fate working at Finch's sense of fairness. A staggering sense of an opportunity lost. A path not taken. An Ambergris where Duncan Shriek was lauded and the Rising had never happened. Or been defeated. A horror at the idea of nothing really changing in a century. The Houses had gone from war to war. The city was more fractured than ever. Would still be fractured even if the gray caps disappeared tomorrow.

All depressingly similar, and yet he remembered the brief years of peace more vividly than the war. No matter how hard he tried to forget. *A better life. A better way.*

Kept searching Duncan's asides for anything that might point to *why* the man would wind up dead a hundred years later in an apartment he'd once lived in. Found a reference to switching apartments to evade the gray caps. Another reference to working as a tour guide while living in an apartment in Trillian Square. The place had been destroyed long before the Rising. Finch wondered if the few children growing up now even knew who Trillian was anymore.

Then there was Shriek's obsession with Manzikert. With the Silence. And with Samuel Tonsure, the monk who accompanied Manzikert underground and who never returned, although his journal—half evidence of an ill-fated expedition, half the ravings of a madman—reappeared sixty years later.

> I became convinced that the journal formed a puzzle, written in a kind of code, the code weakened, diluted, only hinted at, by the uniform color of the ink in the copies, the dull sterility of set type.

A quote from a book Duncan had found helpful called A *Refraction of Light in a Prison* had an uneasy resonance with the desert fortifications from Shriek's memory bulb:

> Where the eastern approaches of the Kalif's empire fade into the mountains no man can conquer, the ruined fortress of Zamilon keeps watch over time and the stars. Within the fortress . . . Truffidian monks guard the last true page of Tonsure's famous journal.

Could Zamilon be the place he had seen in the memory bulb vision?

He read, too, about Duncan's own explorations underground, following in Tonsure's footsteps:

> I could disguise myself from the gray caps, but not from their servants—the spores, the parasites, the tiny mushroom caps, fungi, and lichen. They found me and infiltrated me—I could feel their tendrils, their fleshy-dry-cold-warm pseudopods and cilia and strands slowly sliding up my skin, like a hundred tiny hands. They tried to remake me in their image.

Like Wyte. A few pages later, a section Janice had taken from Duncan's journal. About doors. About a door. A kind of recognition from deep within that stirred him to read carefully.

> A machine. A glass. A mirror . . . But it hasn't worked right since they built it. A part, a mechanism, a balance—something they don't quite understand . . . Ghosts of images cloud the surface of the machine and are wiped clean as if by a careless, a meticulous, an impatient painter. A great windswept desert, sluggish with the weight of its own dunes. An ocean, waveless, the tension of its surface broken only by the shadow of clouds above, the water such a perfect blue-green that it hurts your eyes . . . Places that if they exist in this world you have never seen, or heard mention of their existence. Ever . . . After several days, your vision strays and unfocuses and you blink slowly, attention drawn to a door . . . The distance between you and the door is infinite. The distance between you and the door is so minute you could reach out and touch it.

Skipped a few pages. Found a section where Janice related a conversation with her brother.

> Duncan: The door in the Machine never fully opens.
> Janice: What would happen if it did?
> Duncan: They would be free.
> Janice: Who?
> Duncan: The gray caps.
> Janice: Free of what?
> Duncan: They are trying to get somewhere else—but they can't. It doesn't work. With all they can do, with all they are, they still cannot make their mirror, their glass, work properly.

And, then, on the Silence:

> You learned it wrong. That's not what happened. It didn't happen like that . . . They disappeared without a drop of blood left behind. Not a fragment of bone. No. They weren't killed. At least not directly. Try to imagine a different answer: a sudden miscalculation, a botched experiment. A flaw in the Machine. All of those people. All twenty-five thousand of them. The men, the women, the children—they

didn't die. They were *moved*. The door opened in a way the gray caps didn't expect, couldn't expect, and all those people—they were moved *by mistake*. The Machine took them to someplace else. And, yes, maybe they died, and maybe they died horribly—but my point is, it was all an accident. A mistake. A terrible, pointless blunder.

Also, mentions of the symbol from the back of the scrap of paper: "Manzikert had triggered the Silence, I felt certain, with his actions in founding Ambergris. Samuel Tonsure had somehow cataloged and explained the gray caps during his captivity underground."

Throughout, Finch caught a refrain by Janice. Didn't know if it was Duncan's refrain echoed by Janice: *No one makes it out*. And near the end, with Duncan apparently lost underground again, this sentence: "There may be a way." What the woman had said to him when he'd blurted out *bellum omnium contra omnes*.

No one makes it out. Yet *There may be a way*. Janice had thought Duncan meant metaphorically. Spiritually. Maybe it was literal.

Couldn't help thinking of the words on the scrap of paper in Shriek's hand: *Never lost*. Like a call and response. *There is a way. Never lost*. Was that what he should have said to the woman?

Absently, he petted Feral, who'd leapt onto his lap, nudging his head up against Finch's chest. Tossed back another shot of whiskey. The alcohol had begun to numb his shoulder. It also helped push worry for Wyte into the back of his mind.

Returned relentlessly to the facts.

A man last seen alive a hundred years before turns up dead in an apartment he once lived in. There's a dead gray cap with him. The gray cap has been cut in half as neatly as if he'd been killed in a slaughterhouse.

The dead man is Duncan Shriek, former discredited historian and explorer of the underground. The Stockton spymaster Stark believes the apartment holds a rebel weapon, but the only thing left in the apartment is the body of Shriek.

Stark kills all of Bliss's men, but leaves Bliss alive. Bliss travels through the city using doors that aren't doors—doors that when you come out the other side, it is the future.

And Shriek, the center of it all, believed the gray caps had built a door to another place, and the Silence was a result of that door malfunctioning.

Finch took out the photo of Shriek the Partial had given him. Stared at the photo on the dust jacket of *Cinsorium & Other Historical Fables*. Hadn't looked at either that closely before. Not like he was looking now. Shadows of light and dark in both. Framing a man with eyes shut, eyes open.

Who is he? Who was he?

Eyes Shut had a beard made of fungus. A hard face. A well-preserved quality to it. Weathered in the way of someone who has lowered his head into the wind too many times. Eyes Open had a close-cropped normal beard. A kind of naive quality to the face. The smile perhaps too self-satisfied. The look of a martyr-in-waiting.

Eyes Shut's smile was that of someone with a secret.

6

Woken by a sudden shifting of shadows. A vague awareness of a figure. A sound like a thousand soft gunshots. Dreamt he'd gone down the hole behind the station's curtain. Into the underground. Found the gray caps there. Sleeping on their sides. Heads down like resting silverfish. Heretic and the *skery* lying peacefully on a mattress made of curling ferns. Finch went to join them and immediately exploded into spores. Was everywhere and nowhere all at once.

Finch had a headache. Mouth felt thick. The sound: a thunderous rain. A woman knelt in the gloom beside his bed.

"Sintra."

The sharp smell of grass and water on her skin. Wanted to fall into her. Hold her like he was holding on to Bliss as they fell into darkness. Not caring in that moment what Rathven had told him.

But couldn't decipher the look on her face. Somewhere between watchful and sad. Made him hold back.

"I could've been anyone," she said. "You're too trusting."

Teasing: "But you're not anyone."

Sintra rose and dropped something onto the bed. He picked it up. The extra key to his apartment.

"Keep it." Offered it back to her.

"No," she said.

Frowned, kept holding it out to her. "It's yours. Not mine." Disturbed by her now. Calm disrupted. *There are doors and there are doors.*

"Someone broke into your apartment," she said. "I don't want you to think it was me. Keep the key. Maybe I'll take it back later."

Finch turned on the lamp next to the bed. Could see her clearly. A white blouse that revealed the curve of her breasts. Black pants that ended in stylish boots she must have bought long ago. Over that, a deep green trench coat ending at the knee. And still that expression on her face. Almost grim. Almost frowning.

Lowered his arm. The key felt cold and small in his palm. Made him weak to think of her without it.

"Are you sure?" Couldn't risk more than that.

"Yes," she said. Folded her arms.

He got up. Reached out to touch her hair. She pulled back.

"What's wrong?"

"I don't want to stay here," she said. "I want to go out." Not looking at him.

So this was how it would go down. What could he do but let her.

"Okay, so we'll go out, then."

"You don't have to," she said. As if suddenly undecided. Thought he under-stood. But he felt reckless. They'd only gone out twice before.

"I want to." And he did. Wanted to be out in the world. Even if that world was completely fucked up.

"I can go out by myself."

Touched her face with one finger, to brush aside a strand of hair. To feel the softness of her cheek. Brought her close. Kissed her on the forehead.

"Let me get some clothes on. We'll go. Wherever you want to go." No matter how far.

Wouldn't burden her with the details of his day. *Wyte erupting from ruins of his own dissolution to save them both. The mad charge to safety. The "snow" falling on them both.* A whole world of torment he wanted to leave behind.

"We'll go wherever you want to go," he said again, from the bedroom as he dressed. Savagely. Like he didn't care. Putting it on her. Apartment wasn't safe anyway. A solid wall could become a portal. A man could die and keep dying for a hundred years.

Came back out and made a show of sticking his Lewden in its holster. Put his arm around her, despite the pain in his shoulder. Opened the door. Feral shot out through the gap and was gone.

Made a show, too, of locking the door behind them with Sintra's key.

"You look rested," she said as they went down the stairs. "That's good."

Didn't feel rested. Not anymore.

Sintra: "There's a black market party tonight. We'll go to that. I know the way. There will be signs."

An urgency to the night. A dangerous pace to it. In the sky at some distance: the green towers, lit up like a glistening festival display. They rose impossibly high. In another city, at another time, that stained, blurry light might have seemed romantic.

The rain made it difficult to look for signs that didn't look like signs. A line of white paint in the gutter. A sudden fracture of light from a door. A muttered phrase from a drunk collapsed on a corner. At night, only about half the streetlamps worked. But all across the skyline phosphorescence draped and bled and hazed in and hazed out again. Ragged groups of camp refugees were gray smudges. A smoke smell, and a strong whiff of acidic perfume that came from a blossoming fungus like a light blue wineglass. No umbrellas. They looked too much like mushroom caps.

They huddled in awnings. Ran across open courtyards. Hugged the sides of buildings. Splashed through puddles. Loosened up enough to laugh about it. Like kids. Like the Rising had never happened. Like she'd never returned the key.

They crossed a bridge over a canal. Lights from both sides careened and cascaded through the water rippling below. Stood there for a few minutes. The rain had let up. Came in waves now, with calm between. The night had turned cooler.

He took her hand. Took in her bedraggled hair, the way the rain had moistened her cheeks. Wanted her. Badly. While another part of him wanted to ask, *"How did you know about Duncan Shriek?"*

"It's almost a normal night," he said.

"What's a normal night?" she asked. But she was smiling. A little.

"A night when my apartment isn't trashed twice," he said.

"What do you think they wanted?"

"Money, probably," he said. Unable to look at her while he was lying.

"What about you?" he asked.

"I had a day like any other." She smiled at him. Revealed near perfect teeth. Wondered again if the Dogghe skill with herbs helped.

Couldn't take it anymore. "Sintra, *what do you do?*" Such a naked question. It split the air like a thunderclap.

She studied him. The light from the canal reflected in her eyes. Anything from rotted leaves to dead bodies could lie at the bottom.

"I could be anyone, John," she said. "I could be someone you wouldn't like very much."

"I might have a better idea than you think."

"No. You don't. What if I have three children? What if I'm a trained assassin? What if I'm a prostitute?" In one swift motion: she had his gun and was pointing it at him. "What if I'm somebody who wants you dead?"

Took a step back, had his hands out in front of him. Too surprised to do more. But a flick of her wrist and she was offering the Lewden back to him, grip-first. While his heart dealt with it.

"Point made," he said. Taking it. Swallowing. Hard.

"Maybe I should tell you I'm a spy for the rebels. I think that's what you'd like me to say, isn't it? But why does it matter. Why now?"

"I don't know," Finch said. Except he did. She'd given back the key. While everything was falling down around him.

They stood facing each other. Like friends, or enemies.

"What do you want to know?" she asked. "And *why*?"

"Whatever you can tell me," Finch said. *Something that makes you more real.*

She looked out over the shimmering water. "You don't really want to know. There's nothing I can tell you that will help you more than what's already in your head."

"What's wrong?" he asked. "What's really wrong?"

She didn't blink or turn away. But she didn't answer, either. Just took his hand.

"Do you still want to follow me?"

She led him past an abandoned factory lit up like a burning ship. As if displaced from the Spit. Windows slick with the spray of rain. Came closer, saw that a neon-red fungus had colonized it. Heard Partials hooting and mocking someone a couple streets over. Even saw a couple of quickly disappearing shadows that might've been gray caps. Part of the risky thrill of finding a bootleg party. Like they were doing something dangerous. Kept his hand on his gun the whole time.

Finally found the guts of a building whose roof had been blown off. Every inch of its exterior glittered with graffiti. Finch had completely lost his bearings. Was trusting Sintra.

The weight and sound of the rain lifted off them. They were sopping, but didn't care. So was everyone else.

"It was a theater," she whispered, moving up against him. "I saw a play here once about Voss Bender's life. I saw it with my father when I was fourteen. Afterward, we got ice cream from a sidewalk vendor. Then we took a long walk down to the park. There were so many people around. The night was beautiful. It was one of the first times I'd dressed up for anything. My mother was sick, so she didn't come along. But I spent all night telling her about it."

"Stop," Finch said.

"A year later, the war broke out again and the park was gone. The people couldn't come out onto the streets. It was too dangerous. My mother had gotten better, but my father had lost his arm to a fungal bullet. He couldn't work for a long time he was so depressed. He'd been a journalist. I knew about my native heritage, but it wasn't until then that I learned more, because my father returned to his roots. It was a way of making himself whole again, I think."

"Stop," he said again. Each detail making her more distant.

"What about you, John?" she asked. "What do you want to tell me? Is there anything you want to tell me?" Tone between bitterness and sympathy. Maybe even affection.

"No."

"Does it make it better or worse if I tell you these things?"

Daring him to look at her. But he wouldn't.

"Worse," he admitted. Defeated.

"Because you can't tell me anything back," she said. "Because you don't trust me. Shouldn't trust anyone."

Because then you're not who I need you to be.

Hugged him then. Whispered in his ear, "Do you understand now? We're alone, John, even when we're together." Kissed his cheek.

Didn't want it, but took it.

"Let's just find the party." Needed a drink. Bad.

Down a stairwell. Through a hallway picked clean of detail. The deeper they went, the more light. From gas lamps. From naked bulbs. From flurries of candles unwinding along their path.

People began to appear out of the half-light. Couples kissing. Sidewalk barbers, driven inside. A man leaning against the wall, offering cigars. More vendors. Wine. Drugs. Food. Candy. Pots and pans. Watches. Fabric. The smell of something spicy.

Finch bought a bottle of wine with three packets of gray cap food. The man popped the cork for them. Finch handed the bottle to Sintra. She took a manly swig, laughed, pulled him close as if in apology. Kissed him, her tongue in his mouth. Connected to every nerve in his body. She pulled away to hand him the bottle, whispered, "Isn't that better than *words*, John?" He drank long and deep. Sweet, full-bodied. Exploding against his taste buds. Coursing into his body. Followed by a bitter aftertaste. But he didn't care. He really didn't care.

Down more stairs. The sounds of the party now muted, now blaring. As if they were getting closer, then farther away. They came to a doorway with a black sheet draped across it. A small man with a slurred, gritty voice and dirty black hair took their payment: three food pods and the pocketknife Sintra had brought. Let them through, into light.

A raised platform, looking down at a huge room that must have been used for storage once. Hundreds of people occupied that space now, the sound of their voices muffled yet deafening. Gray archways surrounded the room. No way to defend the space. From anything. Oil lamps hung from each archway, made a buttery light that created shadow even as it swept away the darkness. A strong smell of sweat.

A band played in the far left corner. Cello. A drum made from trashcan lids. An old accordion. People were exchanging pieces of paper nearby. Probably stories, poetry, artwork. The gray caps didn't care, but the Partials did. Noticed a few silent, large men at the fringes. Probably bouncers hired by the vendors.

Finch took another swig of wine. The last time he'd seen so many people in such a small space he'd been fourteen and his father had taken him to a reception thrown by the Frankwrithe viceroy three months after an armistice with House Hoegbotton. Stiff and cramped in a suit. His father had introduced him to each dignitary, and afterward, while they were distracted, Finch had snuck into the viceroy's rooms and taken the papers his father needed.

Recklessly, he crushed Sintra to him, put his arm around her neck, let his hand touch her breast. She turned into him. Shouted in his ear, "Should we go down there?"

He nodded, and they descended into the chaos. Relaxed into it. Despite seeing the tawdry cheapness of it. Too good at playing a role not to know when another role was being played out in front of his eyes.

The frantic, almost hysterical dancing of the women. The faces rising toward them masklike in that half-light. The hesitant rhythm of the band. As if the Partials would break in at any second. How much alcohol everyone was drinking. Quickly, just in case.

More wine. Another kiss from Sintra. Thought he saw on her face a look close to desperation. Or was it resignation?

They made their way to the far end. Next to the band. Joined the dancers. A man and woman, both shirtless, careened into them. Disappeared again in a whirl of arms. Another couple up close to each other, slow as the music was fast. The pungent tang of some drug. A smell like incense. The bodies around them became like one body. Only to fall apart, like the limbs in the rebel safe house. Heads. Legs. Arms. *Wyte charging out to meet the Partials.*

Finch needed more wine, then. For both of them. Smiles from people around them. A shared secret. *Life could be good. If you could only get far enough out of yourself.* Abandoning. Forgetting.

A song ended. As it had ended before, and before that, too. But this time Sintra said, "Follow me." Led him by the hand into the darkness of a doorway where a lamp had failed. The sudden touch of cold stone. On the other side, a catacomb of rooms. The light from the party already receding. Snuffed out. Men and women had paired off here. Moans, murmurs, a sudden heat.

They found a section of wall around a corner. Drank the last of the wine. Let the bottle fall, and, broken, roll to the side. She was unbuttoning her white blouse, a wild light in her eyes. He was helping her, suddenly frantic in his need. His mouth was on her breasts. Tongue on her delicate brown nipple. Coming back up to her mouth with his. She gasped. Unbuttoned his pants. His cock throbbing as she took it in her hand. He let out a long sigh. His fingers curled through her hair.

He pushed her up against the wall. Pulled her pants down. Got his arms under her, ignoring the pain in his shoulder. Slid into her tight wetness. Groaned. Her hand against the back of his head. Her arm around his back. Nails digging into him ecstatically. Thrust hard up into her like an animal, muttering obscenities into her ear. While she encouraged him. His tongue into her mouth. Finding her tongue. Pulling back to look at her sweat-tinged face in the dark. A shadow. A wraith. Those eyes. She leaned into him, both arms around him, and sucked on his ear in a way that drove him mad. Everything receded to just that point at which he was entering her. Then expanded until he was everywhere at once. Suddenly she came, biting his shoulder and he, snarling, telling her to bite harder. The feel of her teeth on his skin made him cry out, come deep into her. Held there by her long after he was spent. She was spent.

With reluctance, Finch let her slide back to her feet. Pulled up his pants as she pulled up hers. Buttoned her blouse. Kissed again. Salty and deep. Shocked him.

They walked until they stood in the archway, staring into the main room. With its loudness. Its light. Its movement.

"Stay here," she whispered. "I'll get more wine and be back."

"Now?"

"Now. I need another drink." She threw her arms around him. Clung to him like a child. Whispered in his ear, "Be careful, John."

When she pulled away she looked so vulnerable Finch almost told her everything he thought he knew. She looked like she was receding from him at a great speed. And he was suddenly frightened.

Then she was gone. Beyond his grasp. Out into the crowd. Lost. And he was standing there. Alone.

He started after her. Didn't know why. She was just going to get more wine. Not leaving for good. But a familiar face stopped him.

Bosun. Entering from the raised stage opposite. Five tough-looking men in trench coats stood behind him. Bosun was scanning the crowd. For him?

Looked again for Sintra but couldn't find her. Decided to step back into the archway. Out of sight.

A hint of movement behind him. A hand over his mouth. A sharp pain in his arm before he could react. Falling as the lamps shuffled through his vision, became the scrap of paper pulled from Shriek's hand, bursting into flame. Became the candles on a cake from his eleventh birthday. Began to blow out the candles. And with each, another clue snuffed out. Shriek going dark. Stark's transcript extinguished. His father's face, hovering just beyond the candles. Mysterious. Shadowed. Smiling.

7

Someone slapped his face.

"Wake up. Wake up."

Finch opened his eyes. Night. Lying on his back. In the grass. Staring up at a field of green stars. He shivered. It looked nothing like the sky over Ambergris.

A woman's face blocked out the stars. For a second, in the gloom, he thought it was the woman from the rebel safe house. She had a gun. Didn't recognize the make.

"You . . ." he said, still woozy.

"Don't make me hurt you," she said, then stepped out of view.

Hands roughly pulled him up. They shoved his arms behind him. Handcuffs slid into place. Cut into his wrists. Felt almost as bad as he had after following Bliss through the door.

"Where am I?" Finch asked.

"Shut up," the woman said.

Wyte, saying to him once, "You know what they say about the rebels? A rebel is just a Hoegbotton who made the mistake of marrying a Frankwrithe."

They stood on the side of a grassy hill. Below them, a crushed tangle of tanks and other military equipment. Glistening darkly. The wind through the hundred metal husks made a distant, warped, singing sound. Beyond, he could see the black silhouette, jagged and *wrong*, of a ruined city. In the middle: a dome of dull orange light.

"Is that Ambergris?" Incredulous.

"Shut up," she said.

Two men appeared to either side of him. They wore dark pants tucked into boots. Camouflage shirts. Ammo belts. Rifles slung over their shoulders. Military helmets.

"Or are we inside the HFZ somehow?" Finch asked. His gun was missing from its holster. His mouth was dry. His arms already ached.

"No one is in the HFZ, John Finch," the woman said.

"Why am I here?" Tried hard to bite down on a rising fear. *I'm here because I work for the gray caps . . .*

"Walk," said one of the men. Shoved him in the back.

"We're going to the top of the hill," the woman said, from in front of Finch. "Don't move too fast, or we'll shoot you. Understand?"

"Yes," he said. "I understand." Understood, too, that Sintra had betrayed him. Realized he'd been expecting that ache for a long time.

Some of the stars in the sky were moving. Slowly moving back and forth. The wind was very cold. The grass whispered around his boots.

They reached the top of the hill. In the shelter provided by the ruined wall of an ancient fortress, a tent served as a windbreak for two chairs. A table with a pitcher on it. Two glasses. A couple of dim lamps, placed so they couldn't be seen from downhill.

A figure beside the chairs. In a long, dark robe. Graying hair lifted slightly by the wind.

The Lady in Blue.

Unmistakable. Finch just stared at her. Disbelieving. Forgot his captors shoving him from behind. Forgot the danger he was in. He had never seen her before, and now he was seeing her by starlight. On a hill under a strange night sky. Surrounded by some kind of dead city.

In the Hoegbotton Irregulars, the promise of meeting her had been held out like a guarantee of better times. As they lay in the trenches. As they went from house to house, rooting out insurgents. As they ate hard, stale bread and molding fruit. Made soup from glue, water, and salt. That whole past life overtaking Finch as they marched him up in front of her.

She was shorter than Finch. Maybe five-six. Late fifties or early sixties. Thin and in good shape. Wrinkles at the corners of her eyes, across her forehead. Accentuated by the lamplight: a near perpetual wry smile, a sad amusement to the eyes. A look that seemed to say she was here, in the moment, but also a dozen other places as well.

The Lady in Blue said, "You are, supposedly, John Finch. And I am, reportedly, the Lady in Blue. You have questions, although I may not have as many answers as you'd like. Let's sit." She spoke with the quiet, weathered quality of experience. Mixed with a bluntness that was nothing like her radio broadcasts. It came as a jolt. Thought for a moment that she might not be the Lady after all.

His captors uncuffed him. Shoved him into a chair opposite the Lady in Blue. Withdrew out of the light.

Finch rubbed his wrists. Sitting in the chair a kind of weight dropped onto his chest. Didn't know if it was some after-effect of how he'd gotten there. Or the presence of the Lady in Blue.

"Where are we? Why am I here?" Aware he sounded weak. *Because I am weak.* Sintra's scent was still on him. Felt trapped.

"Where are we?" echoed the Lady in Blue. "Maybe it's a place you know. Maybe it's, to pick somewhere random, a place called Alfar. Or one version of Alfar. Does it matter? No. We could be anywhere. That's one thing you'll learn."

She leaned forward, poured a clear liquid from the pitcher into a glass. Offered it to him. He took it but didn't drink.

"Go on. If I wanted you dead, you never would have woken up."

"Maybe you're cruel," Finch said. But he drank. The water was cool on his throat. Drove away the lingering nausea.

"Do you know why you're here, 'Finch'?" she asked, leaning back. An appraising look.

"Only you know that." The way she said "Finch" made him feel naked, exposed. His awe was fading. Replaced by a kind of perverse resentment. This woman had helped ruin his father.

"*Bellum omnium contra omnes*," she said, and the little hairs on Finch's neck rose. "Maybe I say those words to you three times and you wake up from this dream you've been living and remember your mission."

"I don't believe you," Finch said. Waking up to the fact that he'd been kidnapped. That he was in a dangerous situation. She'd hinted she knew his real name. She knew he worked for the gray caps. Knew he'd been at the rebel safe house.

The Lady in Blue laughed. "Of course you don't, because, unfortunately, you're correct. You're not a secret agent for the resistance."

"What do the words mean?" Asking questions meant he didn't have to answer any.

"Maybe it's in a language from another place, a place the gray caps don't know about. Maybe we're the only ones who can understand it. 'War of all against all,' that's what it means. Though we won't be using it again after today. You've made sure of that."

"*Never lost* is the countersign."

"*Part* of the countersign." She wasn't smiling.

"We were just doing our jobs," Finch said. "We were going to ask some questions and leave. We wanted to stay alive."

The wind coming from the city below had faded. Finch could hear strange mewls and moans. Then a sound like a million leaves rustling.

The Lady in Blue folded her arms. "Maybe we should talk about your murder investigation instead. Such as it is."

"You're not the first to be interested."

Her smile was as humorless as a knife blade. "Then one more won't hurt, will it? Tell me what you know."

Remembered the transcript Stark had given him: "There's a weapon in the apartment where we found the dead man. You, the rebels, lost a weapon there."

"We lost an agent there, Finch," the Lady in Blue said flatly.

Duncan Shriek.

"What's his name? The man?" Finch asked.

A look of profound displeasure from the Lady in Blue.

"Now that is disappointing, Finch. Disappointing in three ways. First because I don't have much time and you're wasting it. Second because I suppose this means you're going to try to survive by giving me scraps. And third because I'm not your unimaginative little gray cap boss." Unable to keep disgust out of her voice.

"You left," Finch said. "You left all of us behind. We've had to live in that city *for six years*. Survive any way we could."

You abandoned us. Curled up inside that outburst all the bottled-up frustration from nearly eight years of playing a role. A role inside of a role.

The Lady in Blue nodded as if she agreed, but said, "Do you think we've been having a party out here, Finch? Do you think we've been sitting out here waiting for the end times? No. We've been learning things. We've been gathering our forces. Waiting for the right moment. It's been as hard for us as for you. Harder maybe."

At least you've had a change of scenery.

When he remained silent, she said, "Tell me the name of the man in the apartment. Think of it as an exercise in trust."

They already knew. He had no leverage.

"It's a man named Duncan Shriek. Except he died a hundred years ago. That's what I don't understand."

The dead man sat in the chair next to him, smiling.

"Was there anyone with him?"

"Half of a dead gray cap."

Falling through cold air and couldn't feel his legs.

"Is the body still in the apartment?"

"Not the gray cap, but Shriek's is."

"Is there any visible sign of injury to Shriek?"

"Not really."

"How did he die?"

"I don't know. He looks like he might have fallen. Twisted his neck a bit."

"Don't you feel better, telling the truth?"

"Yes," he said. Meant it.

She paused for a moment, as if marshaling hidden forces. Then said, "While we're telling the truth, Finch, I should let you know something: I knew John Crossley. *John Marlowe Crossley.*"

A sharp intake of breath he couldn't control. Too long since he'd heard that name spoken. Hadn't uttered it in years, either. Had tried to unthink it.

The Lady in Blue continued: "John had a strange idea of honor. He had genuine disagreements with us. With everyone, really. That's why he fell so hard. Why no one could protect him. It would have been easier if he'd been a simple spy, one side against another, not working for the Kalif."

"I don't know what you're talking about," Finch said. Although he knew it was hopeless. He felt like a hermit crab being pulled from its shell.

The Lady in Blue nodded, but not to Finch.

A slamming blow came down on Finch's bad shoulder. He cried out, fell from his seat into the grass. Moaning in pain. Turning to protect his shoulder.

The Lady in Blue had risen. Stood next to him. Suddenly more threatening, more terrible, than anyone he had ever seen. "You *do* know what I'm talking about, James Scott Crossley. *You do know.*"

Like looking in a mirror and seeing a double that didn't really match up. He'd been Finch for so long that he didn't know James Scott Crossley anymore. Not really. Some stranger who hadn't survived the Rising. Some poor bastard who'd never made it back, like so many others.

She pulled the chair away from the table and sat down. "Do I have your attention?"

Through gritted teeth. "Yes." He didn't want to remember Crossley. Crossley was dead. Both of them.

"You've changed your look. Your hair is lighter, and you've shaved the beard. You're heavier. Older, of course. But it's still you. What would people *do* if they knew? With your father's reputation for treachery? Even now, maybe they'd be firmer with you. Maybe they'd stop what they're up to long enough to settle old scores. One thing to protect the key to a weapon. Another to find out the key has close ties to someone who betrayed the city to a foreign power. Maybe you'd wake up to a bullet in your brain. And know this, too, John: your father brought it on *himself.* Don't delude yourself about that."

"Fuck you," Finch said. "Fuck you, *Alessandra Lewden.*"

Got a kick in the ribs for that. Lay there, saying nothing. Pinned to the ground by her words. Shoulder knifed through with broken glass.

She relented then. Said in something close to a kindly tone, "But that's not why you're here, 'Finch,' if that's what you'd prefer I call you. A year ago? Maybe. But now? No."

Through gritted teeth, "What do you want, then?"

"We've time enough to talk about that," she said. "Soon we'll be leaving here. It's never safe to stay in one place for long. Get up."

Finch stood. Holding his shoulder.

"Look," the Lady in Blue said, pointing out past the ruined hulks of tanks. Toward the dull orange dome.

"What am I looking for?"

"Just wait."

As she spoke, the dome exploded. A thousand streamers rising in intense shades of red and orange. Like some kind of land-bound sun. The tendrils arched into the sky. Hung there. Then disintegrated into a vast cloud. A roiling mass of particles. Discharging light until a steady humming glow suffused the city in a kind of dawn. There came in reply from the city a hundredfold bestial roar. Strange fractal creatures began to grow at a frenetic pace across every surface. Straining up toward the light. While the orange dome, much reduced, seemed to breathe in and out. Beyond the particle cloud the darkness continued unabated.

"Dawn, Finch," the Lady in Blue said. "That's the kind of dawn they have here."

"Yes, but what is this place?" Finch asked, almost pleading. "Where am I?"

"It's a place where the echo of the HFZ—*just the echo of it*—destroyed a city. Subjected it to this perpetual artificial dawn. There's no one living down there now. No one. Just flesh that serves as fertile soil . . . for something else. The HFZ is like a wound where the knife cut through more than one layer. And that's really all you needed to see. No, it hasn't been *fun* out here for six years, Finch. Not really."

She nodded to someone behind him. A man came up and got Finch in a choke hold. He struggled against it. Kicked his legs. Frantic. The woman came around front. Stuck a needle in his arm.

The stars swirled into a circle, then a haze.

The world disappeared all over again.

✻

James Crossley had been callow, self-absorbed, impatient, a ladies' man. Finch was none of those things. Finch was direct, brusque, had a dark sense of humor.

Crossley had been, for a while, finicky about food. Finch had cured him of the last of that during the worst times, with stew made from leather belts, made from dogs and rats.

Crossley never swore. Finch had trained himself to swear to fit in. To break up the rhythm of his normal speech patterns. Crossley liked the river. Finch kept waiting for something to leap out of it. Both liked cigars and whiskey. Both were as dependable as they could be, indifferent to music, and hated small talk. Although Crossley had had more chances to hate it than Finch.

Crossley had been part of his father's network as a youth, something he'd only known later. Even if he'd had an inkling.

His father passed information on Frankwrithe to Hoegbotton, and information on Hoegbotton to Frankwrithe. Built things for Hoegbotton only to give Frankwrithe the intel to blow them up. Used the contacts to feed Hoegbotton sensitive information on troop movements from supposed "sources." Neither side having any sense of the level of betrayal until they came together to fight the gray caps. After which it became clear John Crossley had been given his orders by someone working for the Kalif. Creating chaos while providing the Kalif's secret service with an inside look at both factions.

And why? *Why?* Neither James Crossley nor John Finch had any idea. Their father had never told them. Just said once that being a powerful man meant you made enemies. "Too many people get the wrong idea," he'd said. While he hid out in an abandoned mansion in northern Ambergris. Coughing up blood from the sickness he'd first contracted while on campaign in the Kalif's territory.

"Look," he'd said to Finch, showing him, "I never knew my face would be printed on playing cards." One of fifty most-wanted men and women. On the rebels' list.

Remembered again the pipe his father had shown him.

Crossley was the past. Finch was the present, waiting for the future. For the air to clear. For all of this to go away.

But two things they agreed on.

Both still trusted in their father, couldn't bring themselves to shun him. Even knowing what he had done.

Both had loved him.

Finch woke with an uneven, sharp surface cutting into his back. Above, a wavery light showed a shelf of rippling black rock. Glittering stalactites pointed down at him.

"We're in an underground cave system," a voice said from nearby.

He sat up. The walls of the cavern glowed a deep, dark gold. Traveling across them, in the waves of illumination, Finch saw what looked like strobing starfish. A smell like and unlike brine came to him. Colder, more muted. He still didn't have his gun. Felt vulnerable, small. *She knows I'm Crossley. And she doesn't care.* Which meant she was going to ask him for something big.

The Lady in Blue stood beside him. Wearing the plain uniform of a private or Irregular, all in muted green. Short-sleeved shirt. Tapered pants. Holding a lantern, staring across an underground sea. It stretched out into a horizon of swirling black shadows and glints like newborn stars. A rowboat was tethered to the shore.

"Stop drugging me," Finch said. He felt sluggish.

"The less you know, the better."

"How long was I out for?"

"It doesn't matter."

"It does to me."

"We drug you because there are things we can't let you know."

"You mean if I'm interrogated. By someone else."

She ignored him, indicated the cave with a sweep of her hand. "This is where the gray caps left Samuel Tonsure," she said. "You know who Tonsure is? Not everyone does."

He nodded. "The monk Shriek was obsessed with. The one who disappeared."

"They took his journal from him right here. Left him to make his own way in their world."

Duncan, in his book: "I became convinced that the journal formed a puzzle, written in a kind of code, the code weakened, diluted, only hinted at, by the uniform color of the ink in the copies, the dull sterility of set type."

"And where exactly is that?" Finch managed with a thick tongue. His head felt heavy. Whatever they'd drugged him with had quieted the pain in his shoulder.

"You might be better off asking *when*, but it's your question. Answer: we're *everywhere*. But at this moment, we're deep beneath the city. Or, at least, *a* city."

The Lady in Blue stepped into the boat, hung the lantern on a hook in the prow. "Come on," she said. "We're going on a journey."

Finch hesitated. Suffered from too many journeys. From a shoot-out on an Ambergris street to falling through a door in time and space. Stepping onto the boat felt like a kind of slow drowning. Into yet another dream.

"You don't have a choice," the Lady in Blue growled. "I don't want to have to force you. But I will."

She was alone. Finch couldn't see a weapon, though she'd picked up a long pole from the boat. But he didn't doubt she could hurt him.

Awkwardly, he got to his feet. Stepped into the boat behind the Lady in Blue. It wobbled beneath his weight.

"Sit down," she said. He sat.

She began to pole them across the little sea, with a strength he hadn't noticed before. He could see the outline of her triceps as she pushed off with the pole.

Over the side, by the lantern light, needle-thin fish with green fins shot through the water. More starfish. A couple of delicate red shrimp. It wasn't very deep; he could see the silver-gold flash of the bottom. The unreal translucent light confounded him. A glimpse of a kind of peace. Fought against relaxing. Was still in danger.

"Where are we going?" he asked. "What does this have to do with Duncan Shriek?"

"Eat something," she said. "Drink something."

Sandwiches and a flask by his feet. He unwrapped a sandwich. Chicken and egg. Ordinary. Normal. Tasted good. The flask had a refreshing liquor in it. It warmed him as it spread through his body.

"And while you eat, listen to me. Don't talk. Just *listen* . . ."

[*She said:*] For a moment, imagine everything from the gray caps' point of view, John Finch. James Scott Crossley.

In the beginning. Once upon a time. A small group of you became separated from your world while on an expedition. In a word, lost. A problem or mistake in the doors between places. Suddenly there are hundreds or thousands of doors between you and home. Suddenly you're adrift. You find yourselves washed up on an alien shore, along the banks of a strange and magnificent river. You can't find your way back to where you came from, even though at first all you do is try. And try and try.

After a while of trying and failing, you decide to settle down where you are, establish a colony that we will later call "Cinsorium." It's a better place for you than other choices for exile. You live a long time but procreate slowly so the isolation is good. No competition. No real threats. You create buildings that remind you of home. No corners. All circles. You bend the local fungus to your will, because you're spore-based and everything you do is based on this fact. Plenty of raw material to use in and around Cinsorium.

But, still, you're always looking for a way back, a way out. You might even have been close at one point—right before Cappan Manzikert sails upriver with his brigands. Because as soon as Manzikert appears, it's back to square one for you. Even less than square one. He destroys your colony, drives you underground. He burns your records, all of the information in your library. Not just the clues you've gathered of how to get home, but your whole knowledge base. Essential things.

Ironic, really, Finch. Because Manzikert's a barbarian. Yet as far as I can tell, he saved us all with that one brutal act. Something even Duncan Shriek didn't understand.

So you stay underground to rebuild. You're cautious, you're far from home, and there aren't very many of you. Will never be very many of you, no matter what you do. You let the people above become comfortable. You lie low, so to speak.

Then you try again. At last. And because you're cautious you build it underground. A door. A machine.

But the door doesn't work. Something goes wrong. Who knows what? It could've been anything. Maybe it's the wrong location. Maybe it was always a long shot. Many of your own people are killed. And everyone in Ambergris disappears, except the ones in the fishing fleet. Either dead or taken *elsewhere*. Scattered across worlds and time. Unable to get back. (Think about that, Finch—somewhere out there, there must be a colony or two of Ambergrisians who survived. Can you imagine what they might be like now, after so long? Stranded. Vague tales of another place, one crueler, kinder, more hospitable, less so.)

Maybe it's then that you believe, *this is the end. We're doomed to die out here, in this backwater. We'll never be found.* But, still, you're patient. You're clever. You're hard working. You spend a long time learning from your mistakes. Sometimes you venture out during Festival nights. You do experiments related to your goal. You even kidnap humans, use them as test subjects. Always trying to convey a sense of dread in those who live aboveground, always trying to make yourself larger in their minds—like a wild cat that puffs itself up in front of an enemy.

When the opportunity comes, it's because Hoegbotton and Frankwrithe have exhausted themselves against each other—sometimes even using weapons you provided to them—and the city lies in ruins. You take a huge gamble. Why a gamble? Because there still aren't enough of you, not compared to the human population.

You pour all of your resources into the Rising. You're hard to kill, but you can't possibly hold a whole city for long against an armed resistance, not if it means a true occupation. But you don't *need* it to last for long. You just need to create the *impression* of overwhelming force.

And it works. You Rise. You use your reengineering skills and knowledge of the underground to flood the city. You use your spores like a kind of diversion, a magic show. Yes, you can kill people, but not all of them, and not as fast as the enemy thinks. Besides, fear is even *more* useful to you—it's how your agents have worked throughout Ambergrisian history. Preying on the imaginations of a people raised to fear you. (Often for good reason.)

You force the combined Hoegbotton and Frankwrithe army arrayed against you to fight on your terms, on your turf. You even leave an escape route so that no one needs to fight to survive. They can just flee.

Again, it works. The resistance retreats—and when they're far enough away, in one more spasm of energy and expertise, you cast the HFZ over your enemy, like a net, and you disperse them across the doors. Thus ending effective armed resistance, and creating more fear.

For the actual occupation, you are clever and resourceful. You enlist the remaining population to police itself, to govern itself—as much as it is able. When the situation is stable except for isolated pockets of unrest, you start to build your final attempt at a door. A way home. Two towers, which aren't really towers but a kind of complex gateway. Situated precisely where you need them to be for success.

Meanwhile, you stall. You go through the motions. You provide electricity, food, drugs on the one hand. Camps, the Partials, and repression on the other. You don't need to control territory in the normal way. You don't see the city from the sky looking down, like humans. You see it from the underground looking up. And you control the underground. That's your homeland away from home. You can choose what you hold on to aboveground and what you don't. So long as you rule everything below. So long as you can *block* access to whatever you like.

You leave the burnt-out tanks on the streets, don't clean up the HFZ *not* as a warning to the human population, but because you don't have the *personnel* to do that and keep working on the towers, too. And because, on some level, you don't really care about any of it. Not any of it. Especially not governing. All you care about are the two towers.

And do you know why? Because we might have called it a door all this time. "A window. A machine." But it's more complex than that. It's not just a door. It's a *beacon*. Because, you see, Finch, they don't need a huge door if they've found a way home. Not according to our intelligence. No, they only need a door this big if they're planning to use it to bring *more* over here. To Ambergris. To the world.

The Silence? All of what Duncan Shriek said in those old books—it's true. Except he was wrong about this one thing. *They've found they like it here.* They want to stay. Permanently. In numbers.

Now, is that *exactly* what happened, and how it happened? No, probably not, because we can't actually imagine how they think, or what they think about. And it might not even be a door yet. It might just be a beacon. If they haven't found their home yet.

But what I've told you is close. Close enough, according to our sources.

. . . You may not believe me, Finch-Crossley, but I don't take any of it personally. Not really. They behave as their nature and their situation warrants. I can respect that. There's a sick kind of honor in that, really. But that still doesn't mean I don't plan on finishing what Manzikert started. Because, as you've guessed, we now have a new weapon. A new weapon that is very old.

They'd reached the far shore, the sea giving way to land. The boat nudged up against a lip of flat rock. Which led to an overhang carved out of the black stone. The ancient fossilized remains of a fireplace out front. Beyond the fireplace, evidence of habitation.

Almost as unreal as the story the Lady in Blue had told him. The air moist and cold. Finch shivered.

Didn't know whether to believe her or not. Didn't know if it mattered. Nothing she'd said sounded any more or less plausible than what Duncan Shriek had written in his books. Understood, too, the weight of everything she had shown him. Knew it in his gut.

Wanted to tell her he lived in a different world. The world where Stark wanted to hurt people he loved, where Heretic could have him killed on a whim. Where Wyte's condition went from bad to worse. All of it gritty and immediate, with immediate consequences. He wasn't Crossley's son anymore. He was Finch, and there was a reason for that. *Survival.*

"You're too quiet," she said.

"I've heard worse theories," Finch said. Because he felt he had to say something. Because he felt overwhelmed.

The Lady in Blue gave him a curious look, head tilted to the side. "Not convinced? That's a shame, because you can disbelieve it all you want. It'll get you nowhere. Now get out of the boat and help me," she said.

The shocking cold of the shallow water woke him up. They pushed the rowboat up onto the shore. The Lady in Blue unhooked the lantern, walked forward.

"What is this place?" Finch asked as his boots found dry land.

"Wait and see," she said. Ushered him toward the overhang.

A cozy little space, sheltered by the rock. A thick layer of dust covered the uneven floor. Looked fuzzy in the lantern light. A welter of numbers and words had been carved into the far wall, all the way up to the ceiling. So many marks that they struck Finch like a cacophony of noise. Made him claustrophobic.

In the far corner, a skeleton on top of a blanket had disintegrated into a thicket of fibers and fragments. Intact. Yellowing. Human. Delicate, almost birdlike. Curled up in a position of sleep. On its side.

Looking at those small bones, Finch felt a sudden, inexplicable sadness. "Is that the monk?"

Words from the man's mouth in the clicks and whistles of the gray caps' language. And then, a sudden and monstrous clarity that can never be put into words.

"Yes, according to Shriek, that's Samuel Tonsure," the Lady in Blue said. "This is where he died. A hermit. In exile. Truff knows why the gray caps left him to this fate. Blind. Alone. He must have gone mad in his last years."

She pointed to the other corner. To a large pockmark in the floor. Light green. With rings within rings. Like a cross section of tree trunk. "And that's where Duncan was found. We didn't even know that he was human, or alive. He looked to us like a gray cap whose legs had been fused into the ground. When he was brought to me, I don't think he even knew who he was. He'd learned to walk among gray caps undetected. He'd traveled through the doors for many, many years. And then he'd come home here, alone, lonely. To give up being human. Half out of his mind.

Attuned to the rhythms of mushroom and spore. Here, by Tonsure's side. Like a dog guarding the grave of its master. I think he thought he'd wake up in a thousand years and everything would be *different*. Or that he'd never wake up at all."

Remembering Duncan's words: *"They found me and infiltrated me—I could feel their tendrils, their fleshy-dry-cold-warm pseudopods and cilia and strands slowly sliding up my skin, like a hundred tiny hands. They tried to remake me in their image."*

"And you found a way to use him." An echo of his voice against the stone. A place more like a memorial than a home.

"Yes. After a while. After we managed to remind him that he was human. Amazing how long that part took."

Finch said, "What happened next?"

Pain in her smile. "Do you want to know a secret?"

He leaned in toward the Lady in Blue, humoring her. This close she looked somehow *off-balance*. Something in her eyes. The faint smell of cigars. Masked by the freshness of some subtle herb.

"Duncan Shriek isn't dead," she whispered.

Then she jabbed something into his neck.

No time for surprise. No time for anything but falling through the gullet of the *skery*. Again.

9

Came to: On the battlements of a fortress at night. Gun emplacements dark and menacing.

Duncan Shriek isn't dead. For a moment he was losing his balance. Then someone propped him up from behind. *I don't believe it.* Not Crossley, not Finch.

Cold, with a wind blowing. Above, the heavens, laced with stars that seemed to be falling in together. A wash of silver and gold across the sky. Beyond the walls, a vast empty space. A desert? In that space, a thousand green fires blossoming. He knew this place—he knew it. It had been in his memory bulb dream. Shriek's memories. *Bliss was here.*

The Lady in Blue stood beside him again. Surrounded by dozens of soldiers. Intent on moving supplies, guard duty, or cleaning weapons.

"This is the monastery fortress of Zamilon, or at least a *version* of it," the Lady in

Blue said, as if reading his thoughts. "Abandoned for many decades, until we came along."

Duncan: *"Where the eastern approaches of the Kalif's empire fade into the mountains no man can conquer, the ruined fortress of Zamilon keeps watch over time and the stars. Within the fortress . . . Truffidian monks guard the last true page of Tonsure's famous journal."*

Below the battlements, the great hulking shadows of some kind of machinery. Engines of war flanking a wide road that led to a huge door. Looked like it was made half of volcanic rock and half of charred book cover. Set in the door, a smaller door, and a small door set into that one.

Painted and carved into every surface, radiating outward, the symbol from the scrap of paper:

Finch pointed to it. "What's that?"

"It's part of how we travel through the doors. Part of the . . . mechanism. But it means something different to the gray caps. It doesn't work the same way for us as for them. Thankfully."

Turned to the scene beyond the battlements. Furtive movement out there. Occluding the fires at times. A suggestion of long, wide limbs. Of misshapen heads.

"And all of *that*?"

"Those are the fires of enemy camps. Not gray caps. Not human. Something else. They don't know what to make of us. And we don't know what to make of them. But we have to hold this positison. Do you want to know why?"

Felt again like he was falling. "I'm not sure."

The Lady in Blue pulled him around. Held him by the shoulders. A viselike grip. An almost inhuman strength. He understood now, on a physical level, how she had held on, and kept holding on, all this time.

"You don't have that luxury, James Scott Crossley. *That* out there is nothing. It's just the latest thing to make us falter, to make us doubt ourselves." She released him. "When we started out, we didn't really understand. We had to learn fast."

"You read Samuel Tonsure's journal?"

"That and other things. Shriek's books after we found him."

"And you learned about Zamilon?"

"Sometimes by hard-earned experience. But now we know: Zamilon is a nexus for the doors. It exists in our world, *but it also exists in many other worlds simultaneously.*"

"And Duncan needed to go through it for his mission? He was on a mission for you?"

"Yes. But he's unpredictable. We think he went somewhere he shouldn't have. Triggered a trap. I'm not sure we'll ever know what went wrong unless Shriek chooses to tell us."

"So it's dangerous to travel through the doors?"

She stared up at the wash of stars. "It can be. We only use doors leading from or to Zamilon. Anything else has resulted in disaster. We don't know why. But Duncan has no such constraint . . ."

Remembering the Spit: *Through many doors . . . The doors smaller then larger, then smaller again. Oval. Rectangular. Square. Inlaid with glass. Gone, leaving only gaping doorway and a couple rusted hinges.*

"Who knows about the portals, the doors?"

The Lady in Blue laughed. "Duncan Shriek knew. Maybe some people have always known. Ambergris's early kings may have had the knowledge and lost it. Every schoolchild used to know. Because every scary story about the gray caps implies that they can move quickly from place to place . . . So far we've kept it from the rebel cells operating in the city. There's too much risk of them being captured by the gray caps and made to talk. And on the other side, the gray caps seem to have kept the doors hidden from the Partials."

"How much do the gray caps know about you?" *How much does Stark know? Or Bliss?*

"They know we're out here. But we're blessed by their concentration on the towers. It makes it easier for us to operate."

"Tell me why I'm here," Finch asked. The question he didn't want answered.

The Lady in Blue's features tightened. She looked away. "What I'm going to ask from you is dangerous. I wanted you to understand fully. So you'd know it in your *gut*. What's at stake. Because the war we're fighting right now isn't in Ambergris. It's out here. It's about opening and closing doors. Holding positions around places like Zamilon. With the few soldiers we have.

"We don't have a functional army here." She gestured around her. "Maybe a thousand well-trained men, if that. The rest are scattered. Twenty thousand soldiers, Finch. Marked by the HFZ and scattered across the doors. Imagine. Each one flung somewhere else, like a pearl necklace shattering on a marble staircase. Only, the moment after that necklace shatters there are thousands of marble staircases and one bead on each."

"They're not dead?" Finch, incredulous.

The Lady in Blue shook her head. "No. Most of them are just lost, and we need to bring them back . . . When Duncan didn't complete his mission, when we figured out where the bodies had turned up, where Duncan was, some wanted to cut our losses. Abandon the mission. Try to sabotage the towers. I said no. I said, I knew your father. I knew him well enough to know that, in this case, we could trust you. That you'd understand. That I'd make you understand."

"Understand what?" Finch said. "What is there left to understand?" A fury rising in him. "Understand that when I go back I have the secret services of not one but two countries working against me? That the gray caps will kill me if I don't solve this case? That my partner is probably dying? *What is it that you want me to understand?*"

The Lady in Blue looked at him in surprise. As if no one had spoken to her like that for a long time.

"I understand, Finch," she said slowly, biting off each syllable, "that you are the only one who can get back to the body while they're watching. It's a trap for anyone else. A fatal trap. And you and I both understand now that Duncan Shriek is alive. And I'm telling you that if you can get to him, you can bring him all the way back and help him complete his mission."

"What kind of weapon is Shriek? Is he a bomb?" Only thing Finch could think of. Like the suicide bombers the rebels had used in the past.

"No. He's the kind of weapon that's also a beacon. Also a door." She smiled. A wide and beautiful smile that cut right through Finch. There on the ramparts.

Overlooking the desert. In a place that might or might not be part of the world. *"There may be a way."*

"Just *say* it."

"We mean to force the door, Finch. To hijack it. To come through in numbers. Duncan Shriek is going to find our lost men and bring them through the gate formed by the towers. Before the gray caps can bring their own people through."

"That's insane. The risk . . ."

"If we had a better plan, we would use it."

"Even if Shriek *is* alive, how do you know he can do it? Bring the soldiers back?"

"He's shown us some of what he can do already."

"How will he find them?" Each question cut him off from one more avenue of retreat.

"They are all marked, or tagged, by the HFZ event. Each man. Each woman. He will find them through the doors, and we will return to Ambergris triumphant."

A strange light had entered her eyes. Like someone who had been dreaming of something that they'd never thought could happen. And now it was happening.

"What if they kill me? Eat my memories?" Finch asked. "What then?"

The Lady in Blue turned the full force of her gaze on him. "What's really bothering you, Finch? Is it fear? Or is it something else?" She turned to look out at the desert again. "Those things out there," she murmured. "They're gray caps, and they're people. Combined. How? I don't know. Maybe they came here during the Silence. Possible. But even though I don't know, I understand. Because *we're changing, too,* Finch. There's no one under my command who hasn't been altered in some way. The question is how much you change. Change too much and you're no different from Shriek, no different from a gray cap. And then even if we win, we lose. But adapt just enough? That's what I need from you. To adapt just enough."

An answer for everything. Yet Finch knew he'd always be searching for the next question. He felt a hundred years old. Like the weight of everything had piled on his back at once.

"What if I say no? What if I want you to just leave me the fuck alone?" *Stop fighting,* some part of him advised. *Just fall into it and keep falling.* But he couldn't. Not yet.

The Lady in Blue sighed. "You know, it's no good for the Kalif, either, if the gray caps come through. I don't care who you are or aren't working for. I don't care about your father's spying. I just know you hate Partials and your father had no love for the gray caps."

"How are you going to protect me?"

"We can't protect you. But we can make sure you don't get caught."

"You mean you can kill me." Feeling ill. Realized that in some ways the Lady in Blue was no different than Stark. *Apply pressure. Squeeze. Get what you want.*

The Lady in Blue looked somehow both stern and compassionate. In a quiet voice, she said, "I mean you know too much, John Finch. Sometimes we have to take the cards we're dealt and make the most of them. You can't throw away the cards now—you've already looked at them."

There it was. Stated directly. Somehow Finch admired her more for it. A bitter laugh of appreciation as he stood there, facing her down. "So I have no choice."

"If it's any consolation, maybe you never had a choice. Maybe there was never a point at which you could have turned back." She had the good grace to look away as she said, "Our man will be in touch when the time comes."

Finch anticipated the needle a second before it entered his neck.

※☀☀

When they released Finch back into the crowd at the black market party, everything was different. The sound soared over him at first. Then it was as if he couldn't hear it anymore. Looked for Sintra but didn't see her. Looked for Bosun but didn't see him, either. Didn't know how much time had passed. But the band was taking a break.

An urgency to the night, but he'd brought it with him. Couldn't get the image of the Lady in Blue out of his head. On a hill. In a boat. At the wall of the fortress. The images stabbed at him, threatened madness. *What didn't she tell me?*

Finch crossed the room on unsteady legs. Wary of Bosun. But still no Bosun. Felt for his Lewden Special. Relief. It had been returned to him.

Made his way through corridors. Gaze unfocused. Seeing nothing. Out into the rain. The towers a steamy green above the tops of buildings. The street nearly empty.

Two steps onto the street and he met an immovable force. Bosun, appearing out of darkness. Pulling his right arm behind him. Inexorable, the man all muscle. Felt Bosun's other hand looking for his gun. Felt it taken. Again.

Bosun's hot breath at his ear as Finch was marched toward a side alley. Helpless as a child.

"Find my carving?" Bosun muttered.

Against the discomfort, twisting, "For Truff's sake, you don't have to break my arm."

"So you didn't find it." Bosun seemed disappointed.

"What carving?" Grunting. Contorting to try to get relief.

"Stop moving. In your apartment. Left it there while we took the place apart. Would've done in your cat if he hadn't hidden."

Another mystery solved. One that didn't even matter anymore.

"Fuck you. Your breath smells like shit."

Bosun just laughed. "Be lucky if yours doesn't begin to smell like blood."

In the alley: Stark. With five other men. Bosun shoved Finch forward, releasing him.

"Finch, what a surprise!" Stark said. "I know you're just coming from a party, but we're having our own little party out here. Glad you could make it."

Bosun punched him in the gut before he could react. Fists like stone. Sent him slumped over onto the ground. Begging for air.

Got to his feet slowly, not sure if he should. Could've used Wyte coming out of the darkness in that moment.

Stark's face was a vicious half-moon in the dimness. Hard to believe Bosun was his brother.

"Where'd you go, Finch? Where'd you go for an hour and a half? Bosun says you were there and then you *weren't*."

The question so much smaller than the answer. Contempt for the interrogator. What kind of spymaster came in person for this kind of ambush? Only someone who'd never gotten past the simple art of the shakedown. Came in hard and fast and thought that was enough.

Not here it isn't.

Secret knowledge gave him strength. "Just enjoying the party."

Stark circled him. "I'll bet you were. Saw your exotic girl leave. She looked well satisfied. Did you give her a good time in there? You should be glad I'm a man of such refinement, Finch, or we might've given her a better one."

"Is that all you came here to say?" Finch asked.

Bosun nodded and two of his men wrenched Finch's arms back. Painfully.

"No, not really. We've some more serious matters to discuss. Like, did you know there's a bounty on the head of the Lady in Blue?" Stark came close, looked him in the eye. "I think you do know that. It applies to anyone who associates with her—on my side or yours."

"I don't know what you're talking about."

Stark nodded. Bosun punched him in the stomach again. Grunted. Fought through the pain. The thugs held him up.

"I think you do, Finch. I think you do. At least, those two thought so. Show him, boys."

They dragged him closer to the wall. Saw four pale feet, the rest of the bodies hidden by shadows.

"The two morons that Bosun saw spirit you away. They didn't say much before they died. But they said enough."

Finch didn't think they'd said anything at all. "I don't even know who they are."

"Of course you don't, Finch," Stark said with disgust. "You never saw their faces. Let alone their feet. So, again, where did you disappear off to?"

"Nowhere."

Stark looked at him a second. "Nowhere? Nowhere. Next you'll be saying you've made no progress on the case."

"There is no progress, Stark."

"Even after I gave you that juicy transcript? I think you're lying."

Finch, reckless: "I think you fed us that address in the transcript. It almost got us killed. For nothing. And I wasted a day. So I've got nothing for you, either."

Stark pulled back a second, as if to get a better look at Finch. "Are you serious, Finch? Because that's not what I heard. I heard Wyte blew it for you. Your man transforms into some huge fucking monster and charges the stage. That's what I'm told. Not exactly proper procedure. Not exactly what you'd expect from a detective. Or maybe it is. Maybe it's the old quick-change comic theater routine. Maybe that goes over big in this shit hole. What is Wyte, anyway? Some kind of secret weapon?"

"He's sick," Finch said.

"Any sicker than Duncan Shriek?" Stark asked, with a knowing leer. "Because I hear Mr. Shriek is dead. And holed up in a certain apartment on Manzikert

Avenue. Writing his ghost memoirs." Stark's refinement was slipping. A rougher voice, with a gutter accent.

"Why not go look for yourself," Finch said. "Maybe you'll turn up some clues."

Stark kneed Finch in the groin. Finch groaned. Couldn't fall down, held by the two men. "Think you're funny? I know that's a kill zone. You don't get me, Finch. Do you think I give a fuck about this sewer of a city?" Stark whispered in his ear. "I don't give a fuck about this dump. I don't care if it all goes up in pillars of flame. It's not my fucking town. But I don't like being lied to. And I don't like people getting in the way of what I want."

Apparently no one did. Not Stark. Not the Lady in Blue. Not Heretic. Finch was tired of it.

Stark wrenched Finch's head back by his hair. "They're working all night on the towers, Finchy. All night. Like there's a deadline suddenly. Driving people past their limits. Until they're dying. Until they're falling from the scaffolding. Why are they doing that, Finch? Why are the towers so important? And what's it got to do with that apartment, Finchy? And what's that got to do with the rebel safe house, Finchy? And how is all of this going to benefit me?"

With every question, Stark seemed smaller. More brutish.

A *wash of stars. An underground sea. A thousand green lights out in the desert.*

"You're the professional spy, Stark. Why don't you figure it out?" Made professional sound small.

Somehow that made Stark laugh. "I'm trying, Finch. Believe me, I'm trying. But people like you make it so difficult." Stark nodded.

They let him fall to the ground. Bosun tossed his gun back to him.

Stark leaned down. "There are no professionals here, Finchy. We're all amateurs. That's what makes us dangerous. Now, you'd better start getting results. You'd better start thinking about your future. What's left of it. Or all the lovely people around you are going to suffer. Starting sooner than you think. And if that doesn't work, we'll just come for you. There's not much time left. This is your last warning."

Had the feel of a well-worn speech.

Stark stalked off, the rest behind him. Leaving Finch beside the two corpses.

Above them all: the towers. Finch saw that the blackness between them was different than to either side. Showed no stars. Blurred, with the vague impression of shadowy nighttime scenes sliding across. Fast.

Now he knew why.

Back in the hotel. Near midnight. Didn't know for sure. Approached the landing below the seventh floor. Heard Feral hissing at something. Saw a flickering, golden light that projected a circle of fire. Elongated and slanted down the hallway. Distorted further by the fungus on the walls. A rank smell, like too-strong perfume.

Bliss? The Partial?

Already had his Lewden out. Slowly walked up the steps. Saw Feral, fur puffed out, standing a few feet from his door. Staring up the source of the light. The thing had attached itself to the door. It looked like a golden brooch with filigree detail extending out in wavy branches or tendrils. From that angle, he could see the transparent cilia underneath. Almost looked like a larger cousin of the starfish he'd seen in the underground cavern.

Came closer, gun aimed at it. Arms shaking a little.

Feral saw him and scurried over to stand next to him. Now a low growl came from the cat's throat.

From ten feet away, the front of the organism had the look of pure gold. A rough flower pattern. In the middle, a closed aperture divided into four parts.

A beam of light flashed out from the thing. Blinded him for a moment. Withdrew.

"Finch!" Heretic's voice. A ghostly quaver.

Finch lowered his gun. Didn't know whether to be relieved or angry. "Not worth your time, Feral." A message from Heretic. A little more dramatic than usual.

The aperture dilated. Out leapt the *skery*. Finch screamed. Stumbled back. The *skery* reached its full length an inch from his face. Receded. Bobbed there, long and black. Curling downward. Until he could see it wasn't the *skery* at all. Just a sick joke. In another second, it broke off and fell to the floor.

Feral came forward. Hissed at it, smacked at it with his claws. Jumping back even as he did so.

No one stirred in the apartments to either side. Finch didn't blame them.

The oval in the middle widened. An approximation of Heretic's face appeared. He looked almost jolly. As if he'd known how horrified Finch would be of the *skery*.

"Finch," Heretic rasped, "you've been gone a long time. Almost long enough for me to suspect you had left us. I thought you'd run. Until you appeared again shadowing Wyte—"

But most of the rest was lost. Whatever it was supposed to be. Reverting to a series of clicks and whistles and moist suppurations. The garglings of a monster. As if Heretic didn't care anymore whether Finch had orders or not. Or something had gone wrong when recording the message. Or everything was falling apart.

Finch listened to the obscene chatter for a minute. Then he put a couple of bullets in Heretic's face. With a sigh the golden organism slid slowly to the hallway floor. Began to curl in on itself.

Picked up Feral, opened the door, locked it behind him, and went to bed.

FRIDAY

I: When did you first realize how deeply you were involved?

F: I didn't. I mean, it wasn't clear. I mean, I never did.

I: That is a lie. You're hiding things again.

F: Then kill me and use a memory bulb to find out the truth. Bastard.

I: We can only kill you once. And once you are dead, all we would have is your bulb. They're unreliable.

F: Then trust me.

I: People lie. They lie and they keep lying. Eventually, they can't remember the truth. Is that your problem, Finch?

F: I'm not really a detective. That's why I can't answer your questions.

I: Once they made you a detective, you *were* a detective. Why did you never understand that?

1

The bed shuddered beneath Finch, almost seemed to gasp. He reached for his gun as a deep thudding vibration shook the hotel. An after-sound like shredding or tearing. Timbers settling and creaking like an old ship. Thought for one sleep-muddled moment it was his damaged shoulder.

Took a moment to realize the impact came from outside the building. He pulled on pants. Ran to the kitchen window as another shuddering thud struck. Looked down through the smudged pane. Nothing on the street below, just a few people running. Checked from the bathroom. No one in the courtyard.

A commotion outside. People on the stairs. All he could think was: fire? Or, worse, Partials rounding up people. Wished Wyte were there with him.

Threw on and buttoned a shirt, put on shoes without socks. Feral meowing round his feet. Agitated. A burning smell in the air now. Or was he imagining it? Shoved his gun into his waistband. Went out the door fast.

Stumbled over the remains of Heretic's message, curled up like a husk. Residents were shoving their way up the stairs to the roof. While his neighbor, the old man, stood watching them from the hall. Framed by a rough stain of blue-gray fungus on the wall.

"What's happening?" Finch asked.

"The towers!" The man spat out the words. "The towers are starting a war. Everybody wants to go watch. Idiots! I'm staying right here."

On the roof the burnt smell was stronger. A cloudless sky. Searing blue. More hotel residents in one place than he'd ever seen before. Black market vendors. Clinic workers. Camp guards. Scavengers. Druggies. All holding on to their gas masks. Just in case. All looking out toward the bay.

No longer muffled, the thud had a growling rasp to it. An immediacy. Like a cannon was going off near his head. With each new thud a murmur rose. Of concern? Of awe? Shoved his way through the crowd until he was near the edge of the roof.

Out in the bay, an emerald light shot out from the tops of the towers, combined into one oddly thick ball of sparks. Hurtled toward the Spit. Smashed into the boats. Sent up steam and fire. Seemed to *cling* there. The Spit. Burning. Some would say "long overdue," but what would come after? A fireworks display to the few children, who were clapping.

A slightly unreal aspect to it. Watching it from afar. The Spit so tiny. Each boat a sliver. A toothpick. Rocking on a vast sea. The tyranny of distance. A few boats had become unmoored and were drifting across the bay. Aimless. Half on fire. Were Stark and Bosun still on the Spit? Desperately moving from boat to boat. Making for shore. Finch didn't think so.

Wondered if Wyte was watching somewhere or still dealing with his condition.

The sky between the towers had become darker, shot through with shades of amber. In the backdrop: a flock of strange birds and the silhouette of an island that shouldn't exist.

The people around him were talking about the green light.

"Getting rid of that nest of spies. Should've done it a long time ago."

"No friends of Ambergris. No friends at all."

"But what's next, then? Where does it stop?"

Finch looked over at the HFZ. Violent strands of strobing orange-red fungal mist rose into the sky. Like an infection running rampant. Remembered the hill he had stood atop with the Lady in Blue. The image came back with a vividness that took over his vision for a moment. A *roiling mass of particles. Discharging light until a steady humming glow suffused the city in a kind of dawn. There came in reply from the city a hundredfold bestial roar.*

"Why do they ever do anything?"

"They're all dead by now. Or dying."

Could the Lady in Blue be both right and wrong? Could Duncan Shriek be alive but the towers have some other purpose altogether? Under that sharp blue sky, he didn't know the answer. What if he was bait? A distraction? Once again, the disconnect hurt him. Between what she'd shown him and Ambergris as he knew it. *An ethereal beauty that no longer lives here.* A dream to believe or deny. A vision as different for him as it was for Wyte or Rathven.

"The city fighting itself. Pointless now . . ."

The Photographer came up next to him. Binoculars hung from his neck. He carried a small pouch by the drawstring. "Breathtaking, isn't it?"

"No," Finch said. "No, it's not. It's fucking awful."

The Photographer said, "Just look at the way the water reacts. Look at the patterns." Almost giddy.

An orange eruption of flames over the Spit. Accompanied by spirals of black smoke. Another blast. Another. The building didn't shake as much now. As if used to it. Or as if Finch were.

"When did it start?"

"Twenty minutes ago? Suddenly most of the workers climbed down from the top of the towers. They're at the base now, still constructing something."

A sudden spark of hope hit him hard. Hadn't realized he still had the capacity for it. "So they aren't finished yet."

"Almost. And so is the Spit."

Finch stared sharply at the Photographer. But there was no hint of triumph in him.

"It's a strong warning," the Photographer said. "They're clearing the way for something."

"I wonder what they'll do when they've finished off the Spit," Finch said, almost to himself.

The Photographer pointed to the east. "What's missing?"

The other camp dome was gone. Had left behind only a kind of ghostly white outline, broken by mottled gray. With that lack, the greens of the Religious Quarter burned even stronger in the sunlight. And through that entanglement lay the distant echo, the distant shadows, of cupolas and minarets. *Like a dream. Like a trap.* Was Sintra watching from there even now?

"Fuck."

A new phase of the Rising.

The crowd had begun to realize the roof might be dangerous. Thinned out. Just a few left. A woman in her fifties dressed in a bathrobe, arms wrapped tightly round herself. A couple in their twenties who had never, Finch realized, known anything but war or the Rising. Three old men in their best clothes, watching solemnly.

Better for most to hunker down in their apartments and not see the end coming. Or go out onto the streets in one last gasp of defiance. *Against what?*

The towers continued to pound the Spit. A white smoke had overtaken the black smoke. It looked now like the thick green spheres slamming into the Spit were dissolving into a cloud bank or a thick mist.

"I have something for you," the Photographer said. Put the pouch in Finch's hand. "It looks just like a memory bulb, but it isn't. Keep it with you at all times."

Finch stared at the pouch. Stared at the Photographer. Taken completely by surprise.

The Photographer said, "If you aren't caught, you'll need it for your mission. If you *are* caught, take a bite. Just one bite."

"And then what?"

The Photographer's face was as blank as the side of a wall. "There will be nothing left of you. Nothing they could trace. Nothing they could *read*."

Nothing left. No pain. No concealment. Nothing.

"We're changing, too, Finch. There's no one under my command who hasn't been altered in some way. The question is how much you change. Change too much and you're no different from Shriek, no different from a gray cap. And then even if we win, we lose."

Instinctively tried to give it back to the Photographer. The man stepped away, hands shoved in his jacket pockets.

"Don't talk about this in your apartment," the Photographer said, as if nothing had happened. "Don't write down anything while in your apartment."

"Why not?"

"The message last night left intruders. We can't run interference on them without leaving a trail."

Didn't even bother to examine that, turn it over in his mind. Just one more intrusion in a life littered with them. No anger left to shed.

The Photographer continued: "Later today someone else will approach you with the rest of what you need."

Assuming I'll do it. But standing there, pouch in hand, it seemed impossible he wouldn't do it. The only way out. To take control of the case before it imploded. *Let it not be a case anymore. Let it be something else.*

"I always thought it would be the madman out front," Finch said.

A thin smile from the Photographer. "He's just a madman."

"Do I need to stay here?"

"Follow your usual routine. You'll be followed. We'll know where you are no matter where you go."

After a pause: "Does Rathven know?"

"No," the Photographer said.

"She's not even your sister, is she?"

"Goodbye, Finch," the Photographer said, and stuck out his hand. A stronger grip than he'd imagined, and more final.

He wasn't coming back.

"What about your photographs?"

"You can have them if you want them. I don't need them anymore."

Then he was gone, walking down the stairs.

In the bay, the towers had fallen silent. There was just the heavy wall of black smoke from the southeast shore. Already he could hear the sound of angry voices from below. Could see, at intersections far below, crowds gathering.

Finch stood there awhile. Looking out over the city. Not sure whether to believe he held its future in his hands.

2

At the station, Blakely had barricaded the door with a couple of filing cabinets and an empty desk. Finch slid through a narrow gap that Gustat quickly closed behind him. Blakely had the smell of whiskey on his breath, masked by coffee. The flushed face of someone trying desperately to get drunk for a long time. Behind him, Gustat was fiddling with his radio, with no luck. No sign of Wyte. Or Albin or Skinner.

"What the fuck is going on?"

Blakely: "You've seen what's happening. We'll be targets. We're thinking we might fortify the bell tower. If things don't get better."

Finch just stared at him. "Fortify the tower?" *Make one last stand.* Wait out the siege in a pathetic excuse for a tree fort, a few dozen bottles of whiskey and beer for comfort. Had a flash of Blakely as a bullying, pimply faced child, strong-arming his way into the local clubhouse.

"You have a better idea?" Blakely asked.

Saw the fear in his face now.

"There are no better ideas," Finch muttered.

But Blakely had a point. The mood on the streets had been fearful, murderous. He'd kept his detective's badge in his hand the whole time. Other hand on his gun. Hating the way the sky made everything so clear, so clean-looking. Hating the weight in his pocket of the thing the Photographer had given him. Partials had been rounding up anyone still in a camp uniform. Bashing in heads. But no statement had been made by the gray caps. By a stroke of bad luck, it was also another drug mushroom day. Everyone wanted them now, to stock up against disaster.

Finch walked toward his desk. Bodies had been stacked in the holding cell. On top: a man of about thirty-five in a lacerated brown suit and a woman in her twenties, wearing a fancy red dress. A platelike lavender lichen had begun to cover up their faces. A dozen others under them. All dead. Thought he recognized one or two from the chapel.

"What's this about?" he demanded.

No response for the longest time. Then Blakely spoke up. "Heretic said they were traitors. With the rebels. Brought them here last night. They had to be liquidated, Heretic said."

Gustat wouldn't look at Blakely. Wouldn't look anywhere.

"So Heretic was here?" Finch asked.

"Yes, he was. Last night."

"And you just plan on leaving the bodies here?" Failing to hide his disgust. *At them? At the situation?*

"He told us to."

Gustat spoke up. "There's talk of the gray caps getting ready to cleanse whole neighborhoods with spore clouds. They've closed off the streets nearest the bay and the towers. The towers will be done in *the next day or two*." The words said with a mixture of awe and dread.

"They're pretty well done already," Finch said. "They took out the whole fucking Spit this morning if you hadn't noticed. Where are the others?"

"Told to go work on the towers, so I guess they aren't done," Blakely said.

Finch sat down at his desk. Anger building in him. For having to go through the motions. At the casual cruelty of his position.

New case notes on his desk. In Blakely's hand. A domestic dispute. A mugging. Someone had stolen someone else's food. Someone's dog had gone missing and the owner had filed a missing person's report. Amazing how the mundane shit never ended. While the world went to hell. Again tried to chart the sequence of events that had led him to this moment. Couldn't.

"Heard anything from Wyte?" he asked, to distract himself.

"He's alive?" Gustat seemed shocked.

"Yes, he's fucking well alive." Then realized he hadn't called in to the station after the shoot-out. *Need to call Wyte.* "Dapple's dead, though. We had a shoot-out with rebels and Partials." The words came out so matter-of-factly. So easily.

"Dapple's dead," Gustat said, hand still on the radio tuner. A blank stare into the distance. Began to cry. As if Dapple had been his best friend, instead of just tolerated.

Harsh laugh from Blakely. "Sorry we didn't have a chance to catch up on your exploits before now. But last night we were too busy sticking it out here in the station next to a pile of corpses."

"It happens, Gustat," Finch said. With a toughness he didn't feel. Ignoring Blakely. Hadn't expected Gustat's tears. Hadn't expected a lot of things. Wondered how much longer he could endure it. When would whatever kept him going run out?

"Look in your memory hole, Finch," Blakely said.

A message? He leaned down. Pulled the pod out uneasily, with the other two watching. Went through the ritual of opening it. Just a note. From Heretic.

PLANS HAVE CHANGED. FILE A FINAL REPORT ON YOUR CASE. THEN REPORT WITH WYTE TO THE TOWERS FOR WORK DETAIL.

A vast improvement over the last message.

Blakely's face held fear and smugness all at once. "You're off the case. He told us before he left. The case is over."

Incredulous: "Who is taking it over, then?"

"No one. Working on the towers is punishment for what happened at the safe house. If you ask me, you got off light. He was in a good mood. Calm. Almost happy. Even when he put them to sleep." A tilt of the head toward the holding cage.

"You've got to work on the towers," Gustat said, still messing with his radio. An odd look on his face, halfway between a frown and a smile. "Thanks for the reminder," Finch said. "Now fuck off."

"Cheer up," Blakely said. "I don't think Heretic's coming back. I don't think anyone's coming back."

The clock ticked. The phone on Finch's desk rang a few times. Mostly people scared because of the destruction of the Spit. Even though the towers had done nothing since. Some of the people who called even had some small hope he could help them. But they were living in the grip of memories of the old days. A past that had never really existed.

Finch worked on his final report. Going through the motions. Sticking to routine. Waiting for someone to tap him on the shoulder and tell him the rest of the plan. He would call Wyte soon, too. Just working up the nerve.

Started out with pen and paper. Wrote drivel. *Fuck you . . . Am I just the bait? . . . There's nothing here you can use . . . You're monstrous . . .*

Paralyzed for a moment by the thought of the look on Sintra's face as she walked away from him for the last time. Clinging now to what she'd told him even as he'd told her to stop before. *"My mother had gotten better, but my father had lost his arm to a fungal bullet. He couldn't work for a long time he was so depressed. He'd been a journalist."*

Threw away his pointless notes. Went to the typewriter. Soon had a real report that while bland made a kind of sense. Was it good enough to satisfy Heretic while he completed his mission? Had no idea. Read it over one last time.

There are no definitive conclusions to be drawn in this murder case. I have found no information on the identity of the dead gray cap. The man may be related to a fringe historian, Duncan Shriek, who lived in the apartment more than a hundred years ago, but this appears to be a coincidence. Two names came up repeatedly in investigating the case: Ethan Bliss, an operative for Morrow, and "Stark," the alias of a spy working for Stockton. Their relationship to the case is oblique at best, but both appear convinced that the man carried a weapon created by the rebels for use against Fanaarcensitii. I remain convinced that the man fell from a great height and was moved to the apartment— that he died elsewhere. Both Bliss and Stark may know more, but they remain fugitives, and we have not been given the resources to track them down. If the dead man was part of a rebel conspiracy, then it appears to have failed. I would suggest that the Fanaarcensitii put all of their resources into tracking down Bliss and Stark. Interrogations of both parties might provide more information. All other intelligence can be found in the attached notes and prior reports.

—Detective John Finch

Short. Protective of those it needed to protect. Giving up those who were asking for it.

Cowardly. Masking death, despair, destruction.

Put it aside.

Typed, pushing the keys down hard:

EVENTS ARE MOVING BEYOND YOU. THERE'S NOTHING YOU
CAN DO. YOU'RE NOT EVEN THE CRAFTIEST BASTARDS IN THE
ROOM. YOU'LL ALL GO DOWN WONDERING HOW IT HAPPENED. I'LL
NEVER UNDERSTAND YOU, BUT YOU'LL NEVER UNDERSTAND US,
EITHER.

Felt like a child. Took that message, too, and walked back to his desk. Pondered both of them, lying there like some kind of judgment on his integrity.

A few minutes later, still thinking, the phone rang.

"Finch." Wyte. The voice barely recognizable. As human. "You've got to help me."

"When the time comes, right, Finch?" "Sure, Wyte. When the time comes."

"Finch. Are you there?"

"Yes."

"It's time."

Every memory of Wyte invincible the day before cracked into pieces. Finch's throat tightened. The world around him spun, lost focus. Blakely hunched over his desk. To the left was a splotch of ruddy white. The windows seemed to contract.

"Are you sure?"

"I'm sure."

"Okay, Wyte. Okay."

"And, Finch, I don't think I'm going quietly. Not like Richard Dorn."

The voice, once so deep and gravelly, had changed since they'd first met. Become soft and liquid, lighter yet thicker.

"Where are you?"

"At my apartment."

"You'll know what to do." "I'll know what to do."

"I'm coming," Finch said.

Wyte hung up.

Sat there a moment. Leaned forward a little over his desk. Elbows digging into the wood. Marshaling his strength.

You can do this. You have to do this. You promised *him.*

Finch raised his arm. Smashed his fist into the desk. Just to feel the pain shoot up through his shoulder. Stood. Swept everything off his desk. Made a sound almost like a roar. Almost like a moan. While Blakely and Gustat, standing now, just stared at him.

Tonsure's bones in the little house by the underground sea. Strange stars. Falling with Bliss into darkness. Emerging into light. Heretic's skery crawling up his leg. Sintra disappearing into darkness.

"What the fuck are you looking at?" Finch snarled. He began to break everything on the floor into pieces small enough to feed into the memory hole. Bits of pencil. Torn paper. The gaping jaw of a stapler. Shoved them into it. The hole rasped and protested.

Then tore up his report and his pathetic message. Put them both down the hole as well.

"Do you like that, Heretic? *Do you?*" Might have been screaming it. Didn't care.

Blakely pulled him away, hand on his shoulder. Finch shrugged it off. Whirled on him. Looked at Blakely like he didn't know him. Saw Blakely had his gun out. Controlled himself, arms outstretched, palms down.

"It's okay, Blakely." But it wasn't okay. How much else could fall apart? What was left? "I just need some things from my desk and then I'm gone."

The Photographer had said they'd be watching him. Now they'd have to watch him deal with Wyte.

Blakely backed away. Didn't put down his gun. "You're crazy, Finch," he said. "You're crazy." Gustat stood there, mouth open.

Finch reached under the desk. Pulled the ceremonial scimitar in its scabbard from its hiding place.

Blakely backed even farther away. "What the hell is that?"

"It's my sword," Finch said. Brought the belt with the scabbard around his waist. "Never seen a sword before, Blakely?" Already had his gun. Didn't really need anything else. Never would again.

At the door, he planned to turn and say something. What, he didn't know. But there was nothing to say. Instead, he just pushed the filing cabinet aside.

Left Blakely and Gustat standing there, looking like two lost boys in a room suddenly grown huge.

3

Wyte's door had a sagging "17" on it. Half shadowed, half in sunlight from the decorative stone wall running parallel to all the apartments. The blue paint had a rust-like stain running through it. An old bullet hole decorated the upper left-hand corner. A faded, torn welcome mat. Sweat and mold and the fading stench of piss. It depressed Finch. He'd only visited Wyte there a few times. Late-night drinking sessions. Bold statements about escape or joining the rebels that nobody remembered in the mornings. Commiserating with Wyte over his estranged wife. His far distant children.

Finch had taken the long route, trying to shake any watchers.

Knocked once. Twice. Gun in one hand. Sword in the other.

Nothing.

Knocked again.

Heard a sound this time. Like a voice. A voice drowning as it spoke. Awash in strange tides. Might've said, "Come in, Finch."

Inside: cracked yellow wallpaper. A photo of Wyte's wife on a rickety table. A short hallway leading to the galley-style kitchen. A couple of crooked paintings showed faded watercolor scenes of Hoegbotton ships hunting the king squid. Fables of a bygone era.

Then the living room. Almost no furniture. As if Wyte were already gone.

But he wasn't. He lay in the corner of the living room, the weak light of an old lamp dribbling across his body. The lamp had come all the way from the Southern Isles, brought by Wyte's grandmother. Shells were still glued into the base.

Wyte dwarfed the lamp. Slumped there. Monstrous. Huge. Spilling out in peculiar ways. As if a mossy hill had been dropped into the room. Wandering tendrils as outliers. Above, looking down at Finch, the face within the face. The tiny eyes. White against the encroaching dark. Staring out.

Who'd laid the trap for Wyte? In the beginning? He'd laid it for himself, in a sense. By falling into it.

Wyte spoke. Guttural. Wet. Dissolving. "Thanks for coming, James." Like everything were normal. *Four days ago we were tracking down Bliss.*

"It's going to be okay, Wyte."

"You don't have to lie to me. It's not going to be okay. It's not. I know that. Even if Otto doesn't." A gruff, coughing laugh.

"You're among friends, Wyte."

A kind of seismic shift from the thing in the corner. Laughter?

"It's nice to call you James again. That might've been the hardest thing. Remembering to call you Finch. Or John."

"You didn't give me up, Wyte. I'll never forget that."

A shambling shrug from the mound in the corner. *From the thing with Wyte's eyes.*

"Tell Emily. Tell her . . ."

"She knows. *I* know, Wyte. No one needs to be told anything." Finch didn't even know where Emily lived anymore.

Creature. Monster. Other.

Finch's hands were shaking. Could he do this? Searching himself. Both Crossley and Finch. *Can either of us do this?* Kept thinking of Wyte behind the desk at Hoegbotton's so long ago. Showing Finch the ropes. Patiently explaining the job.

A world extinguished as thoroughly as a spent match in the gutter.

"James?"

"Yes?"

"Like I said on the phone, I can't control myself anymore. There's not much of me left. The rest might fight back. But you have to know that's not me."

Telling Finch in a candid moment months ago, "I don't want to hurt anybody. I don't want to lose control but still be there, knowing what I am doing."

"I know, Wyte," Finch said. Grinding his teeth. Biting his cheek until the blood came. A soundless scream building inside of him. "It's going to be okay."

But it wasn't.

Finch closed the door behind him.

Drew his sword, tears streaming down his face.

What it took to kill a man transformed that way was almost what it took to kill a gray cap. Finch had killed a gray cap once. Before the Rising. When he was James Crossley. When it was just House Hoegbotton against House Frankwrithe & Lewden. Just poorly trained Irregulars patrolling neighborhoods. Making sure the enemy didn't take hold in the cracks. Weeding them out from derelict, firebombed houses. Abandoned theaters. Courtyards that still held memories of massacres. Official Hoegbotton policy called gray caps "noncombatants" unless a unit felt under threat. Unofficial policy encouraged patrols to engage and drive off, "damage," or kill. Back then, the gray caps supplied arms and ammo to Frank-writhe & Lewden.

Crossley was in charge of the patrol that night. They'd emerged from a warren of streets into a junkyard, surrounded by burnt-out buildings, that had once been a playground. Right after detaining and then releasing three youths without papers. The three had done enough to convince Crossley they belonged. Or enough for him to not want to arrest them and have them wind up in a holding cell where they might not last until morning.

They had only the light of a half-moon and the reluctant streetlamps burning a hundred feet away. But Crossley caught sight of something moving herky-jerky through the junkyard.

Seven in the patrol. Exposed. He wasn't sure what he was seeing at first, because gray caps rarely came out into the open. It was like seeing a dolphin in a public pond. So he'd given the signal to spread out without knowing what they faced. Circle round. Converge.

He crept up, over broken girders and garbage, to find: a gray cap. Wandering in a circle. Talking to itself. No obvious injury. But something wrong. Like it was drunk.

When the gray cap saw them, it broke off its wandering dance. Tried to escape. But they had it hemmed in by then. Its teeth, needle sharp. Claws on its fingers. It expelled a fungal mist, but they were already wearing gas masks.

Crossley was the first to shoot it. It lurched. Righted itself. Ran toward another point of the compass. Two bullets. Another lurch. But absorbed. A cry. A leap like a dancer, then. As if finally realizing the danger. Crossley-Finch would never forget. It whirled past one man and then another. But instead of escaping, it turned to close the distance. As if enraged. Or sick. The light in its eyes green and everlasting. Tore into one man with its claws, slapping away his rifle. Took another bullet for its efforts, but scooped out the Irregular's throat. The man crumpled to the ground. Crossley, scrambling to aim and fire, thought he saw a glint of a smile from the creature.

Darted. Flitted. Was gone. Then back again. Far then close. Each of them struggling to keep up with that speed. Grunting and cursing and sweating, as if it were something normal. Like digging a ditch or a grave. Too invested now. Knowing they couldn't retreat, and that the gray cap had decided to fight.

Wherever the thing stepped, a golden dust rose up from its tread. Clouds of red-and-green spores radiated out from it like steam. Their gas masks protected them.

Low on ammo. They kept shooting it, and it kept taking the bullets.

Knives out. Finch shouted the order to fix bayonets. Down to four. Against one. Reminded them not to let the bayonets get stuck in gray cap flesh. It would reel them in, finish each of them off. But, still—one man's rifle got stuck. Forgot to let it go. The gray cap jerked him forward, disemboweled him, then turned, stung by fresh cuts from all sides. Down to three men. Flesh sloughed off its body, but no blood. It did not wince. Kept shouting in its language. Sometimes mixing in human words. In a hissing, sibilant voice.

They kept at their task. Too busy to be afraid. Too busy to scream. Inside, its flesh was black, accordioned. Crossley saw as he came in close at its back. As it bit and kept biting another man. Finch brought his hunter's knife down across the back of the gray cap's leg. Felt the blade cut through something hard and thick. He pulled it out, taking a wedge of black flesh with it. The gray cap limped away. No longer as agile. A snarl. Finch and the others shot it in the face, the chest, the arms, the legs.

Still, it kept coming. Dancing in and out, its face a discolored mess. Eyes peeking out from the ruined flesh. Crossley lunging, driving his blade deeper into the leg as it turned to face one of his men. Dashed out as the creature tried to turn.

There was a *give*, and a wash of purple blood.

He stood back. Saw the gray cap standing on one leg.

"Murderers," the gray cap crooned. "Murderers. In our city."

Crossley wanted it dead in that moment. To shut it up. Caught in a bloodlust so primal that the enemy looked fey and beautiful in the moonlight. Distant and removed from what they were doing to it.

Now they converged, the three of them. It couldn't evade them. Did it weep as they tore it to pieces? Did it make any human sound to make them stop? No. All it did was stare up at the hard stars as if they were but an extension of its eyes. Arms hacked and pulled off. Cut at. Peeled away. Tossed to the side. The red of its leg. While still it stared. While a cloud of spores erupted from the top of its head, puffing away, disappearing. Hacked, too, at the torso until there was just a head attached to a wreckage of neck. Still the thing smiled. Still it seemed to live. The reflexive life of a gecko's tail.

Now they cursed and sobbed. Unable, as the bloodlust left them, to understand how they had been brought to this. How they could have done this. Even as they still wanted to kill it. Screaming. Shouting. Not caring if an enemy could hear them. Just wanting to keep on killing it until it was dead.

Finally, they burnt it, until it was just dead eyes laughing, asking if it had been worth it.

Soon even that burst into spores.

4

Nothing remained of Finch when he was done with Wyte. Not really. Blood or something like blood drenched him. His left hand gripped the sword tightly, the guard thick with gore. Wyte wouldn't get a funeral. Wouldn't get much of anything. He'd already begun the short, sharp process of becoming one of the forgotten. Nothing anybody could've done to save him from that.

Finch's left shoulder sang with pain from the blow Wyte had given it. Left knee unsteady from having his legs taken out from under him. Toward the end. One last reflexive lunge from a creature that didn't want to die. The whole time it had felt like it was happening to him. His steps were heavy from the weight.

The sounds had been horrific. Something had lived inside of Wyte. When it came out, Finch shot it. Then sliced it apart as it squealed. Was it part of Wyte? Was it the remnants of Otto? Finch didn't care. He had just wanted it dead. Wanted to make sure Wyte wasn't coming back.

No relation to the family man and husband Wyte had once been, before the Rising. No correlation between his life then and his death now. Something crazy. Something beyond prediction. Never sat on the stoop of Wyte's former house, drinking out of his silver flask, and said, casually, "You're going to turn into a monster, Wyte, and I'm going to kill you with a ceremonial sword forged by the Kalif's empire."

Would the resurrection of Duncan Shriek be the opposite of this? Better or worse?

The phone rang inside Wyte's apartment as Finch was leaving. He hesitated. Went back inside. Closed the door. Locked it.

The phone was in the kitchen. He avoided looking in the corner. The stillness was oppressive. The smell thick, physical. Had to pull his shirt collar to his nose.

Picked up the phone with his bloody hand. Waited.

"Hello. Finch?" Stark. Almost cheery.

"What do you want?"

"You sound a little shaky. What's wrong?"

"What do you want?"

Realized then that Stark's people had followed him there. Told Stark where he was. *And that Stark knew Wyte's phone number.*

"It's not what I want," Stark said. "It's what you want. And, apparently, you want me to *keep hurting you.* Apparently if I keep hurting you more and more, I'll get what I want."

A barking laugh from Finch. "The city's fucked. The Spit's destroyed. The towers are almost done. Whatever you want won't matter in a day or two."

"My dear Finch, that's exactly my point. You need to tell me *everything you know*—by the end of today. Otherwise, don't waste your breath lecturing me about the state of this shitty city," Stark said in a silky voice. "Because what you should be worried about is: we could've gotten to Sintra easily enough. If you don't reveal all by nightfall, she's dead."

The same Sintra who betrayed me to the rebels. The one who is still in my head, fucking up my thoughts. Giving me this pain in my chest.

"But you didn't get to Sintra yet," Finch said. "Which means you don't know where Sintra is." *Any more than I do.* Finch's voice had risen to a shout. The back of his throat hurt. Every part of him hurt. *How had Stark known Wyte's number?*

A long, low laugh. "Finchy, I want whatever's in that apartment with Shriek. Today. So make it happen. Or Sintra's next. Or Rathven. I don't care which. Look what we did to Wyte. True, he was almost there already. We just gave him that final push. Want to know how? Look around before you leave. Maybe on the counter, maybe in the sink. Just take a look. Get a sense for just how desperate your friend really was. And who you're up against."

"There's nothing in that apartment but Shriek," Finch said.

"Then bring me Shriek," Stark said.

Finch hung up.

Hated himself for looking, for taking Stark's suggestion. Found nothing on the counter. Nothing in the sink. In the garbage under the sink, though, he found a small white envelope and a note.

In an embellished script, the note read, "Take these, Wyte. They'll help. As promised. Love, Stark." Inside the envelope, the crumbly remains of something fungal. Something that hadn't helped Wyte at all.

Forced himself to imagine it. Wyte. Terrified by the quickening change.

Making a deal to trade information, even though Finch had warned him against it. Wyte maybe thinking that giving Stark some of what he wanted would take the pressure off Finch.

Then Stark had given Wyte some kind of mushroom he knew would drive Wyte over the edge. The note was dated two days earlier, so that meant Wyte had come back to his apartment two straight nights. Looked at Stark's note, the possible solution. Trusting it. Not trusting it. Desperate for something that might save him for a time. Driven to it by the gun battle. Driven to it by every careless, cruel comment by his supposed friends, Finch included. Wyte, too embarrassed, too ashamed, to tell Finch what he'd done. How stupid he'd been. Even at the end. Especially at the end.

For a moment, Finch's self-disdain was boundless. Threatened to bring the ground crashing in on him.

The phone was ringing again. Finch ignored it.

Blood dripped down from his hairline into his eyes. His blood. A claw must've caught him in the scalp as Wyte was shifting from shape to shape near the end. Wiped it away. Went back to what remained of Wyte. Wasn't much. Already beginning to rot. But he rummaged in his jacket pocket. One last thing he had to do now. It wouldn't change anything. Not really. But it might, in the end, satisfy his sense of justice.

Now it was time to take care of Stark.

Ambergris Rules. Take out the immediate threat.

Two hours later, Finch was done. He pulled the curtain back a sliver. Looked out with one eye shut against the glare. Dazzling sunlight. The grainy gray of the wall and a curving narrow strip of archway. Showing the street beyond. Weeds between sidewalk tiles. A row of dank, rotting warehouses on the other side. A lone tree. Crooked and bare of leaves.

If he had watchers, they'd be impatient by now. They'd have to come in closer. Especially if they had another reason.

Took out his gun. Fired a single shot into the room behind him. Lodged in the wall next to the kitchen. The sound was loud, like the others had been. Now they'd heard him with Wyte. Seen him come out, then go back in. Heard the shot. Followed by silence.

That might be enough to bring them.

Thirty seconds passed. Then two men came into view on the sidewalk. Dark clothes. The bulge of weapons under their jackets. Tallish. If Stark had a team on him, say four, they'd split up. Two would keep watch outside. Another one would walk up to the door, with the fourth covering him from the wall. Or they'd have one on the back window. Except Finch had checked the back, and there was no cover. Just a long, narrow alley filled with parts from motored vehicles. No one watching from what he could see poking his head out. Too dangerous. They probably didn't know the area, either. Might not even realize there was a back window. Beyond the narrow alley lay a taller building, more apartments.

They'd be coming right about now. Imagined he could hear footsteps. He went into the bathroom. Stood on the toilet. Hoisted himself up and through the window, ignoring the ache in his shoulder. Dropped into a crouch in the alley. Surrounded by worn tires and metal viscera. Everything but the motored vehicles themselves. Smell of rubber. Distant smell of oil. The long, tall wall of the building next door close enough to reach out and touch. No one watching. Unless they waited out of sight.

Gun drawn, heart beating fast, he made for the far end. The slice of blue sky above. The dull gray-brown of the buildings beyond. Made it, peeked around the corner. No one. Ran parallel to Wyte's apartment complex, into the streets beyond. Doubled back until he was looking around a corner at the wall of archways that hid Wyte's apartment.

Just in time to see, in glimpses, broken up by the wall, a man come out the front, walk down the corridor. Short. Muscular. Looked oddly burnt. Then another man came out from around back, where Finch had just been. Taller, thinner, bald. Weapon out. Finch drew back into the shadow of a stoop until the man was safely past a line of sight where he could see Finch.

The shorter man was now clutching at the front of the taller man's jacket. But the taller man gave way, and suddenly the shorter man was down on his knees, being sick into the ruins of the garden. Wyte had made an impact.

A hand signal from the taller man brought the two lookouts to their side. A quick conference. A few nervous gestures. A head bowed in exasperation or pain or some emotion Finch couldn't interpret. Either way, they'd lost their man and now had to report their failure back to Stark.

After a few moments, they headed off down the street, away from Finch. With as much stealth as possible, he followed. Erring on the side of too much distance between them rather than too little. Until the streets around them began to get more crowded. Mostly former camp prisoners. Still wearing their uniforms. Some had crutches. A few bandaged around the head or arms. Most with that pinched, withdrawn look around the eyes from hunger, stress, or worse. Birthmarks they'd picked up in the camps shone mossy and bright.

They made it much easier. Buried. Following.

As he walked, Finch saw hints of Wyte in the faces of passersby. It sustained his anger, and his grief. *Living against the odds.*

5

Stark was using a mushroom house as his headquarters. Off Aquelus Street. About a half mile from Albumuth Boulevard. About a mile from Wyte's apartment. Maybe a little more back to the station. Positioned so Stark would also have a straight shot, as straight as he'd get, back down to the Spit. A route that meant nothing now.

Using a mushroom house hinted at a rough genius in Stark, and a kind of insanity. It was three stories high. Light green with striations of metallic blue that gave it an ethereal sheen. Except for the tendency of the walls to curl and curve, the windows to flutter without a breeze, it shared a close resemblance to the normal houses on either side.

Finch stood on the opposite side of the street. Four houses down. Hidden by the stoop behind him and in front by a few high bushes with leaves shaped like shovels. An F&L neighborhood before the war. Protected from the worst predations of the wars. A quiet street. Little foot traffic. The mushroom house had probably scared people off. Or Stark's people had done it.

The men he'd followed had gone in. A few minutes later, Stark and Bosun had come from the opposite direction. They stood for a moment on the steps in front of the house. He couldn't hear what they were saying, but it sounded violent, like flames or swords. Then they went inside. He'd been waiting ever since. Going through the options. No way he could storm the house by himself. There were no guards at the front door, but that would've drawn too much attention. They'd even left garbage and debris out front. Let the fungus overgrow everything in sight.

He could just see the shadow of two men sitting back from the windows on the third floor. More men inside, of course. Possibly in the house opposite, on Finch's side of the street. Watching. Finch didn't particularly care. You could defend whatever position you wanted, but if the enemy hit you somewhere else, you were still fucked. He cared more that most of Stark's men would be muscle bought after he'd arrived. Take care of Stark somehow and many of them wouldn't be too keen to hunt Finch down. Too busy looking after their own interests.

An hour later, Stark and Bosun emerged from the house. With the short man who'd gone into Wyte's apartment. The tall man who'd come out the back. Headed his way, on the other side of the street.

"You never gave me up, Wyte. I'll never forget that."

"I can't control myself anymore. There's not much of me left. The rest might fight back. But I don't mean it if I do."

Quick and neat is how he wanted it. But that's not quite how it went down.

They passed by his position. He ran out firing, the sound so loud it shocked him. Put the bodyguards down. One shot in the chest, crumpling into oblivion. The other from a leg wound, blood spurting out. Screaming. Spasming.

Bosun turned at the same time as Stark, in time to get clipped in the shoulder. Registered extreme surprise, but recovered. Took off running, hunched over, cursing.

Bad luck. Finch didn't have time for another shot. Stark had about gotten his gun out. Finch smashed into Stark, twisted the gun out of his hand. Then hit Stark across the face. Saw the pain and anger as Stark bent to one knee.

"Bosun!" Stark shouting it like an order.

Slammed Stark against the side of the head. Started to drag him away as the other two lay on the ground. Grunted with the strain of Stark's bulk. Stark muttering, trying to get his senses back. Couldn't see where Bosun had gotten to. Had to get off the street quick.

A bullet kicked up dirt near his feet. Turned with Stark partially shielding him, the weight more awkward than he anticipated.

Bosun was across the street. Using a lamppost and a pile of junk for cover.

"Let him go and I won't kill you!" Bosun shouted. Had a gun in each hand. And not shitty knockoffs. Looked like custom-made revolvers.

Stark, muttering: "Go ahead, Bosun. Take the chance now."

Finch pulled Stark up. Shoved his Lewden Special against Stark's head. Other arm around Stark's waist. The man was still dazed.

"I'll kill him," Finch shouted back. "I'll kill him right here."

"You'll kill him anyway!" Bosun, anguished.

Backtracking toward the alley. Hoping nothing nasty waited there. Stark's weight awkward, hard to control. Didn't want to fall during this crude shuffle. Bosun would be on him in an instant.

Bosun fired off a couple of shots over his head. "You're a dead man if you hurt him."

Could already hear a commotion coming from the mushroom house. It had all happened in a couple of seconds. But Stark's men were good.

"Come after me, and I've got bullets enough for both of you, you bastard!" Finch shouted back.

Made it to the alley. Got off a couple of rounds to keep Bosun back.

The alley split into three directions just a hundred feet back. Hustled Stark around a corner. Pulled Stark's left arm behind his back. To the point of breaking as Stark groaned. Shoved the muzzle of his gun under the taller man's chin.

"Just keep going. Keep walking." Didn't want to talk. Didn't want to hear.

Guided Stark through a welter of back streets as confusing as any number of doorways on the Spit. Until they were far enough away that Finch felt comfortable stopping. Bosun didn't know Ambergris as well as Finch. And he'd know he had to be careful looking for his brother.

Finch released Stark face-first against a plain brick wall on a tiny side street. Windowless walls of fire-scarred buildings, rectangular and unimaginative. Crowding out the light from above. Stairwells running up their sides like rusting spines. Water on the pavement. A leering shelf of pink fungus jutting from the wall a couple inches from the ground. Stark's boots had cut into that ridge, the fungus staining the leather.

Stark started to talk. Finch came at him from the side. Punched him in the kidneys. Stark crumpled forward, air driven from his lungs. Wobbled, regained his balance. Breathing heavy.

"If you've killed Bosun, I swear . . ." The verbosity had left him for the moment. As if he'd been playing a role.

"Your brother was coming after me the last I saw. With just a nick in his shoulder. But you've got worse problems."

"So do you, Finch, unless you let me go."

But Finch was past that point. "If you just hadn't kept pushing, Stark. If you hadn't *kept at it*, maybe you wouldn't be here now. Take off your shoes."

"What?" A kind of pulsing rage threatened to make Stark's face unrecognizable.

Finch put the gun up against Stark's temple. "Now!"

With a show of repugnance and disdain, Stark removed first one shoe, then the other.

"Empty your pockets."

"Why?"

"Just do it." Realized he was shouting. Realized his hair was still clotted with Wyte's blood.

Stark spat as he pulled out his pockets. He didn't have much. Some money. A photograph of an old woman. A few keys.

"I don't like to be weighed down," Stark said.

Nothing there to tell Finch anything more about Stark.

Finch took a memory bulb out of his packet pocket. "Do you know who this is?"

A kind of savage, jaded amusement at seeing the bulb. Which faded. Quickly. Replaced by something Finch hadn't seen in Stark before. Uncertainty.

"It's from Wyte. Wyte's memory bulb. Now why do you think I made it?"

"Fuck you," Stark snarled. "Fuck you. Why don't you eat it, Finch. Eat it and be damned."

"You wanted information. You wanted me to help you. So I'm going to help you. You're going to live inside of Wyte's head for a while."

"I won't eat it," Stark said. He'd gone pale. The eyes flickered from side to side. Looking for a way out.

"Why didn't you kill Bliss, Stark? What did the two of you talk about?" Still curious.

"We talked about petunias, Finch," Stark said. "We talked about art and literature and what the weather was going to be like. What the fuck do you think we talked about? We talked about why I shouldn't kill him."

"And how'd he convince you?"

"Said he'd get me information, money, influence. Gave me the address of that rebel outpost for starters. He was going to help me clean out the whole area. But I haven't seen him since, the bastard."

Regarded Stark for a moment. Looked him in the eye. Believed what he found there. Or believed if it wasn't the truth he'd never get it out of Stark anyway.

"On your knees."

"No."

Finch pressed the gun up against Stark's cheek. "Guests get to choose. You're new here, so you're a guest. Bulb or bullet? Bullet or bulb?"

Slowly, Stark sank to his knees. Tried again. "I can make you a rich man, Finch. I can even get you out of Ambergris. There are still a lot of choices here."

"Do you think so? I don't."

"Do you know who I am, back in Stockton? Do you know what happens to you if you hurt me?" Stark's lower lip was quivering.

"No, I don't know. Because you won't tell me who you are. Open your mouth."

Stark's stare in that moment contained a kind of limitless, unhinged hatred. A kind of poison that willed itself to close the distance. To enter Finch. He grabbed the bulb from Finch. Crunched down on it with a kind of arrogant defiance. Finch realized Stark thought he could survive it. That he was bigger than whatever might happen to him.

A minute for the bulb to take effect. Finch placed the gun's muzzle against Stark's face. "Any last words before you don't remember who you are?"

Stark gave out a little crumpled laugh. A kind of regal contempt. "Not a one for you, Finchy. Except you'll pay for this, one way or the other. I'm the crown prince incognito. I'm an enchanted frog. Somebody will come after you."

The man's hostility began to fade as the memory bulb took effect. Finch looked into his eyes. Found nothing there. Nothing worth saving. Just an outsider who'd decided he wanted to profit off of the city's misery. A thug who thought he was tougher. Playing a game where his only strategy was to keep turning the screws. Finch didn't care who he was anymore. Just wanted him gone. Wondered without interest what Bosun would do now.

Stark's pupils had begun to dilate. Eyelids flickering like hummingbird wings. Said, as if from a faraway place, "No, I won't. I don't want to." Fell back on his heels. Arms slack.

Finch came close. Held Stark's head back. Took out another pouch. Poured preservation powder all over Stark's tongue. Like sand. Held his mouth shut even as Stark struggled, lethargically. Made him swallow. Once. Twice.

Released him. Stood back. Both times Finch had seen Heretic force a bulb and the powder on a prisoner, they'd died within an hour.

Stark convulsed, smashed his head back against the wall. So hard he left blood and hair on the brick. His eyes rolled back. Fell over on his side. Began to thrash. Blood poured out of his nostrils. Began to talk in a low voice. Very fast. No distance between sentences.

Then Stark began to laugh. Quietly at first. Almost like a gasping whisper. But rising in volume, until he was shrieking. Rolling around on the ground guffawing his brains out. With blood still looping out from his nostrils. Arms tight around himself. Mouth in a half-moon of involuntary mirth. It didn't really sound like laughter anymore. It sounded like screaming. Someone screaming as they were cut apart by knives.

A voice drowning as it spoke. Awash in strange tides.

What did Stark see? Was it Wyte? Wyte's memories? Distorted further by the powder? Or something else entirely?

Finch stepped back, in a firing stance. But he could not fire. All the rage in him had left. The madness.

Finally, lowered the gun. Left Stark there. Writhing in the mud and water. Feet kicking. Fighting with himself. The laughter raw and rasping. Like something had gone wrong in his throat.

Stark would not come back from this. And before the end he'd be in a kind of hell, like the hell Wyte had experienced. Like the hell Finch was in now. Would Bosun come after him? Didn't know. Didn't care at the moment.

Ambergris Rules.

⁂

You could close your eyes forever and still never be anywhere but where you had always been. Finch saw his father's capacity for violence only once. When he was twelve. *A hot night.* Made so by the rumbling excesses of heavy artillery off to the south. Brown smoke highlighting gouts of orange flame erupting around the silhouettes of buildings. The distant whumping sound of shells and tank retort. House Hoegbotton and House Frankwrithe engaged in a struggle none yet knew was pointless. The cease-fire hadn't held.

They'd had to move from their house, gotten caught in a war zone. Finch was hunched down by the window of the third-story apartment they'd taken refuge in. Waiting for his father to return from hours of scavenging for food and other supplies.

The window, with its grimy gray frame, had become a kind of moving painting for Finch. As intense as any zoetrope. Below, Albumuth Boulevard, once one of the richest arteries of trade in the world, had become little more than a mass of rubble and ripped-apart bodies. A day before men and tanks had fought across that landscape, the light red-green at their backs. The moans and screams matched to the cruel intensity of colors. He would watch, unblinking. Sometimes catch glimpses of gray caps running along the periphery.

Behind him, the door burst open.

A sniper with the insignia of House Hoegbotton. Framed by the doorway. Only five years older than Finch. Face already ancient.

"Down on the floor," the sniper ordered, walking into the living room. He had long, delicate fingers. Golden stubble on his cheeks. Smelled of sweat and gunpowder. "Get under that chair."

Finch scuttled out of the sniper's way across the floor. Under the chair as ordered. Watched as the sniper pulled the curtains across the window, opened the pane a crack, and shoved the long, steel muzzle of his automatic rifle through the crack. From Finch's perspective on the floor, the sniper looked huge. The recoil of the rifle made a dull, satisfying sound. Discarded shells rolled across the floor toward Finch. Touched one. Brought his finger away burned.

The man cursed when he missed. Said nothing when he hit his target.

"Shouldn't you be in the militia?" the sniper asked him while reloading, back against the wall. No one had shot back yet. Later, Finch would wonder if the sniper had been shooting at shadows. "You're old enough."

He had no answer. No one had ever told him he was old enough before.

Then his father appeared in the doorway, pistol in his hand. The bright green eyes. The neatly trimmed beard and mustache. The broad shoulders. The callused palms.

The sniper turned, began to raise his rifle.

His father shook his head. A grim, single-minded look. Finch had never seen that look on his father's face before. It wasn't the expression of an engineer. It came from somewhere more primal.

The young sniper saw it, too. Lowered the rifle. Stood up. Walked stiff-legged past Finch's father and out into the hall. Like a dog trying to make itself bigger.

Finch saw his father turn and aim at the back of the sniper's head. Saw him struggle with the decision. Then lower the gun and lock the door.

For a moment, Finch didn't want to come out from under the chair. Didn't know this person who looked like his father.

6

Finch headed back to the station. Wyte's death lodged like a heavy stone in his throat. Constricting his breath. Making him reckless.

A mob came at him out of nowhere, around a corner. Broke around him like a summer storm. A torrent of shouting. Of sweat and dirt and fear. The armbands of a long-dead neighborhood militia reborn. Some dared to show the rebels' blue band on their arms. Sensing that their time had come. Had it? Finch didn't know. So many camp uniforms he began to wonder if the gray caps had released them just to create chaos. To somehow *obscure* what was going to happen. Focused on some objective other than him. Or they didn't like the look of him. Numb. Staring straight ahead. Gun in its holster, sword in his right hand.

Ambergris come alive again, but into tribes, not a city. Finch wondered what old scores would be settled first.

Less than a quarter mile from the station, a shuddering thud and crack rumbled through the world. A series of them, from everywhere. Some near, some distant. Followed by silence. The sounds jolted Finch out of a walking trance. The shock reverberated in his bones.

Had the towers unleashed their weapon again? Couldn't confirm that. Couldn't see the towers from there. Hidden by the dirty green marble of old luxury hotels taken over by lichen and flanked by tall trees with yellowing leaves. People leaned out of windows on the fourth, the fifth floors, holding flags and shouting. Pointing to the northeast, the northwest.

In the street, a tiny old woman in a faded flower dress. A grubby boy gnawing on a shriveled apple stood beside her. Three Partials staring at the sky. All waiting for the next blow.

But there was no green light. No second series of explosions.

Instead, a curling trail of black smoke began to rise into that perfect blue sky. Finch recognized it. Had seen it before when a rebel bomb left a signal to the rest of the city. Heard shouts and screams rising like the smoke. Muffled. Distant. Disguised.

Had an odd premonition. An awful tightness in his stomach.

Finch began to run toward the smoke. Past wounded storefronts. Past the abandoned wooden box and scissors of a sidewalk barber. Past a huge red drug mushroom whose shade snuffed out the sky, the gentle sighing of its gills both ominous and calming.

He crossed onto Albumuth Boulevard, and approached the station.

The remains of it.

Transformed into a couple of side walls. Smoldering blocks of stone. The kindle of shattered, crackling wood. A blackened hole near the back, expelling blacker smoke. A smell like kerosene. A smell like meat cooking.

A roiling mass of particles. Discharging light until a steady humming glow suffused the city in a kind of dawn. There came in reply from the city a hundredfold bestial roar.

Finch rushed to the edge of that broken space. Stopped short. Saw the scattered remains of bodies. A pant leg. A foot. A torso tattooed with dirt and blood. A pile of something he could not identify. Realized some of it came from the people Heretic had killed and left in the holding cell.

The tubes of the memory holes, torn and bleeding, glistened as they thrashed, whipping the ground back and forth. Others lay still and dusty in the rubble.

A couple of men Finch didn't know staggered through the mess. Looking for survivors even though they were both bleeding. Both marked by fire. Searching like they might find something alive.

Finch took a step forward. Then another. Walked through the rubble, still holding his sword. Became aware of a dull, booming roar from deep inside the smoldering black hole in the back. Through the swirling whoosh of the rising smoke.

Became aware, too, of someone laughing from the wreckage of the wall to his left. The bricks still went up maybe twelve feet high, ending in a broken snarl. Sheltering the table with the typewriter, which stood as if indestructible. Beside it, slumped against the wall: Blakely, hurt in ways beyond a doctor's care. But still alive.

Worse than war. Worse than stab wounds.

There would be no putting Blakely back together.

"The typewriter," what was left of Blakely gasped, between laughs. "The typewriter. It's still there. It's still there."

Finch knelt down beside him. The closer he got, the less he was forced to see what had happened to Blakely. Not a scratch on the man's face. But Blakely's eyes knew. Finch could see death in them.

"What happened, Blakely?"

"Albin," Blakely said. "Albin happened." Laughed again. "Blew it all to hell. Came by to talk, he said. Had explosives strapped to him. Stood by the curtain, said something I didn't catch. Stepped inside. Blew himself apart. Threw me all the way across the room. Albin. Can you believe it? Can you believe it? Can you believe it? Can you believe it? Can you believe it? Can you believe it? Can you—?"

Finch returned his gun to its holster. Blakely's face matched his body now. No kinder mercy. The world getting smaller and smaller, even as it expanded.

Stood up shakily, feeling the shock in his legs. Waved to the men searching the rubble. "Get the hell out of here."

They saw his gun and his sword, woke as if from a trance. Picked their way through the rubble, the interrupted flesh. Disappeared as if never there.

More curls of black smoke now. Rising all around. Other stations hit. Felt a conflicting sense of loss and freedom. People were dying who'd just tried to feed themselves. Just wanted to stay alive.

The Lady in Blue: "We don't use suicide bombers anymore." But they did.

Partials would be on their way to the station. Gray caps. Struggling to dig out of the rubble of their underground headquarters. Maybe the sound Finch heard was just a subterranean fire or maybe it was some *fanaarcensitii* beast clawing its way to the surface. Finch knew his imagination couldn't compete.

Was it coincidence he hadn't been there when it happened?

Left the station to whatever demon was fighting its way out from under the bricks and stone.

❧

The madman danced on the steps near his favorite statue like nothing had ever gone wrong in his life. Even while the black smoke continued to rise over the city. In the hotel lobby, people had gathered as if seeking shelter from a thunderstorm. They stood there, strangers to him, and parted before him and his sword. He barely saw them.

Unfinished business. Loose ends. Needed to know his back was secure.

Stood in front of Rathven's door in the basement shadows. A sudden need for his father to be alive, to be counseling him, canceled out an impulse to smash in that door. To pound on it until his fist was raw.

Tried to wipe the crusted blood from his face. Held the gun behind his back. The sword safely at his side. He knocked, gently.

No answer.

Knocked again. Smiled into the peephole. Knew it might come off as a crazed leer.

Finally, muffled: "What do you want?"

"Just to talk." Just a quiet talk. *With my sword and my gun, if it comes down to that.* Then, "Wyte's dead." Investing his voice with a grief that he didn't feel. It had already shot through him and left him numb. *Wyte charging the Partials like some immortal hero. Wyte huddled in the corner of his apartment, scared shitless. The truth somewhere between.*

The door opened. Finch resisted the urge to shove it open. The urge to hit her. To hit someone.

Rathven looked paler than he'd ever seen her. She was aiming that heavy revolver at him. Fought to steady it as the gun dipped and wavered slightly in her two-handed grip. Sudden flash of insight based on nothing real: Rath as a girl, an awkward tomboy with a sense of humor, who couldn't laugh at herself. Uncomfortable in a skirt. Smart. Hopeful. Easily disappointed.

"Your 'brother' sell you that relic?" Contemptuously brushed past her, the image of her as a girl dulling his anger a bit. Brought his gun forward, into the shelter of his body. Holstered it. Found a seat by the table. Facing the door. Didn't like the tunnel behind him, but liked the sound of the water. Figured he'd hear someone long before they came creeping up out of it.

Still holding the gun, she turned to him. In the flickering light. The cavern lit up in faint cascades of green. Made him think of the Lady in Blue. *In a boat. Crossing an underground sea.* Ethereal. A faraway kingdom, too delicate to exist in the real world.

"Wyte's dead," Finch said. Each time he said it, it seemed more remote. Then came back to him fast and unbearable. Like something rising suddenly out of the dark that was both friend and foe.

"You said that." Rathven knew Wyte as someone Finch had talked about. Maybe half a dozen times. Had kept Wyte from her. Why? "What happened to you. You're covered in blood."

"Sit down, Rathven," Finch said. "Try to relax." Talking to himself.

"What happened?"

"Stark gave Wyte a mushroom that put him over the edge. I had to take care of Wyte." Said as calmly as he could manage. *Give her something to think about.*

It surprised Finch when she lowered the gun. Some part of him had thought she would shoot him.

Rathven sat down opposite him. Rested the gun on her knee.

"I'm sorry," she said.

"Why?" Finch asked. "You had nothing to do with it, right?"

A fire in her eyes. "No, of course not."

A feeling of *hurt* came over Finch. A sense of betrayal. It fascinated him. Worried at it like a piece of gristle between his teeth.

"You should've been a detective," Finch said. "Down here with all of your books. With that tunnel as an escape route."

"I should have been," she said, dutifully. But there was nothing playful in her expression. "What do you want from me, Finch? The city is falling apart. They've even disbanded the camps." Said it with a mix of regret and wonder. "I might have to—"

"What? Leave? Like your 'brother'?"

She had the grace to look away. "I'm in a different place than you. You never went to the camps. You don't really know what they were like. It was a white lie. You wouldn't have helped him otherwise. He was still a friend."

"You mean, if I knew he worked for the rebels."

"Everyone works for the rebels," she snapped.

"Even Sintra?" *Even me?*

"Sintra I know nothing about," Rathven said. "Nothing. Except what I told you."

"Who else do you work for?" Finch asked.

"No one. Everyone. You. Myself." Wriggling in the trap. She softened her tone. A kind of misdirection: "I did check out those aliases for you. The Bliss aliases."

"Find anything?"

"Just that 'Dar Sardice' might not be an alias."

"What do you mean?"

"I mean, if you go through some of the books about the wars, and the books I have about it from the Morrow/Frankwrithe side, you don't find Ethan Bliss's name anywhere until after the first mention of 'Dar Sardice.'"

"Do you mean that Dar Sardice is his real name?"

"Either that," Rathven said, "or he killed Dar Sardice and took his name. And then his real name isn't Bliss or Sardice. Or, my sources aren't complete enough."

Bliss pointing him toward Stark. Bliss bringing him into the next day while Bosun trashed his apartment. Bliss throwing him off the scent.

"How about Stark?"

Thought he sensed a hesitation before she said, "No."

"That's funny, because when I mentioned Stark before you didn't even stop to ask me who he was. Like you knew."

"I thought you'd tell me soon enough," she said. "For Truff's sake, *you were telling me your friend was dead!*"

"A lot of people come to you down here in the basement, don't they?" Finch said.

"You knew that already. Don't do this, Finch," Rathven said. Almost convincing him. But the ache was too great.

"A lot of people the gray caps wouldn't approve of," he said, pressing on.

"You're tired, you're grieving," she said.

"People who want things from you," he continued.

She changed tactics, said, "Am I under arrest?" Was it disdain or an echo of hurt he saw on her face? Were they insulting each other or wounding each other?

"No," he said. "Where would I take you? The station was bombed today. It's gone. Matchsticks and stones. Everybody's gone."

She had no answer to that, must've known "I'm sorry" would just set him off.

"Wyte's dead," Finch said, "because Stark took him over the edge. Stark got hold of certain information to try to make me help him. How did he get it?"

For a moment, Wyte sat beside him, saying, "How far are you going to take this?"

"Finch." Pleading. For what, though? For him to trust her? To stop questioning her? To keep things the way they'd always been?

Finch leaned forward, reached out, and pulled her chin up when she tried to look away. She let him do it. "Listen carefully. Stark knew about Sintra. *You* told him. He found out about you from his predecessors, the Stockton agents he liquidated once he got here. He came, or he sent Bosun. They either threatened you or paid you, or both. And you told them about Sintra. About me. Maybe you tried to protect me, and that's all you gave them. You might even think you helped me. But you gave them *something*. I know you did. You're the only one who could. If I'm wrong, tell me. Tell me I'm wrong. Right now. *But don't lie to me.*"

Her lower lip quivered. She pushed his hand away. "You have to choose a side, Finch. Eventually you have to choose a side, even if you pretend to be neutral. Even if you think giving out information is like selling smokes or food packets."

"And you chose Stark's side?" Incredulous.

"No! But Stark would've killed me if I didn't give him something. And he hates the gray caps as much as I do. And I didn't think it would hurt to tell him what he could've found out about you in a couple of days anyway." She looked small, miserable, utterly alone. But right then he didn't care.

"Stark's a psychopath," Finch said. "Only out for himself." Repeating what Bliss had told him.

"Maybe. Maybe not. Maybe I just told myself it was okay because I didn't want to die."

"Couldn't your 'brother' and his friends help you?"

Rathven shook her head. "Everyone comes to me for information. Everyone sees me as neutral because I give everyone *something*."

"And you don't know Bliss?"

"I know of him. He visited the Photographer a few times, but he never wanted anything from me."

Bliss. The Photographer. How did that work? And why?

"Finch?" she said, and he realized he'd been lost in his thoughts. "What are you going to do?"

It took an effort of will. But knew he had to do it. For himself as well as for her. There was no one else. Told himself: She delivered Duncan Shriek to you. She helped you when the memory bulbs brought you low. She never lied to you before. *There is no one else.* Not a soul.

"Stark's as good as dead," Finch said. "And, Rath, I'll forget the rest if you'll do me a favor. I need a favor."

"What kind of favor?" Abject relief in her voice.

He placed his extra apartment key on her table. "Take care of Feral for me. Take care of the things in my apartment. If I don't come back." Wasn't looking forward to saying goodbye to Feral. Wasn't sure that wouldn't be the final stupid little thing that broke him.

"Where are you going?"

Finch smiled. "Nowhere. Everywhere."

7

But he didn't get very far. Bliss waited for him in the courtyard. Came out into the late afternoon light. One arm shoved into the outer pocket of his short brown jacket. Wore matching pants. A wide-brimmed black hat. A dark green scarf. Face flushed. Almost disguising a thin line of dull red that ran up across his right cheek.

Another wound around his hairline, disappearing under the brim. Another remarkable recovery.

Frost clung to his boots. Fast melting. A damp, wet smell to him. Where'd he been? Not here.

"Put the gun away, Finch. And don't even think about drawing the Kalif's sacred steel."

Finch had no illusions about the hand shoved into the pocket. Could see something bulky there. He holstered his weapon. Stood in the gloom with Bliss.

With Dar Sardice.

"Now what?" Tried to push away the thought that Rathven had set him up somehow.

"Now we go up to the Photographer's apartment."

"Not mine? I think you know where it is."

"I don't trust yours." Bliss motioned with the gun in his pocket. "After you." His face closed, angular, serious.

Finch walked past him, tensing for a blow. But it never came. Bliss followed a step behind. Thought about turning on him, but had no illusions about what Bliss would do.

The spy's voice went cold, condemning. "When you see me again, it will be because I want you to see me. And not before."

On the fifth floor, they walked to the end of the hall. Apartment 521. Half hidden by the long stalks of slender lime-green mushrooms. Bliss tossed a key on the floor.

"Open the door."

Carefully, Finch bent down to pick up the key, unlocked the door. Went inside, Bliss following.

The room was empty, except for a stout table in the center. A bottle of whiskey and two glasses.

Photographs covered the walls. Nailed there. A half-dozen in frames were stacked against the far window. Which was blacked out with paint. Some of the photographs were larger than Finch, made up of many smaller pieces of contact paper. All showed water. In puddles. In waves. Close up. From far away. Noticed now how many of them had the towers as a backdrop. How many seemed to have been taken from areas of the shore the gray caps had blocked off.

"Now lock the door."

Finch did as he was told.

Turned to find that Bliss had taken off his hat. Taken out a cigar. Lit it with a quick scrape of a match against the table. Poured two glasses of whiskey. Moved to a position behind the table. Put his own glass down. Returned his left hand to his pocket.

Bliss took a puff of the cigar, said, "Whiskey?"

Finch moved uncertainly forward. "A last drink for the condemned man?" Took a glass.

It was good stuff. Smashing Todd's, twenty-one years. Put into barrels near the end of one of the worst periods of fighting between F&L and H&S. Better than what he had in the apartment. So smooth it only burned a little on the back end. Tasted of Morrow peat. The River Moth.

"No, Finch," Bliss said. "A celebration. A kind of christening, even."

"What do you want?" Snapped it out. No patience left.

"*Bellum omnium contra omnes*," Bliss said in a thin, reedy voice.

"*You're* my contact?" *Rathven saying "Everyone works for the rebels."*

"You're supposed to say, 'Never lost.' Then I'm supposed to give you what you need."

"I thought you worked for Morrow."

A quizzical look from Bliss. "I do? Did I ever say I did? There are no Morrow interests in this city anymore. Only Ambergrisian interests."

"What's your real name, Bliss? Is it Graansvoort? Or maybe it's Dar Sardice?"

"You must believe everything you're told." Said almost without scorn.

"Why were you really in my apartment?"

Bliss's head tilted to the left. Considering Finch. "Checking you out. Seeing how you checked out. I found a lot of familiar books on those shelves. Familiar to me, at least. A curious lack of photographs. That's what really gave you away."

"Me catching you wasn't part of the plan."

"No. I'll never tell you."

"So what do you think you found out?"

A bit of the old facile cleverness shone in his eyes. "Familiar books. No photos. I told her, 'He's changed his look. Shaved the beard. The hair is lighter. He's older, but still *him*. James. The son John helped hide."

"How did you know my father?"

Bliss sidestepped the question. "Your father knew how to keep a secret. I always admired that about him. He had his head on straight. He knew what was important. And what wasn't. I think you do, too. Your father would have agreed to this mission without a second thought."

"My father is dead," Finch said through gritted teeth. Put down his whiskey. Bliss knowing didn't shock him. It was the rest. "You still haven't answered my question."

"I trusted your father," Bliss said. "And he trusted me. If that wasn't the case, I'd have suggested one of the others. Blakely. Maybe even Wyte. But your boss did make you the lead on the case. Much easier for you to get in there."

"Dar Sardice," Finch said. Didn't know if he pursued it because he really believed it was important.

Bliss nodded. Didn't seem surprised. "I met your father while using that name. Out in the desert. It was a complicated time. Many conflicting allegiances." Seemed ready to say more. Stopped himself. Head tilted down. Eyes still on Finch. "But I'm telling tales when we don't have much time. You need to focus on the present."

He carefully laid the cigar on the edge of the table. Kept his other hand on the gun. Pulled something out of a pocket on the inside of his jacket. Put it down on the table. On Finch's side.

A piece of metal, about ten inches long. Segmented, it looked like it folded out into something larger. Like one of the surveyor rulers his father had always carried with him. Except it was made of a strange alloy, the color deep blue, almost gray. With the rainbow hues when the light caught it that meant it was very old. Odd symbols had been etched into every inch of it. None of them familiar. They didn't even look like what he'd seen of gray cap writing. The metal seemed heavy, substantial. But Bliss had lifted it from his pocket like it weighed nothing at all.

Finch said, "What is that? It doesn't look like something made by us. Or by the gray caps."

"It's not."

"Oh." Again, the world opened up. Became larger, wider, deeper, than before. *Let it flow over and through you or you'll be lost.*

"Now give me the memory bulb the Photographer gave you," Bliss said.

"Why?" Sarcastically: "How am I supposed to kill myself without it?"

"Just do it. Trust me." In a pinched, irritable tone. Like Finch should know what was good for him.

Finch placed the pouch on the table.

From his pocket, Bliss took out a small glass vial with a blue crystal stopper. "Watch and learn," he said, finishing his whiskey. Puffing furiously on his cigar.

He retrieved the memory bulb from the pouch. Broke it into pieces in his whiskey glass. Filling it to the top with a hill of colored dirt. Puffed on the cigar again. Blew away the ash column until there was just the blazing tapered tip.

"They call that a dog's dick," Bliss said, laughing.

"Here we call it the Kalif's cock," Finch said.

Bliss stopped laughing. Applied the tip to the memory bulb dust. "Yes, well, they call *this* . . . well, they don't call this *anything* because your normal sort of person on the street never does this . . ."

The dust began to smoke, then liquefy. In a minute or so, the whiskey glass was filled with a pale blue liquid. Bliss carefully shepherded it into the vial. Stoppered it. Put it on Finch's side of the table. Hard to think of backing out faced with something so specific. A procedure so matter-of-fact.

"In this form, it has a completely different effect," Bliss said. "You'll prop Shriek up when you get into the apartment and pour it down his throat, making sure he doesn't choke. He won't have a gag reflex, of course. It will complete the process of regeneration, taking maybe a minute."

Complete the process of regeneration. Shriek awake. An image of everything happening in reverse. Of corpses getting up, walking backward to wherever they'd come from. Unliving their lives. Becoming children. Forgetting how to walk. Returning and returning and returning until they were gone. *Never seeing Shriek or the dead gray cap. Never having to kill anyone, for any reason.*

"What then?" Finch asked.

"You will give him the piece of metal. He'll know what to do. Afterward, he'll leave it behind and you will take the piece of metal with you. And I will come to get it from you.

"Just know that in all of this *you must be fast*. You won't have much time. You'll get in because you work for *them*. And that still means something. For a day or two, at least. They've had distractions thrown at them all day. Dividing their attention. But you can't count on that. We don't have eyes or ears inside of that apartment complex. Too risky. They'd find their way back to the Lady."

"And what do I do then? Confess all? Throw myself on the mercy of the gray caps?"

Bliss shrugged. "If you have to, give yourself up, yes. If all goes well, you won't have long to wait. We'll be watching. But there's always that risk."

Up close, what appeared immaculate about Bliss was actually shopworn, threadbare. His pants. His shoes. A button missing on the jacket. Was it noble or sad that he was still out in the field, running games, networks, schemes?

"Who *are* you, really?" Finch asked.

The old eyes stared out from the well-preserved face. "Any spy worthy of the name would figure that out. *Any spy.* For *anyone.*"

Bliss came around the table, too fast for Finch to warn him off. Then stood there looking at Finch.

"Sometimes you have to take a leap into the unknown, John. Sometimes you just have to trust that, plan or no plan, you have limited control over the situation. Now, it's almost dusk. Leave when it's dark. Take the route you think gives you the most cover. That means people, Finch. Lots of confused, frightened people. Not back alleys. *They* can see a lone man. A crowd's more difficult, even for them. But stay away from Partial checkpoints. They're on edge, and that means they're more dangerous and less predictable. Even with your badge."

Finch felt for a moment out of his league, Bliss growing in stature with each word. Had nothing to say in return.

Bliss took something out of his pockets. Put it on the table. "Last thing. Sandwiches. Eat before you leave. And *don't* go back up to your apartment. It isn't safe."

"But I have to change. I'm covered in blood."

Bliss's expression was grim. "You'll fit in better that way."

He walked to the door. Turned there, surrounded by photographs of water. Gave Finch a salute. "Good luck, Finch. And some advice: be prepared to kill."

Said it casually. Almost as if he'd said it many times before.

8

Back in front of apartment 525. Where it had started. Only five days ago. Everything was different. Everything was the same.

Had fought his way through chaotic streets. *Grim-looking men and women careening past in forbidden motored vehicles. Armed with everything from pitchforks and kitchen knives to rifles and semiautomatics.* Then passed through the double doors. *Bodies slumped on the steps outside the building. Strewn. Spasming in something between agony and ecstasy. An acrid smell lingered from whatever had poisoned them.*

Inside, no one in the corridors. The floor no longer slick. No one on the landings.

No sign of any Partials. Distant sounds of conflict from outside only made it inside as a thud or rumbling echo. Could hear his own heartbeat. Couldn't hear any sounds from inside the apartments around him. Held the gun up, two-handed grip, but it was the weight of the sword at his side that comforted him.

Same gray cap symbol glowing on the door.

Same hesitation, but more pain behind it. The light in the hall flickered crazily.

Finally mastered his fear. Held the gun in one hand while he turned the doorknob and pushed with the other. The door was unlocked. A prickle of unease up his spine.

He walked into the darkened hall with the empty bedroom ahead. A yellow, artificial light leaked into the hall from the doorway on the left.

No sound but his tread on the wooden floor. Just an expectant pause. Realized he was holding his breath. Let it out. An absurd whistling through his nose that was worse.

He came out into the living room. A lantern on a chair by the balcony window provided the light. Cast everything in buttery shadows.

The sofa. The chairs. The empty kitchen behind. A shape on the rug. As his eyes adjusted, he saw it was the familiar shape of Shriek, under the blanket. The rebels' great hope. *A weapon. A beacon. A human being.*

He walked into the living room.

A movement from behind. Before he could turn, the muzzle of a gun had been shoved into his back. Flinched. Felt like something alive was crawling onto him from the gun.

"Drop your weapon, Finch. The bag, too." A familiar voice. The Partial.

"I'm here on official business," Finch snapped.

"We both know that's a lie. Drop it now."

Heard the click of the safety.

Finch dropped the gun.

"Now the sword. Undo the belt. Let it drop."

Finch obeyed, trying to breathe slowly, not let panic take him. What moment should he choose? *This one? The next?*

The sword made a dull clank against the floor. The slap of the belt leather.

The gun muzzle withdrew from his back. "Now turn and face me."

He turned. Fast. Meant to rush the Partial. Get under his guard. Too late. Saw the Partial's gun coming down for far too long. The thin white wrist behind it. A thudding pain in his forehead. The buttery light became death-white, intense. Then faded out.

⚜

He woke facing the window and the lantern, the end of the couch to his right. Tied to a chair. Wrists and ankles burned from the tightness of the rope. Shoulders ached from having his arms wrenched behind his back. Head throbbed. Could taste blood. The jacket with the piece of metal and the vial had been tossed to the side.

The balcony was empty. So was the kitchen. What he could see of it. A series of knives had been set out on the counter. A pot of water boiled on the burner. A hammer had been tossed onto the couch.

Tested the rope, but it just bit in deeper. Tried rocking, but could tell he'd never get to his feet. He'd just fall over.

Heard footsteps. Winced. Expecting Heretic and the *skery*. But only the Partial walked into view. Started rehearsing lines in his head.

"Hello, Finch," the Partial said. He'd brought a second lantern, placed it to the side.

The same sneer. Same recording eye. Same ugliness. As thin and pale as something dead.

"I've disabled the cameras in here, Finch," the Partial said. "I've told the other Partials to give us some privacy, too."

"Why? We're on the same case," Finch said. "Untie me and we can go our separate ways, no harm done."

The eye clicked and clicked. The Partial moved to his left. Finch could see the gun now. Held in the Partial's right hand. A nasty hybrid. An older Hoegbotton revolver altered to fire fungal bullets. The faint red-green tips of the bullets naked in the barrel. Seemed to breathe as they expanded, contracted.

"You should have checked the bedroom first, Finch. You would have found me," the Partial said. "But I'm not surprised. You've been very sloppy. Take the shoot-out at the chapel. A lot of my people died there."

"That was Heretic's decision, to send us there. And this is still an open investigation. I'm the lead detective on it. Untie me and I won't mention this to Heretic."

"But it's not open, Finch," the Partial said. "You closed it yourself. I have your final report. Or bits of it. It doesn't mention a lot of things. Killing Wyte, for example."

Making Stark eat a memory bulb.

"Wyte was dying," Finch said. "It was a mercy."

"Convenient you weren't at the station when the bomb went off."

"I wouldn't call it that." Struggling with the ropes. Getting nowhere again. Had to get free. Reach the pouch. Help Shriek.

"When does Heretic get here?"

"Interesting question, Finch. When will Heretic get here? He's already been here. With his fucking *skery*. I killed them both."

"*What?*" At sea. In a new country. One where he didn't know the rules.

"You may be stupid, Finch, but you're not deaf."

"I don't believe you." And he didn't.

The Partial put the gun down. Picked up the hammer. Leaned forward. Brought it down on Finch's left knee. Fracturing pain. Finch screamed. Cursed. Jerked up and down in the chair.

"Fuck! All right! I believe you. I believe you." Rode through the aftershocks.

The Partial said, "It's easy enough to kill a gray cap. If you can just find a way to push them off a five-story balcony. It's all about breaking down what's inside them. Just pretend they're a sack full of meat and wineglasses. Then imagine that crashing down five stories. Banging into fire stairs. Smacking hard against the pavement. There's a good chance they won't get up again. It's the damn *skery* that was the hard part."

Pointed to the corner nearest the kitchen. Finch saw something long and black. Half-hidden by the drawn-back window curtain. Still twitching. Relief that the *skery* was dead. Followed again by panic. No time. There wasn't time.

"Imagine this, Finch," the Partial said. "Those things were going to *replace* us."

"Untie me. Untie me and I'll leave. Like I was never here."

The Partial slapped Finch across the face. It stung, but nothing like the pain in his knee.

"Bad idea, Finch," the Partial said. Went over to the kitchen. Took the pot of water off the burner. "I think that's hot enough."

"Why are you doing this? Why kill Heretic?"

"You know, Finch, we're almost on the same side," the Partial said, cheerily. Pulled up the side table. Set the pot on it. A hissing sound.

"I don't understand," Finch said. Still in shock.

"Heretic's a disappointment. All of his kind are. Traitors to our cause. Not committed to it, Finch." He went back for the knives. "They can travel by uncanny means. But won't tell us how. They can make spores do whatever they want. But won't tell us how. We only get to be walking, talking cameras. That wasn't the deal. Now they plan to abandon us. Having first made us. Heretic said as much. And I am not interested in letting it happen."

"I still don't get it."

The Partial looked for a second like he would slap Finch again. Instead, he placed the knives on the table. Next to the pot of water.

"They're bringing more of their kind here. They've already begun to abandon us. We have no orders. We're having to create our own purpose, our own orders. Because they don't care anymore. They have no need of us. Any more than they need Unrisens like you."

"Is that what you call us?" Trying not to look at the boiling water. The knives. The hammer.

The Partial sat back. "You should thank me. Heretic would have killed you outright. But I want you alive. I want you alive to tell me what you really know. To tell me what Heretic would never tell me. What you've found out. All those times you went missing this week. Where I couldn't see you."

"I don't know anything that can help you."

The Partial frowned. "That's not true. I think you're just stalling. Maybe you still don't really believe me about Heretic. Maybe you think he's going to come walking through that door."

"No, I believe you!" Anticipating the hammer.

But the Partial stood up anyway. Got behind Finch. Pulled his chair around until he was facing Shriek's body under the blanket.

Stooped. Pulled the blanket away.

Revealing Heretic, and a couple of pillows. The hat missing. A head stippled with tiny mauve mushroom caps. His neck twisted. His face crumpled and torn. Eyes closed. One of his feet was on the wrong way. As if he'd fallen from a great height.

From a suffocating distance, Finch heard the Partial say, "See? Just like I told you."

Heard someone say, "Where's the body? Of the dead man."

Heard the response through the singing of the blood in his ears: "Oh, we destroyed that yesterday. Too big a risk to their plans. Heretic's orders. When he was still giving orders. We spread the ashes over the base of the towers."

Then, thankfully, the Partial was hitting him with the hammer again.

And he was losing the thread again.

Going under.

Going deep under.

SATURDAY

I: Try to see it from my point of view. Because I'm trying to see it from theirs. They've got a vision that's extraordinarily deep and wide. A long view.

F: How you must admire that.

I: Does an ant mourn the passing of another ant?

F: Maybe. I don't know.

I: They see everything, everywhere, over thousands of years. And they work with spores and things smaller than spores—on a microscopic level. What's it to them if they reduce a life from a macroscopic to microscopic level. To its different parts. It's just life in a different form. Nothing's been killed. Nothing's ended because something else has begun. I find it liberating. If only they'd kept their word.

F: Does that excuse them?

I: After all you've done over the past week, Finch. Do you really think *they* need an excuse? Believe me, it's nothing personal. Now, I'm going to have to hurt you again.

1

Woke to a sack over his head. Woke to the Partial whittling a tattoo into his leg. Woke to his own shrieks. Wondered if the Lady in Blue had spirited him away. Waking and drugging him. Waking and drugging him. *Never lost.*

And always, the Partial asking him questions. *Who was Ethan Bliss? How did the doors work? Had he met the Lady in Blue?* Kept answering sideways, but after a while didn't remember what he'd said. Or not said.

After midnight. Maybe. Pitch black except for the lanterns. Except for the pale face of the Partial.

Part of his mouth didn't work right. Jutted out. Swollen. His vowels came out slurry. Couldn't feel his feet or hands. A kind of mercy. Because early on the Partial had cut off one of Finch's toes. Had busted up his knee again. Cut a slit in his right cheek that bled into his mouth.

"Confess," the Partial kept saying. "Confess."

Was he ready to confess? And to what? Duncan Shriek was dead. The mission dead with it. Changing his name, leaving Crossley behind, now seemed as pathetic as the plan to revive Shriek. What had he been doing but playing sides off against each other? Buying time working for one, working for the other. For what? More of the same? Maybe even less of it. And if he confessed that, would the Partial do more than blink in confusion? Half the time the Partial wanted information. Half the time he just wanted to inflict pain.

The Partial said, "My name is Thomas. You should call me Thomas. That's my name."

Laughter gushed up from deep inside Finch at the absurdity of that. Laughter he couldn't stop.

"I confess," he said. Screamed it. As the Partial went back to work.

The chair slowly rocking, rocking back and forth.

Rocking. Rocking. Back and forth.

Finch sat on the upper deck of a houseboat in the Spit. From the towers across the bay, green fire gathered. It leapt out at them. Became huge and sparkling over their heads. Burned into boats all around them. Splintered timbers. Sent up waves of flame. A fire that never seemed to reach them. And yet was inside him.

Wyte and Finch's father sat on a whitewashed bench opposite him. His father was the hunched-over specter he'd been at the clinic, in the last days. Coughing up blood. Wyte was, mercifully, as he'd been before the vainglorious charge from the chapel.

"Getting close," his father said.

"Getting close," said Wyte.

"Hang on," his father said.

"Soon it will be your turn," Wyte said. "Will you be ready?"

"Ready for what?" Finch said.

"Never lost." Now it wasn't Wyte sitting beside his father, but Finch as James Crossley. Youthful. Neatly trimmed beard. Eyes bright with confidence. The James Crossley who'd worked as a courier for Wyte.

Finch smiled. "It's been a long time since I've seen you. Could've used you earlier, James."

His father had disappeared. Duncan Shriek was sitting next to James now. Flickering in and out like a faulty bulb.

Finch stared at them both. While the Spit burned down around them.

Shriek said, "You can't survive much more of this. You've got to find a way out."

Finch grinned painfully. With each new bolt of green light another part of him was disintegrating. Falling away.

"Easy for a dead man to say. I'm still in the world," he said.

Something was calling. Some noise was exploding in his head.

"You'll be back," Shriek promised, fading into darkness.

Woke, finally, to the sounds of combat. Rockets. Gunfire. The recoil of a tank blast?

Through the window, through the blood in his eyes, Finch saw intense flashes of light. Nothing like the gray caps' spore clouds. Or their fungal displays. That light was more like a mist. This was harsh and sudden. Unforgiving.

Blood tickled his throat. The Partial had taken teeth. Each a raging agony in his mouth.

The Partial sat on the couch, tapping his foot. He'd turned the chair so it faced him.

Finch laughed. An unhinged laugh that ended on too high a note. Thought, "Could the interrogation be getting to the fucker?" But had said it aloud. The Partial crept behind him. Felt a soft sawing around his numb hand. A sudden flowing release.

Still the rockets went off. So they must be real. Not hallucinations.

No one's coming for me. No one.

The Partial placed Finch's bloody pinkie finger on the table. It looked like a white worm.

"Don't disrespect me again," the Partial said. Breathing hard. Something almost sexual in the way he swallowed. Let the tip of his tongue show through his teeth. "Or there's more where that came from."

A chuckle or the low sound of a moan? "Only eight, or nine. But I won't. I won't. I won't. Just untie me. I can't feel my hands. I can't feel my legs."

The Partial ignored him. Which meant slapping him a few times.

Nothing he'd told the Partial had stopped him. Nothing. Not once. Not any more than Stark had stopped Finch. Saw Bliss at the table in the Photographer's apartment, carefully creating the vial of liquid. Saw Sintra's face against the wall as they made love. Rathven's hesitant smile at their detective joke. None of it mattered anymore.

Began to cry. To weep. Slumped over. Head leaning toward his lap.

"Oh, there's nothing to cry about, Finch. Nothing at all," the Partial said. "We're just having a conversation. A kind of meeting of the minds. If it makes you feel any better, those sounds you hear—they're your rebels, Finch. They've abandoned you. They're attacking the tower. It won't work, but I almost wish it would. Except there's no place for me in their new world, either."

"I'm sorry the gray caps. Betrayed you." Mangled the words. Parched. As if he could drink forever and not be satisfied. But the Partial had only given him boiling water.

"Are you?" the Partial asked. "Really? Because all I ever got from you before was contempt. An aura of deep contempt."

"Not contempt. Ignorance."

"Ignorance?" Incredulous.

"Of what. You had to go through. To become a Partial."

At some point during the interrogation, if that's what it still was, Finch remembered consoling the Partial. Couldn't keep it straight in his head. His brain felt like it was outside of his body. Exposed and raw.

"It's nice of you to pretend," the Partial said.

If I ever get free, I am going to put out your eye with my hands.

Another flash. A recoil. But the attack seemed blunted. The explosions of light less frequent. Saw the Partial's serious, pale face in the half-light.

"I've told you all I know," Finch said. "Anything you needed to know." But not Sintra. Not Rathven. Not the Lady in Blue. Hadn't given them up. Still, couldn't be sure anymore.

She said she'd have watchers on me. She lied.

The Partial ignored him. "Don't worry, Finch. We're almost to the end. Almost to dawn. Just another couple of hours. You might even make it."

Couldn't help himself. "Fuck you. Fuck you. You psychotic little prick. You cock-sucking psychotic bastard. *You fucking coward!*"

Thrashing in his chair until it fell over onto its side.

Silence then. Waiting.

The Partial lowered himself against the floor next to Finch. Looked him in the eyes. Said, "We'll keep going until I see all of you. *All of you.*"

Finch tried to spit in his face. All that came out was a trickle of blood.

Am I dying? Is this what death is like?

The rest dissolved into a kind of distant burning.

A kind of despairing, raging ache.

᠅᠅᠅

Back on the Spit. On the roof of the houseboat. Dusk now, the sun almost gone, but lingering.

The Spit smoldered. Thick with flame and smoke. The towers were silent. From that angle, he couldn't see what lay between them. But strange birds flew out between them. Like parrots, but different. Flashes of green-blue-orange. Beyond that, the city, in an agony of bronzing light.

Opposite him on the bench sat Duncan Shriek. This time he had a long gray beard, white hair down to his shoulders. His beard writhed, alive. His overcoat wasn't made of cloth at all. Concealed a mountain of a body, reminding Finch of Wyte. No shoes. Shriek's feet seemed to blend into the wood of the floorboards as if rooted there. His image flickered in and out. Could not seem to settle into flesh and blood.

"Hello again, Finch," Shriek said.

Finch, bitter: "They burned your body. Spread your ashes over the towers. You're *dead*," Finch said. "You failed us. Thousands and thousands of people are going to *die* because of you." Angry at himself.

Shriek said, "Your body is shutting down, Finch. You cannot take more torture. You have to do something. All I can do for now is numb the pain."

Finch's legs were on fire. He couldn't put out the flames.

"There's nothing I can do."

Shriek pulled him close. Until his face was inches from Finch's. Drawn into the power of those eyes that were both more and less than eyes. Into the magisterial force of the experience and pain there. "Find a way. And when you've done it, *drink the vial you brought with you.* Even if you do kill the Partial you'll die there on the floor, otherwise."

"The Photographer said the vial is poison."

"It is. But it's life as well. You'll die, and then I'll bring you back."

"You can't do anything," Finch said. "You're just in my head."

"So are you," Shriek said.

He picked Finch up by the shoulders. Raised him high. Pushed and released him in the same motion. So violently that he was sent flying over the city. Where Shriek's hands had touched him, a healing numbness. Spreading.

Below, the fires crackling on the Spit were snuffed out. The black smoke turned white and then broke apart. Still he soared, over the twinkling green of the Religious Quarter, over the dull white remains of the camps, over everything.

So this is how it ends. How it really ends. But at least it ends.

Woke to darkness. Woke to blood caked around his eyes. To a broken nose. To the knowledge that his bowels had loosened. That he'd pissed himself. Dribbling hot down his thighs, itching through the numbness. Was able to move his legs a little. A veil now between him and the pain. It registered as an even, serrated glow around his body. No part of him hurt more than any other part. Allowed him to concentrate. Gave him energy.

"Not done with you. Not the right answers." Mumbled like a prayer from somewhere in front of him.

Right eye was swollen shut. Opened his left enough to squint.

The Partial's face was up close through that slit of vision. The abyss of the fungal eye. The orange lichen of the other. The stark white landscape of that face. Staring at him. A hand shaking him. Trying to see if he was still alive.

Too close.

The gun was on the table. The knives were on the table.

Erupted hard up and out. Caught the Partial on the chin with the top of his head. A grunt of surprise. Of pain. Finch fell on top of the Partial. Legs still too rubbery. Brought his forehead hard onto the fungal eye. Could feel it give. The Partial screamed. Tried to push Finch off him. Battered his sides with his fists. But Finch felt none of it. Bit into the Partial's left cheek. Pulled back. Spit out the flesh. The Partial shrieking. Finch kept smashing his head into the right side of the Partial's face. Until the eye socket sagged and the Partial was moaning. The beating of hands at Finch's sides now more like the wings of a bird.

Finally, the Partial stopped moving. Maybe he'd been saying something. Screaming something. Finch didn't know. Didn't care. The warm glow that surrounded him muffled sound. Muffled everything but itself.

Was the Partial dead? He would be. Finch picked up a knife off the table with his mouth. Positioned it between his teeth. Knelt. Bent his head to the side. Came down hard. Jammed it hilt-deep in the Partial's throat. Got out of the way as the blood came quick and heavy. The Partial convulsed once, twice, back bucking. Then nothing.

The pain was coming back. Everywhere. The veil fading. He backed up to the table. Got his hands around a knife. Tilted it downward. Cut himself free after a minute. Didn't care what he had to cut through to do it.

Stumbled past the Partial. Past Heretic. To his jacket. Found the vial. Opened it. Stood there, trembling.

The Photographer had said it was poison. Bliss had said in liquid form it would rejuvenate Shriek. Shriek was gone. But the figment in his mind had been right about one thing: one way or the other, he was going to die without help.

Downed it in one gulp. Tasted like dirt and chocolate. Sprinkled with some sharp yet familiar herb.

Fell heavily to the floor. Sat there as the energy left him. As his wounds laid him out flat on his back. As he gasped. Every inch of his body crying out in an endless agony.

2

Finch and Shriek stood in the cavern by the underground sea. In front of Samuel Tonsure's one-room shelter.

"You're a hallucination," Finch said. Wouldn't look at Shriek. "I'm dying. I'm having a conversation with myself."

Shriek said, "Remember how Wyte had Otto inside of him? In a different way, you have me inside of you. I entered your mind when you ate my memory bulb."

Something had lived inside of Wyte. When it came out, Finch had shot it. Then sliced it apart as it squealed.

"That's impossible."

"Do you *really know* what's impossible anymore?" Shriek asked. "Are you in a position to have an opinion that means anything anymore? You will still die there, on the floor, Finch, if you don't believe in me." Felt an immense pressure in his skull. A kind of pulse. "That's me," Shriek said. "Me, trying to get out." His eyes burned with a deep and abiding fire. "I was still regenerating. Healing. But I altered the memory bulb. I encoded it with a copy of me. When you ate it, I entered your brain. If my body had lived, if the real me had lived, I would have eventually become less than an echo. A stray thought. An impulse for tea instead of coffee. Unexpected sadness or joy. You would have carried me, decaying, for the rest of your life. But that didn't happen. They've killed me and I'm all that's left. Now it's my mission."

Tea not coffee. The strange surge of energy during the shoot-out. Sadness or joy. Emotions not his own. Not Crossley's, either.

"There is no mission now."

"You're wrong, Finch. Very wrong."

Finch, disgusted: "Like Wyte and Otto. I'll die and you'll come out of me. Like a fucking parasite."

Shriek frowned. "No. Not like Wyte and Otto. Not like that at all. Otto ate Wyte from the inside out. I'm just a passenger, gone soon enough. If you help me."

"Help you do what?"

"Manifest in the real world. Become flesh and blood. Complete the mission while there's still time."

"But you're just a . . . an *imitation.*"

"It's not the best way. It's just the only way now."

"My mind's playing tricks on me."

"Listen to me, Finch. It was Bliss who found me in this cavern. Who brought me to the rebels. I wasn't even human anymore. I wasn't, in any sane sense, alive. I had learned so much about the world that I had decided to withdraw from it. If I could come back from a hibernation of so many years, then maybe you'll understand why a copy of me might be able to reenter the world."

Bliss again. On the walls of Zamilon. Finding Duncan Shriek. Bending the ear of the Lady in Blue.

"When I wake up, you'll just be a memory of a dream."

"You're not hearing me. *You won't wake up.* Your body is shutting down."

"Then take over. It's a weak enough machine," Finch said with self-contempt. "How can I stop you?"

Shriek waved his hand. They stood on the battlements of Zamilon. No one there but them. Cold and windy. Out in the desert: shadows gathering.

"I can't force you. It would take too much time. We don't have that kind of time. You'd die first. And right now the Lady in Blue is holding off the invaders at Zamilon. She's waiting for a miracle. I'm that miracle."

"And if I said no? If I said no, you'd just fade away and this would all be over?"

"Yes."

Thinking again about Wyte. About Stark under the influence of Wyte's memory bulb. *At what price?* And: *You knew you might die. Why aren't you willing to do this?*

Because it's not real.

Looked out at the green lights beginning to appear. Above, the blurred gleam of stars obscured by dust.

"It's up to you, Finch," Shriek said.

"How do we do it?" Finch asked. "I cut open my own head and you pop out?" *And what happens to me then?*

"It's nothing like that," Shriek said. "Nothing like that. You open yourself to me, and then I open myself to you. Then you sleep for a while. When you wake up, I am out of you. I can feed off moisture. Off the air. What I take from you will be no larger than the weight of a baby. And I will do the rest. Then we go our separate ways. You'll never see me again." *Except when I look in the mirror.* "I know you're afraid. But what happened to Wyte was invasive. Hostile. He had a parasite inside of him. Something made possible by the gray caps."

This isn't invasive?

The green lights were closer. He could almost make out the forms of the creatures gathered out there in the desert. Waiting to take Zamilon for themselves. Who could say their cause was any less just? The Lady in Blue didn't even know what they were.

"How do I know you're not hostile? I 'open up' and you take over."

"I won't. I promise. I can't. It wouldn't last for long."

"What's the risk if I say yes?"

Shriek hesitated. Then said, "I won't lie to you. It's a sacrifice. I will be doing things to your body to make my own. Stealing from your tissue. Robbing you while you're already weak. You won't be the same afterward. Even after you recover from the torture. You'll have dizzy spells. Headaches. You may not sleep for a while. When you do sleep, there will be nightmares as your mind flushes out my memories. But you'll be setting me free. And I won't take it from you unless you let me."

"You're saying it'll almost kill me."

"And heal you, too," Shriek said. "In the short term, I can make your flesh knit faster. I can shield you from the aftershock of what the Partial did to you. And a part of you will always be with me. Even after you die, you will live on because I will still be alive." Shriek grinned, showing his teeth. "I'm hard to kill."

Lost time. Lost worlds. A man who had lived for more than a hundred years, only to die in a crappy apartment as part of a larger game by a species that had come from a place so distant they'd spent centuries trying to find it again.

A giving up. A giving in. That's what Shriek was offering him. It tempted him. He had nothing left. Nothing of worth. No master plan. No better life waiting. Just his own death. Too much for him, and too little, standing there on the battlements of a place re-created by a passenger in his brain.

Finch searched the face of the dead man for honesty or deceit. Saw himself reflected back.

"How do we start?" he asked.

"For you, it's easy," Shriek said. "A mental trick. Just think back to the time when you went from being Crossley to being Finch. Imagine that instant as exactly as you can. Every detail you can remember. While you concentrate on that, I will enter through the 'gap' created. That's as simply as I can put it . . . The rest you won't feel."

A hopeful expression on Shriek's face.

The thought that maybe this was happening in the seconds before his death.

That the last week had taken place in a single moment in his head. That none of it was real. Even the parts that seemed real. Those least of all.

Finch shuddered. Closed his eyes.

"Let's get this over with."

⁂

The creation of John Finch happened at night. Cold for once. The flares and tracers of battle over the darkened skyline. The roar of the tanks. The gunfire of attacking infantry. A percussive music playing all over southeast Ambergris. Near the Religious Quarter. Heavy losses for the Hoegbotton side. A series of tactical mistakes.

They stood on the street behind the clinic, he and his father. Next to a burning trashcan. His father was a hunched figure who kept coughing up blood. By then his father had been very sick.

John Crossley had a folder full of documents for his son. James had a suitcase stuffed with identity cards, certificates, incriminating photographs. Had checked John Crossley into the clinic under the name "Stephen Mormeck." Someone they'd picked out of the phone book.

A clinic in Frankwrithe territory. Because of the rash of refugees. Because F&L had less reason to hate John Crossley.

"Is there anyone you want me to contact?" he'd asked his father.

A shake of the head, the great mane of gray hair. "No, no one. Make a clean break. For both of us." A gruff laugh. By then, he was self-medicating with whiskey early in the day. That night next to the trashcan, John Crossley had been drunk for two days.

But his eyes were clear. His arm steady as he handed the folder to his son. "Everything you'll need. For John Finch. Including a way to rejoin the Hoegbotton Irregulars."

Two years before the Rising. Six months after Hoegbotton and Frankwrithe had joined forces against the gray caps. Five months since his father had been denounced as a Kalif spy and they'd had to go on the run. The posters were everywhere. One of a row of traitors.

"I didn't do what they say I did. Not the way they say I did it. I never got anyone killed. I never . . ."

His father had never told James how they'd come to be betrayed. Which of the many people who had come to the house in the valley over the years. And James didn't have a clue, because his father kept pushing him further and further away from that part of his life.

James reached down, opened the suitcase. Felt the click of the clasps against his fingers. "It's all here. Every last document. Every last photograph." From the old house in the valley. James had gone there earlier that night, snuck in. Returned to the clinic in an army truck, along with a few other civilians with ties to Hoegbotton's trading arm. Wyte had stood watch for him, then gone out the back way and melted into the night. Wyte knew every street in the city. He'd have been back home with his wife before midnight.

Two in the morning now.

"What are you waiting for? Start shoveling this stuff into the fire," his father said.

Still, he hesitated. Watched the smoky flames rising into the darkness, the sparks mimicking the flares in the distance.

"If we burn all of the photographs, I'll forget what you look like."

His father didn't miss a beat. "But not who I am. And if you don't do it, there's no clean break, son."

His father reached down, picked up a handful of documents and IDs. Shoved them into the fire. Which flared up for a moment.

"This is the best way." John Crossley had said it a dozen times that day.

Anything else of value that couldn't tie the son to the father had been put in a storeroom on the edge of the merchant district. A neutral area. James could retrieve it at any time. The whiskey. The cigars. The books. The map. The ceremonial scimitar his father had gotten while fighting against the Kalif. "*Keep it hidden, son, but use it when you have to.*"

After a moment, James joined him. Started tossing handfuls into the flames. Photographs from the offensive into Kalif territory. John Crossley on a tank. In a window. Walking through the desert. Old journal entries. Even the little tobacco pipe he'd shown James as a youth.

"*They'll never forget, never forgive, no matter who the enemy is, son. Better just to start a new life. Be someone else.*"

They'd never talked about his betrayal. The son had felt that asking would have meant admitting that the father had done something horribly wrong. He didn't want to let that into their world.

"*Is there anyone you want me to contact,*" he'd asked his father. "*No, no one,*" the old man had insisted.

When the suitcase was empty, James stood back. Beside his father. Watched the flames die down. Then hugged his father close. Sour breath. Shaking arms. The rasp at the back of his throat. Knew he was going to lose him soon.

"Welcome to Ambergris, John Finch," his father whispered in his ear.

3

Still dark when he woke, except for the lanterns. Except for a hint of gray from the window. He lay on the floor. Felt hungry. Thirsty. As much as he'd ever felt in his life. Hollow, too. As if he were made of spores. Would blow away. Over all of that, the constant complaint of his nerves. Reporting pain. Everywhere.

The Partial lay facedown beside the gray cap. Arms out to the sides. On the table, the bloody knives, the pot of water. The empty vial.

He sat up and saw himself, naked, propped up on two elbows opposite. Feet almost touching. Shock. Sudden horror. Even in the dim light, the same dark hair. The rakish yet thickening features. The solid build on the edge of fat. But Shriek's features rose out of his own. The cheekbones a little higher. The eyes different. This other Finch had green eyes. This other Finch had a strange smoothness to him, a blankness. None of Finch's scars had manifested on him. Few of the wrinkles. Finch shuddered. Shriek-Finch looked like a man who had reached middle age without the physical signs of experience.

"The resemblance will fade," Shriek said. "I'll be able to take any form I like, soon." A scratchy voice. As if getting used to his vocal cords.

Shriek rose, and Finch rose with him. An imperfect reflection. Shriek held himself differently than Finch. Shoulders hunched from some invisible weight. A stare less guarded. More expressive hands. Light gathered around Shriek in unnatural ways. A gentle iridescent strobing rippled across his body. It reminded Finch of the starfish in the cavern by the underground sea.

"How do you feel?" Shriek asked.

"I feel light . . . and yet heavy," Finch said. Could sense Shriek's overlay lifted from his mind. Its presence only confirmed by absence.

While all of those things he'd thought himself numb to came rushing back in with a near-fatal intensity. Sintra. Wyte.

Teetered on the edge of an abyss.

Shriek's voice brought him back: "Let it wash over you. Let it wash out of you. It's not real. It's like a dam breaking."

Finch nodded. Vague resentment: How could Shriek know how it felt?

Shriek wrapped his nakedness in the blanket. Muted the strobing. A shimmer across the face. The arms.

"What now?" Finch couldn't stop staring at himself.

"Just what Bliss gave you. Just that."

The piece of metal was still in his jacket pocket. He handed it to Shriek. Shriek nodded. "Perfect."

Perfect for what? An unease in Finch. That he hadn't thought it all through. An urge to pick up his gun and shoot Shriek.

A spark in Shriek's eyes that originated there. Not a reflection from the light.

"What *are* you?" Finch asked.

A low, wheezy laugh from Shriek. As if his lungs were filled with spores.

"Just someone who knows too much."

Finch watched Shriek assemble the metal strip. Must've been some button or other mechanism hidden in the symbols. Because in Shriek's hands the strip of metal clicked, and like some kind of magician he began to pull more metal out of it. Until he had a length of metal as tall as a man. As tall as Shriek.

"Whoever created this also created the doors," Shriek said as he worked. "But I've never found them. Granted, I was more interested in the gray caps."

"Where did you find it?"

"Bliss found it. Somewhere far, far away."

Bliss, again. Finch beyond surprise.

"What does it do?"

Shriek pulled it sideways, with a motion almost like pulling apart something soft, crumbly. A piece of bread or a biscuit. A frame began to appear.

"It focuses my abilities. Like a lens."

When he had persuaded it into a rectangular shape, roughly door-like, Shriek knelt. Pressed the frame into the air like he was hanging a painting.

Let go of it.

It didn't fall. Made a snapping sound and it stayed there. About two feet off the ground. No flicker or waver. Static. Solid. Still. An intense but narrow gold-green light invested the edges of the metal. Made the symbols glow. The space inside the frame continued to show the window beyond it.

"It will be a minute or two before I can leave," Shriek said. *Finch said.* As Finch had watched, it had almost been like watching himself do it. A ghost watching its body move about the apartment.

"What happens next?" Finch asked.

"I complete the mission. Time doesn't work the way we think it works. Not really. I'll go into the HFZ to pick up the trail. From there, I will journey years and worlds away and return. An army gathered with me. I will be the beacon, the light, that guides them."

Words came tumbling out Finch hadn't known were there. "Why? Why do it? What does it matter to someone"—*something*—"so old. Who is so . . . removed"— *alien*—"from all of this."

The intensity of his need to know shocked him.

A sad, lonely smile. "The truth? None of my books ever changed anything. Nothing I did changed *anything*. I always tried, and I always failed. But Bliss helped me to see that failing a hundred times didn't mean you had to fail every time."

"And you trust Bliss?"

"About this? Yes. Even if I am just an echo, this is the last chance."

"It's too late to put things right," Finch said. "Too much has gone wrong." Ruined neighborhoods. The vacant stares of the people from the camps. The fighting in the streets. The effects of decades of near-constant war.

"As much as they can be put right, Finch," Shriek said.

"And after? What then?"

Shriek's dark gaze, from a dark place. The rectangle hanging in the air like a magic trick. A terrible power. Something in between.

"After? After, I'll be gone. Somewhere. Everywhere. Nowhere. A pile of ashes at the base of the towers . . ."

"And I'll still be here," Finch said. It came out like an ache.

Shriek, forceful: "You are a man who did the best he could in impossible circumstances. That's all."

After Shriek left, he would be alone. Terribly injured. In an apartment with two dead bodies. In a war zone.

The door lit up. Became a reflecting mirror.

"I'm leaving now, Finch," Shriek said.

"Wait!" A last burst of curiosity. "Tell me what happened. How did you end up in this apartment?"

Shriek's features softened. "I tried something dangerous. Something impossible. I tried to use the nexus at Zamilon to go back in time. I tried to change the past so I wouldn't have to change the future. But you can't do that. And the past caught up with me. The attempt almost killed me."

The door had begun to hum. An intense white light shot from it, silhouetting Shriek. The hum became a kind of unearthly music.

"And the gray cap?"

"He got caught in the door I'd made."

"What does that mean? I don't know what that means," Finch said.

"You might ask yourself who Samuel Tonsure really was," Shriek said. Then nodded at Finch, and stepped through the door. Disappeared into the light.

The light went out.

The rectangle clattered to the floor.

The metal fell in on itself.

Just a bar of metal again, as before.

Finch knew he would never be able to make it do what Shriek had done. Knew that he would never see Shriek again.

4

Sunlight. Warm against his battered face. Curled up on the couch. His ankles and wrists seemed made of broken glass. Could feel the fragile bones shifting. Sending the glass up into his arms, his legs. His whole body hurt. Ached. His jaw was sore. Couldn't feel his nose anymore.

A vast and formless rush of city sounds from beyond the window. Sporadic gunfire. The thud and shift of something heavier. Like a giant striding across Ambergris. But distant. So distant.

Someone had applied field dressings to the stumps of finger and toe using torn fabric.

Tried to get up. A hand held him down. A voice he knew said, "Don't get up yet." The accent more pronounced. As if she were no longer acting.

An arm propped up his head so he could drink from a cup of water. It tasted good. Even though he had trouble getting it down. Even though it mixed with the blood inside his mouth.

Sintra's face came into view. He looked up at her with what he knew was a stupid, childlike dependence. Everything stripped away from him. Couldn't raise his arm far enough to wipe his eyes.

"Just lie there," she said. An oddly clinical concern in her voice. She wore forest green. Camouflage pants and shirt. Brown boots made out of something soft. A long knife sheathed at her waist. A rifle in the crook of her left arm, muzzle pointed toward the floor.

"Sintra," he said. Turned his stiff neck to follow her as she got up for more water. Saw again the bodies on the floor. A moment of disorientation. A man and a gray cap. Looking like they'd fallen from a great height. Except the Partial, facedown, was sporting the remains of his fungal eye out across the floor. An army of tiny, black, fernlike mushrooms with golden stems had traveled from the eye to colonize the back of his head.

A croaking raven's laugh at the unexpected sight. Even as he realized there'd still be a recording there, somewhere, in the mess.

Tried to say to Sintra, "How did you find me?" Wasn't sure it came out right.

Sintra gave him more water to drink. Perched beside him on the armrest. "The city is catching its breath this morning. There is no one in this building now. Not a single Partial. No eyes left in this apartment. Their attention is elsewhere."

"How did you know? To look here."

Her voice from above him, matter-of-fact: "I've followed you here before."

"When?"

He felt her shrug. "I've followed you everywhere. Especially the last few months. Before the towers started firing on the Spit. I have followed you so much I know more about you than you do." Not said like a joke. More like she was weary of it. Tired of being a shadow.

The words lay there, in the sunlight. Finch picked over them again and again. Didn't find what he was looking for.

"Did you kill them?" she asked. Motioning toward the bodies.

"One of them."

"But not before he got to you." Said it like he was a problem to be solved. Like a threat.

Finch thought for the first time about the sword on the floor. Looked toward it. His own gun appeared in her hand. Again.

"Finch . . ."

"Are you here to finish me off?"

"No, just to stop you from doing anything stupid." She held out a pill to him. "You'll feel better if you take it. Maybe long enough to get back to your apartment."

Took the pill gladly. Willingly. A test both of him and of her. Swallowed. A vague warmth spread through his limbs.

The old absurd idea crept up on him with the warmth. *It still isn't too late. We can get out of Ambergris. Cross the river. Make it to Stockton or Morrow . . .* Readying himself to make the argument again. That if they left together they could leave their old selves behind, too. But he couldn't get the words out. Dust on his tongue. To say them would mean he was delusional. That he was pursuing a ghost.

"What happened to the man who was here before? Your case?"

A deep, shuddering breath. "First, tell me the truth," he said. Had no cleverness, no deception, left to him. "Whatever it is."

She considered the question for a moment.

"We work with the rebels sometimes, in exchange for other favors. Who was the man in this apartment? Was it Duncan Shriek?"

"Who is 'we'?"

"The Dogghe. My people. Who was the man in this apartment?"

The Dogghe. The Religious Quarter. She was part Dogghe, part Nimblytod. Had no known address. Came to him in the night. Seemed to move around the city with ease. Of course she worked for the Dogghe.

"Yes, Duncan Shriek," he told her, because it didn't matter anymore. "Someone who is an expert with . . . doors. Why me? Why not Blakely or Dapple. Or even Wyte?"

The words still came out slowly. Mangled. It took her time to recognize them and respond.

"You had no record up until two years before the Rising, John. That made us curious . . . What was Duncan Shriek's mission?"

"To stop more gray caps coming through. What were your orders with regard to me?"

"Coming through what?"

"The towers. Was it always that way? Between us?" *From the beginning?* An ache now that wasn't from his wounds. A slow-motion treachery. A life concealed.

"Finch, what can you tell me about Ethan Bliss?"

"I *loved* you." Let go of the words now, while she couldn't really see his face. When it didn't matter anymore. He had nothing to say to her about Bliss.

Her slow response: "And I liked you, John. I really did. I wouldn't have slept with you, otherwise. No matter the mission."

A childish bitterness, but he was too weak to keep the poison out of his mind: "You left behind some of your notes once. I had suspicions, but I never went to the gray caps with them. I never told anyone."

A mistake. He could feel the retreat in her words: "You might never have had to find out. We could have continued having our fun. The mystery of it. You liked that very much, I know. But a normal life? Like regular people? We aren't regular people. We were playing roles."

"What roles?"

Her voice took on a harshness that he knew shielded her as much as him. "You were the protector. I was the exotic native girl you liked to fuck."

"That's not true." Wanted no part of what she was doing.

"Isn't it? None of you really *see* us, John. Only what you want to see."

"And what do the Dogghe want? What do they want out of Ambergris?"

Anger in her voice. Desire and need, too. Just not for him. "This was *our* place, John. Before your people came. Before the gray caps. And maybe it will be again."

"The rebels will never let that happen, no matter how you help them," Finch said. "Neither will the gray caps."

"Maybe they won't have a choice. Maybe this time we will just *take* it."

Saw it now. In the chaos of conflict between gray caps and rebels and the Partials. The Dogghe might hold on to the Religious Quarter. If they were lucky. If others weren't.

"I won't answer any more of your questions," he said. "You already know the answers, I think."

He sat up. Took her in while he still could. A beautiful but tired-looking woman in her early thirties. Hair messy, face long and pinched from stress.

"Did your father ever recover?" he asked.

"What?" The question, after all the others, seemed to take her by surprise.

"From his trauma. Did he recover?"

She looked down, away from him. "Yes, he did." Was that a tremor in her voice? "He's passed on now, but he had as good a life as anyone."

He reached out, touched her shoulder. Her skin warm. Like he remembered it.

She clasped his hand. Eyes bright as she met his gaze. "Clean yourself up.

Find someplace safe to be, Finch. The next time I see you, I might be forcing answers from you. And I really wouldn't like that."

He nodded.

A flash of those green eyes. She put his gun down on the table. "I'm leaving it for you, but I'm taking this." Held up the metal strip Shriek had used. Unmistakable that it, ultimately, was what she'd come for.

"You shouldn't." But beyond caring. "It'll do more harm than good." *To me.*

"John, I don't think you really know the difference." Then she was walking out the door, down the hallway. Gone for good.

Finch stared after her for a moment. Then hobbled to the window. Looked out.

The towers were complete. They shone with green fire in the light. Between them, impossible scenes flashed so fast he caught only glimpses. A vast blue dome like an observatory. Replaced by a mountain topped by a tower. A city of gleaming buildings taller than any he'd ever seen. A forest of vine-like trees. A roiling sea over which egg-shaped balloons floated, trailing lines of shimmering light. And on it went. Almost beyond comprehension.

At some point soon, the scenes would stop changing. They would settle in on one scene. They would settle in on the gray caps' home.

Would he know by then if he'd done the right thing?

5

The way home. So heavy, so light, he almost didn't feel the pavement. Wearing one shoe. Only a sock over his other foot because it hurt too much. Somehow easier to hold the sword. The gun shoved into his belt. Head felt like a balloon stuffed with rags. Ached all over, with eruptions of pain in the places most sorely used by the Partial.

Through a haze, saw:

Partials gathered in a black squadron, marching toward a barricade manned in part by a truck weighted down by a cannon that had to be a century old at least. Two anemic mules whose ribs stuck out stood placidly behind the barricade. Along with the pale, uncertain faces of the defenders.

Gray caps approaching, at their back a huge cloud of spores, gliding and shifting, a thousand shades of green. Of red. Of blue. Suffocating the street. A last few stragglers running out before them, anonymous in their gas masks.

The huge drug mushrooms transformed. Hoods drawn down to the ground, the red surface once so soft become hard as brick. Wavering lines of green energy sparked from their minaret-like tops. Shot out toward the green towers. Gray caps stood watch from tiny circles of windows. Across the sides of each stem, unending repetitions of the symbol Shriek had carried with him on the scrap of paper. Over and over again in a kind of madness. No flow of food or drugs now. No pretense of even caring. Just a sense of waiting. For what?

He took a side street, then an alley. Crept through a courtyard and walked into an apartment complex as a shortcut. Kept his face turned to the wall. If someone wanted to kill him, they could.

Finally reached the hotel steps. The madman lay sprawled there. Someone had slit his throat. His arms were thrown out to either side as if in welcome. Just another body. Already a sly fringe of tiny green-and-white mushrooms had sprouted up through his pant legs, his shirt, his face. In another day, he'd be a fucking flower bed.

Next to the madman's left hand Finch saw a little round carving. He picked it up. Crudely drawn, but unmistakably Stark's face, with its sharp features. The deep-set eyes.

Rathven telling him, "You have to choose a side, Finch. Eventually you have to choose a side, even if you pretend to be neutral. Even if you think giving out information is like selling smokes or food packets."

Through his fuzziness, a terrible thought.

Dropped the carving. Hobbled fast up the steps.

At Rathven's door. One more time. Only it was open now. Had forced the Lewden Special into his left hand, over the bandaged finger. Held the sword in his right.

Hobbled inside, trying to focus his fading attention. Through the hallway. Entered the room ringed by bookshelves. In one chair, facing him, Bosun. He'd abandoned his custom-made revolvers. Held a fungal gun on Rathven. Her back was to him, but he could see her raised arms. The glint of her own monstrous revolver. A standoff.

"You are fucking late," Bosun said. "We've been waiting for a while."

Didn't reply. Just walked around until he stood to the right side of them both. Bosun's bald head was bloodstained. Other people's blood? A yellowing bandage over his shoulder where Finch had clipped him. A nervous tic working its way across the corner of his left eye. Wore a dark shirt and darker pants, tucked into boots. Taken from a Partial? Some perverse form of camouflage?

Rathven was pale but composed. Gaze never wavering from Bosun. The battered old gun trembled only a little in her grip. A smell of sweat and fear came from both of them.

"Finch!" Relief in Rathven's voice. That someone was there. That she wasn't alone with the madman. "I didn't let him in. He took me by surprise." As if Finch might, even now, accuse her. Stress crackling into her voice as she glanced over. "But he didn't know I had the gun . . ." Her look turned to dismay at his condition.

"This is my fault, Rathven," Finch said. "I'm sorry."

Bosun: "Your fault? Because you didn't kill me when you had the chance?" An odd expression of sadness and contempt.

Not for lack of trying.

"No, because I ever went after you. I should've left you alone."

A snort from Bosun. "I don't believe you."

I don't believe myself.

The fungal gun complicated things. Even if Finch got a shot in first, Bosun's gun could go off in an unexpected way. Infect them both.

"Where's Stark?" he asked. Knew the answer. Had to start somewhere.

Flat, emotionless: "Gone, but you knew that. You didn't hide him well enough. I found him all crumpled up in the alley, thinking he was someone else. Then he died. There was nothing I could do . . . He's somewhere safe. For now."

A wave of dizziness washed over Finch. Let it come, bent at his knees to stop from falling. As if he were back on the boat with Wyte, heading out to the Spit to meet Stark and Bosun for the first time.

Said: "I wasn't trying to hide him. I didn't want to hurt him. But he, you, kept coming at me."

Bosun ignored that. "I came here to kill you, maybe kill her, too. I still could." In a speculative tone. Like weighing whether to skip stones across a river or keep their smooth weight in his pocket.

"You didn't bring your muscle." To remind him it was two-to-one odds.

A sharp, curt laugh from Bosun. "No muscle left. They wouldn't follow with Stark gone. Now it's just like old times. Or would have been."

Finch, in an even tone: "Why don't you just leave? No one gets hurt then. Because you'll get hurt even if you manage to take out one of us. You know that."

Could see Rathven was having a harder and harder time holding on to the revolver. Didn't want her to drop it. No idea what Bosun would do then. Even with Finch ready to put a bullet in his head.

Bosun looked up at Finch for a second. Nothing there but a low animal cunning. But unmoored somehow. The eyes older than before. "Here's a deal for you: give me the memory bulb powder and then I'll leave." Could sense the intent.

Something in Finch rebelled at that. Wyte resurrected, even as a shadow. Along with Stark and Otto. Each haunting the other inside of Bosun's mind. Dead but not put to rest.

"That might drive you insane, Bosun. All kinds of things might happen."

"*He's my brother!*" A shriek. A scream. Something horrible and lost rising out of Bosun. Finger twitching on the trigger. Finch saw now the incredible control Bosun was exerting over his own impulses. To kill. To strike out. Weighed against that the promise of seeing his brother again. No matter how perverse the homecoming.

Could hear Rathven's sudden intake of breath in the aftermath.

Finch nodded. "I'll give it to you." Took the last pouch of powder out of his jacket. Turned sideways, gun still trained on Bosun. Tossed it toward the open door. "All you have to do to get it is leave."

Mouth dry. Legs still shaky. Holding it together for Rathven.

Bosun: "Tell her to put her gun down. And put down your sword."

"Rathven, put the gun down," Finch said. Let the sword clatter out of his hand. Couldn't risk squatting to place it on the floor. Might just fall over.

"I don't want to put the gun down, Finch."

"Just do it. I've got him covered."

She hesitated, then, hand shaking, placed her gun on the table between them.

"Now I'll get up and move around you to the door," Bosun said.

"Be careful, Finch," Rathven said.

Bosun got up. Came around the table toward Finch. Stepping over the fallen sword.

Gun to gun. Bosun inches away from him in that enclosed space.

"Let's not see each other again," Finch said.

A map of anger and frustration on Bosun's face. "No promises," he hissed.

A hint of a movement as Bosun passed him, back to the door. A blossoming agony Finch couldn't at first identify because of all of the other pain. Then he realized it came from his side.

Knew he was reeling, losing his balance.

Bosun, at the door, stooping to pick up the pouch just as Finch realized he was bleeding. Rathven lunging for her revolver, turning to shoot at Bosun as he ran out the door. Missing. Tearing a chunk out of the ceiling. Rathven scrambling to lock the door behind Bosun.

Finch looked down to see bright red blood welling up from a cut in his side. Saw Bosun's long, thin knife there on the floor. It had been the lightest of touches. Not even a touch. A whisper.

Vaguely knew Rathven was next to him as he slumped to the ground. Felt the touch of his own sword against his exposed foot as he slid, her arms around him.

"Finch! *Finch!*" Her voice, keeping him awake when he didn't want to be awake.

She brought him close. Her body warm and solid and real. He thought she was shaking. Realized she was sobbing. Then she was pulling his shirt away from his side. Pushing something up against it. Felt something wet and sticky next to his left arm.

"What's wrong?" he thought he asked.

"You've been stabbed, Finch," he thought he heard her say. Her face way up near the ceiling, looking down. Her arms impossibly long.

A coughing laugh. "Have I?" A kind of lurching dislocation.

Rathven was wrapping something around his side. Gauze? Urging him onto his feet.

"You're going into shock. I need to get you somewhere I can help you," she said.

"I deserve better." A dry laugh. Everybody deserved better.

Lurched up, almost falling forward onto his face. Leaned into her.

Glints and glimmers in a dark pool. Past the battered, weathered book stacks. Past her little kitchen. Past her bedroom. A glimpse of green and purple. The brightness of a single bulb. Like a sentry.

A rough-hewn doorway. Water on the floor. Curved walls. Moisture. A cockleshell of a boat. Strange pale-blue eyes of mudskippers in the shallows. Glowing in the light from a lantern.

She said something to him he didn't understand. Took his arm. Guided him until he was lying with his back against the prow, legs out in front like useless matchsticks. She took off the oars, began to row.

Glimpses of roots, brick, and wood in the ceiling. His mangled hand trailing through the water. The wound in his side like a rip in a stuffed animal. All the sawdust coming out. Lulling him to sleep. Closed his eyes. She shook him awake. Nodded at her as if she'd said something he agreed with. But there was nothing left to say.

A thud as the boat knocked against something.

"We're here," she said.

Opened his eyes. Saw her tying a rope to a lock embedded in old stone steps. Beyond, a worn archway.

She forced him to his feet. Helped him up the steps.

A single large room at the top, dark except for Rathven's swinging lantern. Caught a glimpse of books, a table.

She led him to a cot at the far end. Fell heavily onto it. She asked him a question. Didn't hear her. Fuzziness around the words. Drifted. Curious about the dryness in his mouth. The way his vision kept blurring.

Said, "The towers are changing. Need to get to the roof."

Rathven saying "No," forcing him back down onto the cot.

Blinks of light and time.

Fading and coming back.

A few hours later. Awake on the cot. Looking out through his good eye. She'd cut his clothes off. Washed him. Bandaged his side. Could feel the edge of the wound like a mouth as he lay there with a towel around his waist.

He was at the back of a large room, looking toward the front and the doors. The archway. Rich, burgundy carpet and rugs worn but clean. The walls covered from top to bottom in bookcases. Every shelf was filled with books. Perfectly preserved. In neat rows. On the floor, more books. In careful piles. Beside boxes and boxes of black market supplies.

Next to him, medicine and food. Two more cots and another table. A one-burner portable kerosene stove and a pot on this second table. Along with a rifle and several boxes of ammo. His sword. His gun.

Between him and the doors: a globe of the known world on a rosewood table. Four ornate wooden chairs. Rathven sitting in one of the chairs. Watching him.

"I brought your maps down here," she said, indicating the table. "A cane to help you walk. A chamber pot. A bottle of your whiskey. You need to stay here. Out of sight," she said. "You need to rest."

"Clean yourself up. Find someplace safe to be, Finch."

"What about Feral? Where is he?"

"I'll bring him later, if the boat doesn't spook him."

Outside, he could lose himself in the fight. Could join the rebels. Could join the militias. Could do something. But, overnight, he had become a broken-down old man. A pensioner well past the days of pensions. Waiting for better days.

I am not a detective.

"What about the towers? Has anything changed?"

"Nothing. Don't worry—I'll let you know."

"What is this place?"

"It's an old library," she said. "From above it's just rubble. You can't get to it. But this one room I found intact. Although it didn't have many books in it to start."

"Found the rest?" he managed.

"Yes. I brought them here from all across the city."

"Why?"

She had the look of the true believer, of someone who still had hope, as she said, "Finch, here you'll find every book I could salvage about the city. Every book by any Ambergrisian author. Every book of history, of politics. Biographies. Novels. Poetry. They're all here. Much of it knowledge that was lost in the wars, because of the Houses. Because of the gray caps. But someday, Finch, when all of this is over . . ."

Finch looked away. Ashamed by her passion when he had so little left.

"Ever afraid of being found out?"

"All the time."

"The cots?"

"Before they disbanded the camps, I'd shelter escapees here. Or people who had been released but were injured."

"And now?"

"Apparently, this is now a haven for cynical detectives."

That made him smile. A little.

She stood. "You lost a lot of blood. But I stopped the bleeding. It's your other injuries I need to work on now. I'm not strong enough to turn you over. I'll need your help."

She got gauze, bandages, and other supplies. Water from the underground channel. A kind of ritual and finality to the way she set the supplies on the table next to him. That made him shudder. Thinking of the Partial with his knives and scalding water.

She saw his look as she set a pot to boil on the little stove. "I have to clean the wounds, Finch," she said.

He nodded. "I know."

She began wiping away any blood that hadn't already come off.

Ignored him when he winced. Stopped only if he cried out.

She looked different in that light. Older. Tougher. More experienced.

"I think two of my ribs are broken," he said.

"Or bruised," she said. "You might be lucky."

Tried not to scream when she washed the places where his toe and finger had once been. Replaced Sintra's field dressings with proper bandages. Cleaned his swollen eye. His broken nose.

He stared at the ceiling as she pulled the towel back and gently dabbed at his thighs. Past modesty.

"Oh, Finch," she said, betraying tenderness that had been disguised by action before. "Who did this to you?"

"A Partial."

"How did you get away?"

"I killed him . . . Will I live?"

Didn't answer. Just replaced the towel, said, "You have deep cuts on your arms and legs." She began to wash and dress the wounds. The warmth stung and comforted all at once. The smell of piss had faded. There was an antiseptic feel to the air.

"Turn over now," she said. "I need to check your back."

With a groan, he managed that delicate maneuver. Ancient, creaky, feather-weak.

"You have more cuts," she announced after a second. Her voice not quite as even. Not quite as under control. She'd stopped working. Knew she was staring at him.

"Is it that bad?"

"I've seen worse," she managed.

"Can't even feel it," Finch said. Shock? Infection? Some last blessing from Shriek?

She worked on him for long minutes. Finally, had him sit up.

Wrapped bandages around his ribs. Her head next to his. Her arms stretched around him.

Slowly reached out to her. Wrapped his arms around her. Though it hurt him. Rathven held him. Held him like a friend. Solid. Comforting.

"Why are you doing this for me, Rathven?"

"You saved my life."

"I put you in danger."

"We both did."

"I have to tell you something," he said.

"Whatever you need," she said.

Understood that she might give him more than he had any right to expect.

It was hard. Halting. But after he began, it was hard to stop. He told her everything. All of it. Leaving nothing out. Sparing no one, least of all himself. As if truly confessing. Needing it out of him.

He told her about the Lady in Blue. About how he'd left Stark. Wyte's death. About Bliss. The Partial. How Shriek had come out of him. About Sintra. Heard his voice. Detached, normal. Wondered how it sounded to her. Rational? Insane?

She said nothing. Just held him. Listened. When he was done, she gave him water. Made him eat a little. Then gently pushed him back onto the cot. Whispered that she would bring him clean clothes soon.

He fell asleep as soon as his head hit the pillow.

SUNDAY

Fading in and out of consciousness. Restless and exhausted. A dryness to his skin. An attenuated feeling. The sense that he could blow away in the wind. Did it come from Shriek? From having given part of himself away? He didn't know.

Lying on a cot or sitting in a chair seemed like a kind of sloth. Also a kind of gnawing ache that was half for Sintra and half, perversely, for what the Lady in Blue had shown him. The sentimental thought that he had never had a chance to tell Wyte about any of it.

Strange, but when he closed his eyes he had an image of the hotel above them restored to its former grandeur. A concierge and porter in the lobby. Someone behind the desk waiting to take his key. Sintra in an evening gown. They'd be about to take a motored vehicle to the opera. The streets would be busy with merchants and people coming home from work. The buildings, the storefronts, would be bright and cheery with lights. Like it had been in those mayfly beautiful moments between wars, before the Rising.

Waiting for a bomb to fall through the ceiling. Waiting for Partials to come up the tunnel to kill or arrest him. Waiting for salvation or disaster to come tumbling out of the space between the towers.

When he couldn't stand what he was feeling, he shook the shadows from his head. Went over to the map of Ambergris and the overlay. Removed the globe and star chart to fit them on the main table. Didn't know if it was Finch or Crossley who liked working on the project. Or both.

Rathven had just left to get some more supplies. She'd told him it was Sunday morning. Ordered him to get back on the cot.

Whatever is coming through the towers, the world will change again.

Still, for now, the world had only changed a little. He used a soft cloth on the map to erase what had been lost. Slowly, with regret, removed the Spit. Knew that even if parts survived, no one lived there now. Erased the station. Removed the words "Wyte's apartment." Removed the words "bell tower." Didn't think any of the detectives would ever go back there. Each red mushroom on his map, he now changed to a symbol indicating a fortified position. Added Stark's mushroom house, whether occupied now or not. Added the towers in the bay, which he had resisted until he knew they were complete. Out of fear? He didn't know.

Question: *How could I know they would burn the body?*
Answer: *Because it would've been stupid for them not to.*

The memory bulbs he'd eaten. The feel of Sintra's body beside him in bed. The full and terrible force of Heretic's gaze. The Partial's scorn for his weakness. The look in the Lady in Blue's eyes as she tried to convince him. The ruined fortress.

Then: disrupting his thoughts, a flash of gold-green light. A fizzling, popping sound. The sounds of footsteps coming up the stairs.

Finch stood up beside his map, grabbed his gun.

Bliss appeared at the edge of the carpet. Dark smudges on his face. The ragged edges of his jacket had a burnt look to them. His dark pants had darker stains on them.

"I should be more surprised," Finch said. And he wasn't. Just scared. *Another test to pass.*

An odd dueling smugness and humility to Bliss's expression. "Rathven has fewer secrets than she thinks, and I have more. You look well."

No indication from those eyes of what to expect.

"I look like shit. I feel like shit."

"Better that than dead," Bliss said, walking into the room. "Since you're still alive, I assume the mission was successful."

"Wouldn't you know already?"

"The towers will be operational very soon. Then we'll know. Where's the piece of metal Shriek used, Finch?"

"You've healed well," Finch said, ignoring him. "Almost as if I never hit you."

Bliss pulled up a chair next to the map. "I took a vacation. Somewhere remote. Somewhere I expected would be a little less . . . exciting . . . than it was." An enigmatic smile. "I see you are busy changing the map. A little premature, don't you think?" Bliss's features hardened. "The mission *is* complete?"

"Yes," Finch admitted. "There were complications. But it's done." Hesitant to tell him just how many complications.

Bliss nodded. "Nothing ever happens the way we think it will. Now, where's that piece of metal?"

"I have a few questions first."

"Questions?"

"I've been doing a lot of thinking," Finch said. "In between passing out. When I haven't been pissing blood. About things like whether or not you really work for the rebels. Maybe Ethan Bliss does, but not Dar Sardice."

A pause, then, as if deciding whether or not to play along with him. Then: "Very good, Finch. Keep going."

"You share information with the rebels, yes, but you don't work for them. Even if they think so."

"Excellent, Finch!" A kind of forced cheeriness. "So who *do* I work for?"

"You were Dar Sardice before you were Ethan Bliss. It's the oldest name you're known by. You knew my father. You said you worked with him. My father was deep in Kalif territory during much of the campaign. Working on engineering projects for the Ambergris army. Often shuttling back and forth behind the front lines. You met him then, I think, not after he returned to Ambergris."

Bliss gave him a look of mingled regret and triumph. "You're right, of course. I gave him that, actually." Nodded at the scimitar on the table behind Finch, beside its scabbard. "A reward for his good service. I was also your father's control in Ambergris. I ran him, along with other sources. But he was the best."

"Ran him for who?" Wanted to hear Bliss say it.

"For the Kalif, of course. Always for the Kalif. The Kalif has a long memory, Finch. And the Kalif never forgets anything. We turned your father in the desert, and he stayed turned. But you knew that."

The question he'd been homing in on, the one he'd never been able to ask his father: "Why did he do it?"

"He never told you? Why does anyone do anything? For money. For love. For our children. Because we think it's right. Your father, he met a woman. He had reservations about the war by then. He'd seen some of the excesses of the Ambergrisian army, had never felt comfortable with the power of the Hoegbottons before the war. And he'd lived in the desert for a couple of years. Observed the traditions of a culture thousands of years old. He was ready to fall in love—with all of it."

"And then what?"

An impassive gaze. "The woman died. Brutalized and killed by Ambergrisian soldiers, apparently. Her body burned in a fire." A kind of triumphant smile. "But you, Finch. You were saved from that fire. You were less than a year old at the time."

A shifting feeling in his stomach. A distant sense of confusion. Stared at Bliss across the maps. "That's a lie. My mother died in childbirth. She was from Stockton. She had no family."

Bliss shrugged. "Believe what you like. Hoegbotton, Frankwrithe—both right. Both wrong. Does it matter in the long run? Your father worked for the Kalif. As for *why*, look around you, Finch. This is a city founded on an attempted *genocide*, and everything that came out of that. The Silence. The Wars of the Houses. The Rising. This place is dangerous, Finch. Its people are dangerous. Ambergris will always need a counterweight. First through Morrow and Frankwrithe & Lewden. Now through the rebels, because the gray caps are in control. Either that, or Ambergris tries to take over the world. One way or the other. That's what the Kalif learned repulsing your offensive."

"Is that what my father believed?"

"That's what I believe. Your father believed that by playing both sides against each other he was serving a greater good. I've never been under that delusion."

Searching Bliss's guarded face for what was true. Trying to reject the idea of further treacheries.

"*You* abandoned him, then. You let him take the fall when Hoegbotton and Frankwrithe joined forces. I was there. He died alone. Except for me."

Bliss shrugged. "I couldn't stop him from being found out. Just from being *found*. Too many people on each side were talking, suddenly. But, Finch, he wouldn't *let* me help him. Wouldn't let me take him out of Ambergris. Because of *you*. And because he was dying."

"But you made sure nobody got to him so he wouldn't talk."

"I did what I could."

Something clicked. Even on the run, when his father was dying, he hadn't wanted Finch to contact anyone. *No help from anyone.* Because he didn't trust anyone.

"He didn't want you getting near me," Finch said.

"I could've found you at any time, James Crossley," Bliss said, leaning back.

"I wouldn't have worked for you. You couldn't have recruited me."

"Haven't I already?" Then shrugged. "But this is all beside the point. Where's the piece of metal, Finch?"

A gun had appeared in Bliss's hand. His regretful look said, *Just in case.*

"Maybe I left it in the apartment. Maybe you should look there."

"Maybe you should just give it to me," Bliss said. "It's not the kind of thing you want to leave lying around." Acid in his voice. A hard glitter to the eyes that chilled Finch. But it didn't stop him.

"Mostly, though, Bliss, I keep thinking about how good you are at *finding* things. You never told me that you were the one who found Shriek. Gave him to the rebels. Do you want to explain that?"

Bliss sat back, tapping his foot against the floor. "You want the truth? Shriek was dumb luck. A wild card. Something to hold in reserve. He was like a spigot once I found a way to pry him out of his protective shell. Like a man left on a desert island for a hundred years. He would've talked to anyone."

"And you found him next to Samuel Tonsure's bones, of all people. And then you 'found' that magical strip of metal. The one that wasn't made by us or by gray caps. You even found the doors before the rebels did. Did you also tell them the soldiers in the HFZ weren't all dead, just lost?"

A sly smile. "It's a skill, Finch. Finding things. Leveraging them. My goals and the goals of the rebels are the same. For the moment. Although it's a very long game we're playing here." The eyes not smiling at all.

"Where did you find the metal?"

A hiss of impatience from Bliss. "I understand, Finch. I really do. You won't be working for me. You don't care who your mother is. Your father is a hero, not a traitor. Now just give me that fucking piece of metal, or we'll do it the hard way. We'll do it the *hardest possible way.*"

Finch turned away from a thought that truly terrified him. That Bliss didn't work for the Kalif at all. That Dar Sardice was just the first of the masks he knew about. That the "long game" was beyond comprehension.

The sounds of oars from beyond the open doors. Of a boat thudding up against the steps.

"That'll be Rathven," Bliss said. "Do you really want to involve her in this?"

No, he didn't.

"I don't have it. Sintra took it from me in the apartment," Finch said. Almost triumphant. Almost proud of Sintra. "There was nothing I could do. The Dogghe have it now. I couldn't stop her."

Bliss erupted from his seat. Suddenly seemed twice as tall. Mouth open in an expression of rage beyond any caricature Finch had ever seen.

Flinched before it. Pushed back in his chair. Waited for the blow, but couldn't look away.

Bliss's eyes were dead. Something else shone through. Something hostile. Something alien. Like a mask had slipped. Peering out through the urbane little man's face was something *other.*

Then it was gone. Bliss was just Bliss. "No matter," he said, with a smile that cut. "A complication soon solved." But Finch didn't think it would be that easy. Hoped it wouldn't.

Footsteps walking up the stairs.

A reptilian smile from Bliss.

"You're just a spectator now, Finch. Just another pawn. But I'll leave you with this: Did you ever stop to think that maybe Wyte represents the future of this city? That maybe you're *the past*. Still living, but the past nonetheless. There will be a day you'll remember this conversation in a much different light."

Then he was walking into the bookshelves. Which turned into a door fringed with green and gold.

Which he stepped into.

And was gone.

Rathven came in, holding her gun and a disgruntled Feral.

"Was someone in here with you, Finch?" She let Feral down. The cat ran to him, rubbed up against his legs.

Finch shook his head. "Talking to myself." Leaned over to pet Feral. Felt like he'd escaped some great danger. Had come across the edge, the outline, of something that his map could not encompass. That neither Finch nor Crossley could ever understand.

Somewhere out there the Lady in Blue was readying for invasion. Somewhere Sintra was bringing the strange piece of metal to her superiors.

Somewhere Shriek was trying to come home.

And he was in a secret room surrounded by books, petting a cat.

From far above, he heard the mutter of mighty engines coming to life. A groaning, rending roar. A rising hum behind it. A metallic scream like the cry of a raptor.

The ceiling vibrated. The floor rumbled. A plume of dust. Feral looked up, concerned.

"I was coming to tell you, John," Rathven said. "The towers are changing. The electricity is out. Everywhere."

Panic and a surge of energy. "I've got to get to the roof to see it."

She shook her head. "No, you don't. You're too weak. We can take the boat instead. The tunnel leads out to the bay."

Wincing, he settled into the boat opposite Rathven. It felt strange to be in a boat not made by the gray caps. The wood so stiff. The lack of give beneath his feet. She lurched onto the seat opposite him. Set the lantern by her feet. Two gas masks there. Binoculars, too. Feral paced on the steps, watching them leave. Rathven had left food just in case.

Ribs of light from the lantern sent across the ceiling made it seem as if they traveled down the gullet of a great beast. Cool, under the earth. Overhead, there might be violence. There might be mobs. Street sweeps by the Partials. Poisonous clouds of fungus. Almost anything. But down here, there was just the shudder from the towers.

Were they entering a new life? Would it be better than the last? He didn't know.

"They'll sing your praises," Rathven said. "If Shriek leads them back." She stared at him as if the enormity of events had finally found her.

Have I done what's best? Have I done the right thing or the wrong thing?

"They won't even remember my name, Rath."

"I will," she said.

An emotion rose up in him that he didn't think he deserved to feel. Facing each other. Two survivors. Gliding through a dark tunnel, headed for the light.

✦✦✦

Now Finch can see the frailty death has lent them. Now Finch can see the vulnerability. The way the light uses them in the same way it uses him . . . and looks out across the damaged face of Ambergris.

The wide expanse of the bay confronts their boat. A stiff, hot wind rising. The Spit just a trace of black smoke. The towers shambly and green to the left. Shuddering and quaking like something alive. Debris falling off of them into the water. On the right, the north shore, and the long arm of the HFZ. Agitated. Alive. A curving hand reaching out across the water toward the towers. A wave of orange-green-red spores. Already torn and jagged at the limits of its reach. Already fading back into itself.

From the towers, an ungodly roar and cacophony. Lines of light reach out from the tops of the towers into the city. Toward the blood-red mushroom stations. As if helping to hold them up. In front of the towers, the tiny shadows of rows of gray caps lined up on the bridge. As if in worship.

In that space between the towers, the gate—the door—has finally found what it was searching for.

A weak white disk in a porous pale sky, poor mimic of the sun beyond the towers. Framed in gray, gigantic living citadels rise in a swirl of glittering dust motes so tightly packed they can only be spores. Two, three hundred feet the citadels rise. Circular. Studded with tiny eyes for windows. A hundred curving causeways run between them. Rising from below, a thick forest of tendrils in constant, rippling motion. Waves of color washing across them, strobing from greens to reds to blues, and back again. Through this landscape, great beasts stride in perpetual gloom. Hunched over. Half seen, half heard. Cities of fungus rising from their backs.

But at the bottom of this scene, a tear or rip. Like a photograph with a flame burning through it in a rough triangle. Turning it to ash.

A green-gold door rising.

They watch from the boat as it lengthens, enlarges itself. Encroaches on the forest of tendrils. A whining sound. A kind of crackling and popping that hurts his ears. And no other sound out across the bay. Or across the city behind them. As if everyone holds their breath. Waiting for this new thing.

The background scene becomes glassy. Vague. Blurry.

The green-gold door stops growing.

The breath goes out of him, and then returns. As if he's been dead and now is coming back to life.

They come in numbers. In legions. Pouring through the door. Across the bridge, overrunning the gray cap positions like an unstoppable river, into the city. He can see them, toy soldiers, through the binoculars. A never-ending torrent running across the surface of the bay. Some wear strange clothes. Carry strange weapons that discharge violet light. Some with gas masks. Some encased in great armored suits of metal sinew and tendon. Others on horses. Some looking human. Others like Wyte at his worst. Some in motored vehicles. Others on foot. A few leading creatures he has never seen before.

The rending sound becomes louder. Vibrating in his ears. He is transfixed. She is transfixed. *People will ask him where he was on this day. He will say, "In a small boat in the bay. With a friend."*

The towers shake and shake but never fall. The men and women and things coming out from the door, their progress does not slacken. They keep spilling out, and as they do, the scene in the background becomes grayer and grayer. Like a smudge. The lines of force from the tops of the towers into the city begin to waver. Until one by one they erase themselves. Slowly. Then more quickly.

Waves now in the bay, like an aftershock. Smacking against the boat. He is holding her tight against the awful wonder of it. He is holding on to her like something familiar.

And still the rebels come, as the backdrop begins to fade. Things from the other side now touch that surface. Fall forward. Into the air. Their shapes that were in that other place graceful or translucent become crumpled and dark. Falling. Extinguished in the bay.

And still the rebels come. Transformed and normal. Through the green-gold door.

Something stirs in him. A hint of a feeling close to pride. Close to horror. Because he knows, and she knows, that the world has changed. And he helped change it.

It may not be better. It may be worse. But it will be different.

He's reached the end of being Finch. Of being Crossley. He's reached the end, and he has no idea who or what he will be next.

He sits in the rowboat next to her and watches the end and beginning of history.

Remembers it all.

Forgets it all.

ACKNOWLEDGMENTS

Over the course of writing these books, numerous individuals influenced my edits and thoughts about the series as a whole. They have been thanked in the original editions. Here I would like to thank Sean McDonald and everyone at MCD / Farrar, Straus and Giroux for their enthusiastic support of this mammoth reprint project. Thanks as well to my wife, Ann, whose suggestions while writing all three books were invaluable. Thanks to Ann also for publishing *Dradin, In Love* as a standalone book. I am also indebted to the thoughts and imagination of old friends Matthew Cheney and Eric Schaller over so many years. Major appreciation to Howard Morhaim, the agent who doggedly found good homes for the *Ambergris* books over the years. Thanks to all the artists who worked on these books over the years. Additional thanks to Sally Harding, Liz Gorinsky, Henry Hoegbotton, and the editors who originally acquired these books for publishers large and small: Sean Wallace, Juliet Ulman, Peter Lavery, Jim Minz, Nicholas Cheetham, and Victoria Blake. I must also mention and thank all of those who hosted *Shriek* movie parties at small theaters around the country on original publication, with special appreciation for Edward Morris for having the brashness to display fresh squid at the premiere in Portland. Huge appreciation to Robert Devereaux, the Church, and Murder by Death for their soundtracks for *Ambergris*. Finally, thanks to all the booksellers and readers who championed the Ambergris Cycle over the years and made this reprint possible. Much love.